T0114584

VIRICONIUM

PRAISE FOR M. JOHN HARRISON

"A Zen master of prose." —Iain Banks, author of *The Algebraist*

"That M. John Harrison is not a Nobel Laureate proves the bankruptcy of the literary establishment. Austere, unflinching and desperately moving, he is one of the very great writers alive today. And yes, he writes fantasy and SF, though of a form, scale and brilliance that it shames not only the rest of the field, but most modern fiction."
—China Miéville, author of *Iron Council*

PRAISE FOR *VIRICONIUM*

"In the best tradition of the finest writing, *Viriconium* is universal and particular together. It is the ultimate city, the very essence of what we understand such a collection of buildings, thoroughfares, monuments, institutions, concerns, inhabitants, lives and fates to be."
—Iain Banks, author of *The Algebraist*

"Exemplary fictions of unease shot through with poetic insight and most beautifully written." —Angela Carter, author of *The Magic Toyshop*

"*Viriconium* is a scintillating kaleidoscope of cities." —*Observer*

"Beautifully written and disconcertingly haunting." —*Time Out*

"The fantasy is grounded in M. John Harrison's sense of reality. . . . It is lifelike. It is also written in the kind of prose which, as you tap a nail on a crystal glass, never rings false." —*Guardian*

"[Harrison] writes with a cool and disciplined hand. His prose is always elegant, but never vain . . . unerringly he seeks the underside of things."
—*Times Literary Supplement*

"A witty and truly imaginative writer." —*Literary Review*

"Enjoyably rancid imagination . . . extraordinary, lively, and moving."
—*Sunday Times*

"M. John Harrison's *Viriconium* series is brilliant, beautiful, and absolutely essential reading. The breadth of vision and imagination alone in these books is unparalleled. It is truly one of a kind and will continue to haunt you in the best possible way for years."
—Jonathan Carroll, author of *White Apples*

"M. John Harrison's *Viriconium* sequence is the jewel in the crown of twentieth-century fantasy, a work that proves irrefutably that fantastic literature can be Art with a capital A, holding its own alongside the very finest writing of our time, or any other."
—Elizabeth Hand, author of *Mortal Love*

"M. John Harrison is a true master of English prose. He possesses the eye of a painter, the ear of a bard, and a rigorous and playful intellect. The *Viriconium* novels and stories are infused with a haunting genius that never falters." —K. J. Bishop, author of *The Etched City*

PRAISE FOR *LIGHT*

PRAISE FROM REVIEWERS

"Profoundly thoughtful, complex, fascinating . . . well worth the wait."
—*Kirkus Reviews* (starred review)

"Harrison's talent for brilliant, reality-bending SF is on display yet again with this three-tiered tale. . . . This is space opera for intelligentsia, as Harrison tweaks aspects of astrophysics, fantasy and humanism to hum right along with the blinking holograms in a welcome and long overdue return." —*Publishers Weekly* (starred review)

"Mind-bending in both its conceptual framework and literary deftness."
—*Entertainment Weekly* (A rating)

"An ambitious, accomplished space opera that brings [Harrison] to the genre's front rank . . . surely one of the best novels of the year, irrespective of genre." —*San Francisco Chronicle*

"A story of wonders, both on the personal and the cosmic level . . . Harrison has done something remarkable. He has turned descriptions of quantum mechanics and astrophysics into a poetry of longing, and awe, with an almost Sylvia Plath–like sense of dread. *Light* is a rare piece of science fiction, and one of the finest I have read. It is also one the best-written books I have read this year." —*Boston Globe*

"Succeeds in evoking the sense of wonder that science fiction readers look for in the best of the genre." —*New York Times Book Review*

"Sentence by sentence [Harrison] is almost certainly one of the most skilled SF writers alive . . . an unusually strong and even, for all its brutality, touching example of how character and physics can illuminate each other in the best hard SF. *Light* is likely to be one of the most rewarding and challenging novels of the year, and goes a long way toward explaining just what it is that Harrison can do that other writers find so astonishing." —*Locus*

"Here we have 'space opera' that brilliantly transcends its humble pulp origins while simultaneously glorying in them. The result is a gripping, thrilling, meditative novel which can be read and enjoyed on multiple levels. . . . In direct line from Cordwainer Smith and Keith Laumer, Michael Moorcock and Norman Spinrad, Harrison has adapted the conceits of space opera until the form is big enough to hold all the marvels he jams within." —*SciFi.com* (Editor's A+ pick)

"M. John Harrison's *Light* is not just among the best SF novels of the year—it's without question the best read of the year. . . . Not since Stepan Chapman's *The Troika* and Iain M. Banks's *Use of Weapons* has a novel managed to so single-handedly revitalize and re-energize the SF field. . . . Harrison has combined his astute, ruthless characterization with the SF form, to create a work that bristles and seethes with energy and intelligence, a work both playful and sublimely serious. . . . Imagine the best pure adrenaline SF novel twinned to a stunning mainstream novel to get an idea of the overall effect. . . . The pleasures of this book are wide and numerous. I cannot recommend *Light* highly enough." —*SFSite*

"A wonderful, playful and solidly genre-based masterpiece . . . Don't hesitate. Buy this book and read it. You will thank me." —*Interzone*

"The ride is uproarious, breath-taking, exhilarating. . . . Gem-like images blink into existence, perfect in their place, both wise and sly. . . . This is a novel of full spectrum literary dominance, making the transition from the grainily commonplace now to a wild far future seem not just easy but natural, and connecting the minimal and the spectacular with grace and elegance. It is a work of—and about—the highest order." —*Guardian*

"An increasingly complex and dazzling narrative . . . *Light* depicts its author as a wit, an awesomely fluent and versatile prose stylist, and an SF thinker as dedicated to probing beneath surfaces as William Gibson is to describing how the world looks when reflected in them. . . . SF fans and skeptics alike are advised to head towards this *Light*." —*Independent*

"Harrison's writing is top-notch and involving. He takes old ideas and mechanisms from early science fiction and invigorates them with a sense of possibility and even, strange within this dark and foreboding book, transcendence and hope." —BookPage.com

"The sort of book that leaves you wondering, in the best way possible, what the heck really happened . . . a wild, satisfying ride."
—Bookslut.com

PRAISE FROM OTHER AUTHORS

"M. John Harrison's *Light* is a remarkable book—easily my favorite SF novel in the last decade, maybe longer—and the image that remains in my head after the book was done is that of light as foam, like the sea foam 'between the water and the dry land' . . . a book that exists in the spaces between things . . . very lovely." —Neil Gaiman, *New York Times*–bestselling author of *Endless Nights* and *American Gods*

"M. John Harrison proves what only those crippled by respectability still doubt—that science fiction can be literature, of the very greatest kind. *Light* puts most modern fiction to shame. It's a magnificent book."
—China Miéville, award-winning author of *Perdido Street Station* and *The Scar*

"M. John Harrison is the only writer on Earth equally attuned to the essential strangeness both of quantum physics and the attritional banalities of modern urban life. This is space opera for these dark times, and *Light* is brilliant."
—Iain M. Banks, author of *Complicity*, *The Bridge*, and *Consider Phlebas*

"I loved it . . . the story is somehow both bewildering and utterly clear, razor-sharp and wide enough to encompass worlds, and the language is beautiful, nailing both the bizarre and the mundane with eerie skill. On every other page there's a line which makes you think 'it can't get better than this,' and then it does. An amazing book: not just a triumphant return to science fiction, but an injection of style and content that will light up the genre." —Michael Marshall Smith, author of *Spares* and *One of Us*

"Post-cyberpunk, post-slipstream, post-everything, *Light* is the leanest, meanest space opera since *Nova*. Visually acute, shot through with wonder and horror in equal measure, in *Light's* dual-stranded narrative M. John Harrison pulls off the difficult trick of making the present seem every bit as baroque and strange as his neon-lit deep future. Set the controls for Radio Bay and prepare to get lost in the K-Tract. You won't regret it."
—Alastair Reynolds, award-winning author of *Revelation Space* and *Chasm City*

"*Light* is a literary singularity: at one and the same time a grim, gaudy space opera that respects the physics, and a contemporary novel that unflinchingly revisits the choices that warp a life. It's almost unbearably good." —Ken MacLeod, author of *The Star Fraction* and *Cosmonaut Keep*

"At last M. John Harrison takes on quantum mechanics. The first classic of the quantum century, *Light* is a folded-down future history bound together by quantum exotica and human endurance. Taut as Hemingway, viscerally intelligent, startlingly uplifting, Harrison's ideas have a beauty that unpacks to infinity."
—Stephen Baxter, award-winning author of *The Time Ships*

ALSO BY M. JOHN HARRISON

NOVELS
The Commited Men (1971)
The Centauri Device (1974)
Climbers (1989)
The Course of the Heart (1992)
Signs of Life (1997)

SHORT STORY COLLECTIONS
The Machine in Shaft Ten and Other Stories (1975)
The Ice Monkey and Other Stories (1983)

GRAPHIC NOVELS
The Luck in the Head (1991) with Ian Millar

VIRICONIUM

M. JOHN HARRISON

DEL REY

NEW YORK

This is a work of fiction. Names, characters, places, and incidents either are
the product of the author's imagination or are used fictitiously.
Any resemblance to actual persons, living or dead, events,
or locales is entirely coincidental.

A Del Rey Books Trade Paperback Original

Copyright © 2005 by M. John Harrison

All rights reserved.

Published in the United States by Del Rey, an imprint of
The Random House Publishing Group, a division of
Random House, Inc., New York.

DEL REY and the HOUSE colophon are registered trademarks of
Random House, Inc.

The Pastel City Copyright © 1971 M. John Harrison
A Storm of Wings Copyright © 1980 M. John Harrison
In Viriconium Copyright © 1982 M. John Harrison
Viriconium Nights Copyright © 1985 M. John Harrison

Library of Congress Catalog in Publication Data
Harrison, M. John (Michael John).
Viriconium / M. John Harrison.
p. cm.
ISBN 978-0-553-38315-7
eBook ISBN 978-0-307-41869-2
I. Title.
PR6058.A6942V57 2005
823'.914—dc22
2005045338

www.delreybooks.com

Book design by Karin Batten

146086900

CONTENTS

INTRODUCTION

On *Viriconium:* Some Notes Towards an Introduction

People are always pupating their own disillusion, decay, age. How is it they never suspect what they are going to become, when their faces already contain the faces they will have twenty years from now?
—"A Young Man's Journey Towards Viriconium"

And I look at the Viriconium cycle of M. John Harrison and wonder whether *The Pastel City* knew it was pupating *In Viriconium* or the heartbreak of "A Young Man's Journey Towards Viriconium" inside its pages, whether it knew what it was going to become.

Some weeks ago and halfway around the world, I found myself in the centre of Bologna, that sunset-coloured medieval towered city which waits in the centre of a modern Italian city of the same name, in a small used bookshop, where I was given a copy of the *Codex Seraphinianus* to inspect. The book, created by the artist Luigi Serafini, is, in all probability, an art object. There is text, but the alphabet resembles an alien code, and the illustrations (which cover such aspects of life as gardening, anatomy, mathematics, geometry, card games, flying contraptions, and labyrinths) bear only a passing resemblance to those we know in this world at this time: in one picture a couple making love becomes a crocodile, which crawls away; while the animals, plants, and ideas are strange enough that one can fancy the book something that has come to us from a long time from now or from an extremely long way away. It is, lacking another explanation, art. And leaving that small shop, walking out into the colonnaded shaded streets of Bologna, holding my book of impossibilities, I fancied myself in Viriconium. And this was odd, only because until then I had explicitly equated Viriconium with England.

Viriconium, M. John Harrison's creation, the Pastel City in the afternoon of the world; two cities in one, in which nothing is consistent, tale to tale, save a scattering of place-names, although I am never certain that the names describe the same place from story to story. Is the Bistro Californium a constant? Is Henrietta Street?

M. John Harrison, who is Mike to his friends, is a puckish person of medium height, given to enthusiasms and intensity. He is, at first glance, slightly built, although a second glance suggests he has been constructed from whips and springs and good, tough leather, and it comes as no surprise to find that Mike is a rock climber, for one can without difficulty imagine him clinging to a rock face on a cold, wet day, finding purchase in almost invisible nooks and pulling himself continually up, man against stone. I have known Mike for over twenty years; in the time I have known him his hair has lightened to a magisterial silver, and he seems to have grown somehow continually younger. I have always liked him, just as I have always been more than just a little intimidated by his writing. When he talks about the process of writing he moves from puckish to possessed. I remember Mike in conversation at the Institute for Contemporary Art trying to explain the nature of fantastic fiction to an audience: he described someone standing in a windy lane, looking at the reflection of the world in the window of a shop, and seeing, sudden and unexplained, a shower of sparks in the glass. It is an image that raised the hairs on the back of my neck, that has remained with me, and that I would find impossible to explain. It would be like trying to explain Harrison's fiction, something I am attempting to do in this introduction, and, in all probability, failing.

There are writers' writers, of course, and M. John Harrison is one of those. He moves elegantly, passionately, from genre to genre, his prose lucent and wise, his stories published as sf or as fantasy, as horror or as mainstream fiction. In each playing field he wins awards and makes it look so easy. His prose is deceptively simple, each word considered and placed where it can sink deepest and do the most damage.

The Viriconium stories, which inherit a set of names and a sense of unease from a long-forgotten English Roman City ("English antiquaries have preferred *Uriconium*, foreign scholars *Viroconium* or *Viriconium*, and *Vriconium* has also been suggested. The evidence of our ancient sources is somewhat confused," a historical website informs us) are fantasies, three novels and a handful of stories which examine the nature of art and magic, language and power.

There is, as I have already mentioned, and as you will discover, no consistency to Viriconium. Each time we return to it, it has changed, or we have. The nature of reality shifts and alters. The Viriconium stories are palimpsests, and other stories and other cities can be seen beneath their surfaces. Stories adumbrate other stories. Themes and characters reappear, like Tarot cards being shuffled and redealt.

The Pastel City states Harrison's themes simply, in comparison with the tales that follow, like a complex musical theme first heard played by a marching brass band. It's far-future sf at the point where sf transmutes into fantasy, and the tale reads like the script of a magnificent movie, complete with betrayals and battles, all the pulp ingredients carefully deployed. (It reminds me on rereading a little of Michael Moorcock and, in its end-of-time ambience and weariness, of Jack Vance and Cordwainer Smith.) Lord tegeus-Cromis (who fancied himself a better poet than swordsman) re-assembles what remains of the legendary Methven to protect Viriconium and its girl-queen from invaders to the North. Here we have a dwarf and a hero, a princess, an inventor, and a city under threat. Still, there is a bitter-sweetness to the story that one would not normally expect from such a novel.

A Storm of Wings takes a phrase from the first book as its title and is both a sequel to the first novel and a bridge to the stories and novel that follow and surround it. The voice of this book is, I suspect, less accessible than the first, the prose rich and baroque. It reminds me at times of Mervyn Peake, but it also feels like it is the novel of someone who is stretching and testing what he can do with words, with sentences, with story.

And then, no longer baroque, M. John Harrison's prose becomes transparent, but it is a treacherous transparency. Like its predecessors, *In Viriconium* is a novel about a hero attempting to rescue his princess, a tale of a dwarf, an inventor, and a threatened city, but now the huge canvas of the first book has become a small and personal tale of heartbreak of secrets and of memory. The gods of the novel are loutish and unknowable, our hero barely understands the nature of the story he finds himself in. *In Viriconium* feels like it has come closer to home than the previous stories—the disillusion and decay that was pupating in the earlier books has now emerged in full, like a butterfly, or a metal bird, freed from its chrysalis.

The short stories that weave around the three novels are stories about escapes, normally failed escapes. They are about power and politics, about language and the underlying structure of reality, and they are about art. They are as hard to hold as water, as evanescent as a shower of sparks, as permanent and as natural as rock formations.

The Viriconium stories and novels cover such aspects of life as gardening, anatomy, mathematics, geometry, card games, flying contraptions, and labyrinths. They have much to teach us about the nature of art.

Harrison has gone on to create several masterpieces since leaving Viriconium, in and out of genre: *Climbers*, his amazing novel of rock climbers and escapism takes the themes of "A Young Man's Journey Towards Viriconium" into mainstream fiction; *The Course of the Heart* takes them into fantasy, perhaps even horror; *Light*, his transcendent twining sf novel, is another novel about failed escapes—from ourselves, from our worlds, from our limitations.

For me, reading *Viriconium Nights* and *In Viriconium* was a revelation. I was a young man when I first encountered them half a lifetime ago, and I remember the first experience of Harrison's prose, as clear as mountain water and as cold. The stories tangle in my head with the time that I first read them—the Thatcher years in England seem already to be retreating into myth. They were larger-than-life times when we were living them, and there's more than a tang of the London I remember informing the city in these tales, and something of the decaying brassiness of Thatcher herself in the rotting malevolence of Mammy Vooley (indeed, when Harrison retold the story of "The Luck in the Head" in graphic novel form, illustrated by Ian Miller, Mammy Vooley was explicitly drawn as an avatar of Margaret Thatcher).

Now, on rereading, I find the clarity of Harrison's prose just as admirable, but find myself appreciating his people more than ever I did before—flawed and hurt and always searching for ways to connect with each other, continually betrayed by language and tradition and themselves. And it seems to me that each city I visit now is an aspect of Viriconium, that there is an upper and a lower city in Tokyo and in Melbourne, in Manila and in Singapore, in Glasgow and in London, and that the Bistro Californium is where you find it, or where you need it, or simply what you need.

M. John Harrison, in his writing, clings to sheer rock faces and finds invisible handholds and purchases that should not be there; he pulls you up with him through the story, pulls you through to the other side of the mirror, where the world looks almost the same except for the shower of sparks. . . .

Neil Gaiman
Narita Airport, July 25, 2005

The pastel city

The pastel city

PROLOGUE
ON THE EMPIRE OF VIRICONIUM

Some seventeen notable empires rose in the Middle Period of Earth. These were the Afternoon Cultures. All but one are unimportant to this narrative, and there is little need to speak of them save to say that none of them lasted for less than a millennium, none for more than ten; that each extracted such secrets and obtained such comforts as its nature (and the nature of the universe) enabled it to find; and that each fell back from the universe in confusion, dwindled, and died.

The last of them left its name written in the stars, but no one who came later could read it. More important, perhaps, it built enduringly despite its failing strength—leaving certain technologies that, for good or ill, retained their properties of operation for well over a thousand years. And more important still, it *was* the last of the Afternoon Cultures, and was followed by Evening, and by Viriconium.

For five hundred years or more after the final collapse of the Middle Period, Viriconium (it had not that name, yet) was a primitive huddle of communities bounded by the sea in the West and South, by the unexplored lands in the East, and the Great Brown Waste of the North.

The wealth of its people lay entirely in salvage. They possessed no science, but scavenged the deserts of rust that had been originally the industrial complexes of the last of the Afternoon Cultures, and since the largest deposits of metal and machinery and ancient weapons lay in the Great Brown Waste, the Northern Tribes held them. Their loose empire had twin hubs, Glenluce and Drunmore, bleak sprawling townships where intricate and beautiful machines of unknown function were processed crudely into swords and tribal chieftains fought drunkenly over possession of the deadly *baans* unearthed from the desert.

They were fierce and jealous. Their rule of the Southerners was unkind, and, eventually, insupportable.

The destruction of this pre-Viriconium culture and the wresting of power from the Northmen was accomplished by Borring-Na-Lecht, son of a herdsman of the Monar Mountains, who gathered the Southerners, stiffened their spines with his rural but powerful rhetoric, and in a single week gutted both Drunmore and Glenluce.

He was a hero. During his lifetime, he united the tribes, drove the Northmen into the mountains and tundra beyond Glenluce, and built the city-fortress of Duirinish on the edge of the Metal-Salt Marsh where rusts and chemicals weather-washed from the Great Brown Waste collected in bogs and poisonous fens and drained into the sea. Thus, he closed the Low Leedale against the remnants of the Northern regime, protecting the growing Southern cities of Soubridge and Lendalfoot.

But his greatest feat was the renovation of Viriconium, hub of the last of the Afternoon Cultures, and he took it for his capital—building where necessary, opening the time-choked thoroughfares, adding artifacts and works of art from the rust deserts, until the city glowed almost as it had done half a millennium before. From it, the empire took its name. Borring was a hero.

No other hero came until Methven. During the centuries after Borring's death, Viriconium consolidated, grew plump and rich, concerned itself with wealth, internal trade, and minor political hagglings. What had begun well, in fire and blood and triumph, lost its spirit.

For four hundred years the empire sat still while the Northmen licked their wounds and nourished their resentments. A slow war of attrition began, with the Southerners grown spineless again, the Northmen schooled to savagery by their harsh cold environment. Viriconium revered stability and poetry and wine merchants; its wolf-cousins, only revenge. But, after a century of slow encroachment, the wolves met one who, if not of their kind, understood their ways. . . .

Methven Nian came to the throne of Viriconium to find the supply of metals and Old Machines declining. He saw that a Dark Age approached; he wished to rule something more than a scavenger's empire. He drew to him young men who also saw this and who respected the threat from the

North. For him, they struck and struck again at the lands beyond Duirinish and became known as the Northkillers, the Order of Methven, or, simply, *the Methven*.

There were many of them, and many died. They fought with ruthlessness and a cold competence. They were chosen each for a special skill: thus, Norvin Trinor for his strategies, Tomb the Dwarf for his skill with mechanics and energy weapons, Labart Tane for his knowledge of Northern folkways, Benedict Paucemanly for his aeronautics, tegeus-Cromis because he was the finest swordsman in the land.

For his span, Methven Nian halted the decay: he taught the Northmen to fear him; he instituted the beginnings of a science independent of the Old Technologies; he conserved what remained of that technology. He made one mistake, but that one was grievous.

In an attempt to cement a passing alliance with some of the Northern Tribes, he persuaded his brother Methvel, whom he loved, to marry their Queen, Balquhider. On the failure of the treaty two years later, this wolf-woman left Methvel in their chambers, drowning in his own blood, his eyes plucked out with a costume pin. Taking their daughter, Canna Moidart, she fled. She schooled the child to see its future as the crown of a combined empire, to make pretense on Methven's death to the throne of Viriconium.

Nurtured on the grievances of the North, the Moidart aged before her time, and fanned secret sparks of discontent in both North and South.

So it was that when Methven died—some said partly of the lasting sorrow of Methvel's end—there were two Queens to pretend to the throne: Canna Moidart, and Methven's sole heir, Methvet, known in her youth as Jane. And the knights of the Order of Methven, seeing a strong empire that had little need of their violent abilities, confused and saddened by the death of their King, scattered.

Canna Moidart waited a decade before the first twist of the knife. . . .

1

tegeus-Cromis, sometime soldier and sophisticate of Viriconium, the Pastel City, who now dwelt quite alone in a tower by the sea and imagined himself a better poet than swordsman, stood at early morning on the sand dunes that lay between his tall home and the grey line of the surf. Like swift and tattered scraps of rag, black gulls sped and fought over his downcast head. It was a catastrophe that had driven him from his tower, something that he had witnessed from its topmost room during the night.

He smelled burning on the offshore wind. In the distance, faintly, he could hear dull and heavy explosions: and it was not the powerful sea that shook the dunes beneath his feet.

Cromis was a tall man, thin and cadaverous. He had slept little lately, and his green eyes were tired in the dark sunken hollows above his high, prominent cheekbones.

He wore a dark green velvet cloak, spun about him like a cocoon against the wind; a tabard of antique leather set with iridium studs over a white kid shirt; tight mazarine velvet trousers and high, soft boots of pale blue suede. Beneath the heavy cloak, his slim and deceptively delicate hands were curled into fists, weighted, as was the custom of the time, with heavy rings of nonprecious metals intagliated with involved cyphers and sphenograms. The right fist rested on the pommel of his plain long sword, which, contrary to the fashion of the time, had no name. Cromis, whose lips were thin and bloodless, was more possessed by the essential qualities of things than by their names; concerned with the reality of Reality, rather than with the names men gave it.

He worried more, for instance, about the beauty of the city that had fallen during the night than he did that it was Viriconium, the Pastel City. He loved it more for its avenues paved in pale blue and for its alleys that were not paved at all than he did for what its citizens chose to call it, which was often Viricon the Old and The Place Where the Roads Meet.

He had found no rest in music, which he loved, and now he found none on the pink sand.

For a while he walked the tideline, examining the objects cast up by the sea: paying particular attention to a smooth stone here, a translucent spiny shell there, picking up a bottle the colour of his cloak, throwing down a branch whitened and peculiarly carved by the water. He watched the black gulls, but their cries depressed him. He listened to the cold wind in the rowan woods around his tower, and he shivered. Over the pounding of the high tide, he heard the dull concussions of falling Viriconium. And even when he stood in the surf, feeling its sharp acid sting on his cheek, lost in its thunder, he imagined it was possible to hear the riots in the pastel streets, the warring factions, and voices crying for Young Queen, Old Queen.

He settled his russet shovel hat more firmly; crossed the dunes, his feet slipping in the treacherous sand; and found the white stone path through the rowans to his tower, which also had no name: though it was called by some after the stretch of seaboard on which it stood, that is, Balmacara. Cromis knew where his heart and his sword lay—but he had thought that all finished with and he had looked forward to a comfortable life by the sea.

When the first of the refugees arrived, he knew who had won the city, or the shell of it that remained, but the circumstances of his learning gave him no pleasure.

It was before noon, and he had still not decided what to do.

He sat in his highest room (a circular place, small, the walls of which were lined with leather and shelves of books; musical and scientific objects, astrolabes and lutes, stood on its draped stone tables; it was here that he worked at his songs), playing softly an instrument that he had got under strange circumstances some time ago, in the East. Its strings were taut and harsh, and stung his finger ends; its tone was high and unpleasant and melancholy, but that was his mood. He played in a mode forgotten by all but himself and certain desert musicians, and his thoughts were not with the music.

From the curved window of the room he could see out over the rowans and the gnarled thorn to the road that ran from the unfortunate city to Duirinish in the Northeast. Viriconium itself was a smoke haze above the eastern horizon and an unpleasant vibration in the foundations of the tower. He saw a launch rise out of that haze, a speck like a trick of the eye.

It was well-known in the alleys of the city, and in remoter places, that, when tegeus-Cromis was nervous or debating within himself, his right hand strayed constantly to the pommel of his nameless sword: then was hardly the time to strike, and there was no other. He had never noticed it himself. He put down his instrument and went over to the window.

The launch gained height, gyring slowly, flew a short way north while Cromis strained his eyes, and then began to make directly toward Balmacara. For a little while, it appeared to be stationary, merely growing larger as it neared the tower.

When it came close enough to make out detail, Cromis saw that its faceted crystal hull had been blackened by fire, and that a great rift ran the full length of its starboard side. Its power plant (the secret of which, like many other things, had been lost a thousand years before the rise of Viriconium, so that Cromis and his contemporaries lived on the corpse of an ancient science, dependent on the enduring relics of a dead race) ran with a dreary insectile humming where it should have been silent. A pale halo of St. Elmo's fire crackled from its bow to its stern, coruscating. Behind the shattered glass of its canopy, Cromis could see no pilot, and its flight was erratic: it yawed and pitched aimlessly, like a waterbird on a quiet current.

Cromis's knuckles stood out white against the sweat-darkened leather of his sword hilt as the vehicle dived, spun wildly, and lost a hundred feet in less than a second. It scraped the tops of the rowans, shuddered like a dying animal, gained a few precious, hopeless feet. It ploughed into the wood, discharging enormous sparks, its motors wailing. A smell of ozone was in the air.

Before the wreckage had hit the ground, Cromis was out of the high room, and, cloak streaming about him, was descending the spiral staircase at the spine of the tower.

At first, he thought the entire wood had caught fire.

Strange, motionless pillars of flame sprang up before him, red and gold, and burnished copper. He thought, We are at the mercy of these old machines; we know so little of the forces that drive them. He threw up his arm to guard his face against the heat:

And realised that most of the flames he saw were merely autumn leaves, the wild colours of the dying year. Only two or three of the rowans were actually burning. They gave off a thick white smoke and a not-unpleasant smell. So many different kinds of fire, he thought. Then he ran on down the white stone path, berating himself for a fool.

Unknown to him, he had drawn his sword.

Having demolished a short lane through the rowans, the launch lay like an immense split fruit, the original rent in its side now a gaping black hole through which he could discern odd glimmers of light. It was as long as his tower was tall. It seemed unaffected by its own discharges, as if the webs of force that latticed the crystal shell were of a different order than that of heat; something cold, but altogether powerful. Energy drained from it, and the discharges became fewer. The lights inside its ruptured hull danced and changed position, like fireflies of an uncustomary colour.

No man could have lived through that, Cromis thought. He choked on the rowan smoke.

He had begun to turn sadly away when a figure staggered out of the wreckage toward him, swaying.

The survivor was dressed in charred rags, his face blackened by beard and grime. His eyes shone startlingly white from shadowed pits, and his right arm was a bloody, bandaged stump. He gazed about him, regarding the burning rowans with fear and bemusement: he, too, seemed to see the whole wood as a furnace. He looked directly at Cromis.

"Help!" he cried. "Help!"

He shuddered, stumbled, and fell. A bough dropped from one of the blazing trees. Fire licked at the still body.

Cromis hurled himself forward, hacking a path through the burning foliage with his sword. Cinders settled on his cloak, and the air was hot. Reaching the motionless body, he sheathed the blade, hung the man over his shoulders like a yoke, and started away from the crippled launch. There was an unpleasant, exposed sensation crawling somewhere in the back of his skull. He had made a hundred yards, his breath coming hard as the unaccustomed exertion began to tell, when the vehicle exploded. A great soundless gout of white cold fire, locked in the core of the launch by a vanished art, dissipated itself as pure light, a millennium after its confinement.

It did him no harm: or none that he could recognise.

As he reached the gates of Balmacara, something detached itself from the raggy clothing of the survivor and fell to the ground: a drawstring pouch of goat shagreen, full of coin. Possibly, in some dream, he heard the thud and ring of his portion of the fallen city. He shifted and moaned. There was at least one more bag of metal on him; it rattled dully as he moved. tegeus-Cromis curled his upper lip. He had wondered why the man was so heavy.

Once inside the tower, he recovered quickly. Cromis ministered to him in one of the lower rooms, giving him stimulants and changing the bloodstiffened bandage on the severed arm, which had been cauterised negligently and was beginning to weep a clear, unhealthy fluid. The room, which was hung with weapons and curiosities of old campaigns, began to smell of burned cloth and pungent drugs.

The survivor woke, flinched when he saw Cromis, his remaining hand clawing at the blue embroidered silks of the wall-bed on which he lay. He was a heavy-boned man of medium height, and seemed to be of the lower merchant classes, a vendor of wine, perhaps, or women. The pupils of his black eyes were dilated, their whites large and veined with red. He seemed to relax a little. Cromis took his shoulders, and, as gently as he was able, pressed him down.

"Rest yourself," he told him. "You are in the tower of tegeus-Cromis, that some men call Balmacara. I must know your name if we are to talk."

The black eyes flickered warily round the walls. They touched briefly on a powered battle-axe that Cromis had got from his friend Tomb the Dwarf after the sea fight at Mingulay in the Rivermouth campaign; moved to the gaudy green-and-gold standard of Thorisman Carlemaker, whom Cromis had defeated single-handed—and with regret, since he had no quarrel with the fine rogue—in the Mountains of Monadliath; came finally to rest on the hilt of the intangible-bladed *baan* that had accidentally killed Cromis's sister Galen. He looked from that to Cromis.

"I am Ronoan Mor, a merchant." There was open suspicion in his eyes and in his voice. He fumbled beneath his clothing. "You have strange tastes," he said, nodding at the relics on the wall. Cromis, noting the fumbling hand, smiled.

"Your coin fell as I carried you from your launch, Ronoan Mor." He pointed to where the three purses lay on an inlaid table. "You will find that all of it is present. How are things in the Pastel City?"

It could not have been the money that worried Ronoan Mor, for the wariness did not leave his face. And that was a surprising thing. He bared his teeth.

"Hard," he muttered, gazing bitterly at his severed limb. He hawked deep in his throat, and might have spat had there been a receptacle. "The young bitch holds steady, and we were routed. But—"

There was such a look of fanaticism in his eyes that Cromis's hand, of its own accord, began to caress the pommel of the nameless sword. He was more puzzled than angered by Mor's insult to the Young Queen. If a man normally given to dreaming of bargain prices and a comfortable retirement (if of anything at all) could show this measure of devotion to a political cause, then things were truly out of joint in the land. Immediately, he found himself thinking: And did you need to know that, Sir Cromis? Is it not enough that the Pastel Towers shudder and fall overnight? There must be further proof?

But he smiled and interrupted Mor, saying softly, "That is not so hard, sir."

For a moment, the survivor went on as if he had not heard:

"—But she cannot hold for long when Canna Moidart's Northern allies join with those patriots left in the city—"

There was a feverish, canting tone in his voice, as though he repeated a creed. Sweat broke out on his brow, and spittle appeared on his lips. "Aye, we'll have her then, for sure! And caught between two blades—"

He held his tongue and studied Cromis closely, squinting. Cromis stared levelly back, endeavouring not to show how this intelligence affected him. Mor clawed himself into a sitting position, trembling with the effort.

"Wise to reveal yourself, tegeus-Cromis!" he cried suddenly, like an orator who singles one man from a crowd of rustics. "Where does *your* service lie?"

"You tire yourself needlessly," murmured Cromis. "It matters little to me," he lied, "for, as you see, I am a recluse. But I admit myself interested in this tale of the Old Queen and her Northern cousins. She has a large following, you say?"

As if in answer, Ronoan Mor's good hand fumbled in his clothing again. And this time, it drew forth a twelve-inch sliver of flickering green light that hissed and crackled:

A *baan.*

He drew back his lips, held the ancient weapon stiffly before him (all men fear them, even their users), and snarled, "Large enough for you, sir. You see"—he glanced sideways at the trophies on the wall—"others may hold forceblades. *Northerners*, they tell me, have many such. With whom does your service lie, tegeus-Cromis?" He twitched the *baan* so it sparked and spat. "*Tell* me! Your evasions weary me—"

Cromis felt perspiration trickling under his armpits. He was no coward, but he had been long away from violence; and though the *baan* was in poor condition, the energies that formed its blade running low, it would still slice steel, make play of bone and butter of flesh.

"I would remind you, Ronoan Mor," he said quietly, "that you are ill. Your arm. Fever makes you hasty. I have given you succour—"

"This to your succour!" shouted Mor, and spat. "Tell me, or I'll open you from crutch to collarbone."

The *baan* flickered like an electric snake.

"You are a fool, Ronoan Mor. Only a fool insults a man's queen under that man's hospitable roof."

Mor flung his head back and howled like a beast.

He lunged blindly.

Cromis whirled, tangled his cloak about hand and *baan.* As the blade cut free, he crouched, rolled, changed direction, rolled again, so that his body became a blur of motion on the stone-flagged floor. The nameless sword slid from its sheath, and he was tegeus-Cromis the Northkiller once again, Companion of the Order of Methven and Bane of Carlemaker.

Confused, Mor backed up against the head of the bed, his slitted eyes fixed on the crouching swordsman. He was breathing heavily.

"Forget it, man!" said Cromis. "I will accept your apologies. Your illness wears you. I have no use for this foolishness. The Methven do not slaughter merchants."

Mor threw the forceblade at him.

tegeus-Cromis, who had thought never to fight again, *laughed*.

As the *baan* buried itself in the trophy wall, he sprang forward, so that his whole long body followed the line of the nameless sword.

A choked cry, and Ronoan Mor was dead.

tegeus-Cromis, who fancied himself a better poet than armsman, stood over the corpse, watched sadly the blood well onto the blue silk bed, and cursed himself for lack of mercy.

"I stand for Queen Jane, merchant," he said. "As I stood for her father. It is that simple."

He wiped the blade of the sword with no name and went to prepare himself for a journey to the Pastel City, no longer plagued by dreams of a quiet life.

Before he left, another thing happened, a welcome thing.

He did not expect to see his tower again. In his skull, there was a premonition: Canna Moidart and her true kinsmen burned down from the voracious North with wild eyes and the old weapons, come to extract vengeance from the city and empire that had ousted them a century since. The savage blood ran true: though Canna Moidart was of Methven's line, being the daughter of his brother Methvel, old quarrels ran in her veins from her mother Balquhider's side, and she had expected the sovereignty on the death of her uncle. Viriconium had grown fat and mercantile while Methven grew old and Moidart fermented discontent in kingdom and city. And the wolves of the North had sharpened their teeth on their grievances.

He did not expect to see Balmacara again: so he stood in his topmost room and chose an instrument to take with him. Though the land go down into death and misrule, and tegeus-Cromis of the nameless sword with it, there should be some poetry before the end.

The fire in the rowan wood had died. Of the crystal launch, nothing remained but a charred glade an acre across. The road wound away to Viriconium. Some measure of order had prevailed there, for the smoke haze had left the horizon and the foundations of the tower no longer trembled. He hoped fervently that Queen Jane still prevailed, and that the calm was not that of a spent city, close to death.

Along the road, grey dust billowing about them, rode some thirty or forty horsemen, heading for Balmacara.

He could not see their standard, but he put down the gourd-shaped instrument from the East and went to welcome them; whether with words or with his blade, he did not much care.

He was early at the gates. Empty yet, the road ran into the rowans, to curve sharply and disappear from sight. A black bird skittered through the leaves, sounding its alarm call; sat on a branch and regarded him suspiciously from beady, old man's eyes. The sound of hooves drew nearer.

Mounted on a pink roan mare fully nineteen hands high and caparisoned in bright yellow, the first horseman came into view.

He was a massive man, heavy in the shoulders and heavier in the hips, with thin, long blond hair that curled anarchically about a jowled and bearded face. He wore orange breeches tucked into oxblood boots, and a violet shirt, the sleeves of which were slashed and scolloped.

On his head was a floppy-brimmed rustic hat of dark brown felt, which the wind constantly threatened to take from him.

He was roaring out a Duirinish ballad which enumerated the hours of the clock as chimed inside a brothel.

Cromis's shout of greeting drove the black bird entirely away.

He ran forward, sheathing his sword and crying, "Grif! *Grif!*"

Grif gathered up the reins beneath the roan mare's bit, hauled her to a halt, and pounded one of the oxblood boots with the heel of his hand.

"Grif, I had not thought to see you again! I had not thought any of us were left!"

2

"No, Cromis, there are a few left. Had you not gone to earth after your sister Galen's accident, and then crept secretly back to this empty place, you would have seen that Methven made due provision for the Order: he did not intend it to die with his own death. A few left, but truthfully a few, and those scattered."

They sat in the high room, Birkin Grif sprawled with a mug of distilled wine, his boots on a priceless onyx table, while Cromis plucked halfheartedly at the eastern gourd or paced restlessly the floor. The chink of metal on metal filtered from the courtyard far beneath, where Grif's men prepared a meal, watered their horses. It was late afternoon, the wind had dropped, and the rowans were still.

"Do you know then of Norvin Trinor, or of Tomb the Dwarf?" asked Cromis.

"Ho! Who knows of Tomb even when the times are uncomplicated? He searches for old machines in deserts of rust, no doubt. He lives, I am sure, and will appear like a bad omen in due course. As for Trinor, I had hoped you would know: Viriconium was always his city, and you live quite close."

Cromis avoided the big man's eyes.

"Since the deaths of Galen and Methven, I have seen no one. I have been . . . I have been solitary, and hoped to remain so. Have some more wine."

He filled Grif's cup.

"You are a brooder," said Grif, "and someday you will hatch eggs." He laughed. He choked on his drink. "What is your appraisal of the situation?"

Away from thoughts of Galen, Cromis felt on firmer ground.

"You know that there were riots in the city, and that the Queen held her ground against Canna Moidart's insurgents?"

"Aye. I expect to break the heads of malcontents. We were on our way to do that when we noticed the smoke about your tower. You'll join us, of course?"

Cromis shook his head.

"A cordial invitation to a skull-splitting, but there are other considerations," he said. "I received intelligence this morning that the Moidart rides from the North. Having sown her seeds, she comes harvesting. She brings an army of Northmen, headed by her mother's kin, and you know that brood have angered themselves since Borring dispossessed them and took the land for Viricon. Presumably, she gathers support on the way."

Birkin Grif heaved himself from his chair. He stamped over to the window and looked down at his men, his breath wheezing. He turned to Cromis, and his heavy face was dark.

"Then we had better to ride, and swiftly. This is a bad thing. How far has the Moidart progressed? Has the Young Queen marshalled her forces?"

Cromis shrugged.

"You forget, my friend. I have been a recluse, preferring poetry to courts and swords. My . . . informant . . . told me nothing but what I have told you. He died a little later. He was in some part responsible for the smoke you saw." He poured himself a mug of wine, and went on:

"What I counsel is this: that you should take your company and go north, taking the fastest route and travelling lightly. Should the Queen have prepared an army, you will doubtless overhaul it before any significant confrontation. Unless a Methven be already in charge of it, you must offer (offer only: people forget, and we have not the King to back us anymore) your generalship.

"If there is no army, or if a Methven commands, then lead your men as a raiding force: locate the Moidart and harry her flanks."

Grif laughed. "Aye, prick her. I have the skill for that, all right. And my men, too." He became serious. "But it will take time, weeks possibly, for me to reach her. Unless she already knocks at the door."

"I think not. That must be your course, however long. Travelling by the canny routes, news of her coming would be a full three weeks ahead of her. An army cannot take the hill ways. With speed, we can hope to engage her well before she reaches Viriconium."

"What of yourself, in these weeks we scatter like minutes?"

"Today, I leave for the city. There I will arrange the backing of Queen Jane for the Methven and also seek Trinor, for he would be an asset. If an army has been sent (and I cannot think the queen as ill-informed as I: there must be one), I will join you, probably at Duirinish, bringing any help I can."

"Fair enough, Cromis. You will need a couple of men in the unquiet city. I'll detail—"

Cromis held up his hand.

"I'll ride alone, Grif. Am I hard-pressed, it will be useful practice. I have grown out of the way of fighting."

"Always the brooder." Grif returned to the window and bawled down into the courtyard, "Go to sleep, you skulkers! Three hours, and we ride north!"

Grif had not changed. However he lived, he lived it full. Cromis stood by him at the window and clapped his meaty shoulder.

"Tell me, Grif: what has been your business all these years?"

Grif bellowed with laughter, which seemed to infect his men. They milled about the courtyard, laughing too, although they could not have heard the question.

"Something as befits a Methven in peacetime, brooder. Or as you may have it, nothing as befits a Methven at any time. I have been smuggling distilled wine of low and horrible quality to peasants in the Cladich Marshes, whose religion forbids them drink it. . . ."

Cromis watched Grif's ragged crew disappear into the darkness at a stiff pace, their cloaks flapping out behind them. He waved once to the colourful figure of Grif himself, then turned to his horse, which was breathing mist into the cold night. He checked the girth and saddlebags, settled the Eastern instrument across his back. He shortened his stirrups for swift riding.

With the coming of darkness, the winds had returned to Balmacara: the rowans shook continuously, hissing and rustling; Cromis's shoulder-length black hair was blown about his face. He looked back at the tower, bulking dark against the cobalt sky. The surf growled behind it. Out of some strange sentiment, he had left the light burning in the upper room.

But the *baan* that had killed his sister he had in an insulated sheath next to his skin, because he knew he would not come again, riding to the light out of battle, to Balmacara in the morning.

Refugees packed the Viriconium road like a torchlit procession in some lower gallery of Hell. Cromis steered his nervous beast at speed past caravans of old men pushing carts laden with clanking domestic implements and files of women carrying or leading young children. House animals scuttled between the wheels of the carts.

The faces he passed were blank and frightened, overlit and gleaming in the flaring unsteady light of the torches. Some of them turned from him, surreptitiously making religious signs (a brief writhe of the fingers for Borring, whom some regarded as a god, a complicated motion of the head for the Colpy). He was at a loss to account for this. He thought that they were the timid and uncommitted of the city, driven away by fear of the clashing factions, holding no brief for either side.

He entered the city by its twelfth gate, the Gate of Nigg, and there was no gatekeeper to issue even the customary token challenge.

His habitually morose mood shifted to the sombre as he took the great radial road Proton Circuit, paved with an ancient resilient material that absorbed the sound of his horse's hooves.

About him rose the Pastel Towers, tall and gracefully shaped to mathematical curves, tinted pale blue or fuchsia or dove-grey. They reached up for hundreds of feet, cut with quaint and complex designs that some said were the high point of an inimitable art, thought by others to be representations of the actual geometrics of Time.

Several of them were scarred and blackened by fire. Some were gutted and broken.

Seeing so much beauty brought down in this way, he was convinced that a change had come about in the essential nature of things, and that they could never be the same again.

Proton Circuit became a spiral that wound a hundred yards into the air, supported by slim and delicate pillars of black stone. At the summit of the spiral lay the palace of the Young Queen, which had been Methven's hall. A smaller building than most in that city, it was shaped like a filigree shell, built entirely of a pure white metal that vibrated and sang. Before its high bright arch stood guards in charcoal livery, who made stringent demands on him to reveal his identity and business.

They found it difficult to believe him a Methven (memories had indeed grown dim, for their chief objection to his claim was that he came with no ceremony or circumstance) and for some time refused him entrance: a circumspection he could only applaud.

He remembered certain pass words known only to the guards of the city.

He made his way along corridors of pale, fluctuating light, passing strange, precious objects that might have been animated sculptures or machines, excavated from ruined cities in the Rust Desert beyond Duirinish.

Queen Jane awaited him in a tall room floored with cinnabar-veined crystal and having five false windows that showed landscapes to be found nowhere in the kingdom.

Shambling slowly among the curtains of light and finely wrought furniture was one of the giant albino megatheria of the Southern forests: great sloth-like beasts, fifteen feet high when they stood upright (which was rarely) and armed with terrible cutting claws, though they were vegetarian and amiable. The Queen's beast wore an iridium collar, and its claws were sheathed in clear thick resin. Seeing Cromis, it ambled up to him in a sleepy manner, and gazed myopically at him. Patterns of light moved across its shining pelt.

"Leave him, Usheen," said a small, musical voice.

Cromis turned his eyes from the megatherium to the dais at the south end of the room.

Queen Jane of Viriconium, Methvet Nian, whom he had last seen as a child at Methven's court, was seventeen years of age. She sat on a simple throne and regarded him steadily with violet eyes. She was tall and supple, clad in a gown of russet velvet, and her skin was neither painted nor jewelled. The identical Ten Rings of Neap glittered from her long fingers. Her hair, which recalled the colour of the autumn rowans of Balmacara, hung in soft waves to her waist, coiled about her breasts.

"Queen Jane," said Cromis and bowed.

She buried her fingers in the thick fur of the megatherium, and whispered to it. The false windows flickered with strange scenes. She looked up.

"Is it really you, Lord Cromis?" she said, a strange expression crossing her pale triangular features.

"Have I changed so much, madam?"

"Not much, Lord Cromis: you were a stiff and sombre man, even when you sang, and you are that still. But I was very young when we last met—"

Suddenly, she laughed, rose from the throne, and came gracefully down to take his hands. Cromis saw that her eyes were moist.

"—And I think I preferred Tomb the Dwarf in those days," she went on, "for he brought me the most wonderful things from his favourite ruins. Or Grif, perhaps, who told questionable tales and laughed a good deal—"

She drew him through the shifting light sculptures to the dais, and made him sit down. The megatherium came to gaze wisely at him from brown, tranquil eyes. Methvet Nian sat on her simple throne, and the laughter left her.

"Oh, Cromis, why have none of you come before? These ten years, I have had need of your support. How many live? I have seen none of you since my father's death."

"Grif lives, madam, for sure. Hours ago, he rode north at my request. He believes that Tomb and Trinor live also. Of the others I have heard nothing. We have come late to this, but you must not think too ill of us. I have come to discover just how late we are. What have been your moves to date?"

She shook her head musingly, so that her bright hair caught the light and moved like a fire.

"Two only, Cromis: I have held the city, though it has suffered; and I have dispatched Lord Waterbeck—who, though well-schooled, has not the strategies of one such as Norvin Trinor—with four regiments. We hope to engage my cousin before she reaches the Rust Desert."

"How long has Waterbeck been gone?"

"A week only. The launch fliers tell me he must reach her within another week and a half, for she travels surprisingly fast. Few of them have returned of late: they report launches destroyed in flight by energy weapons, and their numbers are depleted.

"Our lines of communication grow thin, Cromis. It will be a Dark Age, should our last machines go down."

Again, she took his hand, silently drawing strength from him, and he knew that her young frame was frail for such weight of responsibility. He blamed himself, because that was his way.

"Cromis, can you do anything?"

"I start immediately," he said, trying to smile and finding the requisite muscles stiff from disuse. He gently disengaged her hands, for their cool touch had disturbed him.

"First I must locate Trinor, who may be somewhere in the city; although if that is so, I cannot say why he has not come to you before now. Then it will take me only a short time to come up with Grif, since I can take paths impassible to more than one rider.

"What I must have from you, my lady, is an authorisation. Trinor or Grif must command that army when it meets the Moidart, or failing one of them, myself—this Waterbeck is a peacetime general, I would guess, and has not the experience of a Methven.

"You must not fear too greatly. Can it be done, we will do it, and fall bringing a victory about. Keep order here and faith with what Methven remain, even though we have not used you well."

She smiled, and the smile passed barriers he had not thought existed in his morose soul. She took off one of the steel Rings of Neap and slid it onto his left index finger, which was hardly of greater diameter than her own, saying:

"This will be your authorisation. It is traditional. Will you take a launch? They are swifter—"

He rose to leave, and found himself reluctant.

"No launch, my lady. Those, you must keep jealously, in case we fail. And I prefer to ride."

At the door of the room with five windows, he looked back through the drifting shapes and curtains of light, and it seemed to him that he saw a lost, beautiful child. She brought to mind his dead sister Galen, and he was not surprised: what shook him was that those memories somehow lacked the force they had had that morning. Cromis was a man who, like most recluses, thought he understood himself, and did not.

The great white sloth watched him out with almost human eyes, rearing up to its full height, its ambered claws glinting.

He stayed in the city for that night and another day. It was quiet, the streets empty and stunned. He had snippets of rumour that the Moidart's remaining supporters skulked the narrower alleys after dark and skirmished with groups of the city guard. He did not discount them, and kept a hand on the nameless sword. He expected to find Trinor somewhere in the old Artists' Quarter.

He enquired at several taverns there, but had no information. He grew progressively more impatient, and would have given up had not a derelict poet he met in the Bistro Californium advised him to take his queries to an address on Bread Street in the poorer part of the quarter. It was said that blind Kristodulous had once rented a garret studio there.

He came to Bread Street at twilight. It was far removed from the palace and the Pastel Towers, a mean alley of aging, ugly houses, down which the wind funneled bitterly. Over the crazed rooftops, the sky bled. He shivered and thought of the Moidart, and the note of the wind became more urgent. He drew his cloak about him and rapped with the hilt of his sword on a weathered door.

He did not recognise the woman who opened it: perhaps the light was at fault.

She was tall, statuesque, and graceful; her narrow face had an air of calm and the self-knowledge that may or may not come with suffering. But her blue robe was faded, patched here and there with material of quite another colour, and her eyes were ringed with tired, lined flesh. He bowed out of courtesy.

"I seek Norvin Trinor," he said, "or news of him."

She peered into his face as if her eyes were weak, and said nothing. She stepped aside and motioned him to enter. He thought that a quiet, sad smile played about her firm mouth.

Inside, the house was dusty and dim, the furniture of rough, scrubbed deal. She offered him cheap, artificially coloured wine. They sat on opposite sides of a table and a silence. He looked from her discoloured fingernails to the cobwebs in the windows, and said:

"I do not know you, madam. If you would be—"

Her weary eyes met his and still he did not know her. She got slowly to her feet and lit a squat hanging lamp.

"I am sorry, tegeus-Cromis. I should not have embarrassed you in this fashion. Norvin is not here. I—"

In the lamplight stood Carron Ban, the wife of Norvin Trinor, whom he had married after the fight against Carlemaker's brigands, twelve years before. Time had gone against her, and she had aged beyond her years.

Cromis upset his chair as he got to his feet, sent it clattering across the floor. It was not the change in her that horrified him, but the poverty that had caused it.

"Carron! Carron! I did not know. What has happened here?"

She smiled, bitter as the wind.

"Norvin Trinor has been gone for nearly a year," she said. "You must not worry on my behalf. Sit down and drink the wine."

She moved away, avoiding his gaze, and stood looking into the darkness of Bread Street. Under the faded robe, her shoulders shook. Cromis came to her and put his hand on her arm.

"You should tell me," he said gently. "Come and tell me."

But she shrugged off the hand.

"Nothing to tell, my lord. He left no word. He seemed to have grown weary of the city, of me—"

"But Trinor would not merely have abandoned you! It is cruel of you to suggest such—"

She turned to face him and there was anger in her eyes.

"It was cruel of him to do it, Lord Cromis. I have heard nothing from him for a year. And now—now I *wish* to hear nothing of him. That is all finished, like many things that have not outlasted King Methven."

She walked to the door.

"If you would leave me, I would be pleased. Understand that I have nothing against you, Cromis; I should not have done this to you; but you bring memories I would rather not acknowledge."

"Lady, I—"

"Please go."

There was a terrible patience in her voice, in the set of her shoulders. She was brought down, and saw only that she would remain so. Cromis could not deny her. Her condition was painful to them both. That a Methven should cause such misery was hard to credit—that it should be Norvin Trinor was unbelievable. He halted at the door.

"If there is help you require—I have money—And the Queen—"

She shook her head brusquely.

"I shall travel to my family in the South. I want nothing from this city or its empire." Her eyes softened. "I am sorry, tegeus-Cromis. You have meant nothing but good. I suggest you look for him in the North. That is the way he went.

"But I would have you remember this: he is not the friend you know. Something changed him after the death of Methven. He is not the man you knew."

"Should I find him—"

"I would have you carry no message. Goodbye."

She closed the door, and he was alone on that mean street with the wind. The night had closed in.

3

That night, haunted by three women and a grim future, Cromis of the nameless sword, who thought himself a better poet than fighter, left the Pastel City by one of its northern gates, his horse's hooves quiet on the ancient paving. No one hindered him.

Though he went prepared, he wore no armour save a mail shirt, lacquered black as his short cloak and leather breeches. It was the way of many of the Methven, who had found armour an encumbrance and no protection against energy blades. He had no helmet, and his black hair streamed in the wind. The *baan* was at his belt and his curious Eastern instrument across his back.

In a day, he came to the bleak hills of Monar that lay between Viriconium and Duirinish, where the wind lamented considerably some gigantic sorrow it was unable to put into words. He trembled the high paths that wound over slopes of shale and between cold still lochans in empty corries. No birds lived there. Once he saw a crystal launch drift overhead, a dark smoke seeping from its hull. He thought a good deal of the strange actions of Norvin Trinor, but achieved no conclusions.

He went in this fashion for three days, and one thing happened to him while he traversed the summit of the Cruachan Ridge.

He had reached the third cairn on the ridge when a mist descended. Aware of the insecurity of the path in various places ahead, and noting that his beast was already prone to stumble on the loose, lichen-stained rock, he halted. The wind had dropped, and the silence made a peculiar ringing noise in his ears. It was comfortless and alien up there, impassable when the snow came, as were the lower valleys. He understood the Moidart's haste.

He found the cairn to be the tumbled ruins of an old four-faced tower constructed of a grey rock quite different from that beneath his feet. Three walls remained, and part of a ceiling. It had no windows. He could not guess its intended purpose, or why it was not built of native stone. It stood enigmatically among its own rubble, an eroded stub, and he wondered at the effort needed to transport its stones to such a height.

Inside, there were signs that other travellers of the Cruachan had been overtaken by the mist: several long-dead fires, the bare bones of small animals.

He tethered his horse, which had begun to shiver, fed it, and threw a light blanket over its hindquarters against the chill. He kindled a small fire and prepared a meal, then sat down to wait out the mist, taking up the Eastern gourd and composing to its eery metallic tones a chanted lament. The mist coiled around him, sent cold, probing fingers into his meagre shelter. His words fell into the silence like stones into the absolute abyss:

"Strong visions: I have strong visions of this place in the empty times. . . . Far below there are wavering pines. . . . I left the rowan elphin woods to fulminate on ancient headlands, dipping slowly into the glasen seas of evening. . . . On the devastated peaks of hills we ease the barrenness into our thin bones like a foot into a tight shoe. . . . The narrative of this place: other than the smashed arris of the ridge there are only sad winds and silences. . . . I lay on the cairn one more rock. . . . I am possessed by Time. . . ."

He put the instrument away from him, disturbed by the echoes of his own voice. His horse shifted its feet uneasily. The mist wove subtle shapes, caught by a sudden faint breath of wind.

"tegeus-Cromis, tegeus-Cromis," said a reedy voice close at hand.

He leapt to his feet, the *baan* spitting and flickering in his left hand, the nameless sword greasing out of its dull sheath, his stance canny and murderous.

"There is a message for you."

He could see nothing. There was nothing but the mist. The horse skittered and plunged, snorting. The forceblade fizzed in the damp atmosphere.

"Come out!" he shouted, and the Cruachan echoed, *out! out! out!*

"There is a message," repeated the voice.

He put his back against a worn wall and moved his head in a careful semicircle, on the hunt. His breath came harsh. The fire blazed up red in the grey, unquiet vapours.

Perched on the rubble before him, its wicked head and bent neck underlit by the flames, was a bearded vulture—one of the huge, predatory lammergeyers of the lower slopes. In that gloom, it resembled a hunch-backed and spiteful old man. It spread and cupped a broad wing, fanning the fire, to preen its underfeathers. There was a strange sheen to its plumage; it caught the light in a way feathers do not.

It turned a small crimson eye on him. "The message is as follows," it said. Unlimbering both wings, it flapped noisily across the ruined room in its own wind, to perch on the wall by his head. His horse sidestepped ner-vously, tried to pull free from its tether, eyes white and rolling at the dark, powerful wings.

Cromis stood back warily, raised his sword. The lammergeyers were strong, and said by the herders of Monar to prefer children to lambs.

"If you will allow me:

"*tegeus-Cromis of Viriconium,* which I take to be yourself, since you tally broadly with the description given, *should go at once to the tower of Cellur.*" Here, it flexed its cruel claws on the cold grey stone, cocked its head, ruffled its feathers. "*Which he will find on the Girvan Bay in the South, a little east of Lendalfoot. Further—*"

Cromis felt unreal: the mist curled, the lammergeyer spoke, and he was fascinated. On Cruachan Ridge he might have been out of Time, lost, but was much concerned with the essential nature of things, and he kept his sword raised. He would have queried the bird, but it went on:

"*—Further, he is advised to let nothing hinder that journey, however press-ing it may seem: for things hang in a fine balance, and more is at stake than the fate of a minor empire.*

"*This comes from Cellur of Girvan.* That is the message."

Who Cellur of Girvan might be, or what intelligence he might have that overshadowed the fall of Viriconium (or, indeed, how he had taught a vul-ture to recognise a man he never could have met), Cromis did not know. He waited his time, and touched the neck of his horse to calm it.

"Should you feel you must follow another course, I am instructed to emphasise the urgency of the matter, and to stay with you until such time as you decide to make the journey to Lendalfoot and Girvan. At intervals, I shall repeat the message, in case it should become obscured by circum-stance.

"Meanwhile, there may be questions you wish to ask. I have been pro-vided with an excellent vocabulary."

With a taloned foot, it scratched the feathers behind its head, and seemed to pay no more attention to him. He sheathed his sword, seeing no threat. His beast had quietened, so he walked back to the fire. The lam-mergeyer followed. He looked into its glittering eyes.

"What are you?" he asked.

"I am a Messenger of Cellur."

"Who is he?"

"I have not been instructed in the description of him."

"What is his purpose?"

"I have not been instructed in the description of that."

"What is the exact nature of the threat perceived by him?"

"He fears the *geteit chemosit.*"

The mist did not lift that day or that night. Though Cromis spent much of this time questioning the bird, he learned little; its answers were evasive and he could get nothing more from it than that unpleasant name.

The morning came grey and overcast, windy and sodden and damp. The sister ridges of the Cruachan stretched away east and west like the ribs of a gigantic animal. They left the third cairn together, the bird wheeling and gyring high above him on the termagant air currents of the mountains, or coming to perch on the arch of his saddle. He was forced to warn it against the latter, for it upset the horse.

When the sun broke through, he saw that it was a bird of metal: every feather, from the long, tapering pinions of the great wide wings to the down on its hunched shoulders, had been stamped or beaten from wafer-thin iridium. It gleamed, and a very faint humming came from it. He grew used to it, and found that it could talk on many diverse subjects.

On his fifth day out of the Pastel City, he came in sight of Duirinish and the Rust Desert.

He came down the steep Lagach Fell to the source of the River Minfolin in High Leedale, a loamy valley two thousand feet up in the hills. He drank from the small, stone-ringed spring, listening to the whisper of the wind in the tall reed grasses, then sought the crooked track from the valley down the slopes of Mam Sodhail to the city. The Minfolin chattered beside him as he went, growing stronger as it rushed over falls and rapids.

Low Leedale spread before him as he descended the last few hundred feet of Sodhail: a sweep of purple and brown and green quartered by grey stone walls and dotted with herders' crofts in which yellow lights were beginning to show. Through it ran the matured Minfolin, dark and slow; like a river of lead it flowed past the city at the north end of the valley, to lose and diffuse itself among the Metal-Salt Marshes on the verge of the Rust Desert: from there, it drained westward into the sea.

Sombre Duirinish, set between the stark hills and the Great Brown Waste, had something of the nature of both: a bleakness.

A walled city of flint and black granite, built twenty generations before against the threat of the Northern clans, it stood in a meander of the river, its cobbled roads inclining steeply among squat buildings to the central fastness, the castle within the city, Alves. Those walls that faced the Rust Desert rose vertically for two hundred feet, then sloped outwards. No welcome in

Duirinish for Northern men. As Cromis reached the Low Leedale, the great Evening Bell was tolling the seventh change of guard on the north wall. A pale mist clung to the surface of the river fingering the walls as it flowed past.

Camped about a mile south of the city, by the stone bridge over the Minfolin, were Birkin Grif's smugglers.

Their fires flared in the twilight, winking as the men moved between them. There was laughter and the unmusical clank of cooking utensils. They had set a watch at the centre of the bridge. Before attempting to cross, Cromis called the lammergeyer to him. Flapping out of the evening, it was a black cruciform silhouette on grey.

"Perch here," he told it, extending his forearm in the manner of a falconer, "and make no sudden movement."

His horse clattered over the bridge, steel striking sparks from flint. The bird was heavy on his arm, and its metal plumage glinted in the eastern afterglow. The guard gazed at it with wide eyes, but brought him without question to Grif, who was lounging in the firelight, chuckling to himself over some internal joke and eating raw calf's liver, a delicacy of his.

"That sort of bird makes poor eating," he said. "There must be more to this than meets the eye."

Cromis dismounted and gave his horse into the care of the guard. His limbs were stiff from the fell journey, and the cooking smells of the encampment had made him aware of his hunger.

"Much more," he said. He hefted the lammergeyer, as if to fly it from his arm. "Repeat your message," he commanded it. Birkin Grif raised his eyebrows.

"*tegeus-Cromis of Viriconium,*" began the bird reedily, "*should go at once to the tower of Cellur, which he will find—*"

"Enough," said Cromis. "Well, Grif?"

"A flock of these things has shadowed us for two days, flying high and circling. We brought one down, and it seemed to be made of metal, so we threw it in a river. A strange thing, that you might be good enough to tell me about while you eat."

Cromis nodded. "They are unlikely to trouble you again," he said. "Their purpose, apparently, has been fulfilled."

He allowed the lammergeyer to flap from his arm, and, massaging the place where its talons had clung to him, sat down next to Grif. He accepted a cup of distilled wine, and let it heat his throat. The camp had become quieter, and he could hear the mournful soughing of the wind about the ridges and peaks of Monar. The Minfolin murmured around the piers of the bridge. He began to feel comfortable as the warmth of fire and wine seeped through him.

"However," he said, "I should advise your men to shoot no more of them, should any appear. This Cellur may have odd means of redress."

From a place beside the fire, the lammergeyer cocked its head, presenting to them a blank red eye.

"You did not find Trinor, then?" said Grif. "Can I tempt you with some of this?"

"Grif, I had forgot how revolting you are. Not unless you cook it first."

Later, he showed Grif the Ring of Neap, and related how Methvet Nian had given it to him; told him of the events in Bread Street, and of the curious desertion of Carron Ban; and narrated his encounter with the lammergeyer in the Cruachan mist.

"And you have no desire to follow this bird?" asked Grif.

"Whatever Cellur of Lendalfoot may think, if Viricon goes down, everything else follows it. The defeat of the Moidart is my priority."

"Things have grown dark and fragmented," mused Grif. "We do not have all the pieces of the puzzle. I worry that we shall solve it too late for the answer to be of any use."

"Still: we must go up against the Moidart, however unprepared, and even though that would seem not to be the whole of it."

"Unquestionably," said Grif. "But think, Cromis: if the fall of Viriconium is but a part, then what is the shape or dimension of the whole? I have had dreams of immense ancient forces moving in darkness, and I am beginning to feel afraid."

The lammergeyer waddled forward from the fire, its wings opened a little way, and stared at the two men.

"Fear the *geteit chemosit*," it said. "*tegeus-Cromis of Viriconium should go at once to the tower of Cellur, which—*"

"Go away and peck your feathers, bird," said Grif. "Maybe you'll find steel lice there." To Cromis, he suggested: "If you have eaten enough, we'll go into the town. A search of the taverns may yet bring Trinor to light."

They walked the short distance to Duirinish by the banks of the Minfolin, each occupied by his own thoughts. A low white mist, hardly chest high, covered the Leedale, but the sky was clear and hard. The Name Stars burned with a chilly emerald fire: for millennia they had hung there, spelling two words in a forgotten language; now, only night-herders puzzled over their meaning.

At the steel gates, their way was barred by guards in mail shirts and low, conical helmets, who looked suspiciously at Grif's gaudy clothes and the huge bird that perched on Cromis's arm. Their officer stepped forward and said:

"No one enters the city after dark." His face was lined with responsibility, his voice curt. "We are bothered constantly by Northmen and spies.

You had best wait until the morning." He studied Grif. "*If* you have legitimate business."

Birkin Grif stared unkindly at him, and then slowly up at the great black sweep of the walls. From far above came the faint ring of footsteps on stone.

"So," he said. "It's either climb that lot, or break your pompous face. The latter seems to me the easier." He flexed his hands suggestively. "Let us in, stupid."

"Hold off, Grif," said Cromis, restraining him. "It's a wise precaution. They are merely doing their job." He held his hands well away from the hilt of the nameless sword and advanced. He slid the Ring of Neap from his finger and held it out for the officer's inspection. "That is my authority. I will take responsibility for your opening the gate, should any question arise. I am on the Queen's business."

He took back the ring, returned the officer's short bow, and they passed into the Stone City.

Inside, the roads were narrow, to facilitate defence, should the gate be taken or the outer walls breached. The gloomy granite buildings—for the main part barracks and weaponaries and storehouses—huddled together, their second storeys hanging out over the streets so that fire could be poured into an invader from above. Their windows were morose slits. Even in the commercial centre, where the houses of the metal and fur trade stood, the buildings had an air of dour watchfulness. Duirinish had never been a gay city.

"The army passed through here some days ago," said Grif. "They must have had a fairly glum time of it."

"More important," Cromis told him, "is that they must be well on their way to Ruined Glenluce by now, even travelling by the old coastal road."

"We'll catch them by going directly north. Straight through the marshes, fast and light across the Rust Desert. Not a pleasant trip, but speedy."

"If the Moidart catches them on that road before Glenluce, the fight will be over before we find it," Cromis muttered, brooding on that thought.

They spent an hour travelling the narrow ways that spiralled up toward Alves, stopping at two inns. There, they found no sign of Norvin Trinor, and fellow customers tended to avoid Cromis and his bird. But in the Blue Metal Discovery, a place in the commercial quarter, they came upon another Methven.

A three-storey inn built for the convenience of the fatter merchant classes, the Blue Metal Discovery took up one entire side of Replica Square, less than a mile from Alves itself. Its façade was lit by soft and expensive blue lights salvaged many years before from the Rust Desert, and its windows were less forbidding than the majority in the town, having white ornamental iron shutters reminiscent of those found on dwellings in the warmer parts of the South.

By the time they came to Replica Square, Birkin Grif seemed to be having some trouble in placing his feet squarely on the cobbles. He walked very carefully, singing loudly and continuously a verse of some maudlin Cladich lament. Even to Cromis things looked a little less sombre. No change of mood was discernible in the bird.

The doors of the inn were wide open, spilling yellow light into the blue and a great racket into the quiet square. One or two customers emerged hurriedly from the place and walked off looking furtively behind them. Shouts mingled with the sound of moving furniture. Birkin Grif stopped singing and swaying and became quite still. A little introspective smile crossed his jowly features.

"That," he said, "is a *fight*." And he hurried off, his stride abruptly sure and steady.

He was halfway across the square before Cromis came up with him. They stood in the wash of light from the open door and gazed into a long room.

At its near end, behind a cluster of overturned trestle tables, huddled two potboys and some wan-looking customers, shifting their feet nervously in a mess of sawdust and spilt food. The innkeeper, plump, red-faced, and perspiring, had poked his head into the room through a serving hatch; he was banging a heavy metal mug repeatedly on its sill and shouting abuse at a group of figures in the centre of the room by the massive stone fireplace.

There were seven of them: five heavily built men with wiry black hair and beards, dressed in the brown leather leggings and coats of metal-scavengers; a serving girl in the blue shift of the house (she was crushed into the chimneybreast, her hand to her mouth, and her grimy face was fearful); and an old man in a ribbed and padded doublet of russet velvet.

All six men had drawn swords, and the greybeard, his whiskers wine-stained about the mouth, held also the wicked stump of a broken bottle. He was snarling, and they were advancing on him.

"*Theomeris Glyn!*" bellowed Grif. The metal-scavengers halted their confident advance and turned to stare warily at him. The landlord ceased his swearing, and his eyes bulged.

"You *silly* old goat! You should be passing your remaining years in decent contemplation, not bickering over dirty girls—"

Theomeris Glyn looked a little embarrassed. "Oh, hello," he said. His grey eyes glittered shiftily above his hooked, red-veined nose. He peered at

Grif. "I'm trying to catch up with the army," he muttered defensively. "They left me behind." His face brightened, thick white eyebrows shooting up into his tangled hair. "Heh, heh. Come and stamp some lice, eh, Grif? Now you're here?"

He cackled, and feinted suddenly toward his nearest opponent with the broken bottle. Breath hissed and feet shuffled in the sawdust. Old he may have been, but he was still viperishly quick: bright blood showed where his sword had made the true stroke, and the man danced back, cursing.

His companions closed in.

Grif hurled himself ungracefully across the floor to forestall them, dragging at his sword. But Cromis held back, wondering what to do with the lammergeyer. It gazed beadily at him.

"To ensure your safety," it said, "I suggest you leave here immediately. It is unwise to risk yourself in a minor combat. Cellur has need of you."

Whereupon it launched itself from his arm, screaming and beating its great grey wings like a visitation from Hell. Astonished, he watched it tear with three-inch talons at a white and shouting face (this was too much for the fat innkeeper; wailing with horror as the bird tore at its victim, he slammed the serving hatch shut and fled). Cromis drew his sword, marked his man. He saw Grif wade in, cutting out right and left, but had no time to watch: a dull blade with a notched edge slashed in high at his skull.

He ducked, crouched, and thrust his sword up with both hands into his assailant's groin. With a terrible cry, the man dropped his weapon and fell over backwards, clutching at himself.

Cromis jumped over his writhing body as a second scavenger came howling at him from behind. He landed in an acrobatic crouch, rolled away. The room became a tumbling blur full of screams and the beating of giant wings.

(In the fireplace, Theomeris Glyn was shoving his enemy's head into the flames. He was a nasty old man. The fifth scavenger had backed up against the serving hatch, blood pouring down his face, and was pushing ineffectually at the screeching lammergeyer: Grif, who had already felled his first man, seemed to be trying to haul the bird off its prey so he could get in a clear swing.)

Cromis moved easily behind a wild stroke. "Stop now, and you go unharmed," he panted. But his opponent spat, and engaged the nameless sword.

"I'll *stick* yer!" he hissed.

Cromis slid his steel down the man's blade, so that they locked hilts. His free hand went unseen beneath his cloak; then, deliberately releasing his pressure on the locked swords, he fell forward. For a moment, their bodies touched. He slid the *baan* into the scavenger's heart, and let the body fall.

His knuckles had been cut and bruised as the swords disengaged; he licked them absently, staring at the corpse. A steel medallion showed at its throat. He felt a touch on his shoulder.

"That last was a pretty filthy trick," said Grif, smiling a queer, strained smile. "You must teach me sometime."

"You're too heavy on your feet. And I'd rather teach you to sing. Look at this—"

He poked with the tip of his sword at the scavenger's medallion. It glinted in the bright light. It was a coin, but not of Viriconium; in high relief, it bore the arms of Canna Moidart: wolf's head beneath three towers.

"Already she prepares to rule," said Cromis. "These were Northerners. We must leave at first light. I fear we shall arrive too late."

As he spoke, shouting and commotion broke out again behind them.

In the fireplace, Theomeris Glyn of Soubridge, the old campaigner, was struggling with the serving girl. Her blue bodice had come awry, but she had placed four neat welts on his left cheek. Her small grubby fists hammered at him.

"A man who may not survive his queen's wars *needs* a little affection!" he cried petulantly. "Oh, *drat*!"

Behind him stood the landlord, wringing greasy hands over the wreckage and demanding payment of his bony, oblivious shoulders.

Birkin Grif wheezed and chuckled. Cromis could raise only a thin, weary smile: he had been much disturbed by his discovery.

"Go and pull the old fool off her, Grif, and we'll take him with us. At least he'll see action again, for what it's worth."

Later, as they passed the gates of Duirinish, old Glyn dawdling drunkenly behind them, Grif said:

"She prepares her way to rule, as you say. Her confidence is immense. What can half a hundred brigands, a poet, and an ancient lecher do to flex a will such as that?"

4

Next morning, in the thin light of dawn, Grif's company wound past the dark, watchful walls of the Stony City and into the North. River mist rose, fading up toward the sun in slender spires and pillars. Duirinish was silent but for the tramping of guards on the high battlements. A heron perched on a rotting log to watch as the tiny force forded the northern meander of the Minfolin. If it found them curious, it gave no sign, but flapped heavily away as the white spray flew from cantering hooves.

They had abandoned their ragged, weather-stained finery for makeshift war gear. Here and there, mail rings winked, and some of them wore odd bits of plate armour, but for the most part, it was steel-studded leather stuff. They were a grim, rough-handed crew, with wind-burnt faces and hard, hooded eyes; their speech was harsh, their laughter dangerous, but their weapons were bright and well-kept, and the coats of their mounts gleamed with health over hard muscle.

Birkin Grif rode with wry pride at their head.

His massive frame was clad in mail lacquered cobalt blue, and he wore over that a silk tabard of the same acid yellow as his mare's caparisons. He had relinquished his rustic hat, and his mane of blond hair blew back in the light wind. At his side was a great broadsword with a silver-bound hilt; in a scabbard hanging from his saddlebow rested his long-axe, to hand in case he should be unhorsed. The roan mare arched her powerful neck, shook her big, beautiful head. Her bridle was of soft red leather with a subtle copper filigree inlaid.

To Cromis, riding beside him hunched against the chill on a sombre black gelding, wrapped in his dark cloak like a raven in its feathers, it seemed that Grif and his horse threw back the hesitant morning light like a challenge: for a moment, they were heraldic and invincible, the doom to which they travelled something beautiful and unguessed. But the emotion was brief and passed, and his moroseness returned.

At Birkin Grif's left, his seat insecure on a scruffy packhorse, Theomeris Glyn, his only armour a steel-stressed leather cap, grumbled at the cold and the earliness of the hour, and cursed the flint hearts of city girls. And behind the three Methven, Grif's men had begun to chant a rhythmic Rivermouth song of forgotten meaning, "The Dead Freight Dirge":

> Burn them up and sow them deep:
>   Oh, *Drive them down*;
> Heavy weather in the Fleet:
>   Oh, *Drive them down*;
>   Oh, *Sow them deep*;
> Withering wind and plodding feet:
>   Oh, *Drive them down!*

Its effect on Cromis was hypnotic: as the syllables rolled, he found himself sinking into a reverie of death and spoliation, haunted by grey, translucent images of a shattered Viriconium. The face of Methvet Nian hung before him, in the grip of some deep but undefinable sorrow. He knew he could not go to her. He was aware of the metal bird of Cellur, gyring and hovering high above him as he rode, the embodiment of a threat he could not name.

He was sinking deeper, like a man in a drug dream, when Grif reined in his mare and called his men to a halt.

"Here we leave the Old North Road," he said. "There's our way: direct but unpleasant."

Before them, the road turned abruptly west and was lost to sight behind the black terminal massif of Low Leedale Edge; from there, it found its way to the coast and began the long journey north.

But straight ahead among the bracken and coarse grass at the mouth of the valley ran a narrow track. Fifty yards from the road, the heather failed, and the terrain became brown, faintly iridescent bog streaked with slicks of purple and oily yellow. Beyond that rose thickets of strangely shaped trees. The river meandered through it, slow and broad, flanked by dense reedbeds of a bright ochre colour. The wind blew from the north, carrying a bitter, metallic smell.

"The Metal-Salt Marshes," murmured Grif. He pointed to the reedbeds by the Minfolin. "Even in winter the colours are weird. In summer, they bemuse the brain. The birds and insects there are peculiar, too."

"Some might find it beautiful," said Cromis; and he did.

Theomeris Glyn snorted. He pinched his beaky nose. "It *stinks*," he said. "I wish I hadn't come. I am an old man and deserve better."

Grif smiled.

"This is just the periphery, greybeard. Wait until we reach the interior, and the water thickets."

Where the valley bracken petered out, a dyke had been sunk to prevent the herd animals of Low Leedale from wandering into the bog. It was deep and steep-sided, full of stagnant water over which lay a multicoloured film of scum. They crossed it by a gated wooden bridge, the hooves of their horses clattering hollowly. Above them, Cellur's lammergeyer was a black speck in the pale blue unclouded sky.

In the water thickets, the path wound tortuously between umber iron bogs, albescent quicksands of aluminium and magnesium oxides, and sumps of cuprous blue or permanganate mauve fed by slow, gelid streams and fringed by silver reeds and tall black grasses. The twisted, smooth-barked boles of the trees were yellow-ochre and burnt orange; through their tightly woven foliage filtered a gloomy, tinted light. At their roots grew great clumps of multifaceted translucent crystal like alien fungi.

Charcoal grey frogs with viridescent eyes croaked as the column floundered between the pools. Beneath the greasy surface of the water unidentifiable reptiles moved slowly and sinuously. Dragonflies whose webby wings spanned a foot or more hummed and hovered between the sedges: their long, wicked bodies glittered bold green and ultramarine; they took their prey on the wing, pouncing with an audible snap of jaws on whining, ephemeral mosquitoes and fluttering moths of April blue and chevrolet cerise.

Over everything hung the heavy, oppressive stench of rotting metal. After an hour, Cromis's mouth was coated with a bitter deposit, and he tasted acids. He found it difficult to speak. While his horse stumbled and slithered beneath him, he gazed about in wonder, and poetry moved in his skull, swift as the jewelled mosquito hawks over a dark slow current of ancient decay.

Grif drove his men hard, aiming to traverse the marsh in three days, but their beasts were reluctant, confused by Prussian blue streams and fragile, organic pink sky. Some refused to move, bracing their legs and trembling, and had to be driven. They turned rolling white eyes on their owners, who cursed and sank to their boot-tops in the mud, releasing huge bubbles of acrid gas.

When they emerged from the trees for a short while at about noon, Cromis noticed that the true sky was full of racing, wind-torn grey clouds, and despite its exotic colours, the Metal-Salt Marsh was cold.

In the evening of the third day, they reached the shallow waters of Cobaltmere in the northern reaches of the marsh. They had lost two men and a horse to the shifting sands; a third man had died painfully after drinking from a deceptively clear pool, his limbs swelling up and turning silver-grey. They were tired and filthy, but pleased with the speed of their progress.

They made camp in a fairly dry clearing halfway round the waterlogged ambit of the mere. Far out on the water lay fawn mudbanks streaked with sudden yellow, and floating islands of matted vegetation on which water-birds cackled, ruffling their electric-blue feathers. As the day decayed, the colours were numbed: but in the funereal light of sunset, the water of Cobaltmere came alive with mile-long stains of cochineal and mazarine.

Cromis was woken some time before dawn by what he assumed to be the cold. A dim, disturbing phosphorescence of fluctuating colour hung over the mere and its environs; caused by some strange quality of the water there, it gave an even but wan light. There were no shadows. The dripping trees loomed vaguely at the periphery of the clearing.

When he found it impossible to sleep again, he moved nearer to the dead embers of the fire. He lay there uneasily, wrapped in blanket and cloak, his fingers laced beneath his head, staring up at the faint Name Stars.

About him humped the grey forms of sleeping men. Horses shifted drowsily behind him. A nocturnal mosquito hawk with huge obsidian globes for eyes hunted over the shallows, humming and snapping. He watched it for a moment, fascinated. He could hear the wheeze of Theomeris Glyn's breathing, and the low sound of water draining through the reed clumps. Grif had set a guard on the clearing: he moved slowly round its edge and out of Cromis's field of vision, blowing warmth into his cupped hands, his feet sinking with soft noises into the dank earth.

Cromis closed his eyes and wondered morosely if they would get clear of the marsh by the end of the next day. He discussed strategies suitable for the various areas in which they might meet the Moidart's host. He thought of Methvet Nian as he had last seen her, in the room with five windows that showed landscapes to be found nowhere in the kingdom.

He was considering the fine, firm set of her mouth when he heard a faint sigh behind him: not close, and too low-pitched to wake a sleeping man, but of quite peculiar strength and urgency.

Calmly, waiting for a moment of fear to pass, he felt for the hilt of the nameless sword. Finding it, he rolled cautiously onto his stomach, making as little unneccessary movement as possible and breathing silently through his open mouth. This manoeuvre brought into view the semicircle of clearing previously invisible to him. Stone-still, he studied the point from which the sigh had come.

He could discern little other than the vague, bent outlines of trees. A darker place marked the entrance to the glade. But there seemed to be nothing threatening there. The horses were quiet black silhouettes issuing a white mist of breath. One or two of them had cocked their ears forward alertly.

He realised that he could neither see nor hear the perimeter guard.

Carefully, he freed himself from his blankets, eased his sword a few inches from its scabbard. Reflex impelled him to crouch low as he ran across the clearing and to change direction several times in case he had been marked by archers or energy weapons. He felt exposed but had no actual fear, until he encountered the corpse of the guard.

It was lying near the gap in the trees: a huddled, ungainly form that had already sunk slightly into the wet ground. Upon closer examination, he found that the man had not even drawn his weapon. There was no blood apparent, and the limbs were uncut.

Kneeling, he grasped the cold, bearded jaw, his skin crawling with revulsion, and moved the head to ascertain whether the neck was broken. It was not. The skull, then. He probed reluctantly. Breath hissing through his clenched teeth, he leapt hurriedly to his feet.

The top of the man's skull was missing, sliced cleanly off an inch above the ears.

He wiped the mess off his fingers on some spongy grass, swallowing bile. Anger and fear flooded through him, and he shivered a little. The night was silent but for the far-off drowsy humming of a dragonfly. The earth round the body had been poached and churned. Big, shapeless impressions led away from it and out of the glade to the south. What sort of thing had made them, he could not tell. He began to follow them.

He had no thought of alerting the rest of the camp. He wanted vengeance for this pitiful, furtive death in a filthy place. It was a personal thing with him.

Away from Cobaltmere, the phosphorescence grew progressively dimmer, but his night vision was good, and he followed the tracks swiftly. They left the path at a place where the trees were underlit by lumps of pale blue luminous crystal. Bathed in the unsteady glow, he stopped and strained his ears. Nothing but the sound of water. It occurred to him that he was alone. The ground sucked at his feet; the trees were weird, their boughs a frozen writhing motion. To his left, a branch snapped.

He whirled and threw himself into the undergrowth, hacking out with his sword. Foliage clutched at his limbs; at each step he sank into the muck; small animals scuttled away from him, invisible. He halted, breathing heavily, in a tiny clearing with a stinking pool. He could hear nothing.

After a minute, he became convinced that he had been lured from the path, and in revealing himself to whatever moved so silently in the darkness he had lost his advantage. His skin crawled.

Only his peculiar defensive skills saved him. There was a baleful hissing behind him: he allowed his knees to buckle, and a cold green blade cut the air above his head; poised on his bent left leg, he spun himself round like a top, his sword slashing a half-circle at the knees of his assailant. Knowing that the stroke could not connect, he leapt back.

Before him loomed a great black shadow, some seven or eight feet high. Its limbs were thick and heavy, its head a blunted ovoid, featureless but for three glowing yellow points set in an isosceles triangle. It continued to hiss, its movements silky and powerful and controlled, leaving those strange, shapeless imprints in the mud beneath it. There was an alien coldness about it, a calm, calculating intelligence.

The great *baan*, that he did not dare meet with mere steel, cut a second arc toward him. He danced back, and it sliced through his mail shirt like a fingernail through cold grease; blood from a shallow wound warmed his chest. Despite its size, the thing was cruelly swift. He went behind its stroke, cutting overhand at the place where its neck met its shoulder, but it writhed away, and they faced one another again. Cromis had measured its speed, and feared he was outclassed.

There was no further sparring. In the dark place by the stinking pool, they went at it, and *baan* and steel performed a deadly, flickering choreography. And always Cromis must evade, hoping for a moment's carelessness: yet the shadow was as fast as he, and fought tirelessly. It forced him slowly to the lip of the pool, and a mist was in front of his eyes. He was cut in a number of places. His mail shirt hung in ribbons.

His heel touched water, and for an instant he allowed the *baan* to catch his blade. In a shower of sparks, the tip of the nameless sword was severed: now he could not thrust, but must use only its edge. Fear crept and coiled in him. The giant, its cluster of eyes pale and empty, loomed above him, chopping and leaping like an automaton. Abruptly, he saw a dangerous remedy.

Beneath his clothing, his right hand found the hilt of the little *baan* that had killed his sister. Clutching it, he feigned an injury, delaying a counterstroke and fumbling his recovery. He felt little hope for the stratagem. But the giant saw the opening, and as its weapon moved back, then down, Cromis whipped out the energy knife and met with it the killing blow.

There was a terrifying flash as the two *baans* engaged and shorted out. Cromis was hurled bodily into the pool by the concussion of ancient energies, his arm paralysed. Its blade dead and useless, the giant reeled drunkenly about the clearing, hissing balefully.

Cromis dragged himself from the water, arm numb with agony. Gagging and retching on the liquid that had entered his mouth, he renewed his attack and found that in the final flurry of blades, the nameless sword had been cut clearly in two halfway down its length. Cursing bitterly, he lashed out with the stump. But the giant turned and ran awkwardly into the trees, lumbering through the pool in a fountain of spray.

Its murderous confidence had been dispelled, its grace had left it, and it was defeated: but Cromis cast himself on the poached earth and wept with pain and frustration.

Shouting broke out near him. On grey wings, Cellur's lammergeyer crashed through the foliage, flapping evilly across the clearing, and, screaming, sped after the fleeing shadow. Cromis felt himself lifted.

"Grif," he muttered. "My blade is broken. It was not a man. I injured it with a trick of Tomb's. There is ancients' work here—

"The Moidart has woken something we cannot handle. It almost took me."

A new fear settled like ice in his bone marrow. He clutched desperately at the fingers of his left hand. "Grif, I could not *kill* it!

"And I have lost the Tenth Ring of Neap."

Despair carried him down into darkness.

Dawn broke yellow and black like an omen over the Cobaltmere, where isolated wreaths of night mist still hung over the dark, smooth water. From the eyots and reedbeds, fowl cackled: dimly sensing the coming winter, they were gathering in great multicoloured drifts on the surface of the lake, slow migratory urges building to a climax in ten thousand small, dreary skulls.

"And there will be killing weather this year," murmured tegeus-Cromis, as he huddled over the fire gazing at the noisy flocks, his sword in three pieces beside him, the shreds and tatters of his mail coat rattling together as he moved. They had treated his numerous cuts and bruises, but could do nothing for the state of his thoughts. He shuddered, equating the iron earths of winter with lands in the North and the bale in the eyes of hunting wolves.

He had woken from a brief sleep, his mouth tasting of failure, to find Grif's men straggling back in despondent twos and threes from a search of the glade where he had met the dark giant; and they reported that the Tenth Ring of Neap was gone without trace, trodden deep into the churned mud, or sunk, perhaps, in the foetid pool. The metal bird, too, had returned to him, having lost its quarry among the water thickets. Now he sat with Theomeris Glyn, who had snored like a drunk through all the chaos.

"You take single setbacks too hard," said the old man, sucking bits of food from his whiskers. He was holding a strip of meat to the flames with the tip of his knife. "You'll learn—" He sniggered, nodding his head over the defeats of the aged. "Still, it is strange.

"It was always said south of the Pastel City that if tegeus-Cromis and the nameless sword could not kill it, then it must already be dead. Strange. Have some cooked pig?"

Cromis laughed dully. "You are small comfort. An old man mumbling over meat and homilies. What shall we do without the Queen's authorisation? What *can* we do?"

Birkin Grif came up to warm his hands over the fire. He sniffed at the cooking meat like a fat bloodhound, squeezed his great bulk carefully into the space between Cromis and the old man.

"Only what we would have done had we kept the thing," he said. "Manufacture dooms in your head and you will go mad. Reality is incontrovertible. Also, it will not be anticipated."

"But to command an army—" began Cromis helplessly.

Grif scraped halfheartedly at the filth on his boots. "I have seen you command before, poet. It appeared to me then that you did so from the strengths of your own self, not from those of some bauble."

"That's true," old Glyn said judiciously, spitting out some gristle. "That's how we did it in the old days. Damned expensive boots, those, Grif. You ought to saddle-soap them to keep the damp out. Not that I ever commandeered anything but the arse of a wench."

Grif clasped Cromis's shoulder, shook it gently. "Brooder, it was *not* your fault."

Cromis shrugged. It made him feel no better. "You buried the guard?" he asked, hoping to change the subject.

Grif's smile vanished. He nodded. "Aye, and found one more piece for the puzzle. I was fascinated by the precise edge of his wound. Examining it more closely, I found—" He paused, prodded the fire with his boot, and watched the ascending sparks. "We buried only a part of that man, Cromis: the rest has gone with the creature you put to flight.

"His brain has been stolen."

There was a silence. The colourful trees dripped. Theomeris Glyn began to chew noisily. Cromis reached out to toy with the shards of his sword, unpleasant visions of the corpse crawling through his head: the huddled limbs in the mud, the congealing broth at the edge of the wound.

He said: "She has woken something from the Old Science. I am sorry for that man, and I see each of us in him—" He slid the shards of the nameless sword one by one into his scabbard. "We are all dead men, Grif." He stood up, his muscles aching from the long night. "I'll make ready my horse. We had best to move on."

Perched on an overhanging bough with pale turquoise bark, the metal lammergeyer eyed him silently.

"Sure you won't have some pig?" offered Theomeris Glyn.

They reached the northerly bounds of the marsh without further loss of men. By afternoon on the fourth day the gaudy foliage had thinned sufficiently to reveal a sky overcast but of more acceptable colour. Their speed increased as the going firmed steadily. The bog broke up into irregular patches separated by wide, flat causeways, tending to the colour of rust as they moved north. A cold wind billowed their cloaks, plucked at Cromis's torn mail, and fine rain dulled the hides of the horses.

Stretching east and west in a great lazy curve, the terminal barrens of the Great Brown Waste barred their way: chains of dun-coloured dunes interconnecting to form a low scarp, the face of which was cut and seamed by massive gully erosion.

"We are lucky to come here in winter," said Birkin Grif, twisting in his saddle as he led the company in single file up the gently sloping cleft worn by a black and gelid stream. Walls of damp russet loess reared lifelessly on either side. "Although the winds are stronger, they carry more moisture to lay the soil. The waste is not a true desert."

Cromis nodded dully. In the Low Leedale it had been autumn yet, but that was hard to believe here. He fixed his eyes on the narrow strip of sky beyond the lips of the ravine, wishing for Balmacara, where the year died more happily.

"There is slightly less danger of earth-falls, you understand, and clouds of dust. In summer, one might choke to death, even here on the edge."

From the uncomfortable sky, Cromis shifted his gaze to the file of men behind him. They were lost in a mist of rain, dim shapes huddled and silent on tired mounts.

At the top of the gully, the entire company halted, and by common, unspoken consent, fanned out along the crest of a dune: each man held solitary and introspective by the bleak panorama before him.

The Waste rolled north—umber and ochre, dead, endless. Intersecting streams with high, vertical banks scored deep, meaningless ideographs in the earth. In the distance, distorted into deceptive, organic forms, metal girders poked accusing fingers at the empty air, as if there the Rust Desert might fix the source of its millennial pain. Grif's smugglers muttered, and found that a narrowed eye might discern certain slow but definite movements among the baffling curves of the landscape.

But tegeus-Cromis turned his horse to face away from the spoiled land, and stared back at the mauve haze that marked the marshes. He was much preoccupied by giants.

5

"We should not strive too hard to imitate the Afternoon Cultures," said Grif. "They killed this place with industry and left it for the big monitors. In part, if not in whole, they fell because they exhausted the land. We mine the metal they once used, for instance, because there is no ore left in the earth.

"And in using it all up, they dictated that our achievements should be of a different quality to theirs—"

"There will be no more Name Stars," murmured Cromis, looking up from the fragments of his sword. Dusk had drawn a brown veil across the wastes, amplifying the peculiar vagueness of the dune landscape. It was cold. As yet, they had seen no lizards: merely the slow, indistinct movements among the dunes that indicated their presence.

"Or any more of *this*," said Grif, bleakly.

They had made camp amid the ruins of a single vast, roofless building of vanished purpose and complicated ground plan. Although nine tenths of it had sunk long ago beneath the bitter earth, the remains that reared around them rose fifty or sixty feet into the twilight. A feeble wind mumbled in off the waste and mourned over their indistinct summits. Among the dunes meandered a vile, sour watercourse, choked with stones worn and scoured by Time.

Two or three fires burned in the lee of a broken load wall. Grif's men tended them silently. Infected by the bleakness of the waste, they had picketed the horses close, and the perimeter guards kept well within sight of the main body.

"There will be no more of anything soon," said Theomeris Glyn. "The Moidart, the Afternoon Cultures—both are Time by another name. You are sentimentalists, lacking a proper sense of perspective. When you get to my age—"

"We will grow bored and boring, and make fools of ourselves with dirty girls in Duirinish. It will be a fine time, that."

"You may not make it that far, Birkin Grif," said the old man darkly.

Since Cromis's fight in the Metal-Salt Marsh, Cellur's mechanical vulture had spent most of its time in the air, wheeling in great slow circles over the waste. It would report nothing it had seen from that vantage. Now it perched just beyond the circle of firelight and said:

"Post-industrial shock effected by the so-called 'Afternoon Cultures' was limited in these latitudes. There is evidence, however, that to the west there exists an entire continent despoiled to the degree of the Great Brown Waste.

"In a global sense, the old man may be right: we are running out of Time."

Its precise reedy voice lent a further chill to the night. In the silence that followed, the wind aged, the dying sun ran down like clockwork in an orrery. Birkin Grif laughed uncomfortably; a few thin echoes came from his men.

"Bird, *you* will end up as rust, with nothing to your credit but unproven hypotheses. If we are at the end of Time, what have you to show for it? Are you, perhaps, jealous that you cannot experience the misery of flesh, which is this: to know intimately the doom *you* merely parrot, and yet die in hope?"

The bird waddled forward, firelight spraying off its folded wings.

"That is not given to me," it said. "It will not be given to you, if you fail the real task implicit in this war: *fear the geteit chemosit; travel at once to the tower of Cellur, which you will find—*"

Filled with a horrible depression, Cromis dropped the shards of his sword and left the fire. From his saddlebag he took his curious Eastern instrument. He bit his lip and wandered past the picket line and the perimeter guards. With death in his head, he sat on a stone. Before him, huge loops of sand-polished girder dipped in and out of the dunes like metal worms. They are frozen, he thought: caught on a strange journey across an alien planet at the forgotten end of the universe.

Shivering, he composed this:

Rust in our eyes . . . metallic perspectives trammel us in the rare earth north . . . we are nothing but eroded men . . . wind clothing our eyes with white ice . . . we are the swarf-eaters . . . hardened by our addiction, tasting acids . . . Little to dream here, our fantasies are iron and icy echoes of bone. . . . rust in our eyes, we who had once soft faces.

"Rust in our eyes—" he began again, preparing to repeat the chant in the Girvanian Mode, but a great shout from the camp drove it out of his skull. He jumped to his feet.

He saw the metal bird explode into the air, shedding light like a gunpowder rocket, its wings booming. Men were running about the encampment, casting febrile shadows on the ancient walls. He made pitiful grabbing motions at his empty scabbard, hurrying toward the uproar. Over a confusion of voices he heard Grif bellow suddenly:

"Leave it alone! Oh, you stupid pigs, leave it alone!"

Obsessed by his fantasies of an alien world, Cromis was for a moment unable to identify the dark, massive shape fidgeting and grunting in the gloom of the dead building. Drawn out of the inhospitable dunes by the warmth or the light and surrounded by men with swords, it seemed to be mesmerised and bemused by the fire—a lean, heavy body slung low between queerly articulated legs, a twenty-foot denizen of his own imagination.

He was almost disappointed to recognise it as one of the black reptiles of the waste, huge but harmless, endowed by the folklore of Viriconium with the ability to eat metal.

"Big lizard," muttered one of Grif's brigands, with sullen awe. "Big lizard."

Cromis found himself fascinated by the flat, squat head with its wicked undershot lower jaw and rudimentary third eye. He could discern none of the spines and baroque crests traditional in illustrations of the beast, simply a rough hide with a matte, nonreflective quality.

"Pull back," ordered Grif, quietly.

The men obeyed, keeping their weapons up. Left to itself, the reptile closed determinedly on the fire: finally, the flames leapt, perfectly reflected, in each of its eyes. There it stood for some minutes, quite still.

It blinked. Cromis suspected that whatever sluggish metabolic desires the fire had aroused were unfulfilled. Laboriously, it backed away. It shuffled back into the night, moving its head slowly from side to side.

As his men turned to follow, Grif said sharply, "I told you *no*. Just leave it be. It has harmed nothing." He sat down.

"We don't belong here anymore," he said.

"What do you suppose it saw in there?" Cromis asked him.

Two days out into the barrens. It seemed longer.

"The landscape is so static," said Grif, "that Time is drawn out, and runs at a strange, slow speed."

"Scruffy metaphysics. You are simply dying of boredom. I think I am already dead." Old Theomeris slapped his pony's rump. "This is my punishment for an indiscreet life. I wish I had enjoyed it more."

Since noon that day they had been travelling through a range of low, conical slag hills, compelled by a surface of loose slate to lower their speed to a walk. The three-hundred-foot heaps of grey stone cast back bell-like echoes from the unsteady hooves of the horses. Land-slips were frequent; limited, but unnerving.

Cromis took no part in the constant amiable bickering: it was as unproductive as the sterile shale. Further, he was concerned by the odd behaviour of the lammergeyer.

Ten or fifteen minutes before, the bird had ceased flying its customary pattern of wide circles, and now hung in the air some eight hundred feet up, a silver cruciform slipping and banking occasionally to compensate for a thermal current rising from the slag tips. As far as he could tell, it was hovering above a point about a mile ahead of their present position and directly on their route.

"The bird has seen something," he said to Grif, when he was sure. "It is watching something. Call a halt and lend me a sword—no, not that great lump of iron; the horse will collapse beneath it—and I'll go and find out what it is."

It was a queer, lonely excursion. For half an hour he worked along the precarious spiral paths, accompanied only by echoes. Desolation closed oppressively round him.

Once, the terrible, bitter silence of the slag hills was broken by a distant rhythmic tapping—a light, quick, mysterious ring of metal on metal—but a brief fall of rock drowned it out. It returned later as he was urging his horse down the last slope of the range, the Great Brown Waste spread once more before him, Cellur's metal vulture hanging like an omen five hundred feet above his head.

At the bottom of the slope, two horses were tethered.

A pile of dusty harness lay near them, and a few yards away stood a small red four-wheeled caravan of a type usually only seen south of Viriconium—traditionally used by the tinkers of Mingulay for carrying their large families and meagre equipment. Redolent of the temperate South, it brought to his mind images of affectionate gypsy slatterns and their raucous children. Its big, thick-spoked wheels were picked out in bright yellow; rococo designs in electric blue rioted over its side panels; its curved roof was painted purple. Cromis was unable to locate the source of the tapping sound (which presently stopped), but a thin, blue-grey spire of smoke was rising from behind the caravan.

He realised that it was impossible to conceal his presence from whoever was camped down there—his horse's nervous, crabbing progress down the decline was dislodging continuous slides of rock, which bounded away like live things—so he made no effort, coming down as fast as possible, gripping his borrowed sword tightly.

On the last five yards of the slope, momentum overcame him: the horse's rear hooves slid from beneath it; it pecked; and he rolled out of the saddle over its shoulder. He landed dazed and awkward in the gritty, sterile sand of the waste, and dropped his sword. Fine, stinging particles of dust got into his eyes. He stumbled to his feet, eyes blind and streaming, unpleasantly aware of his bad tactical position.

"Why don't you just stand there quietly," said a voice he thought he knew, "and make no attempt to regain that rather clumsy sword? Eh?" And then: "You caused enough fuss and furore for ten men coming down that hill."

Cromis opened his eyes.

Standing before him, a power-axe held in his knotty, scarred hands, was a thin figure no more than four feet high, with long white hair and amused, pale grey eyes. His face was massively ugly—it had an unformed look, a childlike, disproportionate cast to its planes—and the teeth revealed by his horrible grin were brown and broken. He was dressed in the heavy leather leggings and jerkin of a metal-prospector, and standing on end the haft of his axe would have topped him by a foot.

"You," said Cromis, "could have done no better. You are as insubordinate as ever. You are a pirate. Put up that axe, or my familiar spirit"—here, he pointed to the vulture spiralling above them—"will probably tear the eyes from your unfortunate face. I have a great deal of trouble in restraining it from such acts."

"You will, however, concede that I've captured you? I'll chop the bloody bird up for dog's meat if you don't—"

And with that, Tomb the Dwarf, as nasty a midget as ever hacked the hands off a priest, did a little complicated shuffle of triumph round his victim, cackling and sniggering like a parrot.

"If I had known it was you," said Cromis, "I'd have brought an army of occupation, to keep you quiet."

Night.

A pall, a shroud of darkness lay over the slag heaps, to cover decently their naked attitudes of geographical death. Out on the waste, the harsh white glare of Tomb's portable furnace dominated the orange flickering of a circlet of cooking fires.

Underlit by a savage glow like a dawn in Hell, the little Rivermouth man's unbelievable face became demoniac, bloodcurdling. His hammer fell in measured, deadly strokes onto the soft, hot steel, and, as he worked, he droned and hummed a variant of that queer "Dead Freight" dirge:

> Burn them up and *drive* them deep;
>   Oh, drive them *down*!

It was Cromis's nameless sword, now whole, that flared in the furnace and sparked on the anvil, and drew closer to its gloomy destiny with every accentuated syllable of the chant.

After the meeting by the caravan, Cromis had called down the vulture and sent it to fetch Grif from his position in the hills. On his arrival, he had bellowed like an ox: it was a wild reunion between him and the dwarf, the one bellowing with laughter and the other capering and crowing. Now Grif was eating raw meat and shouting at his brigands, while Tomb and Cromis worked the forge.

"You interrupted me," shouted the dwarf over the roar and wail of the bellows. "I was repairing that."

And he jerked his thumb at a tangle of curved, connected silver-steel rods—resembling nothing so much as the skeleton of some dead metal giant—which lay by the furnace. Small versions of the motors that powered the airboats were situated at the joints of its limbs, and a curious arrangement of flexible metal straps and stirrups was attached halfway down each of its thighbones and upper arms. It looked like the ugly, purposeful work of long-dead men, an inert but dangerous colossus.

"What is it?" asked Cromis.

"You'll see when we get a fight. I dug it up about a month ago. They had some beautiful ideas, those Old Scientists." The light of Tomb's sole enthusiasm—or was it simply splashback from the furnace?—burned in his eyes, and Cromis had to be content with that.

Later, the four Methven sat round a fire with a jug of distilled wine. The reforged sword was cooling, the furnace powered-down, the brigands noisily asleep or dozing in their smelly blankets.

"No," said Tomb, "we aren't too far behind them." He displayed his repugnant teeth. "I'd have been up with Waterbeck and his well-disciplined babes by now, but I wanted to get that power-armour in good order."

"It won't be the same as the old days," complained old Glyn. He had passed rapidly into the sodden, querulous phase of drunkenness. "Now *there* was a time."

Tomb chuckled. "Why did I saddle myself this way? A greybeard with a bad memory, a braggart, and a poet who can't even look after his own sword. I think I might join the other side." He leered down at his hands. "Time I killed somebody, really. I feel like killing something."

"You're a nasty little beast, aren't you?" said Birkin Grif. "Have some more wine."

Cromis, content to have found Tomb if not Norvin Trinor, smiled and said nothing. More roads than this lead to Ruined Glenluce, he thought.

But in the end they had no need to go as far as Glenluce, and Tomb's prediction proved true: two days later, they came upon Lord Waterbeck's expeditionary force, camped several miles southeast of that unfortunate city, in a spot where the waste had heaved itself into a series of low ridges and dead valleys filled with the phantoms of the Departed Cultures.

Time is erosion: an icy wind blew constant abrasive streams of dust over the bare rock of the ridge; it had been blowing for a thousand years.

His black cloak flapping about him, tegeus-Cromis gazed down on the ancient valley; at his side, Grif stamped his feet and blew into his cupped hands. Beneath them spread the tents and bothies of Waterbeck's army— multicoloured, embroidered with sigils and armorial bearings, but hardly gay. Canvas whipped and cracked, the wind moaned in the guylines, and armour clattered as the message runners hurried to and fro between piles of gear that lay in apparent confusion around the encampment.

The tents radiated as a series of spokes—each one representing a division of foot or horse—from a central pavilion surrounded by a complex of ancillary bothies: Lord Waterbeck's command centre. There, canvas was replaced by oiled scarlet silk, shot through with threads of gold wire.

"He has a fine sense of his own importance," said Grif scathingly. "We had better go down and upset it."

"You are too harsh. Don't prejudge him." Cromis felt no enthusiasm for the task ahead. He fingered the hilt of the reforged sword and tried to shrug off his reluctance. "Tell Tomb to settle your men well apart from the main body, while we do what we can."

They rode down one of the wide avenues between the tents, Grif resplendent on his yellow-caparisoned mare, Cromis crow-black in the cold, old wind. They drew a few stares from unoccupied foot soldiers, but, in general, interest was reserved for Grif's smugglers, who were setting up camp around Tomb's gaudy caravan. It was an unconscious parody of Waterbeck's deployment, with the wagon replacing his showy pavilion. They looked like a travelling road show.

Cromis caught threads and tail ends of conversation as he rode:

"The Moidart . . ."

". . . and you can't trust a rumour."

"Twenty *thousand* Northmen . . ."

". . . the Moidart . . ."

". . . and bloody airboats. Bloody scores of them!"

"What can you do about it?"

". . . glad to get it over and done."

". . . the *Moidart*."

At barely thirty years of age, Lord Waterbeck of Faldich had imposing grey hair—cut short and smoothed impeccably back from his forehead—and an urbane manner. His features were bland and boneless, his skin unwrinkled but of a curiously dry, aged texture. He wore a neat, tight jacket of tasteful brown cord, quite unadorned, as were his well-shaped, unobtrusively manicured hands. Cromis imagined that it would be difficult for him to offend any of his peers, and that it was precisely this inability that had earned him his present position.

When they entered the pavilion (it was less opulent than its outer appearance suggested, and draughty) he was sitting behind a small, cluttered camp table, adding his signature to a sheet of white vellum covered with careful grey script. He raised his head, nodded brusquely, and gave his attention to his work again.

"There *is* an official recruitment booth just along the way," he said, his voice crisp and pleasant. "But never mind, now you're here. I'll call an orderly and have him deal with you here."

He looked up and smiled very briefly.

"From your appearance, I'd say you've come some distance to serve. Encouraging to see newcomers, although there won't be many more. Well done, men."

Birkin Grif stepped forward, simultaneously puzzled and antagonistic. "This is Lord tegeus-Cromis of Viriconium," he said, "a knight of the Order of Methven. We are here on the Queen's business. It is imperative that—"

"Just one moment, please."

Waterbeck consulted a small ledger, nodded to himself. He folded his dispatch and began to address it.

"Perhaps Lord Cromis would prefer to speak for himself, eh?"

He offered them his brief little smile.

"You understand that I have many things to occupy my time. Battle will be joined within a week, and fifteen thousand men out there rely on me. If you could—"

He made an apologetic gesture. "I have been advised of no airboat landings recently. If you could give me the meat of your message now, perhaps we could discuss an answer later?"

"I am not a courier, Lord Waterbeck," said Cromis. "My purposes are military, and may be embarrassing to us both."

"I see. I've never run in to you in the city, my lord. Our haunts must be different. Each man to his own, hm?"

He stood up and extended his right hand across the table, palm up.

"You will have some identification provided by Her Majesty, I take it?"

"I began my journey with such proofs," said Cromis, aware of how foolish he must sound. The man was giving him no help at all. "But due to a failure of my own, they were lost. However, the Queen will vouch for me. I suggest you dispatch an airboat to the—"

Waterbeck laughed. He sat down. He shook his head slowly.

"My dear man," he said. "My *dear* man. I might be addressing a simple adventurer. Or even, though I am most reluctant to suggest it, a Northman. I cannot spare an airboat merely to check the credentials of every wanderer who comes in here with a mysterious—and unexplained— proposition.

"If you wish to *fight*, well then, I will sign you on; but I cannot even listen to whatever it is you propose without some concrete, immediate proof of your identity."

Birkin Grif scowled hideously. He leaned over the desk and put his face close to Waterbeck's. He hissed:

"You are a damned fool, or you would use different words to a Methven. At least listen to what we have to say. Lord Cromis led the sea fight at Mingulay—and won it, too—before you were able to lift a practice sword—"

Waterbeck got to his feet.

"There is an official recruitment booth a few steps away from here," he said quietly. "I do not wish to hear any more of this."

Later, they sat on the tailboard of Tomb's caravan, watching the dwarf as he made final adjustments to his peculiar device.

"He knew," said Grif. "He *knew* why we were there. He sensed it."

"You cannot tell that for sure. He was within his rights, if shortsighted. I did not have the ring, and even with that to ease the way it would have been a difficult meeting. He would have resented our command."

Grif made a chopping motion in the air, both hands locked together. He spat into a swirl of dust raised by the wind.

"He knew, all right. If he'd heard us out, he'd have been forced to dispatch that boat."

Tomb the Dwarf chuckled obscenely. He put down his tools and wiped his hands on the back of his leggings.

"Watch this here," he said. "When I've got this thing together, I'll visit Lord Waterbeck. I'll cut his onions off. I'll slice them thinly with my axe."

He had spread the immense skeleton on the ground, so that its legs stuck straight out and its arms were set close to its sides. Now, he lowered himself gently down until he lay supine on its cold bones.

He slid his feet into the stirrups on its thighs, and tightened the metal straps round his ankles. A complicated harness fastened his upper body into its rib cage.

"A cold embrace," he said.

He positioned his hands so as to reach certain levers that projected from the bones above its elbow joint. Its jawless skull he hinged forward to fit over his head like a helmet. He lay there for a moment, strapped to the thing like a man crucified on a tree of insane design.

"I power it up now," he explained. He worked levers. A low, distinct humming filled the air. A smell of ozone reminded Cromis of the airboat disaster at Balmacara. "Ah," said Tomb. He manipulated studs and switches.

The skeleton twitched its huge steel bones.

Tomb sniggered.

He moved his arm, and a fleshless metal hand rose into the air. It made grasping motions. It flexed its fingers.

Tomb bent his legs, and came slowly to his feet. He was eleven feet tall.

"Where's my chopper?" he said. And, having found that weapon, he broke into a grotesque, capering dance, swinging it round his head in ecstatic but deadly figures of eight, lifting his new legs high to display them, pointing his nimble silver-steel toes.

"I'll *shorten* them!" he screamed, the wind whistling through his mechanical limbs. He ignored the helpless, delighted laughter of his friends. "I'll cut the sods!" He didn't say who. "Beautiful!" he crowed. And he stormed off, a gigantic paradox suspended on the thin line between comedy and horror, to test his machine by completing a full circuit of the encampment under the amazed eyes of fifteen thousand sensible fighting men.

Neither the Methven nor their tiny force of brigands ever signed up officially with Lord Waterbeck's army. His estimation of the Moidart's rate of progress toward Duirinish proved to be a little optimistic. An hour before dawn the next day, ten airboats bearing the sigil of the wolf's head and three towers howled over the northern ridge, their motors in overdrive.

Cromis was to be haunted for the rest of his life by his failure to understand how a general could become so concerned with the administration of his men and the politics of his war that he neglected the reports of his own reconnaissance corps.

6

Cromis was asleep when the attack began. In the soft, black space of his head a giant insect hovered and hummed, staring gloomily at him from human eyes, brushing the walls of his skull with its swift wings and unbearable, fragile legs. He did not understand its philosophy. The ideographs engraved on its thorax expressed a message of Time and the Universe, which he learned by heart and immediately forgot. The whine of the wings deepened in pitch, and resolved itself into the monstrous wail of the Moidart's aircraft.

Birkin Grif was punching his shoulder repeatedly and yelling in his ear. He stumbled up, shaking the dream from his head. He saw Tomb the Dwarf scuttle out of the caravan, fling himself onto his exoskeleton, and begin powering up. All around, men were shouting, pointing at the sky, their mouths like damp pits. The noise from Waterbeck's camp was tremendous; fifteen thousand simultaneous inarticulate cries of anger and fear.

He strapped on his sword. "We're too exposed!" They could do nothing about it. Long, fast shapes gyred above them, dim in the light of false dawn.

Evil red flares lit the valley as a section of the attacking squadron located Waterbeck's airboat park and began to bombard it with barrels of burning pitch and large stones. The remainder of the fleet separated and shrieked low over the encampment, dropping their loads at random to panic men and horses.

A detachment of Waterbeck's troops began firing one of the only three operative power-cannon that remained in the kingdom, its pale violet bolts flaming up like reversed bolide trails against a dark sky.

Grif harried his men. Between them, they regained control of the horses.

Despite the efforts of Waterbeck's own airboat men, two machines were destroyed—their spines broken, their ancient energies earthing away—before the rest of his meagre wing hurled into the sky. The energy cannon ceased firing immediately once they were airborne, and the battle moved away from the ground.

Two boats, locked together and leaking strange pastel fireflies of released energy, drifted slowly over the encampment and vanished behind the southern ridge. Cromis shuddered: small dark shapes were falling from them, soundless and pathetic.

"Had I made a different choice, I might be up there now," murmured Tomb the Dwarf, looming up out of the red glare of the pitch fires. He sounded almost wistful.

"Cromis, there's something wrong with your vulture."

The bird was strutting to and fro on the roof of the caravan, where it had perched during the night. It extended its neck as if to vomit, beat its great iridium wings together, and squawked insanely. It made short, hopping sallies into the air. Suddenly, it shrieked:

"Go at once! Go at once! Go at once!"

It launched itself off the roof and fastened its talons on Cromis's arm. It bobbed its head, peered into his face.

"tegeus-Cromis, you should leave here at once and go to—"

But Cromis hardly heard. He was watching Canna Moidart's captains as they swarmed down the face of the northern ridge and into the valley—their standards raised high, thirty thousand Northmen at their backs, and the *geteit chemosit* coming on in dark waves before them.

Time bucked and whipped like a broken hawser in Cromis's head, and for a moment he existed at two separate and distinct points along its curve—

In a dark glade by a stinking pool, he fought a great black shadow some seven or eight feet high. Its limbs were thick and heavy, its head a blunted ovoid, featureless but for three glowing points set in an isosceles triangle. Its movements were powerful and controlled. It hissed as it wielded its enormous energy-blade, and left strange, shapeless imprints in the mud beneath it. There was an alien coldness about it; a calm, calculated intelligence—

Simultaneously, in the irrefutable present of the Great Brown Waste, he observed with unemotional preciseness the terrible skirmish line that advanced into the valley ahead of the Moidart's horde. Each of its units was a great black shadow seven or eight feet high, wielding an immense energy blade. Their movements were alien and silky and controlled, and their unpleasant triplex eyes glittered yellowly from blunt, ovoid heads—

"Beware the *geteit chemosit*!" cried the vulture on his arm.

Sick and shaking, he explored an understanding that had been open to him since his fight in the Metal-Salt Marsh.

"I should have listened," he said. "We have no chance," he whispered.

"We have more than poor Waterbeck, perhaps," murmured Birkin Grif. He put a hand on Cromis's shoulder. "If we live, we will go to Lendalfoot and see the metal bird's owner. They are golems, automatic men, some filthy thing she has dug up from a dead city. He may know—"

"Nothing like this has been seen in the world for a thousand years," said Tomb the Dwarf. "Where did she *find* them?"

Unconcerned by such questions, Canna Moidart's black mechanical butchers moved implacably toward the first engagement in the War of the Two Queens: a war that was later to be seen as the mere opening battle of a wholly different—and greatly more tragic—conflict.

Their impact on Waterbeck's army was brutal. Already disorganised and disconcerted by the airboat raid, scattered, separated from their commanding officers, the Viriconese milled about their ruined encampment in a desperate and feeble attempt to form some sort of defensive position.

Faced by a human antagonist, they might have held their shaky line. Certainly, there burned in all of them a hatred of the Northmen which might in other circumstances have overcome their tactical weakness and stiffened their resistance. But the *chemosit* slaughtered their self-possession.

They sobbed and died. They were hastily conscripted, half-trained. Powered blades cut their swords like cheese. Their armour failed to armour them. They discovered that they did not belong there.

In the moment of first contact, a fine red mist sprayed up from the battleline, and the dying inhaled the substance of the dead while the living fought on in the fog, wondering why they had left their shops and their farms. Many of them simply died of shock and revulsion as the blood arced and spurted to impossible heights from the severed arteries of their fellows, and the air was filled with the stink of burst innards.

When the Moidart's regular troops joined the battle, they found little but confusion to check them. They howled with laughter and rattled their swords against their shields. They flanked Waterbeck's depleted force, split it into small, useless detachments, overran his pavilion, and tore him to pieces. They ringed the Viriconese and hammered them steadily against the grim anvil of the still-advancing *chemosit*. But there was resistance—

In the dead airboat park, someone managed to depress the barrel of the

energy cannon enough to fire it horizontally. For some seconds, its mete-
oric bolts—almost invisible in the daylight—hissed and spurted into the
unbroken rank of the mechanical men. For a moment, it looked like it dis-
comfitted them; several burned like torches and then exploded, destroying
others. But a small squad detached themselves from the main body, and,
their power-blades chopping in unison, reached the gun with ease. It sputtered and went out, like a candle in the rain, and the gunners with it—

And, from a vantage point on the roof of Tomb's caravan, Lord tegeus-
Cromis of Viriconium, who imagined himself a better poet than swordsman, chose his moment. "They make their own underbelly soft. Their only
strength lies in the *chemosit*." His head was full of death. The metal bird
was on his arm. "To the south there, they are completely open." He
turned to Birkin Grif. "We could kill a lot of them if your men were
willing."

Grif unsheathed his sword and smiled. He jumped to the ground. He
mounted his roan mare (in the grey light, her caparisons shone bravely)
and faced his ugly, dishonest crew. "We will all die," he told them. He
bared his teeth at them and they grinned back like old foxes. "Well?"

They stropped their evil knives against their leather leggings. "What are
we waiting for?" asked one of them.

"You bloody fools!" yelled Grif, and roared with laughter. "Nobody
asked you to do this!"

They shouted and catcalled. They leapt into their saddles and slapped
their knees in enjoyment of the joke. They were a gangrel, misfit lot.

Cromis nodded. He did not want to speak, but, "Thank you," he said
to them. His voice was lost in the clangour of Waterbeck's defeat.

"I am already halfway there," chuckled Tomb the Dwarf. He adjusted
some of his levers. He swung his axe a couple of times, just to be sure.

Theomeris Glyn sniffed. "An old man," he said, "deserves better. Why
are we wasting time?" He looked a fool, and entirely vulnerable in his battered old helmet. He should have been in bed.

"Let's go then," said Cromis. He leapt down from the roof. He
mounted up, the iridium vulture flapping above him. He drew the nameless sword. And with no battle cries at all, forty smugglers, three Methven,
and a giant dwarf hurled themselves into a lost fight. What else could they
have done?

The dead and the half-dead lay in mounds, inextricably mixed. The ancient, unforgiving dust of the Great Brown Waste, recalling the crimes of
the Departed Cultures, sucked greedily at these charnel heaps, and turned
into mud. Some five thousand of Waterbeck's original force were still on
their feet, concentrated in three or four groups, the largest of which had

made its stand out of the bloody morass, on a long, low knoll at the centre of the valley.

The momentum of the charge carried Cromis twenty yards into the press without the need to strike a blow: Northmen fell to the hooves and shoulders of his horse and were trampled. He shouted obscenities at them, and made for the knoll, the smugglers a flying wedge behind him. A pike-man tore a long strip of flesh from the neck of his mount; Cromis hung out of the saddle and swung for the carotid artery; blade bit, and, splashed with the piker's gore, the horse reared and screamed in triumph. Cromis hung on and cut about him, laughing. The stink of horse sweat and leather and blood was as sharp as a knife.

To his left, Tomb the Dwarf towered above the Northmen in his exo-skeleton, a deadly, glittering, giant insect, kicking in faces with bloodshod metal feet, striking terror and skulls with his horrible axe. On his right, Birkin Grif whirled his broadsword unscientifically about and sang, while murderous old Glyn taunted his opponents and stabbed them cunningly when they thought they had him. "We did things differently when I was your age!" he told them. And, like a visitation from Hell, Cellur's metal vulture tore the eyes from its victims but left them living.

They had cut a path halfway to the knoll, yelling encouragement to its labouring defenders, when Cromis glimpsed among the many pennants of the Northern tribes the banner of the wolf's head. He determined to bring it down, and with it whatever general or champion fought beneath it. He hoped—vainly—that it might be the Moidart herself. "Grif!" he shouted. "Take your lads on to the hill!"

He reined his horse around and flung it like a javelin at a wall of Northerners who, dropping their gaudy shields in panic, reeled away from the death that stared out of his wild eyes and lurked in his bloody weapon.

"Methven!" he cried.

He couched the butt of a dead man's pike firmly underneath his arm and used it as a lance. He called for the champion under the standard and issued lunatic challenges. He lost the lance in a Northman's belly.

He killed a score of frightened men. He was mad with the horror of his own bloodlust. He saw no faces on the ones he sent to Hell, and the face of fear on all the rest. He spoke poetry to them, unaware of what he said, or that he said it in a language of his own invention—but his sanity re-turned when he heard the voice of the man beneath the wolf's head.

"You were a fool to come here, tegeus-Cromis. After I have finished, I will give you to my wolves—"

"Why have you done this?" whispered Cromis.

The turncoat's face was long and saturnine, his mouth wide and mobile, thin-lipped under a drooping moustache. A wrinkled scar, left long ago by the knife of Thorisman Carlemaker, ran from the corner of one deep-set grey eye, ruching the skin of his cheek. His black, curling hair fell round the shoulders of a purple velvet cloak he had once worn at the Court of King Methven. He sat his heavy horse with confidence, and his mouth curled in contempt.

"Waterbeck is dead," he said. "If you have come to sue for peace on behalf of his rabble"—here, the surrounding Northmen howled and beat their hands together—"I may be lenient. The Queen has given me wide powers of discretion."

Shaking with reaction to his berserk fit, Cromis steadied himself against the pommel of his saddle. He was bemused. A little of him could not believe what was happening.

"I came here for single combat with Canna Moidart's champion. Have I found him?"

"You have."

The traitor nodded, and the Moidart's foot soldiers drew back to form an arena. They grinned and whistled, shook their shields. Elsewhere, the battle continued, but it might have been on another planet.

"What did she offer you? Was it worth the pain you caused Carron Ban?"

The man beneath the wolf's head smiled.

"There is a vitality in the North, Lord Cromis, that was lost to Viriconium when Methven died. She offered me an expanding culture in return for a dead one."

Cromis shook his head, and lifted the nameless sword.

"Our old friendship means nothing to you?"

"It will make you a little harder to kill, Lord Cromis."

"I am glad you admit to that. Perhaps it is harder for the betrayer than for the betrayed. Norvin Trinor, you are a turncoat and a fool."

With the jeers of the encircling Northmen in his ears, he kicked his horse forward.

Trinor's heavy blade swung at his head. He parried the stroke, but it had already shifted into a lateral motion which he was forced to evade by throwing himself half out of his saddle. Trinor chuckled, locked his foot under Cromis's left stirrup in an effort to further unseat him. Cromis dropped his reins, took his sword in his left hand, and stuck it between the heaving ribs of the turncoat's mount. Blood matting its coat, the animal swerved away, compelling Trinor to disengage.

"You *used* to be the best sword in the empire, Lord Cromis," he panted. "What happened to you?"

"I am ill with treachery," said Cromis, and he was. "It will pass."

They fought for five minutes, then ten, heedless of the greater conflict.

It seemed to Cromis that the entire battle was summed up here, in a meeting of champions who had once been friends, and at each brief engagement, he grew more despairing.

He saw Carron Ban's hurt, disdainful face through the shining web of her traitor-husband's blade, but it gave him no strength; he understood that she had felt pity for him that night in Viriconium, knowing that this confrontation must take place. He saw also that he was unable to match the hate she felt for Trinor: at each encounter, something slowed the nameless sword, and he was moved to pity rather than anger by the sneers of his opponent.

But finally, his swordsmanship told, and in a queer way: Trinor's horse, which had been steadily losing blood from the wound in its side, fell abruptly to its knees in the disgusting mud. The turncoat kept his seat, but dropped his sword.

He sat there, absolutely still, on the foundered animal. The Northmen groaned, and moved forward: the combat circle tightened like a noose.

"You had better get on with it," murmured Trinor. He shrugged. "The wolves will have you anyway, Lord Cromis—see how they close in!—and the Pastel City along with you. They are a hungry lot."

"You had better get it over with."

tegeus-Cromis raised the nameless sword for the fatal stroke. He spat down into the face before him: but it was still the face of a friend. He shuddered with conflicting desires.

He raised his eyes to the ring of Northmen who waited to take his blood in exchange for Trinor's. He moaned with rage and frustration, but he could not drown out the voices of the past within him. "*Keep* your bloody champion!" he cried. "Kill him yourself, for he'll betray you, too!" And he turned his horse on its haunches, smashed into their astonished ranks like a storm from the desert, and howled away into the honest carnage of the battlefield as if the gates of Hell had opened behind him.

A long time later, at the foot of the knoll in the centre of the valley, two Northern pikemen unhorsed him, and wondered briefly why he apologised as he rolled from his wrecked animal to kill them.

"I could not kill him, Grif."

It was the second hour after dawn. A cold, peculiar light filtered through the low cloud base, greying the dead faces on the corpse heaps, striking mysterious reflections from their eyes. The wind keened in off the waste, stirring bloody hair and fallen pennants. Four wallowing Northern airboats hung beneath the clouds like omens seen in a dream. The entire valley was a sea of Northmen, washing black and implacable against one tiny eyot of resistance.

Up on the knoll, Birkin Grif led perhaps two hundred of Waterbeck's troops: all those who had not died or fled into the waste. A score of his own men still lived: their eyes were red-rimmed and sullen in worn, grimy faces. They stank of sweat and blood. They stared silently at one another and readied their notched and broken weapons for the last attack.

"I could not do it."

Cromis had fought his way to the top of the hill on foot, aided by Tomb the Dwarf and a handful of the smugglers. The metal bird had led them to him, hovering above him as he fought with the men who had unhorsed him. (Now it perched on his arm, its head and talons covered with congealed blood, and said: "Fear the *geteit chemosit*—" It had said nothing else since he reached the knoll, and he did not care.) He was smeared with other men's brains, suffering from a dozen minor wounds, and there was a pit of horrors in his head. He did not know how he had survived.

"At least you are alive," said Grif. His fat cheeks were sagging with weariness, and when he moved, he favoured his right leg, laid open from knee to ankle in the death struggles of his beautiful mare. "Trinor could have killed any of the rest of us with ease. Except perhaps for Tomb."

Of them all, the dwarf had suffered least: hung up there on his dented exoskeleton, he seemed to have taken strength from the slaughter; his energy axe flickered brightly, and his motor-assisted limbs moved as powerfully as ever. He chuckled morosely, gazing out across the valley.

"I would have done for *him*, all right. But to what point? Look there, Grif: that is our future—"

Out among the corpse heaps, black, huge figures moved on a strange mission, a mechanical ritual a thousand years old. The *geteit chemosit* had lost interest in the fight. Their triplex eyes glittering and shifting as if unanchored to their skulls, they stalked from corpse to corpse. They performed their curious surgery on the lifeless heads—and robbed each Viriconese, like the dead smuggler in the Metal-Salt Marsh, of his brain.

"They will come for us after the Northmen have finished," said Cromis. "What are they *doing*, Tomb?"

"They are beginning the destruction of an empire," answered the dwarf. "They will hack the brains out of the Stony City and eat them. They will take a power-knife and a spoon to Viriconium. Nothing will stop them.

"Indeed, I wonder who are the actual masters of this battleground—it is often unwise to meddle with the artefacts of the Afternoon Cultures."

"*tegeus-Cromis should go at once to the tower of Cellur,*" said the metal bird, but no one listened to it.

Theomeris Glyn, the old campaigner, sat some distance away from the rest of the Methven, hoping to reinvigorate his sword by stropping it on a dead man's boot.

"I think it is starting," he called cheerfully. "They have licked their privates for the last time down there, and gathered up their courage."

With a wild yell, the Northerners threw themselves at the knoll, and it shook beneath the onslaught. A spearcast blackened the air, and when it had cleared, pikemen advanced unimpeded up the lower slopes, gutting the survivors and treading in their wounds.

Behind the pikers came a never-ending wave of swordsmen, and axemen, and berserk metal-prospectors from the northmost reaches of the waste, wielding queer weapons dug from pits in the ground. The shattered, pathetic remnant of Waterbeck's expeditionary force fell back before them, and were overcome, and died. They hit the summit of the hill like some kind of earthquake, and they split the Methven, so that each one fought alone—

Tomb the Dwarf sniggered and swung his greedy axe. He towered above them, and they ran like rats around his silver-steel legs—

Birkin Grif cursed. His sword was shattered at the hilt, so he broke a Northman's neck and stole another. He called to his smugglers, but all that brave and dirty crew were dead—

Old Glyn lunged. "You've never seen this one before," he cackled, as he put his hidden knife in, "eh?" His opponent was astonished—

Cromis ducked and rolled like a fairground acrobat. The metal vulture was above him, the nameless sword was everywhere—

They came together, and made their stand.

"Methven!" cried Cromis, and they answered him. "Methven!"

Something in the grey air caught his eye, a movement beneath the cloud base. But a blade nicked his collarbone, and death demanded his attention. He gave it fully. When he next looked up, there were seven airboats in the sky where there had been four, and three of them bore the arms of Methvet Nian, Queen Jane of Viriconium. "Grif! Up there!"

"If they are couriers," said Grif, "they come a little late."

The crystal launches clashed with a sound like immense bells. As Cromis watched, the Northern squadron commander closed to ram: but the sky exploded suddenly around his ship, and burned, dripping cold fire; and, tail-first and crippled, it dropped out of the sky. Faint violet bolts chased it down.

"There's a cannon aboard one of those ships," said Tomb the Dwarf wonderingly. "It is the Queen's own flight."

Confused by this sudden renaissance in the air, the Northmen drew back from their prey and craned their necks. The dying airboat ploughed through them and blew up, scattering limbs and bits of armour. Howling with rage, they renewed their attack, and the Methven on the hill were hard put to it.

Up above, one of the Viriconese boats left its sister ships to a holding action against the remaining three Northern craft, and began to cruise up and down the valley. But the Methven were unaware of this until its huge shadow passed over them, hesitated, and returned. Tomb crowed. He tore off Cromis's tattered black cloak with a huge steel hand and waved it about above his head. The airboat descended, yawing.

Ten feet above the top of the hill, it swung rapidly on its own axis, and fell like a stone. The energy cannon under its prow pulsed and spat. A hatch opened in its side. Its motors sang.

It was a difficult retreat. The Northmen pressed in, determined to claim what was due to them. Tomb took a blow from a mace behind the knees of his exoskeleton: a servo failed, and he staggered drunkenly, flailing about him.

Cromis found himself some yards away from the open hatch, the old campaigner at his side. They fought silently for a minute.

Then Theomeris Glyn put his back squarely against a pile of corpses and showed the Northmen his teeth. "I don't think I'll come, Cromis," he said. "You'll need some cover." He sniffed. "I don't like flying machines anyway."

"Don't be silly," said Cromis. He touched the old man's arm, to show his gratitude. "We'll make it."

But Glyn drew himself up. His age sloughed away from him. He had lost his helmet, and blood from a gash in his head had clotted in his beard; his padded doublet was in ruins, but the pride in his face shone out clear.

"tegeus-Cromis," he said, "you forget yourself. Age has its privileges, and one of them is to die. You will do me the honour of allowing me to do that in my own way. Get into the ship and I will cover your back. Go. Goodbye."

He met Cromis's eyes.

"I'll gut a few of them, eh?" he said. "Just a few more. Take care."

And Theomeris Glyn, a lord of the Methven despite his years, turned to face his enemies. The last Cromis ever saw of him was a whirling rearguard of steel, a web such as he used to spin when the Old King ruled, and his blood was young.

Trembling violently, blinded by the old man's courage, Cromis stumbled through the hatch. The metal bird rocketed in after him. It was still screaming its useless message of warning: he suspected that its mechanisms had been damaged somehow during the fight. He slammed the hatch shut. Outside, the Northmen were beating their weapons on the hull, searching for another entrance, grunting like frustrated animals.

The ship lurched, spun, hung five or ten feet off the ground. In the green, undersea gloaming of its command bridge, lights moved like dust motes in a ray of alien sun. Navigation instruments murmured and sang. "I'm having some trouble here," said the pilot, conversationally. "Still, not to worry." He was a rakish young man, his hair caught back with a pewter fillet in the fashion of the Courier Corps.

Birkin Grif lay on the vibrating crystal deck, his face white and drained. Bent over his injured leg, a woman in a hooded purple cloak was attempting to staunch the bleeding. He was saying weakly, "My lady, you were a fool to come here—"

She shook her head. Russet hair escaped her hood. Her cloak was fastened at the neck with a copper clasp formed to represent mating dragonflies. Looking at her, Cromis experienced a terrible premonition.

Sprawled in a tangle of silver spars at the base of the navigation table, Tomb the Dwarf struggled with his harness. His ugly face was frantic. "Take her up! Take her up!" he shouted. "Help me out of this, someone—"

"We can expect a bit of fuss when we get up there," said the pilot. "Ah. Got her. Do hold tight—" He opened his throttles. The ship began to climb steeply.

Cromis, stumbling toward the dwarf, was thrown to the deck. He dropped his sword. He hit his head on the fire control of the energy cannon. As he passed out, he recognised the woman in the purple cloak: it was Methvet Nian herself, the Young Queen.

We are all insane, he thought. The Moidart has infected us all with her madness.

7

Shortly after Cromis came to his senses, the airboat was rammed.

Clinging grimly to a stanchion as the daring young courier flung his ship about the dangerous sky, he felt as if he were sitting behind the eyes of a tumbler pigeon: earth and air blurred together in a whirling mandala of brown and grey, across which flickered the deadly silhouettes of the Northern airboats. He was aware that Tomb had finally escaped the embrace of his own armour, that Grif and the Young Queen had wedged themselves against the rear bulkhead of the command bridge.

But his concern with events was abstract—since he could in no way influence the situation—and he had something else to occupy his mind: a speculation, a fear stimulated by the sudden appearance of Methvet Nian—

Abruptly, the portholes darkened. The ship gave a great shudder, and, with a sound like destroyed bells, its entire prow was torn off. Shards of crystal spat and whirred in the gloom. Five feet in front of the pilot, leaving his controls undamaged only by some freak of chance, an enormous hole opened in the hull: through it could be seen briefly the tumbling, receding wreck of the craft that had accomplished the ramming. An icy wind rushed in, howling.

"Oh," murmured the courier. A twelve-inch spike of crystal had split his skull. Three fingers could have been got in the wound with ease. He swayed. "We still have power—if anybody can fly this thing—" he said, puzzledly. "I am sorry, my lady—I don't seem to be—" He fell out of his seat.

Tomb the Dwarf scuttled on all fours across the listing deck to take his place. He fired off the energy cannon, but it tore itself away from the wreckage. "Benedict Paucemanly should see me now," he said. He turned the ship in a wide loop, swung once over the battlefield. He flogged and cajoled it and nursed it over the waste, losing height. Beneath the cloud base, the sole uncrippled ship of the Queen's flight fought a doomed action against the two remaining Northerners.

"Look down there," said Tomb, as they veered over the scene of Waterbeck's rout. "What do you think of that?"

The valley was a gaping wound filled with Northerners and dead men and thick white smoke which surged up from wrecked airboats, obscuring the dark figures of the *geteit chemosit* as they performed their acts of skull rape. The waste surrounding the battlefield was crawling with reptiles: hundreds of stiff, dust-coloured forms, converging slowly from south, east, and west, their motions stilted and strange.

"Every lizard in the Great Brown Waste must be down there. What are they doing?"

"They seem to be watching," said Cromis. "Nothing else." And, indeed, the ridges that flanked the valley were already lined with them, their stony heads unmoving as they gazed at the ruin, their limbs held rigid like those of spectators at some morbid religious observance.

"We fascinate them," said Birkin Grif bitterly. With the boat's return to stability, he had regained his feet. His leg was still bleeding freely. "They are amazed by our propensity for self-destruction." He laughed hollowly. "Tomb, how far can we get in this machine?"

The ship drifted aimlessly, like a waterbird on a quiet current. The waste moved below, haunted by the gathering reptiles.

"Duirinish," said the dwarf. "Or Drunmore. We could not make Viriconium, even if Paucemanly had postponed his flight to the Moon, and sat here at the controls in my place."

Methvet Nian was kneeling over the dead courier, closing his eyes. Her hood was thrown back and her autumn-rowan hair cascaded about her face. Cromis turned from the strange sight of the monitor lizards, his earlier fears returning as he looked at her.

"There is nothing for us in Duirinish," he said, addressing himself only partly to Tomb. "Shortly, it will fall. And I fear that there is little point in our going to the Pastel City." He shook his head. "I suspect you had a reason for coming here, Your Majesty?"

Her violet eyes were wide, shocked. He had never seen anything so beautiful or so sad. He was overcome, and covered his emotion by pretending to hunt in the wreckage of the cabin for his sword.

He came upon the limp carcass of Cellur's metal vulture: like the young courier, it had been torn open by a shard of crystal; its eyes were lifeless, and pieces of tiny, precise machinery spilled out of its breast when he picked it up. He felt an absurd sympathy for it. He wondered if so perfect an imitation of organic life might feel a perfect imitation of pain. He smoothed the huge pinions of its wings.

"Yes, Lord Cromis," whispered the Young Queen. "This morning, the rebels rose again. Canna Moidart will find resistance only in Duirinish. Viriconium is in the hands of her supporters—

"My lords," she appealed, "what will become of those people? They have embraced a viper—"

And she wept openly.

"They will be bitten," said Birkin Grif. "They were not worthy of you, Queen Jane."

She wiped her eyes. The Rings of Neap glittered on her thin fingers. She drew herself up straight and gazed steadily at him.

"You are too harsh, Birkin Grif. Perhaps the failure was not in them, but in their queen."

They drifted for some hours over the waste, heading south. Tomb the Dwarf nursed his failing vehicle with a skill almost matching that of his tutor and master (no one knew if Paucemanly had actually attempted the moon trip in his legendary boat *Heavy Star*: certainly, he had vanished from the face of the earth after breaking single-handed Carlemaker's air siege of Mingulay, and most fliers had a fanatical faith in the tale . . .) and brought them finally to Ruined Drunmore in the Pass of Methedrin, the city thrown down by Borring half a century before.

During that limping journey, they discussed treachery:

"If I had Norvin Trinor's neck between my hands, I would break it lightheartedly," said Birkin Grif, "even with pleasure, although I liked him once."

He winced, binding up his leg.

"He has blackened all of us," murmured Cromis. "As a body, the Methven have lost their credibility."

But the Queen said, "It is Carron Ban who has my sympathy. Women are more used to betrayal than men, but take it deeper."

It is the urgent and greedy desire of all wastes to expand and eat up more-fertile lands: this extension of their agonised peripheries lends them a semblance of the movement and life they once possessed. As if seeking protection from the slow southward march of the Rust Desert, Ruined Drunmore huddled against an outflung spur of the Monar Mountains.

In this, it failed, for drifts of bitter dust topped its outer walls, spilling and trickling into the streets below every time a wind blew.

The same winds scoured its streets, and, like an army of indifferent housekeepers, swept the sand through the open doors and shattered roofs of the inner city, choking every abandoned armoury and forge and barracks. The erosion of half a millennium had etched its cobbled roads, smoothed and blunted the outlines of its ruins, until its once-proud architecture had become vernacular, fit for its equivocal position between the mountains and the waste.

Even as a ruin, Drunmore was pitiful: Time and geography had choked it to death.

Towards the end of the flight, a wide rift had appeared suddenly in the deck of the airboat, exposing the ancient engines. Now, as they hovered over the city, flecks of coloured light, small writhing worms of energy, rose up out of the crack, clung to the metal surfaces of the command bridge, fastened on the inert carcass of the mechanical vulture, and clustered about the Queen's rings.

Tomb grew nervous. "Corpse lights," he muttered. He brought the machine down in Luthos Plaza, the four-acre field of Time-polished granite from which Borring had organised the destruction of Drunmore so many generations before.

Grif and Cromis dragged the dead courier from his ruined ship and buried him in a deep drift of loess on the southern side of the plaza. It was a queer and sombre business. The Queen looked on, her cowl pulled forward, her cloak fluttering. They were impelled to work slowly, for they had only their hands for shovels. As they completed the interment, great white sparks began to hiss and crackle between the shattered crystal hull and the surrounding buildings.

"We would be wiser out of this," suggested Tomb, who had been carrying out salvage work, as was his nature, and promptly rushed back into the wreckage to steal more tools and retrieve his exoskeleton. After that, they made their way through the bone-smooth streets until Grif could walk no further, the damp wind mourning about them and Tomb's armour clanking funereally as he dragged it along.

Under the one unbroken roof that remained (like a static stone haunting, like a five-hundred-year memory) in the city, amid piles of dust younger than the waste but older than the empire, they lit a fire and prepared a meal from the miserable stores of the wrecked machine. Shadows danced crudely, black on the black walls. The sun had gone down in a gout of blood.

At the prompting of some impulse he did not quite understand, Cromis had rescued the corpse of Cellur's bird from the ship. While they ate, he explained its nature to the Young Queen, and Tomb probed its mechanisms with a thin steel knife.

"... We know nothing more of this man. But by sending the bird, he warned us—the fact that I did not heed the warning in no way devalues it—of the *geteit chemosit*. It may be that he has some way of dealing with them."

Birkin Grif chewed a strip of dried meat. He laughed.

"That is pure conjecture," he said.

"It is the only hope we have. Grif. There is nothing else."

"He is very clever with his hands," cackled Tomb the Dwarf, poking at the innards of the bird. He thought for a moment. "Or, like Canna Moidart, good at digging."

"So, if you do not object, my lady, we will travel to Girvan Bay and solicit his aid. Should there be some secure place to which we can deliver you first—"

"Places do not guarantee security, Lord Cromis, only people"—here, she smiled at him—"a thing we have both learned recently, I think." He reflected ruefully that it was unwise to forget the astuteness of the House of Methven. "And, besides, I have been safe for seventeen years. I think I would like to be at risk for a while."

A huge, urgent lurching motion manifested itself on the other side of the fire like a local geological disturbance. Birkin Grif had heaved himself to his feet. He looked down at the Young Queen, mumbling subterraneanly to himself. He bowed from the waist.

"Madam," he said, "you have the courage of your father. That is a brave attitude." He sat down again. "Mind you," he added in a low voice to Tomb, "it's a bloody long trip for a man in my condition."

Queen Jane of Viriconium laughed for the first time since she had lost her empire. Which shows at least, thought Cromis, the resilience of youth. He did not mean to condescend.

They stayed in that city for five days. A processing centre in the heyday of the Northmen, perhaps it welcomed the ring of Tomb's hammer as he worked on his damaged armour—a loop in Time, a faint, distorted echo from a past in which other mechanics had beaten the subtle artefacts of the Afternoon Cultures into cruder, more vital forms.

Grif's leg was slow to heal; exertion reopened it; the blood seemed slow to clot, and he found walking difficult. Like a convalescing child, he was prone to brief, silly rages. He limped and fretted about, railing at his own limitations. Finally, he forced himself to walk to the wreck in Luthos Plaza, tear a slim cobalt girder from the destroyed engine housing, and bend it into a crutch.

It was an unfortunate admission. His gait thereafter was laborious, unsteady—and Tomb, a cruel humourist, imitated it gleefully, stumbling and capering like a crippled acrobat. That parody was a horrid work of art.

Grif lost his temper, and implied that the power-armour was a less respectable kind of crutch. They went for one another murderously, all hooked hands and cunning blows, and had to be separated forcibly. They took to cutting each other dead in the bleak streets.

"You are preposterous," Cromis told them.

To Methvet Nian he said, "They are bored with inaction; we will leave here tomorrow," but later that day two airboats bearing the Moidart's sigil ghosted in off the waste and hung over the plaza. Northmen swarmed down rope ladders to examine the burnt-out launch, kicked noisily through the wreckage, looking for souvenirs.

Cromis took his small party to earth in the archaic suburbs of Drunmore. But it became apparent that the airborne force was the vanguard of an attempt to reoccupy the city after half a millennium's absence, so they left the place that night, and went undetected into the cold spaces of the Pass of Methedrin.

They began their journey down the Rannoch:

It was a land of immense, barely populated glacial moors, flanked by the tall hills—of bogs and peat streams—of granite boulders split from the Mountains of Monar during slow, unimaginable catastrophes of ice, deposited to wear away in the beds of wide, fast, shallow rivers;

Of bright green moss, and coarse, olive-green grass, and delicate, washed-out winter flowers discovered suddenly in the lee of low, worn drumlins—of bent thorn and withered bullace, of damp prevailing winds that searched for voices in stands of birch and pine;

Of skylines, wrinkled with ridges;

Of heather and gorse, grey cloud and *weather*—of sudden open stretches of white water that would swell in spring, dwindle and vanish with the coming of summer—mysterious waterways;

It was green and brown, green and grey; it grew no crops; it constituted one quarter of the Empire of Viriconium.

At dawn each day, Cromis would leave his blankets, shivering, to inspect whatever snares he had set the night before: generally, he caught rabbits and waterlogged his boots, but he took a morose pleasure in these solitary outings. Something in the resigned, defeated landscape (or was it simply waiting to be born? Who can tell at which end of Time these places have their existence?) called out to his senses, demanded his attention and understanding.

He never found out what it was. Puzzling, he would return with his catch, to wake the camp and initiate another day of walking.

They were a ragged crew, a queer crew to be walking down the Rannoch like that: Tomb crucified in his leather leggings against the metal tree of his exoskeleton, never tiring, going like a machine over bog and river, leaping ravines and cutting down whole spinneys with his axe; Birkin Grif in the ruins of his splendid cobalt mail, hopping and lurching, cursing his crutch like a mad scarecrow; Cromis, his beautiful black hair lank in the damp wind, the dead metal bird dangling limply by its neck from his belt, stopping to gaze at waterworn stone by the hour—

And Methvet Nian in her purple cloak, discovering a portion of her lost empire, and of herself. "Towers are not everything, Lord Cromis!" she laughed, and she took his arm. "They are *not*!" She brought him flowers and was disappointed when he could not identify them for her. He showed her crows and mountains, and expected no identification at all. He smiled; he was not used to that. They were thrown together by small observations.

In this way, they covered twenty miles a day.

During the third week, it snowed. Ice crusted the rivers, rock cracked and broke above the thousand-foot line of the flanking hills. Cromis found his traps full of white hares and albino foxes with red, intelligent eyes. Birkin Grif killed a snow leopard with his crutch: for ferocity, it was an even match until the last blow.

For a week, they lived with a community of herders, small, dark-haired folk with strange soft accents, to whom the war in the North and West was but a rumour. They gave the Queen a sheepskin coat; they were shy and kind. As a measure of gratitude, Tomb the Dwarf cut wood from dawn to dusk, while Grif sat with his bad leg stretched in front of him and split it into enough kindling for a year (they became friends again as a result of this: neither of them loved anything better than cutting and chopping).

Everything began to seem distant: the snow was an insulator. Cromis forced himself to keep in mind the defeat in the North. It was important to his brooding nature that he remember the terrible blades of the *geteit chemosit*. He imagined them. He saw them lay siege to Duirinish in his head. Would the winter halt them at all?

After seven days of that, and a further fortnight of travel in the grim mountains at the southern end of the Rannoch, he was glad to see the arable lands around Lendalfoot and catch a glimpse at last of the grey sea breaking on the dark volcanic beaches of Girvan Bay.

Lendalfoot was a fishing town built of pale fawn stone, a cluster of one-roomed cottages and long drying sheds, their edges weathered, blurred by accumulations of moss and lichen. Here and there rose the tall white houses of local dignitaries. In the summer, fine pink sand blown off the shifting dunes of Girvan Bay filled its steep, winding streets; the fishwives argued bare-armed in the sun; and creaking carts carried the catch up the Great South Road into Soubridge.

But now the waves bit spitefully the shingle beach. The sea heaved, the mad black gulls fought over the deserted deep-water jetties, and the moored boats jostled one another uneasily.

Determined that news of the Young Queen should not travel north by way of the fish route, Cromis sent Tomb into Lendalfoot to pose as a solitary traveller and gather certain information (he stumped off sulkily, stripped of his power-armour so as not to alarm the fishermen, but refusing to give up his axe), then retired with Methvet Nian and Birkin Grif to a barren basalt hill behind the town.

The dwarf returned jauntily, throwing up and catching a small, wizened apple, which had been given to him (he said) by an old woman. "She was as dried up as her fruit," he laughed. "She must have thought I was a child." More likely, he had stolen it.

"It was a good thing I went alone: they are frightened and surly down there. News has come down the road to Soubridge." He crunched the apple. "The Moidart has taken Low Leedale, thrown down Duirinish—with great loss of life—and now marches on Viriconium.

"Between the Pastel City and Soubridge, the *geteit chemosit* are abroad by night, killing with no reason."

He ate the apple core, spat the pips impudently at Birkin Grif—who was sharpening his sword with a piece of sandstone he kept in his belt for that purpose—and lay down on his exoskeleton. "They have given me directions, more or less precise." He strapped himself up, rose to his feet, once more a giant. He pointed out over the basalt cliffs, his motors humming.

"Our goal lies east and a little inland. The fishermen cooled further toward me when they learnt of my destination: they have little like of this Cellur. He is seen rarely, an old man. They regard him superstitiously, and call him 'The Lord of the Birds.' "

8

In each of them had grown a compulsion to avoid roads and centres of population: by this, they were driven to travel the wilderness that stretches from Lendalfoot to the Cladich Marshes—a hinterland ruined and botched when the Afternoon Cultures were nothing but a dream in the germ-plasm of an ape, a stony wreckage of deep ravines and long-dormant volcanic vents.

"It is a poor empire I have," said Methvet Nian, "win or lose. Everywhere, the death of the landscape. In miniature, the end of the world."

No one answered her, and she drew her hood over her face.

It had not snowed in the South, but a continual rain lashed the grey and leafless vegetation, glossed the black basalt and pumice, and made its way in the form of agitated streams through the ravines to the sea. At night, electrical flares danced about the summits of the dead volcanoes, and the columnar basalt formations took on the aspect of a giant architecture.

As they went, they were shadowed and haunted by birds—ominous cruciform silhouettes high against the angry sky.

They reached the tower of Cellur in the evening of the second day. Cresting a ridge of pitted dolerite, they came upon the estuary of one of the unnamed rivers that ran from the mountains behind Cladich. Luminous in the fading light, the water spread itself before them like a sheet of metal. High black escarpments dropped sheer to its dark beaches; the cold wind made ephemeral, meaningless patterns on its surface.

Set in the shallows near the western bank was a small domed island, joined to the mainland by a causeway of crumbling stone blocks. It was barren but for a stand of white, dead pines.

Out of the pines, like a stone finger diminished by distance, rose the tower. It was five-faced, tapering: black. A tiny light shone near its summit, a glow that flickered, came and went. Birds wheeled about it, wailing mournfully, dipping to skim the water—fish eagles of a curious colour, with wings like cloaks in a gale.

"There is nothing for us here," said Birkin Grif abruptly. "Only a lunatic would choose to live here. Those fishermen had the right of it."

But Cromis, who understood isolation, and was reminded of his own tower among the rowans of Balmacara, shook his head. "It is what we came for, Grif. Those birds: look, they are not made of flesh." He touched the corpse of the iridium vulture hanging from his belt. "We will go down."

The estuary was filled with a brown, indecisive light, the island dark and ill-defined, enigmatic. The creaking of the dead pines came clearly across the intervening water on the wind. From a beach composed of fine basalt grit and littered with skull-sized lumps of volcanic glass, they mounted the causeway. Its stones were soapy and rotten; parts of it were submerged under a few inches of water.

They were forced to go in single file, Cromis bringing up the rear. As they drew nearer the island, Tomb the Dwarf unlimbered his axe, and Grif, drawing his broadsword a little way out of its scabbard, scowled about him as if he suspected a conspiracy against his person on the part of the landscape.

With damp feet, they stood before the tower.

It had been formed in some unimaginable past from a single obsidian monolith two hundred feet long by seventy or eighty in diameter; raised on its end by some lost, enormous trick of engineering; and fused smoothly at its base into the bedrock of the island. Its five facets were sheer and polished; in each was cut twenty tall, severe windows. No sound came from it; the light at its summit had vanished; a stony path led through the ghostly pines to its door.

Tomb the Dwarf chuckled gently to himself. "They built to last," he said proudly to Cromis, as if he had personally dug the thing up from a desert. "You can't deny that." He strutted between the trees, his armour silver and skeletal in the dusk. He reversed his axe and thundered on the door with its haft.

"Come out!" he shouted. "Come out!" He kicked it, and his metal leg rang with the blow, but no one came. Up above their heads, the fish eagles made restless circles. Cromis felt Methvet Nian draw closer to him. "Come on out, Birdmaker!" called Tomb. "Or I'll chop your gate to matchwood," he added. "Oh, I'll *carve* it!"

Soft but distinct in the silence that followed this threat, there came a dry, reedy laugh.

Birkin Grif cursed foully. "At your backs!" he bellowed, lugging out his heavy blade. Horrified by his own lack of foresight, Cromis turned to meet the threat from behind. Sweat was on his brow, the nameless sword was in his hand. Up above, the fish eagles gyred like ghosts, screaming. The pathway through the pines yawned—a tunnel, a trap, a darkness. He aimed a savage overhand stroke in the gloom, a cut that was never completed.

It was Cellur of Lendalfoot who stood there, the Birdmaker.

The Lord of the Birds was so old that he seemed to have outstripped the mere physical symptoms of his age and passed into a Timelessness, a state of exaltation.

His long, domed skull was fleshless, but his skin was smooth and taut and unwrinkled, so fine and tight as to be almost translucent. His bones shone through it, like thin and delicate jade. It had a faint, yellow tint, in no way unhealthy, but strange.

His eyes were green, clear, and amused; his lips were thin.

He wore a loose, unbelted black robe—quilted in grouped arrangements of lozenges—which was embroidered in gold wire patterns resembling certain geometries cut into the towers of the Pastel City: those queer and uneasy signs that might equally have been the visual art or the language or the mathematics of Time itself.

They had this property: that, when he moved, they seemed to shift and flow of their own accord, divorced entirely from the motions of the cloth of which they were a part.

"Hold your weapon, my lord," he murmured, as the point of the nameless sword hovered indecisively at his old throat. He eyed the dead lammergeyer dangling from Cromis's belt.

"I see by my bird that you are tegeus-Cromis. You have already left your visit too long. It would be a pity if you were to compound the error by killing the one you came to see."

He laughed.

"Come. We will go in—" He indicated his tower. "You must introduce me to your energetic friend with the power-axe. He would like to kill me, I feel, but he must save that pleasure. No dwarf likes to be made a butt. Ah well."

Stubborn Grif, however, would have none of it. When Cromis put up his sword, he showed no sign of following. He confronted the old man.

"You are either fool or malefactor," he said, "to risk death, as you have just done, for such a silly trick. In coming here, we have killed more men than you have eaten hot meals, and many for less than that practical joke.

"I should like proof that you are the former, senile but well-meaning, before I enter your house.

"How, for instance, would any of us know that you *are* Cellur of Lendalfoot, and not some reproduction as cunningly fashioned as the bird?"

The old man nodded. He smiled.

"You would know by this, perhaps—"

He raised his arms and tipped back his head until he was gazing up into the darkening spaces where the fish eagles flew. The diagrams on his robe appeared to fluoresce and writhe. From his throat he forced a wild, loud cry, a shriek compounded of desolation and salt beaches, of wind and sea—the call of a seabird.

Immediately, the eagles halted their aimless gyring about the summit of the tower. One by one, they folded their great ragged wings, and, returning the cry, fell out of the sky, the wind humming past them.

For a moment, the air about the Birdmaster was full of sound and motion. He vanished in a storm of wings: and when he reappeared, it was with an eagle perched on each of his outspread arms and ten more on the earth before him.

"They have been constructed, you see," he said, "to respond to a vocal code. They are very quick."

Birkin Grif sheathed his weapon. "I apologise," he said.

From the shadows by the door, Tomb the Dwarf sniggered quietly. He shifted his flickering axe to one shoulder, and came forward, his armour clanking dismally. He held out one huge metal hand to the old man.

"Fool or no, that is a trick I should like to learn." He studied the perfect iridium plumage of the birds. "We will make a pact, old man. Teach me to build such things, and I will forget that I am a sensitive and evil-minded dwarf. I am sorry I threatened to mutilate your door."

Cellur inclined his head gravely.

"I regret that it would have been impossible anyway. You shall learn, my friend. It is necessary that one of you be taught . . . certain operations. Come."

He led them into the tower.

It was an ancient place, full of the same undersea gloaming that haunted the airboats of the Afternoon Cultures. There were ten floors, each one a single pentagonal room.

Three of these were given over to personal space, couched and carpeted; the remainder housed equipment of an equivocal nature, like the sculptures unearthed from the waste. Light curtains hung and drifted; there were captured electrical voices whose function was obscure—

"Green," they whispered. "Ten *green*. Counting."

Tomb the Dwarf walked among them, his expression benign and silly.

Suddenly, he said, "I have wasted forty years. I should have been *here*, not picking over the detritus of deserts—"

Incomplete carcasses of metal birds lay on the workbenches: there were eagle owls, and martial eagles, and a black-shouldered kite complete but inert, awaiting some powering-up ritual that would put life into its small and savage eye.

And in the last room, at the summit of the tower, there were five false windows, most precise duplicates of those that lined the throne room at Viriconium and showed landscapes to be found nowhere in the Empire. . . .

There, after they had refreshed themselves, Cellur the Birdmaker told them in his dry manner of the *geteit chemosit,* and his own strange life:

I have (he said) waited for some time for your arrival. You must understand that there is very little time left. I must have your cooperation if my intervention in this affair is to become concrete and positive. I should have had it earlier. Never mind.

Now: you are aware of the threat posed to Viriconium by Canna Moidart. You are not, however, aware of the more basic threat implicit in her use of what the Northmen—from their trough of ignorance and superstition— have called *geteit chemosit,* that is to say, "the brain stealers."

This threat I must make clear: to do that—and, simultaneously, to set your minds at rest about my own position—I must tell you a little about myself and my queer abode. Please, sir, do not interrupt. It will speed things if you save your questions until I have outlined the broad picture.

Well.

Firstly, I want to make it clear that my involvement in this war is in no way political: the victory of Viriconium is as unimportant to me as the victory of the Northmen, except in one particular—please, Lord Grif, sit down and listen—with which I shall deal presently.

What concerns me is the preservation of the human race on earth, by which I mean, on this continent, for they are one and the same thing.

Certainly, you may ask who I am, my lord—

It is my tragedy that I do not know. I have forgotten. I do not know when I came to this tower, only that I have been here for at least a millennium.

I have no doubt that I was here during the collapse of what you would call the Afternoon Cultures—that, at that time, I had already been here for at least a century. But I cannot remember if I actually belonged to that rather mysterious race. They are lost to me, as they are to you.

I have no doubt also that I am either immortal or cursed with an extreme longevity: but the secret of that is lost in Time. Whether it was a disease that struck me, or a punishment that was conferred upon me, I do not know. My memory extends reliably for perhaps two hundred years into the past. No further.

That is the curse of the thing, you see: the memory does not last. There is little enough space in one skull for a lifetime's memories. And no room at all for those of a millennium.

I do not even remember if I am a man.

Many races came—or were brought despite themselves—to earth in the prime of the Departed Cultures. Some stayed, marooned by the swift collapse of the environment that gave rise to the Rust Deserts, caught when the global economy could no longer support a technology and the big ships ceased to fly.

At least two of them survived that collapse, and have since successfully adapted to our conditions.

It may be that I represent a third.

However.

That is secondary to our purpose here. If you will consider the screens that face you, I will attempt to give you some idea of what we may expect from the mechanical servants of the Old Queen.

Yes, madam, the "windows," as you call them, have been here at least as long as myself. I may have constructed them, I cannot remember. Until I discovered certain properties of light and sound, they, too, showed only fixed views of places not to be found in the kingdom. Now, each one is connected—by a principle of which I have recently gained a little understanding—to the eyes of one of my birds.

Thus, wherever they fly, I see.

Now. We will operate the first screen. As you can see, Canna Moidart had little trouble in taking Duirinish—

The huge metal doors are buckled: they swing to and fro in a wind that cannot be heard. Beneath the overhanging walls, a mountain of dead, Northmen and Viriconese inextricably mixed. The battlements are deserted. Moving into the city, a patrol of scavengers, dressed in looted furs. Fire has blackened the squat armouries of the city. On the edge of Replica Square, the Blue Metal Discovery lies in ruins. A dog sniffs at the still, huddled, headless figure in the centre of the square. It is a dead merchant. . . .

There, she left the small holding force we have just seen returning to Alves after a foraging expedition, and moved on to Viriconium—

The Pastel City. Five thousand Northmen march the length of Proton Circuit, their faces flushed with triumph. A tavern in the Artists' Quarter: spilt wine, sawdust, vomit. A line of refugees. The Pastel Towers, scarred in the final battle, when the last ship of the Queen's Flight detonated the power-source of the last remaining energy cannon in the empire, in a vain attempt to repeat Benedict Paucemanly's relief of the seige of Mingulay . . .

She was quick to move south. Here, we see the *geteit chemosit* in action against a group of guerillas, survivors of the Soubridge massacre—

That terrifying black skirmish line, moving up a steep hillside, energy blades swinging, in unison. The dead, sprawled about in agonised attitudes. A sudden close-up of a black, featureless face, three yellow eyes set in an isosceles triangle, unreadable, alien, deadly . . .

Mark that. That is the real enemy of Viriconium. I am sorry, Lord Cromis: I did not intend to cause Her Majesty so much distress. We will dispense with the fourth screen, my lady, and move on to the most important. This is taking place *now*, in Lendalfoot, the town you have just left—

Night. The unsteady flare and flicker of torches in the main street of the town. Their light outlines a group of fishermen, bending over something laid out on the cobbles. The scene jerks. An overhead view; a white, shocked face; tears; a woman in a shawl. There on the cobbles, a child, dead, the top of its head cut neatly away, its skull empty . . .

Finally, let us examine the history of what you know as the *chemosit*, and discuss my purpose in inviting you here. No, Lord Grif, I will be finished shortly. Please hear me out.

During a period of severe internal strife towards the end of the Middle Period, the last of the Afternoon Cultures developed a technique whereby a soldier, however hurt or physically damaged his corpse be, could be resurrected—*as long as his brain remained intact.*

Immersed in a tank of nutrient, his cortex could be used as a seed from which to "grow" a new body. How this was done, I have no idea. It seems monstrous to me.

The *geteit chemosit* were a result of escalation. They were built not only to kill, but also to prevent resurrection of the victim by destroying his brain tissue. As you remark, it is horrifying. But not a bad dream, those are not words I would use: it is a reality with which, a millennium later, we have to deal.

It is evident that Canna Moidart discovered a regiment of these automata in the north of the Great Brown Waste, dormant in some subterranean barracks. I became aware of this some years ago, when certain elements of my equipment detected their awakening. (At that time, I was unsure precisely what it was that the detectors *were* registering—a decade passed before I solved the problem; by that time, the war was inevitable.)

Now, Lord Cromis.

My tower's records are clear on one point, and that is this: once awakened, those automata have only one in-built directive—

To kill.

Should Canna Moidart be unable to shut them down at the end of her campaign, they will continue to kill, regardless of the political alignment of their victims.

The Old Queen may very well find herself in full possession of the Empire of Viriconium.

But as soon as that happens, as soon as the last pocket of resistance is finished, and the *geteit chemosit* run out of wars to fight, they will turn on her. All weapons are two-edged: it is the nature of weapons to be deadly to both user and victim—but these were the final weapon, the absolute product of a technology dedicated to exploitation of its environment and violent solution of political problems. They hate life. That is the way they were built.

9

Silence reigned in the tower room. The five false windows continued to flicker through the green twilight, dumbly repeating their messages of distant atrocity and pain. The Birdmaker's ancient yellow face was expressionless; his hands trembled; he seemed to be drained by his own prophecy.

"That is a black picture—" Tomb the Dwarf drank wine and smacked his lips. He was the least affected of them. "But I would guess that you have a solution. Old man, you would not have brought us here otherwise."

Cellur smiled thinly.

"That is true," he said.

Tomb made a chopping gesture with one hand.

"Let's get to the meat of it then. I feel like killing something."

Cellur winced.

"My tower has a long memory; much information is stored there. Deciphering it, I discover that the *geteit chemosit* are controlled by a single artificial brain, a complex the size of a small town.

"The records are ambiguous when discussing its whereabouts, but I have narrowed its location down to two points south of the Monadliath Mountains. It remains for someone to go there—"

"And?"

"And perform certain simple operations that I will teach him."

Cellur stepped into a drifting column of magenta light, passed his palms over a convoluted mechanism. One by one, the false windows died, taking their agony with them. He turned to tegeus-Cromis.

"I am asking one or all of you to do that. My origin and queer life aside, I am an old man. I would not survive out there now that she has passed beyond the Pastel City."

Numbed by what he had witnessed, Cromis nodded his head. He gazed at the empty windows, obsessed by the face of the dead Lendalfoot child.

"We will go," he said. "I had expected nothing like this. Tomb will learn faster than Grif or I; you had better teach him.

"How much grace have we?"

"A week, perhaps. The South resists, but she will have no trouble. You must be ready to leave before the week is out."

During the Birdmaker's monologue, Methvet Nian had wept openly. Now, she rose to her feet and said:

"This horror. We have always regarded the Afternoon Cultures as a high point in the history of mankind. Theirs was a state to be striven for, despite the mistakes that marred it.

"How could they have constructed such things? Why, when they had the stars beneath their hands?"

The Birdmaker shrugged. The geometries of his robe shifted and stretched like restless alien animals.

"Are you bidding me remember, madam? I fear I cannot."

"They were stupid," said Birkin Grif, his fat, honest face puzzled and hurt. It was his way to feel things personally. "They were fools."

"They were insane towards the end," said Cellur. "That I know."

Lord tegeus-Cromis wandered the Birdmaker's tower alone, filled his time by staring out of upper windows at the rain and the estuary, making sad and shabby verses out of the continual wild crying of the fish eagles and the creaking of the dead white pines. His hand never left the hilt of the nameless sword, but it brought him no comfort.

Tomb the Dwarf was exclusively occupied by machinery—he and Cellur rarely left the workshop on the fifth floor. They took their meals there, if at all. Birkin Grif became sullen and silent, and experienced a resurgence of pain from his damaged leg. Methvet Nian stayed in the room set aside for her, mourning her people and attempting to forgive the monstrousness to which she was heiress.

Inaction bored the soldier; moroseness overcame the poet; a wholly misplaced sense of responsibility possessed the Queen: in their separate ways they tried to meet and overcome the feeling of impotence instilled in them by what they had learned from the Lord of the Birds, and by the enigma he represented.

To a certain extent, each one succeeded: but Cellur ended all that when he called them to the topmost room of the tower on the afternoon of the fifth day since their coming.

They arrived separately, Cromis last.

"I wanted you to see this," Cellur was saying as he entered the room.

The old man was tired; the skin was stretched tight across the bones of his face like oiled paper over a lamp; his eyes were hooded. Abruptly, he seemed less human, and Cromis came to accept the fact that, at some time in the remote past, he might have crossed immense voids to reach the earth.

How much sympathy could he feel for purely human problems, if that were so? He might involve himself, but he would never understand. Cromis thought of the monitor lizard he had seen in the waste, and its fascination with the fire.

"We are all here then," murmured the Birdmaker.

Birkin Grif scowled and grunted.

"Where is Tomb? I don't see him."

"The dwarf must work. In five days, he has absorbed the governing principles of an entire technology. He is amazing. But I would prefer him to continue working. He knows of this already."

"Show us your moving pictures," said Grif.

Ancient hands moved in a column of light. Cellur bent his head, and the windows flickered behind him.

"A vulture flew over Viriconium this morning," he said. "Watch."

A street scene in the Artists' Quarter: Thing Alley, or Soft Lane perhaps. The tottering houses closed tight against a noiseless wind. A length of cloth looping down the gutter; a cat with an eye like a crooked pin flattens itself on the paving, slips out its tongue and devours a morsel of rancid butter. Otherwise, nothing moves.

Coming on with an unsteady rolling gait from the West End of the quarter: three Northmen. Their leather leggings are stiff and encrusted with sweat and blood and good red wine. They lean heavily against one another, passing a flask. Their mouths open and shut regularly, like the mouths of fish in a bowl. They are oblivious.

They have missed a movement in a doorway, which will kill them.

As crooked and silent as the cat, a great black shadow slips into the road behind them. The immense energy blade swings up and down. The silly, bemused faces collapse. Hands raised helplessly before eyes. Their screams are full of teeth. And the triangle of yellow eyes regards their corpses with clinical detachment. . . .

"It has begun, you see," said the Birdmaker. "This is happening all over the city. The automata fight guerilla engagements with Canna Moidart's people. They do not fully understand what is happening as yet. But she is losing control."

Birkin Grif got to his feet, stared at the false windows with loathing, and limped out.

"I would give an arm never to have come here, Birdmaster," he said as he left the room. "Never to have seen that. Your windows make it impossible for me to hate the enemy I have known all my life; they present me with another that turns my legs to water."

Cellur shrugged.

"How soon can we move?" Cromis asked.

"In a day, perhaps two. The dwarf is nearly ready. I am calling in all my birds. Whatever your Lord Grif thinks, I am not some voyeur of violence. I no longer need to watch the Moidart's fall. The birds will be more useful if I redeploy them over the route you must shortly take.

"Make sure you are watching when they return, Lord Cromis. It will be a sight not often seen."

Cromis and Methvet Nian left the room together. Outside, she stopped and looked up into his eyes. She had aged. The girl had fallen before the woman, and hated it. Her face was set, the lips tight. She was beautiful.

"My lord," she said, "I do not wish to live with such responsibilities for the rest of my life. Indirectly, all this is my fault. I have hardly been a strong queen.

"I will abdicate when this is over."

He had not expected such a positive reaction.

"Madam," he said, "your father had similar thoughts on most days of his life. He knew that course was not open to him. You know it, too."

She put her head on his chest and wept.

For twenty-four hours, the sky about the tower was black with birds. They came hurling down the wind from the north:

Bearded vultures and kites from the lower slopes of the Monar Mountains;

Eagle owls like ghosts from the forests;

A squadron of grim long-crested hawk eagles from the farmlands of the Low Leedale;

A flight of lizard buzzards from the reaches of the Great Brown Waste;

A hundred merlins, two hundred fish hawks—a thousand wicked predatory beaks on a long blizzard of wings.

Cromis stood with the Young Queen by a window and watched them come out of night and morning: circling the tower in precise formation; belling their wings to land with a crack of trapped air; studding the rocks and dark beaches of the tiny island. They filled the pines, and he saw now why every tree was dead—Cellur had had need of his birds some long time before, and their talons had stripped every inch of bark, their steel bodies had shaken every branch.

"They are beautiful," whispered the Queen.

But it was the birds, despite their beauty, that destroyed their maker.

. . . For in the stripped lands south of Soubridge, where the villagers had burned their barns before the enemy arrived, a hungry Northman fired his crossbow into a flock of speeding owls. A certain curiosity impelled him: he had never seen such a thing before. More by luck than judgement, he brought one down.

And when he found he could not eat it, he screwed his face up in puzzlement, and took it to his captain. . . .

Dawn came dim and grimy over the basalt cliffs of the estuary. It touched the window from which Cromis had watched all night, softening his bleak features; it stroked the feathers of the birds in the pines; it silvered the beaks of the last returning flight: seventy cumbersome cinereous vultures, beating slowly over the water on their nine-foot wings.

And it touched and limned the immense shape which drifted silently after them as they flew—the long black hull that bore the mark of the wolf's head and three towers.

Cromis was alone; the Queen had retired some hours earlier. He watched the ship for a moment as it trawled back and forth over the estuary. Its shell was scarred and pitted. After two or three minutes it vanished over the cliffs to the west, and he thought it had gone away. But it returned, hovered, spun hesitantly, hunting like a compass needle.

Thoughtfully, he made his way to the workshop on the fifth floor. He drew his sword and rapped with its pommel on the door.

"Cellur!" he called. "We are discovered!"

He looked at the nameless blade, then put it away.

"Possibly, we can hold them off. The tower has its defences. It would depend on the type of weapon they have."

They had gathered in the upper room, Methvet Nian shivering with cold, Birkin Grif complaining at the earliness of the hour. Dry-mouthed and insensitive from lack of sleep, Cromis found the whole situation unreal.

"One such boat could carry fifty men," he said.

It hung now, like a haunting, over the causeway that joined the tower to the mainland. It began to descend, slowed, alighted on the crumbling stone, its bow aimed at the island.

"Footmen need not concern us," said Cellur. "The door will hold them: and there are the birds."

Beneath the weight of the boat, the causeway shifted, groaned, settled. Chunks of stone broke away and slid into the estuary. In places, a foot of

water licked the dark hull. Behind it, the hills took on a menacing gun-
metal tint in the growing light. Cellur's fish eagles began their tireless
circling.

Five false windows showed the same view: the water, the silent launch.

A hatch opened in its side, like a wound.

From it poured the *geteit chemosit,* their blades at high port.

Birkin Grif hissed through his clenched teeth. He rubbed his injured
leg. "Let us see your home defend itself, Birdmaker. Let us *see* it!"

"Only two humans are with them," said the Queen. "Officers: or
slaves?"

They came three abreast along the causeway; half a hundred or more
energy blades, a hundred and fifty yellow, fathomless eyes.

The birds met them.

Cellur's hands moved across his instruments, and the dawn faltered as
he lifted his immense flock from the island and hurled it at the beach. Like
a cloud of smoke, it stooped on the *chemosit,* wailing and screaming with
one voice. The invader vanished.

Blades flickered through the cloud, slicing metal like butter. Talons like
handfuls of nails sought triplet eyes. Hundreds of birds fell. But when the
flock drew back, twenty of the automata lay in shreds half in and half out
of the water, and the rest had retreated to their ship.

"Ha," said Grif in the pause that followed. "Old man, you are not
toothless, and they are not invulnerable."

"No," said the Birdmaster, "but I am frightened. Look down there. It
seems to me that Canna Moidart dug more than golems from the
desert—"

He turned to Cromis.

"You must go! Leave now. Beneath the tower are cellars. I have horses
there. Tunnels lead through the basalt to a place half a mile south of here.
The dwarf is as ready as he ever will be. Obey his instructions when you
reach the site of the artificial brain.

"Go. Fetch him now, and go! His armour I have serviced. It is with the
horses. Leave quickly!"

As he spoke, his eyes dilated with fear.

Despite repeated attacks by the birds, the *chemosit* had gained a little
space on the causeway beside their ship. In this area, four of them were assembling heavy equipment. They worked ponderously, without haste.

"That is a portable energy cannon," whispered Birkin Grif. "I had not
thought that such things existed in the empire."

"Many things exist *under* it, Lord Grif," Cellur told him. "Now go!"

The tower shuddered.

Violet bolides issued from the mouth of the cannon. Rocks and trees vaporised. Five hundred birds flashed into a golden, ragged sphere of fire, involuntary phoenixes with no rebirth. Cellur turned to his instruments.

The tower began to hum. Above their heads, at the very summit, something crackled and spat. Ozone tainted the air.

Lightning leapt across the island, outlined the hull of the airboat with a wan flame.

"I have cannon of my own," said the Birdmaker, and there was a smile on his ancient face. "Many of those birds were so complicated they had learned to talk. That is as good a definition of life as I have ever heard."

The water about the causeway had begun to boil.

Cromis took the Queen's arm.

"This is no place for us. The old weapons are awake here. Let them fight it out."

The rock beneath the tower trembled ominously.

"Should we not bring the old man with us? They will kill him in the end—"

"I do not think he would come," said Cromis, and he was right.

Tomb the Dwarf was dull-eyed and bemused.

"I have wasted fifty years of my life," he said. "We must go, I suppose."

One hundred steps led to the caverns beneath.

It was a queer journey. The horses were skittish from lack of exercise, the tunnels ill-lit. Moisture filmed the walls, and fungus made murals from the dreams of a madman. Huge, silent machines stood in alcoves melted from the living rock.

The vibrations of the battle above died away.

"We are beneath the estuary. It is the underside of the world, where the dead men lose their bones."

They were forced to ride through a column of cold fire. They discovered these things:

The white skeletons of a horse and its rider; a sword too big for any of them to lift; an immense web; the mummified body of a beautiful princess.

Sounds that were not echoes followed them down the twisted corridors.

"I could believe we are out of Time," said tegeus-Cromis.

Finally, they came up out of the earth and stood on the lip of the western cliffs, gazing down. The tower of Cellur was invisible, wrapped in a pall of coloured smoke, through which the lightnings flashed and coruscated. The causeway had sagged; in places its stones were melted. Steam hung over the estuary.

A cold mist drew round them as they turned their horses south and west, making for Lendalfoot, and then the Forest of Sloths. As they left

Cellur to his vain battle, one fish eagle was hanging high above the smoke: circling.

Tomb the Dwarf never spoke to anyone of his sojourn on the fifth floor, or of what he had learned there. It is certain that he absorbed more than the knowledge required by his task, and that the Birdmaker found him an apt and willing pupil. Nor could he be persuaded to say anything of Cellur, the man who had forgotten his age and his origin. But in his later life, he often murmured half to himself:

"We waste our lives in half truths and nonsense. We waste them."

10

Canna Moidart's long thrust into the South reached Mingulay and guttered. The town fell, but in the bleak streets behind the sea front, the
chemosit sensed there was nowhere further to go: they slaughtered the
civilians, and then, quite without purpose or emotion, turned on their
masters, who died in a smell of blood and fish . . .

While, in the back alleys of Soubridge and the Pastel City, death wore
precise, mechanical limbs . . . A greater war had begun . . . Or perhaps it
had never finished, and the automata were completing a task they had
started over a thousand years before . . . The Northmen desperately
needed *enemies*. . . .

"A forbidding prospect."

tegeus-Cromis and Tomb the Dwarf stood at the summit of a rainswept
ridge in the south of that narrow neck of land which separates the
Monadliath Mountains from the sea.

The country around them was alkaline and barren, an elevated limestone region seamed and lined with deep gullies by the almost constant
rain: in areas, rock strata that had resisted the erosion of millennia made
tall, smooth, distorted columns which stood out above the surrounding
land.

"An old road runs through it, according to the Birdmaster. What we
seek is at the end of it—perhaps. You are sure you will recognise it?"

Above the grotesque spires and limb shapes of the terrain, grey clouds
were flung out across a drab sky, and the wind was bitter. Tomb tapped
enormous steel fingers impatiently against the left leg of his exoskeleton.

"How many times must you be told? Cellur taught me."

They had been five days travelling. On the first night, the successful skirting of Lendalfoot and its uneasy garrison of Northmen, the fording of the major estuary of the Girvan Bay at low tide: but the next afternoon, crofters living in the southwestern shadow of Monadliath had warned them of *chemosit* advance parties operating in the area, and their movements had been cautious thereafter.

Now, the vanguard of the South Forest barred their path.

The land sloped away from them for five miles, growing steadily less tortured as the limestone faded out. Low scrub and gorse made their appearance, gave way to groves of birch: then the black line of the trees—dark, solid, stretching like a wooden wall from the thousand-foot line of the mountains to the chalk pits by the sea.

"Well," said Cromis, "we have no choice."

He left the dwarf staring ahead and made his way down the greasy northern slope of the ridge to where Birkin Grif and Methvet Nian huddled with the horses under a meagre overhang, rain plastering their cloaks to their bodies and their hair to their heads.

"The way is clear to the forest. Hard to tell if anything moves out there. We gain nothing by waiting here. Grif, you and I had better begin thinking of our way through the trees."

Within half a day they were lost among the green cathedrals.

There was no undergrowth, only trunks and twisted limbs; their horses stumbled over interlaced roots; the going was slow. There was no movement or sound among the lower branches, only the slow drip of moisture percolating from the groined grey spaces above. Pines gave way to denser plots of oak and ash, and there was no path: only the aimless roads their minds made through the trees.

Mid afternoon.

In a clearing of gigantic, wan hemlock and etiolated nettle, Tomb the Dwarf left them.

"It is a bitch that I have to do your work, too," he muttered. "Stay here." And he strode off, chopping a straight route with his big axe, uprooting saplings out of spite.

Shaggy mosses grew on the southern faces of the trees that ringed the glade; wet fungoid growths like huge plates erupted on their cloven massive trunks, bursting putrescently when touched. The light was lichen-grey, oppressive.

"We have come too far to the west," said Birkin Grif, glancing round uncomfortably. "The land begins to slope." After a pause, he added in his own defense: "The Birdmaker was less than explicit."

"The fault is also mine," Cromis admitted.

Methven Nian shivered. "I hate this place."

Nothing more was said: voices were heavy and dead, conversation fell like turf on a grave or the thud of hooves on endless leaf mould.

At dusk, the dwarf returned, a little less sullen. He bowed to the Queen.

"Tomb, my lady." He explained: "An itinerant dwarf of menacing demeanour. Mechanic *and* pathfinder"—here, he glanced witheringly at Cromis and Grif, who had both become interested in a thicket of nightshade—"at your service."

He sniggered.

He led them to a poorly defined path overshadowed by great rough blackthorn, the light failing around them. As the sun died without a sound somewhere off behind the trees and the clouds, they came to a broad, wasted space running to north and south in the mounting gloom.

Fireweed and thistle grew thickly there, but it could not disguise the huge, canted stone slabs, twenty yards on a side and settling into the floor of the forest, that had once made up a highway of gargantuan proportion. Nor could the damp moss completely obscure the tall megaliths, deeply inscribed with a dead language, that lined the way to the city in the forest: Thing Fifty, a capitol of the South in days beyond the memory of Cellur's marvellous tower.

They camped on the road, in the lee of an overgrown slab, and their fire, calling across Time, perhaps, as well as space, brought out the sloths. . . .

"Something is out there," said Birkin Grif.

He got to his feet, stood with the flames flickering on his back, looking into the terrible silences of the forest. He drew his broadsword.

Flames and stillness.

"There," he hissed. He ran foward into the shadows, whirling the long blade round his head.

"*Stop!*" cried Methvet Nian. "My lord—leave them be!"

They came shambling slowly into the light, three of them. Grif gave ground before them, his weapon reflecting the flames, his breath coming slow and heavy.

They blinked. They reared onto their great stubby hind legs, raising their forepaws, each one armed with steely cutting claws. Patterns of orange firelight shifted across their thick white pelts.

Fifteen feet high, they stared mutely down at Grif, their tranquil brown eyes fixed myopically on him. They swayed their blunt, shaggy heads from side to side. Grif retreated.

Slim and quick as a sword, her hair a challenge to the fire, Methvet Nian, Queen and Empress, placed herself between him and the megatheria.

"Hello, my Old Ones," she whispered. "Your kindred sends you greet-
ings from the palace."

They did not understand. But they nodded their heads wisely, and
gazed into her eyes. One by one, they dropped to their haunches and ambled to the fire, which they examined thoroughly.

"They are the Queen's Beasts, my lord," said Methvet Nian to Birkin
Grif. "And once they may have been more than that. No harm will come
to us from them."

In two days, they came to Thing Fifty. It was a humbled city, ten square
miles of broken towers, sinking into the soft earth.

Squares and plazas, submerged beneath fathoms of filthy water, had
become stagnant, stinking lakes, their surfaces thickly coated with dead
brown leaves. Black ivy clutched the enduring metals of the Afternoon
Cultures, laid its own meandering inscriptions over bas-reliefs that echoed
the geometries of the Pastel City and the diagrams that shifted across the
robe of Cellur.

And everywhere, the trees, the fireweed, the pale hemlock: Thing Fifty
had met a vegetable death with thick, fibrous, thousand-year roots.

Between the collapsed towers moved the megatheria, denizens of the
dead metropolis. They lived in sunken rooms, moved ponderously
through the choked streets by night and day, as if for millennia they had
been trying to discover the purpose of their inheritance.

Tomb the Dwarf led the party through the tumbled concentric circles
of the city.

"At the very centre," he said, "a tower stands alone in an oval plaza."
He cocked his head, as if listening to a lecture in his skull. "To descend
into the caverns beneath the plaza, we must enter that. Certain defences
may still be operating. But I have the trick of those, I hope."

The ground sloped steeply down as they went, as if Thing Fifty had
been built in the bowl of a tremendous amphitheatre. They were forced to
cross pools and unpleasant moats. Running water became common,
springs bubbling from the cracked paving.

"I had not counted on this. The bunkers may be waterlogged. Runoff
from the foothills of the Monadliath has done this. Help for the trees, but
not us."

He was near the mark, but how near, he could not have imagined: and
when they reached the plaza, none of his new skills were of any use.

For at the hub of the city of Thing Fifty lay a perfectly oval tarn of clear
water.

At its centre, like the stub of one of Tomb's own broken teeth, rose the
last few feet of a tall tower. In its depths, they could see luxuriant water

plants rooted in the thick black silt that had covered and blocked the entrance to the bunkers.

Into their stunned silence, Birkin Grif murmured, "We are finished here before we begin. It is drowned."

Methvet Nian looked at Tomb. "What shall we do?"

"Do?" He laughed bitterly. "Throw ourselves in. Do what you like. I can accomplish nothing *here*."

He stalked off a little way and sat down. He threw lumps of dead wood and stone into the water that mocked him.

"We cannot get down there," said Cromis. "We will sleep in a drier part of the city tonight, and in the morning move on.

"Cellur told us that the siting of the artificial brain was uncertain. We had warning of that. We will try our second goal, in the Lesser Rust Desert.

"If that fails, we can come back here—"

Tomb the Dwarf sniggered.

"And dive like ducks? You are a fool. We have lost the game."

Cromis fondled the hilt of his sword. "We lost the game a long time since, in the Great Brown Waste," he said, "but we still live. It is all we can do."

"*Oh, yes indeed,*" said a soft, ironical voice from close behind him. "*It is your place to lose, I think.*"

Cromis turned, horror blooming in his skull, his sword sliding from its leather scabbard.

Norvin Trinor stood before him.

Twenty Northmen were at his back, forceblades spitting and hissing in their hands.

"You should have killed me when you had the chance, my lord," he said. He shook his head theatrically and sighed. "Still, perhaps it was not meant to be that way."

He looked from Cromis to Grif. The scar left by Thorisman Carlemaker's knife immobilised one side of his face, so that when he smiled only one eye and half his mouth responded. He still wore the cloak and mail Cromis had last seen on the battlefield. Like the leather garments of the Northmen, they were stained with blood and wine.

"Hello, Grif," he said.

Birkin Grif exposed his teeth.

"Arselicker," he said, "your lads will not save you, even though they kill me after I have gutted you." He showed Trinor a few inches of his broadsword. He spat on the floor. He took a step forward. "I will have your bowels out on the floor," he promised.

Cromis put a hand on his shoulder.

"No, Grif, no."

Trinor laughed. He swept back his cloak and slid his own blade back into its sheath.

"tegeus-Cromis sees it," he said. "Heroism is useless against a strategist: Methven taught us all that many years ago."

"You learnt quickest of all," said Cromis dryly. "Grif, we could kill him four times over: but when we have finished, we will face twenty *baans*. Even Tomb could not stand against them.

"However well we fight, the Queen will die."

Norvin Trinor made a sweeping bow in the Young Queen's direction.

"Quite. A splendid exposition, my lord. However, there is a way out of this for you. You see, I need your dwarf.

"Let me explain. I am on the same quest as yourselves. I am able in fact to tell you that you are wasting your time here in Thing Fifty unless your interest is purely archaeological.

"For some time now, we have been a little worried about our allies. During certain researches in our good queen's library"—he bowed again—"in the Pastel City, I discovered what an unreliable weapon the *chemosit* are. Quite like myself, you understand: they serve only themselves. (Hold still a moment, Lord Grif. It will not hurt you to listen.) You have learnt this, of course. I should like very much to know where, by the way.

"I came also upon part of the answer to the problem: the exact whereabouts of the machine which will . . . turn them off, so to speak.

"Now, I gather from your conversation here that the dwarf has been given information I was unable to obtain. In short, I need him to do the business for me. I could not *take* him from you without killing him. Persuade him that it is in the best interests of all of us that he work for me in this matter, and I spare you. The Queen, too."

Throughout this monologue, Tomb had remained sitting on the edge of the tarn. Now, he unlimbered his axe and got to his feet. Norvin Trinor's wolves stirred uneasily. Their blades flickered. The dwarf stretched to the full eleven feet his armour lent him and stood towering over the traitor.

He raised the axe.

He said: "I was born in a back alley, Trinor. If I had suspected at the battle for Mingulay that you would do this to three men who fought alongside you, I would have put a *baan* between your ribs while you slept. I will do your job for you because it is the job I came to do. Afterwards, I will cut off your knackers and stitch them into your mouth.

"Meanwhile, Methvet Nian remains unharmed."

And he let the axe fall to his side.

"Very well. We declare a truce, then: precarious, but it should not stain your finer feelings too much. I will allow you to keep your weapons." He smiled at Cromis's start of surprise. "But a man of mine stays by the Queen at all times.

"I have an airboat parked on the southern edge of the city. We will leave immediately."

Later, as they entered the black ship, its hatch opening directly beneath the crude, cruel sigil of the wolf's head, Cromis asked:

"How did you discover us? You could not have followed us through the forest, or even through the barrens without being seen—"

Trinor looked puzzled. Then he gave his crippled smile.

"Had you not realised? It was pure luck: we were here before you entered the city. That's the beauty of it. We had stopped for fresh meat. At that time, I anticipated a long sojourn in the desert."

And he pointed to the great heap of carcasses that lay beside the launch, their white pelts stained with gore, their myopic eyes glazed in death. Crewmen were preparing to haul them into the cargo hold, with chains.

Cromis looked out at the tangled landscape of Thing Fifty.

"You are an animal," he said.

Norvin Trinor laughed. He clapped Cromis on the shoulder. "When you forget you are an animal, my lord, you begin to *lose*."

11

Brown, featureless desert slipped beneath the keel of the drifting airboat: the Lesser Waste, in all respects similar to the great dead region north of Duirinish, the spoliated remnants of an industrial hinterland once administrated from Thing Fifty.

tegeus-Cromis, Birkin Grif, and Tomb the Dwarf, locked in the cargo hold with the dead megatheria, paced restlessly the throbbing crystal deck. With a power-blade at the neck of Methvet Nian, Norvin Trinor had forced the dwarf to give up his armour, although he had allowed him to keep his axe. He looked like an ancient, twisted child.

"A chance may come when I breach the defences of the organic brain," he said. He fondled the axe. He shrugged. "Indeed, I may slip, and kill us all."

The boat lurched in an updraught: white carcasses slid about the hold. Cromis stared from the single porthole down at the desert. Unknown to him, his fingers plucked at the hilt of the nameless sword.

"Whatever is done, it must not involve a fight. You understand that, Grif? I want no fighting unless we can be sure the Queen will remain unharmed."

Grif nodded sulkily.

"In other words, do nothing," he said.

As he spoke, the bulkhead door opened. Norvin Trinor stepped through, two of his wolves flanking him. He pulled at his drooping moustache.

"A commendable plan," he said. "Most wise." He looked at Grif for some moments, then turned to Tomb. "Dwarf, we have arrived. Look down there and tell me if this place was mentioned in your information."

Tomb moved to the porthole.

"It is a desert. Deserts were indeed mentioned to me." He showed his rotting teeth. "Trinor, you are displaying a traditional foolishness. I can tell nothing for sure until we land."

The traitor nodded curtly, and left. A few moments later, the airboat began to descend, bucking a little as it entered a low level of wind.

Trinor's pilot settled the ship on a bare shield of black rock like an island in the rolling limbo of the dunes. The engines ceased to pulse, and a soft, intermittent hissing sound commenced beyond the hull. Time is erosion: an icy wind blew streams of dust across the surface of the rock. It had been blowing for a millennium.

They stood in the lee of the vehicle, eddies of wind wrapping their cloaks about them. Dust in their eyes and mouths, Cromis looked at the thin, hunched shoulders of the Queen. We are nothing but eroded men, he thought, wind clothing our eyes with white ice. Benedict Paucemanly flew to the *earth*. It is we who live on the barren moon. . . .

"Well?" said Trinor.

A hundred yards away reared the curving flank of a dune. From it poked the ends of broken and melted load girders, like a grove of buckled steel trees. They were bright, polished, and eroded. Cromis, eyeing the desolation silently, became aware that beneath the muted cry of the archaic wind was a low humming: the rock beneath his feet was vibrating faintly.

Tomb the Dwarf walked about. He bent down and put his ear to the rock. He got up again and dusted his leather leggings.

"This is the place," he said. "Begin digging at the base of the dune." He grinned cockily at Cromis. "The wolves become moles," he said loudly. "This would have taken us weeks without them. Perhaps we should thank Lord Traitor." He strutted off to examine the girder forest, his long white hair knotting in the wind.

With surly grunts, the Northmen were set to work, and by noon of the following day, their labours had exposed a rectangular doorway in the flank of the dune: a long low slit sealed with a slab of the same resistant obsidian stuff as had been used to construct the Birdmaker's tower.

The maker of the door had cut deep ideographs in it. Time and the desert had been unable to equal him in this respect: the slab was as smooth and the ciphers as precise as if they had been made the day before. It seemed a pity that no one could read them.

Trinor was jubilant.

"We have a door," he said, pulling at his moustache. "Now let us see if our dwarf can provide a key." He slapped Tomb jovially on the shoulder.

"You forget yourself," murmured the dwarf.

He stood before the door, his lips moving silently. Perhaps he was recalling his apprenticeship on the fifth floor. He knelt. He passed his hands over a row of ideographs. A red glow sprang up and followed them. He murmured something, repeated it.

"NEEDS YOU," intoned the door abruptly, in a precise, hollow voice: "NEEDS YOU. BAA, BAA. BAA. OURO-BUN-DOS—"

The gathered Northmen dropped their spades. Many of them made religious signs with their fingers. Eyes round, they clutched their weapons, breathing though their open mouths.

"DOG MOON, DOG YEARS," moaned the door. "BAA, BAA, BAA."

And to each ritualistic syllable, Tomb made a suitable reply. Their dialogue lasted for some minutes before silence descended and he began again the process of moving his hands across the ancient script.

"GOLEBOG!" screamed the door.

A brief, intense flare of white light obscured the dwarf. He staggered out of it, beating at his clothes. He chuckled. His hair reeked, his leggings smouldered. He blew on his fingers.

"The door mechanism has become insane over the years," he said. "It"—here, he said a word that no one knew—"me, but I misled it. Look."

Slowly, and with no sound, the obsidian slab had hinged downwards until it rested like the lower lip of a slack mechanical mouth on the dust, compacting it; and behind it stretched a sloping corridor lit by a pale, shifting pastel glow.

"Your door is open," he told Trinor. "The defences are down."

Trinor rubbed the scar on his cheek.

"One hopes that they are," he said. "tegeus-Cromis enters first. If there should be a misunderstanding between him and the door, the Queen will follow."

There were no accidents.

As Cromis entered the bunker, the door whispered malevolently to him, but it left him alone. The light shifted frequency several times as he stood there staring at the vanishing point of the gently sloping passage. Vague, unidentifiable musical sounds were all around him. Growing from the walls were clumps of crystal that reminded him of the Metal-Salt Marsh; they pulsed regularly.

He felt no fear.

"Remain where you are, Lord Cromis." Trinor's voice seemed muffled, distant, as though affected by passage through the open door. "I shall expect to find you when I come through—"

He entered with sword drawn. He grinned.

"Just in case you had planned . . . Well, of course, I'm sure you hadn't." He raised his voice. "Bring the Queen through first."

When they had assembled, the Northmen sullen and silent, keeping their eyes fixed on the floor and mishearing their orders, he made Tomb take the lead. "Any . . . defences . . . you should disarm. Remember where the knife is held, dwarf, and who holds it."

That corridor stretched for two miles into the earth. Shortly after they had begun to walk, they found that the incline had levelled off. The nature of the walls changed: the clumps of crystal were replaced by yard-square windows, arranged at four-foot intervals. Nothing could be clearly discerned through them, but they were filled with a milky light in which were suspended vague but menacing organic shapes.

There were no turnings. Their footfalls echoed.

There were no junctions or side passages. They did not speak.

They came eventually to a great circular chamber, in the centre of which columns of light and great rods of shadow wove patterns impossible to understand, like spectral dancers at the end of Time. Its roof and walls, all of green diamond, made a perfect half-globe. Twelve corridors, including their own, led off it from twelve vaulting arches. Otherwise, it was totally featureless.

Those columns and cylinders of light and darkness flickered, intertwined, exchanged their substance, reversed their directions of motion. Motes of brighter light appeared suddenly among them, hovered like insects, and vanished. A single musical chord filled the place, a high cathedral resonance.

Cromis saw nothing he recognised as a machine.

"You had better begin," said Trinor to the dwarf, looking uneasily about. His voice was taken by the diamond walls and flung about. As if in response, the visual display of the brain increased its activity. "It is aware of us. I would like to leave here as soon as possible. Well?"

For a moment, the dwarf ignored him. His ugly features had softened, there was a gleam in his knowing eye. He was enraptured. He sniggered suddenly, swivelled slowly on his heel to face the traitor.

"My lord," he said satirically, "you ask too much. It will take a century to understand this." He shrugged. "Ah yes, you hold the knife, I remember." He shook his head sadly. "I can shut it down in a week—perhaps a little more. It is a matter of finding the right . . . combination. A week: no less."

Trinor fingered his scar.

For the next few days, Cromis saw nothing of Tomb or the Queen: they were kept in the central chamber of the complex, constantly under the eyes and swords of the reluctant Northmen, while he and Grif were limited to the cargo hold of the airboat, and lived out a dreary captivity among the dead sloths.

Each day, a Northman brought them food.

Cromis's in-turning nature enabled him to come to terms with this—he made verses while gazing from the porthole at the unchanging waste—but it betrayed him also in the end, in that it kept him unaware of Birkin Grif's shift of mood.

Confinement chafed the big Methven. He grew irritable and posed questions without answer. "How long do you suppose we will live after the shutdown? Tell me that." And: "The dwarf cares only for his machines. Are we to rot here?"

He took to sharpening his broadsword twice a day.

Later, he lay morose and withdrawn on a pile of bloody pelts, humming songs of defiance. He tapped his fingers dangerously.

Each day, a Northman brought them food.

On the sixth day after the discovery of the central chamber, Birkin Grif stood behind the door of the hold, honing his sword.

The door opened; their jailor entered.

He had an energy blade in his right hand, but it did him no good.

Grif stood over the folded corpse, eyeing with satisfaction its pumping stomach wound. He wiped his broadsword on the hem of its cloak, sheathed it. He wrested the flickering power-blade from its tightening grip. A terrible light was in his eye.

"Now," he said.

Cromis found himself dulled and slowed by horror.

"Grif," he murmured, "you are mad."

Birkin Grif stared levelly at him.

"Have we become cowards?" he said.

And he turned and ran from the hold, quick and silent.

Cromis bent over the ruin that meant death for the Queen. In the distance, cries of pain and surprise: Grif had come against the Northmen in the forepart of the ship, berserk.

The nameless sword in his hand, Cromis followed the trail of slaughter. On the command bridge, three dead men. They sprawled grotesquely, expressions of surprise on their faces, their blood splashed over the walls. The place stank. The open hatch yawned. Wind blew in from the desert, filling the dead eyes with fine dust.

Outside, the wind tugged at him. A fifth corpse lay at the entrance to the bunkers. The door moaned and hissed as he entered. "OUROBUN-DOS," it said. It snickered. Cromis caught up with Grif halfway down the corridor that led to the brain chamber—too late.

His ragged cobalt mail was smeared with blood, his hands were red with murder. Over the corpse of his final victim, he faced Norvin Trinor. And behind the traitor, their blades spitting, stood ten Northern wolves.

Trinor acknowledged Cromis's arrival with an ironical nod.

"I did not expect quite such stupidity," he said. "I will make no more contracts with you. I see they are worthless."

Birkin Grif ground his heel into the chest of the dead Northman. His eyes sought Trinor's, held them.

"You have killed your queen," Trinor said. "Yourself, too."

Grif moved a pace forward.

"Listen to me, Norvin Trinor," he whispered. "Your mother was had by a pig. At the age of ten, she gave you a disease. You have since licked the arse of Canna Moidart.

"But I will tell you this. There is *still* Methven enough in you to meet me now, without your dirty henchmen—"

He turned to the Northerners. "Make a combat ring," he said.

Trinor fingered his scar. He laughed. "I will fight you," he said. "It will change nothing. Four men are with Methvet Nian. They have instructions to kill both her and the dwarf if I do not shortly return to them. You understand: die or live, you or I, it will change nothing."

Birkin Grif dropped the stolen energy blade and slid his broadsword from its scabbard.

The dead Northman was dragged away. In the strange milky light from the windows of the corridor, the combatants faced each other. They were not well matched. Grif, though a head taller, and of longer reach, had expended much of his strength in the cabin of the airboat: and his slow, terrible rage made him tremble. Trinor regarded him calmly.

In the days of King Methven, both of them had learned much from tegeus-Cromis—but only one of them had ever matched his viperish speed.

They clashed.

Behind the windows, queer objects stirred and drifted, on currents of thick liquid.

Two blades made white webs in the air. The Northmen cheered, and made bets. They cut, and whirled, and leapt—Grif cumbersome, Trinor lithe and quick. Fifteen years or more before they had fought thus side by side, and killed fifty men in a morning. Against his will, Cromis drew closer, joined the combat ring, and marked the quick two-handed jab, the blade thrown up to block . . .

Grif stumbled.

A thin line of blood was drawn across his chest. He swore and hacked.

Trinor chuckled suddenly. He allowed the blow to nick his cheek. Then he ducked under Grif's outstretched arms and stepped inside the circle of his sword. He chopped, short-armed, for the ribs.

Grif grunted, threw himself back, spun round, crashed unharmed into the ring of Northmen.

And Trinor, allowing his momentum to carry him crouching forward, turned the rib cut into an oblique, descending stroke that bit into the torn mail beneath his opponent's knees, hamstringing him.

Grif staggered.

He looked down at his ruined legs. He showed his teeth. When Trinor's sword couched itself in his lower belly, he whimpered. A quick, violent shudder went through him. Blood dribbled down his thighs. He reached slowly down and put his hands on the sword.

He sat down carefully. He coughed. He stared straight at Cromis and said clearly: "You should have killed him when you had the chance. Cromis, you should have done it—"

Blood filled his mouth and ran into his beard.

tegeus-Cromis, sometime soldier and sophisticate of the Pastel City, who imagined himself a better poet than swordsman, clenched his long, delicate fingers until their rings of intagliated, non-precious metal cracked his knuckles and his nails made bloody half-moons on his palms.

. A huge, insane cry welled up out of him. Desolation and murder bloomed like bitter flowers in his head.

"Trinor!" he bawled. "Grif! *Grif!*"

And before the turncoat's hand had time to reach the energy blade his victim had discarded—long, long before he had time to form a stroke with his arm, or a word with his lips—the nameless blade was buried to its hilt in his mouth. Its point had levered apart the bones of his neck and burst with a soft noise through the back of his skull.

tegeus-Cromis shuddered. He threw back his head and howled like a beast. He put his foot against the dead man's breastbone and pulled out his blade.

"You were never good enough, Trinor," he said, savagely. "Never."

He turned to face his death and the death of the world, weeping.

"Come and kill me," he pleaded. "Just come and *try.*"

But the Northmen had no eyes for him.

12

His face fired up with hate and madness, the nameless sword quivering before him, he watched them back away, toward the chamber of the brain. So he kicked the stiff, bleeding face of their dead captain. He crouched like a wolf, and spat: he presented them with lewd challenges, and filthy insults.

But they ignored him, and stared beyond him, their attitudes fearful; and finally he followed the direction of their gaze.

Coming on from the direction of the door, moving swiftly through the milky light, was a company of men.

They were tall and straight, clothed in cloaks of black and green, of scarlet and the misleading colour of dragonfly armour. Their dark hair fell to their shoulders about long, white faces, and their boots rang on the obsidian floor. Like walkers out of Time, they swept past him, and he saw that their weapons were grim and strange, and that their eyes held ruin for the uncertain wolves of the North.

At their head strutted Tomb the Dwarf.

His axe was slung jauntily over his thick shoulder, his hair caught back for battle. He was whistling through his horrible teeth, but he quieted when he saw the corpse of Birkin Grif.

With a great shout he sprang forward, unlimbering his weapon. He fell upon the retreating Northmen, and all his strange and beautiful crew followed him. Their curious blades hummed and sang.

Like a man displaced amid his own dreams, Cromis watched the dwarf plant himself securely on his buckled, corded legs and swing his axe in huge circles round his head; he watched the strange company as they flickered like steel flames through the Northmen. And when he was sure that they had prevailed, he threw down the nameless sword.

His madness passed. Cradling the head of his dead friend, he wept.

When Methvet Nian discovered him there, he had regained a measure of his self-possession. He was shivering, but he would not take her cloak.

"I am glad to see you safe, my lady," he said, and she led him to the brain chamber. He left his sword. He saw no use for it.

In the centre of the chamber, a curious and moving choreography was taking place.

The brain danced, its columns of light and shadow shifting, shifting; innumerable subtle graduations of shape and tint, and infinitely various rhythms.

And among those rods and pillars, thirteen slim figures moved, their garments on fire with flecks of light, their long white faces rapt.

The brain sang its single sustained chord, the feet of the dancers sped, the vaulting dome of diamond threw back images of their ballet.

Off to one side of the display sat Tomb the Dwarf, a lumpen, earthbound shape, his chin on his hand, a smile on his ugly face, his eyes following every shade of motion. His axe lay by his side.

"They are beautiful," said tegeus-Cromis. "It seems a pity that a homicidal dwarf should discover such beauty. Why do they dance in that fashion?"

Tomb chuckled.

"To say that I appreciated that would be a lie. I suspect they have a method of communication with the brain many times more efficient than crude passes of the hand. In a sense, they *are* the brain at this moment—"

"Who are they, Tomb?"

"They are men of the Afternoon Cultures, my friend. They are the Resurrected Men."

Cromis shook his head. The dancers swayed, their cloaks a whirl of emerald and black. "You cannot expect me to understand any of this."

Tomb leapt to his feet. Suddenly, he danced away from Cromis and the Queen in a queer little parody of the ballet of the brain, an imitation full of sadness and humour. He clapped his hands and cackled.

"Cromis," he said, "it was a master stroke. Listen—"

He sat down again.

"I lied to Trinor. Nothing was simpler than dealing with the *geteit chemosit*. Those golems stopped operating twenty minutes after I had entered this room. Wherever they were, they froze, their mechanisms ceased to function. For all I know, they are rusting. Cellur taught me that.

"What he did not tell me was that a dialogue could be held with the brain: that, I learnt for myself, in the next twenty minutes. Then—

"Cromis, Cellur was wrong. One vital flaw in his reasoning led to what you have seen today. He regarded the *chemosit* as simple destroyers, but the Northmen were nearer to the truth when they called them the brain-stealers. The *chemosit* are harvesters.

"It was their function in the days of the Afternoon Cultures not to *prevent* the resurrection of a warrior, but to bring the contents of his skull here, or to a similar centre, and give it into care of the artificial brain. This applied equally to a dead friend or a foe actually slain by the *chemosit*—I think they saw war in a different way to ourselves, perhaps as a game.

"When Canna Moidart denied the *chemosit* their full function by using them solely as fighters, she invited destruction.

"Now. Each of the 'windows' in this place is in reality a tank of sustaining fluid, in which is suspended the brain of a dead man. Upon the injection of a variety of other fluids and nutrients, that brain may be stimulated to re-form its departed owner.

"On the third day of our captivity here, the artificial brain reconstructed Fimbruthil and Lonath, those with the emerald cloaks.

"On the fourth day, Bellin, and Mader-Monad, and Sleth. See how those three dance! And yesterday, the rest. The brain then linked me to their minds. They agreed to help me. Today, we put our plan into effect.

"Twelve corridors lead from this chamber, like the spokes of a wheel miles in diameter: the Resurrected Men were born in the northwestern corridor. At a given signal, they issued from their wombs, crept here, and slew the guards Trinor had left when he went to his death. The fourteen of us stepped into the light columns. From there, by a property of the brain complex, we were . . . shifted . . . to the desert outside.

"We waited there for Trinor and his men. By then, of course, he was . . . otherwise involved. We eventually reentered the bunker, and arrived in time to save you from yourself."

tegeus-Cromis smiled stiffly.

"That was well done, Tomb. And what now? Will you send them back to sleep?"

The dwarf frowned.

"Cromis! We will have an army of them! Even now, they are awakening the brain fully. We will build a new Viriconium together, the Methven and the Reborn Men, side by side—"

The diamond walls of the chamber shone and glittered. The brain hummed. An arctic coldness descended on the mind of tegeus-Cromis. He looked at his hands.

"Tomb," he said. "You are aware that this will destroy the empire just as surely as Canna Moidart destroyed it?"

The dwarf came hurriedly to his feet.

"What?"

"They are too beautiful, Tomb; they are too accomplished. If you go on with this, there will be no new empire—instead, they will absorb us, and after a millennium's pause, the Afternoon Cultures will resume their long sway over the earth.

"No malice will be involved. Indeed, they may thank us many times over for bringing them back to the world. But, as you have said yourself, they have a view of life that is alien to us; and do not forget that it was them who made the waste around us."

As he gazed at the perfect bodies of the Resurrected Men, a massive sadness, a brutal sense of incompleteness, came upon him. He studied the honest face of the dwarf before him, but could find no echo of his own emotion—only puzzlement, and, beneath that, a continuing elation.

"Tomb, I want no part of this."

As he walked toward the arch from which they had issued, his head downcast so that he should not see that queer dance—so that he should not be ensnared and fascinated by its inhumanity—Methvet Nian, Queen Jane of Viriconium, barred his way. Her violet eyes pierced him.

"Cromis, you should not feel like this. It is Grif's death that has brought you down. You blame yourself, you see things crookedly. Please—"

tegeus-Cromis said: "Madam, I caused his death. I am sick of myself; I am sick of being constantly in the wrong place at the wrong time; I am sick of the endless killing that is necessary to right my mistakes. He was my *friend*. Even Trinor was once my friend.

"But that is not at issue.

"My lady, we regarded the Northmen as barbarians, and they were." He laughed. "Today, *we* are the barbarians. *Look* at them!"

And when she turned to watch the choreography of the brain, the celebration of ten thousand years of death and rebirth, he fled.

He ran toward the light. When he passed the corpse of his dead friend, he began to weep again. He picked up his sword. He tried to smash a crystal window with its hilt. The corridor oppressed him. Beyond the windows, the dead brains drifted. He ran on.

"You should have done it," whispered Birkin Grif in the soft spaces of his skull; and, "OUROBUNDOS!" giggled the insane door, as he fell through it and into the desert wind. His cloak cracking and whipping about him, so that he resembled a crow with broken wings, he stumbled toward the black airboat. His mind mocked him. His face was wet.

He threw himself into the command bridge. Green light swam about him, and the dead Northmen stared blindly at him as he turned on the power. He did not choose a direction, it chose him. Under full acceleration, he fled out into the empty sky.

And so tegeus-Cromis, Lord of the Methven, was not present at the forming of the Host of the Reborn Men, at their arming in the depths of the Lesser Waste, or their marching. He did not see the banners.

Neither was he witness to the fall of Soubridge, when, a month after the sad death of Birkin Grif, Tomb the Giant Dwarf led the singing men of the Afternoon Cultures against a great army of Northmen, and took the victory.

He was not present when the wolves burned Soubridge, and, in desperation, died.

He did not see the Storming of the Gates, when Alstath Fulthor—after leading a thousand Resurrected Men over the Monar Mountains in the depths of winter—attacked the Pastel City from the northeast;

Or the brave death of Rotgob Mungo, a captain of the North, as he tried in vain to break the long Siege of the Artists' Quarter, and bled his life out in the Bistro Californium;

Nor was he there when Tomb met Alstath Fulthor on the Proton Circuit, coming from the opposite end of the city, and shook his hand.

He was not present at that final retaking of Methven's hall, when five hundred men died in one hour, and Tomb got his famous wound. They looked for him there, but he did not come.

He did not break with them into the inner room of the palace, there among the drifting curtains of light; or discover beneath the dying wreck of Usheen the Sloth, the Queen's Beast, the cold and beautiful corpse of Canna Moidart, the last twist of the knife.

It is rumoured that the Young Queen wept over the Old, her cousin. But he did not see that, either.

EPILOGUE

Methvet Nian, the Queen of Viriconium, stood at early evening on the sand dunes that lay like a lost country between the land and the sea. Swift and tattered scraps of rag, black gulls sped and fought over her downcast head.

She was a tall and supple woman, clad in a gown of heavy russet velvet, and her skin was neither painted nor jewelled, as was the custom of the time. The nine identical Rings of Neap glittered from her long fingers. Her hair, which recalled the colour of autumn rowans, hung in soft waves to her waist, coiled about her breasts.

For a while, she walked the tideline, examining the objects cast up by the sea: paying particular attention to a smooth stone here, a translucent spiny shell there, picking up a bottle the colour of dragonfly armour, throwing down a branch whitened and peculiarly carved by the water. She watched the gulls, but their cries depressed her.

She led her grey horse by its white bridle across the dunes, and found the stone path to the tower which had no name: though it was called by some after that stretch of seaboard on which it stood, that is, Balmacara.

Balmacara was broken—its walls were blackened, it was like a broken tooth—and despite the spring that had brought green back to the land after a winter of darkness and harsh contrasts, the rowan woods that surrounded it were without life.

Among them in the growing gloom of twilight, she came upon the wreck of the crystal launch that had brought down the tower. It was black, and a wolf's head with wine-red eyes stared at her from its buckled hull— quite without menace, for the paint was already beginning to peel.

She passed it, and came to the door; she tethered her horse.

She called out, but there was no answer.

She climbed fifty stone steps, and found that night had already taken the husk of the tower. Dusk was brown in the window arches, heaped up in great drifts in the corners. Her footsteps echoed emptily, but there was a strange, quiet music in the tower, a mournful, steely mode, cadences that brought tears to her violet eyes.

He sat on a wall-bed covered with blue embroidered silks. Around him on the walls hung trophies: a powered battle-axe he had got from his friend Tomb the Dwarf after the sea fight at Mingulay in the Rivermouth Campaign; the gaudy standard of Thorisman Carlemaker, whom he had defeated single-handed in the Mountains of Monadliath; queer weapons, and astrological equipment discovered in deserts.

He did not look up as she entered.

His fingers depressed the hard strings of his instrument; its tone was low and melancholy. He recited the following verse, which he had composed on the Cruachan Ridge in Monar:

"Strong visions: I have strong visions of this place in the empty times. . . . Far below there are wavering pines. . . . I left the rowan el-phin woods to fulminate on ancient headlands, dipping slowly into the glasen seas of evening. . . . On the devastated peaks of hills we ease the barrenness into our thin bones like a foot into a tight shoe. . . . The narrative of this place: other than the smashed arris of the ridge there are only sad winds and silences. . . . I lay on the cairn one more rock. . . . I am possessed by Time. . . ."

When he had finished, she said, "My lord, we waited for you to come."

In the gloom, he smiled. He still wore his torn cloak, his ragged, dented shirt of mail. The nameless sword was at his side. He had this mannerism: that when he was worried or nervous, his hand strayed out unknown to him and caressed its hilt.

He said with the grave politeness of his time, "Lady, I would have come had I felt there was any need for me."

"Lord Cromis," she answered, "you are absurd." She laughed, and did not let him see her pity. "Death brought you here to sulk and bite yourself like an animal. In Viriconium, we have ceased to brood on death."

"That is your choice, madam."

"The Reborn Men are among us: they give us new arts, new perspectives; and from us they learn how to live in a land without despoiling it. If it brings you satisfaction, Cromis, you were correct—the empire is dead.

"But so are the Afternoon Cultures. And something wholly new has re-placed them both."

He rose, and went to the window. His tread was silent and swift. He faced her, and the sun bled to death behind him.

"Is there room in this new empire for an involuntary assassin?" he asked. "Is there?"

"Cromis, you are a fool." And she would allow him no answer to that. Later, he made her look at the Name Stars.

"There," he said. "You will not deny this: no one who came after could read what is written there. All empires gutter, and leave a language their heirs cannot understand."

She smiled up at him, and pushed her hair back from her face.

"Alstath Fulthor the Reborn Man could tell you what it means," she said.

"It is important to my nature," he admitted, "that it remain a mystery to me. If you will command him to keep a close mouth, I will come back."

A STORM
OF WINGS

A STORM OF WINGS

1

THE MOON LOOKING DOWN

In the dark tidal reaches of one of those unnamed rivers which spring from the mountains behind Cladich, on a small domed island in the shallows before the sea, fallen masonry of a great age glows faintly under the eye of an uncomfortable moon. A tower once stood here in the shadow of the estuarine cliffs, made too long ago for anyone to remember, in a way no one left can understand, from a single obsidian monolith fully two hundred feet in length. For ten thousand years wind and water scoured its southern face, finding no weakness; and at night a yellow light might be discerned in its topmost window, coming and going as if someone there passed before a flame. Who brought it to this rainy country, where in winter the gales drive the white water up the Minch and fishermen from Lendalfoot shun the inshore ground, and for what purpose, is unclear. Now it lies in five pieces. The edges of the stone are neither shattered nor worn, but melted like candle wax. The causeway that once gave access here—from a beach on the west bank where lumps of volcanic glass are scattered on the sand— is drowned now, and all that comes up it from the water is a strange lax vegetation, a sprawl of giant sea hemlock which for some reason has forsaken the mild and beneficial brine of the estuary to colonise the beach, spread its pale and pulpy stems over the shattered tower, and clutch at a stand of dead, white pines.

In this time, in the Time of the Locust, when we have nothing to ourselves but the hollowness within us, in the Time of Bone, when we have nothing to do but wait, nothing human moves here. Nothing human has moved here for eighty years. Fire, were it brought here, would be pale and dim, hard to kindle. Passion would fade here on a whisper. Something in the tower's fall has poisoned the air here, and drained the landscape of its power. White and sickly and infinitely slow, the hemlock creeps out of the water to run sad rubbery fingers over the rubbish in the fallen rooms. The collapse of the tower seems complete, the defeat of artifice accomplished.

Yet in the Time of the Locust are we not counselled to patience? Eighty years have passed since tegeus-Cromis broke the yoke of Canna Moidart, since the Chemosit fell and the Reborn Men came among us; and in the deeps of this autumn night, under the aegis of an old and bitter geology, we witness here in events astronomical and enigmatic an intersection crucial to both the earth and the precarious foothold on it of the adolescent Evening Cultures. "Wait! Things are. Things happen. Only wait!" The estuarine cliffs impend, black, expectant; the air is full of frost and anticipation . . .

It is the hour of our old enemy, the moon. Her fugitive reflections shiver on the water amid the cold unmeaning patterns of the wind. Above, her tense circle aches across the sky (imprisoned there within it, staring down, the pocked face of our mysterious crone, our companion of a million-million years). Somewhere between midnight and dawn, in that hour when sick men topple from the high ledges of themselves and fall into the darkness, suddenly and with no warning, something can be seen to detach itself from the edge of that charmed circle and, through the terrible spaces surrounding, speed towards the earth. It is only a tiny puff of vapour, a cloud of pollen blown across a single ray of light in some darkened, empty room—gone in the time it takes to blink, to rub the eyes and rearrange the waiting brain—but nothing like this has been seen for ten thousand years; and though all might seem unchanged, and the moon hang never so white and hard over the rim of the cliffs, like a powdered face yearning from a vacant doorway, and the memory decide the eye has played it false—nothing will ever be the same again.

Not many hours later, as the thin, uncertain light of day spreads like smoke between the soft fat stems, limning the fallen column of the tower, a figure emerges from the hemlock thickets—puzzled and reluctant as if harried from a deep sleep—to scan the southern sky where the moon is still a bone-white image, the cankered face which lingers in a dream. The old man shivers a little, and settles his cloak about his shoulders; they confront for a time, man and planet. But then in an instant, sunrise proper has splattered everything below with blood—the sea, the shore, the hemlock, and the old man's cloak all smeared and dappled with it—and he turns urgently away to drag from cover a small crude wooden boat. Its keel grates on the shingle, oars fall whitely on the water. The day brightens, but as he rows, the old man winces from the ominous sky. Beaching his boat on the western shore, muttering and panting with the effort, he pauses at the water's edge for a final glimpse of the tower, locked in its long struggle with decay, then shrugs and hurries up a flight of steps cut long ago into the cliff. While behind him, a single fish eagle with wings of a curious colour beats up out of the bright south and swoops over the island like a valediction.

In the Time of the Locust it is given to us to see such things.

The Reborn Men do not think as we do. They live in waking dreams, pursued by a past they do not understand, harried by a birthright which has no meaning to them: taunted by amnesia of the soul.

Alstath Fulthor, the first of them to be drawn by Tomb the Iron Dwarf from millennial interment in the Lesser Rust Desert, remembered nothing of his previous life: instead, his steps were dogged by a suspicion he could not make plain even to himself. His body, his blood, his very germ cells knew (or so it seemed to him), but could find no everyday language in which to tell him what his life had been like during the frigid lunacy of the Afternoon. Dark hints reached him. But the quivering fibrils of his nervous system were adjusted to receive messages dispersed a thousand or more years before, intimations faded on the winds of time.

In the months following his revival he dreamt constantly: sometimes of a large silver insect, clicking and metallic, the life cycle of which he was able to observe in all its main aspects; at others of a woman (who sat alone in a room so tall that its ceiling was a web of shadow, spinning a golden thread which, of its own accord, rose and flickered from her hands until it filled all that mysterious, immense, whispering space above her). In the ruck and ruin of Soubridge, with its warehouses full of rotting fish and massacred children, during the long icy march through the Monar Mountains in winter, and at the storming of the Northeast Gate, these images came repeatedly between him and the battle: the insect with its expressionless faceted eyes, the woman with her jewelled spinaret. (Often he inflicted dreadful cuts on its carapace; or smeared her sleeve with blood; and once, as he fought his way through the streets of Viriconium to shake the hand of Tomb the Dwarf over a heap of Northmen's corpses, the flames along the Proton Circuit merged for a moment with the woman's strange writhing skein, so that his past and his present crackled in a lightning arc through his mind and he fell on his face blinded, and was taken for dead, no longer able to tell which was real—the airy whisper of the city fires or the roaring of that golden cloud. . . .) Steadily though, as if he were leaving the haven of some second childhood, even these reference points seemed to be withdrawn from him, to be replaced by a rushing chaos, the sense of an act of memory continually performed without relief, a hidden river in the night, from which might sometimes surface unbidden some fragment of an event drifting like a dead branch amid the unidentifiable rubbish of the tides. . . .

A face stalked him between the twilit stacks of the ancestral library, bobbing like a balloon. It came very close to his, twitching and dissolving under the impact of some deeply felt emotion, then retreated with a hiss of indrawn breath.

"What are you doing?" someone asked him. They were outside the walls but he didn't know where. . . .

He stumbled through the arteries of his home, his brain buzzing and vibrating with a new vigour, discovering chambers and oubliettes he had never seen before. At every turn hands beckoned him in. . . .

Here, organic towers, tall shapeless masses of tissue cultured from the plasm of ancient mammals, trumpeted and moaned across the abandoned wastes of another continent, their huge cynical voices modulating on the wind, now immensely distant, now close at hand. *Natural philosophy,* they maintained (holding him to be in heresy), *is a betrayal of invention. It is an edifice of clay.* It was always night there. . . .

A city spread itself before him in the wet, equivocal afternoon light like interrupted excavations in a sunken garden. It could be reached by a ladder of bone. "I will go down into that place!"

With these poor and misleading relics of a dead culture he tried to create a past for himself and so achieve, like any other human being, some experiential perspective from which to judge his own actions, crouching, as it were, on the banks of his own internal stream and scooping from the water those things which floated closest. They rarely helped him in dealing with the new reality of the Evening Cultures. And at least one of the catches he made in this manner came to haunt him, a dead thing risen from the bottom mud of one incarnation to infect his perception of the other. It was not a normal memory, rendered as an image—a sound, a scent, a vision of a face or place. Rather it came as an act he felt compelled to perform—or one which his body might perform quite of its own accord, as if his muscles remembered what he did not—and in performing, recall.

Eighty years, then, had passed since tegeus-Cromis broke the yoke of Canna Moidart, since the Chemosit fell and dragged the North down with them; and Alstath Fulthor, first among the Reborn Men, heir to a technology whose power he could not really appreciate, a lord respected among the councils of the Pastel City, was running through the foothills of the Monar as if his life depended upon it, without any knowledge of why he ran or what compelled him to do it.

He was a tall man, as are all the Reborn, and a thin one, clad in tunic and trousers of black satin, the contorted yellow crest or ideograph of his House writhing over his breast. On his feet were the curious flimsy shoes his race wore in preference to boots, and at his waist hung a short forceknife, or *baan,* dug up along with its ancient ceramic scabbard from some desert. His long coarse yellow hair was tangled and damp, and sweat filmed his prominent birdlike features. He came into Dyke Head Moss

over the steep and dangerous ground at the head of Rossett Gill, the low
rounded hills about him browned with autumn; shot the screes at
Surgeon's Gate with arms windmilling to keep his balance and grey dust
exploding round him as he went; and gained the valley path in a few long,
energetic strides. That the pace he set would have crippled an ordinary
man he was unaware. His queer green eyes were blank and unfocused, but
with a psychic rather than a physical weariness. In the more foolish and
fashionable salons of Viriconium he was held to be the "most human" of
the Reborn, but this was a silly expression (not to say a meaningless one),
and if there was anything more or less human in his face now it was only
despair.

Thirty-six hours before, black and incontrovertible, the madness had
driven him from his comfortable house on the edge of Minnet-Saba,
dragged him through the silent predawn streets of the city, along Proton
Circuit to the Northeast Gate, and so up into the icy gullies of the Monar,
where it showed him the evil landscapes of quite another country (in his
ears was a prolonged metallic moan rising on a *föhn* wind, while against the
horizon moved tall and cumbersome shapes) and drove him on with
"Run! Run!" whispered in every chamber of the heart, shrieked in the
skull's deep recess and echoed in each atom of his pounding blood. The
known world fled away from him. The running hours became simply
the spaces between dreams. The great fault between "now" and "then"
opened itself on him like a chasm and he ran along its rim—poised, taut,
forever . . .

A hundred and forty miles he had come, or more, in a long loop through
the hills, old landscapes fomenting in his brain: but the fit was leaving him
as he descended Dyke Head Moss, and his senses were returned to him
one by one. A stream glittered beside him. Sheep were bleating distantly as
the shepherds drove them down from the upland turf to winter pasture in
the valley. The air was harsh with the scent of peat and ling heather, and
below him the path fell away in a series of curves and re-entrants and gentle descents to the distant city. Weariness was replacing the mixture of elation and dread which had filled him while he ran. From a state of black
exultation he tumbled into one of puzzlement. He had run like this a
thousand years before: but from what? Where had he run to? What fears
had pullulated in his brain? What curious joy?

Under the brow of Hollin Low Moor he slowed to a walk. His feet and
ankles hurt. He sat on a rock by the path to massage them, and his attention was captured by the city, waiting there in its mantle of stillness and
distance. Light flared through the haze: heliographing from the riverine
curves of the Proton Circuit; phosphorescing from the pleasure canal at

Lowth where, under a setting sun, banks of anemones glowed like triumphal stained glass; signalling from the tiered vivid heights of Minnet-Saba, from the inconceivable pastel towers and plazas of the Atteline Quarter. All was immaculate—illuminated, transfigured, miniature. It attracted him not as a refuge (although he saw himself as a refugee), nor by its double familiarity, but by its long strangeness and obstinacy in the face of Time, celebrated here in the generation (or so it seemed) rather than the reflection of light. Viriconium, the Pastel City: a little cryptic, a little proud, a little mad. Its histories, as forgotten as his own, made of the air a sort of amber, an entrapment; the geometry of its avenues was a wry message from one survivor to another; and its present, like his own, was but an implication of its past—a dream, a prediction, a brief possibility to be endured.

Thus he fell into a reverie of dispossession, a thin man sitting on a rock in the red wash of sunset, heraldic yellow blazing across his chest, while in his face puzzlement contended with weariness and a certain awe. The light began to fail about him. The valley sounds intensified then died away. A cool wind sprang down from Rossett Gill to rustle like a small animal in the bracken. When he looked up again the city was lost, the evening grey and chilly, and an old man in a long cloak was walking up the path towards him.

He got to his feet and stretched his stiff limbs. Covertly he studied the newcomer's apparel for the Sign of the Locust. When he could not find it he let his hand drop from the hilt of his *baan*.

"Hello, old man," he said.

The old man stopped. He was barefooted and dusty, bent as if from a long journey undertaken in haste and poverty, and his face was hidden in the depths of his hood. Fulthor would have taken him for a tenant farmer, or one of the small shopkeepers of the south, called away from Soubridge or Lendalfoot to bring a dowry to the wedding of a favourite daughter (copper in the shape of a dolphin, long-hoarded; a small piece of steel equal to the profits of one fig tree), tears and unbleached cloth to the funeral of a younger son. But his cloak was of good fabric, and woven with odd mathematical designs which seemed to ebb and flow in the receding light. And, "You cannot always be running, Alstath Fulthor," he whispered, his eyes glittering brightly from the darkness of the hood. "Why do you waste your time—and the time of your adopted city not less!—away in the brown hills like this?"

Fulthor was intrigued, and a little taken aback. It was a strange place for such a meeting. He shrugged and smiled.

"Why do you waste yours in asking, old man?" he answered.

The old man shivered, and with a quick unconscious movement of the head glanced up at the southern sky before he spoke again. The high, naked shriek of a fish eagle echoed over the fells, but there was no moon yet in the sky.

In a palace like a shell—in Methven's hall where the Proton Circuit draws itself up into a spiral on a hundred pillars of thin black stone—Methvet Nian, Queen Jane, Queen in Viriconium, who in her youth had taken to the windy birch stands and glacial lakes of the Rannoch Moor, hunted away by the Chemosit and wild as any moss-trooper's daughter (with the last of the Methven limping and scarred to guard her, a poet and a dead metal bird to guide her, and a giant dwarf to expedite her passage), sat before five false windows in a tall room floored with cinnabar crystal. She was surrounded by precious, complex objects of forgotten use—machines or sculptures excavated from ruined cities in the Rust Desert beyond Duirinish. Curtains of pale, fluctuating light drifted irregularly about the chamber like showers of rain, and through the dreamlike shadows thus created shambled the Queen's Beast—one of the great white sloths of the Southern forests, who are said to be the fallen remnants of a star-faring race invited or lured to earth during the madness of the Afternoon.

Eighty years had passed since Usheen, the first of her beasts, died on Canna Moidart's knife, and in dying sealed the final defeat of the North. tegeus-Cromis lay two decades still and dead beneath the fields of sol d'or at Lowth. Methvet Nian was no longer young, even by the standards of the Evening. Still, in her purple eyes there might yet be discerned something of the girl who in the space of one year lost and gained the Last Kingdom of the world: and in the dreaming light where those five false windows showed landscapes to be found nowhere in Viriconium, her age weighed only lightly on her—like the hand of some imaginary child. Inside, the windows flickered. Outside it was autumn, and under a cold moon processions of men with insect faces went silently through the streets.

A curious thing happened to her.

Often in that flickering room the past had come to touch her with quiet persistence, tugging at her sleeve in the effort to capture her attention: white hares in the twilight at Shining Clough Moss or Torside Naze; the long brown sweep of the Rannoch peat moors like a brush stroke in some enormous written language; desert dust piling itself noiselessly in the bleak plazas of Ruined Drunmore. But these were no more or less than the sad fingerprints of memory on her brain (she remembered the verses tegeus-Cromis made, the ancient cry of the fish eagles, and his voice out of night and morning): tonight it was something more. The windows flickered; the windows shimmered; the windows said,

"Methvet Nian."

All five went blank and dark.

"Methvet Nian!"

Smoke and snow filled them, a pearly grey light like dawn over the tottering seracs of some marine glacier in the north beyond the North. It shivered and was wrenched away—

"Methvet Nian!"

Fused sand, and a sky filled with mica, the rolling dunes and dry saline wadis of the sempiternal erg. In the fierce air hung a perfect mirage of the city, pastel towers tall and mathematical, cut with strange designs. The wind stooped like a hawk—

"Methvet Nian!"

She approached the windows fatalistically, and with a sense of being drawn or invoked (seeing herself perhaps walk complaisantly through them and out into some other time). Now they poured out on her a green and submarine radiance, as if the palace she stood in truly were a shell, or a ship full of drowned sailors spinning forever beneath the ancient clammy sea. All other lights in the throne room were dimmed; the sloth whimpered, rearing puzzledly up on its hind legs, great ambered claws extending and retracting nervously.

"Hush," she said. "Who wishes to speak to me?" and was still.

"Methvet Nian."

The deep-sea gloom surged, foamed, blew away, like spindrift off a wave in the invisible wind, only to be replaced by the image of a cavernous, ruined room which seemed to be full of dusty stuffed birds. Moonlight filtered through rents in the walls. An old man stood before her, pentadic, five-imaged. His long domed skull was yellow and fleshless, his eyes green and his lips thin. His skin was so fine and tight as to be translucent, the bones shining through it like jade. His age, she thought, has outstripped mere physical symptoms, and exalted him. His robe was embroidered with subtle gold designs having this property, that in every draught of air they seemed to shift and flow, responsive to each movement of the cloth but independent of it.

She trembled. She put out a hand to touch cold glass.

The cry of gulls rang in her ears, and the sound of a cold grey sea lapping on black sand far away and long ago.

"Do the dead live in that country, then?" she whispered, twisting her fingers in the white fur of the sloth. "Beyond the windows?"

"Methvet Nian."

East and south of Monar runs a strip of heathland whose name, when it still had one, was a handful of primitive syllables scattered like a question into the damp wind. It is a deserted and superseded country, that one, full of the monuments and inarticulate ghosts of a race older than Viriconium, younger than the Afternoon Cultures, and possibly more naive than either: a short-lived nation of tribal herdsmen who buried their dead once-yearly in tiered barrows and knew nothing more of their heritage than that it should be avoided. Of the future they knew nothing at all. Worked metal was the death knell of them, tolling from the crude and ceaseless smithies of the North. Their works, ridge path and necropolis alike, have now taken on the air of natural features and, overgrown with gorse and young beech, become one with the sombre expanse of long mounds and shallow valleys sloping away to merge imperceptibly with the Rannoch beyond.

This place avoided the poisoned hands of the Afternoon only to age and grow enfeebled instead. Curlews make free of its sad desuetude; hares play in the deep cloughs and sheltered hollows of a land which has quietly exhausted itself; it ignores the traveller, and gently seeks the night. Here on many an evening in the latter part of the year darkness visits the earth while the pale wreck of the sunset still commands the sky. The air is suffused with brightness yet somehow lacks the power to illuminate. In a moment each declivity has brimmed up with shadow and become the abode of mumbling wind and the shy thin ghosts who never dreamed of the Afternoon or knew its iron, at first or second hand. On just such an evening one autumn, eighty years after the Fall of the North, grey smoke might have been seen issuing from the chimney of a small red caravan parked on an old ridgeway deep in the heart of the heath; and from a considerable hole newly dug in the ground nearby, the chink of metal on metal—

It was a four-wheeled caravan of the type traditionally used by the Mingulay tinker to move his enormous family and meagre equipment along the warm summer roads of the South. Indeed, the South vibrated in it, every panel and peg, lively atrocious designs in electric blue rioting over its sides, its thick spokes picked out in canary yellow, the curved roof a racy purple to throw back the last of the light in a challenge to the sombre crawling umbers of the heath. The hilarious, slovenly children, it seemed, were not long departed, run off snot-nosed to go blackberrying among the brambles. Smoke rose, and a smell of food. Two dusty ponies tethered to the backboard with a bit of frayed rope cropped the short ridgeway turf in noisy self-absorption, lop ears cocked to catch the voice of their master, who, though rendered invisible by the embankment of fresh sandy soil surrounding his pit, could be heard from time to time punctuating with vile threats and oaths the low monotonous humming of some Rivermouth dirge. But no children returned from the bracken (we hear their voices fade and recede across the long darkness of the heath), and this impatient excavation continued unwearyingly until the light had almost left the sky.

Long shadows engulfed the caravan; its chimney ceased to smoke; the ponies shuffled at the end of their tether. Fresh showers of earth added height to the ramparts. Then a peculiar thing happened.

The sound of digging ceased . . .

A great white light came up out of the pit and flared soundlessly into the sky like a signal to the stars . . .

(Simultaneously an enormous voice could be heard to shout, "OOGABOURINDRA! BORGA! OOGABOURINDRA-BA!")

And a small figure dressed in the leather leggings of a metal-prospector was hurled out of the hole, cartwheeling like a horse-chestnut leaf in a March wind, to fall heavily in a heap of harness near the tethered ponies (who bared their old yellow teeth in brief contempt and immediately resumed their greedy pulling at the turf), its beard smouldering furiously, its long white hair alight, and all its accoutrements charred. For a moment it sat on the ground as if stunned; beat feebly at itself, muttering the foulest of marsh oaths from Cladich; then sank back, insensible, silent, smoking. All around, the light that had come up from the earth was fading from white and the invisible colours through a strange series of violets and pinks to darkness and vanishment. A small breeze searched the rowan and thorn for it; shrugged; and departed.

Tomb the Iron Dwarf, acting at the lean end of his life on an impulse he didn't fully understand, had left the Great Brown Waste, his longtime prospecting ground, and in his one hundred and fiftieth year travelled through Methedrin in the spring, where amid the tumbling meltwater and short-lived flower meadows he recalled other times and other journeys. Surprised by his own sentimentality and suddenly aware he was seeking something special, he'd dawdled south down the Rannoch, warming his old bones. "One last discovery," he had promised himself, one last communion with ancient metal, and then an end to arthritic nights; but this seemed a strange place to make it. What he might find in a land that hadn't known industry for millennia, what he might return with for the last time to the Pastel City, he couldn't imagine. He had not seen the city for twenty years, or his friend Fulthor. He had never seen the Sign of the Locust.

When he woke up, it was dark, and he was inside his caravan. A tall old man in a hooded cloak bent over him like a question mark in the orange lamplight. Strange designs worked into the weave of the garment seemed to shift and writhe as he moved.

Tomb winced away, his thick gnarled hands yearning for the axe he had not used in a decade (it lay beneath his bed; his armour was there too, packed in a trunk; so his life had gone since the Fall of the North). "Why have you come here, old ghost?" he said. "I'll cut off your arms!" he whispered as he lost consciousness again, feeling an old cruelty sweep over him like a familiar pain; and then, waking suddenly with his wide astonished eyes staring into that aged face, skin like parchment stretched over a clear lemon-yellow flame, he remembered! Ten thousand grey wings beat down the salty wind like a storm in his head!

"We thought you were dead," he said. "We thought you were dead!" And slept.

2

GALEN HORNWRACK AND THE SIGN OF THE LOCUST

Autumn. Midnight. The eternal city. The moon hangs over her like an attentive white-faced lover, its light reaching into dusty corners and empty lots. Like all lovers it remarks equally the blemish and the beauty spot—limning the iridium fretwork and baroque spires of the fabled Atteline Plaza even as it silvers the fishy eye of the old woman cutting fireweed and elder twigs among the ruins of the Cispontine Quarter, whose towers suffered most during the War of the Two Queens. The city is a product of her own dreams, a million years of them. Now she turns in her sleep, so quietly you can hear the far-off rumour of the newest: white bones, the Song of the Locust, dry mandibles rubbing together in desert nights . . . or is it only a wind out of Monar, and autumn leaves filling the air, to scrape and patter in the side streets?

In the Artists' Quarter it is that hour of the night when all and nothing seem possible. The bistros are quiet. The entertainments and smoking parlours are all closed. Even Fat Mam Etteilla the fortune-teller has shipped her wicked pack of cards, put up for a few hours the shutters of her grubby satin booth, and waddled off with her aching ankles and her hacking cough, which is bad tonight. Canker, the *Dark Man* of the cards, has her by the lungs; she leans against a wall to spit in a puddle of moonlight, whispering the word that will hold him back; it falls hollowly into the vibrant, vacant street. The canker, she confides to her shadow, will take her in its own good time; at present she is less concerned about herself than her last customer of the evening. She has a wan belief in her own efficacy, and tells the silent Quarter, "I did my best, I did my best—"

She did her best—

"There is nothing good in the cards spread thus.

"Bogrib, NOTHINGNESS, crosses you, and here is NUMBER FOUR, called by some 'the Name Stars': beware a fire.

"A woman shadows you, POVERTY lies behind you, the Lessing; and before you a discussion, or it may be water.

"Nothing is clear tonight—who is that, running in the alley? I heard steps for a moment in the alley—but see the MANTIS here, praying at the moon beneath three arches. The first is for something new; the second for injustice; under the third arch all will be made different. Something taken away long ago is now returned.

"These are your thoughts on the matter, to turn this card I must have something more. Thank you. FIVE TOWERS! Do nothing, I beseech you, that you might regret. Fear death from the air, and avoid the North—

"Wait! We have hardly begun! Three more cards remain to be turned!"

—but he went all the same, rapidly down the street and into the Alley of Bakers: a dark self-sufficient figure whose face she never clearly saw, going with a light and dangerous tread.

Once in the alley and out of Mam Etteilla's earshot (for fear perhaps she might pursue him, predicting, haranguing, or merely coughing up her lungs), he allowed himself to laugh a little, baring his teeth wryly to the grim city, the walls which contained him, the towers which had failed him, the night which covered him; and he quickened his pace, making for the Bistro Californium, that home of all errors and all who err. The air had stilled itself; it was sharp and cold, and his breath hung about him in a cloud. He did not enter the Californium at once but hung like a bird of prey on the edge of the lamplight to see who might await him inside. In this bright, static quadrant of the night's existence the city seemed shattered and fragmentary, tumbled into hard meaningless patterns of light and shade, blue and grey and faded gamboge, grainy of texture and difficult of interpretation. Stray beams of smoky lemon-yellow barred his harsh worn features, his tired hooded eyes. When a dog barked down in the Cispontine Quarter—desultory, monotonous, distant—he seemed to stiffen for a moment; pass his hand over his face; and look puzzledly about him, for all the world like a man who wakes from a nightmare to an empty, buzzing dream, and wonders briefly how his life has led him *here*. . . .

Fear death from the air!

His name was Galen Hornwrack. He was a lord without a domain, an eagle without wings, and he did not fear the air, he loved it. The War of the Two Queens had ended his boyhood without hope, and he had spent the slow years since hidden away in the mazy alleys of the Artists' Quarter, the better to regret an act of fate which (so it appeared to him) had robbed his existence of any promise or purpose before it was fairly begun. Out of spite against himself or against the world, he never knew which, he had not taken up a profession, learning to use the steel knife instead to cut a living from the streets, shunning his peers and watching himself turn from a young man full of dreams into an older one stuffed with emptiness and fear. Fear death from the air! He feared it at every corner—it yawned at him from every alley's mouth—but never from there, where he would willingly have burned or bled or hung like a corpse from the million-year gallows of his own pain!

Presently he shook himself, laughed harshly, and, certain that the Californium contained no obvious trap or enemy, abandoned the shadows like a viper. One hand hung visible by his side while the other, beneath his threadbare grey cloak, rested on the hilt of his good plain knife. In that manner he made his way through the notorious chromium portals behind which Rotgob Mungo, a captain of the North, had in the last days of Canna Moidart's rule laid his vain and valiant plans to break the siege of the Artists' Quarter, only to bleed out his life—albeit more honourably than many of his kin—under the strange axe of Alstath Fulthor.

Californium! The very word is like a bell, tolling all the years of the city—tolling for the mad poets of the Afternoon with all their self-inflicted wounds and desperate drugged sojourns at its rose-coloured glass tables; tolling for their skinless jewelled women who, lolling beneath the incomprehensible frescoes, took tea from porcelain as lucid as a baby's ear; tolling for Jiro-San and Adolf Ableson, for Clane and Grishkin and the crimes which sickened their minds in the rare service of Art—their formless, quavering light extinguished now, their names forgotten, their feverish stanzas no more than a faint flush on the face of the world, a fading resonance in the ears of Time!

Californium!—a knell for the new nobles of Borring's court, the unkempt rural harpists who only five centuries ago filled the place with sawdust and thin beer and vomit, beating out their sagas and great lying epics like swords on a Rivermouth anvil while Viriconium, the only city they had ever seen, refurbished itself around them (remembering, perhaps, its long declining dream) and, at the head of Low Leedale, the cold stronghold of Duirinish levered its way upward stone by stone to bar the way to the wolves of the North. They were here!

Here too came the young tegeus-Cromis, a lord in Methven's halls before the death of his proud sister, morose and ascetic in a bice velvet cloak, eager to stitch the night through with the eerie self-involved notes of a curious Eastern gourd . . . Californium! Philosophers and tinkers; poetry, art, and revolution; princes like vagrants and migrant polemicists with voices soft as a snake's; the absolute beat and quiver of Time, the voice of the city; millennia of verse echo from its chromium walls, drift in little dishonest flakes of sound from that peculiarly frescoed ceiling!

Tonight it was like a grave.

Tonight (with the night in the grip of the Locust, at the mercy of a poetry as icy and formal as an instinct) it was filled with the singular moonlight, bright yet leaden, arctic and elusive, that seeped in from the street. It was cold. And from its windows the city was a broad ingenuous diorama, blue-grey, lemon-yellow, textured like crude paper. Each table cast a precise dull shadow on the floor, as did each table's occupant, caught in frozen contemplation of some crime or moral feebleness—Lord Mooncarrot, he with the receding brow and rotting Southern estates (gardens filled with perspiring leaden statuary and wild white cats), pondering the blackmail of his wife; Ansel Verdigris the derelict poet, head like an antipodean cockatoo's, fingering his knife and two small coins; Chorica nam Vell Ban, half-daughter of the renegade Norvin Trinor, forgiven but shunned by the society she craved—the persistent moon illuminated them all, and shadows ate their puzzled faces, a handful of rogues and poseurs and failures watching midnight away in the security of their own sour fellowship.

Lord Galen Hornwrack found an empty table and settled himself among them to drink cheap wine and stare impassively into the lunar street, waiting for whatever the long empty night might bring.

It was to bring him three things: the Sign of the Locust; a personal encounter wan and oblique enough for the bleak white midnight outside; and a betrayal.

The Sign of the Locust is unlike any other religion invented in Viriconium. Its outward forms and observances—its liturgies and rituals, its theurgic or metaphysical speculations, its daily processionals—seem less an attempt by men to express an essentially human invention than the effort of some raw and independent Idea—a theophneustia, existing without recourse to brain or blood: a Muse or demiurge—to express *itself*. It wears its congregation like a disguise: we did not so much create the Sign of the Locust as invite it into ourselves, and now it dons us nightly like a cloak and domino to go abroad in the world.

Who knows exactly where it began, or how? For as much as a century (or as little as a decade: estimates vary) before it made its appearance on the streets, a small group or cabal somewhere in the city had propagated its fundamental tenet—that the appearance of "reality" is quite false, a counterfeit or artefact of the human senses. How hesitantly they must have crept from alley to alley to confirm one another in their grotesque beliefs! How shy to confide them! And yet: the war had left our spirits as ruinous as the Cispontine Quarter. We were tired. We were hungry. The coming of the Reborn Men was disheartening, unlooked-for, punitive. It left us with a sense of having been replaced. How eagerly in the end we clutched at this pitiless, elegant systemization of one simple nihilistic premise!

"The world is not as we perceive it," maintained the early converts, "but infinitely more surprising. We must cultivate a diverse view." This mild (even naive) truism, however, was to give way rapidly—via a series of secret and bloody heretical splits—to a more radical assertion. A wave of murders, mystifying to the population at large, swept the city. It was during this confused period that the Sign itself first came to light, that simple yet tortuous adaptation of the fortune-teller's MANTIS symbol which, cut in steel or silver, swings at the neck of each adherent. Ostlers and merchant princesses, soldiers and shopkeepers, astrologers and vagabonds, were discovered sprawled stiffly in the gutters and plazas, strangled in an unknown fashion and their bodies tattooed with symbolical patterns, as the entire council of the Sign, elected by secret ballot from the members of the original cabal, tore itself apart in a grotesque metaphysical dispute. A dreadful sense of immanence beset the city. "Life is a blasphemy," announced the Sign. "Procreation is a blasphemy, for it replicates and fosters the human view of the universe."

Thus the Sign established itself, coming like a coded message from nowhere. Now its apologists range from wheelwright to Court ascetic; it is scrawled on every alley wall to fluoresce in the thin bluish moonlight; it rustles like a dry wind—or so it's said—even in the corridors of Methven's hall. Its complicated subsects, with their headless and apparently aimless structures, issue many bulletins. We counterfeit the "real," they claim, by our very forward passage through time, and thus occlude the actual and essential. One old man feeding a dog might by the power of his spirit maintain the existence of an entire street—the dog, the shamble of houses with their big-armed women and staring children, the cobbles wet with an afternoon's rain, the sunset seen through the top of a ruined tower—and what mysteries lie behind this imperfect shadow play? What truths? They process the streets impulsively, trying to defeat the real, and hoping to come upon a Reborn Man.

Such a procession now made its way toward the Bistro Californium, given up like a breath of malice by the night. It was quick and many-legged in the gloom. It was silent and unnerving. The faces which composed it were nacreous, curiously inexpressive as they yearned on long rubbery necks after their victim. Surprised among the Cispontine ruins not an hour before, this poor creature fled in fits and starts before them, falling in and out of doorways and sobbing in the white moonlight. A single set of running footsteps echoed in the dark. All else was a parched whisper, as if some enormous insect hovered thoughtfully above the chase on strong, chitinous wings.

Since their condition allows them no deeper relief, the merely selfish are raddled with superstition; salt, mirror, "touch wood" are ritual bribes, employed to ensure the approval of an already indulgent continuum. The true solipsist, however, has no need of such toys. His presiding superstition is himself. Galen Hornwrack, then, cared as much for the Sign of the Locust as he did for anything not directly connected with himself or his great loss: that is to say, not in the least. So the first clue to their coming confrontation went unrecognised by him—how could it be otherwise?

Glued to its own feeble destiny in the leaden blue moonlight, the clique at the Bistro Californium regarded its navel with surprised disgust. Verdigris the poet was trying to raise money against the security of a ballad he said he was writing. He bobbed and hopped fruitlessly from shadow to harsh shadow, attempting first to cheat the fat Anax Hermax, epileptic second son of an old Mingulay fish family, then a sleepy prostitute from Minnet-Saba, who only smiled maternally at him, and finally Mooncarrot, who knew him of old. Mooncarrot laughed palely, his eyes focused elsewhere, and flapped his gloves. "Oh dear, oh no, old friend," he whispered murderously. "Oh dear, oh no!" The words fell from his soft mouth one by one like pieces of pork. Verdigris was frantic. He plucked at Mooncarrot's sleeve. "But listen!" he said. He had nowhere to sleep; he had—it has to be admitted—debts too large to run away from; worse, he actually did feel verses crawling about somewhere in the back of his skull like maggots in a corpse, and he needed refuge from them in some woman or bottle. He nodded his head rapidly, shook that dyed fantastic crest of hair. "But listen!" he begged; and, standing on one leg in a pool of weird moonlight, he put his hands behind his back, stretched his neck and recited,

> My dear when the grass rolls in tubular billows
> And the face of the ewe lamb bone white in the meadows
> Sickens and slithers down into the mallows
> Murder will soothe us and settle our fate;
> Hallowed and pillowed in the palm of tomorrow
> We tremble and trouble the hearts of the hollow:
> The teeth of the tigers that stalk in the shallows
> Encrimson the foam at the fisherman's feet!

No one paid him any attention. Hornwrack sat slumped at the edge of the room where he could keep an eye on both door and window (he expected nobody—it was a precaution—it was a habit), his long white hand curled round the handle of a black jug, a smile neglected on his thin lips. Though he loathed and mistrusted Verdigris he was faintly amused by this characteristic display. The poet now choked on his horrid extemporary, mid-line. He was becoming exhausted, staring about like a bullock in an abattoir, moving here and there in little indecisive runs beneath the strange Californium frescoes. Only Hornwrack and Chorica nam Vell Ban were left to importune; he hesitated then turned to the woman, with her pinched face and remote eyes. She will give him nothing, thought Hornwrack. Then we shall see how badly off he really is.

"I *dined* with the hertis-Padnas," she explained confidentially, not looking at Verdigris as he bobbed uxoriously about in front of her. "They were too kind." She seemed to see him for the first time, and her imbecile smile opened like a flower.

"Muck and filth!" screamed Verdigris. "I didn't ask for a social calendar!"

Shivering, he forced himself to face Hornwrack.

A grey shadow materialised behind him at the door and wavered there like some old worn lethal dream.

Hornwrack flung his chair back against the wall and fumbled for his plain steel knife. (Moonlight trickled down its blade and dripped from his wrist.) Verdigris, who had not seen the shadow in the doorway, gaped at him in grotesque surprise. "No, Hornwrack," he said. His tongue, like a little purple lizard, came out and scuttled round his lips. "Please. I only wanted—"

"Get out of my way," Hornwrack told him. "Go on."

Scarlet crest shaking with relief, he gave a great desperate shout of laughter and sprang away in time to give Hornwrack one good look at the figure which now tottered through the door.

A thin skin only, taut as a drumhead, separates us from the future: events leak through it reluctantly, with a faint buzzing sound, if they make any noise at all—like the wind in an empty house before rain. Much later, when an irreversible process of change had hold of them both, he was to learn her name—Fay Glass, of the House of Sleth, famous a thousand and more years ago for its unimaginably oblique acts of cruelty and compassion. But for now she was a mere faint echo of the yet-to-occur, a Reborn Woman with eyes of a fearful honesty, haphazardly cropped hair an astonishing lemon colour, and a carriage awkward to the point of ugliness and absurdity (as if she had forgotten, or somehow never learned, how a human being stands). Her knees and elbows made odd and painful angles beneath the thick velvet cloak she wore; her thin fingers clutched some object wrapped in waterproof cloth and tied up with a bit of coloured leather. Muddy and travel-stained, there she stood, in an attitude of confusion and fear, blinking at Hornwrack's knife proffered like a sliver of midnight and true murder in the eccentric Californium shadows; at Verdigris's disgusting red crest; at Mooncarrot and his kid gloves, smiling and whispering delightedly, "Hello, my dear. Hello, my little damp parsnip—"

"I," she said. She fell down like a heap of sticks.

Verdigris was on her at once, slashing open the bundle even as her fingers relaxed.

"What's this?" he muttered to himself. "No money! No money!" With a sob he threw it high into the air. It turned over once or twice, landed with a thud, and rolled into a corner.

Hornwrack went up and kicked him off. "Go home and rot, Verdigris." He gazed down thoughtfully.

Perhaps a decade after the successful conclusion of the War of the Two Queens it had become apparent that a large proportion of the Reborn could not manage the continual effort necessary to separate their dreams, their memories, and the irrevocable present in which they now discovered themselves. Some illness or dislocation had visited them during the long burial. No more, it was decided, should be resurrected until the others had found a cure for this disability. In the interim the worst afflicted would leave the city to form communes and self-help groups dotted across the uplands and along the littorals of the depopulated North. It was a callous and unsatisfactory solution, except to those who felt most threatened by the Reborn; ramshackle and interim as it was, however, it endured—and here we find them seventy years on, in deserted estuaries full of upturned fishing boats and hungry gulls, under fretted fantastic gritstone edges and all along the verges of the Great Brown Waste—curious, flourishing, hermetic little colonies, some dedicated to music or mathematics, others to weaving and the related arts, others still to the carving of enormous mazes out of the sodden clinker and blowing sands of the waste. All practise, besides, some form of the ecstatic dancing first witnessed by Tomb the Dwarf in the Great Brain Chamber at Knarr in the Lesser Rust Desert.

The search for a cure is forgotten, the attempt to come to terms with Evening abandoned. They prefer now to drift, to surrender themselves to the currents of that peculiar shifting interface between past, present, and wholly imaginary: acting out partial memories of the Afternoon and weaving into them whatever fragments of the Evening they are able to perceive. Privately they call this twilight country of perception "the margins," and some believe that by committing themselves wholly to it they will in the end achieve not only a complete liberation from linear Time but also some vast indescribable affinity with the very fabric of the "real." They are mad, to all intents and purposes: but perfectly hospitable.

From one of these communities Fay Glass had come, down all the long miles to the South. The weird filaments of silver threading the grey velvet of her cloak; her inability to articulate; her palpable confusion and *petit mal*: all spoke eloquently of her origins. But there was nothing to explain what had brought her here, or why she had failed to contact the Reborn of the city (who without exception—full of guilt perhaps over their abandonment of their cousins—would have fêted and cared for her as they did every visitor from the North); nothing to account for her present pitiable condition. Hornwrack touched her gently with the toe of his boot. "Lady?" he said absently. He did not precisely "care"—he was, after all, incapable of that—but the night had surprised him, presenting him with a face he had never seen (or wanted to see) before: his curiosity had been piqued for the first time in many years.

The city caught its breath; the blue hollow lunar glow, streetlight of some necrotic, alternate Viriconium, flickered; and when at last something prompted him to look up again, the servants of the Sign were before him, filing in dumb processional through the chromium Californium door.

Chorica nam Vell Ban left her table hurriedly and went to sit beside Lord Mooncarrot, whom she loathed. Her shoulders were as thin as a coat hanger and from the folds of her purple dress there fluttered like exotic moths old invitation cards with deckled edges and embossed silver script. Mooncarrot for his part dropped both his rancid smile and his yellow gloves—*plop!*—and now found himself too rigid to pick them up again. Under the table these two fumbled for one another's shaking hands, to clasp them in a tetanus of anxiety and self-interest while their lips curled with mutual distaste and their curdled whispers trickled across the room.

"Hornwrack, take care!"

(Much later he was to realise that even this simple counsel was enmeshed in incidental entendres. Not that it matters: at the time it was already too late to follow.)

"Take care, Hornwrack!" advised a voice of wet rags and bile, a voice which had plumbed the gutters of its youth for inspiration and never clambered out again. It was Verdigris, sidling up behind him to hop and shuffle like a demented flamingo at the edge of vision. What abrupt desperate betrayal was he nerving himself up for? What unforgivable retreat? "Oh, go away," said Hornwrack. He felt like a man at the edge of some crumbling sea cliff, his back to the drop and the unknown waves with the foam in their teeth. "What do you want here?" he asked the servants of the Sign.

By day they were drapers, dull and dishonest; by day they were bakers. Now, avid-eyed, as hollow and expectant as a vacuum, they stood in a line regarding the woman at his feet with a kind of damp, empty longing, their faces lumpen and ill-formed in the hideous light—moulded, it seemed, from some impure or desecrated white wax—weaving about on long thin necks, grunting and squinting in a manner half-apologetic, half-aggressive. Their spokesman, their priest or tormentor, was a beggar with the ravaged yellow mask of a saint. A surviving member of the original cabal, he wielded extensive financial power though he lived on the charity of certain important Houses of the city. A rich bohemian in his youth, he had refuted the ultimate reality even of the self (staggering, after nights of witty and irreproachable polemic, down the ashen streets at dawn, afraid to destroy himself lest by that he should somehow acknowledge that he had lived). He no longer interpreted but rather embodied the Sign, and when he stood forward and began to work his reluctant jaws back and forth, it spoke out of him.

"You do not exist," it said, in a voice like a starving imbecile, articulating slowly and carefully, as if speech were a new invention, a new unlooked-for interruption of the endless reedy Song. "You are dreaming each other." It pointed to the woman. "She is dreaming you all. Give her up." It swallowed dryly, clicking its lips, and became still.

Before Hornwrack could reply, Verdigris—who, filled by circumstance with a bilious and lethal despair, had indeed been nerving himself up, although not for a betrayal—stepped unexpectedly out of the shadows. He had had a bad afternoon at the cards with Fat Mam Etteilla; verse was scraping away at the wards of his skull like a picklock in a rusty keyhole; he was a rag of a man, in horror of himself and everything else that lived. To the spokesman of the Sign he offered a ridiculous little bow. "Pigs are dreaming you, you tit-suckers!" he sneered, and, squawking like a drunken juggler, winked up at Hornwrack.

Hornwrack was astonished.

"Verdigris, are you mad?"

"You're done for, at least!" was all the poet said. "It's black murder now." A perverted grin crossed his face. "Unless—"

Suddenly he extended a dirty avaricious claw, palm upwards, calloused and ink-stained from the pen. "If you want her you'll have to pay for her, Hornwrack!" he hissed. "You can't fight them on your own." He glanced sideways at the Sign, shuddered. "Those eyes!" he whispered. "Quick," he said, "before my guts turn to prune juice. Enough for a bed, enough for a bottle, and I'm your man! Eh?" As he watched Hornwrack's incomprehension dissolve into disgust, he shivered and sobbed. "You can't fight them on your own!"

Hornwrack looked at him. He looked down at Fay Glass, insensible yet invested—a mysterious engine of fate. He looked at the spokesman of the Sign. He shrugged.

"Peddle your knife somewhere else," he told the poet. "These people have never had cause to quarrel with me. They should remember that. They have made a simple mistake in the identity of this unfortunate woman (who is a cousin of mine, I now see, from Soubridge), and they are leaving."

He stood there feeling surprised. He had meant to say something else.

"You do not exist," whispered the Sign.

Ansel Verdigris chuckled.

Shadows flickered on the wall. Knives were out in the eerie light.

"Oh, very well," sighed Galen Hornwrack. "Very well."

Possessed by the sudden instinctive cannibalism of the baboon (our unshakable mahout, seated in the skull these million centuries), the combatants throw themselves at one another: the flesh parting like lips, wounds opening like avid mouths, precious fluids of the heart spent in one quick salivation; the bloody flux . . .

Hornwrack watches at the celebration of his own genius, helpless and a little awed. He has done nothing during his self-imposed exile from humanity if not learn his trade. A cold, manufactured rage, counterfeit of an emotion without which he cannot do his work, laps him round. The good steel knife, conjured from its sheath like a memory, settles comfortably in his hand. He can no longer influence himself, and treads the measures of his trade—the cut, the leap, the feint. Like a juggler in the Atteline Plaza he tumbles to avoid the despairing counterstroke (the blade whickering in beneath his cheekbone, the displaced air brushing feather-like his hollowed cheek). Blood fountains in the mad Californium light, the colour of old plums. That is no new colour. (All the while the girl lay between his shuffling feet like a stone, her eyes full of pain and disbelief.) The knife goes home, and goes home again in the queasy gloom. His blood is now inextricably mixed with that of the Sign, daubed on his bare forearms, greasy underfoot, a fraternity of murder and pain. . . .

Somewhere behind him Verdigris was struggling, his face luminous with terror, his mouth a gargoyle's spouting a filth of verses, some drainpipe lyric of relaxing sphincters and glazed eyes. "Remember this, Hornwrack!" he shouted. "Remember this!"

Hornwrack never heard him. Three, perhaps four, fall before him, and then the mouthpiece of the Sign squeezes into view from the bloody mêlée like a face surfacing from the bottom of a dream—long, yellow, smeared with blood, triangular and expressionless as a wasp's—the breath huffing in and out like dry inhalations of some machine, the breath of the insect whispering the deadly symbolic secrets of the cabal, the arid rustling visions of bone and desert—until Hornwrack's knife thumps him squarely in the hollow between collarbone and trapezius with a sound like a chisel in a block of wood, to end eighty years of fear and doubt. At the point of

his death, electricity flares between them, as if the whole cabal gave up its
heart in the one despairing, vomited word,

"No,"

which was simultaneously his warning and his triumph.

Hornwrack supported the corpse by its throat, struggling to pull out his
knife. The yellow face grinned at him, laved by its own punctured carotid.
He let it slip away, back down into his nightmares.

For a moment he felt quite old and hopeless. All around him shadows
were slipping from the place in defeat—silently, like sapient grey baboons
quitting some foggy midnight rock in a warmer latitude, fur blood-
streaked, the game up. In the middle of the room Verdigris had fallen to
his knees and, clutching one gory thigh to stem the bleeding, was slashing
feebly at retreating hamstrings. As Hornwrack watched he fell on his face
and dragged himself off into a corner. Hornwrack ran out into the street,
shouting. Brought up short by the dazzle of moonlight, he could hear
only the rapid patter of feet. He stood there for a long time, shaking his
head puzzledly, growing cold as the clock moved from midnight to one,
the knife forgotten in his hand; then he went back inside.

Verdigris had gone, through the rear entrance and out into the thousand gutters of the Quarter, the girl's bundle with him; even now he
would be trying to sell it in some derelict shambles at the dark end of an alley. Mooncarrot and Chorica nam Vell Ban were gone, to spend the rest of
the night together in grey, narcissistic embrace, each seeing in the other's
unresponsive face a mirror—and to part with revulsion as the spasm of fear
which had briefly united them faded in the spreading light of dawn. The
Sign had gone, and its dead with it. The queer Californium frescoes
looked down on an empty and echoing space, and, standing awkwardly at
the hub of it, staring about her in characteristic frozen panic, the Reborn
Woman Fay Glass, a harbinger, a messenger in a velvet cloak. Her cropped
yellow hair was spiky with congealing blood and she was trying desperately
to speak.

"I," she said. "In my youth," she whispered. Her eyes were blue as acid.

"Look," he told her, "you had better leave before they come back." A
place in his left side ached unbearably. He felt dull and fatigued. "I'm sorry
about the bundle," he said. "If I see Verdigris . . . but I expect your people
can help you." He put his hand through the rip in his soft leather shirt. It
came out warm and sticky. He bit his knuckles. "I'm hurt," he explained,
"and I can't help you anymore."

"In my youth I—"

She was plainly mad (and attracted madness too, focusing all the long lunacies of the city like a glass catching the rays of some ironic invisible sun). He wanted no dependents. He put out a hand to touch her shoulder.

Immediately he experienced a shocking moment of blankness, a lapse like the premature tumble into sleep of an overtired brain. It was accompanied by something which resembled an intense flash of light. He heard himself say, quite inexplicably: "There are no longer any walls." Shadows rushed out of the Californium corners and swallowed him: the Afternoon was vibrating in him like a malign chord. Somewhere out there in the millennial dark night, tall ancient towers howled on a rising wind. He approached them over many days, fearfully, across tracts of moorland and dissected peat, scoured ridges and deep sumps. The water was corrupted and undrinkable, the paths difficult to find. Finally the hidden city composed itself before him like a dream, but by then it was too late. . . . Simultaneously (in a vision overlaid like delicately coloured glass) he was in some other place. A settlement huddled on the verge of the Great Brown Waste. Behind it steep slopes covered with sickly dwarf oak swept up to an extensive gritstone escarpment running north and south, its black bays and buttresses looming up against the fading light. A few flakes of snow hung in the bitter air, and, silhouetted against the pale green sky, enormous insectile shapes marched in slow processions across the clifftop.

"No," cried Galen Hornwrack. He shook himself like a dying rat and pushed the woman away. "What?" he said, staring at her. He was trembling all over. Then, with his hand clapped to his left side and his face haggard, he staggered out of the Californium, feeling the dry, febrile touch of wings or madness on his skin.

Behind him the Reborn Woman moved her lips desperately, a child making faces into a mirror.

"In my youth," she said to his retreating back, "I made my small contribution. Venice becomes like Blackpool, leaving nothing for anybody. Rebellion is good and necessary. I—" The Californium became silent about her. There was nothing left but the doorway, a trapezium of blue and grey and faded gamboge—the reflection of the city in a deep well of moonlight on an autumn night. Nothing was left but the wind out of Monar, a little blood, the falling leaves. She began to weep with frustration.

"I—"

Viriconium. Hornwrack. Three worlds colliding in his head. As he ran aimlessly up and down the alleyways at the periphery of the Quarter, dark, viscid peat groughs yawned like traps beneath his feet. The wind hissed in his ears. Looming against an electric sky, that terrible haunted crag with its slow purposeful visitation! In the shattered moonlight of the city he stum-

bled into doors and walls, his limbs jerking erratically as if the vision accidentally vouchsafed him had been accompanied by some injection of poison into his nervous system. His clothes were torn and he was caked with
blood; he couldn't remember where he lived; he couldn't imagine where
he'd been. It was this fatal disorientation which camouflaged the sound of
footsteps following him, and by the time he had remembered who he
was—by the time those other landscapes had faded sufficiently for him to
appreciate his situation—it was too late.

Out of the shadows that curtained the alley wall another shadow hurled
itself; across a band of moonlight a white perverted face was launched at
his own; he was carried to the floor by a tremendous blow in his damaged
side, as if someone had run full-tilt into him in the bruised yellow gloom.
Thin, hispid arms embraced him, and close to his ear a voice that smelt of
wet rags and bile—a voice pulped by self-indulgence and curdled with
vice—hissed, "Pay up, Hornwrack, or you'll rot in the gutter! I swear it!"

The hands which now scuttled over him were lean and fearful, full of
horrible vitality. They discovered his purse and emptied it. They stumbled
on his knife, retreated in confusion, then snatched it up and drove it repeatedly against the flagstones until it shattered. Overcome by this ambitious tactic they abandoned him suddenly, like frightened rats. Something
heavy and foul was flung down on the pavement near his head. A single exotic shriek of laughter split the night: running footsteps, the signature of
the Low City, faded into echoes, stranding him sick and helpless on this
barren, reeling promontory of his empty life.

Now he realised that he had been stabbed a second time, close to the
original wound. He grinned painfully at the ironical shards of his own
blade, winking up at him from the cracked flags, each one containing a
tiny, perfect reflection of the mad retreating figure of the balladeer, coxcomb flapping in the homicidal night. "I'll have your lights, you bloody
cockatoo, you rag," he whispered, "you bloody poet!" But now he wanted
only his familiar quarters in the Rue Sepile, the dry rustle of mice among
the dead geraniums, and the murmured confidences of the whores on the
upper stair. After a while this hallucination of security became so magnetic
that he hauled himself to his feet and began the journey, clinging to the alley wall for comfort. Almost immediately he was enveloped in a foul reek.
He had stumbled over Verdigris's abandoned rubbish: the Reborn Woman's
bundle, still wrapped in its waterproof cloth. For the life of him he couldn't
think why it should stink so of rotting cabbage.

When he unwrapped it to find out he discovered the hacked-off head of
an insect, rotting and seeping and *fully eighteen inches from eye to globular eye.*

He dropped it with a groan and fled, through the warrens behind
Delphin Square, past the grubby silent booth of Fat Mam Etteilla and the

crumbling cornices of the Camine Auriale, his feet echoing down the empty colonnades, his wounds aching in the cold. Things pass behind me when my head is turned, he thought, and he knew then that the future was stalking him, that a consummation lay in ambush. He stared wildly up at the Name Stars in case they should reflect the huge unnatural change below. From Delphin all the way to the Plaza of Unrealised Time he went, straight as an arrow across the Artists' Quarter to the narrow opening of the Rue Sepile, to those worm-eaten rooms on the lower landing with the ceilings that creaked all night . . .

. . . Where the dawn found him out at last and his eighty-year exile ended (although he was not to know that at the time).

All night he had lain in a painful daze broken by short violent dreams and fevers in which he received hints and rumours of the world's end. Fire shot from the ruined observatory at Alves, and a great bell tolled where none had hung for millennia. *A woman with an insect's head* stuffed his wounds with sand; later, she led him through unfamiliar colonnades scoured by a hot dry wind—the streets crackled underfoot, carpeted with dying yellow locusts! Mam Etteilla, sweating in the prophetic booth—"Fear death from the air!"—opened her hands palm upwards and placed them on the table. He was abandoned by his companions in the deep wastes and crawled about groaning while the earth flew apart like an old bronze flywheel under the wan eye of a moon which resolved itself finally into the face of his boy, impassive in the queasy light of a single candle.

"What, then?" he whispered, trying to push the lad away.

It was the last hour of the night, when the light creeps up between the shutters and spreads across the damp plaster like a stain, musty and cold. Outside, the Rue Sepile lay exhausted, prostrate, smelling of stale wine. He coughed and sat up, the sheets beneath him stiff with his own coagulating blood. Pulling himself, hand over hand, out of the hole of sleep, he found his mouth dry and rancid, his injured side a hollow pod of pain.

"There are people to see you," said the boy. And, indeed, behind his expressionless face other faces swam, there in the corner beyond the candlelight. Hornwrack shuddered, clawing at the bloody linen.

"Do nothing," he croaked.

The boy smiled and touched his arm, with "Better get up, my lord," the gesture ambivalent, the smile holding compassion perhaps, perhaps contempt, affection, or embarrassment. They knew nothing about one another despite a hundred mornings like this, years of stiff and bloody sheets, delirium, hot water, and the stitching needle. How many wounds had the boy bound, with pinched face and capable undemonstrative fingers? How many days had he spent alone with the dry smell of the geraniums, the Rue Sepile buzzing beyond the shutters, waiting to hear of a death?

"Better get up."

"Will you remember me?"

He shivered, and his hand found the boy's thin shoulder. "Will you remember me?" he repeated, and when no answer was forthcoming swung his legs over the edge of the bed.

"I'm coming," he said with a shrug; so they waited for him in the shadows of his room, silent and attentive as the boy bathed and dressed his wounds, as the candle faded and grey light crept in under the door. Fay Glass the madwoman with her message from the North; Alstath Fulthor, lord of the Reborn and a great power in Viriconium since the War of the Two Queens; and between them the old bent man in the hooded robe, who peered out through a chink in the mouldy shutter and said dryly, "I can connect nothing with nothing today. But look how the leaves fall!"

3

A FISH EAGLE IN VIRICONIUM

Tomb the Dwarf's return to Viriconium, his adoptive city, was accomplished at no great pace. The passage of two or three days placed the site of his abortive excavations and near-incineration behind him to the southeast. The Monar massif was on his right hand (its peaks as yet no more than a threat of ice, a white hanging frieze hardly distinguishable from a line of cloud), while somewhere off to his left ran that ancient, paved, and—above all—crowded way which links the Pastel City with its eastern dependencies—Faldich, Cladich, and Lendalfoot by the sea. This latter route he avoided, preferring the old drove roads and greenways, out of sentimentality rather than any conscious desire to be alone. He remembered something about them from his youth. Although he was not quite sure what it might be, he sought it stubbornly in the aimless salients and gentle swells of the dissected limestone uplands which skirt the mountains proper, haunted by the liquid bubble of the curlew and the hiss of the wind in the blue moor grass.

He gave little thought to his rescuer from the past. The man had vanished again while he slept, leaving nothing but a half-dream in which the words *Viriconium* and *Moon* were repeated many times and with a certain sense of urgency. (Tomb had woken ravenous in the morning, abandoned the new pit immediately, despite its promise, and gone in search of him—full at first of a curious joy, then at least in hope, and finally, when he failed to find so much as a footprint in the newly turned earth, with a wry amusement at his own folly.) He was, as he had put it more than once, a dwarf and not a philosopher. Events involved him utterly; he encountered them with optimism and countered them with instinct; in their wake he had few opinions, only memories. He asked for no explanations.

Still, curiosity was by no means dead in him, and since he could not go to the moon he moved west across the uplands instead, toward Viriconium. In a region of winding dales a further queer event overtook him.

Fissuring the high plateau, so that from above it looked like a grey and eroded cheese, these deep little dry-bottomed valleys were dreamy and untenanted. Hanging thickets of thorn and ash made them difficult of access (except where some greenway deserted impulsively its grassy sheep run to follow an empty streambed, plunge through tumbled and overgrown intake walls, and nose like a dog among the mossy ruins of some long-abandoned village), and each was guarded by high, white, limestone bastions. Into one such came the dwarf at the end of a warmish October afternoon, the wheels of his caravan creaking on a disused track drifted with ochre leaves. Reluctant to disturb the elegant silence of the beech-woods, he descended slowly, looking for a place to pass the night. The air was warm, the valley dappled with honey-coloured light. Summer still lived here in the smell of the wild garlic, the dance of the insects in the steep glades, and the slow fall of a leaf through a slanting ray of sun.

The curves of the track revealed to him first a forgotten hamlet in the valley floor—then, swimming above that in a kind of amber glow, the enormous cliff which dominated it.

The village was long dead. Past it once had flowed a stream called the Cressbrook, but there was no one left now to call it anything, and it had retreated shyly underground leaving only a barren strip of stones to separate the relics of human architecture from the vast limestone cathedral on its far bank. There was no water for his ponies, but Tomb turned them out of their shafts anyway; he felt magnetized, drawn, on the verge of some discovery. For this they bore him no more or less ill will than usual, and he could hear them tearing at the damp grass as he pottered along the bank of the vanished brook. But he couldn't get comfortable there, or amid the contorted and lichenous boughs of the reverted orchard with its minute sour apples—and after a while he shook his head, staring puzzledly about him. Something had attracted him, and yet the place was nothing more than a collection of bramble-filled intakes, grassy mounds, and heaps of stone colonized by nettle and elderberry, its air of desuetude and loss magnified by the existence of the cliff above—

That cliff! That aching expanse of stone, with its ancient jackdaw colonies, its great ragged swathes of ivy, and its long, mysterious yellow stains! It hung up there, every line of it precise in the amber glow, every scalloped overhang thick with brown darkness, every leaning ash tree, golden and exact against its own black shadow. Every buttress was luminous. The gloomy and suggestive caves worn in its face by a million years of running water seemed more likely places of habitude than the pitiful handful of relics facing it across the dry stream. The shadow of a bird, flickering for a moment across an acre of vibrant white stone, invested it with some immemorial yet transitory significance (some distillation or heirloom of a thousand twilights, a billion such shadows fossilized impalpably in the rock): it was like a vast old head—imperial, ironic, and compelling.

Eventually he cooked himself a meal and ate it squatting comfortably on the step of the caravan. Smoke from his fire became trapped in the inversion layers and drifted down the little valley. Evening came closer and yet never seemed to arrive—as if the valley and its great white guardian were removed from the ordinary passage of Time. The sun dipped forever into the greyness and yet never sank. The air cooled, but so slowly. No wind came. Tomb the Dwarf scratched his crotch, yawned. He stood up to massage the deep ache of an old back wound.

He fed the ponies. Then he went to look at the cliff.

At first, a little out of breath after the ascent of the vegetated scree beneath, he was content merely to stand at the bottom of it and crane his neck to watch the jackdaws. The rock was warm: he placed the palm of his hand against it, flat. The earth beneath his boots was filled with the smell of autumn: he breathed deeply, cocking an eye at a hanging rib, a soaring corner, an ivy-filled crack.

He stood there at the beginning of it where every line led upward, then he began to climb.

He had remembered what was haunting him.

He climbed slowly and amiably, placing his feet with care, here jamming a fist into a crack, there balancing his way across some steep slab while empty space burnt away beneath him like a fuse; and with him as he climbed went the long barren limestone scars of his youth, burning and distant under a foreign sun: the baking hinterlands of the Mingulay Peninsula in summer—the stones so bright at midday they hurt the eyes—the tinkers' caravans string themselves out like gems across the Mogadon Littoral—the sea cliffs blaze in a fifty-mile arc from Radiopolis to Thing Ten while, high above the stone heaps and the thorny rubbish in the dry gullies, patrols a single lammergeyer, a speck on the burning bowl of the air! Each place or event he now saw miniaturised and arid, as if sealed in clear glass. He regretted none of them—but he was glad on the whole to have exchanged them for the softer airs of the North; and the memory identified, the haunting laid, he let it slip away. . . .

Soon he was able to rest on a shaggy platform some three hundred feet from his starting point and perhaps two hundred more above the caravan on the valley floor. Here there was a cool breeze, and he could watch the jackdaws pursue their millennial evening squabble beneath him; harrying one another from roost to roost, then exploding away into the clear air in a clatter of wings and sneers—to soar and drift and drop like stones into the treetops below before returning to the bramble ledges to begin the whole tedious argument over again. . . . He took off his belt and with it anchored himself among the roots of the yew with which he shared his perch. The air around him cooled; the light began imperceptibly to fade; the long shoulders of the plateau receded north before him, horizon after horizon like grey pigeon feathers set against the enamelled blues and yellows of the sky. Across the valley he could no longer distinguish individual ash trees—crowned with a continuous lacy fretwork of branches, the sun red and unmoving above it, the far slope rose dark and sullen like a vast earthwork.

And as he watched, a head began to raise itself above that earthwork.

It was such a brief glimpse that later he was unable to describe it coherently—by then, of course, it no longer mattered. The thing revealed itself in total silence, and by parts. First the drooping, jointed antennae, in constant nervous motion, were lifted above the trees; then the great globular eyes followed them, dull and faceted, set in a wedge-shaped carapace like the stained and polished skull of a dead horse; finally came the mouthparts, working like a machine. Two trembling, oddly curved forelimbs appeared, and, braced against the earth's dark edge (although they left not the slightest mark), levered this shocking mask high above the dwarf's stance. He never saw the rest of the creature. The valley winked out below him; the cliff lurched and spun; he shuddered, and heard a thin piping noise coming out of his own mouth—

Then it was gone.

He retained the impression of something *fading*, of a noise he had never actually heard gradually diminishing from some unimaginable crescendo—as if an invisible energy dissipating itself like water dribbling away under a stone—then he felt the rough powdery bark of the yew against his sweating hand; the cry of the jackdaws came back to him (faint at first, as though from a vast distance); the valley of the Cressbrook was once more as it had been—

Such a brief glimpse.

The sun sank, the dark welled in, but the small hunched figure on the cliff remained—chin on knees, singed grey hair moving in the night wind, expression quizzical. When he eventually got up to leave his ledge and begin the careful retreat, he saw suddenly that it was scattered with hundreds of little luminous insects. Leaping and glittering in an excess of life and energy, they scuttled over his feet, flickered between the roots of the yew, and tumbled in a constant rain over the edge, spilling into the depths like sparks. He could not see where they came from, and when he tried to pick some of them up they evaded him.

During his descent he had expected to see them falling past him into space, but when a few minutes later the difficulties eased and he was able to look up, they had gone, and he couldn't even see the ledge.

In a languor of puzzlement and dried blood, then, his wounds gaping at him every time he closed his eyes, Galen Hornwrack abandoned his familiar rooms, his stale but bearable captivity. Nothing was said. Nothing was explained. The shrewd whores watched him go (moving abstractedly from window to window, fingers raised to a drooping underlip, a leaded cheek, a favourite comb). The boy, too, followed him with uncommunicative eyes. Did he understand what had happened? Would he wait for as much as a day before drifting away into some desperate, motiveless new liaison? Hornwrack could not care for him (both of them bore too obviously the signature of the city, the impassive self-indulgence, the narcissism which precludes compassion), but he had a sudden quick vision of the boy's thin shoulders hunched against a corrosive yellow lamplight; of dripping brickwork and energetic shadows; and he found himself searching for something to say in farewell, some gift or acknowledgment. Nothing came, so he said nothing, and let the inevitable profitless curves of the Rue Sepile carry him out of sight.

Eventually, he knew, his present inertia would be replaced by a faint bitterness, a sense of betrayal which, though directed away from himself, would yet be experienced on behalf of the boy. In this way he managed his crippled emotions. For now he could only watch covertly the faces of his unwelcome companions, waiting for some indication of their purpose. Beneath his cloak he had hidden his second-best knife, a thing with a peculiar hilt and an old black stain he could not remove.

They had fetched him a horse, though he hated that method of travel, and urged him silently to get up on it. Now, the Plaza of Unrealised Time and its shabby dependencies behind them, they shepherded him through the Low City. Alves passed like a dream, its breached copper dome and sprawling rookeries lapped in the silence of desuetude. Along the Camine Auriale a drizzling rain commenced. The earthy wounds of the Cispontine Quarter opened before them like a freshly dug graveyard.

Eastward, where the Artists' Quarter huddles up to the skirts of the High City (and Carron Ban, it's said, deserted by her sour daughter, still waits for Norvin Trinor in the inexpressibly sad shadows beneath the heights of Minnet-Saba), dawn had filled the streets with faces Hornwrack knew. The curdled horizontal light picked out a wicked jaw, an eyebrow like a punctuation mark—here a blanched cheek, there a goitre like a pregnancy or some prodigal carious baring of the teeth. Deformed and weary, furtive or gleeful, they were the faces of usurers and wastrels, of despairing cannibals and blemished martyrs, all corroded in the moral marrow and burnt to the underlying bone with the city's mark: Equipot, the one-eyed merchant, with his sardonic grin and rotting septum; pale Madam "L," her haematitic eyes full of fever, hurrying to keep an appointment in the

Boulevard Aussman; Paulinus Rack, the undertaker's agent, his very large head covered with broken veins, carrying a short jade cane. . . .

They were customers of his for the most part, though none of them seemed to know him now. It was as if the events of the night had removed him from his proper sphere.

No such sleight had operated in the case of Alstath Fulthor, however much he might have wished it otherwise. From booth and gutter the eyes of the Low City stared out, to pass incuriously over Fay Glass and her outlandishly cropped hair; dwell a little longer on the old man who rode by her side (puzzled perhaps by the strange geometries on his robe, and briefly disconcerted by his tranquil yellow features and impenetrable smile); then fasten greedily on the Reborn Man like the eyes of communicants or at least the spectators at an execution.

Fulthor, that myth!

He was the enigma of the Low City, the meat and drink of their gossip. In the streets beneath Minnet-Saba all motion ceased at his comings and goings, whatever the hour. The constant bedlam of the gutters abated as he rode by, wrapped in his queer diplomatic status and his queerer armour with its strangely elongated joints at knee and elbow and its tremulous blood-red glow. Who was he? Did he serve the city, or it him? He was like some living flaw in time, through which leaked faint poisonous memories of the Afternoon—its fantastic conspiracies and motiveless sciences, all its frigid cruelties and raging glory. Since his triumphant entry at the head of the Reborn Armies eighty years ago (the Northern wolves driven before him to be caught at last between his hammer and the anvil of Tomb the Giant Dwarf), he had gone about Viriconium like the courier of a god, the very beat of his heart a response to some lost prehistoric cue. He was a miasmal past and an ambivalent future, a foreign prince in a familiar city. He was, and always had been, the repository of more fears than hopes.

So they quietened as he passed. It was like an embarrassment in them. A few smiled up at him. Some spat. Others fingered thoughtfully the metal pendant at their necks and wished, perhaps, for the night.

If Hornwrack was disposed to a certain cynical amusement at this reception of the Queen's favourite advisor, it was dispelled when their destination became plain. Fulthor led his little group first to Minnet-Saba by a northward traverse—the precipitous Rivelin Way being at this hour impassable for the stalls of a makeshift but flourishing fish market—then on to the Camine again, and by this indirect and ill-chosen route (like a man remembering quite another city) brought them finally to the Proton Circuit: a road which has only one ending, there in the great filigree metal shell of Methven's hall. Dwarfed by the vast curve of that airy way, spiralling above the lesser thoroughfares on its hundred fragile stone pillars, they inched their way towards the palace under a sky like red lead, four small figures imprisoned in a monstrously beautiful geometry. Above them orbited a solitary fish eagle, raucous and lost here on the edge of the mountains, making long white arcs against the clouds.

Hunched up on his horse in the wind and the rain, Hornwrack perceived simultaneously his destination and his mistake. He nodded bitterly to himself. He looked up at the fish eagle to remind himself of old freedoms cruelly taken away. Then he reached deliberately over to his left where the old man rode by his side, hooked one arm round the ancient neck, and brought his second-best knife smoothly from its place of concealment beneath his wet woollen cloak. His own horse halted in confusion, but the old man's continued to move in a nervous circle. This had the effect of dislodging him from its saddle, so that his weight was completely supported by Hornwrack's stranglehold—while Hornwrack's flawed blade, flickering in the ashy light, pricked his yellow skin, and Hornwrack's flawed laugh died in his face like a poisoned dog.

"I'll go no further on this bloody road," cried Hornwrack, "until you tell me why, Alstath Fulthor! What have I ever had here but disappointments?"

Above him, closer now, it seemed, the fish eagle screamed. Its cries caused a kind of elation to spill through him, briefly anaesthetising the ache of his wounds and strengthening him if need be for another murder.

"I've not ridden this road for eighty years. I know you, Fulthor. Give me a reason why I should come with you now!"

But a chill went through him as he spoke, and though his words were for the Reborn Man, he found himself staring into the parchment face of his impassive hostage. The old man had spoken not once since his cryptic greeting of the dawn in Hornwrack's rooms—not once in all that long ride across the city—but now he opened his mouth and gave vent to a sudden mewing wail, a cry with no speech in it at all, which rose inhumanly into the sky and fled away like an ancient bird. This done, he became still again, his lips dry and bluish, his rheumy eyes fixed vacantly on the empty air. The queer geometrical embroidery on his robe seemed to settle itself slowly, as if a moment before it had been in violent and independent motion.

Hornwrack clung tightly to him and shuddered, as the victim clings to his assassin. His wounds hurt him suddenly. He felt sick and he felt very old.

Alstath Fulthor, caught between one tepid nightmare and the next:

For two days a scene from his previous life had hung at the outside edge of perception, giving him the impression that he was accompanied everywhere by one or two partly visible companions. They were tall and whitish—candle-like figures resembling the drawings of the insane—and whenever he turned his head they vanished immediately. At unexpected moments the scene would submerge him completely, and he would become aware that they were walking in some sort of sunken ornamental garden planted with flowers whose names he could not remember and filled with a smell of horsehair and mint which varied in intensity with the wind from beyond the walls. Across it floated the voices of his companions, engaged in some half-serious philosophical or religious dispute. His relationship to them, whilst not precisely sexual, could be described in only the most complex and emotional of terms, and his constant attempts to see them more clearly had given his head a slight sideways tilt, and lent to his expression an even more withdrawn quality than was usual.

It was symptomatic, perhaps, of a sudden self-doubt. The old man in the embroidered robe—guarded as to his immediate origins, secretive of purpose though evidently benign—had issued from the recent history of Viriconium with all the force of a living myth. And on that high path under the brow of Hollin Low Moor, less than a week before (night coming on, the sweat drying on him, and the distant shriek of a fish eagle making alien the bleating of the autumn flocks), Alstath Fulthor had relinquished to him what he secretly saw as the stewardship of the empire. He did not quite understand how this had come about. Only that he had fought so long against the quicksand of his Afternoon memories (because after the passing of tegeus-Cromis and the vanishing of Tomb the Iron Dwarf, who else was left to advise the Queen?) and now the fight was failing and he was tired to death. Only that the old man's charisma was immense, his frail old figure looming somehow over every foreseeable future, a warning or a threat.

So, even before the appearance at his house in the early hours of the woman Fay Glass, incoherent and alone, he had begun to act in a stupor, consumed by the feeling that there was nothing to choose between the fevers of his skull and those of the world outside it. When he closed his eyes strange waxen figures moved through a garden; when he opened them again he found that he had allowed the girl (like some demented diviner) to lead him halfway across the city in search of a cheap assassin. Somewhere along the way he had collected the old man, who now watched him sardonically and offered him no assistance—"I can connect nothing with nothing. . . ." The tenement in the Rue Sepile filled him with disgust for the people among whom he must now make his life. Its stairways wound like a tedious argument, luring part of his brain along with them until he found himself thinking, apropos of nothing, If the dead have a city it is like this one, and it smells of rats and withered geraniums. . . .

"But look how the leaves fall . . ." While his boy bled him patiently, the assassin groaned and whispered from the disordered bed. Fulthor eyed the process with distaste, noting how the boy's face, delicate and womanish in the unsteady light, filled with a strange detached sympathy. Later, watching the assassin dress, he felt only impatience at the Low City swagger of him, and missed the hidden knife. . . .

Now Hornwrack closed on his victim like a rat trap.

There was a sudden hiss of indrawn breath. A flurry of hooves. The knife flickered out from somewhere, a blemished steel tongue in the grey light. The old man gasped once and was silent. They remained locked together for a long moment, like lovers. Above them, somewhere up in the dark morning, a huge bird shrieked. The madwoman began to ride round them in circles, whimpering and waving her arms. Hornwrack laughed madly. "I'll go no further, Fulthor! I've been this way before. It's a road to nothing!" Suddenly he stared into the face of his hostage as if he saw his own death there. "What?" Fear stretched his thin brutalised features.

The old man opened his throat, retched, squawked inhumanly, then seemed to smile.

"Oh! Oh! Oh!" cried Fay Glass, staring upward.

Alstath Fulthor, his brain an empty beach across which were scattered the bones of understanding, felt, rather than saw, something detach itself from the racing clouds above.

It fell slowly at first, toppling languidly off one great wing, giving vent to a high wailing cry (thus do the fish eagles of the Southern Marches plummet almost lazily a thousand yards into the cold salt water of their native sea lochs: but this one was fully five feet from wingtip to wingtip, and of an odd grey colour); plunged quicker and quicker until Fulthor was sure it must bury itself in the paving of the Circuit; then in the final instant shot horizontally across his field of vision in a rush of displaced air, to smash into the assassin's rib cage with a noise like an axe going into an oak door. Shouting in rage and fright, Hornwrack fell backwards off his horse. He lost his hold on the old man, hit the wet road, and was bowled over in a mist of blood and feathers.

Relieved—if astonished—at this turn of events, Fulthor drew his powered blade and cursed his horse in close, found that he could get a clear stroke at neither assassin nor bird, and swept the old man up to safety instead. This gave him the illusion, at least, of participation.

In the immediate aftermath of its strike the hawk had the advantage of momentum: with its talons fastened in his face, Hornwrack went rolling and bellowing about the roadway, knife arm flailing while he tried with the other to protect his eyes and throat. There was little to choose between them for ferocity. The bird shrieked and croaked; the man groaned and wept; rain fell on them both. Alstath Fulthor stared, appalled. Eventually, blood streaming from his face and forearms, the man wriggled into a kneeling position. He grasped the bird by its neck and pulled it off him. Time after time he drove the knife into its body, but it was like stabbing a brick wall. The huge wings buffeted him. Their faces were inches apart, and both of them were screaming now as if they had finally recognised one another from some other country and were continuing a quarrel begun there long ago. . . . Suddenly the man threw his knife away, transferred both hands to the bird's neck, and twisted it once.

They raised their bloody heads and shrieked together. The man choked. The bird was still.

Fulthor rode over, dismounted, and watched Hornwrack get unsteadily to his feet. His cloak was ripped, his shoulders a mantle of blood. He looked round him like an idiot, empty-eyed. "Yours, I suppose," he said to Fulthor, his voice thick and dull. He hardly seemed to notice the powered blade flickering and spitting at his throat. He held out the dead bird. "Some bloody thing dug up out of the ground."

The Reborn Man stared at it in silence. It was a perfect image of *a bird made all in metal*: a fantasy with armoured wings, every feather beaten from wafer-thin iridium, the fierce raptorial beak and talons forged from steel and graven with strange delicate designs. It hung from Hornwrack's hand, though, like anything newly dead—loose of limb, open-mouthed, and vulnerable (as if in the moment of death it had been surprised by some truth which made nothing of beaks and claws), one great wing hanging in a slack double curve. He shook his head stupidly and turned away.

The old man seemed little the worse for his adventure, though the strain seemed to have accentuated something not quite human in the set of his features, the way his almost-saffron skin clung to cheekbone and jaw, taut as an oiled-silk lampshade. "You had better tell him why we need him, Alstath Fulthor," he whispered hoarsely. He massaged his scraggy neck and chuckled. "I believe he will not come except of his own accord. And I would rather he destroyed no more of my property."

Fulthor failed to hide his surprise. "You made the bird?" he said.

"Long ago. There may be a few more left"—he looked up into the grey sky—"but they have grown shy since the war. They are less dependable, and no longer speak." He nodded to himself, remembering something. Then: "Tell him why we need him."

Fulthor could think of nothing to say. He looked from the old man to the ruined bird and back again, then at Hornwrack (who, far from show-ing any further signs of fight, had begun to shiver volcanically).

"The girl," he began. "She was sent here with a message, we think, vital to the city, to the empire. To all of us in these peculiar times. But look at her! The rest of her party must have wandered off somewhere between here and the Great Brown Waste: they are far along the road to the Past in her village, and it is hard for them to concentrate for long on what they judge to be nine-tenths dream." (Waxen figures were at that moment processing through his own skull, carrying something wrapped in a fantastically decorated sheet, all of them leaning at thirty degrees to the vertical; they were singing. Nine-tenths dream! He had placed her by the weave of her cloak. He could find the place, but would he ever leave it again?) "You must know what they are like out there."

The assassin seemed preoccupied. With the hem of his cloak he was dabbing at his lips, his cheeks; the lobe had been torn off his left ear. He fought off a fresh bout of shivering (looked for a second hunted and afraid, like a man who suspects in himself a fatal disease). "She said nothing to me. Nothing but gibberish." He touched white bone where his jawline had been laid open, winced. "Look at me! I am already bleeding for her. Three times now she has brought me to this, though that bastard Verdigris had his dirty hands in the matter." He sneered. " 'The face of the ewe lamb bone white in the meadows'! Gibberish!"

Fulthor could follow little of this. He thought privately that the man was mad.

"It is not what she has said," he explained carefully, "but what she brought with her, that is of significance. Had she anything with her? I thought as much! You are the only one who saw it. We must know. You owe us this, if only because you were the cause of its loss!"

This seemed to enrage the assassin.

"Then ask her, Reborn!" he shouted. He spat blood into the road at Fulthor's feet. "It is I who am owed. I killed five of the Sign last night on her behalf and my palm is empty. One of them at least would have fetched twenty pounds of steel in the open market. Martin Fierro under my knife! That was a black madness. Here!" He stuck out his cupped right hand. "Black bloody madness! I am sick of doing the work of the High City and reaping only their sanctimonious stares!" He turned away disgustedly and made to pick up his knife. When Fulthor's weapon pricked the small of his back, he froze. He looked back over his shoulder, a sneer spreading across his lacerated face. "Are you frightened of a steel knife now, up there in the High City? You could chop me like an onion with that thing if I had fifty knives like this!" He bent down quickly and snatched it up. "Look, blunted at the tip." It had vanished under his cloak before Fulthor could protest. He had sensed now to what extent he was needed; to what extent safe.

"She cannot tell us, Hornwrack," said Fulthor tiredly. "You can. That is why she brought us to you. It was her only means of communication. At least come to the palace to discuss it. I agree that you may have been treated unfairly."

Hornwrack ignored him. He shook the carcass of the metal bird. He put it to his ear. "It hums still. It hummed even as I strangled it." His hands trembled, then stilled. "I feel my death in all this." He walked off a few paces and stared up at the palace, a mile distant and misty through the blowing rain. "Methven's hall!" they heard him say. He seemed to be listening. "I was once one of you," he said. "I was one of the rulers. I chose to become one of the ruled." Then: "To hell with all of you," he said. "I'll come because you have the weight of that behind you"—pointing to the palace—"and because you have the *baan*. But I'll tell you nothing." He regarded Fulthor with a cold smile, drew his ragged sleeve across his red-daubed face. "You had better watch me, Reborn Man," he threatened. "You had better watch me all the time."

I would rather be a ghost than play such hollow games, thought Alstath Fulthor.

Hornwrack:

The horse had run off and he refused to try and catch it on foot.

"Then walk," the Reborn Man told him.

He writhed his bruised lips and spat. (If he shut his eyes the bird came at him still, tearing long elastic strips of flesh from his chest until the ribs showed through.)

"So," he said. He shrugged.

Lord Galen Hornwrack, scion of a respected—if relict—House, one-time officer and pilot of the Queen's Flight, now a professional assassin of some repute in the Low City, made his way for the first time in eighty years to the palace at Viriconium. He walked. His wounds throbbed and chafed. Memories of the night gnawed him. But at his belt hung a metal bird he had ruined with his own bare hands, and he felt this to be the symbol of a continuing defiance: though he now had to admit that control of his own destiny had passed from him. Occasionally, small wheels spilled from somewhere deep within the bird to run soundlessly in diminishing circles until the wind whirled them away like chaff across the Proton Circuit. Before he went into the hall of Methven he looked up at the sky. What had begun at least in light was now dull and unpromising. Even the deadly litharge stain of dawn had faded from the cloud layer, so that, grey and solid, it capped the earth like an enormous leaden bowl, a single thin crescent of silver showing at its tilted northern extremity. And as he watched even that faded.

4

IN THE CORRIDORS

Tomb the Dwarf came in through the southeastern or Gabelline Gate of the city, just before dawn, some two weeks after his strange meeting on the edge of the Rannoch. A fine rain was falling as he led his ponies beneath the heavy seeping curve of masonry—more tunnel than arch—where the guard dozed in a wicker cubicle and old men, woken by the rattle of wheel on cobble, squatted under their dripping felt hats and stared incuriously at him as he passed. Here, in an alcove in the wall of the arch, had once hung the notorious Gabelline Oracle, sought out and yet dreaded by all who entered or left the city: the severed head of a child hanging from a hook, beneath which had been constructed an alchemical "body" composed of yew twigs bound together by certain waxes and fats. A lamp being lit beneath the oracle, or in more special circumstances an inscribed wooden spatula being forced under its tongue, it would give in a low but penetrating voice the fortune either of the consultant or of the city itself. No one who had ever heard that voice could forget it; many would take the Gate of Nigg to avoid it.

Tomb heard nothing, though he cocked his head for echoes; but a breath of the past followed him a little way beyond the gate, a cold and depressing air generated in those outer regions, overflowing into the alleyways and peeling demimonde avenues of the suburbs where geranium leaves were turning ochre and a faint smell like cat's urine issued from the mouldy brick. Viriconium, sump of time and alchemical child, sacrificer of children and comforter of ghosts—who can but shiver and forgive in the damp theatrical airs of dawn?

A red stain grew in the sky above the Haunted Gate. Against it floated the airy towers, suspended as if in water glass, while below were conjured shabby reflections—a glitter of fish scales, olive oil, broken glass, and the west wind shivering the wide shallow puddles in the empty squares. Asleep one minute and aware the next, the Pastel City woke like a whore, to commerce and betrayal, to pleasure and misery—to rare metals and offal, velvet and sackcloth, lust and holiness, litharge, lithia salts and horse cures. The red stain spread until it had filled the sky. Worm-eaten floorboards groaned. Gummy eyes gazed forth, half-blind already with boredom and disgust, to watch the dawn drop dead among the sodden chestnut leaves in the Rue Montdampierre! Tomb the Dwarf, recognizing in this suburb the same slut who had emptied the pockets of an impressionable Mingulay tinker's son a hundred years before, was overcome by sentiment. He took deep delighted breaths, spoke almost kindly to his ponies, and grinned about like a juggler.

Beneath Minnet-Saba the Rivelin market spilled across his path like the encampment of a besieging army, dotted with paling flares and the little warm enclaves of charcoal braziers. It was a good-natured, anarchical siege, noisy and stinking, full of laughter and mock acrimony. Fish stalls predominated, but among them were distributed the kerbside pitches of tattooist and juggler, prostitute and priest; together with the booths of those deft-fingered old women who are equally happy to play at the cards for whatever stakes you name, or with them tell your fortune to the accompaniment of a practised homily. The gutters were filled with fish heads, with sneaking cats and unconscious thieves. Fishwives rubbed elbows with boys selling anemones from neck trays (while others offered filthy marzipan, or caramelized locusts like intricate jewellery from the forgotten towns of the dusty East). Over it all hung a marine reek, a pall of hot cooking fat and reedy, disconnected music.

Into this came the dwarf's caravan like a spirit of chaos—pushing aside tottering stalls, running over unguarded feet, impervious to abuse, drawing forth as it passed each brazier the ironic catcalls of idlers and the shrieks of fishwives (who required that the dwarf come behind a booth with them and there bash the dents out of a pot they would show him). The anemone-boys rode his tall yellow wheels, grinned into his face, lost their balance, and fell into the street. All the while he moved steadily up the hill toward Minnet-Saba, the crowds eddying in his wake, until he came to the upper limit of the market; and there, on the precise interface of High and Low Cities, chanced on the booth of Fat Mam Etteilla.

Despite the coming and going about the booth, it had attracted few onlookers. Wan torches set at its corners guttered in the growing light. Its greasy satin curtains were drawn back to reveal the Mam herself, billowing over her three-legged stool and coughing like a horse in the raw air. In her vast lap sat a small drunken man with a depraved triangular face, from the top of which stuck straight up a stiff brush of almost crimson hair. His bottle-green jerkin was not only encrusted with old filth, but was sticky besides with new foulness, and he seemed to be confessing his part in some brawl or murder the night before. Tears were running down his cheeks; great twitches racked his body; odd spasms of free verse left him now and then like vomit. ("I renounce the blessed face," he intoned, "the silent sister veiled in white and blue," and made a sound like a choking cat. "What else could I do? He was no friend to me!")

Before them on a flimsy baize-covered table were arranged the cards—four Urns above him; behind him the Conjuror reversed; the MANTIS crossing him; and many others. Each strange little scene glowed up from the grubby pasteboard as if viewed in a reducing mirror—leaning columns clustered beneath a vanished constellation, extinguished suns and naked supplicants, the shadowy hierarchical figures of a symbology as old or older than Viriconium, legacy perhaps of some Afternoon parlour game. "This," she whispered, "is your card, MALADIE; and here are three towers and a dog, the future as yet unrevealed, also disgrace. (Another account speaks of greed frustrated.) Look! Here's a deserted beach, and in the tide a hermit crab. Above fly three swans: APPUI. Between the alternatives there is no marriage possible—on the one hand magnificence; on the other, disease. (Also a certain clouded joy.)" The man with the red hair, though, would look anywhere but at the cards. If his glance fell on them by accident he would pretend to see someone he knew in the crowd.

But the dwarf saw little of this, and of what he saw retained only fragmentary impressions: a white, bony face; the scattered cards like pieces of coloured glass. He heard a voice like the outfall of a sewer say, "A locust the size of a man; a head two feet across!"

At this Fat Mam Etteilla shook herself as if surfacing from a dream. She looked down at the little drunk in her lap and put one of her great fat hands over his. "I wish I could help you, dearie," she said with a sigh, and set him carefully on his feet. A fit of coughing overtook her as he bobbed about in front of her trying to bow. "Piss and blood!" he screamed suddenly. "I saw it!" He ran off into the market and vanished.

"Wait!" cried Tomb, any talk of insects having recently become of interest to him. "Stop!"—more to himself than to the retreating figure. The caravan was being carried forward, despite his best efforts, by the sheer weight of humanity behind it. He stood up on his seat to get a better view: nothing but a red coxcomb and a despairing cry. "Its head twice bigger than a man's!" And then nothing at all but heads, bobbing and eddying; the market had ejected him and he was alone in the bleak formalistic spaces of the High City. The wind ruffled the puddles, and the Proton Circuit rose like a question mark into the air before him.

———

No one recognised him at the palace gates. An officer made him wait while they verified a complex sequence of passwords given him twenty years ago by someone who might have been dead for ten of them. His ponies fidgeted, and furtively bit one another. Servants came and went, but none of them looked at him. "It won't take long. Look, can you move the caravan? We really need the room." The city's sudden indifference hurt him, although he pretended to take it with a certain stoical amusement. "Oh, well," he told the officer. "Oh, well." Then he jumped out of the caravan, ducked the presented arms of the gate guard, and ran off into the palace. Old wounds had given him a dragging, unsteady gait so that he looked from behind like some escaped ape. After a shocked silence a lot of shouting began.

A little while later he stopped to get his breath back in a corridor where the light fell as if strained through muslin. He had lost himself quite quickly in the maze of passageways which riddled the outer regions of the building like the interstices in a piece of pumice—quickly enough at any rate to evade the detachment which had tried to catch him at the front door. He grinned. He could still hear them faintly, crashing about in the empty lobbies and forgotten storerooms of quite another quarter, moving away from him all the time. But he realized now that he couldn't reach the Queen without moving into the more frequented passages and thus being sighted. An undignified homecoming. His chest hurt. He leant against the back wall of the alcove, staring at some old machine and trying to remember with half his mind whether he or someone else had dug it up and brought it back here; and when finally he decided he did indeed recognise it, he found he had forgotten which desert had given it up to him, back when he was young. Whole sections of the palace were "his" in this respect, which only galled him further. . . .

He was upset by his own actions and could hardly explain them to himself. An ironic game with the palace guard, conceived out of impatience and hurt pride—so it had seemed at the time—but now he felt like a man who, falling down a hole in a familiar street, discovers some artful yet not quite successful mimicry of the world he has known above. In his new subterranean existence he quarrels with familiar objects or alienates his friends—he yearns for escape but quickly finds he can no longer control events; cause and effect separate like worn-out old lovers. But it was not simply that he was out of temper with himself. The temper of the palace puzzled him, too.

Its previous calm beauty, ordered and formalistic, had become icy; monstrous passions seemed about to crystallise in its interstices. Something had invaded the corridors where the whispering light sculptures drifted about (their laughter so ancient and inscrutable that it no longer recalled anything human); something was abroad in the sudden nautiloid spaces, chilly and nacreous. Stumbling along in his dusty leather gear he had experienced a sudden *gauntness,* the feeling that he had allowed to go unnoticed some change which, though vast, showed itself only in the subtlest of signs: the dream of an old dwarf in a high place; a red-haired man in a market; footsteps in an empty passageway. The sounds of pursuit had for a moment mutated into a strange dry rustle, the geometry of the corridor into a mathematics, pure and bony and beyond him, and he had fancied himself the last human survivor on some craft spinning slowly through infinite space, rigging full of frozen sailors and royal faces staring from the windows at its stern. . . .

I am a dwarf, not a philosopher. He touched the cold wall behind him. He had got his breath back. Since his arrival in the alcove the old machine had been making soft, persuasive little noises at him, as if it needed his help to attain some self-fulfilment he could never imagine; now it abandoned him abruptly. *Oogabourundra!* it whispered. *Mourunga!* it laughed, and extended a curious yellow film of light like a wing. Tomb stuck his head out and peered down the passage. A figure appeared, strange at first, warped by the unsteady yellow gleam into a shape like a praying mantis; the dwarf waited until it had become that of a young guard—a boy still, self-conscious in lacquered black mail and pewter-coloured cloak, new boots ringing on the worn flagstones, and on the thin chain round his neck a peculiar silver medallion—then withdrew. His grinning and apparently disembodied head snapped back into the corridor wall to leave a tunnel of bland saffron light, a throat down which the boy strode unaware. Tomb let the footsteps come level with him. He waited for perhaps fifty heartbeats, then slipped out.

The machine clucked disappointedly after him.

From corridor to corridor went the boy, up and down narrow flights of stairs and through abandoned halls—all the while moving towards the centre of the palace. Flickering columns of light accosted him, but he ignored them; the soft pleas of old machines he ignored. And after him came Tomb the Dwarf, hands like two bunches of bones and a grin like death—alert for the sound of voices, sidling round corners and hanging back at intersections, hoping the boy would flush up any guard that might be mounted there. The corridors were as cold as an omen, haunted by an ancient grief. Here, stairs spiralled into the upper gloom of the shell; there, faint footsteps vibrated in another passage, footsteps that might have been made in another age. As his confidence increased, Tomb began to play with the boy: scuttling up until he was only a few inches behind him, making obscene faces and gestures (and once touching the hem of his cloak) before falling back again. Success only whetted his appetite. He dodged in and out of alcoves, his head poked like a gargoyle's round each new corner. He aped the boy's stiff walk, pointing his toes extravagantly and sticking his nose in the air. He quite forgot about using him to reach the Queen unchallenged and set about tormenting him instead.

He hid behind a sculpture. He sniggered softly. When the boy looked round: nothing.

He let his feet scrape, with a horrible purpose.

He made quiet animal noises.

He was everywhere and nowhere; it was a cruel charade. The boy knew. He hurried: stopped: listened: stared over his shoulder, his hand feverishly clutching the pommel of his brand-new sword. He said nothing, because that would have been an admission. His eyes were round, glistening in the white like a boiled egg, boiled and shelled like a fresh egg. He touched the silver insect medallion at his throat; he began to run. Tomb only let him hear another chuckle. Their merged shadows fled away beneath them as they crossed a high elegant bridge, parted at a crossroads unused for two hundred years, only to join again and vanish at the moment of joining in a silent flare of purple light vented from some ancient artefact. Tomb grew careless. Swaggering along like the tame midget of some Southern prince in cockerel-coloured doublet and yellow stockings, he came abruptly face to face with his victim, who—finding himself confronted by an old mad dwarf with a knife in his gnarled hand and a series of peculiarly childish grimaces chasing themselves across his features—stared, appalled.

"I—" said Tomb. He looked down at his hand. He wondered how long he had been carrying the knife without knowing it.

The boy meanwhile trembled despairingly. His eyes were watering. He made a painful effort to draw his sword.

"Don't!" said Tomb. "I didn't mean—" And it might have rested there had he not heard the sound of feet coming along the corridor toward them.

"I'm sorry," he told the boy, kicking him beneath the left kneecap. The boy lay on the floor, motionless, looking up at him like a hurt animal. Tomb hauled the new sword from its scabbard and tried it for balance. He had some idea of using it in the absence of his axe. "Rubbish," he said, and threw it clattering across the passage out of harm's way. "Get something decent as soon as you can afford it." He knelt on the floor close to the boy, who made no move to stop him, set the point of his knife against his throat, and stared into the round hopeless eyes. "What's this round your neck?" But the boy couldn't speak. "Don't worry," said Tomb, "please." In this manner both of them awaited the arrival of the footsteps.

Not long after, a Reborn Man came striding towards them down the corridor. He had on the fantastic blood-red plate armour of an important House, its contorted yellow ideograph flaming on the black cloak that billowed out behind him. The trembling glow of the armour made his image seem mythical, transitory, as if he flickered in and out of Time as we know it; its curious blunt shoulder spikes and elongated joints gave him the look of some mutated crustacean. His head was bare, his expression beleaguered, and his companions were an ill-assorted lot, comprising a woman of his own race, bitterly thin, shaven-headed, her gait awkward and ungraceful, as if her skeleton worked in a new, untested way (her smile was empty, and she was singing softly, *We are off to Vegys now, Fal di la di a*); a gutter bravo from the Low City, with the walk of a frustrated predator and the spoilt features of a minor aristocrat; and a dark silent figure wrapped like a corpse in an embroidered cloak.

Tomb started up with a cry. He took a pace forward, blinking and confused.

"Cromis?" he whispered.

Pain filled him and he forgot the boy on the floor. He went up close to Galen Hornwrack (for it was him, of course, morose as a wolf, petulant as an adolescent girl at finding himself so unmoved by his ancient bugbear the palace, which after all was only a place) and touched the wrecked metal bird that hung from his belt in lieu of a sword. He looked up into the assassin's face for a moment, then sighed: there was little similarity once you looked closely, and he could find there only an anguished savagery he had never found in the face of the dead poet-hero. He shook his head and turned to Alstath Fulthor.

"I'm sorry, old friend. I thought for a moment—"

Fulthor smiled absently down at him.

"I know," he said. "The similarities are superficial. What were you doing on the floor with that boy?"

He tilted his head to one side as if he were listening to something no one else could hear, and seemed to forget what he had been saying. There was an awkward pause. Then he went on. "You should be more patient, Dwarf. I heard there was a maniac or an ape of some kind loose in the corridors. When I saw the little caravan, I"—Fulthor shook his head as though to clear it of some double image—"I knew it must be you. Are you going to murder this lad, or can he get back to his post?" His tone was curious, friendly but ironical: absent.

Tomb bared his rotten old teeth. He was a little disconcerted by such a reception after twenty years. "I'm too old for patience, Reborn," he said gruffly. "Are you all right?" When no answer came he turned his attention almost gratefully to the boy (who had risen to his knees: colour was coming back into his face), thinking: the whole city is in a dream which it will not share with me; these corridors are cursed. "Get up," he told him. "What *is* that thing round your neck?" When the boy wouldn't answer he asked Fulthor, but Fulthor didn't hear.

Light streamed suddenly down the corridor, the colour of murder. It rushed over them like smoke, to be sucked away into the outer maze and there dissipate; their shadows followed it. The old machine from which it had issued, so long denied its proper function, began to shriek in horror and frustration, flailing its corroded limbs as if waking after millennia to the truth of its position. Echoes fled like bats.

Out of this abrupt madness crept a party of ten or fifteen men. A squad of the palace guard, they wore the same black and pewter uniforms as the boy, but their faces were distorted by the unsteady glare—salient features drifting into repulsive new relationships—and they came on not with a military gait but with a curious tiptoed tread, their eyes fixed on the dwarf with a feral yet somehow inorganic intensity. Had they shadowed him even as he shadowed the boy, passage to passage, all the way from the outer halls? How had he not felt those eyes like the empty lambent eyes of animals on a dark night? (Or perhaps he had.)

"Fulthor?"

But Fulthor was gazing emptily into the air again, his lips moving silently. There was no help there.

The dwarf shuddered, ambushed by circumstances. The city's web was now complete, and he found himself enmeshed. It wasn't much of a homecoming. Yet it would not be the first time he had fought his way down these corridors. He stood forward a little so as not to prolong the waiting. Nothing much was in his mind.

They were almost upon him when Fulthor whispered, "Stop." His voice seemed to come from a long way off, and he looked almost surprised to hear it. "Stop!" For a moment nothing changed. Tomb snarled; Fulthor touched the hilt of his sword, faced with the motiveless slaughter of his own men. But then the world shook itself and threw off the nightmare. The old machine wailed despairingly, sagged, and was silent (in its frenzy it had melted parts of its own spine, and now, bent double like a crone, it twitched and contracted as the hot metal cooled). The evil light faded. The approaching men looked uncertainly at one another and put up their swords.

It was little enough, and grudgingly done: their captain nodded woodenly, staring straight ahead, while behind him they shuffled into two columns, looking embarrassed and elbowing one another sullenly. Each wore a medallion like the boy's, a curious complex twist of silver the meaning of which retreated from its seeker like a vacant perspective. "Call off the search," Fulthor ordered them. He spoke reluctantly, like a man hard put to control some pain or intense desire. "A mistake has been made. This is the Iron Dwarf, who has returned to help the city in its hour of need." They regarded him warily for a few seconds, then turned their heads away as one man and marched off. When they had gone some distance down the corridor the boy leapt abruptly to his feet, flung the

Reborn Man a glance of bitter hatred, and was off, flying down the passage after them, his sword abandoned where Tomb had thrown it. Tomb picked it up. "What do you make of all this?" he asked Fulthor. Fulthor stared blindly after the boy, his thin hands like a layer of white wax over bone.

"I am lost," he said, and turned his face to the corridor wall. "They no longer accept my leadership. Soon one of them will disobey and I shall have to kill him." He made a noise that might have been a laugh or a sob.

Through all this, Fulthor's companions had hardly moved, but looked on with fear or irony or whatever emotion seemed appropriate. Now the Reborn Woman, sensing his distress, came forward and put one hand uncertainly on his shoulder. "I—" she said, and then something in a language Tomb could not follow. "*Mein Herz hat seine Liebe.* In my youth I made—" It was clear she could not help him, which distressed her in her turn. She shook him. She looked around for help. "In my youth I made my small contribution. Blackpool and Venice become as one. Above the night the stars revolve, in circuits of the shuddering bear!" This last a shout. She wept. Oddly enough it was the assassin from the Low City who moved to comfort her. He touched her hand and his bloody, spoilt features writhed briefly: after a second's puzzlement Tomb decided this was an attempt to smile. The woman smiled back, and her face was transfigured—where the dwarf had previously seen only a chilling vacancy there now flared delight, and an intelligence like a lamp uncovered. She let go of the assassin's hand and danced away from him, singing,

> We are off to Vegys now
> Fal di la di a
> We are off to Vegys now
> Fal di la di a
>
> On the shores of the diamond lake
> We shall watch the fishes
>
> On the summits of the mountains
> Cry "Erecthalia!"
>
> Fal di la di a
> Fal di la di a
> Di rol

Hearing this, Alstath Fulthor put his hands over his ears and groaned. "I cannot forget the people in the beautiful gardens!" he exclaimed. He hit the side of his head with the heel of his fist. "Arnac san Tehn! How long is it since I saw your sweet mad face at midnight, or trod with you the pavements of the Rue Morgue Avenue?" And still groaning, he ran away down the corridor toward the outside world, stripping off his armour as he went.

A thin wind passed down the corridor, smelling of dust and hyacinth; with it came silence—a substance, not an absence—to fill the ears with empty rooms and abandoned stairs and the motionless unspeaking figures of the earth's innocence. In this silence Tomb the Dwarf sought desperately for reassurance. But the woman had retreated into her own memories, shoulders hunched and eyes hooded secretively, a ghost of tenderness playing about the corners of her mouth; nothing she said made sense anyway. And the assassin merely smiled sardonically, shrugging as if to absolve himself of this responsibility at least (the movement appeared to hurt him somewhere in the region of his lower ribs, and his expression immediately became sour and self-involved).

"Is everybody insane, then?" Tomb asked himself irritably, turning in the end—though something made him reluctant—to the man in the shroud-like cloak, who stood a little way off examining the distraught machine as if it might help him break the universe's last mad code. The machine was crooning to him out of its incomprehensible pain, and he, standing like a mysterious parcelled statue, was whispering back; neither of them would ever understand the other. Tomb went up and stood between them, arms akimbo, staring aggressively into the unrelieved darkness of the man's hood.

"Leave that, sir," he said, "although I'm sure it must be very interesting, and tell me: has the city lost its senses?"

Silence.

"Very well, then: if you are a friend of Fulthor's, at least tell me when *his* illness began. I am the Iron Dwarf (of whom you may have heard), who woke him from his aeon sleep to help defeat the North (which I did by means of knowledge gained from an old man)."

He craned his neck, but no face was visible despite that he felt eyes focused on him from somewhere under the hood. At this, his temper went. He pulled out his knife.

"Say something, you cold pudding, or I'll serve you up in slices! Are you all ignorant or loony in here?"

But the man only chuckled and said, "You knew me last time we met, Dwarf, with your beard on fire and your broken head! Have you forgotten so soon? I would have asked you then, only there was no time: how has it been with you since our other fateful parting, there beneath the sad tower eighty years ago? What a change you and I have wrought in the world by our doings then! Do you see any of my children as you go about from desert to desert, from waste to waste?"

And he threw back his hood, laughing his dry old enigmatic laugh, and became Cellur, the Lord of the Birds. . . .

5

GALEN HORNWRACK AND METHVET NIAN

Cellur the Bird Lord: he has lived for aeons in a five-sided tower full of undersea gloaming. Instruments flickered and ticked about him all that time, while his sensors licked the unquiet air, detecting new forms and seasons. Out of the cold reaches of salt marsh and estuary, out of the long cry of the wind, out of the swell of the sea and the call of the winter tern he comes to us now: out of the War of the Two Queens, with his thousand dying metal birds; out of the long-forgotten dream of the Middle Period of the earth, shaking his head over the pain and beauty, twin demiurgi of mankind's enduring Afternoon!

What has he witnessed, that we shall never see? Forgotten, that we could hardly imagine?

The lines and figures on his marvellous robe writhe and shiver like tortured alien animals. Geometry remembers, though he may not. "Nothing is left as it was," they sigh, "in that final perfect world. The towers that ruled these wastes have fallen now. The world, which they halted for a millennium in its tracks, has begun to turn again. We find here no compassion as savage and sterile as theirs; no cruelty as structured or formal; no art. The vast air is stilled, where they lowed beneath five artificial planets, trumpeting verse into the frozen distance. Their libraries lie open like the pages of a book abandoned to the desert wind, their last dry whispers fade; philosophers and clowns alike, fade; that febrile clutching at the stars . . ."

Cellur. Ten thousand seasons once were his, years beating like hearts! These geometries could tell us. They are the spoor of Time itself, did we but know. Cellur the Bird Lord! Now he speaks—

All are assembled in the throne room but Alstath Fulthor.

(Rumour has him running through the filthy alleys of the Artists'

Quarter, up the hill at Alves, and through the grounds of the derelict observatory, expressions of madness eroding his proud features; rumour had him leaving Viriconium for the third time in a month—no horse, no armour, only his heaving lungs, and his past in close pursuit. The Low City is entranced.)

The Queen sits with her calm hands in her lap; at her feet kneels Tomb the Dwarf, picking his teeth with the point of his knife; Fay Glass of the vanished House of Sleth, dressed in a new cloak, whispers nonsense to the Queen's Beast: while Galen Hornwrack stands apart, with a face like death. All wait, except perhaps the madwoman. Round them hover curtains of mercurial light, twists of mirror'd air. Before them five false windows tremble with views of a landscape to be found nowhere in the kingdom.

In the Time of the Locust it is given to us to see such things. "My lady" (began Cellur, bowing to Methvet Nian): "I had, as you know, some small part in the war against the North. But that war was almost my death—as I shall tell—and it destroyed both my refuge and my birds, which hurt me grievously. I have been many years coming to terms with this, and my life has been a curious one since then. I return to find the kingdom much changed, and I am afraid my very coming heralds further uncertainty. It is eighty years since I sent the iridium vulture to tegeus-Cromis in his tower at Balmacara among the rowan woods: I wish he were here today to answer a similar summons. Although I believe he thought of himself as a poet, he had a great gift for murder. Events again require such a captain. If I am to explain why, I must return for a moment to the War of the Two Queens. . . .

"That I survived the onslaught of Canna Moidart's forces was as much a surprise to me as it is to you, who last saw me beleaguered and without hope. My birds were long dead, or else scattered. The Geteit Chemosit held the causeway. Their airboat, though grounded during the early part of the exchange, mounted weapons of which I could not conceive. I was trapped in my tower, whose armoury I had never had the wit to investigate. A battle began in which the sole true flesh and blood at stake was mine, yet I looked on impotently, terrified. Stone dripped and sputtered in the face of their cannon; the estuary brine boiled and threshed with the power of mine! The watching cliffs echoed and roared with it, dust trickling down their immemorial buttresses like mortar from a rotten wall. All across the water hung a pall of glowing smoke, through which I caught brief glimpses of those dreadful automata coming and going about their vessel, their yellow eyes baleful. A curious armour seemed to protect them against my beams.

"Day gave way to a long night of blue fogs and drifting corrosive lights. The tower began to show signs of strain. It hooted mournfully into the wrack. Its summit revolved erratically, threatening nonexistent enemies. Every five or six minutes its armaments blazed forth like crooked lightning, but every time a little duller. Soon its foundations began to shift. It was doomed. I knew I could not survive a night above ground, even if it should achieve some Pyrrhic victory: two hours after tegeus-Cromis had led you to safety over the estuarine cliffs, the air and water had become contaminated with some energy which poisons the fish even now, so many years on. The tower moaned, its trapped electrical voices pleading with me in strange militaristic languages, whether for advice or relief I could not tell. I could do nothing. I left it, feeling like a traitor, for the cellars beneath, reasoning that I might make my escape through the very tunnels you had used on the previous day.

"It was useless. The estuary floor had subsided. Those passages which had not collapsed were blocked with hot mud or full of boiling water. Only one would admit me, and down that I wandered for some time, the distant thud of weapons to spur me on, until I realized I had entered a part of the system unknown to me. I say little of what I found there. Much I did not understand. Much I would not even wish to remember. The sounds of conflict above grew steadily more muffled, progressively more dreamlike, until I could hear it no longer. How long it continued I do not know. Which side had the victory, I am at a loss to say. By the time I found my way back to the surface the melted stone was cold again, the tower like a snuffed candle, the Chemosit and their weapons gone. Two fish eagles patrolled the grey water; the cliffs were quiet. This was much later.

"I had known for some time of the existence of such regions beneath the tower. They had lain beneath me like a new continent, but something had kept me from exploring them. They were, I sensed, still too close to the millennial past. Echoes of the Afternoon had not yet died in them. But such echoes are not, after all, confined beneath the surface of the earth; they move above it, too: wherever one goes there is always that sense of a door closed but a moment since. And I had little choice, for only my death waited above. Therefore I went down.

"The architecture below was cold and complicated. The staircases, of which there were many, bent back on themselves, to peter out at florid, blind arches, or deliver me bemused into some hanging gallery from which I could find no exit. There was no sense of being under the earth; rather I felt that I had stumbled into some empty city or vast deserted museum. Hundreds of small cubical storerooms led off the major passageways, each one containing an eccentric object the height of a man, wrapped against the effects of time in grey sheeting. Dust covered everything. For the most part these chambers and corridors were dark, although not silent. Instruments ticked, or clattered suddenly into life as I passed. I was afraid, which seems strange now, for it was shortly made clear to me that I had built most of these things, or at least collected them, against some contingency I have now forgotten. Eventually I reached a lighted section: at first a hundred yards of corridor strung with dim green beads; then a part of one room, full of submerged blue light from an unseen source; finally a whole suite as bright as day, haunted like a summer afternoon by an insectile hum, and full of drowsy voices!

"In these nitid quarters I was to spend many years. Here I confronted myself (although this meeting was more metaphorical than literal, and ultimately barren. I remain an enigma). Here also I learned the thing which has brought me to you today. It was here that I came to curse the monstrous burden of immortality and the fatal snare of compassion. For I am sure now that I am immortal, though I have no idea of where or when my life began. I no longer believe myself to be human. But it is human beings who have kept me here for so long.

"I entered, then. I was tired and hungry. The place was full of moving lights which took the form of columns, diffuse spheres, or dancing lampyrines. My uneasiness communicated itself to them immediately. They flickered in the cold sour air, drifting agitatedly about and whispering in secret electrical voices. Each was the outward form or "personality" of a different machine. One might listen to the earth, another the air, while a third measured the stars themselves: they were possessed of an excitable, nervous curiosity, like thoroughbred horses. An endless ritual interweaving allowed them to exchange information or—should the situation demand it—compound their functions, so multiplying their great native percipience. One, however, was supreme above the rest. It was a magnificent ivory column over twenty feet tall. Out of the hubbub of voices—which by now rose like flood water or the wind at night among alders—this one addressed me. All the others ceased immediately, as though in deference.

"I was astonished, for it spoke with my own voice. It maintained its superiority over the others by virtue of being *the keeper of my memory*. The skull, you see, cannot contain the years. Memory fades or is destroyed in periodic bouts of madness and self-disgust. Before this happens the best must be consigned to some archive. Luck or perhaps an instinct brings me to that room every hundred years or so, to be relieved of the burden. In that column of ivory light reside the dry fragments of all my former selves, like a cache of earthenware shards in the foundations of an old house. I learned this with horror (and with what horror have I contemplated it since!): an emotion that was as nothing to the misery with which I confronted the incompleteness of the record itself. . . . For more than ten millennia this machine has lodged beneath the estuary—gaps have now appeared in its own memory! Something in the machine is broken; many times too I have lost the material before it could be transferred, and there have been, it seems, deliberate deletions. A decade is missing here; there a century has slipped quietly away, leaving no clues. At the beginning of the record (if it can be said ever to have had one) only tantalising glimpses remain to imply a period half as long again as its entire span! What remains is like a tapestry holed and flimsy with age (torn, too, here and there, in senile rage), through which one must stare forever at the great void. In each new incarnation. I must learn afresh how to operate the machinery. That is not hard. But to understand my purpose in being here at all . . . I can review ten thousand years, but I have no identity beyond that which I can scrape together in any one incarnation. I am, in short, nothing but what you see before you, an old man who has wandered into the city from the past. . . .

"The years I have spent in that cavern burn me! The machines with their strange lights and their voices like dead leaves; the sour underground air; the Past rampant. I watched it all, on windows that formed out of the empty air at a word of command! Saw myself from many angles—a hand extended, a new robe, speaking to a crowd, watching my first awkward creation as it hawked above the waters. I watched the Afternoon, of which I shall not speak, with its madness. I learned: but I have still not learned who or what I am, and from vague clues must build up a fleeting image, a memory which slips away even as it forms. Worse, my present memory is becoming unequal to the years. I become uncertain of my own name. Soon I shall find it hard to remember why I owe you an explanation of all this, or of myself. The void reaches out.

"Do not pity me, my lady. I have pity enough for myself.

"Months passed. I learned. The machines cared for me. They passed their secrets on to me, willingly. During the long hopeless nights I sought an image of myself in the foxed mirror of the past, but by day I learned to interrogate the natural world. I became an inexpert ear cupped to that silence which has overcome the earth since the end of the Afternoon. Where once the air sang, now only thin electrical noises came from my instruments, like the cries of dead children. When Tomb the Dwarf disarmed the great brain in the Lesser Rust Desert, I overheard. Lights flickered in my cavern. All over the empire clusters of signals faded abruptly—the Chemosit going out like corpse candles. Later I followed his triumphant progress across the continent, Alstath Fulthor with him. From site to secret site they went, awakening the Reborn Men. For a while the aether was full of voices. Then, as the tragedy became apparent and the rebirth complexes shut themselves down one by one, silence fell again. It lasted until ten or eleven years ago when I picked up the first of the transmissions that have brought me here.

"I could hear it only when the moon was in the sky. It came as a hollow whisper, filling the stony subestuarine chambers. It was a strange, unreliable, inhuman voice, speaking a dozen made-up languages. Had it not so obviously belonged to a man I might have taken it for the monologue of some stranded alien demiurge, leaking accidentally into the void between earth and her wan satellite. I cannot tell you how it excited me, that voice! Feverishly, I interrogated my machines. They knew nothing; they could not advise me. I answered it, on all wavelengths: nothing!

"*Septemfasciata*, it whispered, over and again: *Guerre! Guerre!* The machines remember every syllable. *Dai e quita la merez . . . a hundred years in the cold side of the moon . . . the veiny wing . . . 'the heaven whose circles narrowest run' . . . I saw the garden that lies behind the world. There the cisterns turn against the men . . . nomadacris septemfasciata . . . colonnes fleuries (douloureux paradis!), temps plus n'adore . . . Oh, the filmy wing! Cold ravages me . . .* And then, dreadfully loud: *Septemfasciata! The outer planets! Methven!*

"For a year I suffered this monologue, with its meaningless warnings, its references to a search for 'the metaphysical nature of space,' to madness and death between the stars. I tired of its chuckled obscenities and cabalistic circumlocutions, its mad prophecies. I despaired of making any sense of it, and began to believe that the moon had been infiltrated by some vast corrupt cosmic imbecile. Attempts to make contact were fruitless: there was never a break in the flow in which to admit of my existence. It ceased as suddenly as it had begun. I rushed to the machines—nothing but an empty hiss. For three days the cavern was silent and dark. The machines would not respond to me. It was as if the ending of the monologue had been a cue. I sensed that they were not so much dormant as fascinated; their attention was focused elsewhere. On the fourth day a purple mist sprang up, a pure and sourceless illumination; through this there danced excited rods and lampyrines of light, spinning, whirling, and interpenetrating in a mad quick ballet. I had never seen them so agitated. They spilled from the cavern and out into the surrounding corridors, whispering hysterically their single message.

"Something had detached itself from the moon and was now making its way toward the earth.

"I have never heard that demented lonely voice again. But every lunar month since then has seen a fresh launching, a new landing. I have watched them, my lady! They are like puffs of white smoke issuing from the moon's bony grin; they are like clouds of pollen. They fall to earth here in the empire. I do not know exactly where. My instruments are confused, their findings incomplete and contradictory. They report interference, of a kind not encountered in ten thousand years of operation. But listen: yesterday I spoke with Alstath Fulthor the Reborn Man, in his house above the Artists' Quarter. From him I learned that some unknown force is harrassing the Reborn communities in the Great Brown Waste. We have agreed—as he would tell you if he were here—that these events must be linked. And though my instruments cannot agree on its location or its origin, they report that a city is being built somewhere in the north and west of Viriconium.

"My lady, it is not being built by men."

Cellur's eye is like a bird's, ironic and bright; his profile aquiline. It was different when we thought him human. His expression betrays so little now that we know he is not. Having delivered himself of his revelation, he drinks some wine and looks about him to gauge or enjoy its effect.

The Queen sits with her calm hands in her lap. At her feet kneels Tomb the Dwarf, his mouth open and his knife forgotten in his hand; he is actually trying to remember something, but it will not come to him until a day or two later. Fay Glass, of the vanished House of Sleth, what is she trying to remember? It is immaterial. She sits singing to an imperturbable sculpture of steel and white light dug up long ago in the ruins of Glenluce, while Galen Hornwrack stands apart—wounds griping, expression cynical and amused. (It's clear he has forgotten the events of the Bistro Californium, and thinks the old man mad.) Round them hover curtains of mercurial light, bright primary colours flecked for a moment—like flawed but vital ores—with the reflected uncertainties of the room.

No one knows what to say.

Viriconium, remarks Ansel Verdigris in his last ironic essay "Allies," *is a world trying to remember itself. The dumb stones perform an unending act of recall.* This pervasive awareness of the past, recent or distant, informed the personality of all its rulers, not least that of Methvet Nian. Cellur had pricked old memories back to life. Her mood, when Galen Hornwrack was brought to her in the side chamber or *salle* she used as a library and sitting room, was already a nostalgic one. This affected her opinion of him, perhaps: although events, in the end, might be said to have borne her out.

She knew little enough about him. Alstath Fulthor, returning wheyfaced and muddy from some unexplained errand only an hour before, had outlined their dependence on him as a witness to the incident in the Low City. "The girl herself found him, by luck or instinct; she insisted that he come with us (though we'd have brought him anyway). It is hard to know why. He seems to have fought on her behalf—and thinks well of himself for it—but he will say nothing about the fate of the message she carried, and that is the important thing. His motives for refusing seem confused."

Of Hornwrack's history he had been reluctant to say anything save, "A disaffected lordling from the midlands near Soubridge. After the war he seems to have wiped the clay off his boots and tried to drink himself to death in the Low City." Nevertheless, when pressed, he admitted, "Hornwrack was the youngest son. His brothers fell with the rest of Waterbeck's ploughboys in the Great Brown Waste. His mother and sisters were murdered later, when the Chemosit invested Soubridge. At the outset of the war he was an apprentice airboatman with the prospect of his own command, but he saw no service as such. Initially he was too young, later—with the destruction of its vessels—the whole corps was dismantled. This he appears to regret more than the deaths of his family. After the defeat of the North he seems to have failed as a farmer, and the family estate was forfeit to the Crown when debts made it unworkable. Now he lives by his knife in the Artists' Quarter, retaining his title perhaps as an advertisement, more likely as an insult to the empire that bestowed it on his grandfather.

"At the last count he had killed more than eighty men, in High and Low Cities. A dozen are presently trying to kill him."

I will at least understand his bitterness, she had thought.

Now she looked up from a sheet of music as he came in. His demeanour was a sham, or so it seemed to her: he affected the braced instep of the professional dancer; his long grey hair he wore gathered in a steel clasp, in imitation of those doomed airboat captains who had flown their final sorties over the Great Brown Waste at the height of the war; his cloak was the crude meal-coloured garment of the hired bravo, tailored for swagger, its hem dyed with sardonic vulgarity to the exact shade of dried blood. How could he mean anything to her, this ageing assassin with bones as raw as a jeer? He filled the sitting room like a murder. His very existence was too much for her delicate little coralline ornaments and collection of antique musical instruments; he overpowered them at once. It cannot be said that she saw through the Low City and the failed lordling, through the trappings to the man beneath: there was, after all, hardly any of him left to see.

Yet rather than simply walking through a door, he seemed to rush out at her from the past. His hair blew back in the wind of time! She saw him for a moment silhouetted against some vanished dawn—the tall thin body held with a helpless formality, the misery in the eyes, the great ruined metal bird hanging from his belt. Only a moment, but in it she mistook self-concern for dignity; wept for the dead poet tegeus-Cromis; and wondered briefly why this tired hooligan should remind her of winter hyacinths blooming in a tower by the sea.

It passed, of course.

Alstath Fulthor followed the assassin in. Beyond the threshold they regarded one another like wary dogs; then Hornwrack shrugged and smiled slightly, and Fulthor turned away, looking disgusted. She offered them refreshment. Fulthor refused, picked up a book bound in olive leather, and stared angrily at it; while Hornwrack stood in front of her, swaying a little.

He would not look at her. He smelt of death. Presently, Cellur and Tomb entered the room. Cellur took a little Mingulay wine, sighed—"These lamps somehow recall my buried life"—and sat down in the shadows. The dwarf made her a pretentious intricate bow, then leant against the wall, one leg bent to rub his calf.

"You feel your House was wronged by mine," she began without preamble. "We confiscated your estates. Our wars robbed you of your family."

Hornwrack favoured her with a bitter smile.

"Houses?" he said. "Madam, my family were farmers." He fingered his jaw where, she saw, something had recently laid it open to the bone. "Every airboat in the kingdom was destroyed so that you might keep your throne." He stared over her head. "It was my freedom you robbed me of."

If she thought she could see the Queen's Flight burning to ashes in his eyes (drifting down into the desert like withered leaves, spilling smoke and queer lights and little silent figures), she was wrong. He had not even seen their last defeat—only stood, sixteen years old, on the phlegmatic earth and watched them fly like greyhounds into the North: vessels, friends, captains all. None had ever returned, nor had he expected them to. The rest of the war he had passed in killing Northmen with a knife in the starving alleys of a captured city, practising unknown to himself the skills of the only trade his imagination had left to him.

"Mornings," he whispered feverishly, "chafe me still. I wake, and look into the empty air, and wonder if throne and empire were worth it—the burning boys and crystal ships."

He curled his lip and looked about him.

"I would not come here again for fear of finding it was not."

His hand went quickly under his cloak.

"Fulthor, do nothing!" he hissed. "I'll kill you here, if I have to!"

He wiped the back of his hand across his lacerated cheeks. Outside in the corridor a cold draught spoke of a change in the wind, a new weather. Inside, Alstath Fulthor let his *baan* drop back into its sheath. The dwarf cocked his head like a starling. The old man looked on from the shadows. Hornwrack relaxed slowly.

"Madam," he said, "your next family quarrel will have to be fought on the ground."

"Yet wrongs are not righted by hiding in the Low City," Methvet Nian told him patiently.

He shrugged.

"Can you give me back the sky? If not, pay me for the service I did you last night and let me go. I believe the girl is worth something to you, and I bled for her. I do not hide in the Low City: I reject the High."

She would not believe him. (How could she?) Instead she offered him a myth of his own: a place among the hieratic furniture and exemplary figures of a long-declining dream—

In a rosewood chest with copper reinforcing bands she kept three things: a gourd-shaped musical instrument from the East; a short coat of mail, lacquered black; and an unpretentious steel sword with a sweat-darkened leather grip. Now she bit her lip, and went over to the chest, and took from it the sword and mail. For a moment she stood uncertainly with them in the centre of the room, facing first the Reborn Man—who would not meet her eyes—then Tomb (the old dwarf glanced at Hornwrack and made a sudden half-amused movement of his head) and Cellur, who only stared impassively at her—and finally the assassin himself.

"Will these serve as payment?" she asked. "They are all I have."

Hornwrack looked surprised. He accepted the sword, hefted it; the mail coat he flexed with experienced fingers. He took a little rat's tail file from under his cloak and nicked them with it.

"They are steel," he admitted, and shrugged. "A fair price, though I'd have preferred it as an ingot." He stared at her, puzzled now. "If that is all, I'll go."

"It is not all!" exclaimed Fulthor. "Methvet Nian, the message!" He stood between Hornwrack and the door. The powered blade came out, evil sparks dripping from it in the gloom.

"Here's a High City trick if you like!" laughed Hornwrack, who hadn't a hope against it. He looked down at the old steel sword in his hand. "Still—"

"Stop!" cried Methvet Nian. "Alstath Fulthor, are you mad?"

His thin face white and sullen with confusion and rage, Fulthor let the *baan* fall to his side.

"Do not touch him. He has done us a service." And to Hornwrack: "My lord, I see you are wounded. Visit the hospitallers before you leave here."

Hornwrack nodded curtly. "Don't come near the Low City after dark, Fulthor," he said. At the door he paused, looked back. "I would prefer to owe the House of Nian nothing," he told the Queen. He threw the mail coat on the floor and dropped the sword carefully on top of it.

"The girl carried a bundle tied up in cloth," he said. "A poet called Verdigris stole it. When he opened it he found an insect's head the size of a melon. He couldn't sell it anywhere."

Methvet Nian gazed at him in horror. He seemed unaware of it, leaning against the doorpost and staring into space. "I don't think I've ever seen him so frightened," he mused. He looked at her. "It's in the gutter now, somewhere in the Low City. I left it there to rot, my lady. Goodbye."

Out beyond Monar the wind was shifting uncertainly, picking the first sleet
of the season from the frigid summits and sea-lanes of the North. Later it
would invest the city with rime, freezing airs, and a faint smell of rust; now
it nosed like a cold black dog among the vast dunes and endless empty rubbish heaps of the Great Brown Waste, visiting the drab stones and
foundered pylons, the half-buried wreckage of ten thousand years. What
else moved up there, throwing its equivocal shadow over the Reborn communes (and mimicking the jerky, hesitant gait of the votaries of the Sign as
they trod at night the streets of Viriconium, the measures of the dream)?
The implications of Hornwrack's statement were colder than any wind.

"What can they have meant?" whispered Fulthor. "To send that?"

But Tomb was intrigued by the departed assassin, and stared pensively
after him. He went over and closed the door. "*Does* he know whose sword
it was?" he asked Fulthor absently. "Did he guess?" But Fulthor only
rubbed his eyes tiredly and said, "He is a liar and a jackal."

The dwarf sniggered. "So am I." He picked up the discarded sword and
mail, smiled at Methvet Nian. "That was a valiant try, my lady. A stone
would have unbent to you. Shall I put these away?"

"One of you go after him and give them to him," she replied. "Wait. I
will do it."

When they stared at her, she laughed. "I meant him to have them." She
would let them say no more, but finished: "He saved the girl out of compassion, though he will never understand that."

But for a peculiar interruption, Fulthor, at least, would have pursued
the matter: indeed his mouth was already open to form a protest when
Cellur—who had been slumped for some minutes in his chair, a variety of
expressions, each more unreadable than the last, chasing themselves across
his face—gave a queer high-pitched cry and struggled to his feet as if he
had woken suddenly from some implacable nightmare. His skin was grey.
His accipitrine eyes were fixed on the door, as though Hornwrack still
stood there; they were bright with anguish. When Methvet Nian touched
his shoulder he hardly seemed to notice her (beneath the odd embroidery
of his robe, the bones were thin and unpredictable; brittle), but muttered
desperately, "Fulthor! Tomb! No time to lose!"

"Old man, are you ill?"

"You did not hear it, Methvet Nian, the voice from the moon, with its
'great wing against the sky.' The insect's head; the landings at night; the
Sign of the Locust: all are one! I must go north immediately. *All are one!*"

"Cellur, what is it?" begged the Queen.

"It is the end of the world if we are too late."

We value our suffering. It is intrinsic, purgative, and it enables us to perceive the universe directly. Moreover, it is a private thing which can neither
be shared nor diminished by contact. This at least was Galen Hornwrack's
view, who, by the very nature of his calling, had been much concerned
with pain. It was a view enshrined in the airless room above the Rue Sepile,
and in his relationship with the boy, whose function had been less that of a
nurse than of hierophant at his master's lustral agonies. As Hornwrack had
grown used to the smell of self-recrimination—which in the Rue Sepile as
nowhere else is compounded of dead geraniums, dry rot, and one's own
blood squeezed out of towels—he had also grown to welcome it, as he
welcomed the black fevers of his deeper wounds, in which he rediscovered
a symbolic reenactment of his crimes.

In Methvet Nian's infirmary, however, he had found none of this, but
instead open casements and cheerful voices and, worst of all, that good-
humoured competence by which the professional nurse—who otherwise
could not bear it—demeans the pain and indignity suffered by her charge.
In short: they had stitched him up but refused to let him brood. Some
three days after the events in the Queen's sitting room, therefore, he had
extricated himself from the place and now stalked the corridors of the
palace in an uncertain temper.

His cloak had been returned to him, washed and mended. Beneath it he
wore the mail of Methvet Nian, and at his side hung the unaccustomed
sword. Both chafed, as did the manner in which he had come by them. He
had, it is true, gone to some trouble to find for the sword a scabbard of
dull moulded leather, and it looked well on him. Nevertheless, the sword
is a weapon chiefly of the High City, and he felt ill-at-ease with it. He had
had little training in its use. As he hurried toward the throne room for
what he hoped would be the last time, he touched the knife hidden beneath his cloak, to assure himself he was not unarmed. As for the Queen's
intentions, he understood none of them. She had first tried to bribe and
latterly to patronize him; he was full of resentment. It was a dangerous
frame of mind in which to encounter the Queen's dwarf, who had on his
face a sardonic grin.

His short legs were clad in cracked black leather, his thick trunk in a
sleeveless jerkin of some woven material, green with age; his bare forearms
were brown and gnarled; and his hands resembled a bunch of hawthorn
roots. Indeed he looked very like a small tree, planted up against the
throne-room doors, stunted and unlovely against their serpentine metallic
inlays and ornamental hinges. On his head was a curious truncated conical
hat, also of leather and much worn.

"Here is our bravo, with his new sword," he said matter-of-factly.

"So the dwarf says," murmured Hornwrack, pleasantly enough. "Let me pass."

The dward sniffed. He looked along the passage, first one way and then the other. He crooked a finger, and when Hornwrack bent down to listen, whispered, "The thing is, my lord assassin, that I understand none of this."

And he jerked his horny thumb over his shoulder to indicate, presumably, the throne room.

"Pardon?"

"Voices, from above. Insects. Madmen, and madwomen too. One comes back from the dead (albeit he's a good friend of mine), while another runs like a greyhound at the sound of a song. Both old friends of mine. What do you think of that?"

He looked around.

"The *Queen*," he said, lowering his voice, "gives away the sword of tegeus-Cromis!"

He laughed delightedly at Hornwrack's start of surprise, revealing broken old teeth.

"Now you and I are plain men. We're fighting men, I think you'll agree. Do you agree?"

"This sword," said Hornwrack. "I—"

"That being so, us being ordinary fighting men, we must have an understanding, you and I. We must treat gently with one another on this daft journey north. And we must look after the mad folk; for after all, they cannot look after themselves. Eh?"

Hornwrack made as if to pass into the throne room.

"I'll make no journey with you or anyone else, Dwarf. As for gifts, they can be easily returned. You are all madmen to me!"

He had not gone so much as a step towards the inlaid doors when a terrific blow in the small of his back pitched him forward onto his face. Tears filled his eyes. Astonished and desperate—he thought the dwarf had stabbed him—he fumbled for his knife and scrabbled into a kneeling position: only to find his tormentor grinning ironically at him, unarmed but for those disproportionate arthritic hands. Before he could haul himself to his feet, the dwarf—whose head was now on a level with his own—had first embraced him lightly, then spat in his ear and hit him again, this time somewhere down below his ribs. His knife clattered away. His breath deserted him. Through his own heaving and choking he heard the dwarf say coldly—

"I like you, Galen Hornwrack. But that is the sword of my old friend, which was given you in good faith."

Hornwrack shook his head and took his chance. He reached forward and clasped with both hands the nape of the dwarf's neck, then pulled him forward sharply. As their heads connected, the dwarf's nose broke like a dry stick. "Black piss," he said surprisedly, and sat down. They went seriously at it then, and neither could get the advantage: for though the dwarf was cunning, old, and hard, the assassin was as quick as a snake; and both of them knew well the cul-de-sacs and wineshop floors where the anonymous chivalry of the Low City settles its quarrels amid the slime and the sawdust.

It was Cellur who discovered them there twenty minutes later. There was a yellow malice in their eyes as they staggered about in the bloody-mouthed gloom taunting one another in hoarse, clogged voices—but it was fading like a sunset, and as he watched, in the puzzled manner of someone who doesn't quite know what it is he's watching, he heard this final exchange:

"I beg my lord the sheep's arse to change his mind."

"My brain is as addled as a harlot's egg. Get me out of this place, Dwarf. It stinks of kindness. North if you like. What do I care?"

6

THE SUDDEN EMBODIMENT OF
BENEDICT PAUCEMANLY

Cellur could not (or would not) articulate his fears more clearly. He questioned Fay Glass, it is true: but nothing was revealed, her contribution being only a babble of archaisms and ancient songs; bits and pieces—or so Alstath Fulthor maintained—plucked from the racial memory as she pursued her lonely temporal descent. "She understands us: but speaks from a vast distance, no longer sure what language to use, or what to say." Despite this, Cellur argued, it was clear that she knew the secret of the insect's head—why else should she show such distress at her own failure to communicate? Since she could not tell them what had happened there, it was, he repeated, essential to follow her back to the North.

"She is in herself the message: and a call for help."

When Fulthor protested that, as seneschal, he could not abandon the Queen while the Sign of the Locust grew so in power, harassing daily the Reborn of the city and infiltrating its prime functions, Cellur only said: "I shall need you. Your people in the Great Brown Waste will not treat with me. They are too far gone on this 'road to the Past' you describe. When we have discerned the meaning of the insect's head, that will be the time; when we have understood the warning from the moon, and discovered the landing sites in the North, then we shall know what to do about the Sign of the Locust."

And Fulthor could only stare out into Viriconium, where at night in a lunar chiaroscuro of gamboge and blue, the long processions wound silently from one street to another, to the accompaniment of a small aimless wind.

The weather deteriorated as he watched, a raw air piling up against the massif of the High City and filling the Low with damp. Beneath a thick

grey sky the watery plazas took on a wan and occult look, while in the pen-
sions of the Rue Sepile the old women coughed all day over their affairs,
and the atmosphere became adhesive with the smell of cabbage. The walls
seeped. It was, all agreed, no time to be living in the Artists' Quarter, and,
perhaps as an addendum to this theory, gossip remarked the sudden disap-
pearance of Galen Hornwrack. Had he indeed quarrelled with Ansel
Verdigris, his erstwhile crony (some said over a coin, though others maintained it was a woman from the North, or even the wording of a verse in a
ballade of smoked fish)? Up and down the hill from Minnet-Saba, huddling closer to brazier and guttering cresset, his enemies and rivals
scratched their heads—or else, distempered, fought among themselves.

The object of this attention, meanwhile, languished in the draughty
corridors of Methven's hall, where he examined his wounds from hour to
hour and honed morosely his knife, gripped by the phthisis and melancholy of early winter. He had little contact with his new companions. He
avoided Fulthor and thus, of necessity, the discussions in the throne room.
Once or twice he heard the madwoman singing in some chamber. Of
Tomb, who had in such a peculiar manner befriended him (at least he supposed it was that), he had no news. Methvet Nian having at last agreed to
an expedition, therefore provision must be made of food, horses, weapons,
and such safe conducts as were necessary. The dwarf had concerned himself with this, and with preparations of his own, and was not much about
the palace.

Hornwrack shrugged, paced the corridors at night, gazing in a sort of
savage abstraction at the old machines and whispering sculptures, and refused to answer his door. On the day of their departure he had to be
fetched from his apartment (he was staring into a mirror). On the day of
their departure, sleet fell, quickly soaking the striped awnings in the street
markets and filling the gutters with a miserable slush. On the day of their
departure a vision was vouchsafed to them; Tomb the Dwarf remembered
a legend at whose birth he had presided long ago; and their ill-fated expedition acquired its tutelary or presiding spirit—

This apparition, which was to remain with them until the peculiar termination of their journey, manifested itself first in the throne room at
Viriconium. Besides Cellur the Birdmaker, only Hornwrack was present.
(Methvet Nian was to watch their departure from the city by the Gate of
Nigg, and had gone there early. Alstath Fulthor fretted in an outer yard
with Fay Glass and the horses. Tomb the Dwarf, having worked all night in
his caravan—white heat flickering out over the tailboard to the accompaniment of a sad hammer—was dozing in some corner.) It was not yet light:
the palace was chilly, echoic, nautiloid. Cellur, hoping to contact his own

machines in their redoubt beneath the Lendalfoot estuary, passed a yellow hand through his beard. "Brown, green, counting," he whispered, and in response a flock of grey images twittered like bats across the five false windows of the throne room. Clearly this was not the result he had forecast. "Do you see nothing?" he said impatiently. "I must have fresh news!"

"Be quick, old man," said Hornwrack neutrally. He yawned and rubbed his face, feeling an obscure tension in the muscles of his neck. This he put down to being woken early. Like Fulthor, for reasons more or less complex, he was anxious to be off. Alone with wound, knife, and mirror over the last twenty-four hours, he had been surprised to find that he no longer regretted his psychic severance from the Low City. He thought now only rarely of the boy in the Rue Sepile, the bitter smell of dead geraniums, instead looked forward with a dry eagerness, curious as to the fate of his obsessions now that their confining frame had been removed. He massaged his neck. The old man muttered fractiously. In the upper air of the throne room the light was becoming stratified, bands of very pale pink and yellow leaking through the high eastern skylights. Dawn had arrived early. Fresh news! "Be quick!"

"*Abrogate all rituals,*" said a soft confidential voice from somewhere above him. He looked up, startled. It sniggered. "*What a lovely piece of meat!*"

Up near the vaulted ceiling a salmon-coloured layer of light had begun curdling into grey muculent lumps and strings which floated about like bits of fat in a lukewarm soup, bumping one another gently. After a minute or two of slow tidal effort, these in their turn merged to form a thick, lobed nucleus, from which presently evolved the crude figure of a man. Hornwrack studied this process with disgust, noting how, as they strained to become arms and legs, the lobes heaved and struggled like something trapped in an elastic bag. He caught the birdmaker staring puzzledly upwards and sniffed sarcastically.

"Have you finished tampering, old man?"

Cellur made an impatient movement with one hand.

"Hush!"

The man hanging in the air above them (if it was a man) wore clothes of some rough faded material, originally black, tailored in a fashion which had not been common in the city for over a century. Where it could be seen, his skin was pallid, greenish, covered in withered silvery patches. Over his face was clamped a kind of mask or breathing apparatus from the black snout of which sprouted many truncated tubes and proboscides; this was attached by four black straps which, cutting into the swollen flesh of his cheeks, met in the straggling yellow hair at the back of his head. He was enormously fat, as if he had passed much of his life in a sphere where human conditions of growth no longer pertained: his hypertrophied buttocks floated over their heads like shadowy moons, accompanied by a thin monologue, cabalistic and futile, of which no sense might be made whatever—

"Here I sit, an old man in the *Neant* of the wind (*Prima convien che tanto il ciel*), stranded for so long in the fractured white spaces, a hundred years of pearly silence in the garden behind the world: there I lay in the biting wind—ABRACADABRA—there ate in the shadow of the veinous wing manna (*perch' io indugiai al fine i buon sospiri*); and what for? WAR! Now they burrow in the great borrowed abracadabra of my surviving soul. Ah! Fear death from the air! What a lovely piece of meat, my dear!"

—And so on, punctuated by roars of pain or rage as, rolling slowly from one corner of the room to another, he attempted to right his huge floundering bulk or adjust its height from the floor. At times he seemed quite solid, while at others an appalling smell filled the throne room and his outlines became vague and mucous again. In moments of solidity he would struggle and thresh; he waved his arms, perhaps for attention, perhaps to keep his balance in whatever grotesque medium he was floating. (It was plain that the air of earth could not support so gross a body—he wallowed rather in some mysterious water glass, some dimension of his own.) When he faded, his voice faded too, becoming feeble and distant and distorted, as if by passage through some inhospitable aether.

Cellur the Birdmaker was transfixed. "This is none of my doing!" he cried, full of an ancient excitement. "Hornwrack, it is the voice from the moon!"

("It's a voice from a sewer," declared Hornwrack, and, *sotto voce:* "A voice from a pantomime.")

Cellur addressed the floating man. "Many nights I listened to you. What have you to tell me? Speak!"

"Blork," said the floating man.

Thereafter he disregarded Cellur, but courted Hornwrack vigorously, his eyes ingenuous and fishy behind the tinted faceplate of his mask. Sidling up to the assassin he would wink coyly and embark on some earnest incoherent suit, only to topple helplessly over on his side before he could complete it, like the corpse of some small decomposing whale. "Listen to me, my lad (black buggery!). I can see you're a flier. Listen, the regenerated word burrows within me! We must have a talk, you and I—" Then, making a terrified pushing motion: "No more, no more of that!" And off he would go, bobbing about the throne room at the height of Hornwrack's head, a sour fluid dribbling from the edges of his mask.

This was too much for Hornwrack, who, eyeing the apparition superstitiously, got out the sword of tegeus-Cromis and followed it about, making lethal cuts at the air. "Back to your sewer!" he shouted. "Back to your madhouse!" while Cellur in an attempt to restrain him plucked feebly at his cloack and the apparition evaded them both, chuckling and sneezing.

Nothing could be got from it. If they left it alone, it harangued them mercilessly, in fragments of infernal languages. When they pursued it, Cellur in a spirit of conciliation, Hornwrack with murderous blows, it merely hiccupped behind its mask and blundered off. For half an hour this pantomime continued, until, in the face of the growing daylight, its periods of stability became fewer, its outline grey and debatable. Its voice faded into an enormous echoing distance in which might be heard quite distinctly the sound of waves on some unimaginable shore. Eventually it vanished into the same odd brew of light as had engendered it, and they were left stranded in the empty throne room, furious and futile.

This was how Alstath Fulthor found them: staring breathlessly into the vacant air. Had he listened carefully, as they begged him, he might have heard a feeble buzzing voice exhorting him to "Fear death from the air!" The sound of waves, or something like it. Silence. But what were voices to him, who now heard them constantly in his head?

"It is long past dawn," he said irritably, "and the Queen will be waiting for us."

In the event they saw very little of her, for it was a brutally cold day: only a white face in a window near the top of a tower; a white hand raised; and then nothing. Alstath Fulthor, his great black horse and blood-red armour glowing heraldically beneath the overcast, drew an ironic cheer from the handful of Low City dwellers who stood in the slush to watch them through the Gate of Nigg. Viriconium foundered across the stream of Time behind them, like some immense royal barge abandoned to winter! This zone of monstrous narcissism and gigantic depressions behind him, Hornwrack sensed the beginnings of the new phase signalled by the manifestation in the throne room. We are all mad now, he thought. On an impulse he unsheathed the old steel sword and held it high. But when he looked back Methvet Nian had already left the tower.

Outside on the low brown foothills of Monar lay the first snow of the season, drifted up against the stone intake walls and sheep enclosures. The pack animals were fractious, the wind bitter. They travelled slowly, but the dwarf, who had been sleeping in some straw, did not catch up with them until much later.

When he did, he said, "This 'bloated ghost' you speak of: he was the finest airboatman of them all."

And that night, huddled by a dying fire in the hills above the distant city, he continued: "At Mingulay he flew one machine against eight. Cooking rats in the sun at noon we watched, my long-dead friends and I, from the beleagured city. His boat was old, his crew haggard; the drugs he took to stay awake had made him shake and stagger; but how that boat spun and turned, how it dropped like a hawk amid the violet bolts of the power cannon! How the brassy light of the South glanced off its crystal hull! Benedict Paucemanly: seven wrecks dotted the arid plain before the siege was lifted; the eighth he rammed afterwards, in an oversight.

"But war was never enough for Paucemanly. When the world was still young (and the Methven still casting their shadows across it) he flew round it. I know, for I was with him, a dwarf of few summers who fancied himself an adventurer. We crossed the oceans, Hornwrack, and all the broken continents! Deserts drifted beneath our hull, rapt in their millennial declining dream. At the poles, aurorae cascaded and roared above us like spectral rivers. We sampled the tropics; the equatorial air burned about us. That was Paucemanly's first flight in the *Heavy Star*. But if war failed to satisfy him, so did the world. He grew bored. He grew melancholy and thin.

"He began to stare each night at the wan and sovereign moon.

"Oh, he yearned after that sad planet. His plan was to go there. 'The mysterious navigators of the Afternoon,' he reasoned, 'had commerce with it daily, in just such boats as these. The space outside the earth was of no consequence to them. Perhaps,' he persuaded himself, 'the boats remember the way.' We watched him leave on a black night, in that famous ship. She rose into the darkness, hunting like a compass needle. Old sense revived in her. She trembled in anticipation, and strange new lights glimmered at her stern.

"We never saw her again, any of us. The *Heavy Star*, the *Heavy Star*! That was a hundred years ago—"

The old dwarf's eyes were red and flat in the gloom, reflecting the firelight like the eyes of an animal.

"Hornwrack," he whispered, "she knew her way. Don't you see? This 'bloated ghost' you describe is Benedict Paucemanly returned to us. He has been a hundred years in the moon!"

Hornwrack stirred the embers with his boot.

"That is all very well," he said a little cruelly (for he envied the dwarf these memories, with which he had nothing to compare). "But what has he brought with him past the gates of earth? And why is he a gibbering idiot?"

The dwarf looked at him thoughtfully.

Later, Cellur the Bird Lord was to describe their journey north in these terms:

"Among the stone crowns and aimless salients of the empty foothills we received hints of some state of being we could not imagine. The world was bleached of its old meanings even for those of us who had previously accepted them. (I do not count myself among these. How could I?) This happened immediately after we left the city. It was as if a protection had been removed from us. Mosaic eyes seemed to observe us from behind the dry-stone walls. In the outline of a ridge or a wayfarer's tree might be contained the suggestion of quite another object—a folded wing, for instance, or the coiled tongue of a moth.

"Alstath Fulthor led the way. Some internal process held him rapt. He had begun, perhaps, to map the paths inside himself which led to the Past. This gave him an absentminded air, and an irritable one, as if by our presence we interrupted some private conversation—although had anyone suggested this he would have rejected it angrily. Attempting to live simultaneously in two worlds, he rode moodily ahead and seemed to see nothing—head bowed into the rain, blood-red armour pulsing like a beacon. If it was madness then it was only the madness that has infected all his people since their Rebirth. They will learn in the end that the journey they long for is impossible, and accept the world as it is.

"The unmarked journeys of the soul: as we descended the foothills, we came upon old roads lined with sagging yews and blunt formless stone beasts. Here there is little left to humanize the debased earth; this is the beginning of the end, where the empire wastes away with its own geography. On the narrow strip between the mountains and the coastal flats only the giant hemlock grows now, and among it the ruins of the Afternoon are rotting, cities made of bloody glass submerged beneath cold and muddy lagoons: the ancient Fen Cities, among whose broken towers now creep the black wherries of the Evening, tacking and creaking from staithe to staithe in pursuit of a bleak diminishing trade. Of the old roads none are whole. The wide fused highways of the Afternoon peter out into shattered flags or limestone cobbles laid in Borring's day, eventually into sheep-trod, nettle, and smallholding.

"The best of them, though, skirting warily both salt marsh and massif, makes its way to Duirinish, that grey outpost of former kings which is gateway to the Great Brown Waste and to the old cities of the North; and along this we took ourselves, under the patronage of the hallucinatory pilot Benedict Paucemanly. Exhorting, demanding, mumbling eternally in its strange self-constructed language, vanishing at intervals only to return refreshed, his ghost (if indeed it was his) had haunted us for a hundred miles or more. Now it wallowed above us like a waterlogged tree; now hid like a girl among the fleshy etiolated hemlock stems; now muttered, 'On the moon it was like white gardens. *Pork*.' It would not answer Alstath Fulthor, which put him out of temper; nor would it speak to me; Tomb the Dwarf it actively avoided, as though embarrassed by his persistence, sidling away down the hemlock glades grinning and breaking wind apologetically. And if he spoke to it of the 'old days' it regarded him with wide panicky eyes and flapped deprecatingly its awkward great hands.

"Galen Hornwrack, however, it courted ardently, trying to capture his attention with a wink or a whistle. 'Land ho, lad!' it would cry, and, bobbing in the air before him, make an elaborate mime of discovering some *terra incognita*: shading its eyes with one hand while with the other it pointed north and west. (Fulthor made light of this mummery, arguing that the thing was mad if it could be said to exist at all: yet after a few repetitions one felt a profound sense of urgency, as if some fading fragment of the original airboatman was struggling to act out or insinuate something he could no longer articulate.) Hornwrack's response was characteristic. He hated to appear a fool. The more the thing wooed him the more he averted his gaze. And at night when he thought himself unobserved he stalked it patiently through the firelight, the partly healed scars on his cheeks burning like the ritual stigmata of some primitive hunter. Each failure to kill or confine it increased his anger: when the girl Fay Glass sang, 'We are off to Vegys now,' and smiled at him—which was some days her only human contact—he would not smile back, which made her fractious and difficult to manage in her turn.

"In this way we came to Duirinish, which we avoided to the west, having no business there. It is a great place, that, the bulk of it being built facing north. We passed it in a pale dawn, the sun striking grave and oblique on the dwarf oaks of Low Leedale. A bitter metallic smell hung in the air, making the horses delicate of temper; the grey stones of the city had a brooding look. Small dour figures could be seen staring down from among its parapets and machicolations, but they had no time for us. For five hundred years the men of Duirinish had kept the border: what they now saw from their fastness as they stared into the North, what strange alterations and diffusions of reality, I do not care to think. On our part we found the world a changeable place.

"Shrewd sea winds courted us. On our right marched a line of tall cliffs. Originally deposited as a limestone reef front some hundreds of miles long, these had been worked during earth's long Afternoon into a chain of quarries broken here and there by little steep-sided valleys with crumbling mossy headwalls. In and out of the hidden caves and sinkholes of this region (in effect the lip of a vast plateau, stretching a mile or so back inland before being buried under the culm measures and doomed black soils of the Great Brown Waste) there flowed whitish polluted streams. The trees were grey and dry. Now we moved deeper into it, and into a kind of psychic dislocation, picking a way through the gummy, lifeless tidal pools while mirages came and went over our bowed heads.

"We had no idea of what might disclose itself from day to day. At

evening we left the beach and lit fires in the tottering mazes where inter-
leaving bituminous strata had made the rock rotten and easily eroded. But
the flames were hard to kindle. They were pale and cool. Later the echo of
falling rocks clattered through the dark like the sound of skittles falling in
a deserted alley. From the upper ledges there drifted down an endless rain
of tiny luminous beetles. All night long the wind shook the skeins of dead
ivy; and in the morning, as the sea fogs cleared, vast insects would appear
in the distance, their reflections perfect in the wet sand of the tidal flats;
they moved ponderously away before we could identify them. All this, as I
have said, was contained at first in the outlines of ordinary things, much as
a shadowy architecture of colonnades and alien galleries can be made out
in the walls of an empty quarry, but as we moved north the landscape itself
became thin and grey, textured like mucus, with the bones of some other
landscape showing more or less clearly through.

" 'The world is coming to bits,' said Galen Hornwrack, and someone
answered dryly, 'The world is being exchanged for something else.'

"It comes to me that each of us suffered during this northern transit an
emptying or bleaching of the identity in preparation for a future we could
not describe. Viriconium was behind us. (Even those of us who returned
there never saw it again, but found a changed city, one in which we were
not comfortable.) In the sense that it no longer filled our day-to-day
thoughts, we had forgotten our purpose. We existed simply to slip through
the rain, a handful of salt-lipped figures beneath the unending cliffs, speaking in low sepulchral voices. Before went, like a banner, the raging glory of
the Afternoon, with its great horse and scarlet armour; while a sniggering
dwarf in a leather hat brought up the rear on a pony no bigger than a dog;
and above us floated the balloon-like form of the ancient airman, chivvied
like a dying whale by gangs of raucous gulls. Cyphers, we pass beneath the
hungry ironic eyes of the gannets and guillemots—the assassin resentful
and disfigured; the woman who believes herself lost in Time; and myself—
a thing, alive beyond its rightful years, far beyond its rightful place! The
landscape, though, anticipates our release: this preparation or interlude is
drawing to a close. . . .

" 'We should turn east soon if we are to find your village,' Fulthor insisted patiently. Fay Glass frowned at him like a child, her hair plastered to
her skull. She wore two or three purple flowers which she had previously
offered to Hornwrack, and due to his refusal of them was agreeing with no
one. 'Nobody who truly cared about hygiene could read the message
above,' she declared with a mutinous dignity. 'How can we prevent abuse
in the first place?' Fulthor could only shrug. Shortly after this exchange it
became evident that we had lost the Glenluce road: the beach became narrow and steeply shelving, the cliffs undercut, and our progress dependent

on the state of the tide, from which we were forced to take refuge twice a day. Eventually we led our horses up the first tottering rake which offered a way to the top of the cliffs.

"That was evening or late afternoon. The light was fading. Squalls of rain blew out of the advancing sea fog, dotted with large wet flakes of snow. A melancholy heath dipped away inland—shadowy, sheep-cropped turf, black gorse, and bent hawthorn trees. Northwards and at right angles to the coast, defile succeeded narrow defile, each one cutting through the limestone to the underlying metamorphic shales and broadening as it reached the sea. The landscape was scattered with old metal bridges. It had a discarded air. We passed the night huddled at the foot of a ruined stone wall, unaware that a mile or so ahead lay the port of Iron Chine, nexus of a strange war, with its weird banners and demented prince. Rusty iron creaked in the wind."

Cellur does not relate how on the next morning they found that Paucemanly's ghost had abandoned them, or how they slumped on their soaked and surly animals staring dully at the desolation which stretched away inland: that half-fertile strip of dissected peat and tough ling heather pocked with lethal seepage hollows which was the merest periphery of the Great Waste. Unpredictable soughs full of brown water threaded its endless slopes of sodden tussocky grass, and queer rocks were embedded along its rheumy skylines, eroded by the wind into vague and organic silhouettes. This was their ultimate destination (it is, in another way, the ultimate destination of everything, as the earth enters its long Evening), or so they imagined: but in the face of its winter they faltered. Instead of turning eastward Alstath Fulthor led them first along the cliffs and then down into Iron Chine. They followed him like a handful of refugees from some chronological disaster, heads bowed against the bitter blow of Time.

The cyclopean quays of Iron Chine are older than the Afternoon. No one knows who built them, or for what crude purpose. The massive untrimmed blocks which comprise them are not native to this coast but cut from granites formed much further north. Who brought them down from there to bind them with iron and pile them in the cold sea, or when, is not known. They are black, and wet with fog, like the vertical walls of the fjord which contains them, the archaean unvegetated slates of which sweep down to an ebon sea. The enormous quayside buildings are also black; their purpose is quite lost and most of them have fallen into decay. The modern port subsists on fish, gulls' eggs, and mutton. Cowed by geography, Time, and the sea, its lime-washed cottages huddle uneasily amid a greater architecture; above them a road has been pushed through the rotting slates, and winds its way perilously up to the clifftop pastures.

Down this Galen Hornwrack now rode (the dwarf beside him croaking tunelessly), puzzled by the mist that lay in the trough of the fjord. It was ashen and particulate. Inner currents stirred it sluggishly. A gust of wind, exploding over the lip of the cliffs and roiling down past him, parted it for a moment, but revealed only black water patterned by the rain. Yet he sensed it was occupied (although he could hardly have said by what): he stopped his horse, stood up in his stirrups, and craned his neck anxiously until the rift had closed again. "What's this then?" he asked himself. He shook his head. "Fulthor," he called back, "this may be unwise." Further down, where the air was calmer, he smelt smoke, urgent and powdery at the back of his nose. Now the dwarf became agitated too, wiping his nose with the back of his hand, squinting and sniffing about him like a nervous dog. Behind the smell of smoke was something sharper, less easy to identify.

Lower still, at the edge of the mist, halted before it like a swimmer at the margin of an unknown lake, he became convinced that people were moving about down there on the water in a panicky and disorientated fashion; and distant shouts came up to him, partly muffled by the mist but discernibly cries for aid. "It may be unsafe, Fulthor." But Fulthor motioned him on, and from then on events seemed to reach him at one remove, as if he was not quite part of them. It was a familiar feeling, and one that recalled the Bistro Californium, the deadly gamboge shadows of the Low City—

Inside the mist was a distinct smell of lemons, and of rotting pears—a moist and chemical odour which sought out and attacked the sensitive membranes of the body. The light was sourceless, and had the effect of sharpening outlines while blurring the detail contained within them: on Hornwrack's right, the dwarf looked as if he had been cut from grey paper a moment before—a tall queer hat, a goblin's profile, an axe head bigger than his own. Beyond this paper silhouette the path fell away into a whitish void in which Hornwrack made out now and then a localized and fitful carmine glow. While he was trying to remember what this reminded him of, Alstath Fulthor took station on his left. Their throats raw, their eyes streaming, and their noses running, they advanced in a cautious formation until the path began to level out and they found themselves without warning on a wide stone concourse bordering the estuary.

Here the mist was infused with a thin yellow light. But for the slap of the waves on the water stair below, but for the silence and the smell of the fog, they might have been in the Low City on any cold October night. Hornwrack led them to the water's edge, the hooves of the horses clacking and scraping nervously across an acre of worn stone slabs glistening with shallow puddles. A languor of curiosity came over them. Despite their forebodings they tilted their heads to hear the distant thud of wood on wood, the faint cries of men echoing off the estuary. Even Fay Glass was quite silent.

Hornwrack narrowed his eyes. "Fulthor, there are no longer fishermen in this place." Distances were impossible of judgement. He wiped his eyes, coughed. "Something is on fire out there."

The smell of smoke had thickened perceptibly, perhaps carried to them by some inshore wind. With it came a creaking of ropes and a smell of the deep sea; groans and shouts startlingly close. Now a node of carmine light appeared, expanding rapidly. A cold movement of the air set the mist bellying like a curtain. Hornwrack shook his head desperately, looking about him in panic: abruptly he sensed an enormous object moving very close to him. The mist had all along distorted his perspectives.

"Back!" he shouted. "Fulthor, get them back from the water!" Even as he spoke the mist writhed and broke apart. Out of it thrust the foreparts and figurehead of a great burning ship.

Its decks were deep with blood. Once it had been white. Now it rushed to destruction on the water stair, spouting cinders. Its strange slatted metal sails, decorated with unfamiliar symbols, were melting as they fell. Captained by despair, it emerged from the mist like a vessel from Hell, its figurehead an insect-headed woman who had pierced her own belly with a sword (her mouth, if it could be called a mouth, gaped in pain or ecstasy). "Back!" cried Galen Hornwrack, tugging at his horse's head. "Back!" Fay Glass, though, only stared and sneezed like an animal, transfixed by the mad carven head gaping above her. Dying men tumbled over the sides of the ship, groaning "Back!" as the lean, charred hull drove blindly at the shore; "Back!" as it smashed into the water stair and with its bow torn open immediately began to sink.

Down it went, with a roar and a shudder. The deep cold water gurgled into its ravaged hull. Ratlines and halyards fell in blazing festoons about its cracked bowsprit. Hornwrack pulled the madwoman off her horse and dragged her away. She wiped her nose. Sparks flew about their heads. The hulk lurched, settled a little lower in the water. A sail fell, showing Hornwrack for a moment a curious symbol—a hexagon with eccentric sides, through which crawled orange-throated lizards—before it hissed molten into the sea. High up in the doomed forecastle a solitary figure stood mantled in blood. "Murder!" it sobbed, staring wildly down at Hornwrack. "They've followed us into the estuary!" It hacked with a blunt shortsword at a flaming spar. "Oh, this damned mist!" Suddenly it was catapulted from its perch and with a thin wail fell into the water.

"Hornwrack!"

The burning ship reminded him of some childhood ritual, some solstitial bonfire lit in the wet dark ploughland. He turned almost reluctantly from it, his face stiff with heat. Fulthor, Tomb, and the old man stood a little way off; toward them across the gleaming concourse men were running. "To you, Fulthor!" he cried, just as he might have done beneath the heights of Minnet-Saba, where the rival factions of the Low City clash without chivalry at night; and, encumbered by the madwoman, promptly dropped the unfamiliar sword. "Black filth, girl. Let go." The weapon tolled like a bell on the worn flagstones. His horse trod on it. A fit of coughing racked him.

As he disentangled himself, though, he realised that the mist was dwindling round him like a dream, to reveal the giant quays and boatsheds; the little town; the slatey cliffs. Seabirds called as they skimmed the water. Even the clouds were blowing away. For all the fears of the dead sailor, nothing floated out there on the roadstead. But for the bubbling wreck on the water stair, the estuary was empty of menace, quite empty. Puzzled, he drew his knife and urged forward his horse.

7

ST. ELMO BUFFIN AND THE
NAVIGATORS OF IRON CHINE

With the mist dispersed, the village smelt of smoked fish and salt. Fulthor and his party stood outnumbered and uncertain at the centre of an un-armed crowd. Hornwrack had put up his knife. Like the survivors of some forgotten colonial war (desultory, expedient, never quite resolved), the oc-cupants of Iron Chine drew round him: thin intelligent women, a few bare-limbed children. There were no young men present, only some old ones who stamped their feet and turned up their heavy collars, faded blue eyes watering in the cold wind. They stared up at him with a defiant incu-riosity and he stared back embarrassed, although he could not have said precisely why. It was a mixed community; at the periphery of the crowd a handful of the Reborn hovered like strange, long-necked animals, their delicate features coarsened a little by an unrelenting deprivation. What had they left behind them in the Afternoon, what mad sophistications ex-changed for the smell of dead fish?

A few sailors who had escaped the wreck now swam ashore.

No one offered them any help, nor did they seem to expect it, but pulled themselves up on to the quay and sprawled there with the blind, open-mouthed look of the exhausted. After a moment two of them got up again and between them pulled out a third. He kept trying to thank them. They knelt by his atrociously burnt head until a trickle of clear fluid ran out of the corner of his mouth; then they left him to stare sightlessly at a flock of gulls tearing pieces off something out on the estuary. They were yellow-haired, guileless, hardly more than children, but their faces were full of de-spair, as if they had fought a lifetime of holding actions and unplanned retreats. Alstath Fulthor observed them gravely for a minute or two, then, finding no other authority and extricating himself with difficulty from the civilian crowd, presented them with his safe conducts.

"Our mission is one of importance," he told them.

Eventually one of them said, "This was not the time to come here." He turned his back and, quietly dismissing the intrusion, vomited up a quantity of seawater. His companion put a placatory hand on his shoulder and reminded him,

"Captain, they come from the capital—"

But he only wiped his mouth and laughed wildly. "Ay, and look at them! Some yellow old man, and a *woman*. Two city lordlings and their dwarf!"

A fit of dry retching shook him. "There will never be any help from Viriconium," he said indistinctly. There was self-pity in his voice, and after a moment or two he acknowledged it with a disgusted twist of his mouth. "Did you see anything out there?" he asked, and when the other shook his head, whispered, "I pity those that did."

He tried to squeeze the salt water from his hair.

"One of our own vessels rammed us, that's certain," he continued thoughtfully. "But by then we were already burning."

He shrugged.

"It was as usual. Those who saw anything were struck mad immediately. Those who did not, got lost in the mist."

Thus the defeated, locked in their dreams of defeat.

"You are bound to help us!" shouted Alstath Fulthor suddenly.

"Leave them alone, Fulthor," advised Hornwrack. Often enough he had been among the defeated himself. His sudden compassion surprised him nevertheless, and that he should recognise it as such surprised him even further. He looked sidelong at Tomb the Dwarf to see if he had noticed anything, but the dwarf wasn't interested—he only grinned pleasantly and unforgivingly down at the sailors and said, "There is no enemy in sight now."

"They are bound by those signatures to help us," said the Reborn Man less loudly.

They regarded him with puzzlement, and some scorn.

"Go up to the new hall," was all they said, "and leave us alone." And they wandered off along the quay to where the remaining mast of the foundered ship poked up at a strange angle from a scum of floating wreckage. There a smell of lemons clung, as if some bitter dew had condensed on that doomed hull during its confused final voyage. It was an unearthly, chemical smell. The horses hated it.

The crowd, sensing a termination, looked on emptily for a minute or two, then began to disperse—the children drawn by a kind of magnetism toward the wreck while their elders took to the cobbled road which wound up into Iron Chine proper, where they vanished in twos and threes among the little two-storey houses with the wet slate roofs, the drying nets, and lines of flaccid laundry. Dulled by the cold and continual privation, they seemed unable to react to a tragedy which, as someone in Fulthor's party pointed out later, must have involved them all. One woman did stand for a time staring out into the estuary, a few tears drying on her cheeks in the wind. Only then did Hornwrack realise that more than one vessel had been involved. A spatter of rain blew out of the west (where like a great ancient fish there lay in wait the island continent of Fenlen) and into his face. He could see the "new hall" on a rise above the village. He felt wretched.

"This wind is prising my joints apart," said Cellur the Birdmaker cheerfully. When no one answered him he gave an impatient shrug. "These people need more help than they could ever give us," he told Fulthor. "When you stop sulking you will see that."

It came on to rain in earnest as they passed through the Chine. The peeling walls had once been gaily whitewashed, the window boxes tended; now pale faces observed them from behind the streaming windows. Higher, they found they could look down into the boatyards of St. Elmo Buffin, from which rose the masts and spars of his white and fated fleet—rakish three-hulled craft fitted with those peculiar slatted metal sails over which rioted orange lizards, green beetles glowing like fresh tattoos, and subtly distorted geometrical figures. Designed by the Afternoon, built by the Evening, blessed by a new madness of both, they were arming for some invisible war. DEATH proclaimed one sail, and LIFE another, in calligraphies rich and outlandish; while on the decks beneath, shipwrights and sailors swarmed like rats.

"No hint of this war has ever come to us in the High City," said Alstath Fulthor wonderingly. "It is no wonder they are poverty-stricken here."

Higher still, the "new hall" hung above them like a threat. Sombre, columnar, mysterious of purpose, it had about it a most appalling air of age, an age which emptied out the cultural luggage of Alstath Fulthor's vanished race—all the moral atrocities and philosophical absurdities and expired technologies—and found it meaningless; rendering meaningless in the end even the deserts which were their only legacy to the Evening. As he approached it, wincing from the weather, huddling into his cloak against a wind a million years old, it spoke to Galen Hornwrack from an age fully as naive but by no means as puzzled as his own. It was a survivor of the Morning.

There was a ramshackle new construction perched on its roof like a greenhouse; from this flags were flying which no one could identify, though Fulthor and the dwarf argued desultorily over their provenance.

And down at its ancient front door, his big-knuckled hands clasped like a bunch of dice, stood the solitary principal of that lost maritime demesne, genius of a doomed fleet, St. Elmo Buffin.

Elmo Buffin, that sad travesty, with his limbs like peeled sticks! He was seven feet tall and a yellow cloak was draped eccentrically about his bony shoulders. Plate armour of a dull-green colour encased him, sprouting all manner of blunt horns and spurs, little nubs and bosses which seemed chitinous and organic. It pulsed and shivered in its colour, for it had come to him from his father, a Reborn Man of the defunct House of medina-Clane, one of the first to be resurrected by Tomb the Dwarf and now dead. What his mother—a dour Northwoman and fishwife of Iron Chine, whose first husband had died in the War of the Two Queens—had bequeathed him is hard to say. Neither strain had bred true, for between Afternoon and Evening there is a great genetic as well as temporal gulf. Epilepsy racked him twice a week. His eyes were yellow and queer in that slack clownish face, which seemed too large for his thin limbs. His brain heaved like the sea; across it visions came and went like the painted sails of his own fleet. Of years he had twenty-six; but his insanity made of that forty or fifty. Since the death of his father (himself an eccentric but principled man, who had consented to the miscegenation in order to cement the two halves of his biracial community) the whole weight of the Chine had rested on his shoulders.

How many of the villagers actually believed in his invisible enemy, or his experimental fleet? It seems immaterial. Those who died at sea knew the truth, as do we. Those that did not were nonetheless inspired by him. And if it did not thrive, well then, the village survived. Buffin's success was as a symbol—queasy but enduring—which enabled past and present to collaborate. (His failure lay in underestimation—in being, if you like, not quite mad enough—but that was not to become clear until later, and who anyway could have been quite so mad as to imagine the actual state of affairs?) Now he stood in the doorway of the ancient hall, with its dreadful disregard for the passage of Time and its rooftop contraptions worn with the air of a rakish hat, watching from the corner of his eye Fulthor's party as it approached. He was dwarfed by the dark columns. He could not keep still. He rubbed his hands to warm them in the cold air. He leant unconcernedly on the doorpost. Then he must look at his feet to admire his boots. Then, muttering to himself, jerk upright and practise a handshake with some imaginary visitor.

" 'News from the city!' " they heard him murmur. "Shall I say that? No. I must not appear so anxious. Shall I then enquire (thus, with a politic solicitude), 'Your journey, it was comfortable?' Manifestly though, it was not—"

He snapped his fingers impatiently.

"Oh, what shall I say!"

Suddenly he dodged back among the columns and was lost to view. (Though it had no basis, Hornwrack retained for some time an impression of him huddled up there somewhere in the gloom the way a child might huddle breathless and white-faced behind the great half-opened doors of some echoing abandoned palace into which it has wandered, that palace being the world.)

After a moment he called querulously, "Hello?"

No one answered. Except for Fay Glass they had all got down from their horses and were staring astonished into the massive fluted shadows. Out popped his head like a crumpled leather bag on a stick, and he tapped the side of it mournfully. "We're all mad here," he sighed, as if the village, the boatyards, and the ancient stones were all in some way contained within it: which, Hornwrack supposed, in a way they were. Now he recovered himself, smiling ironically, came forward and clasped Fulthor's hands. "The briefest of aberrations," he apologised (at this the madwoman pursed her lips enviously, and sniffed); "Please forgive me," and never referred to it again. "Viriconium has sent observers then, at last!"

Under this misapprehension he led them up a monstrous flight of stairs. They could not correct it because he would not let them speak. He had, he explained, given up hope of ever getting help from the capital. He did not blame the High City for this. Messengers had been sent every six months to Duirinish, which was the regional centre, but patently the messages had not been sent on. This was understandable. In Duirinish they semed to believe that he was quarrelling with some other coastal village. This had not been at all uncommon in the years immediately following the war. What could he do but maintain a philosophical attitude?

Up the vast stairs they went behind him, listening to his monologue float down. His laughter was strained. "Still, now you have come—"

His rooms were full of bald light, strange navigational instruments, clutter. In one room the charts had peeled from the wall and lay all along its foot in odd folds. He took them to a thing like a conservatory built right out on to the roof—"From here I can see twenty miles out to sea." He smiled proudly, a little pathetically. "I expect you have more profound instruments in the South." There was a great maze of tubing made of brass into which he invited them to look. They bent one by one to the eyepiece. When it was Hornwrack's turn to look, all he saw was a sad reticulated greyness, and, suspended indistinctly against it in the distance, something like a chrysalis or cocoon, spinning and writhing at the end of a thread. "Success is slow to come with this particular instrument." Hornwrack shook his head, but Cellur seemed to be fascinated. As they moved from exhibit to exhibit like reluctant tourists in some artist's studio, Buffin sat

on a stool with his limbs tense. He was like an exhibit himself in the direct
odd light filtering through the whitish panes, legs wound tensely round
one another, his face like an apologetic bag. "It is not an ordinary telescope." Out to sea nothing moved.

The rooms were draughty and seemed deserted. When he ordered refreshments they were brought by an old woman but he served them himself. "Would you like some of this dried herring?" Money and men were
his most urgent requirements, he said (there was besides a shortage of timber). The fleet was fitted but under-crewed. "Pardon?" He showed them
charts, designs, plans for a strategy they could not comprehend. On these
maps an unconventional symbol depicted "mist." The island continent of
Fenlen was not marked. Hornwrack looked for it but he could not find it.

"The war," Alstath Fulthor managed to say. "What is its exact nature?"
Buffin looked surprised.

"Why, it is precisely as you have seen. That is the extent of it."

He thought for a long time. Then he said that his ships went out well-
armed. They were captained by crafty men. At sea they encountered first
rough water and adverse currents: then a mist. In the mist was some enemy no one had ever seen. "A madness comes over them, and they throw
themselves into the water." Those that did not drown were destroyed by
fire, by unimaginable weapons. Some returned. A strange smell clung to
their vessels, and they spoke of sounds so appalling as to be beyond description (though they were not loud).

Fulthor began to show signs of impatience. This sort of conjecture was
not to his taste. He looked sideways at Hornwrack, who shrugged. Cellur
the Birdmaker, however, had been listening to every word. "Have you
ever been attacked on land?" he asked.

"For ten years now," Buffin said absently, "we have fought a war we
cannot see. Since the death of my father something has been out there."

Fulthor stirred, drew in his breath. "I can make nothing of this," he said
brusquely to Cellur. "We cannot concern ourselves with this."

Buffin blinked at him and went on, "When the mist rolls inshore at
night we can sometimes sense them down there in the fjord, sailing
stealthily inland. Where they are going we do not know." He smiled
tiredly. "I'm sorry, the fish is awful." Momentarily sponged of its lines, his
face regained a young and pliant air. "I'm glad you've come at last."

Fulthor got up. He handed over his safe conducts and his letters of introduction. "Our mission is urgent," he said. "I should like fresh horses if
you have them. Otherwise nothing. I'm sorry we cannot help."

There was a silence.

"That was badly done, Alstath Fulthor," said Cellur.

Buffin looked at them both. Sleet tapped the milky panes of the greenhouse. Outside, the wind tossed the strings of pennants, and set to swaying the distant mast tops of the half-completed fleet. A mist was coming in off the sea.

"I dreamt last night of a fatal blunder made while asleep," said Cellur as they made their way back up to the clifftop in the blowing sleet. "A sleepwalker murdered his own son."

"We have done nothing decent here," agreed Hornwrack a bit absently. Watching with horror the torment of St. Elmo Buffin, he had suddenly begun to think of his own youth, a faithless season spent in the wet plough of the midlands. He could not quite connect the two except in their antithesis. "That's certain. Only cooperate in one more High City betrayal." It was later in the day. They were all mounted on fresh animals. Out of his reverie he gave Alstath Fulthor a look of dislike. (He remembered when it came to it only a touch of dead chrysanthemums on the skin in some still-aired room; rooks sweeping over the heavy earth. What he had taken to be unsentimentality with regard to this had turned out to be quite the reverse. In turn, this caused him to think about the Rue Sepile, and all that implied.)

"I thought I recalled the man," Cellur said. "Perhaps it was a story heard long ago. And yet the face was very familiar."

"Quite."

"I cannot shake off a sense of foreboding."

At the top of the cliff, about to turn inland, they were accosted by the spectre of the ancient airboatman. Opening and shutting its mouth like a deformed goldfish, it approached them out of the eddying sleet, rotating slowly about its vertical axis. Although, as before, it appeared to maintain only the most precarious contact with the world, a thin grey snow seemed to be settling on its shoulders, the ghostly precipitate of some foreign continuum. It was agitated. It came very close to Hornwrack and plucked at his cloak. (He felt nothing until he tried to beat it off with the flat of his hands, when there was some slight, gelatinous resistance.)

"Few lawn!" it shouted through its cupped hands, as from a great distance. "Fog . . . Forn . . . Fenling. Oh, crikey." It pointed desperately out to sea. It looked inland and shook its head. "FENGLIN! nuktis 'agalma . . . 254 da parte . . . ten cans for a boat load . . . *Fengle!*"

And it took up station above his head like a fat angel, staring tragically backwards as they moved inland and signing madly whenever it caught his eye.

Still later, Tomb the Dwarf rode up to his side. He held out the weapon Hornwrack had lost on the quayside.

"You dropped your sword, soldier."

Hornwrack said bitterly, "Listen, old Dwarf, I thought I had got rid of that. *I am not him.* Whatever he was to you. Don't you understand that?"

The dwarf grinned and shrugged, still holding the sword out expectantly.

Hornwrack looked up at the thing floating above him. Seeing this, it steered itself rapidly toward him, clearing its throat. He groaned, accepted the sword. Both his spectres had returned to haunt him.

The weather now changed. Low cloud and sleet rolled away east and south to be replaced by a pale sky and good visibility. A wind like a razor blew from the north. On a succession of bright but bitterly cold days they penetrated the habitable margin of the Great Brown Waste, to find a frozen crust over deep, wet peat. Progress was slow. If a bird called, *tak tak,* like an echo in a stony gully, the madwoman followed it with her eyes, tilting her head, smiled. She was nervous, but now rode ahead of Alstath Fulthor. She had led them into a region of high dissected plateaux over which hummed the icy wind, and then cast about over the bleak hillsides for a while like a lost bitch. Little paths ran everywhere, contouring the salients. As far as anyone could make out she followed them randomly. They led her in the end to a stone-crowned, steep-streamed escarpment which sheltered among its boulder fields sparse woods of stunted oak. On its lower slopes might be discerned the lanes and enclosures of a settlement, the walls toppled, the sheepfolds in poor repair. Behind the village rose the eroded shapes of the Agdon Roches, from which it took its name: a string of gritstone outcrops quarried long ago for building stone so that they formed a succession of bays and shattered promontories.

"This is a vile bloody place."

Hornwrack: Paucemanly's ghost had left him alone for a while, vanishing with a wet pop and a feeble grin as if remembering a prior appointment. He was relieved, but found himself with nothing to think about but the cold. He was used to the city, where winter is episodic. The wind whistles across the junction of the Rue Sepile and Vientiane Avenue. The women clutch their shawls tightly and dash laughing from house to house. There is always a window to watch them from while you drink mulled wine prepared by a boy. Not so here: his fingers were welded to the reins like the fingers of a stone horseman falling apart in some provincial square. He had been miserable for days.

"I've seen worse," said the dwarf speculatively, as if he wondered whether he had. He wore his leather hat at a queer angle; his arms were empurpled with the cold.

The wreckage of an ancient landscape lay across their path.

The metaphysical disputes of the late Afternoon Cultures, raging here across the floodplain of some vanished river, had turned it into a corridor of black ash strewn with rounded stones. It was zoned and undulating; in places stripped to the underlying rock, ten or twenty feet thick in others. Every summer a little more of it dried up and blew away into the waste. Some of the stones were quite large, some no bigger than a fist, and each stood on a little pediment of wind-smoothed ash. Some isolated colonies of bilberry and ling grew here and there, raised by the same erosive process until they resembled a chain of hairy islets. Outlier or prefigurement of the deeper waste to come, it was a little less than two miles wide, and across it could be seen the cracked buttresses of the Agdon Roches, brushed at their summits with rosy light. A thin white mist flowed down the gullies and stony cloughs at their feet, drifting through the hanging oakwoods and filling up the village street so that only the roofs and upper storeys of the cottages were visible. Through the still air a dog could be heard barking; sheep bleated from the intakes. In a small field stood one cow. All this one might almost have touched, so precisely enamelled did it seem on the bright surface of the air: but Fay Glass would make no move towards it.

"She is frightened of the maze."

"And yet," said Fulthor, returning from a brief foray, "her own people must have made it." Damp ash was caked between the fingers of his gauntlets. The discovery of the earthwork had filled him with an obscure excitement. Her subsequent refusal to enter or even pass it seemed only to have sharpened this. "They were obsessed by patterns, those who came north in the final desperate days of the Resurrection determined to discover a way back." He smiled whitely. "As if the fingers of the Past do not already brush our cheeks, waking or sleeping—" He stared back into the maze. "She is a child, I'm afraid."

("We gave them life," the dwarf said. "How were we to know they would go mad?" No one answered him.)

"It is not just the woman," said Cellur. "I feel it too." And he looked out over the little strip of land. "Error is piled on error."

"Nevertheless, we go through," announced Fulthor, setting the madwoman on her horse.

"There. You shall sit safely. It was bravely done to guide us so far."

She looked at him as if he were a stone.

The basic earthwork, cut into the compacted ash, was supplemented partly by piles of stones, partly by raised banks or dykes: the whole being roughly radial in character and some fifteen feet deep. Are we to guess its purpose? In the Time of the Locust sign and substance become fatally blurred together: it was not so much a maze, perhaps, as a great ideogram, a design representing some barely achievable state of mind; but this said, we have said nothing. Down in the trenches the ash showed evidence of regular traffic, and cold, damp airs moved purposelessly. Fulthor's motives

were unclear. He could equally well have crossed the plain to reach the village. He would not discuss this. He became lost but was slow to admit it.
When he did, the girl would not help him, though she had plainly been in
the maze before. He set Tomb to climbing one of the walls, but the stuff
fell away in fibrous lumps when he was near the top and he slid down in a
shower of it without having seen anything. "I seemed to be facing south."

Thereafter, they travelled at random.

An hour passed (they came upon the hoofprints of their own animals,
travelling in the opposite direction) and then another.

A bird flying overhead; the exchange of arguments at a junction; all normal events receded and became stripped of meaning. Queer contractile
sensations in Hornwrack's skull recalled to him his colourless Low City
fevers with their intimations of failure and death. (At these times a desultory buzzing had filled his ears, as of a wasp trapped among the dry geraniums in some airless attic: he heard it now.) Looking uncomfortably
round he saw that the others were similarly affected. The whole party had
halted. Near him the dwarf was shaking his big head about and blinking
desperately. Fay Glass had somehow fallen off her horse and lay on the
ground glaring madly up at the sky. The walls of the maze began to mutate, and beckoned Hornwrack with limbs like the first delicately curled
fronds of a fern in spring. Now the world toppled sideways with a jolt, as it
sometimes does on the verge of sleep. Simultaneously he began to perceive
it as if through a cluster of tiny hexagonal lenses: for a moment he looked
out with horror onto a faceted universe. He could make nothing of it. He
thought he was dying.

Fay Glass vomited suddenly, leapt to her feet, and ran off down the passage. Hornwrack followed more slowly, leading his horse, concentrating
very carefully in case the ground should tilt further and spill him off into
the mosaic void he now conceived to be surrounding him. He could hear
the other three tottering along behind him, crying out like the newly
blind.

The maze, he now understood, had lain in wait for him since his flight
from the Bistro Californium, its centre coexistent with the hub of that affair. As he struggled down its cindery passageways he imagined himself
stabbed again and again, a half-successful execution presided over by the
mad laughter of the poet Ansel Verdigris. He lost his horse. Clutching the
phantom wound in his side he groaned and drew his flawed steel knife (as
if a gesture remembered from one maze might release him from the com-
plexities of another). Despairing, he stumbled out into a circular space
about thirty feet across, where he was relieved abruptly of the mosaic universe and saw normally again. This central stage or arena was raised a few
inches above the level of the surrounding maze, and in the middle of it
there waited an *insect larger than a man—*

The violation, if there was one, was hieratic, notional. Fay Glass lay like a corpse. *The creature crouched over her.* It resembled no insect Hornwrack had ever seen but was rather a *composite of all insects.* From its *segmented thorax,* which was of a curious *smoky yellow colour* and as shiny as lacquered bamboo, sprang the veiny *wings of the ichneumon fly,* the wedge-shaped mask of the common wasp, the mysterious *upcurved abdomen of the mantis like a symbol* from a forbidden language. Its *eyes* were lit from within, or seemed to be. They were *pale green,* and streaked with orange. A mass of palps and maxillae hung beneath its head, clattering spasmodically. He thought of the wasteland grasshopper with its serrated legs and arid stridulations. He thought of flight through vast abandoned regions, and the world he knew fell away from him so suddenly that he was sick. When he could see again, the madwoman had come back to life.

She made no attempt to get from beneath the insect, but, like something emerging painfully from a larval stage, groped and writhed about until she lay on her stomach, her neck twisted so that her white motionless face was turned to the assassin.

"I," she said, and retched dryly. She licked her lips. "We."

"I can't help you," said Hornwrack.

The insect, he saw, was damaged. The raised and elongated prothorax from which issued its frail forelimbs was covered in cuts and gouges, some of them deep enough to reveal the whitish stored fat beneath. Crusted secretions rimmed its unearthly eyes. From time to time it scraped aimlessly in the ashes at its feet or beat wildly its filmy wings.

"We see your world," said the madwoman. "Killing is all dead world. World killed. We are all killed here."

Her voice was flat and mournful. It seemed to come from a huge distance away. In the pauses between the words Hornwrack himself became an insect. He flew through the great derelict spaces, shaken by compulsions he did not understand. Many others were there with him. A hunger drove them, presiding and unproductive. They fell into a choking air and were consumed.

"We now press your heads. Our words are pressing your heads. Your world presses us. Oh. Gah."

The creature flailed its forelimbs against the ground until one of them fell off.

"Gah," said Fay Glass. "Help. Oh."

Hornwrack rushed forward and tried to haul her from under the clattering mandibles. She would not come. He felt the huge triangular mask dip toward him. He shouted and ran away again, slashing out blindly with his knife. Tomb the Dwarf came out of the maze and touched his elbow. They both ran forward and this time pulled her out. The dwarf lost his hat. "I. We. Oh," whined Fay Glass, while the insect's nervous system underwent some fresh deterioration, causing it to writhe, fan the air, and curl its abdomen repeatedly over its head. These spasms were replaced by a curious immobility, which in turn affected the madwoman. She lay on the floor like a pupating grub, the ends of her fingers bleeding where she had bitten them. The insect looked like a great enamelled brooch dug up from some depraved old city. Hornwrack and the dwarf watched it warily. It stared back, its eyes enigmatic, crusted. A faint smell of lemons hung about it, and behind that, rotting cabbage.

"It sees us," whispered Tomb. He licked his lips. "What did she say?" Then: "Can it see us?"

Hornwrack was too out of breath to speak.

The Reborn Men do not think as we do, but live—pursued by an incomprehensible past—among distempered waking dreams. Alstath Fulthor wandered into the centre of the maze from quite another entrance, his gait stilted. He stared at the insect in astonishment, flung a hand up in front of his face; a long groan came out of his mouth. He looked like some exotic mantis in his blood-red armour. Attracted perhaps by this, the insect turned with a *clack clack* of coxal joints to face him. (Hornwrack and the dwarf were now able to see the curious markings on its abdomen, the three black diagonal bars or fascia running across each wing.) He walked round it, groaning, his head working as if his neck contained bent clockwork. Plainly he thought he was in a dream of the Afternoon, for he murmured to himself of Arnac san Tehn and the "Yellow Gardens." Now they faced one another again, and if Fulthor looked like an insect, then the thing before him with its hacked yellow prothorax resembled an armoured man. Fulthor glanced down at the energy blade spitting and fizzing in his hand. He hit the insect across the head with it, bursting an eye, cutting into the thorax, and shearing off one of its legs.

It fell over on its side and dragged itself round in a circle, a high whining sound coming from its wings. Fay Glass darted about, shrieking. Fulthor hit it again; watched its redoubled frenzies with his head tilted intelligently on one side; then dropped his weapon, which immediately began fusing the ash around it into glass. "Oh, the great cups!" he cried. "The thousand flowers and roses! The thought with the force of a sensation!" He stared imploringly over at Hornwrack, then picked up his sword again and ran off into the maze, his eyes wide and his body leaning at an incredible angle to the vertical.

The mutilated insect had fetched up against one of the cindery walls and was trying to climb it. Ash showered down. Fay Glass wept, "Wait, we are killed here. Vienna, Blackpool, Venice, drown in their own tears. Press our world. Oh. Oh." Above her head there materialised suddenly the ghost of Benedict Paucemanly, flabby face full of fear. It grimaced apologetically— "Fenlen! Fenlen!"—and was carried away on some psychic current, waving its arms. Dark clouds had blown up from the west, and now a scatter of hard snow filled the grey air, pattering off the carapace of the insect, which lay motionless in a corner, a flicker of orange animating its remaining eye. The ground was ploughed up all around it. Fay Glass, exhausted, was walking round and round the central area with her hands over her face, moaning.

Hornwrack stared at the churned earth, the wreckage of the insect. He shuddered.

"Look after her," he told Tomb the Dwarf. "Try and find Cellur. Tell him about this. He may understand what is happening here." And with that he set off into the maze in search of the Reborn Man.

8
GALEN HORNWRACK AND THE NEW INVASION

Down ran Alstath Fulthor, last representative of his House, a scarlet figure with a stride like an ostrich's; and down ran Hornwrack the assassin after him, the breath rattling in his lungs. The maze was behind them, the village before. In the maze, fearing the hidden junction, the sudden mad leap and mantid clutch, the bared teeth of an ambush, Hornwrack had drawn the old sword; out there on the plain it dragged down his arm. Westward the land was all as dark as the sky, long black salients reaching back beneath the cold clouds, their flanks scored by steep-sided valleys and dotted with piles of haunted stones. In the east a little of the early brightness remained to pick out the shattered towers of the Agdon Roches, to touch the escarpment and its oakwoods with a lichenous grey. Mist still choked the village beneath, thick and slow, but a new wind had stirred out in the waste and was beginning to tease its edges out in streamers, like sheep's wool caught on a fence. The light infused these strands with a delicate yellow, and they smelt strongly of lemons.

Alstath Fulthor flung up his arms and was engulfed. Hornwrack followed, with a desperate cry.

The mist enwrapped them; it stuffed their lungs with cotton wool. They passed like two coughing ghosts along the silent village street. The cottages that loomed on either side were tenantless, dusty, and cold, their front doors lodged open and creaking in the small winds which seemed to inhabit the inside of the mist. From the empty rooms behind issued dry smells. Birdlime was spattered beneath the eaves, and the gutters were choked with old nests. Sacking lifted in the wind; lifted, dropped, and lifted again.

Alstath Fulthor drew ahead. He became a shadow, and then only a thud of footfalls. Hornwrack ran on, isolated and a little afraid. Death, he saw, had been there before them; perhaps a month, perhaps two months before. A dead man hung half in and half out of a broken window beneath the spattered eaves. Another sat like a bundle of sticks propped up in the angle of a stone wall. They observed one another dryly, as if some old joke had recently passed between them. Their weapons were orange with rust but their bodies, instead of decomposing, seemed to have shrunk, and were as intact as tight old sheaves of straw tied up in ancient sacking; as though the mist in advancing one process of decay had retarded the other. The village was full of corpses, staring out of doorways, caught in contorted attitudes on the grass round the horse trough—looking surprised or complacent or out of breath. Others had drawn their knives and had been about to throw themselves on some enemy. A few children had fallen down during a game in which they followed one another stealthily among the houses, hands held hooked above their heads.

"They sail inland all night," thought Hornwrack, and for a moment the face of St. Elmo Buffin came into his mind, decent, puzzled, wistful. "*Where they are going we do not know—*"

They had been coming here. Wherever they had come from they had ended up here, standing at salient junctions like abandoned machines, their broken antennae and cracked wings dangling in the wind, their compound eyes as dull as stones. Patches of corruption darkened the ground beneath them like tarry shadows, as if vital fluids had bled slowly from abdomen and thorax to fertilize a crop of bluish mushrooms and unearthly moulds before drying up altogether. With this desiccation had come the slow retreat of the intelligence into the husk, the drying up of the violent insectile telepathies received by Hornwrack and the others in the maze, those incidental broadcasts from the mosaic universe which had driven Buffin's sailors to burn their own ships or drown themselves in the fogbound sea.

At night, its mad energy not quite spent, a disembodied head bounced down the gutters of Hornwrack's Low City dreams, accompanied by the laughter of the crackpot poet: plainly it had originated here among these dilapidated hulks, one out of three of which had fallen under the energy blades of the Reborn villagers and, curious viscera exposed in section, now lay surrounded by a litter of amputated limbs. Someone had cut it off and sent it south as a call for help. The rest of them, though they showed a few shallow cuts and scrapes made by less-exotic weapons—like violent scribbles on a lacquered screen—had evidently succumbed to the same disease as the lone survivor in the maze. Crusted discharges had swollen their joints. Strings of hardened mucus hung from the curious appendages attached by leather straps to their facial parts. They faced one another in the mechanistic postures of their death, and a faint whisper of telepathy was draped about them like a cobweb. It touched the inside of his skull as he ran dreaming between them, afraid they would come back to life if he lingered.

He ducked beneath a complicated snout. He pushed aside a canted crackling wing. He waved the old sword about until his arm ached. Later he might recall this: now he knew nothing. The wings of the wasteland locust rustled uneasily in his head, gathering for some vast migration. He no longer cared about Alstath Fulthor, running ahead in the mist. He leapt and sang like a grasshopper, and his progress had become a flight.

Alive or dead, he managed to think, they have altered the earth; they have changed it manifestly. Something has come into it . . .

. . . And thinking this, emerged from the village. It was like a door opening and closing. When he looked back the mist was streaming away along the foot of the escarpment in the new wind, and the three small figures of Cellur, Tomb, and Fay Glass, issuing uncertainly from the maze, had begun to cross the plain.

Hornwrack and Fulthor confronted in a stony cleft among dwarf birch and oak. A chalky light, slanting down between the brittle boughs onto banks of heather and bilberry, revealed the Reborn Man sitting quietly on an unfinished millstone, his features as white and careworn as those of a praying king. A pied bird absorbed his attention: it hopped from stone to stone, tilting its small bright eye to watch him. Chill airs rattled the twigs above his head, stirred his yellow hair. The *baan* in his hand flickered like a firework in the hand of a child; he had forgotten it. Votive and calm in his scarlet armour, he looked like the invalid knight in the old painting; and the overhanging towers of the Agdon Roches, with their silent gullies and damp sandy courses, rose up behind him through a screen of black branches like the buttresses of an ancient chapel.

When Hornwrack pushed his way through the oaks, old leaves and lichenous dust showered down, and the little bird flew away.

"Fulthor?"

The wounded king wakes and stares about him with a new fear. He has risen from the devotions of one nightmare into the ruins of another. "Where is this place?" he'll whisper. None will speak. "Back, then!" he'll cry, sweeping the great baan *round his head in an arc which makes the sound of panicked wings. Shadows fly like wounded doves from horizon to horizon. Precarious flowers bloom in his secret heart . . .*

"Hornwrack! Am I mad?" A bitter laugh. "Another dream. More days lost in the absolute abyss of Time. Oh, the fiery woman, with her expressionless eyes! How long have I been away?"

And he advanced dreamily on Hornwrack, still swinging the energy blade.

"Fulthor!" screamed Hornwrack, who saw no magical king (who could blame him? He had been born three millennia too late) and who failed to hear the hum of that long-declining dream: "It's me!" He ducked the lethal stroke, offered the old steel sword (its tip was lopped off instantly), stepped in desperately close, and hammered Fulthor's wrist with the pommel of his trusty knife. Nerveless, the white hand opened. The *baan* fell. Fulthor gave a howl of despair and sat down suddenly. "Must I always choose between there and here?" He regarded Hornwrack from between his hands. "Kill me then." He looked round. "Where are we?"

Hornwrack, however, was no longer interested.

The ghost of Benedict Paucemanly had reappeared, to float over the oakwood mouthing like a drowned sailor; and through its unsteady, half-transparent shape he had caught a sudden glimpse of the horizon. There, insectile silhouettes processed slowly against a greenish sky, full of bitter snow. They seemed to carry with them an unquiet cobalt halo; along their sides flared sphenograms of an acid green; they held their forelegs delicately raised. Over the summits of the Agdon Roches they went, southwards, with an exquisite mechanical concentration, looking neither left nor right.

The world started to melt like candle wax.

Hornwrack got Fulthor somehow to his feet. Unspeaking, they descended the hill.

Snow whirled round them. Roots caught at their feet. Paucemanly encouraged them with whistles and farts.

"I really mean it, you blokes—ten thousand nights were put in one! There I lay, listening to the winds gathering in the dry places, the abandoned places. We're all in it now, us and them, raw-blind on the water stair at Shadwell Pier like burnt rats! Phew! The white moon makes thus 'the stair of our descent' . . ." There was more of this. "Ooh, what you must think of me I don't know," he would exclaim fishily, and then, screwing up his eyes behind the faceplate of his abominable mask, bawl—

"Felneck! Fandle! FENLEN!"

—his queer epicene voice hooting across the hillside like a signal while, above, the insectile procession moved on imperturbably: south, south, south . . .

The new wind, rushing blindly out of the east under a cavernous overcast, had brought black obscurity to the village, whose streets were now full of flying chemical ice blown in from the Deep Waste. The dead insects at each corner creaked and shifted in the gale. Their eyes were pitted and stony. Above them splinters of chitin, sections of antennae and shattered veiny wing floated and spun in the rooftop eddies like the rubbish of the Low City rattling round the chimneys below Alves on a blustery night. Hornwrack leaned on Alstath Fulthor, his eyes rimed with urgent ice, the words blown out of his mouth and every thought out of his skull. They came down the main street like drunks in the weak glow of Fulthor's armour. All else was shadowy, hard to interpret. Dead men leaned conversationally forward as they passed, then toppled onto empty faces, limbs breaking away like the rotten limbs of scarecrows to go bounding off down the road and lodge in a fence.

Cellur the Birdmaker awaited them at the centre of the village, where the wind was whipping spray off the horse trough and the front doors were banging on rooms inhabited only by mice and suffocated children. He had with him Tomb the Dwarf. From the debacle in the maze they had retrieved three horses and the pony, which now stood in the street shifting bad-temperedly with each fresh gust of wind: Tomb was redistributing the surviving baggage between them as if in preparation for a further journey into the deep madness of the world. This activity made an island of humanity in the rushing gloom, at the approaches of which hovered the madwoman, wrapped from head to foot in a thick whitish garment and turning aimlessly this way and that like something hanging from a privet branch.

Alstath Fulthor looked emptily at this scene as if he recognized no one in it, then sat down in the road. Hornwrack, tugging at his arm, heard the birdmaker shout, "Ride! West, for your life!" He shook his head. "Wait!" He wasn't sure he had heard correctly. The old man had got up on his horse now and was watching them impatiently, his embroidered cloak streaming in the wind. The dwarf ran round checking saddlebags, tightening girths, and urging the inert Fay Glass into her saddle by means of pantomimic threats. The wind rose and fell cynically, tugging at the dry husks of the insects. The horses milled about, sensing an imminent departure. Hornwrack let go of Fulthor's wrist ("Black piss! Stay there, then, if you must!") and caught at the birdmaker's stirrup instead. The horse dragged him off his feet, the old man's yellow face swam above him, alive with what he took to be fear. They were in an eddy or pocket in the gale.

"In the maze," said Cellur, "my errors were made plain. Much, if not all, is now clear to me. I cannot yet explain the ghost"—he prodded Hornwrack's shoulder, pointed up into the wrack where Paucemanly bobbed, smirking and bowing like a butler—"but I have at last learnt what he was trying to tell us.

"You must go and rouse Iron Chine. Pray that St. Elmo Buffin, a man ill-used by circumstance, is not as mad as he seems! Tell him the time has come to launch his fleet. Tell him help is on its way." He smiled bitterly. "Lunatics and ghosts—all along they have had the right of it!" For a second he stared slack-faced and frightened into the west, his hooded eyes human for once. (After all, he is out in the world now, thought Hornwrack—who sympathized, being newly out in it himself—like a crab out of its shell: what guarantees has he left? And again: What can he fear after ten thousand years?) He made a cutting motion with his hand. "Still, I was slow to connect these things. I have been too content to sit by and let Fulthor lead. Now Fulthor has failed me, and there it is.

"Fenlen, the island continent, is infested. They have been established there since they poured down from the moon eleven years ago. (I looked on like a fool. What else could I have done? I forget.) But they cannot bear earth's airs: and when their scouts fly inland low over the sea, which they do night and day, they do so surrounded by an atmosphere of their own manufacture. By day they blunder into Buffin's sailors. They are as motiveless and mad as the men they kill. They do not belong here."

He gestured at the empty village, the creaking husks. "Can you doubt it? Yet they are trying to make the air over to suit them. This is only the beginning." He shuddered. "They will remake the earth, if they can. Rouse Iron Chine, Hornwrack. I ride now to the capital. Delay me no longer!"

Hornwrack hung on to the stirrup. All he could think of to say was, "Something is the matter with Alstath Fulthor. Up on the escarpment he tried to kill me."

"Oh, I am in Hell," said Alstath Fulthor, shaking his head. He had come up behind them silently, the *baan* like a live thing in his hand. "I am not myself." Tomb the Dwarf, who had tightened the final strap, tried to take the weapon away from him for his own good. "Come on, old friend." They rolled about in the road, cursing and biting. Fulthor wriggled away and got up again. "Come down off your horse," he ordered, "and explain all this. Why, up there, great *cock-a-roaches* walk along the ridge!" He pointed in the wrong direction. (The dwarf crawled away, holding his face and spitting.) "Or is it in my head?" He shrugged, smiled shyly, lurched off. Fay Glass woke up and looked at him sharply. Keeping a wary eye on the dwarf, she got off her horse.

Suddenly they both began singing, "We are off to Vegys now." Hornwrack looked on, appalled. "Fal di la di a."

(When he fled through the High City like a bleeding king, in a sweat of fear in the middle of the night, and hoped no one would notice; when he muttered in the palace the nine long alchemical names of his House, and hoped no one would hear: all heard, all knew but himself. Alstath Fulthor: the past was pulling him down.)

"When we first met," said Cellur, "he spoke to me often of memory, which he conceived of as a hidden stream, himself perched on its bank looking into the water. Also of something which hovered like a dragonfly over the moment of his reawakening in the desert at Knarr." He sighed. "What did he kill down there in the maze? Nothing you or I saw. All this has hastened the inevitable.

"Soon he will be as mad as the woman. She will help him. You must help them both. It is why I brought you."

"I brought myself, old man."

"Be that as it may."

"What am I to do?"

"Earn what you were given," said Tomb the Dwarf, and meant, perhaps, the sword. "I believe you'll get no other pay." He was in a bad temper. He wiped his pocked old nose on the back of his hand to show what he thought of it all, and pushed his sodden conical hat firmly down onto his head. "You were not brought but bought," he said with a hard grin. "Goodbye, Hornwrack." Hauling himself up into his saddle he added, "We'll go back across the waste to Duirinish—for it's quicker if you know the paths and don't mind old battles or old lizards—and thence to Viriconium. Cellur fears the Sign of the Locust. He fears for the Queen. He does not quite know what he fears." He looked about him like a man expecting rain. "I fear this. Still: one way or another I daresay we shall all have some heads to cut off before long. Do you look after the mad folk." And he gave the pony vigorous kicks until it consented to move off into the weather. Teetering on the edge of visibility for a moment, dwarf and pony made a curious uncouth silhouette, a composite creature above which flew like a flag on its long haft the curved evil blade of the power-axe. "Never say I disliked you!" The eyes of the pony before it turned its head away were a flat and empty green.

Out there Cellur waited impatiently, staring west or south. "Rouse Iron Chine!" came a faint cry through the crack and belly of the gale. Hornwrack never saw either of them again. "On the shores of the diamond lake," sang the madwomen in a weird voice,

> "We shall watch the fishes,
> On the summits of the mountains
> Cry Erecthalia!
>
> We are off to Vegys now."

The weather closed in. He was alone. Even the ghost of Benedict Paucemanly, part at least of its purpose accomplished, had gone out like a candle. In the deserted village it might as easily have been evening as afternoon. Out of the crepuscular sky issued a thin snow which drifted up behind the dry corpses, blew into the empty rooms, and plastered itself to the windward eaves. Every so often the wind from the Deep Waste mingled with it a scatter of old ice, flinging it down the street like two handfuls of dirty glass beads. He rubbed the back of his neck. How had he come to be stranded in the cold North with two lunatics, and no option but to go and look for a third? After Iron Chine he would make his way south along the coast, since he knew no other route (that inhospitable strand, with its distant illusions and tottering cliffs, now seemed familiar and comforting); he would lose himself again in the Low City. Perhaps he would find the boy. He would kill the dwarf if he ever had the chance.

All this time, off at the edge of his awareness, faint telepathies crawled like maggots round the rim of a saucer. Up there on the Agdon scarp was a stealthy and purposeful movement, too far away to hurt him yet, too close for comfort. Suddenly he became frightened that they would come down unexpectedly and discover him among their dead. What delicate revenge might they take? In any case he could not bear their thoughts in his skull. Two horses had been left him for three people. Feverishly he urged the madwoman up onto one of them, and then with his hand on his knife approached the Reborn Man, wishing the dwarf had captured the *baan* during their brief scuffle beneath the horse. Eyeing him with a sad amusement, Fulthor said, "I will run beside you. It is not so far."

The ramshackle conservatory of St. Elmo Buffin, with its invented flags and fantastic telescopes, teetered high above the fish docks of the port, full of silence, brackish air, and the smell of the food they had been served there a week or more ago. Buffin sat as if he had not moved since then, in a high-backed chair surrounded by plates of congealed herring. He had taken off his father's armour and underneath was swathed in some dirty white stuff, linen or flannel, as if he suffered with his joints. He was staring at nothing, his long thin legs thrust out in front of him and crossed as though they belonged to someone else, his bag-like face crumpled and desperate. His instruments lay smashed. They were no more or less meaningful for it: nests of bent brass tubing, complex coloured lenses pulled apart like sugared anemones underfoot. The charts he had ripped down, to reveal the walls beneath. He had lost his patience with them, perhaps.

Hornwrack wiped the condensation from a cracked pane, looked out.

"You need not have done this to yourself," he said.

It was such a waste. He felt hot and angry, cold and remote, all at once.

"What happened here?"

Buffin did not answer for a long time. The Afternoon had betrayed him again, and the old powered knife with which he had tried to kill himself now lay sputtering feebly in his lap, its energies spent at last. Some blood had flowed, then dried brown. He did not seem to be able to move his head. The silence drew out. Wondering if he was already dead, Hornwrack waited, breathing evenly and trying to make out what was happening in the port below.

"What does it matter?" came the eventual answer. Then, after another long pause: "Of the fleet I ordered the uncompleted part destroyed. It is of no use now. Viriconium will never help us now." He laughed quietly. "The rest has sailed, into madness and death. The mist surrounds us (can you not hear it? It is like bells!) and all has failed."

He bit his bottom lip. "I dare not move my head," he said, staring forward at nothing, fingering the hilt of the useless knife. "Can you see what I have done?"

"Your throat is cut," said Hornwrack, breathing on the glass. "But not well."

If he wiped a circle on the glass with the palm of his hand he could see framed in it the black original buildings of the fjord squatting like toads on the lower slopes. To his right a cliff swept up, also black, and laced for five hundred feet with icy ledges. Until recently ice had locked the harbour; now churned and broken sheets of it bobbed in the black channels cut by the departed fleet. Beneath him banks of white vapour hung, drifting sluggishly down the cobbled slopes toward the shrouded quays. In places it was deep enough to cover the upper casements of the cottages as it was driven reluctantly between them by the bitter intermittent wind; in others, where it was shallower, he thought he could see heads and torsos going about above it on some cryptic dislocated errand. The suggestion of movement beneath it he tried to ignore. Above all this in the green subarctic sky, aurorae flickered, and great streaks of red and black cloud mimicked the flame and smoke beneath, where men ran despairingly among the boatyards with torches, setting fire to their labour of years.

Death was written in the scrollwork at the bows, death on the painted sterns and the ornate brass bells. DEATH, proclaimed the painted sails, while the white decks beneath bubbled and charred, generating a heat fierce enough to melt the metal masts. Ash whirled into the air, unknown incandescent alloys showered down, last fruit of that doomed collaboration between Afternoon and Evening (which now pursue their separate courses, as we know). Rolling into the flames, the mist turned them instantly green and blue, and was itself transformed with a roar into a greyish powdery smoke which, sucked up in the merciless updraughts, bellied out above the doomed craft in a choking spherical cloud. Spars flared and fell. Ratlines parted with the sound of a broken violin. Here and there a man was trapped in a tangle of ropes, or caught among the stays beneath a blazing bowsprit with no one to hear his cries. At the height of the fire a single painted sail escaped its ties, unfurled, billowed upward. For a brief moment a pair of great illusory lizards danced in the air!—only to sink with a regretful whisper and be consumed, writhing amid the smoke in a counterfeit of the pain in St. Elmo Buffin's frigid, frightened stare.

"I had no life," said Buffin, "even as a child." Hornwrack bent close to the cold lips to hear. "My father bade me, 'Watch the sea.' "

"I've had no life, either," said Hornwrack.

He forced himself to look through the one surviving telescope. At first he could see nothing. A sailor rushed into the room behind him, shouting, "Buffin, they are among us in the fog!" Seeing Hornwrack he halted uncertainly. A pleading note entered his voice. "Buffin, only one ship remains. Let us take you aboard her!"

"He is dead," said Hornwrack, who now discerned a sad grey ground, and against that something spinning at the end of a thread. "What's happened here?"

"A fog followed us ashore this morning. The women and children are all dead of it." He stared at Hornwrack's back. "Great *locusts* inhabit it!"

"They are your longtime enemy. Where does this last ship sail?"

"West, after the fleet, as he would have wished."

Spinning, spinning.

"Take me then," said Hornwrack, "instead."

He turned from the telescope and went out of the door. In the empty room a masked figure materialised briefly in the air above the corpse, and was gone.

During the journey from Agdon Roches, Alstath Fulthor had regained a measure of his sanity—that is to say he now remembered where and, to an extent, who he was; but the girl had chopped his hair to a ragged stubble one night while he slept, giving him something of her own hollow-eyed, perpetually surprised expression, and his skin had taken on a bleached unearthly look, like a saint's. They were often together, reciting the rhymes that comprised her vocabulary, practising the scraps of meaningless dialogue and lists of nonexistent cities which seemed to be her "keys" to the Past. Fulthor was learning, in the way the child of an exile learns those bits and pieces of its heritage that remain (and which, after so much repetition, undergo a sea change, bearing less and less relationship to a vanished culture in a land it has never seen). Hornwrack tried to ignore their public tendernesses, their strange, almost unemotional sexual contacts, and clothed his embarrassment in a characteristic surliness.

He found them now down in the port, two tall, awkward figures wrapped in cloaks, standing uncomfortably near the burning boatyards.

Despite the heat and smoke they were waiting exactly where he had left them, the flames reflected in their calm odd eyes. Later, at the rail of the last ship, watching the sailors warp her sadly from the bleak shore, Fulthor seemed disposed to talk. He was lucid, polite, aware; but each new immersion in the stream of memory had carried him further from his Evening existence and its events, and he had forgotten his earlier shoddy treatment of St. Elmo Buffin. So when he asked, "How then did the shipwright die?" it was cruel of Hornwrack to reply,

"He cut his own throat, but it was you he died of."

Iron Chine would not survive him. Fires had now sprung up among the cottages, set by the sailors before they left, and small flames danced behind the panes of the dilapidated conservatory above the town. The strip of black water between the boat and the quay grew wider. The frigid cliffs slipped past; the curious flags and strips of coloured rag flying over the conservatory blazed up one by one; above everything burned the clouds, like the bloody auroral sunset of some other planet.

What happened to the fleet of St. Elmo Buffin? It was not provisioned well. He had given small thought to navigating it. Much of it was lost immediately amid the white water and foul ground, the atrocious currents and uncharted islands which outlie the jagged coast of Viriconium. Much of it, hampered by the ice which formed on decks and rigging, turned quietly turtle in the gelid sea. There were fogs, too, lying in hundred-mile banks across the straits which separate Fenlen from Iron Chine; and in these the greatest loss was incurred. Each ship fought alone, wrapped in a dream-like shroud of pearly light. Ice burned like alum on the ratlines and stays. There were collisions, mutinies, accidental fires, and shouts as of other men desperate and dying beyond the nacreous wall of fog. It was in all aspects a lost venture. The fog smelled of rotting fruit; and at the sound of wings men leapt overboard or cut their own throats, staring dumbly for a last few seconds at a universe faceted like an insect's eye. One ship survived.

Imagine a low dark coastline shelving back through a series of eroded fossil beaches into a desolation which makes the deepest waste of Viriconium seem like a water meadow. Nothing lives about these beaches but limpets and kelp, a few curiously furtive terns which survive for the most part by eating one another's eggs, and in season a handful of deformed seals. Chemical rivers make their way here from the continental marshes north and west; tars and oils from sumps a thousand years old and a thousand miles inland trickle sluggishly down the terraces of black pumice, staining them emerald green, ochre, purple. Imagine a glaucous ocean; a low swell at the freezing point, lapping at the brutal shore. Strings and bulbs of mineral pigment wave beneath the water like weed, growing from the chemical silt. There is no wind to speak of. Out to sea about a mile, a bank of mist is rolling south, parallel to the coast.

Imagine a white ship: rudderless, masts bent beneath their load of ice.

Her deck plates are up, buckled like lead foil, her wheelhouse blackened by the same fire which lately ate into her hull amidships. Her figurehead hangs loose in a wreck of stays, a partly human form difficult of exact description. She is down at the stern and listing to starboard. Silently, captured by some current invisible from the shore, she is drawn in toward the beach, quicker and quicker until she rams the stained pumice shelves with a groan and, ripped open, goes over by the bow and begins to sink. A few birds fly up from her yards. Chips of ice rattle down. A sail, partly unfurled by the shock of the collision, shows a great drunken beetle to the empty beach. Bedded in the poisonous silt, she will settle no further, but nudges the shore with every wave.

After a few minutes a grotesque shape begins to form in the cold air above her shattered deck, like a crude figure of a man projected somehow on a puff of steam.

9

THE EXPLANATIONS OF THE ANCIENT AIRBOATMAN

Midwinter clutches the Pastel City, cold as thought.

In the Cispontine Quarter the women have been to and fro all day gathering fuel. By afternoon they had stripped the empty lots to the bare hard soil, bobbing in ragged lines amid the sad induviate stems of last year's growth, their black shawls giving them the air of rooks in a potato field. Not an elder or bramble is left now but it is a stump; and that will be grubbed up tomorrow by some enterprising mattock in a bony hand. At twilight, which—exhaled, as it were, from every shattered corner—comes early to the city's broken parts, they filled the nearby streets for half an hour, hurrying westwards with their unwieldy bundles to where, along the Avenue Fiche and the Rue Sepile, Margery Fry Road and the peeling old "Boulevard Saint Ettiene," the old men sat waiting for them with souls shrivelled up like walnuts in the cold. Now they sit by reeking stoves, using the ghost of a dog rose to cook cabbage!

Cabbage! The whole of the Low City has smelt of this delicacy all winter. It is on everyone's breath and in everyone's overcoat. It has seeped into the baize cloth of everyone's parlour. It has insinuated itself into the brickwork of every privy, coagulated in alleys, hung in unpeopled corners, and conserved its virtues, waiting for the day when it might come at last to the High City. This evening, like an invisible army, it filtered by stages along the Boulevard Aussman, where it woke the caged rabbits in the bakers' backyards and caused the chained dogs to whimper with excitement; flowed about the base of the hill at Alves, investing the derelict observatory with an extraordinary new significance; and passed finally to the heights of Minnet-Saba, where it gathered in waves to begin its stealthy assault on the High Noses. On the way it informed some strange crannies:

inundating, for instance, a little-used arm of the pleasure canal at Lowth, where its spirit infected incidentally a curious tragedy on the ice.

The air was bitter inside the nose, the sky as black as anthracite. The Name Stars glittered cynically, commemorating some best-forgotten king. Down below on the frozen canal a grubby satin booth was pitched, its yellow shutters up, its cressets cold. From its door a long-legged brazier, kept fed with frigid horse dung, looked out like a red eye. In it, under the zodiacal representations and the testimonials to its proprietor's efficacy, a poet and a fortune-teller sat, cheating one another feverishly at "blind Michael."

The poet was a rag of a man, little, and hollow-cheeked from a life of squalor, with his bright red hair stuck up on his head like a wattle and greed lurking in the corners of his grin. He gave his small hands no rest— when he was not trying to palm cards or filch the bottle, he was flapping them about like a wooden puppet's. At slow moments during the play he would stare silently into the air with his face empty and his mouth slack, then, catching himself, leap up from the three-legged stool on which he sat and go jigging round the booth until by laughing and extemporizing he had got his humour back. In mirth, or delivering doggerel, his voice had a penetrating hysterical timbre, like a knife scraped desperately on a plate. He had made a "ballade of stewed cabbage" earlier that evening, but seemed to hate and fear the smell of the stuff, grimacing with dilated nostrils and turned-down mouth when a wave of it passed through the booth. His name was Ansel Verdigris, and the fat woman across the card table was his last resort.

Fat Mam Etteilla, with her aching ankles and her fatal cough, was known to be the wisest woman in the Low City: yet she paid the poet's debts; admired his verses without in the least understanding them; and, though he gave her nothing in return for it, forgave both his perversions and his frequent distempers. All is made possible in the shadow of the *Dark Man*. On his calmer days Verdigris sat on her knee and ventriloquised her customers. When his nerves were bad, and he drove them away by spewing on the cards, she slapped his head. He made her laugh. She feared death, but he feared everything: and the closer to death she came, the better she looked after him. One of her great soft hands made three of his! They were an odd pair to be keeping the night alive like that down on the deserted pleasure canal while worthier people slept. There was a cemetery behind the booth, and Verdigris could not keep his eyes off it.

At midnight he scratched his armpits and parted for the hundredth time the grubby satin curtains. The gravestones seemed to stretch back indefinitely under the moonlight. Where they ceased the Artists' Quarter began, its piebald roofs hanging on the dark skyline like an evil conundrum. Up the slope went his eyes, through the graves and into the city; back again. "You sleep well enough out there!" he jeered, and then said a name the fortune-teller could not catch. His narrow angular shoulders shuddered convulsively. She called him back but he hardly heard. He had not slept well himself since the night he murdered Galen Hornwrack. It was a yellow night, that one, grimed into his raddled brain and smelling of that unspeakable bundle with its rotting eyes. Ever since, he had had a feeling of being followed around. "Someone walked over my grave," he said. He laughed. "Well, I'll not mourn!" The moonlight flooding past him into the booth was of a peculiar cast: in it, as we shall soon see, things seemed almost more solid than they did in broad daylight. "They sleep well enough out there on All Men's Heath," he said, and made to draw the satin closed.

Instantly the reek of stewed cabbage redoubled, rooting him to the spot. A lethal claustrophobia overcame him. "Hornwrack!" he shrieked. He spun round, blundered past the fortune-teller (who had got laboriously to her feet and spread her arms in an elephantine gesture of comfort), and tumbled out onto the ice, where his feet slipped from under him. In an attempt to keep his balance he grabbed the brazier by one of its iron legs. This only served to upset it over him. Squealing with pain and fear, he slid out of the light, plucking feverishly at the glowing embers in his clothing.

The Fat Mam was used to his convulsions. Grumbling hardly at all, she righted the table. Queer little scenes glowed up at her from the scattered cards, ancient hieratic conjunctions of tower and insect stimulating her to worn prophecies. A good marriage, she thought, and a bad one; and there a blond-haired man. (Each card was like a small bright doorway at the end of a corridor. She was perhaps too old now to step through and be enshrined in pasteboard with a hermit crab and a flight of swans.) On her way to the back of the booth to see what had upset him this time, she stopped to turn one card at random; stare at it for a moment, panting; and nod heavily to herself. Then she parted the curtains and looked out.

For a month or more, agents and emissaries of the Sign of the Locust—now grown massively in power though its outlook became daily more esoteric, and seeking revenge for (among other things) the bloody confrontation in the Bistro Californium—had sought Ansel Verdigris through the warrens of the Low City. They were oblique but patient. Every clue had pointed to the pleasure canal. Now, their gait curious in the extreme, they raced silently down the slope of All Men's Heath toward the quivering Mam. They were wrapped in rags and bandaged about their peculiarly misshapen heads, and as they hopped high in the air over the graves, their arms flew out at odd angles and their knives were white in the moonlight.

Verdigris, with one short anticipatory gurgle, squirmed further into the shadowy undergrowth on the far bank of the canal. . . .

Soon after they had entered it the booth began to agitate itself in a violent and eccentric fashion, lifting its skirts and tottering from side to side as if it was trying to remember how to walk—while out of it came a steady rhythmical thumping sound, like two or three axes hitting a wet log. A dreadful astonished wail rose up in accompaniment to this, modulating with each blow. Verdigris bit his lips and drew back further into the weeds. He put his hands over his ears, but this changed nothing. The knives of the Sign rose and fell regularly; and the booth, like some remarkable engine in the night, continued to propel itself with an uncertain shuffling motion this way and that across the ice. After a little while, having reached the centre of the canal (where only lately it had been all boiled chestnuts and skating anemone boys), it collapsed. Amorphous figures struggled momentarily beneath it; then it gave them up and they poured away through the cemetery in a quiet tattered wave, like the shadow of a cloud crossing a stony field. The booth gurgled and was still. It had somehow become tangled in the legs of the spilt brazier. Fire licked, reluctantly at first, at its grubby skirts. Then it was engulfed in a sudden silent rush of flames.

Ansel Verdigris stood on the ice in the unsteady yellow glow. He drew his knife and, in an access of some emotion he did not quite recognise, went off shouting up the hill and was ambushed and killed among the gravestones.

Not far away from All Men's Heath in the sharp and cabbagey night, Tomb the Dwarf kicked at his pony. His feet were cold. He had recently entered the city through the Gate of Nigg after three or four weeks in the deep wastes with Cellur the Bird Lord. Adventures and privations had attended him there, as they always did: old lizards following his steps, blinking at night in the small light of the fire; the pony quagged perpetually to its elbows in seepage hollows; and a great bird, first hanging high up in the air above them, then settling nervously on a rock to inspect them from intelligent puzzled eyes, every feather made of metal! He had a friend buried in every acre of the North—knights of the Methven, sour old prospectors, all the thieves and princes who had traipsed with him at one time or another the useless places of the empire. They had followed him, too, as night drew in across the old battlefields of the Great Brown Waste.

The season now teetered on the cold iron pivot of the solstice, and Viriconium was asleep for once, huddled against the cold; you could hear its catarrhal snores from upper windows. The mosaic of its roofs, whited by moonlight and last week's frozen snow, lay like the demonstration of some equivocal new geometry. The Low City had retreated from him even as he entered it (dogs shivering outside the gatehouse, no other sign of life; the tunnel smelling of pee, black ice, and that merciless vegetable), so that he seemed always to view it at a distance. He did not understand its mood. A muted expectancy, a cold glamour resistant to his dwarfish intuition, vibrated in its surfaces: he had for a moment (it was a moment only) a sense of *two* cities, overlapping in a sprawl of moonlit triangles and tangled thoroughfares. This conceit caused him to smile but remained with him nevertheless, quite distinctly, as if he had seen the future as a composite city uninhabited by human beings.

More beggars were abroad than a single city had a right to, moving quietly about in ones and twos, the deformities that would by day be displayed up on Chamomile Street outside the pot-house doors now half-hidden under scalloped rags and strange tight bandages—as if when left to themselves they sought a finer aesthetic of suffering, and a subtler performance of it. Tomb stood up in his stirrups to see over the parapet of a bridge. (*Toc toc* went the pony's hooves, little and sharp on the cobbles.) "Someone at least is keeping the night alive," he observed. Underneath him the Pleasure Canal diminished toward Lowth in an icy curve, its surface tricked out with dim reflections of the moon. "The ice is miraculously hard. They've lit a brazier down there on it." Cellur, though, seemed preoccupied. "Now it's split!" Faint shouts and wails, as of laughter, floated up. "Look here, Cellur—some fool's set fire to a conjuror's booth!"

"I see nothing."

"You wish to see nothing. You are a dreary companion, I can tell you that. It's all gone dark now anyway," said the dwarf disappointedly. He craned his neck. Nothing. His pony drifted to a standstill. When he caught up again the old man was hemming and clucking nervously.

"Those alms-men are following us now. Be ready with your axe. I do not believe they are what they seem."

"Arms-men! Bloody beggars, more like." He shifted the axe from one shoulder to the other. "Black piss!" He had looked back and got a glimpse of the beggars hopping after him, soft-boned and rickety-kneed, their arms flying out this way and that for balance. It was a horrible sight. "There are not that many beggars in the entire world!" They were all humps and goitres. Their misshapen heads were concealed under crusty swathes of muslin and hats with ragged brims. Up in the Artists' Quarter and all around the derelict observatory at Alves they were gathering in large groups, lurching crazily about in white-breathed circles, watching idly as Tomb and Cellur rode past, joining the quiet procession behind. An occasional soft groan came from amongst them. Cellur's horse slithered and stumbled from rut to frozen rut; and though the pony was surer-footed they still went slowly up the Rivelin Hill between the shuttered booths and empty taverns.

Into the High City they went, but it proved to be no sanctuary. When they quickened their pace, the beggars quickened theirs, breaking into the parody of a run. Through the elegant deserted plazas of Minnet-Saba (where the road is made of something that muffles the sound of hooves and the wind has mumbled puzzledly for millennia round the upper peculiarities of the Pastel Towers) they poured, and out onto the great exposed spiral of the Proton Circuit, reeling from side to side, jumping and hopping and tripping themselves up, always out of the power-axe's reach: maintaining a zone of quarantine about the old man and the dwarf, sweeping them along by the mere promise of contact. Tomb bit his lip and belaboured the pony's sides. All around him was a sort of dumb rustling noise, punctuated by the gasps and quiet desperate groans of the deformed. (Above and behind that he thought he heard a parched whisper, as if some enormous insect hovered above the chase on huge thoughtful wings.)

Ahead, lights glimmered. In the gusty winds at the summit of the spiral, the overlapping filigree shells of the palace creaked as if they were part of some flimsier structure. Methven's hall: the moon hung above it like a daubed head. "Look!" For a moment its image wavered—two palaces were superimposed; behind it another landscape showed through. Blue particles showered from its upper regions, a rain of tiny luminous insects. They galloped toward it nevertheless. Where else could they go? It trembled like a dragonfly's wing; was refracted like something seen through running water on a sunny day; and accepted them almost reluctantly. New Palace Yard was almost deserted. Tomb's caravan still stood there, its shafts empty and its colours dimmed by the smoke of winter. No guards were there to observe the sparks fly up from the pony's hooves or watch the dwarf—axe in hand and white hair streaming out behind—tumble to the ground and hurl himself back through the gate they had just come through, determined to hold it at all costs.

The beggars, though, had forgotten about him the moment he entered the palace, and now idled about outside, staring blankly at one another. They were not beggars, he saw: they were bakers and greengrocers, in the remnants of striped aprons; they were dukes and moneylenders; they were butchers. The Sign of the Locust peeped through their curious rags. They stood in the bluish moonlight and they seemed to be waiting for something; he couldn't tell what. (They no longer had any reasons for the things they did, but he wasn't to know that. A white and single instinct had them now, like a thin song in the brain.) He watched them for five or six minutes, feeling the sweat dry on him as the seconds stretched uneventfully out and his body relaxed. Cellur came up behind him and looked over his head. "You can put up the axe," he said with a certain morose satisfaction. "The city is theirs, High and Low." And he strode rapidly off into the outer corridors, heading for the throne room. Tomb backed away from the gate with a halfhearted snarl and, stopping to collect the bundle of long silver rods he had carried behind his saddle to the Agdon Roches and back, followed him.

The corridors were full of rubbish, mounds of decaying vegetables and heaps of ashes. Everywhere were the discarded uniforms of the palace guard. Much of the food was spoiled, half-eaten, as if whoever had prepared it was unused to human provisions, or had forgotten what to do with them. Cellur shook his head.

"They have let us in," he said, "but they will not let us out again so easily. I wonder what they are waiting for."

Methvet Nian, Queen Jane, waited also, in a cold room with five false windows. It had been a long time to wait at the heart of emptiness, nothing human moving in the corridors outside.

Elsewhere, three figures cross our field of vision like the vanguard of an as-yet-distant refugee column. The deep wastes of Fenlen roll away from them in the weak, variable light of late afternoon, hollow as a fevered cheek. Their faces are haggard but human. They walk—if *walk* is the word for this slithering, staggering progress through the mud—heads down into the rain and some yards apart. They rarely speak to one another. Madness and pain have divided them and they will not now be brought back together. All day long they have followed a fourth figure (there!—bobbing in the saturated air above them, like some great inflated spectral frog!) through a belt of derelict factories. Often they half and stare anxiously about, in case this floating guide has abandoned them: for they are forty days out from the wreckage of Iron Chine, and they have almost forgotten who they are. The moor ahead of them is scattered with interlacing ash-pits, chancred with shallow albescent tarns, and strewn as far as the eye can see with broken earthenware pipes—the detritus, it may be, of some ancient ill-fated reclamation project. From the continental marshes and sumps to the north, the wind brings a deadly metallic reek, and mixed with that more often than not comes the faint smell of lemons, to usher in another period of delirium.

The woman imagines she is the spokesman of some alien race. Her cropped hair is daubed with mud, and she makes complicated motions of the fingers to symbolize the actions of wings or antennae. She speaks of a city on the plain. "We did not wish to come here," she says reasonably, "this is not our place!" There is a cold sore at the corner of her mouth. For the last half hour her gait had grown steadily more disconnected. "Your breath burns us!" she exclaims with a light laugh, as if stating some principle so obvious as to need no demonstration, and she collapses into the mud. Her limbs move feebly, then stop. Broken pipes are dislodged and roll down onto her. Her companions continue their ascent of the low ridge before them. At last one of them looks back.

"Fulthor," he says dully, "she can't go any further unaided," and the other replies, "I see the great-breasted chimerae with their ironic eyes, but I cannot go to them! This morning early I had a vision of Arnac san Tehn—him with the head like a god—sitting in a garden."

He strikes himself repeatedly about the face and head. "Dust and hyacinths in my father's library; dust and hyacinths my proud inheritance!" This litany seems to give him doubtful comfort. For some time he runs in erratic circles in the mud, his neck bent and his face pulled over to one side of his skull as if he has suffered a stroke. Eventually he joins the first figure (who has sat down wearily to watch him) and with much fumbling they raise the woman by her legs and shoulders. Their farting guide, meanwhile, hectors them in a language not heard on earth before or since. He waves a fat, admonitory hand and they must follow; slower than before, up the dip of the long low ridge, sliding into peat groughs and shallow hidden pools, their eyes on their feet and the woman slung between them like a rotting hammock. . . . Imagine that our field of vision is static, and that they have almost moved out of it, creeping across from left to right as the light fades. They crest the ridge. We see only their uncomprehending faces, made tiny and grey by distance, while they see only the city which spreads itself suddenly below them like excavations in a sunken garden.

A mist drifts over the scene—particulate, sullen, smelling of lemons.

The throne room at Viriconium, on a cold and desultory afternoon three or four days after the death of the Fat Mam: three o'clock, and the night was already closing in, diffusing through the draughty passages where the old machines muttered and drew about themselves their meagre shawls of light. Methvet Nian: nine steel rings glittered cold and grey on her thin stiff fingers. She wore a cloak made from white fur clasped with amber and iron, and took her chocolate from a rare grey china cup. Her eyes were purple and depthless. Cellur the Birdmaker sat with her, leaning forward a little, his face beaky and hollow in the weak light admitted by the clerestory windows high above. Their murmurs echoed in the chilly air. "We know nothing but that the world is invaded." "Our fate in St. Elmo Buffin's hands." "Nothing seen from the outer wall." "Great insects, marching south." The Queen held out one hand, palm flat, to the small blue flames of the fire, feeling an uncertain, transitory warmth.

Around them the palace was quiet, though not unpopulated. The Queen's guard had, it turned out, destroyed itself some weeks before in a series of bloody, motiveless purges and episodic defections to the Sign of

the Locust: the day after his arrival, Tomb the Dwarf had brought his caravan in from the courtyard, established himself like a nomadic warlord
somewhere in the littered outer corridors, and taken charge of the handful
of disoriented survivors he found living rough in the guardrooms and
abandoned mess halls. It was a situation which suited both his inclinations
and his experience. At night the dull ring of his hammer penetrated the intervening walls; he was rearming his little force. During the morning he
made the round of his defences—which consisted mainly in barricades
constructed from old machinery—or stared from the judas-hole he had
contrived in the main gates at the silent "beggars" without. In the afternoons he would knock on the throne-room door and allow Methvet Nian
to serve him lukewarm chamomile which he compounded with a violent
brandy from Cladich. "I expect an attack soon," he would report, and
another day would pass without event. "It can't be long in coming." He
was happier, he explained, with something to do. Nevertheless he dreamed
a lot, of the lost excitements of his youth.

Leaving the palace for the city was like entering a dark crystal (especially
at night, under the "white pulpy spectre" of the moon); the shape of
things became irregular, refracted; sudden astonishing mirages swallowed
the Pastel Towers or engulfed the denizens of the streets beneath them. It
was as if Viriconium (the physical city, that is, the millennial artefact which
sums up a thousand dead cultures) had suffered some sort of psychic
storm, and forgotten itself. Its very molecules seemed to be creeping
apart. "As you walk," the dwarf tried to explain after a single clandestine
excursion to the Artists' Quarter, "the streets create themselves around
you. When you have passed, everything slips immediately back into chaos
again." Many of the Reborn had abandoned their houses in Minnet-Saba
and were making their way north, a trickle of great horses, big-wheeled
carts, and vibrantly coloured armour: they carried their strange weapons
with care. Down in the Low City the alleys were empty and stuporous—no
one was coming out except for coke or cabbage. Outside the palace waited
the devotees of the Sign, becoming more misshapen beneath their cloaks
and bandages every day. . . .

In the room at the centre of the palace the light had almost gone.
Draughts ran about like mice in the corners. White stiff fingers retreated
beneath the fur cloak she clasped about her: "It is so cold this afternoon.
On the Rannoch Moor when I was little more than a child, Lord Birkin
Grif killed a snow leopard. It was not so cold then. He spun me round by
the arms, crying, 'Hold on, hold tight!' (That was earlier still.) The dwarf
is late this afternoon."

"It isn't yet four. He never comes sooner than four."

"He seems late this afternoon."

As the clerestory dimmed, weighting the upper air with shadows, and the chocolate cooled in its china cups, the flames in the hearth achieved a transitory, phthisic prominence; and, one by one, like the compartments of a dream, the five false windows of the throne room were filled with a grey and tremulous glow. Against this fitful illumination moved the silhouettes of Cellur and the Queen, nodding murmurous figures of a shadow play. The bird lord's success in controlling the windows—through which it was possible to see sometimes long lines of insects moving across an unknown terrain—had been only partial. He could turn them neither on nor off. And though three out of five of them could lately be compelled to show some recognizable part of the empire, how these views were selected was not clear to him. Since coming here he had sought:

Contact with his own machines beneath the estuary at Lendalfoot;

Views of St. Elmo Buffin's fleet;

Some intimation of the circumstances in which Hornwrack and his charges now found themselves.

Luck had not been with him. This was now to change, but not in a way he could have foreseen.

The windows were arranged in a high narrow bay which resembled the stern lights of an old ship. The glow in them grew gelid and shifty. In the third pane from the left (for two hundred years prior to Methven's reign it had depicted the same view, becoming known as the "Pane of Jars" and giving rise to a common proverb) it condensed into three or four muculent lumps, drifting like fish in a polluted tank. After a moment this activity had spread to the four other panes, and a further refining or condensation had revealed the lumps to be the salient features of five deformed heads—or five images of the same head (two of them upside down). The head was in pain. A dark rubbery device had been forced over its nose and mouth. The straps securing this gag or mask cut deeply into the plump flesh of its cheeks, which was of a mouldy, greenish-white colour patched with silvery acne. Whether the expressions that contorted the visible features reflected hope or fatalism, anger or panic, it was impossible to tell. Its eyes, though watery, were urgent.

For some minutes this apparition struggled silent and unnoticed behind the glass as though trying to escape into the throne room. A psychic gulf of such vastness separated spectre from substance that it seemed to be maintained in focus only by its own desperation, by some debilitating and debasing act of will. It could see Cellur and the Queen and it was trying to speak. Eventually it whispered a little, a syllable like a trickle of vomit in a voice quite at odds with the amount of effort needed to produce it.

Gorb, it said.

Its eyes widened triumphantly. *Gorb.* Cellur and the Queen murmured on. The cups clinked, the day darkened and slipped inevitably into night;

thin blue flames danced in the hearth, leaving delicate indelible images on the surface of the eye.

Gorb.

The head flung itself about, its hidden mouth gaping, until

"GORB!"

fell into the room like a corpse.

The windows flickered dementedly, shuffling views of the head like Fat Mam Etteilla shuffling the trumps. Cellur jumped to his feet, his cloak knocking the china onto the floor. "It sees us! At last the windows have come to their full function!" (This was a guess: he was still in the dark.) Five panes showed the awful mutated face of the ancient airboatman—left profile, right three-quarter profile. They showed sudden random close-ups of individual features—an ear, an eye, the mask with its proliferating tubes and cilia. Pentadic, huge, it winked down into the throne room. "Is it the man from the moon? Speak!"

Speak?

All this time he has been struggling to speak!

Now at last he masters the language—Benedict Paucemanly with his message from a white and distant planet:

"Gorb," he said. "*Fonderia di ferro in Venezia* . . . mi god guv . . . nonarticulated constituent elements . . . Here lie I in the shadows of the veinous manna, burrowed into the absolute ABRACADAVER of the earth . . . Earth!—all things are one to the earth . . . mi god guv im all swole up . . . *Fear death from the air!*"

He giggled weakly and shook his head. "It's simpler than that." He tried again. "In the Time of Bone, in the Time of Dreams, when, on the far side of the moon, I lay like a cheese, blue-veined and with a loop of blue wire for a brain . . . No. Simpler than that, too—

"Look, as a young man I flew to the moon. I would not do such a thing now. Something happened to me there, some transformation peculiar to the airs of that sad planet, and I fell asleep. I fell into a rigor, sank without trace into a trance in which I perceived for a hundred years the singing latticework of my own brain. It was a gift, do you see, or a punishment. (I no longer care which, though the question perplexed me then for its metaphysical implications if nothing else.) There, I was no longer a man at all but a theory; I was a thought received with the clarity of a sensation—hard, complex, resonant with proof. I was a crystal set, and I thought that I could hear the stars.

"I lay on a marble slab in a paved garden among formal perspectives, my naked body citronised by the light falling down from space. At my side a single rose grew like an alum cyst on a long stem. Sometimes it emitted a quiet but intolerably beautiful melody comprising four or five notes on a vanished musical scale. The frozen air filled my mouth. I soon forgot my ship, the *Saucy Sal*. I communicated with the spare, bony winds of that region, blowing in from between the stars. The moon is a strange place. Up there, shadows fall motionless and subtly awry. It is a nexus. It was changed by many races who tried to come to earth (or to leave it) during the long downfall of the Afternoon Cultures. It is a listening ear. It is an outpost."

In the throne-room hearth the small blue flames were exchanged mysteriously for a heap of orange embers. Dark seeped in through the clerestory windows. The dwarf did not come. Outside, the evening wind had brought more snow into the numbed city, hurrying it along as a guide hurries tourists down the picturesque but dangerous streets of some revolution-torn capital. (Streets that would turn later into black and silver geometrical proofs under the sovereign influence of the moonlight.) Benedict Paucemanly whispered like the waves on a distant beach, sometimes audible, sometimes not. He suffered frequent bouts of aphasia. Obscenities, mingled with a dubious lyricism, still made up much of his vocabulary. He still confused the grammar of a dozen old languages with that of a score of invented ones. But the backbone of his monologue was comprehensible. Cellur and the Queen, hypnotised by his awful pentadic image, listened to it and later reported it:

"The moon, or some secret relic of the Afternoon which still inhabits it, had captured the aviator on his arrival and made him into a sort of ear by which to listen to the populated universe (though *listen* is perhaps not the word to use). This, we learnt from him, had been a common practice at one time. He was paralysed and placed on a slab. Messages poured through him like a clear fluid. Around him rows of other slabs diminished into the distance, and on them he could see the empty shells of other 'ears' abandoned millennia ago when their long sleep turned finally into death. Many of the bodies were broken; they were like hollow porcelain figurines. He found himself able to eavesdrop on the transmissions passing through him, but it was like eavesdropping on Babel. The material universe, it would appear, has little absolute substance. It hardly exists. It is a rag of matter, a wisp of gas, a memory of some former state. Each sentient species perceives the thin evidence of this state in a different way, generating out of this perception its physical and metaphysical *Umwelt*: its little bubble or envelope of 'reality.' These perceptual systems are hermetic and admit of no alternative. They are the product of a particular set of sense organs, evolutionary beginnings, and planetary origins. If the cat were to define the world, he would exclude the world of the housefly in his mouth. Each species has its fiction, and that fiction is to all intents and purposes real; and the actual thin substance of the universe becomes more and more debatable, oneiric, hard to achieve, like the white figures that will not focus at the edge of vision. . . .

"Ten thousand sentient races populate the stars. All their mad jargons lace the aether. Paucemanly listened, but was unable to answer them. 'All were distant, dreadfully distant. Their voices were a fading, incomprehensible whisper; a sickening rumour of otherness.' Thus he lay there on his catafalque: far enough from the human *Umwelt* to perceive the myriad realities of the cosmos; not far enough to be able to forget his own humanity. This state persisted for a hundred years or a little less, until new, strong transmissions invaded local space.

"At first, new voices sang to him. This was the first feathery touch of their spiritual envelope or atmosphere. Latterly, he saw them, as a great filmy wing stretched across the cruel lunar meridian. Closer, they were a vast wave. He was soon inundated, sodden with their new 'reality.' All other transmissions ceased. The rose which had bloomed beside his slab shattered with a sound of unearthly grief. A fine tracery of cracks appeared in the slab itself. The white gardens fell to dust around him. He was free. In that moment he lost his humanity for good. (But could not as yet attain any other form. The flesh has an inertia.) His broadcasts to the earth were begun too late: by then, the tenuous wave fronts of the new consciousness had brushed the Pastel City, and in its gutters and alleyways and great Houses was conceived the 'Sign of the Locust'—immaculate and ravishing, a philosophy like a single drop of poison at the centre of a curved mirror, an imperfect intuition of the alien *Umwelt* and of its implications for our own; the first infection of the human reality!

"They were insects long ago. They need no vehicles, but slip like a swarm of locusts down the faults and cleavage zones of space (which they conceive of as an extensive empty wasteland littered with the stony rubbish of planets and echoing with their own dry stridulations). Their motives are unclear: instinct—or something resembling it—compels them to search the continuum endlessly for some solution they cannot even define to themselves. Now, that cold passion is in ruins, and they are trying to live on the earth. They were never meant to come down here and build a city. It is their tragedy as much as ours.

"This was how the great aviator put it to us. Out of confusion he had offered to lead them to the earth. (Who can blame him? Woken from apparent death on the far side of the moon, he had found himself neither insect nor human nor anything he had once been! They were all he had to cling to.) Out of a greater confusion they had followed him. Now—totem or deity or mere interpreter—he was encysted at the heart of their new city, passing his immobile hours in the blue mosaic flicker of his half insectile dreams, involuntary amplifier of the swarm's *Umwelt*.

" 'Already it is too late for human consciousness ever to fully repossess the world; the new dream pours out like mist to envelope and mutate it.' Yet the swarm had been contaminated in its turn: 'Where once it boasted the horny membranes of the locust, the mantis, or the wasp, now it imagines flesh, skin, hair. It regards itself with horror. It is losing the struggle to maintain its inner vision, its hermetic certainty in the face of the void.'

"In the grip of this perceptual stalemate the very substance of the planet had begun to fade, stretch, and tear, like an old net curtain at a window in the Boulevard Aussman. If it continued, the conflict between Man and Insect would become nothing more than a jumble of meaningless shadowy events pivoting round a decaying point in space and Time. In areas of major confrontation, matter, in its attempts to accommodate both 'realities,' was already distorting, drifting into new forms and miscegenations. New ranges of mountains had appeared in the North; coastlines had taken on new forms, plastic, curious, undependable, draped with a new vegetation which had come up out of the sea along the flight paths of the insects and now assumed a grey, etiolated, mucoid transparency; vast hallucinatory displays filled the skies at night, great shifting modular curtains like the view from a mosaic eye. All this had been added to the minor symptoms already observed—the Sign of the Locust, the rains of lights. In addition, the conflict of two dreams had woken older dreams: the factories of the Afternoon rebuilt themselves fragmentarily in the Great Wastes, producing clouds of corrosive vapour; strangely dressed figures speaking ancient languages were posturing in the streets of Lendalfoot and Duirinish.

" 'The world,' whispered Benedict Paucemanly, 'is desperately trying to remember itself . . . blork . . . *nomadacris Septemfasciata!* . . . what a lovely bit of meat . . .' "

Embers settled in the hearth. The doors of the throne room rattled suddenly, their brass motifs of coelacanths and mermen shifting uneasily in the bluish gloom, and were still. It was the wind, perhaps; or perhaps something had fallen against them. From the passage outside was heard briefly an indistinct groaning; a dull clamour far off; silence. Something was happening out there, but those within were captivated by the wavering pentadic spectre of the old airman, his voice faint and his flesh tortured by the mask which, he explained, was now his sole means of perceiving the "real," the human, world. Methvet Nian said nothing, but only watched in horror and compassion the nodding of that wounded, debased head, and gently shook her own, while Cellur the Birdmaker tugged his robe tighter round his thin chest and shivered. His head ached with the cold, and with the effort of following that faded cloacal whisper. He had recognized in the spectre's antics a certain self-consciousness. There was an archness in its winks and gross nods; the narcissism of the confessional informed its breakings of wind.

"What must we do, then?" he asked, a little impatiently.

Paucemanly gave a loud belch. His image swam, retreated, and was replaced by something quite new: great dragonflies, jewelled and crippled, dragged themselves across the shivering panes while behind them the landscape heaved and humped itself into shapes nascent and organic. "They mutate and die in the new vapours of earth: but their breeding cells are full." Wingless and melting, the insects were swallowed by the curious hills about them. These in turn folded back to reveal a face, brown and bony-looking like the stripped and varnished skull of a horse into which had been inserted two half-pomegranates for eyes. It stared into the throne room. "Oops," it said. "Green, brown, testing. Hello?" Paucemanly reappeared in a glutinous yellow fog, looking puzzled. "Whatever emerges from them," he went on, "will wrest the world to its own purposes . . . testing? . . . *Septemfasciata* . . ." A high fluting sound came out of the windows. One of them shattered. Glass fell into the room. Nothing was revealed except a dusty hole which later proved to contain only some gold filaments and a few small bones. (Cellur, though, winced away as if he expected some alien limb to reach out of it.)

In the remaining panes a tarry smoke obscured intermittently the greenish image of the airman. A clump of fat sinister fingers—his own—appeared, feeling their way over his face as if trying to remember it from some previous encounter. They rested thoughtfully on the mask, then with a quick, predatory motion clutched it by the straps and tugged it off. Vomit sprayed from the defaced features beneath. Paucemanly vanished instantly.

"Is the world ending, then?" asked Cellur.

"I want only death," came the answer, a distant whisper clogged with self-pity and guilt. "A hundred years in the moon! Only death."

In the windows appeared a series of faded pictures of ordinary insects, the dry husks of wasps crushed underfoot in an attic long ago, and hawk moths like flower pressings in an old book. A wind stirred them. They darkened one by one until there was nothing left at all. Cellur stood for a long time in the gloom, thinking of nothing. He could not make himself say anything to the Queen.

The dwarf came in with his axe in one hand and a bundle of thin shiny steel rods in the other. He was out of breath and there was blood in his hair. He drank his lukewarm chamomile with a grimace. When he noticed the dark windows and broken glass he nodded grimly. "They had the signal to pass the gates half an hour ago," he said. "We're done for in here."

He dropped the steel rods on the floor and, with a packet of tools he took from under his jerkin, set about assembling them. It was quick work. Soon he had in front of him a half-human skeleton ten or eleven feet tall—his famous "mechanical wife," grubbed up long ago from some frigid desert in the far North. It was quiet in the room as he coupled its metal bones. Nevertheless he paused every so often to tilt his head on one side and listen; and at one point said casually: "Someone will have to bolt the doors. I can't reach them, and the lads out there won't last much longer." (Cellur did not answer. Little motes of blue light like luminous beetles had begun to spill from the shattered window. They fell faster and faster, like rain. They filled the room with a queer glow which lit the white cheek of Methvet Nian as she sat staring silently at nothing.)

A distant shout filtered through from the beleaguered outer corridors. The whole palace seemed to shudder. The dwarf scratched his head. After a long life his understanding of such situations was preternatural. Steel scraped on steel, on stone, as he hurriedly spread the mechanical wife on the floor so that its legs stuck straight out and its arms were set close to its sides. He did something to it until it hummed and sent up motes of its own. Then he lowered himself down so that he lay limb for limb on its cold bones. A harness fastened his upper body into its flaring rib cage; its jawless skull he hinged forward to fit over his head like a helmet. "It is my cold companion, that I thought I would never embrace again," he murmured. Certain levers enabled him to control it, but for the moment he lay still in the curious blue light, performing some act of memory. Ozone, and a low buzzing, filled the air. The skeleton snapped its fingers inadroitly. It shivered and stretched, and of its own accord made grasping motions; but when he moved the levers at last, it failed to respond.

Something threw itself with a crash against the throne room doors.

The dwarf was stuck in the harness. He writhed about. "Bolt the doors, one of you, or it's the end of us!" He got free and addressed himself feverishly to the machine. Sparks came up from it; it gave up slow yellow fireflies to join the flow of blue light from the broken window. A smell like burnt horsehair filled the air. As for Cellur and the Queen: neither of them seemed to be able to move. Their faces were waxy with despair, their eyes like lemurs'. For Tomb it was only a physical disaster, it was only another war; for them it was a disaster of *meaning*. They murmured in low, slurred voices to one another, like old intelligent animals—"Saint Elmo Buffin"; "a fatal chance." Tomb broke his nails on the ancient machinery. He was a dwarf, not a philosopher; it was just another war: and he thought he still had time to win it. . . .

He strapped himself back into the harness. The mechanical wife lifted itself from the flagstones with a groan and an ungainly lurch, like an over-loaded camel. It was worn out, like all the other machinery in Viriconium. No one knew what it had been used for all those centuries ago in the doomed Afternoon Kingdoms. It flailed clumsily about, smashing pieces of furniture in its efforts to stay upright. It fumbled on the floor until it came up with the dwarf's power-axe, which it proceeded to swing in dangerous, humming arcs. "Ha ha," laughed the dwarf. He pulled the skull piece down over his head. His old eyes blinked redly. He felt alive. He only had to stamp his feet and the walls shook. He moved his levers. Trailing creamy white motes like cabbage moths, the mechanical wife shambled over to the doors, one enormous hand reaching triumphantly for the upper bolts. . . .

Outside in a victorious gloom, the remnants of the palace guard bubbling to death at their feet, were gathered the devotees of the Sign. Since the murder on the Pleasure Canal they had lost touch with their ruling echelon in the fluorescing windy mazes of the Artists' Quarter; their ideological priorities had become unfathomable, even to themselves; and their very flesh had suffered violent and useless evolutions. In their endless quartering of the Low City they had uprooted railings, constructed wooden clubs studded with bits of broken glass, helped themselves to butchers' cleavers and old kitchen knives black with corrosion, gathering an army fit for the mutated, the motivationally bankrupt, and the burst. The pain of their transformation had caused them to loosen or unwind the bandages which had previously disguised their humps and tumours, and these now flapped about them in crusty strips as they hopped and sprang erratically along the palace corridors on their strong, bent legs.

Their eyes were puzzled and full of agony. They could not become insects. The flesh, ultimately, resists: there is a conservatism of cell and marrow. But they would never again be human—

From wounds like women's lips had bloomed a fantastic, irrelevant anatomy: drooping feathery antennae, trembling multi-jointed legs, a thousand mosaic eyes, vibrating palps, and purposeless plates of chitin. Where these new deformed organs merged into the original flesh was a transitional substance, pinkish grey, weeping like an unsuccessful graft. None of them were in the right place. From a mutilated torso sprang six thin legs, rattling like dry sticks in a wind. (They seemed to be beckoning. The man from whom they had grown screamed involuntarily whenever he caught sight of himself.) Here rubbery, saw-edged mandibles had burst from flower-like lesions at knee or nape and were now speaking unknown languages in reedy, creaking voices; there a gristly membrane flapped like a mantle, dotted with the abortive stumps of wings. For the genitals of a magistrate from Alves had been substituted a coiled moth-like tongue which poked out uncontrollably at intervals. Some of them leapt and sprang about unpredictably, like grasshoppers on a sunny day; others had lost completely the power of upright locomotion and dragged themselves round in circles like crippled blowflies. This degradation was not wholly their own: behind the desperate murmurs that escaped them could be sensed the rustling whisper of some crippled demiurge, the pain of the Idea striving to clothe itself.

Propelled by a black horror of their own state, dimly but bitterly aware of the humanity they had willingly discarded, they broke down the doors and bore the mechanical wife of Tomb the Dwarf back across the throne room, beating at it with their old shovels and broken swords. Hung up there among its gleaming limbs he swung his axe; tottered; retreated. While behind him Cellur the Birdmaker woke from a dream of dissolution and found it to be real.

10

ALL THE WOUNDS OF THE EARTH

Galen Hornwrack came down into the mysterious city like some legendary failed conquistador. (Fever and magic have defeated his skills. The wastelands he set out to cross in his youth have shown him no enemy but his own ambition. All wells were poisoned; sand has swallowed his troops and his hopes. He lurches back alone into the country of his birth only to find that it too had become shifting, unreliable, changed forever. . . .) The scars left by his fight with the metal bird, an encounter which he recalled only dimly, had diverted and hardened the characteristic lines of his face, so that a strange asceticism now modified his habitual expression of petulance and self-involvement. His nose was running. The sword of tegeus-Cromis he carried in his left hand, having lost its scabbard somewhere in the rotting landscapes behind him. His torn cloak revealed the mail the Queen had given him, now rusty. His eyes were empty and his gaze appallingly direct, as if, tiring of the attempt to winnow the real from the unreal, he now assigned exactly the same value to every object entering his visual field: as if he had suspended judgement on events, and now merely lived through them.

His desire to see the city had kept him from sleep.

Alstath Fulthor followed him, supporting the woman and her endless prophecies. A radiance, colourless in itself, issuing no doubt from his horned and lobed crustaceal armour, appeared to fill both their bodies, illuminating from beneath the things they wore, crimson and blue, as in some old painting. The alien presence of the city, its equivocal contract with "reality," had lent new energy to their madness. "In my youth," sang the woman, "I made my small contribution. Blackpool and Chicago become as nothing; their receding colonnades echo to the sound of vanished orchestras." At this they stopped to regard one another half in delight, half in horror, their cropped spiky hair and long restless hands giving them the air of children caught in some game of conspiracy. (It was only that they hoped to manipulate Time, as we know: believing that by combination and recombination of a few common images—which are themselves only the symbols rather than the actual memories of acts peculiar to the Afternoon Cultures—they might obtain the "code" which would liberate them from the Evening. Thus Mam Etteilla, shuffling her pasteboard cards . . .)

They dawdled, and Hornwrack sat tiredly in the mud to wait for them.

"That's enough of that!" he said sharply. He treated them for the most part with a gruff indulgence, but tried to prevent their odd and embarrassing sexual encounters, chasing the woman away with the flat of his sword while being careful to keep his eye on Fulthor's own great weapon.

"That's enough!" they mimicked. "That's enough!"

He did not know why he was here, heading into the world's deep wound. Bankrupt of purpose when they had fetched him that morning from the rooms in the Rue Sepile, he had maintained himself on the energy of old betrayals and resentments, none of which had survived the journey through the Deep Wastes. He shrugged. He was a husk. Above him hung the torpid and corrupt manifestation of Benedict Paucemanly, which was his only hope. Since dawn it had been undergoing a crisis of will, dissolving sporadically into a mass of greyish curds and losing the power of speech. It would reassemble itself slowly after such a bout, beckon Hornwrack on toward the city, belch tragically. "I want only death," it would explain. And Hornwrack with a sigh would lead his mad protégés a little closer.

This city had appeared on the plain with the descent of the insects a decade before, growing from the worn stone nubs, tilted columns, and submerged pavements of an ancient Afternoon site. They had not so much built it as expected it. It was not so much a city as a response of ordinary matter to their instinctive metaphysical demands, the warping pressures of their "new reality." Originally it had consisted of a number of large but flimsy structures arranged without apparent thought on and around a low mound. The biggest of these were perhaps a hundred feet tall. They were like dry wasps' nests, and of the same papery, cellular construction. They rustled in the wind. The insects went leaping among them on curiously aimless pathways, along the sides of which had been built up over the years peculiar crystalline accretions, hanging reefs and tottering spires, galleries composed of crumbling metallic oxides veined with serpentines and alien glasses. Smaller structures had eventually grown up in the shadows of this development: partly roofed eccentric hexagons formed of impacted sand mixed with certain bodily secretions of their inhabitants, who forced themselves in and out of small openings in the walls.

But if the insects had first begun to change the earth at this spot, so it had begun to change them; and matter's accommodating plasticity had turned suddenly into a trap.

Gravity had imprisoned them: here they had first felt its pull, and lost the power of extra-atmospheric flight. It had suddenly become necessary for them to breathe, yet they could not breathe air, and must invent some substitute: here they had built the chugging machinery to disseminate it. (It never worked very well.) Fluids had been unknown to them during their frigid millennial migration through the barren spaces: here they had first filled their tissues with them as a buffer against the poisons of earth. Here they had put on their breathing masks and built their weapons, seeing themselves as beleaguered, unwilling colonists, victims of a cosmic accident: which they were. Here the human *Umwelt* had first penetrated their strange nervous systems, working a madness on them so that they could not understand what they saw or felt, and began to die of a new disease.

At the time Galen Hornwrack met his end here, all order and sense of purpose had vanished from the place. The buildings, alien to begin with, had begun to subside like hot glass, as if searching for a new centre of gravity. A partly transparent architecture of nightmarish balconies and overhanging walls that had formed as matter, struggling to find a compromise between human and insect demands, began to teeter and grope toward verticals and horizontals that satisfied neither. Streets laid down under no wholesome plan ended in pits, or in staircases which themselves petered out after a turn or two up the sides of some enormous windowless cylinder. The towers shuddered and quaked, vibrating between human and alien states, then slumped and dissolved like jelly. A languorous buzzing sound accompanied this process, and beneath that the clangour of enormous bells, as if matter were trying to toll itself apart. Appalling winds howled down the changing thoroughfares. Streams of tiny blue motes tumbled from the higher cornices; out in the open squares (through which, as in a dream, could be discerned the equivalent plazas of Viriconium—opposite pole, node of nightmares, sister city) struggled the changed individuals of the swarm; while among the alleys of this disintegrating province proliferated the thick, yellow stems of some mutated plant.

Above, vast clouds of the insects hung in the throbbing purple sky, making adventive, meaningless patterns as they attempted to replicate or restart the endless spatial pilgrimage. They hurled themselves into huge pits dug in the desert. They invented useless vehicles which rolled like mouldy grapefruit between the dunes, rising a few feet above the ground to emit foul gases. ("Regretfully," whispered the madwoman, "it is part of a scheme you cannot understand.") Into this chaos Galen Hornwrack was persuaded to lead his party, unaware that circumstances were about to return to him a fragment or two of his distant—indeed by now almost imaginary—adolescence.

Under a sky like a glass mantle, at an intersection in the disintegrating ground plan of the city, two insects performed a dance in the suicidal light. Disease had maimed them, their eyes were like rotting melons yet vivid heraldic insignia flared along their blue and green flanks like the lights of deep-sea fishes. Stiff and quivering, with curled abdomens and spread wings, moving one damaged limb at a time, they had the air of being painted on one of Elmo Buffin's sails, or tattooed in glowing inks on an upper arm. Clouds of coloured vapour streamed through the galleries which curled over them in a flaking mineral wave. Balancing on their rear legs they curled themselves backwards into the annular symbols of some organic alphabet; they dragged themselves between the bone-like pillars of the colonnades, following the veins of serpentine and obsidian as if they were cooling streams; they tore with their forelimbs at the masks they wore—perhaps to obtain relief, for part of the function of these was to enable them to perceive the world they found themselves marooned in.

"Let me kill them," advised Alstath Fulthor.

His periods of sanity, rare since the departure from Iron Chine, were now characterised by a dreamy, idle cruelty, an echo, Hornwrack believed, of the unimaginable and stylized sadisms of the Afternoon Cultures.

"No."

Galen Hornwrack, living in two worlds: he was hopping and whirling despite himself down the million fractured perspectives of the mosaic universe, the thin stridulous hymn of the swarm filling the waste spaces about him. Suns baked him. The void froze him. Infinity drew him on like a promise. Sad stony planets spun beneath him, their cisterns barren. He understood none of it. . . . Simultaneously he was aware of Fulthor coughing and choking at his side, hollow face underlit by the eerie, transfiguring flicker of the powered sword. They stood in the shadow of a huge dead locust, or perhaps it was a mantis. Its forelimbs were folded hieratically above them, clutching something they couldn't see. Leathery curtains of dried mucus hung down from its ventral joints and openings. Its fading telepathies trickled through Hornwrack's skull in a reedy counterpoint to the perceptual disorganisation that swelled over him like triumphant organ music from the city's living inhabitants. His eyes were watering in the lemon fog from the exploding atmospheric distilleries; his nose was running. A tarry fungus flourishing in the shade of the great corpse had begun to corrode the soles of his boots.

"Let me kill them," said Fulthor.

"They may not remain here for long."

He was right. After a while they left their barren exercises and crawled away deeper into the gloom of the reefs, following the glittering veins of mineral.

"They were trying to remember how to fly."

The spectre of Benedict Paucemanly seemed cowed by the city. A corrupt whitish colour when it was visible at all, it wallowed through the upper galleries, losing definition like a piece of wet soap. There seemed to be taking place a dissolution not only of its image but of its personality. This grew more marked the deeper it penetrated the city's confusion. Index finger raised to its lips (or where they would have been), it peered furtively over the sagging balustrades, edging shyly away if an insect appeared in a distant plaza or stood vibrating like a delicate engine at the end of some dark alley. It feared an inevitable meeting.

Nevertheless it would allow them no respite. Fulthor trembled on the edge of his old madness, his armour changing colour eerily, taking on the ribbed greys and greens of the wasteland grasshopper. Hornwrack reeled along beside him, dizzy and vomiting. (His flesh was itching on the bone. He could feel it yearning to grow into new and extravagant shapes.) Soon they were dragging the madwoman along by her armpits. Waves of distortion emanating from the chaos ahead had flung her into a rigor from which she woke only to bite her tongue or make meaningless noises with her slack lips. Her heels furrowed the ground behind, which was now compacted sand, now the sodden peat of the continental sumps. Brown water leaked slowly into the furrows. Was the city there at all? At the peak of each wave the earth tolled and boomed; the buildings deliquesced, revealing for an instant the disfigured waiting towers of Viriconium (which, a thousand miles away, was trying to become a city of dried wasps' nests); and blue particles swirled out of air like luminous rain. The world was being rhythmically eroded; underneath could be discerned the bony grin of nothingness, the *Neant* of Fat Mam Etteilla's grubby pack.

Paucemanly's ghost slipped like a tadpole between the collapsing columns, a blob of mucus propelling itself through this architecture of melting wax by small energetic movements of its finny hands.

Evening came, and with it a purple gloom through which darted curious flames.

Out of this, wreathed in a glutinous yellow fog, some clumsy insects dragged themselves. There were three or four of them. Alstath Fulthor put his hands to his head and fell down. "Oh oh oh," he cried. "Oh, oh," whispered the insects. They approached with a peculiar reluctance, dipping their great masks. Their grey wing cases and armoured yellow underparts were crosshatched with self-inflicted wounds. From these wounds were growing like buds a variety of pink new half-human limbs, joined to the pricked and rotting carapaces by a transitional substance, membranous, neither flesh nor chitin. There were clumps of little hands with mobile, perfect fingers, each one having a tiny fingernail like mother-of-pearl. There were the faces of very young children with closed eyes. There were eyes alone (as indeed there were legs and torsos and internal organs), gummy with postnatal sleep, and of a very distinct blue like enamelling on an old brooch. Some of the faces murmured drowsily.

Whether these insects were ambassadors or soldiers was not clear. They had recognised Hornwrack's party as human, and been attracted by the magistral lustre of the Reborn Man's scarlet armour. (When they approached him their own insignia flared up along their sides, orange and emerald.) They could not speak, though, and he could not help them. They remained immobile, at once heraldic and debased. It was the madwoman who sat up suddenly to speak on their behalf.

"We did not ask to come here," she said. She watched Hornwrack, who in his turn licked his lips and stared at the travesty of a baby's head.

"What?" he said.

"Go away and wait," she begged. "Leave us to be finished here. We cannot live here much." She opened her mouth and blood trickled from her lacerated tongue. "Give us in peace," she whispered, holding her head on one side in a listening attitude, her mouth full of crushed flowers. "Oh!"

At the end of this speech she was standing with her back to the insects, her eyes bright with a horrifying intelligence. Their own great faceted orbs observed Hornwrack calmly over her shoulders. They were motionless. Hornwrack began to back away, laughing. "No more of this!" he heard himself exclaim. He held up his hands. "I don't want to hear any more." He looked round for guidance, but Fulthor was grunting on the floor, and the spectre of the ancient airman had inconveniently vanished. Suddenly a kind of fake anger overcame his fright. He dragged the sword of tegeus-Cromis from his belt, shoved the woman aside, and waded into them with it. But it was only steel, and quickly broke in half. The ambassadors fell back without resisting him, rustling, bearing their dreadful human buds. (One of the heads woke up. *"Leave us alone,"* it whispered, looking directly at him.) Then another wave of disintegration surged out of the core of the city, which was now very close. Hornwrack staggered. The ambassadors writhed and thrashed, their joints gouting fluid. Fay Glass screamed.

"Leave us alone! We will soon die here!"

Hornwrack could bear no more of it. He was used to a less equivocal violence. Retching, he stumbled over to Fulthor's inert body and got the powered broadsword from its ceramic sheath. He had never used one before. He went back and cut inexpertly at the flailing forelimbs and compound eyes of the ambassadors. This time they made a halfhearted fight of it as they backed into the purple gloom. But their odd, gnarled weapons only sputtered feebly in the damp air, gave up strings of pale light, and failed utterly. They tumbled onto their sides as he chopped off their legs. They whirred round in circles, pushing the earth up into irregular mounds. Soon they were all dead. He stared at them in astonishment; at the artefact fizzing in his hand; at Fay Glass. At the last moment they had tried to direct his attention away from the hulk of Benedict Paucemanly's airboat, the *Heavy Star.*

The hull of this ship loomed over him, crawling with the enigmatic corrosions of its hundred-year sojourn in the moon. It was embedded in a tall bulwark of compacted sand, which curved away right and left like the shell of some huge stadium. Hornwrack walked round it, awed, exultant. That famous machine! Lights were dimly visible through its fissured outer skin; pulpy vines enwrapped it; a few flakes of black and silver paint adhered to its stern—the colours of the House of Methven, set there at the height of the air siege of Mingulay.

" 'Fear death from the air!' " shouted Hornwrack. He laughed. He took hold of the madwoman's wrist in his enthusiasm and pulled her along after him. " 'Fear death from the air!' " He thought of Fat Mam Etteilla, and the Bistro Californium with its clientele of perverts and poseurs. He thought of the dwarf who had beaten him up in the palace and then abandoned him in the shadow of the Agdon Roches. He thought of the High City, which had wooed him merely to betray him. He thought of the Low City, of the boy in the Rue Sepile, the drifts of sodden chestnut leaves in the late-afternoon light of November, the women laughing in the upstairs rooms. He thought of the candle at night, a cat sneaking into the room, the smell of geraniums—one dawn following another until they made eighty years of wounds and fevers. None of it meant anything. It was as if he had been relieved of these things, only to have them changed somehow and given back to him merely as memories. "If I can rip her loose we'll fight our way out of this madhouse!" he said. He would fly down to the Pastel City in the last airboat left in the kingdom. There he would speak with the dwarf, perhaps even the Queen. There he'd state his terms. "She'll never take to space again," he said, rubbing his thumb over the thin, whitish, lichen-like growths, the network of tiny cracks that dulled the crystal skin. Even this slight contact made him shiver with excitement. He kicked at a door in the stern to see if it would open, and was rewarded by a hollow boom. "But her motors still work. Look!"

He dropped the High City sword suddenly, grasped the girl by her upper arms. She stared blankly at him. "Once I flew such vessels!" he cried. "Don't you believe me?" And then: "That ghost has given me back the sky. It has given me back the sky!"

Alstath Fulthor came up behind him on all fours and picked up the
discarded *baan*. Some nightmare of the past had him by the head. He
sniggered.

"I'll suffer nothing at the hands of those beautiful philosophers," he
said. "I'll promenade no more in *their* metallic gardens!"

He jumped to his feet, whirling the blade in sputtering arcs round his
head. Sparks showered from it into the dead wet air. Discovering no other
enemy he advanced on Hornwrack, who produced defensively his steel
knife, shouting, "Fulthor, no more grudges! Stop!"

Fulthor could not stop. Hornwrack allowed him to get in close; ducked
the *baan* as it swung in towards his collarbone; and slashed out at
Fulthor's hand, taking off two fingers and severing all the major tendons.
Fulthor dropped the power-blade. He studied his hand in wonder.

"That hand will never annoy me again," he said.

Before they could stop him he had run off into the gloom, singing.

Hornwrack said, "I did not mean to do that. This knife has betrayed
me." He threw it down and stepped on it, but the blade would not break
despite its flaw, and after a moment he forgot it. He retrieved the *baan* and
set about chopping his way into the *Heavy Star* through the stern door.
His blows set up a resonant groaning in the crystal hull. He pulled the
madwoman in after him. She stared back over her shoulder.

The boat was abandoned and empty. Its motors sent up slow violet
motes through a rift in the deck: small worms of light that clung to the
metal surfaces, fastened on Hornwrack's mail shirt, and clustered round
the steel fillet which bound back his hair. Further in, navigation instruments ticked and sang; he could hear them. It was thick with dust in there.
He moved about quietly, touching the things with which he was familiar.
He shivered a little. In the command bridge was a light like sunshine filtered through bottle-green glass. "Go and sit down," he told Fay Glass.
(An insect had entered through the damaged hatch; he could hear it moving about in the hold.) The bow of the boat projected right through the
wall of the "stadium" he had seen outside, but nothing was visible through
the portholes, which seemed to be covered by some gelatinous medium
like agar. Aft, the insect scratched its way across the hold; paused. Its wings
whirred faintly. It departed. Hornwrack let out his breath.

He swallowed.

"Sit still," he told the woman.

He tried to remember what to do.

Under his clumsy hands the vessel groaned and shook. (It was old. In
the moon something vital had gone out of it; some millennial reservoir
had been emptied.) Down below, its motors pulsed, leaking light and generating a rapid percussive shudder. This continued for some minutes and,
transmitted to the outer hull, split it open with a high ringing sound.

Splinters of dark glass flew about the bridge; a fissure twenty inches wide appeared in the wall beside Hornwrack's shoulder, admitting foetid gases; Fay Glass was picked up and flung against a bulkhead, and thereafter lay on the deck like a discarded towel, her thin bruised legs drawn up under her chin. The boat lifted an inch or two and was stationary again. Gelatinous fluids streamed off the forward portholes and slopped into the bridge, where, mixed with the sand from the wall outside, they formed a foul and slimy secretion. Hornwrack clung to his seat.

"You bitch," he said. "You old bitch."

Outside, sand could be seen fountaining up against a purple sky. With a despairing groan *Heavy Star* pulled free of the retaining wall and hurled itself into the mad airs above. Hornwrack sobbed with relief. Around him, instruments were demanding his attention in hysterical whispers, but he had forgotten what most of them were for. The smell of the stuff in the cabin was making him feel sick. He leaned forward to look out of the portholes. The boat was wallowing above an elliptical walled pit about a hundred yards long. This was filled with a grey, viscous, partly organic substance which was now leaking from the breached wall like the white of an egg. As the level of this putrid stuff fell, it revealed by stages a colossal human figure stretched out in the pit.

Benedict Paucemanly!

A monstrous and corrupt flowering of his flesh had taken place in all those white years on the moon. Constrained by a thick rubber suit in case he burst, studded with new sensory organs, whorls and ropes of flesh which reported only mutation and pain, he lay there prostrate. He had tried to become something else and failed. His arms were by his sides and his vast corpulent legs apart. It was from here that he had broadcast his despairing spectre, to Viriconium and beyond. "I want only death." Teetering between two realities, he could perceive neither of them except as an agonizing dream—and yet here he was half a god, a demiurge or source, out from which spread like the ripples on a stagnant pond all the new nightmares of earth: he had become, unwillingly enough, the amplifier of the swarm's *Umwelt*, as he had once been an ear that listened to the stars. He had lain like this for ten years, groaning and whimpering and vomiting into the mask which had long ago been forced over his bloated head so that he could see something of the world surrounding him. Worse: through his great corroded bulk burrowed the parasitic larvae of the swarm, deposited there when gravity first sucked them down and mortalized them. A thousand miles away, in the false windows of the throne room at Viriconium, his other image was telling Cellur: "The breeding cells are full. Whatever emerges will wrest the earth to its own purposes."

He was the breeding cell. It was a strange end for a legendary man.

A gust of wind caught the airboat, causing it to spin slowly through a few degrees of arc. A smell came up. Hornwrack shuddered. The enormous half-corpse swung beneath him, displaying its fermented sores, the cratered flesh that bulged between the straps. The larvae forced themselves in and out. How long had it sought him, before it came upon him in Methven's hall? What psychic bond now linked them? As he stared down, the spectre formed again behind him, attempting to attract his attention by snapping its fingers and coughing softly. He knew it was there. He didn't dare look back.

"Bugger me, lad," it said, "but we've seen some queer berths, you and I."

He turned against his will to face it. It was bobbing about under the ceiling, making embarrassed washing motions with its fat hands.

"Now you've seen me as I am, lad, would you do me a favour?"

"Go away. Why have you brought me here?"

"Pork!" it choked. "*Porcit me te bonan* . . . Death! . . . There's only the jungle out there, son. The water barrel's contaminated and the captain's got the clap . . ."

"What are you saying? Leave me alone!"

". . . hung up there raw-blind in the ratlines like the corpse of a dog." The spectre quivered suddenly, sniffed, as if scenting something new in the air. "The lee shore!" it screamed. "The lee shore!" Then, quieter: "And only we two left aboard, matey."

It put its head intelligently to one side.

"Christ, listen to those parrots!" it said in a hoarse whisper.

(While down in the pit, trapped among these metaphors and invented languages, Paucemanly strove to overcome his madness and communicate. His colossal limbs, partly submerged in milky grey slime, kicked and waved. Behind the eyepieces of his mask—which, like the panes of an aquarium abandoned in some dusty room, were occluded by a green deposit—his weak blue eyes rolled and bulged. The wind stank of delirium, gangrene, and false compass bearings. A tear of self-pity trickled down his cheek. He was adrift between universes.)

"Kill me," the spectre implored at last. "Kill me, lad. You can do it."

Hornwrack advanced on it with flailing arms. It shied away from him, belching morosely.

"Is that why you led me here?" he asked it.

It faded abruptly and he never saw it again. He bit his lip and went back to the controls.

"I'm commandeering this boat," he said.

He sent the *Heavy Star* lumbering away from that city and out into the calm emptiness beyond. He could not bear the ancient airman's degradation. He could not bear his own despair (which he conceived of as compassion). Behind him in the pit a great hand came up, fumbled, ripped away the tormenting mask: and with a terrible lowing sound that echoed across the shallow poisoned tarns and endless peat hags of the continental waste, Benedict Paucemanly plunged into the full nightmare of his own decay.

A single erratic line of footprints crossed the waste. Along it at intervals were strewn items of plate armour which lay like shards of scarlet porcelain amid the blowing dust, glowing faintly as if by their own light. It was night now, or the end of the world. The sky, drained of its aching purples except where the enigmatic city festered on the horizon, was of a green so dark as to be almost black; it had the shine of a newly cracked flint. Beneath this pall, files of insects entered the city from all directions, accompanied by occasional enormous mirages and flashes of rose-coloured light. The silence of the caesura was over everything; judgement in abeyance. Hornwrack, remote and unimpassioned, allowed the vessel to drift along at walking pace above the footprints while the madwoman, recovered from her latest malaise, pressed her face to the portholes and sang in a small bruised voice,

> On the shores of the diamond lake
> We shall watch the fishes
>
> Fal di la di a

All decisions were postponed. After half an hour of this they came upon the Reborn Man.

He was running north among the deep peat groughs which here wind their way back to a flat and boggy watershed dotted with foundering cairns and rotten wooden posts. His limbs were shadowy, but on the loose black stuff he had worn beneath his armour there flared like a beacon the ideograph of his House. For some minutes he seemed unaware of the arrival of the *Heavy Star,* and ran on ignoring it, his arms windmilling for balance as he picked his way among the steep-sided channels and fibrous mounds. Then he looked up, staggered, and shook his fist. His mouth opened and shut angrily. He swayed, cupping his ears with his hands, and fell into the bed of a narrow stream, where he lay with his head in the peaty water for a moment or two, looking confused. By the time Hornwrack, having landed the machine a little way off, had found him again, he was back on his feet.

"Where have I been?" he asked.

"I don't know," said Hornwrack. "Look, I am sorry to have cut off your fingers. I no longer bear you any grudge." (He examined this statement with surprise. It was true.)

Fulthor looked down at his maimed hand.

"My mind feels very clear," he said. "Where is the dwarf?"

He had forgotten everything, and could not take in Hornwrack's explanations. Causality meant nothing to him. "Have we been to Iron Chine already, then?" he would ask. "Or have we yet to see those burning sails?" Or, holding his head tenderly as if he could feel Time coiled and knotted there in it like purple braid, "We've to meet Arnac san Tehn. Tonight, in the Garden of Empty Wounds!" Smiling secretively, the madwoman took his hand and affected to count the fingers. He bore this calmly. The two of them stood there against black waste and obsidian sky; and in Hornwrack's imagination a light surrounded them. It was as though they had already separated themselves from the world in preparation for their descent into the past. He was filled with a deep resentment of their beauty (in response to which images of the Rue Sepile passed through his brain like fatal playing cards, or the lines extemporised by some bad poet in the purgatorial night—"Here is the smell of fog; I see dead geraniums on your windowsill, and women whisper in the lighted rooms"), but this was suppressed immediately by a corresponding urge to protect them, both from the world and his own envy.

"You will have to look after each other now," he told Fulthor. He stared at the city fulminating like a spot of phosphorus on the horizon. "I don't know how you'll get back to Viriconium, even if you want to go there."

He tried to think of something else to say.

"Good luck."

They watched puzzledly as he trudged back to the *Heavy Star*, which was sinking a little under its own weight in the mud. For a moment it looked as if the madwoman might run after him. An expression of ordinary human intelligence crossed her face. Then she laughed. The old machine rose gracelessly into the air and turned towards the city.

The city! Its end is near. It expands and contracts, like a lung. Regular spasms of dissolution shake it like the vomits and distempers of a dying king. It is full of fires, not all of them real; memories of a history never achieved, a future unrealised. Sketchy and counterfeit, the towers of its sister city Viriconium advance and recede through a roseate smoke. Up from the buildings come fountains of earth! They pour into the sky as if gravity had been reversed, and where they fall on the surrounding plain a litter of insects is deposited, bits of dead insects which lie like ruined machinery amid the crude stones. At the height of each spasm the ground tolls like a bell; deep in the streets inexplicable phantoms stalk (headless women, their jewelled sandals sinking into a carpet of dusty grasshopper husks; rains of stinking skulls and luminous beetles; a sail moving down some nonexistent Pleasure Canal: failed dreams of a compromise with the bony skeleton of earth); and a great mad hooting goes up from the heart of the city, a groan of pain and horror in which may be distinguished the voice of the mutated airboatman calling to the assassin he has lured across a thousand miles to serve him—

Kill me.

The insects ignored this lowing call—as of some large but delicately organised animal being disembowelled—and forced themselves in and out like wasps round a rotting apple. They buzzed erratically across the plain; hurled themselves into the pits they had dug; and gathered in the dark air in diffuse humming clouds. Meanwhile, the *Heavy Star*, stern down, fabric wounded by the curious stresses of space, floundered toward them with blue lights leaking from its engine rooms. They were aware of it. It fascinated them. They made sudden abortive darts and forays in its direction. Did they link it with their flight down from the moon? Did they perceive Galen Hornwrack encysted at the heart of its simple nervous system? Some of the more daring individuals threw themselves against its hull, only to topple away into the convection currents and streams of floating debris, which consumed them. This agitation grew as Hornwrack approached the erupting city. Their forays became more purposeful, and more prolonged. The city pulsed and heaved, generating a savage mauve glare, and they came up from it like smoke.

Up on the watershed Fulthor and the madwoman, interrupted in some partial rite of the Afternoon, some fragment of an old sin, shaded their eyes against the novel light. (Their iconic calm now representing a wiser— or at least more ordered—station of the world, a culture which would surely have taken such fireworks in its stride. . . .) The plain was alive with crippled insects, tiny as aphids and bathed in the magnetic radiations of the city. A cold wind sprang up, lashed the boggy waste, and—rolling their wingless corpses before it like the discarded regalia of a mystery play— rushed away into the North; while above, the *Heavy Star*, a wobbling black mote in the hectic air, rose to meet the spreading swarm, and was engulfed.

They fastened themselves on to its outer hull like locusts on a branch. It strained forward as if the air had solidified around it, and was brought to a standstill above the perimeter of the city, where the hulk of Benedict Paucemanly greeted it with booms and roars of self-pity, waving his infested limbs. (From up on the watershed this activity seemed like the movements of some tiny damaged mechanical toy.) He had replaced his mask but was unable to secure it, so that it hung awry on his blubbering tub-like head like the woollen cap on the head of a retarded child. His new organs pulsed, engorging themselves in time to the rhythms of the city. "In the moon," he said, "it was like white gardens." He begged for freedom in an abandoned language. He blinked up, watching the insects as they continued to alight on his old ship. When they could find no further space to settle, they attached themselves to one another in a parody of copulation. Beneath this rustling layer the *Heavy Star* struggled to gain height. Suddenly, violet bolides arced from its bows! Caught up in the discharge of the ancient cannon, many of the insects dropped away, crackling and roasting and setting fire to their neighbours, so that they fell about the ears of the decaying airboatman like burning leaves.

Fear death from the air! Up there, we can see, Hornwrack fears nothing. He makes the boat his own. Power plants enfeebled by its unimaginable journeys, substructure creaking like an old door, it nevertheless wriggles ecstatically under his hands, light flaring off its stern. We see it even now, long after the fact, rolling and spinning against the southern quadrant of the sky. The patterns it is making are gay, adventive, dangerous. It tumbles off the top of a loop and falls like a stone. It soars eighteen hundred feet vertically upwards, spraying violet fire almost at random into the dark green varnished sky. Persistence of vision makes of it a paintbrush, violet strokes on an obsidian ground, while the insects fall like comets all around it, trailing a foul black smoke, to shatter and burst pulpily on the plain beneath! Even the watchers on the watershed have abandoned their cruel calm. He may yet escape! something whispers inside them. He might yet escape! . . . But now the energy cannon has stopped working, and he seems to have undergone a fatal faltering or change of heart. They bite their lips and urge him on. Some listlessness, though, prevents him: something inhaled from the cabbagey air of the Low City long ago. Now the *Heavy Star* drifts immediately above Paucemanly's carcass like an exhausted pilot fish. The insects descend. All Hornwrack's efforts have made no impression on their numbers. One by one they approach the wallowing vehicle. One by one they settle on its creaking, riven old hull and commence to bear it down. . . .

Fay Glass, shading her eyes, looked out across the plain.

The city was a throbbing sepulchre of light. At the height of every spasm, light vomited from it into the world, bringing a chaotic new reality and causing vast attenuated shadows to flicker across the stony plain; while above it hovered the swarm like an antithetical twin, a giant shadowy planet composed of interlocking wings, curled abdomens, and entangled insectile legs, from which glittered thousands of mosaic eyes. Deep inside it was buried the *Heavy Star,* the whine and groan of its engines overlaid by an unearthly stridulation—a dry, triumphant song like the song of the wasteland locust as it rushes over the bony spaces of the South. Lulled by its own barren psalm, the swarm basked in the light of its coming transformation, anticipating the day when its larvae, made over entirely, should leave the refuge of the mutated airman and come forth into a reality neither human nor insect, and themselves bask in the warmth of a totally unknown sun.

"Such a long way," she said dreamily (and apropos, perhaps, of something else: for what could she know?). "Such a long way, and so many wings."

But now the *Heavy Star* tapped some final resource. The swarm, caught unawares, shook itself out into the density of a cloud of winter smoke. From this burst Galen Hornwrack and his legendary craft—which, devouring its own substance, was spilling a lemon-yellow light from every rift and porthole!

There was a thoughtful pause, as if he were surveying his chances.

Then, before the swarm could act again, he switched off the motors, and the boat began to fall straight down toward the city; slowly at first, then faster and faster.

What of Viriconium—Pastel City and erstwhile centre of the world—at this desperate conjunction, amid the mass abdication of real things and the triumph of metaphysics? Twin sister of the city on the distant plain, she nevertheless approaches her dissolution with a kind of fatalistic calm (stemming perhaps from a sense of history—"an irony in the very stones"—and the feeling that it may all have happened before. Who has lived here for long, Ansel Verdigris asks us, in the fragmentary polemic *Answers*, without experiencing some such sensation?). Her cold plazas and antique alleys reeking of cabbage accept their fate. Her geometries accept their fate. Her people accept their fate: they are so superstitious that they believe almost everything, and so vulgar they have noticed hardly anything.

In the Artists' Quarter, in the Bistro Californium, they stare at one another and the door; sitting in the blue and gamboge shadows like wax figures waiting for a murder, for their own long-sensed termination which at once fascinates and frightens them. "I *dined* with the hertis-Padnas." "Oh, shut up." Unearthly structures have insinuated themselves between the towers on the hill at Minnet-Saba: hanging galleries under the fat white moon, like veins of quartz; sandy domes and papery things like wasps' nests. All have an immaterial feel, the air of an intrusion from some other imagination, but the Low City streets are generally so cold that there is nobody in them to notice. And the Reborn have gone. (All night long on the high paths of the Monar their columns move uneasily north. Many will die of cold. Out among the tottering seracs of the glaciers, their advance parties report mirages.) So there is no one abroad in the High City to see the palace of Methvet Nian pulsing like a great alchemical rose up there at the summit of the Proton Circuit, its filigree outer shell warping with light. No stars are visible above that hall; only there is a feeling of some heavy weight, some great uncommon cloud balanced above it. Its corridors are deserted but for the crawling survivors of the Sign trying to become insects—

The palace awaited its end, breathing like an old woman: and with every shallow inspiration a yellow cabbagey air was drawn in from the city outside, to trickle down the passageways, chill the devotees of the Sign where they crouched in corners over their dragging abdominal sacs or quivering elytra, and come eventually through a region of old machines in niches, to the throne room of the Queen—that room which Tomb the Dwarf had barricaded with corpses, and in which he now lay unable to get up.

In the end it hadn't been much of a fight; better than some he'd had, worse than many. The usual shouts and stinks; some hot work with the axe in a corner; the room frozen at sudden odd angles as the mechanical wife bore him to conclusions in the bluish gloom; shadows teetering on the walls. When it came down to it the servants of the Sign had behaved more like its victims—curiously lethargic and self-involved, as if trying to recover their human state. Those lucky enough to be unimpeded by their deformities had been preoccupied with them nevertheless, and had found it difficult to defend themselves against the axe; the rest had welcomed it quite openly. That axe! He remembered it now. How it hissed and sputtered in the dark, dripping with St. Elmo's fire! He recalled its evil light in the dim depopulated Soubridge streets at the conclusion of the War of the Two Queens. It had been with him on the Proton Circuit, when he stood on a heap of corpses to shake the hand of Alstath Fulthor; it had been with him at Waterbeck's rout, when with tegeus-Cromis the legendary swordsman he had watched a thousand farmboys slaughtered in ten minutes: and both these friends now lost to him through death or madness. He remembered distinctly how he had first dug it up, but he could not think where. . . . At any rate it had been a terrible thing to unleash on a handful of deformed shopkeepers, who could meet it only with kitchen knives and nightmares, in a shadowy room at the "smoky candle end of time." He could not understand how they had brought him down.

There was a strong smell of death in the room, and his view of it was obscured by the dead themselves. They surrounded him like an earthwork topped with a fringe of stiffened limbs which framed part of a tapestry here, there a broken high-backed chair; and the blue light lay on their waxy skin like a bruise. The mechanical wife embraced him. Her delicate spars had snapped like icicles when she fell; her spine was cracked; and up from her mysterious centres of power came a thin stream of whitish motes, interrupted every so often by a sluice of yellow radiation and a momentary lifelike twitching of her limbs. Cellur and the Queen had tried and failed to free him, passing to and fro in front of him, their distracted expressions like those of illuminated figures on a grubby pasteboard playing card.

———

Now they were waiting calmly for the end, staring into the invisible North as if they might by force of will understand what was happening there; as if they sensed Galen Hornwrack perched there on the edge of his long fall. Their voices were desultory in the gloom.

"Birds no longer come to see me out of the high air," whispered one; while the other smiled regretfully and said, "A dead bird swung at his belt during all that journey down the Rannoch. I did not hate my cousin, but it was a hard winter."

Tomb licked his lips. He was dying. The excitement of murder, which had come back to him like a familiar old pain, was now ebbing. He was stranded on the shore of himself, hollowed out yet filled with enigmas which he recognised dimly as the evidence of his own unwounded psyche. He had made few judgements, before or after the fact: thus the events of his life, and the figures in it, retained their wholeness, remaining—he was surprised to find—like icons in the brain, sharp and brightly lit. Now they presented themselves to him as a series of unexpected gifts—a spring shower making paste out of the pink dust of the Mogadon Littoral, where the enamelled hermit crabs run up sideways out of the sea; the smell of whitebait frying in some café on the Rue Montdampierre; someone saying, "Here the anemone boy spilt wine on her cloak"—shy, unbidden, peripheral little memories. He was captivated. While he waited, he reviewed them. He attended them with a shyness of his own, a pure and unironic affection for his own past.

(Tomb the Dwarf! Much later, Methvet Nian discovered his caravan undamaged in Old Palace Yard. Its vulgar colours were still bright beneath the winter's grime. The inside of it was very clean. She could find in none of its cleverly designed cupboards and hiding places anything personal to him, anything he might have kept out of sentiment. His old spade was there, but it was simply a spade. His belongings were utilitarian, or else had myths—and thus existences—of their own: the little furnace, for instance, which had reforged the Nameless Sword all those years ago. There was nothing here to remember him by—this was how she put it to herself. Nevertheless, rather than leave she turned over the cold bed linen, or touched a small pewter cup. Out in the courtyard there was clinging rain; yellow light and footsteps on the cobbles; night drawing in. Sitting alone in the dark she wondered what had become of his ponies.)

City, dwarf, Queen: all waited.

Cellur the old man, alien millennia fading in his brain, waited.

Up in the North, Fay Glass and Alstath Fulthor waited on the quaking plain. Demented, pained, tortured by the persistence of the universe, Benedict Paucemanly could only wait.

Hornwrack himself waited, falling eternally toward the mysterious city.

He had pulled his hair ruthlessly back and fastened it with a steel clasp in imitation of the doomed captains of a now-forgotten war. About him he had drawn the meal-coloured cloak of the Low City bravo (which with its grotesquely dyed hem signifies that he has wallowed in the blood of fifty men). His hands, he discovered, had betrayed him over the breaking of the knife. They had hidden it in his cloak. Now it lay in his lap, flawed blade black and enigmatic. In all, he was as the Queen had seen him last, in her drawing room at Viriconium. He had rejected the myth she had offered him and adhered to his own. These symbols of the pose which had sustained him through eighty years of wet dawns in the Rue Sepile now served, perhaps, to reassure him of that.

The ship fell. He would not touch the controls. He held the knife tightly to keep his hands occupied. One moment his thin face was in eclipse. The next it had been thrown into prominence by a flash of rose-red light from the decaying node beneath.

We are not talking of his motives. All his life he had looked not for life itself but for some revelation to unify it and give it meaning: some—any—significant occurrence. Whether he was able or willing to recognise it now it had come, we cannot say. It is immaterial anyway. In the event he sacrificed himself to release the old airboatman from an undeserved nightmare. It was a rescue.

At the instant of impact the boat split open around him like an empty gourd, but he did not feel it.

Instead, as the crystal splinters entered his brain, he experienced two curious dreams of the Low City, coming so quickly one after the other that they seemed simultaneous. In the first, long shadows moved across the ceiling frescoes of the Bistro Californium, beneath which Lord Mooncarrot's clique awaited his return to make a fourth at dice. Footsteps sounded on the threshold. The women hooded their eyes and smiled, or else stifled a yawn, raising dove-grey gloves to their blue, phthisic lips. Viriconium, with all her narcissistic intimacies and equivocal invitations, welcomed him again. He had hated that city, yet now it was his past and it was all he had to regret . . . The second of these visions was of the Rue Sepile. It was dawn, in summer. Horse-chestnut flowers bobbed like white wax candles above the deserted pavements. An oblique light struck into the street—so that its long and normally profitless perspectives seemed to lead straight into the heart of a younger, more ingenuous city—and fell across the fronts of the houses where he had once lived, warming the rotten brick and imparting to it a not unpleasant pinkish colour. Up at the

second-floor casement window a boy was busy with the bright red geraniums arranged along the outer sill in lumpen terra-cotta pots. He looked
down at Hornwrack and smiled. Before Hornwrack could speak he drew
down the lower casement and turned away. The glass which now separated
them reflected the morning sunlight in a silent explosion; and Hornwrack,
dazzled, mistaking the light for the smile, suddenly imagined an incandes-
cence which would melt all those old streets!

Rue Sepile; the Avenue of Children; Margery Fry Court: all melted
down! All the shabby dependencies of the Plaza of Unrealised Time! All
slumped, sank into themselves, eroded away until nothing was left in his
field of vision but an unbearable white sky above and the bright clustered
points of the chestnut leaves below—and then only a depthless opacity, behind which he could detect the beat of his own blood, the vitreous humour of the eye. He imagined the old encrusted brick flowing, the glass
cracking and melting from its frames even as they shrivelled away, the
shreds of paint flaring green and gold, the geraniums toppling in flames to
drop like comets through the fiery air; he imagined the chestnuts fading to
nothing, not even white ash, under this weight of light! All had winked
away like reflections in a jar of water glass, and only the medium remained,
bright, viscid, vacant. He had a sense of the intolerable briefness of matter,
its desperate signalling and touching, its fall; and simultaneously one of its
unendurable durability.

He thought, Something lies behind all the realities of the universe and
is replacing them here, something less solid and more permanent. Then
the world stopped haunting him forever.

It is so hard to convey simultaneity:

As Hornwrack dreamed, so did Tomb the Iron Dwarf, dying a thousand miles away in his one hundred and fiftieth year, old friend of kings
and princes; as Cellur and the Queen stood in the chilly throne room, staring into the North and whispering in the dry voices of the old, so Fay
Glass and Alstath Fulthor stood in the distant waste and watched Benedict
Paucemanly open his arms as if to embrace the falling airboat. His voice
hooted morosely across to them on the wind. "You've come home," he
tried to say: to whom or what is unclear, unless it was himself. It was too
late anyway. The *Heavy Star* buried itself in the bloated arch of his chest
and broke apart with a muffled thud. He rolled like a stricken whale with
this enormous blow, making a soft, almost female noise of grief or pleasure; and a white light issued suddenly from him, a nimbus which filled the
pit and spread so rapidly that within a minute the whole of the city had
been transfigured, its alien arcades and papery constructions appearing to
glow from within.

This light rippled out over the earth, thinning as it went. By the time it had crossed the bitter coasts of Fenlen it was nothing more than a faint disturbance of matter which, speeding through the very stones of the world, liberated everything in its path from the "new reality." It cleansed the ruins of Iron Chine, where for a month great green beetles had fumbled through the whitish remains of Elmo Buffin's ill-starred fleet. Spilling over the battlements of the cold city of Duirinish, it relieved the proctors there of their visions—crane flies stalking distant fantastic littorals, trees into men, men into geometrical figures. It swept between the shattered buttresses of the Agdon scarp, and when it had passed the stunted oakwoods on the slopes below were untenanted again. It flickered among the high passes of the Monar, scouring them with a glacial light, and finally crossed the walls of the Pastel City to empty those ancient streets of all illusions but their proper human ones.

(Out there on the alien plain, Fay Glass and Alstath Fulthor felt it pulse through them, and were pulled away into the past. "Arnac san Tehn!" he called triumphantly. "We meet in the Garden of Women! Midnight!" But she whispered, "So many wings," a little sad, perhaps, to leave. "So many wings," seeing the cruelty of it all. They lingered for a while as grey phantoms amid the sinking cairns of the watershed, the Afternoon Cultures reclaiming them by degrees. Now they are lost to us for good.)

Benedict Paucemanly writhed silently as if determined to vomit something up. All was done but this one thing: his death. He groaned and strained. Abruptly the larvae of the swarm burst out of his distended pores, fell off him into the pit, and dried up like dead leeches. He hooted in triumph. The light fountained up from him for some minutes more, all the light he had absorbed during his long imprisonment in the moon, all his pain. He was beatified, dissolving in his own light. Repository and symbol, he released all the energies of the two realities colliding within him: and in releasing them released the earth.

The plain darkens. We see it from a long way off. The old airboatman is dead. There is a slow fading of the sky, a cold wind springing up; a deeper night arrives. The mysterious city winks like an ember on the edge of the plain, fading from white to purple to a dim red and then nothing. For a moment the swarm hangs above this, its first and last stronghold, forming itself into a complex grid-like pattern in the obsidian air—some last attempt to communicate with the human world, a glowing symbol, meaningless yet full of import against the darkness. Down floats its stridulant hymn, bony celebration of the waste spaces of the universe. Then, its ontological momentum lost, its position in the material continuum untenable, the life goes out of it. Those individuals which survive will become mere insects and wander about the plain forever with folded wings, as lost as all the other races that ever came down to the earth, and whose descendants now inhabit the Deep Wastes. When they meet they will stare lengthily at one another as if trying to remember something; or, copulating hopelessly beneath a black rain, become suddenly immobile, so that they resemble tangled silver brooches mislaid on the desert by the hetaerae of some vanished civilisation. . . .

EPILOGUE

Viriconium.

Its achingly formal gardens and curious geometries; its streets that reek of squashed fruit and fish; its flowers like purple wounds on the lawns of the "Hermitage" at Trois-Vertes; its palace like a shell: how can one deal with it in words?

Viriconium.

If you go and stand up in the foothills of Monar you can see it hanging below you wrapped in a mantle of millennial calm. From the brow of Hollin Low Moor you may watch it fade into another night. Its histories make of the very air about it an amber, an entrapment. Light flares from the vivid tiered heights of Minnet-Saba, from the riverine curve of the Proton Circuit, the improbable towers and plazas of the Atteline Quarter; under a setting sun banks of anemones and sol d'or planted about the graves of tegeus-Cromis and Tomb the Dwarf glow like triumphal stained glass; and someone far off in the still twilight is reading aloud a verse of Ansel Verdigris, the poet of the city.

Viriconium.

Spring. Down in the Cispontine Quarter the vegetation has begun to flourish again. The fuel-gathering women are no longer seen. Ragwort clothes all the fallen walls and earthy scars, its stems already infested with black and yellow caterpillars (later in the year these become an attractive crimson moth which was once the symbol of the city). Up at Alves, jackdaws are squabbling all day over nesting sites in the cracked dome of the observatory. And in that demimonde which has its centre at the Plaza of Unrealised Time, the women smile down from their casement windows, lifting a hand to pat newly washed hair. Humanity has recolonized the inconceivable avenues of the High City—gaping up open-mouthed at the inexplicable architecture of the Afternoon Cultures while it empties its bladder in their millennial gutters—and hung out its washing again in the Low. The "Winter of the Locust" is over. Only a sudden increase in the number of beggars (some of whom have the most novel deformities) along the Rivelin Way persuades us that it ever took place, that we ever listened to that white thin song.

We hear that Lord Mooncarrot is seen about with Chorica nam Vell Ban, that cold fish. He has received her mother at his house in Minnet-Saba: rumour is rife. We hear that the feverish Madam "L" has ceased her visits to the Boulevard Aussman, is cured of all but her bad taste, and this week reopens her salon. We hear that Paulinus Rack, the fat poetaster and undertaker's agent, has come by a packet of manuscript in not-unquestionable circumstances, and plans soon to edit a volume of the cockatoo's work. He can be seen any day, with his fat hands and jade cane, drinking lemon gin at the Bistro Californium. (He has a theory of the Locust Winter and its madness. Who does not? Invite him to dinner and he will spill it on his waistcoat with the custard.) As for the rest of the Low City: the younger poets favour a Bistro gnosticism—the world, they say, has already ended, and we are living out hours for which no chronology allows. They cut atrocious figures as they swagger about the Artists' Quarter practising their polemic. And these days so many poseurs are wearing the meal-coloured cloak that the bravos have taken in defence to yellow velvet.

In short, the Eternal City stands as it once did, infuriating, beautiful, vulgar by turns. Only the Reborn are missing. You do not see them now in the Atteline Quarter, or on the Proton Circuit hurrying from the palace on an errand of Alstath Fulthor's. (He has never returned. The Low City always knew something like this would happen. It taps the side of its nose; sniffs.) After the persecutions they endured at the hands of the Sign, the majority of them will never come here again. They will live now in the deserts for many generations, their germ-plasm becoming as alien as that of the big lizards of the Great Brown Waste, refining their theory of Time, redefining their heritage, growing mad and strange.

In the evenings Queen Jane, Methvet Nian of Viriconium, sits in the side chamber or *salle* she uses as a library and drawing room, sometimes meditating this loss, which is one of many in her life. "A world trying to remember itself": surrounded by her sheets of music and delicate little corals, she has the wry but supple calm of an ageing danseuse; keeps in a rosewood chest with copper reinforcing bands a gourd-shaped musical instrument from the deep East; hears the past in every passing footstep; and wonders often what became of the sword and the mail and the assassin she gave them to.

"I had hoped for so much from the Reborn," she confides to her new advisor, the old man who is so very rarely seen in public. "We might have rebuilt our culture. Yet they were perhaps too concerned with their own salvation to teach us . . . and we always too uncomplicated for their delicate nerves . . ."

She closes her eyes.

"They enriched us even so. Can you still see them, Cellur, when Tomb woke them first? What a pageant they made, there in the brain chamber at Knarr, with all their strange weapons!"

He can see nothing. He was not there. But he has forgotten even that (or perhaps he realizes that she has) and with a small diffident movement of his hands says, "I am sure I do, my lady," then, remembering something else, smiles suddenly. "Did I not live then in a tower by the sea?"

Ten thousand grey wings beat down the salty wind, like a storm in his head!

In Viriconium

IN VIRICONIUM

THE FIRST CARD

DEPOUILLEMENT

This card indicates an illness of uncertain severity. Apprehension, fear, and indefinite delay. Expect difficulties in your business.

"There is correspondence everywhere; but some correspondences are clearer than others."

CHARLES WILLIAMS, *The Greater Trumps*

Ashlyme the portrait painter, of whom it had once been said that he "first put his sitter's soul in the killing bottle, then pinned it out on the canvas for everyone to look at like a broken moth," kept a diary. One night he wrote in it.

The plague zone has undergone one of its periodic internal upheavals and extended its boundaries another mile. I would care as little as anyone else up here in the High City if it were not for Audsley King. Her rooms above the Rue Serpolet now fall within its influence. She is already ill. I am not sure what to do.

He was a strange little man to have got the sort of reputation he had. At first sight his clients, who often described themselves later as victims, thought little of him. His wedge-shaped head was topped by a coxcomb of red hair which gave him a permanently shocked expression. His face accentuated this, being pale and bland of feature, except the eyes, which were very large and wide. He wore the ordinary clothes of the time, and one steel ring he had been told was valuable. He had few close friends in the city. He came from a family of rural landlords somewhere in the midlands; no one knew them. (This accident of birth had left him a small income, and entitled him to wear a sword, although he never bothered. He had one somewhere in a cupboard.)

She must be got out of there, he continued, writing a little more quickly. *I have thought of nothing else since this evening's meeting with Paulinus Rack. Rack, with his fat lips and intimate asides! How did he ever come to be her agent? In his oily hands he had some proof sketches of her designs for his production of* Die Traumunden Knaben—The Dreaming Boys. *I stared at them and knew that she must be preserved. They are inexplicable, these figures in their trance-like yet painful attitudes. They suggest a line and form quite foreign to us warmer, more human beings. Could she have understood something about the nature of the crisis that we have not?*

He bit his pen.

But how to persuade her to leave? And how to persuade anyone to help me?

This was rhetoric. He had already persuaded Emmet Buffo the astronomer to help him. But what is a diary for, if not effect? The world has already seen too much history dutifully recorded: that was the unconsciously held belief of Ashlyme's age.

When the ink was dry he locked the book, then picked up the light easel he used for preliminary studies and went downstairs. "Come sometimes at night," she had said when he accepted the commission, and laughed. "A lamp can be as unflattering as daylight." (Touching his sleeve with one mannish hand.) At the bottom of the stairs he stood still for a second or two, then let himself out into the empty street and echoing night. From here he had a view of the Low City, some odd quality of the moonlight giving its back and foreground planes equal value, so that it had no perspective but was just a clutter of blue and gamboge roofs filling the space between his eyes and the hills outside the city.

He made his way down the thousand steps which in those days gave access to the heights of Mynned, hidden behind the façade of the Margarethestrasse and its triumphal arches, winding among the fish markets and pie shops where the Artists' Quarter rubs up against the High City like someone's old unwanted animal. There were people who did not want to be seen coming and going between High City and Low. They could be heard ascending and descending this stairway all night, among them those curious twin princes of the city, the Barley brothers. (How are we to explain them? They weren't human, that's a fact. Had Ashlyme known his fate was mixed up with theirs, would he have been more careful in the plague zone?) At the bottom they would let themselves through a small iron gate. It was constructed so as to permit only one person through at a time, and its name commemorated in the Low City some atrocity long since forgotten in the High. Ashlyme had his own reasons for keeping off the Margarethestrasse. Perhaps his nightly visits to the plague zone embarrassed him.

He was inclined to hurry through the Artists' Quarter. Blue light leaked from the chromium doors of the brasseries and estaminets as he passed. In the Bistro Californium, beneath Kristodulos's notorious frescoes, some desperate celebration was in progress. Out came the high-pitched voice of a poet, auctioning the dull things he had found in the back of his brain. There was a peculiar laugh; a scatter of applause; silence. Further on, in the Plaza of Unrealised Time, beggars were lounging outside the rooms of the women, curious bandages accentuating rather than covering their deformities as they relaxed after the efforts of the day. One or two of them winked and smiled at him. Ashlyme clutched his easel and quickened his pace until they had fallen behind. In this way, quite soon, he entered the infected zone.

The plague is difficult to describe. It had begun some months before. It was not a plague in the ordinary sense of the word. It was a kind of thinness, a transparency. Within it people aged quickly, or succumbed to debilitating illnesses—phthisis, influenza, galloping consumption. The very buildings fell apart and began to look unkempt, ill-kept. Businesses failed. All projects dragged out indefinitely and in the end came to nothing.

If you went up into the foothills outside, claimed Emmet Buffo, and looked down into the city through a telescope, you could see the affected zone spreading like a thin fog. "The instrument reveals something quite new!" The Low City streets, and the people you could see in them (and he had an instrument which enabled them to be seen quite clearly) were a little faded or blurred, as if the light was bad or the lenses grimy. But if you turned the identical telescope on the pastel towers and great plazas of the High City, they stood out as bright and sharp as a bank of flowers in the sun. "It is not the light at fault after all, or the instrument!" Whether you believed him or not, few areas south of the Boulevard Aussman remained safe; and to the east the periphery of the infection now threatened the High City itself along the line of the Margarethestrasse, bulging a little to accommodate the warren of defeated avenues, small rentier apartments, and vegetable markets which lay beneath the hill at Alves. Buffo's observations might or might not be reliable. In any case they only told part of the story. The rest lay in the Low City, and to appreciate it you had to go there.

Ashlyme, who was there and didn't appreciate it, put down his easel and massaged his elbow. With the onset of the plague all the streets in this corner of the city had begun to seem the same, lined with identical dusty chestnut trees and broken metal railings. He had walked down the Rue Serpolet ten minutes ago, he discovered, without recognising it. The houses on either side of Audsley King's were empty. Piles of plaster and lath and hardened mortar lay everywhere, evidence of grandiose and complicated repairs which, like the schemes of the rentiers who had instituted them, would never be completed. Speculation of this kind was feverish in the plague zone: a story was told in the High City in which a whole street changed hands three times in one week, its occupants remaining lethargic and uninterested.

Audsley King had a confusing suite of rooms on an upper floor. The stairs smelt faintly of geraniums and dried orange flowers. Ashlyme stood uncertainly on the landing with a cat sniffing round his feet. "Hello?" he called. He never knew what to expect from her. Once she had sprung out on him from a closet, laughing helplessly. He could hear low voices coming from one of the rooms but he couldn't tell which. He set his easel down loudly on the bare boards. The cat ran off. "It's Ashlyme," he said. He went from room to room looking for her. They were full of paintings propped up against the neutral cream walls. He found himself staring down into a square garden like a cistern, full of darkness and trailing plants. "I'm here," he called—but was he? She made him feel like a ghost, swimming idly around waiting to be noticed. He opened what he thought was a cupboard but it turned out to be a short hall with a green velvet curtain at the end of it, which gave on to her studio.

She was sitting there on the floor with Fat Mam Etteilla, the fortune-teller and cardsharp. One lamp gave out a yellow light which was reflected from the upturned cards: threw the women themselves into prominence but failed to light the rest of the room, which was quite large. Consequently they seemed to be posed, in their strained and graceless attitudes, against a yellow emptiness in which hung only the faintest suggestions of objects— a pot of anemones, the corner of an easel, or a window frame. This lent a bewildering ambiguity to the scene he was later to paint from memory as "Visiting the women in their upper room." In the picture we see the Fat Mam sitting with her skirts pulled up to her thighs and her legs spread out, facing the cards (these are without symbols and, though arranged for divination, predict nothing). Crouched between her thighs and also facing the cards is a much thinner woman with hair cropped like an adolescent boy's and a body all elbows and knees. Ashlyme's treatment of these figures is extraordinary. Their arms are locked together and they seem to be rocking to and fro—in grief, perhaps, or in the excesses of some strange and joyless sexual spasm. A few brutal lines contain them; all else is void. There is some humanity in the way he has coloured the skirts of the Fat Mam. But Audsley King is looking defiantly out of the canvas, her eyes sly.

They remained in this position for thirty seconds or so after he had pulled back the curtain. The studio was quiet but for the hoarse breathing of the fortune-teller. Audsley King smiled sleepily at Ashlyme; then, when he said nothing, reached out deliberately and disarranged the cards. Suddenly she began coughing. She put her hand hurriedly over her mouth and turned her head away, writhing her thin shoulders in the attempt to expel something. "Oh, go away you old fool," she said indistinctly to the fortune-teller. "You can see it hasn't worked." When Ashlyme took her hand it was full of blood. He helped her to a chair and made her comfortable while the Fat Mam put away the cards, brought water, lit the other lamps.

"How tired I am," said Audsley King, smiling up at him, "of hearing my lungs creak all day like new boots." She wiped her mouth with the back of her hand. "It makes me so impatient."

The haemorrhage had left her disoriented but demanding, like a child waking up in the middle of a long journey. She forgot his name, or pretended to. But she would not let him leave: she would not hear of it. He would set up his easel like a proper painter and work on the portrait. Meanwhile she would entertain him with anecdotes, and the Fat Mam would read his fortune in the cards. They would make him tea or chocolate, whichever he preferred.

Ashlyme, though, had never seen her so pale. Should she not go to bed? She would not go to bed. She would have her portrait painted. In the face of such determination, what could he do but admire her harsh, mannish profile and white cheeks, and comply? After he had been drawing for about an hour he put down the black chalk and said carefully,

"If you would just come to the High City. Rack is a charlatan, but he would have you well cared for, if only to safeguard his investment."

"Ashlyme, you promised me."

"It will soon be too late. The quarantine police—"

"It's already too late, you stupid man." She moved her shoulders fretfully. "The plague is here"—indicating herself and then the room at large, with its morosely draped furniture and empty picture frames—"and in here. It hangs in the street down there like a fog. They will make no exceptions, we have already learned that." For a moment a terrible hunger lit up her eyes. But it turned slowly into indifference. "Besides," she said, "I would not go if they did. Why should I go? The High City is an elaborate catafalque. Art is dead up there, and Paulinus Rack is burying it. Nothing is safe from him—or from those old women who finance him—painting, theatre, poetry, music. I no longer wish to go there." Her voice rose. "I no longer wish them to buy my work. I belong here."

Ashlyme would have argued further. She said she would cough herself to death if he did. He went miserably back to his work.

A curious listlessness now came over the studio—the dull, companionable silence of the plague zone, which stretched time out like a thread of mucus. Mam Etteilla shuffled the cards. (What was she doing here, this fat patient woman, away from her grubby satin booth in the Plaza of Unrealised Time? What arrangement had been made between them?) She set the cards out; read them; gathered them up without a word. She did this sitting on the floor, while Audsley King looked on expressionlessly, for the present indifferent to her condition, as if she were dreaming it. The feverish energy of the haemorrhage seemed to have left her; she had sunk into her chair, eyes half closed. Only once did the symbols on the cards attract her attention. She leaned forward and said,

"As a young girl I lived on a farm. It was somewhere in the damp, endless ploughland near Soubridge. Every week my father killed and plucked three chickens. They hung on the back of a door until they were eaten. I hated to pass them, with their small mad heads hanging down, but it was the only way to get to the dairy." One day, opening the door, she had seen an eyelid fall suddenly closed over an eye like a glass bead. "Now I dream that it is dead women who hang behind the door: and I imagine one of them winks at me." Catching Ashlyme's astonished glance she laughed and ran her hand along the arm of her chair. "Perhaps it never happened. Or not to me. Was I born in Soubridge, or have I been here all the time, in the plague zone? Here we are prone to a fevered imagination." She watched her hand a moment longer, moving on the arm of the chair, then seemed to fall asleep.

Ashlyme, relieved, immediately packed his chalks and folded his easel.

"I must go while it is still dark," he told the Fat Mam. She put her finger to her lips. She held up one of the cards (he could not see what was on it, only the yellow reflection of the lamp), but did not answer otherwise. I will return, he pantomimed, tomorrow evening. As he passed her chair the dying woman whispered disconcertingly, "Yearning has its ghosts, Ashlyme. I painted such ghosts, as you well know. Not for pleasure! It was an obligation. But all they want in the High City is trivia." She clutched his hand, her eyes still closed. "I don't want to go back there, Ashlyme, and they wouldn't want *me* if I did: they would want some pale, neutered shadow of me. I belong to the plague zone now."

The fortune-teller let him out into the street. The cat rubbed his legs. As he made off in the direction of the High City he heard something heavy falling in an upper room, and a confused, ravaged voice called out, "Help me! Help me!"

He continued to visit the Rue Serpolet once or twice a week. He would have gone more frequently but he had other commissions. An inexplicable lethargy gripped him: while he still had access to the dying woman he found it hard to finalise his plans for her rescue. Still, the portrait was progressing. In exchange for his preliminary sketches and caricatures, which had delighted her with their cruelty, she gave him some small canvases of her own. He was embarrassed. He could not accept them; compared to her he was, he protested, only a talented journeyman. She coughed warningly. "I would be honoured to take them," he said. He came no closer to understanding her relationship with the fortune-teller, who was now seen only rarely at her yellow booth in the Artists' Quarter, and spent her time instead laundering bloody handkerchiefs, preparing meals which Audsley King allowed to cool uneaten, and endlessly turning over the cards.

The cards!

The pictures on them glowed like crude stained glass, like a window on some other world, some escape. That the fortune-teller saw them so was plain. But Audsley King looked on expressionlessly, as before. She was using them, he thought, for something else: some more complex self-deception.

All his visits were made via the Gabelline Stairs. There was a considerable volume of traffic there during the plague months. Ashlyme made an oddly proper little figure among the poets and poseurs, the princelings, politicians and popularists who might be found ascending or descending them at dawn and dusk. But his peculiar red coxcomb gave him away as one of them. One morning just before dawn he encountered two drunken youths on the stairs where they went round behind Agden Fincher's famous pie shop. They were a rough-looking pair, with scabby hands and hair of a dirty yellow colour chopped to stubble on their big round heads. They wore outlandish clothes, which were covered with food stains and worse.

When he first saw them they were sitting on each side of the stair, throwing a bruised melon back and forth between them. They were singing tunelessly,

> "We are the Barley brothers.
> Ousted out of Birmingham and Wolverhampton,
> Lords of the Left Hand Brain,
> The shadows of odd doings follows us through the night,"

but they soon stopped that.

"Give us yer blessing, vicar!" they called. They staggered up to Ashlyme and fell at his feet, bowing their heads. He had no idea who they had mistaken him for. Perhaps they would have done it to anybody. One of them gripped his ankles with both hands, stared up at him, and vomited copiously on his shoes.

"Oops!"

Ashlyme was disgusted. He ignored them and walked on, but they followed him, trying out of curiosity to prise his easel from under his arm.

"You should be ashamed of yourselves," he told them fiercely, avoiding their great sheepish blue eyes; they groaned and nodded. They accompanied him in his fashion about a hundred steps toward Mynned, winking conspiratorially when they thought he wasn't looking. Then they seemed to remember something else.

"Fincher's!" they shouted.

They began to pelt each other furiously with fruit and meat.

"Fincher, make us a pie!"

They tottered off, falling down and knocking on doors at random.

Ashlyme quickened his pace. The reek of squashed fruit followed him all the way up to the High City, where his shoes attracted some comment.

Who were these drunken brothers? It is not certain. They owned the city, or so they claimed. They had come upon it, they said, during the course of a mysterious journey. (Sometimes they claimed to have created it, in one day, from nothing but the dust which blows through the low hills of Monar. Millennia had passed since then, they explained.) At first they appeared in a quite different form: two figures materialising once or twice a decade in the sky above the Atteline Plaza of the city, huge and unrealistic like lobsters in their scarlet armour, staring down in an interested fashion. Mounted on vast white horses, they had moved through the air like a constellation, fading away over a period of hours.

Now they lived somewhere in the High City with a Mingulay dwarf. They were trying to become human.

This is a game to them, or seems to be, wrote Ashlyme in his diary: *a curious and violent one. Not a night passes without some drunken imbroglio. They hang about all day in the pissoir of some wineshop, carving their initials in the plaster on the walls, and after dark race along the Margarethestrasse stuffing themselves with noodles and pies which they vomit up all over the steps of the Mausoleum of Cecilia Metalla at midnight.*

Were they responsible for the city's present affliction? Ashlyme had always blamed them. *If they really are the lords of the city,* he wrote, *they are unreliable ones, with their "Chinese take-away" and their atrocious argot.*

While the Barley brothers wrestled with their new humanity, the plague was lapping at the foot of the High City like a lake. An air of inexplicable dereliction spread across the entire Artists' Quarter. The churchyards were full of rank marguerites, the streets plastered with torn political posters. Dull ironic laughter issued from the Bistro Californium and the Luitpold Café. In the mornings old women stared with expressions of intense intelligence into the windows of pie shops along the Via Gellia in the rain. While, up in the High City and all down the hill below Alves, dismayed servants were pulled across the roads by dogs like wolves on jewelled leashes. These were the secret agents of the Barley brothers. *Everyone knows them,* Ashlyme told his journal. *They pretend to be harassed and have receding hair, pretend to be exercising these gigantic dogs. On whom are they spying? To whom do they report? Some say the brothers, some their dwarf, who has recently granted himself the title of "The Grand Cairo." Now that the Barleys are among us nothing is reliable.*

Other police enforced the quarantine of the affected area. They were strangely apathetic and unpredictable. For a month nobody would see them; suddenly they would put on smart black uniforms and arrest anyone trying to leave the zone, taking them away to undergo "tests." People detained this way were released erratically and under no obvious system.

I cannot take them seriously, Ashlyme wrote. *Are they police at all?*

They were. The next time he went to see Audsley King they stopped him at the foot of the Gabelline Stairs before he could even enter the zone. It was a new policy.

They were polite, since he had obviously come down from the High City, but firm. They took his easel from him so that he would not have to be bothered carrying it. They led him back up the steps and into a part of the city which lay behind the fashionable town houses and squares of Mynned, where the woody parks and little lakes, the summery walks and shrubberies of the Haadenbosk merged imperceptibly with that old and slightly sinister quarter which had once been known as Montrouge. Here, they said, he would have a chance to explain himself.

He looked anxiously about. In Montrouge the great characteristic towers of the city, with their geometrical inscriptions and convoluted summits, had been allowed to fall into disrepair after some long-forgotten civil war. Their delicate pastels were faded or fire-blackened, their upper storeys inhabited by birds; and though the bustle and commerce of the Margarethestrasse was only a stone's throw away, no one lived here anymore. When Ashlyme reminded them of this, his custodians only smiled and inquired after the satchel in which he kept his colours and brushes: was it too heavy for him? Soon he began to notice signs of recent construction work, trenches dug across the avenues, walls half-finished among the ragwort and willow herb, low courses of brick lying abandoned amid the excavations. Here and there a raw new building, looking like a town hall or civic centre, had been completed. But no one seemed to be working now, and the majority of the sites lay unfinished, dwarfed and depressed by the ancient structures tottering above them.

Ashlyme had to go into one of the towers to be questioned. From the outside it looked like a charred log, but it was habitable enough. New wooden partitions, still smelling of carpenter's glue, had reduced its internal spaces. In the narrow corridors there was a good deal of coming and going. A gloomy, ill-dressed man took charge of Ashlyme and ushered him through a succession of small bare rooms, in each of which he had to explain to different officials why he had been trying to get into the plague zone. They watched him indifferently as he spoke, and his story began to sound feeble and rehearsed.

Did he not know, they asked him, that the zone was closed? "I'm afraid not. I had a commission there." Posters had been stuck up on every wall for weeks, they said: had he not noticed them? "Sorry, I'm a portrait painter, you see, and I had a commission in the Low City." He did not mention Audsley King by name. "I always go in the evening. Shall I have to pay a fine?" They received this bit of naïveté emptily. All at once he saw that, having got him there, they didn't really know what to do with him. Oddly enough this made him even more anxious. They searched his bag perfunctorily, and examined his easel. Suddenly they began asking him questions about the Barley brothers; had he seen them lately in the Low City? Were they with anyone? What was his opinion of them?

"Everyone sees the Barley brothers," he said puzzledly. He shrugged. "I have no opinion of them at all," he said.

Were they practising these obliquities to frighten him? Ashlyme couldn't tell. When he coughed and asked if he could go home, no one answered him. Each time they transferred him to another room it seemed to him that he was taken deeper into the building. Its inner architecture had a curious hollow quality which the dreary new passages and staircases could not quite fill up. If he closed his eyes he could easily imagine himself afloat on a ringing emptiness, in which strange old languages were being spoken. And he could get no idea of who lived here: empty bottles and rotting apple cores rolled about underfoot, yet every so often he glimpsed through some half-open door a richly furnished suite of rooms, or observed fleetingly a servant hurrying along the landing with a dog on a jewelled lead. Finally he found himself in an office equipped with a brass voice pipe, into which his answers were conveyed. When he mentioned his profession, this apparatus set up a tinny, excited squawking. He could not catch its drift, but his custodians listened carefully and then conferred among themselves.

"Ask him his name," they advised one another, and after it had been given for the hundredth time, and repeated twice into the voice pipe, told Ashlyme: "His nibs would like to see you."

The Grand Cairo was a very small man of indeterminate age, thick-necked, grown fattish in the middle. "I like to think of myself as a fighter," he was always saying, "and a veteran of strange wars." He did move with a light, aggressive tread, much like that of a professional brawler from the Plaza of Unrealised Time, and sometimes quite disconcerting: but he had too sly a glance even for a common soldier; and drinking bessen genever, a thick black-currant gin very popular in the Low City, had ruined his teeth, lent his eyes a watery, spiteful caste, and made his forearms flabby. Nevertheless he had a high opinion of himself. He was proud of his hands, in particular their big square fingers; showed off at every opportunity the knotted thigh muscles of his little legs; and kept his remaining hair well oiled down with a substance called "Altaean Balm," which one of his servants bought for him at a stall in the Tinmarket.

Ashlyme found him waiting impatiently by a window. He had on a jerkin with heavily padded shoulders, done in gorgeous dull red leathers, and he had arranged himself in the curious hollow-backed pose—hands clasped behind his back—he believed would accentuate the dignity of his chest.

"Come here, Master Ashlyme," he said, "and tell me what you see."

By now it was dark outside. The windowpanes reflected the lamplight and furnishings like a pond. If he strained his eyes, Ashlyme could make out rooftops, some of them quite close, which he took to be those of the less fashionable side of Mynned, near Cheniaguine and the Hospital Coictier. Off to the left, hardly visible at all and looking like the preparations for some long-drawn-out nocturnal war, there were the strange trenches and abandoned foundations which had been visited on the district of Montrouge.

"If it were not for *their* interference," said the Grand Cairo, giving the word a particularly virulent emphasis and at the same time glancing over his shoulder as if he suspected someone might be listening, "this part of the city would have been transformed by now. Transformed!"

"I know very little about town planning," said Ashlyme, careful not to enlist himself in some quarrel between the Barley brothers and their dwarf.

The Grand Cairo tilted his head alertly on one side. "Just so," he said in a flat voice.

Suddenly he threw open the window, letting in the warmish air from a small balcony, where some early roses, planted in curious old baptismal fonts and trained to the wrought-iron railing, gave off a heavy vulgar scent.

"Come out here and see if you can guess how I do this," he invited. He gave a low, plaintive whistle, *oulouloulou*, which echoed away across the housetops like the call of a summer owl. Nothing happened. He laughed and tried to catch Ashlyme's eye.

Ashlyme, embarrassed, avoided this by looking out over the balcony. "We're not at all high up here," he said, and found himself slightly disappointed.

"Look! Look!" said the dwarf gleefully. "See?"

The balcony was full of cats, purring and mewing, lifting themselves up momentarily on their hind legs to rub their heads against his knees. The dwarf picked them up one by one, chuckling and saying their names: "This is Nounoune . . . Sexer . . . here's Zero with his bent tail . . . and here's my fierce Planchette . . . Namenloss . . . Eamo . . . Elbow," and so on, an eerie list spoken thoughtfully into the scented night. More than a dozen lean little animals had come to him out of the darkness. It was in its way quite impressive.

"Not one of these cats is mine," he said. "They come from all over the city, because I speak their language." He looked intently at Ashlyme. "What do you think of that? Of that possibility?"

"What lovely animals!" exclaimed Ashlyme evasively. He tried to stroke one of them but it turned on him such a cold, knowing glance that he moved his hand away at once. "Very impressive," he said.

At this, the dwarf seemed to lose interest. He required Ashlyme to come and sit down next door in what he called his "side chamber," a monstrously tall room, original to the tower, in which he looked like a spoiled child wandering about a palace at night. Even the furniture was too large, huge wing chairs and armoires with pewter fitments. There were intricately carved circular tables, old, heavy brocade curtains, and cushions embroidered with metallic thread. The walls had been done out in black and dull gold, with panels of red in which were mounted paintings by Audsley King, Kristodulos, and Ashlyme himself. "I am a collector, you see!" said the dwarf proudly. There was even a sentimental watercolour signed by Paulinus Rack, almost invisible against its overblown setting. The room smelled of incense and stale cakes, the smell of great age. The cats loved it: they filed in one by one and filled up the air with a drugged purring, but Ashlyme felt dizzy, and—when he saw his own work hung in those ancient spaces—a little uneasy.

The Grand Cairo sighed. He stared thoughtfully at an Audsley King landscape, done in oil and pencil, which showed an old swing bridge being mended at Line Mass Quay.

"What do you see when you look at me?" he said at last. "I'll tell you. You see a man who has rubbed hard against the corners of the world; a man who has had to endure privations and attacks, and constantly fulfil the role of outcast." He laughed scornfully. "Outcast!" he repeated, and went on: "Perhaps you look admiringly round this room and tell yourself, 'A streak of the sinister is mixed in this man's composition with many good qualities.' You are right!" And he gave a satisfied nod, as if this dramatic assessment had indeed been Ashlyme's. "Nevertheless: I am a man of strong sensibilities—do not forget that—who might once himself have been artist, athlete, mathematician!"

He gave the Audsley King a last admiring glance.

"If only we could be as she is! Still, we can only do our best. I'll order some refreshments, then stand—or sit—wherever you want me to. Will you have the right profile or the left?"

And, when he saw Ashlyme staring at him helplessly:

"I want you to do my portrait, Master Ashlyme. You are the one to catch me as I am!"

He was an exasperating subject, full of nervous energy and forever dissatisfied with his pose. He began by standing up, one hand stretched out like a populist orator. Then he sat down and put his chin on his hand. But soon that was not good enough for him either and he had to stand up again to display the muscles of his upper back. At first he thought too much light was falling on him to emphasise the essential duality of his character, then too little to bring out the line of his jaw. He smiled until he remembered that this would reveal his teeth, then frowned. "I cannot decide how to present myself," he admitted, with a sigh. He was talking constantly.

"Do you know why I am so handsome?" he would ask. "It is because of the straightness of my legs."

It was clear that he hated and feared his masters. One of his favourite topics was the steel ring he wore on the thumb of his right hand. It was a wicked object, with a sharpened spur mounted on it instead of a stone. His employers, he hinted darkly, had attacked him before; the day would come when he would have to fear them again. Suddenly he leapt to his feet and cried, "Imagine the scene! I am attacked! I slash at the forehead of my opponent! Immediately *his own blood* fills his eyes, and I have him where I want him!"

He accompanied this explanation with a violent sweep of his arm, which knocked over a little pewter vase of anemones.

This was how they passed the rest of the night. Extra lamps were brought in at Ashlyme's request, and at the dwarf's a tray of aniseed cakes and a preparation he called "housemaid's coffee," made of heavily sugared milk heated slowly while buttered toast was crumbled into it and then browned until it formed a thick crust. This he drank with great gusto, rolling his eyes and rubbing his diaphragm, while Ashlyme watched him covertly from behind the easel, yawning and pretending to draw. As the room cooled, the cats crowded round him, or ran about picking up the pieces of food he threw them.

Towards dawn there was a dull crash outside the building. The dwarf got up and went hurriedly into the adjoining room. Ashlyme found him standing on tiptoe on the little balcony, looking down at the Barley brothers. "Give us a tune, dwarf!" they shouted. "Give us a story!" Drunken singing came up, mixed with laughter and dry retching sounds. They tried to scale the rotten wall below the balcony. They redoubled their efforts to get the door open, and a hollow booming echoed away across the deserted building sites of Montrouge. The dwarf greeted this without a word, staring out over the rooftops, his jaw muscles twitching spasmodically. Ashlyme, intimidated, kept quiet.

Doors opened and closed elsewhere in the tower. Servants ran about. Eventually it was quiet again, but the dwarf stood on at the railing. When he turned away at last it was apparent that he had expected to find himself alone. He regarded Ashlyme with blank hatred for a moment, then said effortfully, "Do you see how they plague me? I won't have them in my portrait. Hurry. It will spoil everything if they find you here!"

Ashlyme nodded and went to fetch his easel.

The dwarf stood in the doorway watching him pack chalks and paper. "What's your game in the plague zone, Ashlyme?" he asked quietly. His expression was detached. When he saw Ashlyme's confusion he laughed. "Go anywhere you like! My men will leave you alone unless I order it. But don't forget your new commission."

Outside, the night was totally silent; and as Ashlyme picked his way between the derelict towers and rubbish-filled trenches, it seemed to him that the whole city had shrunk to a black dot on the vast featureless map of the end of the world.

This week, he wrote in his journal, *the High City can think of nothing but the Barley brothers. What they wear, where they go, what they do when they get there, all this is suddenly of paramount interest. The most vexing question is: where do they live? Yesterday at Angina Desformes's I was told in confidence that the Barleys live in a workman's hut in the cisPontine Quarter; this morning I learned to the contrary that they stay on a houseboat down at Line Mass and spend their time throwing things in the canal. Tomorrow I expect to hear that they have bought all the houses on Uranium Street, where, in a grave beneath the pavement, they have secretly arranged a sepulchre for themselves and their dwarf . . .*

It was a silly preoccupation, he felt, and one which could only confirm the Barley brothers in their bad behaviour. *Now that I have visited the tower in Montrouge, and seen the curious roadworks beyond the Haadenbosk,* he added, *I do not encourage such speculation.* To the extent that he could, he pushed his encounter with the Grand Cairo out of his mind. He was not anxious to admit, perhaps, that the pattern of his life could be so easily disturbed. As an antidote he worked hard at his round of commissions in Mynned.

Most of these, he recorded, *are middle-aged women, bored, educated, "artistic." I am quite the fashion with them. At present, of course, they are besotted by the Barley brothers, and filled with delighted fear by the proximity of the plague zone: but they remain eager to talk about Paulinus Rack, who is still their darling despite the growing row over* Die Traumunden Knaben, *which many of them consider too risqué a production to be put on the High City. Like all of us, Rack relies for his funding on these women, and his feet are getting colder by the minute. If the play fails, Audsley King will fail with it.* The Dreaming Boys *are her last link with the High City, her last investment in life rather than death. The women of Mynned, who have not thought about this, are scandalised by what they imagine her plight to be. May they send her money? they enquire of me. "I'm afraid it is against quarantine regulations," I tell them. They find this quite unsatisfactory.*

He always lost two or three of these clients when the finished portrait turned out a little less "sympathetic" than they had expected.

"La Petroleuse" complains that I have made her look provincial. I have not. I have given her the face of a grocer, which is another matter entirely, and in no way a judgement. There are so many other things to think about that I cannot regret it. Audsley King seems lower in spirit every time I see her. Emmet Buffo is anxious about his part in our plan, and lately has sent me several letters on the subject of disguises. He does not want to enter the zone without one. He thinks we should both have one. He knows where there is an old man who can get them for us.

After some thought Ashlyme decided, *I don't care for this idea.*

Nevertheless, to Buffo he wrote, *I will meet you to see this man as soon as I can get away.*

It was a cool, bright morning in the High City.

"How lucky you are to live up here!" exclaimed Buffo. "The plague hardly seems to have changed anything."

"I don't know about that," said Ashlyme.

"Well, I love to come here," Buffo insisted, "especially if I've been working all night. Look: there's Livio Fognet on his way to lunch at the Charcuterie Vivien." He waved cheerfully. "Not a care in the world!"

Buffo was tall and thin, with a loose, uncoordinated gait which made him look as if the wrong legs had been attached to him at birth. His face was clumsy and long-jawed, he had limp fair hair and a pale complexion. Years of staring through homemade lenses had given his eyes a sore and vulnerable look. His researches, which had something to do with the moon, were regarded with derision in the High City. He did not suspect this. Lately, though, he had been short of funds. It had made him absentminded; when he thought no one was watching him his face became slack and empty of expression.

"You even have better weather in Mynned," he went on, stretching, expanding his chest, and blinking round in the weak sunlight. "It's always so windy where I live." He had bought himself a pound of plums and was eating them as he went along. "I don't know why I like plums so much," he said. "Did you see the sky just after dawn today? Extraordinary!"

They were on their way to the cisPontine Quarter, a Low City district as yet untouched by the plague. To get there they had to cross Mynned and go down to the canal. It had rained quite heavily an hour or so before. As they made their way between the deserted quays and warehouses, the eggshell colours of the sky were reflected in the puddles on the towpath. A coolish breeze blew across the lock basin at Line Mass, giving it something of the windy spaciousness of a much larger body of water and reminding Ashlyme without warning of the Midland Levels, where he had been born. He thought suddenly of bitter winter floods, eels coiled fat and unmoving in the mud, and herons standing motionless along the silvery margins of the willow carrs. He shivered.

Buffo was describing the man they were going to meet.

"He is a great collector of stuffed birds. He makes them, too. He sells, among other things, the clothes the beggars wear. He lives behind 'Our Lady of the Zincsmiths,' and thinks as I do that the future of the world lies with science." (Ashlyme, hearing only the word *future*, looked guiltily in the direction Buffo happened to be pointing. He saw only an old lock gate, behind which had collected a creamy brown curd full of floating rubbish.) "His researches take him into the old towers of the city, and their derelict upper floors. You will not believe this, Ashlyme, but there among the jackdaw colonies and sparrows' nests he claims to have found living birds whose every feather is made of metal!"

"He should avoid those old towers," said Ashlyme. "They can be dangerous."

"It's interesting work, though. Do you want the last plum or can I have it?"

Presently they came to the cisPontine Quarter and found the old man at home in his shop. The small dusty window of this place was full of birds and animals preserved in unrealistic poses, and above it hung a partly obliterated sign. It stood on one side of an old paved square, entry to which was gained through a narrow brick arch. Fish was being sold from a cart at one end of the square; at the other rose the dark bulk of "Our Lady of the Zincsmiths"; children ran excitedly about between the two, squabbling over a bit of pavement marked out for the hopping game "blind Michael." As Ashlyme stepped through the arch he heard a woman's voice, shrill, nasal, singing to a mandolin; and the air was full of the smells of cod and saffron.

The old man was watery-eyed and frail. He stood amid the clutter at the back of the shop, clutching one stiff hand with the other and smiling uncertainly. The skin was stretched over his long skull like yellow paper. He had on a faded dressing gown which had once been embroidered with fine silver wire. A few twists of this still poked out of its lapels and threadbare elbows. He took Emmet Buffo by the arm and drew him away from the door.

"Come and look!" he whispered excitedly.

In a garret near Alves he had found a metal feather. It was the first proof of his theories. Smiling and nodding, he held it out for Buffo to examine. He cast quick, anxious little glances over his shoulder at Ashlyme. Ashlyme looked away and pretended to be interested in the stuffed birds which stood on the shelves as if they were waiting to be revived. The gaze of their small bright eyes made him shift impatiently. The old man looked like a bird himself, with his thin bones and nodding skull. He is frightened I will steal his discovery, thought Ashlyme. Buffo should have come on his own.

"Hurry up, Buffo." But Buffo was engrossed.

Ashlyme picked his way between the bales of rags and secondhand clothes which made up the shop's stock-in-trade. He found what he thought was a nice piece of brocade, folded into a thick square and heavy with damp. When he shook it out and held it up to the light from the doorway, it turned out to be a decomposing tapestry, in which was depicted a city at night. Huge buildings and monuments stood under the moon. Along the wide avenues between them, men dressed in animal masks were stalking one another from shadow to shadow with mattocks and sharpened spades. He dropped it quickly and wiped his hands. He heard the old man say, "The clue I have been looking for."

"What do you think, Ashlyme?" asked Buffo.

"It looks like an ordinary feather to me," said Ashlyme, more bluntly than he had meant to. "Apart from the colour," he amended.

"These birds are real!" said the old man defensively. He came closer to Ashlyme, holding the feather tightly. "Would you like a cup of chamomile tea?"

"I think we'd better just look at what we came to see," said Ashlyme. Buffo and the old man bent down and began to root through a pile of disintegrating bandages. Ashlyme watched uneasily. "What are you looking in there for?" he said. "Who would wear things like that?" He walked off irritably.

"Don't you want to choose your own disguise?" Buffo called after him in a puzzled voice.

"No," said Ashlyme.

He stood outside in the square, watching the children run about in the chilly sunshine. Above him the partly obliterated sign creaked. If he studied it carefully he could make out the word SELLER. The fishmonger was pulling his barrow out under the archway; the woman was still singing. Ashlyme closed his eyes and tried to imagine how he would paint if he lived here rather than up in Mynned. He decided that one day he would find out. The smell of the food being cooked was making him hungry. Suddenly he realised how rude he had been to Buffo and the old man. He went back inside and found them drinking chamomile tea. "Can I have a look at that feather?" he asked.

The old man held it out. "You see?" he said. "Look at the craftsmanship. These birds were built long ago, by whom and for what purpose is as yet unclear." He leant forward. "I believe," he said, in a whisper so quiet that it forced Ashlyme to lean forward, too, "that one day they will speak to me."

"It's interesting work," said Ashlyme.

Later, as they were preparing to leave, the old man touched his sleeve. "This will surprise you," he said. "I don't know how old I am." Suddenly his eyes filled up with tears. He rubbed them unembarrassedly with the back of his hand. "Can you understand what I mean?" He gazed at Ashlyme for a moment or two, with a look in which could be read only a vague anxiety, then turned away.

"Goodbye," said Ashlyme. And outside, to Buffo: "Do you know what he was talking about?"

"It means nothing to me," admitted Buffo, hefting the brown paper parcel which contained their disguises. "I can't wait to get these home and try them on." But on the way back to Mynned through Line Mass he stopped suddenly. "Look," he said. "That's the fishmonger following us. I saw him in the High City this morning, and he had some nice hake. I think I'll cook a bit of that for tea." He was unlucky. For some reason, as soon as he saw Buffo approaching, the fishmonger went into a side alley and made off, his barrow clattering on the cobbles.

THE SECOND CARD

THE LORDS OF
ILLUSIONARY SUCCESS

This card implies a transaction which leaves you unsatisfied. Be prepared for unexpected events. If it comes next to No. 14 you will lose a favourite overcoat.

"Viriconium is all the cities there have ever been."

AUDSLEY KING, Reminiscences

Ashlyme seldom took his own meals at home. Before the plague he had eaten with his friends at the Luitpold Café in the Artists' Quarter. Now, more often than not, he could be found at the Vivien, or one of the other charcuteries on the Margarethestrasse, eating a chop.

One night he had supper there with Mme. Chevigne, who wanted him to design the programme for a production called *The Little Humpbacked Horse*. This had been devised as a vehicle for Vera Ghillera, the city's newest principal dancer, illegitimate daughter of a laundress, with a lyrical *port de bras*, and would run as a rival to *Die Traumunden Knaben* if that play was ever produced. Ashlyme was not enthusiastic but allowed himself to be persuaded. (Later he was to make two or three sketches for this commission; but they were of young dancers caught unawares during exercises often far from graceful, and they were never used.) The sharp-nosed little Chevigne, who in her time had danced as well if not better than Ghillera, amused him with her scandals until late. When he got home a bluish moon was shining through the roof lights of the studio, giving an odd look of frozen motion to his easel and lay figure, as if they had been moving about just before he came in.

A note had been pushed in through his front door and lay on the mat. *Come at once*, it said, in a self-assertive script. It was unsigned, but with it the Grand Cairo had sent a massive silver signet ring which he treated nightly in powdered sulphur to maintain its tarnish. Ashlyme sighed, but he set out immediately for Montrouge.

The night was quiet and dry. A wind had got up and was scattering dust over the surface of the puddles. In Montrouge the Barley brothers had fallen out over a white geranium in a pot, which they had stolen in some midnight adventure along the Via Gellia. They were rolling about in the moonlight among the half-finished brick courses of the dwarf's municipal estate, kicking over stacks of earthenware pipes and biting one another when they got the chance. Ashlyme found himself watching them silently from the shadows on the other side of the road. He could not have said why. Presently Gog Barley got on top of his brother and gave him a punch in the chest.

"You bit of snot," he said. "Give us me rose back."

He twisted Matey's arm until he got the geranium. It was more foliage than flower. He jumped up and made off with it, but Matey gave him the "dead leg" and he fell into a trench. They scuffled stealthily in there for a minute or two, then bolted out of it with enraged howls. Suddenly they spotted Ashlyme.

"Oh, gor," said Matey. "It's the vicar."

He dropped the flower and stood there breathing heavily, wincing and squinting and shading his eyes as if Ashlyme had unexpectedly held up a bright light. He nudged his brother in the ribs and they both ran off shouting in the direction of the Haadenbosk. After a moment the night was quiet and empty again. The geranium pot rolled slowly across the road until it came to rest at Ashlyme's feet. He bent down to pick it up and then thought better of it. One ghostly white floret remained among the leaves of the geranium, luminous in the moonlight; a musty smell came up from it and surrounded him.

He got into the tower by showing the dwarf's ring.

Pride of place in the *salle* had been given over to a delicate little drawing by Audsley King. It was of boats, done in charcoal and white chalk on grey paper, and Ashlyme had not seen it on his last visit there.

He found the dwarf pacing impatiently to and fro, dressed with a kind of ignominious majesty in a studded black jerkin. A pair of spectacles gave him a judiciary air. His hair gleamed with Altaean Balm. Despite his new acquisition he was in a dangerous temper, and he greeted Ashlyme brusquely. "Begin drawing," he said, taking up immediately a stiff seated pose which threw into prominence the tendons of his ageing neck. Confused by the lateness of the hour and the vertiginous spaces of the old building, Ashlyme made some attempt to set up his easel. The dwarf watched disapprovingly, fidgeting about in his chair as if the pose had already become intolerable to hold, and said as soon as Ashlyme had settled down,

"What fresh secrets have you found it necessary to hide from me today, Master Backstabber?"

He gave Ashlyme no time to answer this accusation. "Say nothing for the moment," he warned, with an irritable gesture. "Don't bother to try and justify yourself to me." Suddenly he gave a sly laugh. He jumped out of his chair and took off his spectacles. "I got these when I lived in the North," he said. "But I can see very well without them. What do you think of this new drawing of mine?"

Ashlyme, unconvinced by this change of mood, swallowed. "I should not like you to think that I had deceived you deliberately—" he began. He saw the dwarf watching him with the patient, ironic eyes of the secret policeman, waiting for an answer. He could not organise his thoughts. "It is very good," he said at last.

"And you recognise the artist, of course?"

Ashlyme nodded.

"Audsley King," he whispered.

The Grand Cairo nodded. "Just so." He sat down again. "Go on with your work," he advised. "I think that would be best for you now." But he was soon back on his feet, rearranging a display of sol d'or. He picked up one of his cats and stroked its greyish fur. Every time he said its name the animal purred loudly and poked its head into his armpit. "You are not a man for secrets, Ashlyme," he said contemplatively as he opened the door and watched the cat run out into the corridor with its tail in the air. "Never imagine you are." He listened for a moment at the door. "I am your man for secrets," he mused. "They're safe with me." He went up to the Audsley King sketch, regarded it with his hands behind his back, then tapped its frame. "Why didn't you tell me about your little scheme to smuggle this woman out of the quarantine zone?"

"I—" said Ashlyme. He was confused and frightened. "She is the great painter of our age. We—"

The dwarf studied him silently for a moment, head on one side. " 'She is the great painter of our age'!" he mimicked suddenly. "Do you know, Ashlyme, I can't quite make you out. That's not a very responsible attitude in the face of our present plight, is it?" He took out a leather notebook. "What about this other man, this 'Emmley Buffold', who is so fond of fish? He gave my man quite a fright, chasing him like that! What does he hope to gain from it?" He laughed at Ashlyme's expression. "Oh, make no mistake. It's all written here. I know who's in it with you." He shut the book decisively.

"I am the man for secrets," he said. "You must always bring them to me. It is the only safe course."

Ashlyme looked at him in dismay. "What will you do with us?" he said.

The Grand Cairo put his notebook away.

"Why, I'll join you!" he answered, and winked.

Nothing would persuade him otherwise. He would listen to none of Ashlyme's arguments. He had the romantic temper, he said. He needed action! Besides: Audsley King was the greatest painter of their age. Only a criminal oversight could have placed her in such jeopardy. She was a resource. He made Ashlyme sit down, poured out two glasses of bessen genever, and insisted they drink to their adventure. "Confidentially," he admitted, "I am bored with all this." His gesture took in the whole of Montrouge. "This morning I woke up wishing I was back in the North again." He emptied his glass. "You can't imagine how appalling it is up there," he said. "Constant intrigue and backstabbing, and black mud in everything you eat. The wind never drops. Ruined cities full of cripples, and insects as big as a horse!"

He shuddered. "Even the rain was black. But I'll tell you something, Ashlyme: at least we were alive then! Our intrigues had bowels. A kingdom was at stake, even if it was a kingdom of mud!"

"But what about your own police?" appealed Ashlyme, who had understood little of this reminiscence, with its implications of habitual conspiracy in a country which could barely support life. "What if they catch you with us?" This was his last argument. The wine had made him feel sick but slightly less frightened. He was sure that the dwarf would never forgive him his deception; he suspected that his position was only slightly less insecure than it had been when he first entered the room. "Won't that put you in wrong with your employers?"

The Grand Cairo laughed scornfully.

"Never mention those brothers to me!" he exclaimed. He shook his head, staring into space. "I argued all along against us coming down here, even in defeat—" He rubbed his hands over his eyes. "Look at them now!"

He refilled Ashlyme's glass, emptied his own.

"Oh, it was hand-to-mouth in those days, it was catch-as-catch-can. You should have seen some of the lads I had with me then; they'd kill a cow with their bare hands! It's all very well for you to be frightened of those imbeciles downstairs: after all, they're here to frighten civilians. But not one of them would have lasted a week up there. Not one of them." He examined this idea with morose satisfaction. "Don't you worry about them. This is a scheme that can't go wrong!" He leaned forward enthusiastically and took Ashlyme's hands. "Imagine the scene—

"Three muffled figures, heavily armed and disguised, support a fourth. (She is unable to walk unaided. Her face is pitiable, pinched, almond white, framed in a great collar of wolf's fur. Under her skin are fine mauve veins like those the clematis sometimes displays beneath its flower. Her eyes are as blue as phosphorus in the gloom.) Like ghosts they cross the end of an alley, passing in silence in the deep night, and make their way stealthily from gravestone to gravestone across Allman's Heath, down to the waters of the Pleasure Canal. Will the boatman be waiting, as he promised? Or has he been enlisted by their enemies? They are almost home now. But wait! Out of the mist at the water's edge comes the pursuit! Now they must fight!"

A dreamy, excited expression had settled on the dwarf's face. He got up and mimicked the weariness of the conspirators, taking the part of each in turn, then the curious lurching gait of the sick woman. He let his eyelids fall half-closed and said in a kind of shrieking falsetto, "I can go no further." He collapsed, and caught himself before he fell to the ground. He pulled forth an imaginary knife and looked warily about. This pantomime took him all round the room and up to a huge wardrobe of black pear wood, its mouldings disfigured where he had struck matches on them. As he reached this he turned towards Ashlyme the sexless, ageless glance of the obsessed, full of incomprehensible irony; and at the word *fight*, he opened it with a quick, powerful tug.

It was full of weapons of all kinds: clubs, truncheons, and loaded wooden coshes; miséricordes and stilettos, with and without sheaths; knuckle-dusters studded and spiked, trick knives whose blades shot out on springs, and strangling cords made of silk or cheese wire, all hanging in rows from pegs. Most of this stuff seemed rusty and ill-kept, although at one time it had been in almost daily use. In a wooden rack were three bottles made of deep blue glass, which had once contained acids. Some rotten-smelling objects in the bottom of the cupboard turned out to be potatoes and cakes of scented soap into which had been embedded bits of broken glass; among them were other homemade devices of less obvious purpose. The dwarf took them out one by one and laid them on the floor, knives in one place, garrotes in another. He beckoned Ashlyme closer.

"Come on," he said. "Have anything you want. We must go prepared."

Ashlyme stared at him dry-mouthed. The dwarf made encouraging sounds. Eventually Ashlyme picked up the smallest knife he could find. It had a curious flaw halfway up the blade. The dwarf started a little when he saw Ashlyme had picked that particular one; but he soon recovered himself and told several stories about it. "I got that knife on Fenlen Island in the North," he said. "There was blood on that knife from the moment I had it." But this was said with such unconvincing bravado that Ashlyme was sure he had simply stolen it from the Barley brothers years ago, and was glad to get rid of it now in case they found out.

Ashlyme was to grow used to this weapon, sharpening his pencils with it, and sometimes fingering the flaw in its blade, which was quite unlike rust and had a satisfying texture to the ball of the thumb: but that night he took it home in horror, wondering what would become of him.

Emmet Buffo lived at the top of an old house at Alves, halfway up the famous hill (the summit of which had interfered with many of his most radical and innovatory observations). Alves was a curious place. It was a windy salient or polyp of the High City flung out into the Low, partaking of the character of both. While its streets were wider than those of the Artists' Quarter, they were no less shabby. Strange old towers rose from a wooded slope clasped in a curved arm of the derelict Pleasure Canal. About their feet clustered the peeling villas of a vanished middle class, all plaster mouldings, split steps, tottering porticos, and drains smelling of cats. Ashlyme trudged up the hill. A bell clanged high up in a house; a face moved at a window. The wind whirled dust and dead leaves round him.

While he waited for the astronomer to open his door, he thought of Audsley King's most popular watercolour, "On the bridge at New Man's Staithe."

In this view of Alves a honey-coloured light seems to rise from the glassy waters of the abandoned canal and enfold the hill behind, giving its eccentric architecture a mysterious familiarity, like buildings seen in a dream. The towers, their pastel colours thickened romantically, glow like stained glass.

Ashlyme smiled. A print of this picture hung in every salon in the High City. The question most frequently asked about it was: "This unmoving figure at the parapet of the bridge, is it male or female?" Audsley King would answer: "I did not intend you to know." She had painted it during a love affair sixteen years before. She now disowned its dreamy lights and sentimentality. "It is untruthful," she complained. "Yet they love it so!"

Emmet Buffo put his head round the door and blinked.

"Come in, come in!" he said.

He took Ashlyme's hand as if he had never seen him before, and, under the impression that he had been sent from some committee to explore the funding of a new telescope, led him up the stairs. He had, he explained, almost given up hope of ever getting money for his experiments. He did not blame the High City for this. "Every six months I go to the patents office and sit for an hour, perhaps two, on the benches with all the others. I understand the needs of the bureaucracy. I understand its inertia. What can I do but maintain a philosophical attitude?"

Up the stairs went Ashlyme behind him, listening to this monologue float down, unable to find any opportunity to speak and in any case hardly knowing what to say. There were pockets of dust in the corners of the landings.

"Still," said Buffo. "They've sent you. That's something!"

He laughed.

He lived in a kind of penthouse, much of which he had built himself. It was cold there even in summer. In one room he cooked his food and slept; it was tidy, but a stale smell hung in the air about the low iron bed and the homemade washstand. He ground his lenses in another smaller room. Little pieces of coloured glass like the petals of anemones littered a table, some set in complex frames made of whitish metal. The astronomical charts had peeled that morning from the wall and lay in folds at its foot. (Mouldy patterns in the plaster suggested that another universe had been hidden behind them.) "It's the damp," apologised Buffo. He showed Ashlyme around like a tourist in the Margarethestrasse. "This is my 'exterior brain,'" he said. "I call it that. I can refer to it at any time. It's more than just a library." He indicated an ordinary set of shelves on which were arranged reference books and instruments, models of telescopes and bits of paper with technical drawings on them.

The adjoining room, where he spent most of his time, was a flimsy structure like a greenhouse, with a complicated system of ratchets and rods that enabled him to lift its roof and poke out his telescopes. It was composed of odd panes of glass, some coloured, some milky; they were cracked, and of different sizes.

"This is the observatory itself. From here I can see twenty miles in any direction."

Ashlyme looked out. A quarter of the sky was obscured by the bulk of Alves, with the cracked, threatening copper dome of the old palace askew on it like a crown. From the other side he could look down across the Pleasure Canal at the famous graves on Allman's Heath. "It was built to my own design, ten years ago," said Buffo. It was full of contraptions. As Ashlyme moved from one to the other, pretending not to have seen them before, Buffo sat on a stool. But he couldn't sit still. He hopped to his feet to explain, "These are the plans for the new device," and sat down again. He was like an exhibit himself in the odd light.

One of the contraptions was a maze of copper tubing into which Buffo had let two or three eyepieces, apparently at random. Ashlyme bent to look through one of them. All he saw was a sad reticulated greyness, and, suspended indistinctly against it in the distance, something like a chrysalis or cocoon, spinning at the end of its thread. Buffo smiled shyly. "Success is slow to come with that one," he admitted. "You'll agree it has vast potential, though?" He went on to explain his experimental method, but soon saw that Ashlyme didn't understand. He left the observatory for a moment and came back with a tray. "Would you like some wine? Some of these pilchards?" Thankfully, Ashlyme sat down and took some. They ate in silence. When he had finished, Ashlyme rubbed his hand over his face.

"Buffo," he said. "You know it's me, not some clerk from the patents office. It's Ashlyme. I've seen all this a hundred times before."

"Pardon?" Buffo stared at him, his expression changing slowly. "I suppose you have," he said thoughtfully. "I suppose you have." He sighed. "I expect I knew all along really. I'm sorry, old chap."

Ashlyme explained how he had become entangled with the Grand Cairo.

"Now this dwarf wants to come with us to the Rue Serpolet," he told Buffo. "He won't take no for an answer. What are we going to do?"

Buffo looked bleakly round the observatory.

"You wake from one nightmare into the next," he said in a quiet voice. He inspected the palm of his hand as if it was his whole life. "I'm sorry, this fish is awful. Leave it if you like." Suddenly he laughed and pushed his plate on the floor with a clatter. "We must lay new plans then!" he exclaimed. He touched Ashlyme's arm. "Come on, Ashlyme, it cheers me up just to see you!"

He had an idea already, he continued. "Let him push the handcart if he is so keen to come! We need someone to do that, after all; and it's our plan, not his."

Ashlyme wiped the condensation off a pane of glass and looked out. The Artists' Quarter was barely three hundred yards away across the Pleasure Canal and Allman's Heath. He stared at the dark loop of water, the jumble of roofs to the west, the leaning gravestones that filled the heath between. (Had Audsley King set her easel up among them to paint "On the bridge at New Man's Staithe," anemones and sol d'or burning at her feet? Now the graveyard was full of briars and plaster dust blown in from the senseless renovations on Endingall Street and de Monfreid Square.) The canal was quite shallow. You could see the bottom on a sunny day. They had intended to wade it after the rescue, and bring Audsley King directly to Alves. His long experience of conspiracies had enabled the dwarf to guess this immediately.

"I don't think he would be content with that, Buffo. Even if we could persuade him, he is untrustworthy. He is subject to moods, fits of enthusiasm, distempers, sudden hatreds. He is in love with plots. Even his masters, the Barley brothers, he believes, are plotting against him."

"Never mind," said Buffo. "We'll think of something."

He went out for a minute and came back with what looked like a bundle of rags, wrapped around something more solid.

"Don't look for a moment," he said.

Ashlyme was forced to smile. He closed his eyes; ran his tongue round the inside of his mouth to dislodge a piece of pilchard. When he opened his eyes again he saw Buffo standing there wearing a kind of varnished rubber mask. It covered his head completely, and resembled the stripped and polished skull of a horse, two pomegranates set in the empty sockets to simulate eyes. It was ludicrous. Buffo had taken off his clothes and wound strips of green swaddling round his body. His arms were like sticks, his rib cage huge. Two great branched feathery horns came up out of the forehead of the mask. He did not look human.

"They're rather well done, aren't they?" he said, his voice muffled by the rubber which was forced down over his nose. "Don't you want to look at yours?" He had another mask in his outstretched hand.

Ashlyme backed away. "No," he said. "I don't want to see it. Why must we dress like that?"

"I thought the old man had done rather well. We will look just like beggars. No one will recognise us!" He pounced on Ashlyme and took him by the shoulders. He whirled him round and round in a clumsy dance. "What an idea!" he crowed. "What a success!"

Ashlyme was helpless. The skull of the horse was thrust into his face. It was hard to believe that Buffo's familiar features were somewhere beneath it. He was as frightened by the strength of the astronomer's thin arms as he was by the sound of breath sobbing in and out of the mask. Then he began to laugh despite himself.

"Well done, Buffo!"

Buffo, encouraged, sang a lively but mawkish popular song. They finished the bottle of wine and even the pilchards. The sun set. Crowing and singing, they pranced about the observatory, bumping into things and falling down, until they were exhausted.

Later, with the proper fall of night, the observatory became cold and uninhabitable; but the two men sat on, talking at first, then contemplating their plan in a companionable silence. They discussed the future. Buffo would move out of Alves and into the High City, where he believed his work would be better appreciated; Ashlyme would share his studio with Audsley King and they would do great work together. The flimsy structure of the greenhouse creaked around them as the wind rose. Damp air blew through the cracked panes, giving Ashlyme the impression of motion, of racing travel through some ramshackle but benign dimension. Where would they end up? He smiled over at Buffo. The astronomer's head had sunk on to his chest; he had fallen asleep with his mouth open and begun to snore. Turned down, the lamps emitted a queer crepuscular light. Ashlyme got his cloak and folded it about him. It was too late to go home. Besides, he felt somehow responsible for the astronomer, who looked even more honest asleep than he did awake. He wandered about for a while, squinting into the eyepieces of the telescopes. Then he sat down and dozed. Once or twice he woke up suddenly, thinking about the pile of clothes and masks on the floor.

For a week he felt debauched and bilious, uninclined to commit himself. Was the dwarf still having him watched? Was Emmet Buffo a broken reed?

The plague, he wrote in his diary, *permeates all our decisions, like a fog.* He put the rescue attempt off again and again, and for the most part stayed in his studio, watching morosely as the unseasonable rain swept across the Low City and lashed the fronts of the houses at Mynned. *This summer is a travesty,* he wrote, as if the trivial might allow him to forget his situation. And, on finding water among his belongings in the attic, *I am appalled, but it is my own fault. I have not repaired the roof.* Neither had he repaired his opinion of the High City art cliques. *Is anything worthwhile being done? In short, no: up here it is all dinner arrangements and affaires. Rack has had the set designs for* The Dreaming Boys *for two months now, yet there have been no auditions, no readings. He wishes (he says) "to consult the artist"; but he never goes to the Low City.*

He could not work on the portrait of Audsley King. Instead he began framing the pictures she had given him. He discovered with delight the early landscape "A fire this Wednesday at Lowth," and what appeared to be an incomplete gouache of the notorious "Self-portrait half clothed," in which the artist is seen peering slyly into a mirror, her long hands touching her own private parts. He hung the paintings in different places to find the best light and stood in front of them for long periods, thrilled by the stacked planes of the landscapes, the disquieting eros of her inner world.

At last an oblique sunshine broke through the clouds above the city and filled it with a shifting, fitful brightness. There was a rush to the banks of the Pleasure Canal. The High City emptied itself onto Lime Walk and the Terrace of the Fallen Leaves, and there, in audacious proximity to the plague zone, took the sun.

Little iron tables were set up and the women drank tea out of porcelain "lucid as a baby's ear"; while those poets who had escaped exile in the Californium and the Luitpold Café recited in musical voices. Everyone had a theory about the plague. Everyone had it from a reliable source. Most agreed it would never reach the High City. Imagine the scene! The women had on their muslin dresses. The men wore swords and meal-coloured cloaks copied carefully from those fashionable among the Low City mo-hocks two or three centuries before. A wet silvery light fell delicately on the white bridges, limning the afternoon curve of the canal and perfectly disguising its shabbiness. Everyone enjoyed themselves thoroughly; while down below, among the ragwort on the towpath, writhed the thousand-and-one black and yellow caterpillars of the cinnabar moth, some fat and industrious, rearing up their blunt, ugly heads, others thin and scruffy and torpid. The Barley brothers ate them and were sick.

Ashlyme, who had been out buying mastic, wandered onto the Terrace of the Fallen Leaves and could not find his way off again. The crowds con-fused him. He ran into Paulinus Rack, who was sitting at a table with Livio Fognet, the lithographer, and their patron the Marchioness "L." A shy young novelist stood behind the Marchioness's chair, admiring the famous curve of her upper arm. They were all delighted to see Ashlyme. What a stranger he was!

"Has the plague lifted, then?" he said, staring puzzledly about him. It was the only reason he could think of for a celebration.

They were amused. Had he never heard of sunshine? He accepted a cup of tea the Marchioness had poured especially for him, but declined to watch the antics of the Barley brothers down on the canal bank. He could not think of them, he explained, as a sideshow.

"Aren't you being a little naive, old chap?" said Livio Fognet. He winked at the Marchioness's novelist.

"After all," chided the Marchioness, "we must think of them as something!" She laughed shrilly and then seemed to lose her confidence. "Mustn't we?"

A bemused silence followed. After a minute her novelist said, "I don't think Rack himself could have put it better." He blushed. He was saved by a general movement toward the railings. A murmur of laughter went up and down the terrace. "Oh, do look, Paulinus!" cried the Marchioness. "One of them has fallen in, right up to the knees!"

Rack gave her a mechanical glance and a twist of his fat lips. He shrugged. "My dear Marchioness," he said, and moved his chair closer to Ashlyme's. He could create a small eddy of intimacy in any crowd. We, he was able to suggest, with a touch of one plump hand, have nothing in common with these people. Why are we here at all? Only because they need us. It was a flattering device, and he owed to it much of his social and financial success. "Fognet's a buffoon, I'm afraid," he murmured, leaning forward a little. "And the Marchioness a parasite. I wish we could have met under better circumstances."

"But I love the Marchioness," said Ashlyme loudly. "Don't you?"

Rack looked at him uncertainly. "You surprise me." He laughed. He raised his voice. "By the way," he said, "how *is* Audsley King?"

"Oh, yes," said the Marchioness plaintively. "We are all appalled by her situation."

The Barley brothers, egged on by the laughter from above, linked arms and jumped into the canal together, showering the tables along the terrace with bright drops of spray. They had found a spot where the water was deeper. It surged and bubbled; then their great red faces appeared, puffing and blowing, above its greenish surface. "Gor!" they said. "It i'n' 'alf cold!" They coughed and spat, they shook their heads about and stuck their fingers in their ears to get the water out. The little screams of the women encouraged them to thrash about (it could hardly be called swimming); to blow bubbles; and to push one another under. Presently they dragged themselves out, water gushing out of their trouser legs and running down the towpath. They grinned stupidly upward, too exhausted now to go back in for their shoes.

Ashlyme was enraged by this display.

"Audsley King is coughing her left lung up, Marchioness," he said bitterly. "She is dying, if you want to know. What will you do about that?" He laughed. "I do not see you abroad much in the plague zone!"

The Marchioness blinked into her teacup. It seemed for a moment she would not answer. Finally she said: "You judge people by unrealistic standards, Master Ashlyme. That is why your portraits are so cruel." She looked thoughtfully at the tea leaves, then got to her feet and took the arm of her novelist. "Though I daresay we are as stupid as you make us appear." She adjusted her dove-grey gloves. "I hope you'll tell Audsley King that we are still her friends," she said. And she went away between the surrounding tables, exchanging a word here and there with people that she knew. Once or twice the young novelist looked angrily back at Ashlyme, but she touched his shoulder in a placatory way and soon they were lost to view.

Paulinus Rack bit his lip. "Damn!" he said. "I shall have to pay for that later." He stared across the canal. "You'll find you've carried this attitude too far one day, Ashlyme."

"What are you going to do when the plague reaches the High City, Rack?" asked Ashlyme with some contempt.

Rack ignored him. "Your work may be less fashionable in future. If I were you I would be prepared for that. Never insult the paying customers." He made a dismissive gesture. "You cannot save Audsley King anyway," he said.

Ashlyme was furious. He grabbed at Rack's arm. Rack looked frightened and pulled it away. Ashlyme caught him by the fingers instead. He twisted them. "What do you know?" he jeered. "I'll have her out of there within the week." Rack only curled his lip. He made no attempt to free his fingers, so Ashlyme, horrified to have committed himself to the rescue attempt in public, twisted them harder. "What do you say to that?" He wanted to see Rack wince, or hear him apologise, but nothing like that happened. They sat there for some time, looking at one another defiantly. Rack must have been in considerable pain. Livio Fognet, who did not seem to understand the situation, winked and grinned impartially at them. It came on to rain. The High City opened its umbrella and took itself off to Mynned, while the Barley brothers put their arms over their heads to protect themselves from the rain and, groaning, watched their shoes float away towards Alves. Ashlyme let Rack's fingers go. "Within the week," he repeated.

"I'll just go and have a word with Angina Desformes," said Livio Fognet.

"There is a certain time of the afternoon," said Audsley King, "when everything seems repellent to me."

The city was unseasonably dank again, the air chilly and lifeless. Tarot cards were scattered across the floor of the studio as if someone had flung them there in a fit of rage. Audsley King lay in a nest of brocade pillows on the faded sofa, her thin body propped up on one elbow. On the easel in front of her she had a grotesque little charcoal sketch, in which a conductor, beating time with extravagant sweeps of his baton, cut off the heads of the poppies which made up his orchestra. It was full of overt violence, quite unlike her usual work. It was unfinished, and she regarded it with flushed features and angry, frustrated gestures. In her preoccupation she had let the studio fire burn down, but she did not seem to feel the cold. This wasn't a good sign.

Ashlyme stood awkwardly in the middle of the room. He felt shy, guilty, inadequate: not so much in the knowledge of the betrayal he had come to effect, as in his inability thereby to make any real change in her circumstances. He had never before been so aware of the bareness of the grey floorboards, the impermanent air of the canvases piled in the corners, the age and condition of the furniture. He opened his mouth to say, "In the High City they would take more care of you," but thought better of it. Instead he studied the two new paintings that hung unframed on the wall. Both were of Fat Mam Etteilla, and showed her crouching on the floor shuffling the cards. Under one of them the artist had written in a slanting hand, *the door into the open!* They were hurried and careless, like the cartoon on the easel, as if she had lost faith in her technique—or her patience with the very medium.

"You shouldn't work so hard," he said.

She was amused.

"Work? This is nothing." She dabbed at the sketch, looked disgustedly at the resulting line, and smeared it with her long thumb. "When I lived in the farmlands," she said, "I would paint from six in the morning until it grew dark."

She laughed.

" 'Six in the morning, and chrome yellow is back in nature!' Do you know that quotation? My eyes never grew tired. The ploughed fields stretched away like a dark dream, covered in mist. Rooks creaked above it, circling the elms. My husband—"

She stopped. Her mouth curved in regret, and then in self-contempt.

"What a masterpiece this is!"

She struck the canvas so hard that her charcoal broke. The easel tottered, folded itself up, and fell over with a clatter.

"That field of poppies is the field we have sown!" she cried, looking vaguely into the air in front of her. "It is like an orchestra in which the players take no notice of their conductor. Am I raving?"

Suddenly she collapsed among the pillows and blood poured out of her mouth. It ran along her arm and began to soak into the brocade. She stared helplessly down at herself.

"My husband was an artist too. He was far better than I am. Shall I show you?" She tried to get up, slumped back, dabbed at herself with a handkerchief. "Nothing of his is left, of course." Her eyes focused on Ashlyme. Tears ran out of them. "No, I am quite all right, thank you."

Ashlyme was dismayed. She had never been married. (Before moving to the city she had lived, as far as he knew, with her parents. This had been several years ago, and no paintings survived from the period.) The haemorrhage had brought to the surface in this inexplicable delusion some deeply buried internal drama. She clutched his wrist and pulled him closer to her. Embarrassed, he stared into the thin face, white as a gardenia, with its harshly cut features and strange voracious lines about the mouth. She whispered something more, but in the middle of the sentence fell asleep. After a moment he detached himself gently from her grip, and, walking like a man in a dream, went out into the passage.

"Come on, Buffo," he said.

It had been their intention to dose Audsley King with laudanum, although neither of them, frankly, had been clear how this might be done. She ate so little. They had discussed putting it in a glass of wine. "But how to make sure she drinks it?" The drug now seemed unnecessary, but Buffo was an inflexible conspirator and insisted she have it anyway. In the event he did not give her enough: as the stuff touched her tongue she moaned and moved her head with the practised obstinacy of the invalid (who fears that every surrender to sleep might be the last), so that most of the dose trickled down her cheek. The little she swallowed, though, had an eerie effect. After a moment she sat bolt upright, and with her eyes firmly closed said clearly:

"*Les morts, les pauvre mortes, ont de grand doleurs.* Michael?"

Buffo gave a tremendous guilty leap and spilled the remainder of the draught on the floor.

"What?" he shouted. "Are we discovered already?"

Ashlyme, who could see that the woman was only talking in her sleep, tried to pull him away from her. He resisted stubbornly, plucking at Ashlyme's clothes and hair.

"The noise!" appealed Ashlyme in an urgent whisper. "Do you want to wake her, you madman?"

They tottered about on the bare boards in the failing light, panting, hissing, pushing at one another, while the thick smell of the drug rose up all around them.

"She has not taken it!"

"Nevertheless!"

Audsley King groaned suddenly, as if seeking their attention, and subsided into the pillows. They stopped struggling and watched her warily. Her mouth fell open. She began to snore.

To Ashlyme's surprise the Grand Cairo had agreed to wait below in the Rue Serpolet with the handcart. Their plan was to carry her down to him in an old linen sheet of Buffo's. Meanwhile he would make sure that no one got into the house. Ashlyme was worried nevertheless. Audsley King's limbs were lax and uncooperative, and she was heavier than her wasted appearance had led him to expect. "Hurry! If he gets impatient he will come up here and interfere!" A fierce heat seemed to radiate from her skin. Upside down, her face, with its bluish hollows and trickle of dried blood, looked accusatory, ironical, amused. They muddled it and could not get her off the sofa and onto the sheet. Ashlyme would not continue. "We've killed her!" he said. The whole idea was mad. He would have nothing more to do with it. "At any moment that creature will be up here with his knives and knuckle-dusters!"

In the end Buffo had to lift her onto the sheet on his own, while Ashlyme stood by with a blunted upholstery needle, ready to sew her in with long, loose stitches.

"Now the disguises. Be quick!"

Buffo took his clothes off in a corner. As he hopped from one foot to the other on the cold floor, trying to conceal himself, a strong smell of camphor wafted from him. Ashlyme, embarrassed by his friend's modesty, turned over the scattered tarot cards or glanced through the window at the yellowish underbelly of the clouds above the Rue Serpolet. He began to believe that the scheme might succeed after all. He would offer Audsley King space in his own studio while she reorganised her life. He would get her away from Rack and the Marchioness "L." There would be other patrons, other dealers, only too willing to take her on. He tapped his fingers on the windowsill. "Hurry," he urged Buffo. "Even now the Fat Mam may be returning."

Buffo, swaddled at last in his disagreeable bandages, pulled the rubber mask over his head and turned to face into the room.

He asked, "Is it on straight?" which Ashlyme heard as a sepulchral and threatening *"Iv id om fdrade?"* Yellow light, reflected from the clouds outside, splashed down one side of the mask. It looked like a horse's head, newly scraped to the bone in a knacker's yard and decked with green paper ribbons for some festival. But its horns and eyes belonged to nothing on earth. The astronomer patted it with one cupped hand like a woman adjusting a hat and came towards Ashlyme, who shuddered and backed away, saying,

"Must I wear such an awful thing?"

Buffo laughed. "Yours isn't half so striking. Here!"

Ashlyme accepted it with distaste. It was damp and sweaty. He forced it quickly down over his face, so as not to give himself time to think, and was at once unable to breathe. Nauseated by its smell, his nose squashed over to one side, his left eye covered, he struggled to tear it off, found the astronomer's hands forcing it back on. "I need no help! Leave me alone!" He was disgusted with himself as much as with Buffo. This foetid confinement, more than anything else, made the plan unbearable. His eyes were streaming. When he could see again he glared resentfully at Buffo's swathed, stick-like limbs.

"I won't be bandaged up like that, whatever you say!"

Buffo shrugged.

"Suit yourself, then."

The lower stairs of the house were bathed in a dim yellow light and strewn with the lath and plaster dislodged daily by the landlord's workmen. Abandoned building materials lay about on each landing. Ashlyme and the astronomer picked their way down through this litter, Audsley King slung between them like a stolen carpet. (While behind their doors the other occupants of the house ignored the furtive thudding on the stairs and spoke in the desultory, argumentative tones of the plague zone, asking one another if it meant to rain, and what they would get from the butcher tomorrow.)

Audsley King shook her head restively and groaned. "I cannot have those great lilies in here," she said in a low, reasonable voice. "You know how hard it is to get my breath." She trembled once or twice and was still.

Ashlyme and Buffo redoubled their efforts. She seemed to have grown heavier with every step, numbing their arms and slipping out of their aching fingers. They weren't used to the work and bickered over it like two old men: if Buffo was not pulling forward too hard, then Ashlyme was hanging back. Neither dared raise his voice to the other, but, trammeled in his rancid helmet, could only curse the thick hiss of his own breath in his ears and wish himself back in the High City. Their feet scraped and slithered on the stairs.

"Don't *pull*!"

"If only you would stop pushing like that!"

Without warning, Audsley King—dreaming perhaps—drew her knees up to her chin, and the sheet contracted like a ghostly chrysalis in the gloom. Ashlyme lost his grip on her shoulders. She slipped forward, knocked Buffo off his feet, and tumbled down the stairs after him, bumping and groaning on every step, to fetch up with a hollow thud among the bags of sand and lime on a landing not far below.

"Buffo!" begged Ashlyme. "Be more careful!"

Buffo stared at him with hatred, his absurd barrel chest heaving beneath its rags. The sheet writhed briefly; snores came from it. They approached it cautiously.

"Where am I?" said Audsley King.

She had regained consciousness, and obviously believed herself to be alone.

"Am I in Hell? Oh, nothing will ever console me for the ghastliness of this condition!"

It was the voice of someone who wakes in a bare room in an unknown city; stares dully at the washstand and the disordered bed; and having pulled open every empty drawer turns at last to the window and the empty streets below, only to discover she has lived here all her life.

"Another haemorrhage. If only I could die."

She considered this, then forgot it.

"My father said, 'Why draw this filth?' " she went on. " 'If you abuse your talents you will lose them. They will be taken from you if you draw filth.' It's so dark in here. I didn't want to go to bed so soon."

There was a small sob. She struggled a little, as if to test the limits of her confinement.

She stiffened.

A piercing shriek issued from the sheet.

Ashlyme tried to get hold of her feet but she tore herself out of his grasp and began to roll back and forth across the landing, knocking into the walls and shouting, "I am not dead! I am not dead!"

At this, doors flew open up and down the stairs and out came her neighbours to complain about the noise. A few ducked back when they saw what was happening, but several of them, mainly women, exchanged ironical if puzzled nods and settled down to watch. Emmet Buffo, who had rehearsed such an eventuality, explained to anyone who would listen: "Official business. Quarantine police. Keep back!" This was so manifestly ridiculous that he was ignored (although in the mêlée that was to develop later it did him more harm than good).

Audsley King, meanwhile, had ripped the sheet open along Ashlyme's rough seam and thrust one of her long powerful hands through the gap to clutch desperately at the air. By now she was so frightened that she had started to cough again, in a series of deep, destructive spasms between which she could only retch and gasp. A red bloom appeared at the upper end of the sheet and spread rapidly. Ashlyme lifted her into a sitting position. "Please be calm," he begged. The convulsion decreased a little. He was ready to confess the whole sordid business to her, but he did not know where to begin. Gently he freed her head and arms from the sheet. The women crowded forward, silent, uncertain, no longer amused; they groaned angrily at the sight of her white cheeks and bloody lips. She blinked up at them. Her hands were hot; she took one of Ashlyme's between them.

"I beg of you, whoever you are, to get me out of this shroud," she said.

Suddenly she caught sight of the thing over his head. She began to scream again, flailing her arms and begging him not to hurt her.

This was too much for the women, who advanced on Ashlyme, jeering and rolling up their sleeves. Emmet Buffo stepped in front of them, making gestures he imagined to be placatory. He took several nasty knocks about the head and chest, and was pushed into a pile of sand, where he lay jerking his long legs ineffectually and repeating, "Official police, official police."

Audsley King thrust Ashlyme away. "Fish into man: man into fish!" she cried, in a thick Soubridge accent—remembering perhaps some solstitial bonfire, some girlhood ritual in the heavy ploughland. "Murderer!"

Ashlyme fell back, astonished.

A fish?

He touched the mask with his fingers. It was the head of a trout, to which someone had added thick rubbery lips and a ludicrous crest of spines. He clapped his hands to his head and, reeling about in disgust, tried vainly to pull the mask off. Its smell grew horrifying. Why had he conspired to make himself so absurd? He could think only of escaping. Audsley King would have to be abandoned. In the High City he would be a laughingstock. He threw himself at the women, who were punching and kicking Buffo with a kind of dazed, preoccupied savagery, and tried to drag the astronomer away from them.

"Bitten off more than you can chew, eh?" they sneered. "Let's have them headpieces off and see who you really are!"

Having won the day, though, they made no attempt to carry out this threat. One of them attended to Audsley King, while the rest stood arms akimbo, sniffing defiantly, or tugged nervous fingers through their ruffled hair.

So it would have remained but for the arrival of the Grand Cairo, who had grown bored with his post at the handcart. He ran lightly up the stairs from the street and approached the women with a brisk tread, as if he was used to taking command of any situation. He was wearing a suit of military-looking brown leather, into the belt of which he had stuck a curious weapon—a knife about a foot long, with a round, varnished wooden handle like an awl's, and a blade nowhere thicker than a knitting needle. From a strap on his wrist dangled a workman-like rubber cosh. His feet were shod in laced boots with steel toecaps. He was well aware of the effect his appearance made. With his hands clasped behind his back and his chest thrown out, he gave the women a long intent look.

"What's this?" he asked. "Are we having some trouble with these people?"

"No," said Ashlyme. "It's all right."

Hearing this, the women laughed sarcastically. They returned the dwarf's scrutiny with bold, interested glances.

Meanwhile Emmet Buffo sat helplessly in a corner, breathing in exhausted gasps, while one of the women bent over him trying to pull off his mask. "Stop that," ordered the dwarf. He swaggered over to her and prodded her buttocks with his truncheon. Her face reddened. "Why, you dirty little bugger," she said, half-amused. She ruffled his hair, wrinkling her nose at the smell of Altaean Balm; then, quick as lightning, knocked him over with a jerk of her elbow. She watched him rolling about on the floor clutching his eye and said, "You'll not do that again in a hurry, will you, my dear?"

"Obscene bitch!" shouted the Grand Cairo.

He sprang to his feet with the unpredictable violence of the acrobat (who moves from rest to motion without any apparent intervening state), dragging the long knife from his belt. Before anyone could stop him he had grabbed her by the hair, pulled her down into a kneeling position, and rammed the knife twice into her open mouth as hard as he could. Her eyes bulged briefly. "That's that, then," he said. Ashlyme fell down and vomited into the fish's-head mask; around him he could hear the rest of the women screaming in panic. Emmet Buffo sat where he was, whispering, "Official police." The dwarf danced about the landing, stabbing at any women who came within reach, until he drove the knife three inches into a doorpost and broke it off. He swung his cosh on its leather thong.

"No more!" shouted Ashlyme. "Why are you doing this?"

Weeping with fear and revulsion, he ran down the stairs and into the street, where rain had begun to pour from the undersides of the clouds, spattering the dusty chestnut trees and making a greasy cement out of the plaster dust and fallen leaves on the pavements. Buffo staggered out after him, confused and bleeding, his rags coming unwrapped and his dreadful headdress knocked askew. Seeing that they were not pursued, they leaned against the handcart. "Those wretched women," panted the astronomer. "They will always ruin your plans."

Ashlyme stared at him speechlessly for a moment, then walked off.

The rain fell.

Buffo called, "What about the handcart? Ashlyme?"

The screams and shouts which continued to come from the house soon drew the attention of the plague police. Buffo saw them in the distance. He gave a start of surprise, grabbed the handles of the cart, and ran erratically down the Rue Serpolet with it until one of its wheels came off. It mounted the kerb and fell onto its side. Buffo looked round in panic, as if he had lost his bearings, then made off with long strides into the gathering darkness between two buildings, calling, "Ashlyme? Ashlyme?"

The plague police went up into the house, two at a time. Shortly afterwards there was silence. Fat Mam Etteilla the fortune-teller then trudged into sight from the direction of the market. The rain had plastered her yellow cotton dress to her billowing breasts and hams. Her eyes were phlegmatic, her arms full of greengrocery. She entered the house. A great wail went up as she discovered Audsley King on the stairs. Doors were banged, the lights came on in Audsley King's studio, there was a great deal of coming and going between floors.

Ashlyme, who had been hiding from Buffo in a wet doorway, waited until the commotion had died down and then went home, soaked.

Later, he stared into the mirror above his washstand, hardly seeing the lugubrious, blubbery-lipped totem that stared back out at him, its eyes popping solemnly and its loose scales dropping into the sink. All the way back he had dreaded trying to remove it, but it came off quite easily in the end.

THE THIRD CARD

THE CITY

You will mix with important people without artistic appreciation. Their tastes differ widely from yours. Beware "the Small Man" coming after this card.

"Angels, it is said, often do not know whether they walk among the living or the dead."

RAINER MARIA RILKE, Elegies

The period that followed was quiet and nerve-racking. He woke guiltily from every sleep. In the middle of stretching a canvas or doing his house-work he would recall some incident of the débâcle and be overwhelmed by a wave of revulsion and shame. He could not turn his clients away when they came to pose, yet dreaded every knock on the door in case it was the quarantine police or—worse still—some message full of contempt from Audsley King, delivered by the avenging fortune-teller. But no summons came from either quarter.

I hear nothing from Emmet Buffo, he wrote in his diary. And went on, perhaps unfairly, *Why should I seek him out? The whole farrago was his fault.* He reminded himself in the same breath, *I must avoid Rack and his clique. How can I face them now, with their sneers and insinuations?*

In fact he had no difficulty. Ironically enough his encounter with them on the Terrace of the Fallen Leaves had only served to increase his standing in the High City. Rumours of the failed rescue attempt—which, when they filtered up to Mynned from the exiles in the Bistro Californium and the Luitpold Café, were mercifully vague—merely added to his new romantic stature. He was popular in the salons. The Marchioness "L" called on him, with a new novelist. He was forced for the first time in his career to turn away commissions. The two or three portraits he completed at this time tended to be kinder than usual. This embarrassed him, and rather disappointed his clients. For once no one wanted an Ashlyme they could live with. They craved his bad opinion. He was their conscience. Not that he could compete with the plague, or the Barley brothers: and of the latter he was soon writing,

In the salons we hear nothing but what clothes they wear, what wineshop they frequent this week, how they have got pregnant some silly young brodeuse from the Piazza of Inherited Tendencies. "Will the Barley brothers dine at home tonight?" the women ask each other. "Or will they dine abroad?" They will dine, as everyone knows, like pigs, in some pie shop behind the Margarethestrasse and then fall down insensible in the gutters. "The Barley brothers have invented Egg Foo Yung!"

When he thought about the Grand Cairo, Ashlyme was filled with a kind of violent disgust which extended to himself. He dreamed about the woman with the gaping mouth and the bulging eyes as if he had been responsible for thrusting the knife into the back of her throat. Nothing like this event had ever happened in his life before; even awake, he could see it over and over again just by closing his eyes. He could also see the dwarf's expression when he had said, "That's that, then." It was one of satisfaction, the ordinary satisfaction of an ordinary need, as if one had just finished breakfast. Ashlyme dreaded another meeting with him if only because the shadow of this expression would lie—as it had always done, but now visible—just under his skin, alongside his vanity or his belief that he understood the language of cats.

Nevertheless a meeting was unavoidable. Ashlyme stayed away from the tower at Montrouge, but one night after his meal at the Vivien he came back to find the front door of his house banging open in the wind and the dwarf waiting for him in the darkened studio.

The dwarf looked tired. He complained, as usual, that the Barley brothers were plotting his downfall. "I do not take them seriously yet—things have not gone that far—but soon I must." He complained of boredom. To alleviate it, he said, he had spent all week with prostitutes in Line Mass. They had called him "my little chancellor" and "my pet cock," but he had got no enjoyment out of it, only migraines and a dry cough. As he told Ashlyme this he was watching him carefully. He sat on a windowsill, kicking his legs. He picked up Ashlyme's lay figure and twisted its limbs into uncomfortable, not-quite-human positions. He laughed. "Come on, Ashlyme, what's the matter? How's old Emmley Burwash? He always looked the feeble type to me!"

Ashlyme stared at him across the studio.

"Well, if you won't talk, you won't," said the dwarf. "I can't make you." He poked about among Ashlyme's things until a rough portrait of Audsley King caught his eye. "What's happened here?"

Ashlyme often saved the money he would have spent on a new canvas by reusing an old one. In this case he had done the painting over a group portrait of the Baroness de B—— and her family which had never been collected from the studio. As the wet summer advanced and the new paint began to fade, the image of the Baroness was beginning to reemerge in the form of a very old woman holding a flower, slowly absorbing and distorting the figure of Audsley King. There was something deliberate and eerie about this act of replacement. It was as if the Baroness, prohibited by her own vanity from collecting the original picture, nevertheless intended to claim the canvas. Ashlyme had followed the process with a sort of fascinated horror.

"It is some failure of the pigments," he said. "The weather. I don't know. It wasn't a very successful portrait anyway." He cleared his throat; swallowed. "It sometimes happens."

Now that he found himself able to speak, he could wait no longer.

"How did you escape the police?" he heard himself ask anxiously. "What did you tell them? I watched from the Rue Serpolet, but you did not come down again. What happened after I went?"

The dwarf, who had been waiting for this, winked cruelly.

"In the Rue Serpolet," he said, in a parody of an official voice, "I surprised two men in the act of smuggling a poor woman out of the quarantine zone against her will. I attempted to arrest them, but they stunned me, stabbed another unfortunate woman in a particularly horrible manner, and made their escape. I cannot describe them. They were wearing the most grotesque disguises. They were obviously very experienced criminals. Oh, don't look so wretched, man! Can't you take a joke?"

Ashlyme bit his lip.

"Even so," he said. "Are you sure they believed you?"

The dwarf stared at him impatiently.

"Why shouldn't they? I am the Grand Cairo. Everything they have, they have from me." He laughed. "Besides, I am now in charge of this very investigation." He gave an insolent shrug, tapped the side of his nose. "I have sworn to catch the offenders. A horrible crime like this is a matter of honour to me, you might say."

"But the testimony of the other women!"

"Unfortunately we had to arrest some of the women. They were confused, and had somehow got hold of the idea that I had injured one of their number."

He gripped Ashlyme's arm suddenly.

"For your own peace of mind," he said, in a low, urgent voice, "I advise you to forget the whole dangerous business. I intend to, which is good luck for you. And another thing, Ashlyme—" He tightened his grip until tears were forced from Ashlyme's eyes. "Never leave me in the lurch like that again, or you'll be the next one to feel that little skewer of mine.

Enemies are all around!" Ashlyme tried to pull his arm away. Contemptuously, the dwarf watched his struggles for a moment or two, then let him go. "Remember!" He was silent after that, staring at Ashlyme as if he couldn't really see him. Then he said in quite a different tone,

"A curious thing happened to me on my way back from Line Mass this morning. I tell you, Ashlyme, it was one of those incidents that make you think! I was walking along the canal bank in a district full of warehouses. Pink-and-brown-brick walls. The smell of old water. Rusty pulleys swinging in the wind above your head. A very old man approached me and, as we drew level, stopped to look into my face. It was an eerie look he gave me. As I stared back at him the sun came out briefly from behind a cloud. An unbearable halo seemed to flare round the edges of his yellowed skull! For a second or two it was very beautiful, this incandescent light burning round the edges of his head, dissolving away the pink brick behind him so that the whole sky seemed to open up like the white page of a book—

"But then the wind came up again and the sun went back in, and I saw that his face was eaten away by some disease contracted in youth. His mouth was trembling. He looked sickly and preoccupied. A vague power emanated from him, like a wind pushing me away. Ashlyme, I think the plague will have us all in the end!"

The dwarf shuddered superstitiously and was silent again. This was a side of his character he had never displayed before. At first Ashlyme suspected he had made the story up, or at least embroidered it to make it more impressive; but when he passed his heavily ringed hands over his face and turned to stare gloomily out of the window, it was quite impossible not to believe that something had genuinely disturbed him in Line Mass. He declined Ashlyme's offer of tea, with a gesture which hinted that he could not be jollied out of his mood. He was plagued, he admitted, with nervous depressions which came and went with the weather. Undoubtedly this new melancholy was of that sort. Abruptly he said, "As a matter of fact I have thought a great deal about a woman I saw when we were in the Rue Serpolet, a big woman who tells fortunes and is said to live with Audsley King. I daresay you know of a woman like that?"

Ashlyme nodded puzzledly.

The dwarf gave him a curious smile, weak-mouthed yet conspiratorial, and drew from inside his studded leather jacket an envelope with a red wax seal as big as a carbuncle. "Just so," he said. "I want this delivered to her." He thought for a moment. "Tell her that I am most interested in the cards. Assure her of my regard. Build me up in her eyes. This is a romantic matter, Ashlyme, and I trust you. Take the letter to the Rue Serpolet as soon as you can."

Ashlyme was filled with panic.

"But what about Audsley King?" he appealed. "She may have recognised my voice in the mêlée on that wretched staircase! How can I face her again?"

The dwarf stared at him expressionlessly, holding out the letter. Ashlyme spent a sleepless night and visited the house in the Rue Serpolet the next day, a dozen lilies waxen and heavy in the crook of his arm.

"How are you?"

"As you see me."

The room was cold. Audsley King lay on the sofa—thin, still, dazed-looking—wrapped in a fur coat with curiously huge sleeves. She spoke reluctantly of "thieves"; her eyes moved apprehensively every time a builder's cart went past the house. Bowls of anemones stood on every flat surface, as if she had begun to mourn herself. The flowers were purple and wine red, the colours of her disease; their necks were bent compliantly. She discussed small things: her domestic arrangements ("I am here in the studio all day now") and her meals. "I have a sudden dislike for fish!" He studied her closely, but she was not laughing at him. "Would you go to the window and look out? We have had thieves break in, and I am very nervous."

No, she said, she had done no new work. There, as he could see, was her easel, folded against the wall. She had drawn some cartoons, but she would not show them to him, of all people. They were not good enough. She had kept them for a day only, then torn them up. Why had he not been to see her? She would be glad to sit for him again, if that was what he wanted. Life seemed so quiet. She hadn't to exert herself. It was not empty, but very quiet. "The fortune-teller is kind, but I miss the High City," she said. Then again, she had so much to think about, there was barely time in the day!

He promised to call again soon. As he went out she was already staring uneasily into the corners of the room.

In the narrow hall with its broken linoleum and stacked canvases, Ashlyme found the Fat Mam bending over a bucket, her great bulk unhappy in a loose, flower-printed dress with little "muttonchop" sleeves. Washing the floor had made her breathe heavily through her open mouth, and there were broad patches of sweat beneath her arms. The hall was lighted only by a fanlight, which opened onto the communal stairs; in the brown gloom this produced she seemed monumental, immovable. But she stood up as he approached, wiping one powerful forearm across her cheek, and made way for him impassively. Steam came up from the bucket. Hardly knowing what to say, he handed her the dwarf's envelope. She turned it over, examined the florid seal, weighed it a moment in her big rough hands as if she was not certain what to do with it.

"Would you like a glass of anisette?" she asked slowly.

"Thank you," said Ashlyme, "but I'll have to go."

It was the first time they had spoken.

He watched her blunt fingers, so unaccustomed to the task, split and dampen the envelope. She saw him watching and turned away with a kind of instinctive modesty to read the single sheet of paper she had found. Her lips moved. Ashlyme, who would have given her greater privacy if he could, looked up at the wall. Out of the corner of his eye he saw a flush of bright red spread slowly up her thick neck and into her pallid cheeks with their downy hairs and faint film of perspiration. This monolithic woman, with her heavy shoulders, stuporous movements, and ox-like calm, was blushing! He tapped the side of his leg nervously and stared at the steaming bucket as hard as he could.

The sound of a builder's cart came dully into the hall through the fanlight. He could smell food cooking down the passage in the kitchen. He had a sudden feeling of ordinariness and stability, then someone shouted in the street and it was gone. At last she folded the letter up and put it, with some effort, carefully back into its envelope. She dropped it down between her huge breasts and patted the place where it had settled.

"Your friend is a fine little man," she said. "And very helpful."

This was not what Ashlyme had expected. Suddenly he could see, superimposed on her face, the face of the woman the dwarf had murdered—head lolling back, mouth agape on that appalling thin knife. He felt he ought to warn her of this.

"You may find that the dwarf is subject to . . . enthusiasms," he said, after some thought. "I mean that he may not be as dependable as you would like."

He saw immediately that he had said both too much and too little. Perhaps the moment was past for him to say anything about the dwarf's behaviour anyway: he had already condoned it by keeping quiet. The fortune-teller eyed him heavily. Then she smiled. For a second her eyes seemed to become a very pure and limpid blue. It was like a signal from the intelligence within, which had disengaged itself briefly to attend to him before returning to the eternal task of sifting sense from the random fall of some internal pack of cards. "I'm sure he is a man of great resource," she said, "and a good man. Thank him for his invitation. But what he suggests is not yet possible."

"I see," said Ashlyme, who did not.

Rather than wait to see her eyes fade again, he gave her a vague nod and went out. When he looked back from the door she was down on her hands and knees by the bucket, scrubbing hard at something on the floor.

He reported this meeting to the dwarf in the tower at Montrouge.

"Good," said the dwarf, rubbing his hands. "Excellent. Better than I expected. But we must press our advantage, eh? She must come here and see me as I am, a man who has organised his life on comfortable lines but who is willing to share it!"

He was in a high good humour. He blinked and winked with contemplative conceit and contentment. He ate a pear with relish, polished his spectacles vigorously. He had a bottle of bessen genever brought in and made Ashlyme toast what he called his "romantic success." Once or twice his gaiety seemed a little tired: he ran his hands continually through his hair, and when he wasn't speaking his eyes had an unfocused look. He got up without warning and threw the door open as if he hoped to catch someone listening outside. Once he said, "Half my men were themselves arrested yesterday morning, due to some administrative blunder up at Uriage and Montdore." He gave a strained laugh. "Can you imagine that?" But generally he was pleased.

"Give these to her next," he ordered. "What flowers are in season? Never mind. Remember, no more 'not yet possible'! No more coyness! Come and tell me her answer." He thought for a moment. "The next time you come we will have a sitting for my portrait." But it was plain that he had lost interest. Ashlyme left the tower carrying a parcel which proved to contain nothing but two freshly killed young rabbits, each with a green paper ribbon tied carefully round its neck. These the fat woman refused to touch, and though the dwarf claimed later that they were a traditional wedding gift in the Mingulay peninsula, Ashlyme had his doubts.

Soon he was back and forth between them once or twice a week.

This was not an onerous duty at first; and though he was conscious that it made him look a fool to play the dwarf's romantic proxy, it suited him well enough in that it enabled him to resume his visits to Audsley King on a regular basis. Recklessly he began using the Gabelline Stairs again to get in and out of the Low City, reasoning that while he was abroad on the dwarf's business he would not be arrested by the dwarf's police. He began the portrait of Audsley King all over again, watching her helplessly as every day another layer of flesh melted away, deepening the bluish hollows underneath her cheekbones. Her face was constantly refining itself, seeking the exact expression of the underlying bone structure to be found in death. She did not seem to be interested in the picture. She stared listlessly at what he had done and urged him to "seek out the forms of things." To entertain her in the long cold hours while he was painting, he told her lies about Paulinus Rack and invented scandalous love affairs for the Marchioness "L"; Livio Fognet he bankrupted. He lied without mercy, and she was eager to believe anything.

For the first time, he sensed, her courage had faltered, and she was sustained in her determination to remain in the Low City only by her ready self-contempt, her appalling strength of will. This disappointed him obscurely where, before the kidnap attempt, it would have given him heart.

Outside the studio the Low City deteriorated daily, its meaningless commerce and periods of stunned lethargy mimicking the dull decline of Audsley King's spirit. Shredded political posters flapped from the iron railings. Rain blew across the muddy grass. The horse chestnut flowers guttered like grey wax candles. The plague cut off first Moon Street, then Uranium Square, making peninsulas then archipelagos out of them—finally it engulfed each little island while its unsuspecting inhabitants were asleep. In the sodden churchyards and empty squares the police of the Barley brothers stood about in small groups, jeering at the police of the Grand Cairo. Poets droned from the abandoned estaminets.

Audsley King seems to observe all this from a dream, Ashlyme wrote, beginning a new page in his journal. *Her expression is terrible: hungry, despairing, hopeful, all at once.*

He could not release himself from a sense of guilt. A self-portrait painted at about this time, "Kneeling with raised arms," shows him, his eyes squeezed closed, apparently crawling and groping his way about his own studio, a whitish empty space. He seems to have come up against some sort of invisible barrier, against which he is pressing one side of his face so that it is distorted and whitened into a mask of frustration and despair. (This obstacle was probably the full-length mirror he had brought with him to the city some years before, as a student. In spite of its size and weight he always took it with him when he moved from studio to studio.) The original oil of the painting has been lost, but a watercolour study shows it to have been one of his most powerful pieces. He disliked it markedly, and wrote, *I have drawn a rather unpleasant thing today after seeing the Grand Cairo. It is because of the outrage he has done my freedom.*

The dwarf's relations with the Barley brothers now underwent a further deterioration. It was not made clear what plots and counterplots were involved. But Ashlyme noted: *He has let himself go. His boots are dirty and he reeks of hair oil. I return home late at night to find him waiting for me. If the Barley brothers are mentioned he flies into a rage, denouncing them for their latest betrayal and shouting, "They were down in the gutters until I dragged them out!" and "What thanks have I ever got for that?" Raving like this seems to tire him out, and then he spends most of his time slumped in a chair remembering the good times he has had in some brothel or other on the Rue des Horlogers.*

Beneath his obliquity and his vile temper he is a child. Though they have done him no harm as far as I can see, he goes in such hatred of his masters that he has even made up a sort of embroidered mythological slander to account for them. The details of the myth vary from day to day, but its basis is always much the same.

The Barley brothers, he claims, are all that remain of a race of magicians or demiurges driven out of Viriconium hundreds or thousands of years ago in a war with "giant beetles." Finding themselves exiled in the inhospitable sumps and deserts to the north, these creatures first built cities of stone cubes "with gaps between them through which the wind rumbles," then set about projecting themselves backwards in time to a remoter, happier period of the world. By now most of them have achieved this aim, and their cities are derelict, inhabited only by mirages, simulacra, or ordinary human beings trying to mimic their culture. The Barley brothers were left behind as a punishment for some moral flaw in their natures, and in their attempts to follow where they are not wanted they have somehow become stuck in our city.

This story shows the complexity and force of the dwarf's feelings. All he has he owes to the Barleys, though he wishes he did not. When he tells it his eyes are glazed and inturned, as if the events were still there in front of him but can only be discerned by a great effort. He makes broad yet hesitant gestures. He is very clever at details, especially architectural ones, and he dwells with considerable ingenuity on the sin of the Barley brothers which has kept them from following their peers into the past. If he did not fully believe his own tale to begin with, he has now left himself no choice.

One night the dwarf spoke of a city built by this race in the North (or perhaps in the sky, although he did not explain how this was possible):

"The people in their black overcoats seemed to drift along a few inches above the pavements. Now and then the wind pulled shadows over them so that the scene trembled like water. Their faces were white with conspiracy. Their eyes were wide open, passive; they had abandoned themselves to the wind between the blocks which pushed them gently along. Now and then there was a laugh, quickly stifled. We had them weighed up. Each one would do anything for you if he believed he had been let into some secret unknown to the rest. In the evenings a new wind howled and screamed in off the waste, bringing with it enormous lizards and insects. Handfuls of ash and ice were thrown down the streets like glass marbles. On Sundays the wet streets were carpeted with dead locusts. The Barley brothers have invented many towns, but this was the worst. I found them in the gutters there, and they soon dragged me down with them!"

He was silent for five minutes. Then he asked to see the knife he had given Ashlyme before the kidnap attempt. He always asked to see it: perhaps it was in his eyes the reaffirmation of a bond.

"I got that knife up there in the North," he said, "and I had to do some quick work to keep it. Quick work! Do you know what we mean when we say that? Quick work is when you have to move your feet or go to the wall!" And he danced round the studio, showing his stained teeth and making clumsy passes with the knife until he was out of breath. "Oh, yes, there was blood on this knife from the moment I had it. I've lived in some queer spots, I can tell you. That knife and I have been in some queer spots!" His eyes took on a distant, romantic look, and he rubbed his thumb up and down the curiously flawed blade before handing it back.

"That knife will serve you well one day," he said portentously. "I can tell you that."

Ashlyme was impressed by his powers of invention. *In the end, though,* he recorded, *I listen without believing. He tires, mumbles, allows his head to fall on his chest, snores. Suddenly he wakes up with a start and goes home biting his nails, afraid that he has contracted a syphilis in the Rue des Horlogers, and forgets everything he has said. By tomorrow he will have invented something else to place the Barleys in a bad light.*

Each night before leaving he gave Ashlyme some new gift for the fortune-teller. He would not hear of abandoning his suit. The longer she resisted him, the more inappropriate his presents became: a hank of hair, signet rings with obscene designs, a rusty flint picked up in some desert long ago. She accepted them expressionlessly, repeating, "What your friend suggests is not yet possible. My responsibilities are here." He lost his temper with Ashlyme. He had reason to believe, he said, that his expensive flowers had been given to Audsley King instead of Fat Mam Etteilla; some of his gifts had been found in a dustbin; his letters were not being delivered. He brushed aside all Ashlyme's explanations. "Bring her to me or it'll be the worse for you," he said.

Unnerved, Ashlyme put this to the Fat Mam the next time he was in the Rue Serpolet. She looked at him sharply, then said,

"Very well."

That morning, Audsley King had suffered a small haemorrhage and was resting with open mouth and bluish lips on the studio *fauteuil,* turning over restively now and again to murmur in some language Ashlyme didn't know. So as not to wake her, they were standing in the passage just the other side of the curtain, talking in low voices.

Ashlyme was surprised. "Do you mean to go and see him in his own house?"

"Yes," said the fortune-teller. "Why not?" Suddenly she blushed, and smoothed her hair with one big, chapped hand. "A strong man will always have his own way in the end," she said complacently.

Ashlyme stared at her.

The meeting took place one evening a week later, in the dwarf's *salle.*

He had worked feverishly to prepare it for the occasion. All week, the teams of carpenters and interior decorators had gone to and fro, working to his precise instructions.

The floor had been stained black and polished. His collection of paintings had been taken down carefully and stored. The walls were covered with white linen dustcloth up to a height of about twenty feet. This had been stretched tight and pinned to make a background for a profusion of objects made from straw, hair, and metal, and also many tools such as pliers, hammers, pincers, and chisels, which hung from coppered nails or braided silk cords or specially made brackets of the dwarf's own devising. There were old sheaves of corn, full of dust and shrivelled mice; samplers woven out of the hair of girls; two or three mantraps black with rust; and a monkey made of twisted jute fibres on a soft wire armature. All these things had been decked with loose spirals of yellow and green ribbon. A greyish light fell on them. Above them lurked the smoky umber void of the original room, a space the colour of time and decay.

The furniture had been dressed similarly. Draped with white cloth, wound about with coloured ribbon, the armchairs, armoires, and cupboards took on the air of huge, vaguely threatening parcels.

It wasn't clear how many people the dwarf was expecting. A long trestle table in the centre of the room was loaded with food, mostly game birds still in their feathers, glazed pies, custards, and large joints of meat decorated with paper frills. Crudely plaited "corn dollies," such as a child may make from raffia or straw on a wet afternoon in the midland levels, had been placed among the baskets of fruit, the bottles of genever, and the thick white plates. In the middle of the table was a full-sized sheep's head, stripped and varnished, with oranges for eyes. On each side of this stood a vase of late hawthorn blossom, filling the room with the thick, soporific scent of the may.

Fat Mam Etteilla eyed these preparations nervously. She had given nothing away as she swept through the Haadenbosk, looking neither right nor left. But the queer environs of Montrouge had puzzled her, and the attentions of the dwarf's police, though friendly, had weakened her resolve. She stared up into the vault of the old room and toyed with the floral trimmings of her hat. She is already wishing she hadn't come, thought Ashlyme, and in an effort to make her feel more at home he said cheerfully,

"Well, he's put on quite a show for you. Look at all this food! Do you think anyone would mind if I had one of these plums?"

When the dwarf arrived he took Ashlyme aside and said in a low voice, "I've dreamed the name of a street two nights in succession, Ashlyme. A street in the North." He slopped some genever into a glass and drank it off. "What do you think of that? It's made me damnably nervous, I don't mind telling you."

He noticed the fortune-teller. Immediately he was all charm. "My dear woman!" he cried, smiling up at her with all his blackened teeth. "Are you well? Are you *fully recovered* from those appalling events in the Rue Serpolet?" He looked slyly over his shoulder at Ashlyme, who turned away and pretended to be interested in something else. "You must tell us as soon as you feel in the slightest bit tired!" The fat woman, holding her hat with both hands in front of her, blushed modestly at the shiny floor and allowed herself to be ushered past the curious collection on the walls.

The Grand Cairo lost no chance to impress her. He turned this way and that to display his best profile. He stood with his spine arched and his chest thrust out and his hands tucked into the small of his back, looking up at her sideways to judge the effect he was having. He had dressed for the occasion in green velvet trousers tied up below the knee with red string, boots whose polished steel toecaps gave back a curved, bemusing reflection of the room at large, and a collarless shirt over which he wore unfastened a shiny black waistcoat. Round his neck he had a bit of green rag; and his hair had been slicked down with repeated applications of Altaean Balm, the powerful smell of which filled the room and mingled oddly with the scent of the may.

They made a strange pair, shuffling from exhibit to exhibit in the grey light. When he had shown her all his pieces of bone, his hair dolls, and blunt iron sickles twined with ribbon like convolvulus, he explained the meaning of each object and also where he had got it. This he had won at cards; that he had dug up in a desert; no value could be put on that one. He spoke coaxingly. "You can have any of these things. They are all very lucky." But she was nervous and looked away. The Grand Cairo would not be downcast. He winked at Ashlyme with the vulgar gallantry of the secret policeman, as if to say, "I'm not finished by a long way yet!"

On a table he had a machine in a box. When he did something to it with his hands it produced a thin complaining music like the sound of a clarinet in the distance on a windy night, to which he tapped his feet and nodded his big head energetically, while he grinned round the room. But this only further confused the fortune-teller, and as soon as he saw that she would not dance, he shrugged and made haste to silence it. "We had a lot of those in the North," he said.

"Look at this," he invited her. "You can have this." He stuck out his hand and made her look at the ring he had on it. "Inside here," he boasted, "I carry the most deadly poison there is, made from the excrement of cats. I always wear this ring, even while I am asleep. And if it ever happened that I found myself in a position intolerable to my pride . . ."

He unscrewed the bezel of the ring. The fortune-teller stared expressionlessly down at the dull powder it contained.

"You can have that," he said, snapping it shut.

She shook her head slowly in her bovine way. He smiled and looked directly into her eyes.

"Tell me my future, then," he ordered.

The night was coming on. Fat Mam Etteilla sat resting her bosoms comfortably on the edge of the little green baize table, two dark patches of sweat spreading slowly under the arms of her dress. She shuffled the cards, spread them, and stared at them in surprise. The dwarf, looking over her shoulder, laughed loudly. He lit a lamp and sat down opposite her. "That's something, eh?" he said. "What do you think of that?" Dull gold light flared off the grubby, colourful slips of pasteboard. He tilted his head to one side and considered them intently.

"Again!" he ordered. The fat woman went on staring at him. "Again!"

Ashlyme sat forgotten in a corner of the room. He had asked if he might go home, but the dwarf would not let him. "I might want you to take a message for me," he said carelessly. The hot food cooled; the sheep's head gazed into the gathering gloom with its bulging eyes; downstairs the dwarf's police came and went, came and went, with their urgent reports from the Artists' Quarter, their rumours from Cheminor, and their suspects from the Pont de Nile. None of this was interesting to the fortune-teller and her client. Only their two heads were visible, leaning avidly over the cards in the gold wash of light. Sometimes they set up a dull murmur: "Two rivers—a message!" "Avoid a meeting!" The room grew chilly. Ashlyme wrapped himself in his cloak and slept uncomfortably.

Later there was a quarrel; or perhaps he dreamed it. Someone knocked the table over in the dark. A stool scraped on the floor. A bottle fell and broke. Ashlyme heard the Fat Mam breathing heavily through her mouth, then the words,

"I am committed in the Rue Serpolet! What you ask is not yet possible!"

He had a confused impression of the cards spilling through the cold air the way a conjuror spills them from hand to hand, each small crude picture bright and cruel and alive and very far away.

When he next woke it was early dawn. If the table had been knocked over, they had righted it again and now sat with their elbows on it, looking first at the cards and then into one another's eyes. The dwarf had disarranged his hair; it stood up in spikes, and beneath it his face was eroded and unhealthy. A half-eaten meal and a jug of "housemaid's coffee" stood at the Fat Mam's elbow, and there was dried milk in the hairs on her upper lip.

They seemed to be talking a language Ashlyme didn't understand. He shook his head, cleared his throat, hoping they would notice him and become less remote. Fat Mam Etteilla gazed at him blankly for a second, an expression of greed fading from her features. The Grand Cairo got up and stretched. He walked over and pulled one of the oranges out of the sheep's head, then went into the other room, peeling it. Ashlyme heard a muffled *oulouloulou* through the wall. A moment later the cats began to come in from Montrouge. They surrounded the card table, rubbing their heads against the fortune-teller's ankles, more and more of them until the room was full of their drugged purr.

"None of these cats is mine," the dwarf told her proudly, finishing his orange. "They come to me from all over the city because I speak their language. What do you think of that?"

She smoothed her hair complacently.

"Very nice," she said.

Ashlyme left them and walked stiffly out into the city, where the thin milky light of dawn was falling across the earthworks and onto the faces of the dwarf's raw new buildings. When he looked back the tower was dark but for a single yellow window, against which he could make out two silhouetted figures. He rubbed his eyes.

THE FOURTH CARD

THE LORD OF THE
FIRST OPERATION

Chaos and uncertainty follow this card. A journey or undertaking of which the outcome cannot be guessed. According to another reading, vacillation.

"I have heard the café philosophers say, 'The world is so old that the substance of reality no longer knows what it ought to be.'"

ANSEL VERDIGRIS, *Some Remarks to my Dog*

If you stood at the window in the studio at Mynned and looked out towards the Low City, you felt that Time was dammed up and spreading out quietly all around you like a stagnant pond. The sky was the colour of zinc.

Ashlyme pursued his life dully, unsure what he might have begun by bringing the dwarf and the fortune-teller together. One night he dreamed he was standing in a gallery which overlooked the ground floor of a large building. *The whole of this floor,* he recorded, *was given over to piles of sec-ondhand clothes, among which wandered hundreds of elderly women with powdered cheeks and wet angry eyes. They turned the clothes over busily: they looked like beetles in their black coats.* Then the Barley brothers had come in, accompanied by the Grand Cairo, who immediately began giving away coloured balloons. *There weren't enough to go round. The women fought over them in the aisles, running over one another furiously, red in the face. I woke up sweating: it was just like being in Hell.*

The popularity of his portraits persisted, but he found his clients distracted and hard to pose. *For the moment,* he wrote, *they are a little subdued. It will pass. They find themselves chafed by their isolation. They say it is like living on an island, and I suppose they are right.*

Something new, in the shape of Paulinus Rack and his difficulties, soon came to take their mind off their predicament. *I have heard*, Ashlyme noted, not without satisfaction, *that he has made unwise property invest-ments in the Low City. If Die Traumunden Knaben is not a success, he will crash, and his patrons will disown him. Yet they constantly interfere with the production, demanding that it be made "more acceptable." They must have sets designed by Audsley King, but they do not want the ones that have already been submitted. These are, it appears, "too gloomy"; they are "drab"; they are at one and the same time "too suggestive" and "too blatant." Rack is driven to dining alone at the Charcuterie Vivien (where he does not speak to me). Meanwhile, somebody has suggested we have a play about the Barley brothers.*

He viewed this with some distaste.

These great fools occupy our minds enough as it is. Nightly they are stagger-ing along the Mynned gutters, gaping at the stars through the branches of the trees. Must we have them paraded in front of us at the Prospekt Theatre, as well, their pockets full of clinking bottles, followed onto the stage by half a dozen barking Dandy Dinmont dogs they have bought from some trader in Line Mass who claims to have trained them on Stockholm Tar and live cats?

And later he added:

The Grand Cairo seems to fear them more than ever. "Their ears are every-where!" he claims, and has sent out orders to increase the vigilance of his own spies. He visits my studio in the early hours and sits down cross-legged in the only good chair, as full of his own importance as ever and heavy with secrets he cannot wait to divulge—the plague zone has shifted again, fifteen people will be arrested at Alves tomorrow for trying to smuggle relatives out, and so forth. But his conspiracies are not going well. He is bilious, quarrelsome, insecure. If he hears a door slam in the distance he gives a guilty start, then tries to pass it off by laughing sarcastically or flying into a rage. He drinks black-currant gin without stopping; and as this stuff inflames his imagination his conversa-tion turns less on how he will outwit his masters, and more and more on escape from the city.

"Tell me, Ashlyme," he sighs. "Will any of us ever get out of this trap we have made for ourselves?" He never mentions the Fat Mam.

As the dwarf's anxieties multiplied, he abandoned his visits to Mynned. But he would not have Ashlyme at the tower in Montrouge. Instead he arranged furtive meetings in Shrogg's Dene, Cheminor, and the Haunted Gate, all the most squalid regions of the Low City, often to no more pur-pose than half an hour's walk in the rain along some old fortification over-grown with willow herb, during which he would pick up and cast aside dozens of bits of leather, rusty saucepans, and other decaying domestic im-plements. One evening on his return from such an outing, Ashlyme found himself on Clavescin Crescent, a street whose name was not familiar to him.

He had come from a depopulated suburb a mile north of Cheminor, where muddy cinder paths lined with poplar trees wound among the empty lazar houses and crematoria. He had hoped to be at the foot of the Gabelline Stairs before darkness caught him: but it was already late, and a heavy blue twilight had set in, confusing him as to distances. He recognised the three-storey terraced houses, with their peeling fronts and cracked casement windows, as belonging to the Artists' Quarter. Which part of it he wasn't entirely sure, although he hoped he might be close to the familiar warren of streets behind Monstrance Avenue and the Plaza of Unrealised Time.

Little arched alleyways led off the crescent at intervals. He was hurrying past the mouth of one of them when he heard a low cry—not quite of pain, but not quite of anguish either.

This was such a strange sound to hear, even in the plague zone, that he stopped and peered into the alley. It was damp and unwelcoming, but it opened out after ten yards or so into a courtyard like a deep well, the sides of which were propped up by huge balks of timber. Night was already advanced there amid the builders' rubble. At the foot of one bulging wall, under a heavily boarded window, bags of mortar stood in a line. Someone had fallen down among them. Ashlyme could see an indistinct figure supporting itself on its hands and knees. Unwilling to enter the alley, he called uncertainly, "Are you unwell?"

"Yes," said a muffled voice. Then: "No."

Ashlyme bit his lip. "Can you move this way?" he suggested.

Silence.

"I can only help you if you come out," said Ashlyme.

A low chuckle came from behind one of the timber balks. Ashlyme said, "Is there someone else in there?" He strained his eyes to see into the courtyard. The man on the floor put his hands on his head and groaned suddenly. "Are you alone in there?" Ashlyme asked him.

The Barley brothers, who had spent all afternoon hunting rats in the overgrown gardens behind the crescent, were unable to keep quiet any longer.

"Nobody in here, yer honour," said Matey in a sepulchral voice. They had never heard anything funnier. They stuffed their handkerchieves into their mouths and rolled about on the floor. They bolted from the shadows which had concealed them and, laughing helplessly, shouldered their way out of the alley. "What a frightful sight!" they shouted, and, "Give him some stick, vicar!" Their grinning faces bobbed over Ashlyme in the twilight like red balloons; they smelled strongly of ferrets and bottled beer. Hard-favoured little Dandy Dinmont dogs milled about between their hobnail-booted feet, yelping hysterically.

"I'm weeing myself," said Gog. "I'm doing it!"

Ashlyme was incensed. "Leave us alone!" he cried. "Go back where you belong and stop all this!" But they only laughed louder and ran away down the crescent, belching and farting and tripping over their dogs.

When the echo of their footsteps had died away at last, Ashlyme went to have a look at the man in the courtyard. He was trembling feverishly. Every so often he let out a groan, then whispered something to himself which sounded like, "Where am I? Oh, where am I?" He had no obvious injuries. His clothes, though crumpled and covered with whitish dust, were of good quality; he still had on a wide-brimmed felt hat of a kind popular in the High City. But he would not say who he was or where he had come from; and when Ashlyme urged him, "If you could just get up—" he only whimpered and pushed himself further in among the bags of cement. Ashlyme knelt down and tried to lift him. He resisted feebly and his hat fell off. Ashlyme found himself gazing into the flabby features and horrified eyes of Paulinus Rack.

"What on earth are you doing here, Rack?" he said.

"I'm lost," whispered the entrepreneur helplessly. "I'm lost."

He clutched Ashlyme's sleeve. "Beggars are all around us," he said. "Do nothing to provoke them." Suddenly he shivered and hissed: "Livio, all these roads are the same! Livio, *they don't lead anywhere!* Livio, don't leave me! Don't leave me!" Breathing heavily, hanging on to Ashlyme's shoulder for support, he pulled himself to his feet and stood there with his mouth hanging open, staring about in a frightened, sightless way.

At the Luitpold Café they were keeping the night at arm's length in a stuporous silence.

Madame sat behind her zinc counter with its shallow glass dishes of gooseberries soaked in lemon genever, thirty years the speciality of the house. A few vague plumes of steam issued from the kitchen door behind her. When she wasn't required to serve she folded her thin hands in her lap and stared at nothing, like an animal waiting at a gate. Insects smacked into the wavering, bluish lamps, blundered off round the room, and flew into the lamps again. A generation before, this place had been the very heart of the Artists' Quarter, the centre of the world: now its walls had an indelible lacquer of dirt into which had been scratched the indecipherable signatures of arriviste and poseur; and in place of the fabulous poets and painters of long ago, only a few fakers and failed polemicists sat at the marble-topped tables, writing endless letters to influential men.

Quarantine was the only word they knew. They could taste it in their mouths. They contemplated it constantly, while the plague, like grey dust, rained down on their shoulders.

Paulinus Rack had recovered his wits, although his eyes were still watery and apprehensive. It was not clear what had happened to him. He contradicted himself at every turn. First he claimed that he had entered the Low City on his own, then that he had been with Livio Fognet and some unnamed friend of theirs, "who cleared off as soon as he saw our plan." He said that they had come in that morning at eleven o'clock, but maintained later that he remembered passing an entire night in the courtyard where Ashlyme had found him. He said that he had been opportuned by beggars, and had to hide from them, but boasted later that they had been members of the plague police in disguise, with a special warrant for his arrest.

Whatever the truth of the matter, the plague zone had frightened and disoriented him. "Trees, buildings, gutters, every street identical, Ashlyme!" he kept saying. "We soon lost all sense of direction." And then, speaking of his ordeal of the courtyard, "You know, I could hear those two foul creatures inside the house for hours, killing things, laughing at me." He shuddered. "The shouting and squealing! It was the worst thing that's ever happened to me!"

Ashlyme eyed him unforgivingly. "You were a fool to come in at all. What happened to Livio Fognet?"

Rack looked down at his fat hands and gave a little smile. "I know," he sighed. "I know it was foolhardy, but that is my nature. How can I ever thank you?" He drank noisily from his glass of tea. "I feel much better now." Of Fognet he would only say, "I stuck with him as long as possible, Ashlyme. But he kept taking his own pulse. He was certain he had caught some disease. Then we quarrelled over the direction of the High City. He hit me. He was blubbering at the end: blubbering."

"You will always get lost in here," said Ashlyme, who privately thought that Fognet might tell a different story. "But you must never panic. When I first started to come in I stuck to the Plaza of Unrealised Time. You get used to it in the end. Will Fognet find his own way back? Or ought I to look for him?"

Rack wiped his lips. "Isn't that Gunter Verlac over there?" he said. He smiled insincerely across the room. "I must go and have a word with him."

And Ashlyme could get no more from him.

At about eleven o'clock they rose to go, chilled by the emptiness and gloom. At the next table, B—— de V—— the poet was busy writing a letter. He raised his white, inoffensive, sheep-like head as they passed by. "We'll never escape from here, any of us," he said matter-of-factly, as if they had asked his opinion. Madame sat beside her counter and watched them leave, her hands in her lap, a cup of bluish chocolate cooling in front of her. Ashlyme saw Rack to the head of the Gabelline Stairs. He shook Ashlyme's hand and trotted off eagerly towards Mynned. *We shall never hear the last of it,* Ashlyme wrote later, *now that he has been in the plague zone*. And: *His only hope was to get Audsley King to redraw her designs for* The Dreaming Boys. *But I don't believe she would have helped him, even if he had got as far as the Rue Serpolet.*

Ashlyme's own visits to Audsley King continued. One afternoon, at her insistence, he lit a bonfire in the small garden at the rear of the house and carried her out to watch it.

"How nice this is," she said.

There was no wind. Within the tall brick walls—which, with their mats of bramble, bladder senna, and reddish ivy, dulled the sounds of construction coming from either side—the air was sharp and rapturous, the light a curiously bleached lemon colour. The smoke of Ashlyme's blaze, of which he was deeply proud and which he fed energetically with dead elder branches and sprays of yellow senna, hung motionless over the house, its scent remaining sharp and autumnal even when it mixed with the smoke of the builders' fires. Audsley King watched him affectionately, smiling a little at some recollection. But when he began to pull down living ivy she chided, "Be careful, Ashlyme, that those tangled stems do not fasten themselves round your dreams. They will have their revenge." But it was plain that her own dreams concerned her more than his. "Let's burn the furniture instead. I shan't need it soon."

He eyed her warily. He could not tell if she was teasing him. All day her mood had been changeable, demanding.

"Paint me!" she ordered suddenly. "I don't know how you can bear to waste this light!"

It was a long, strange afternoon.

The too-large collar of Audsley King's fur coat conspired with the bleached light to diminish and soften the mannishness of her features until she looked, as she stared into the fire, like a child staring out of a familiar window. Ashlyme, encouraged, worked steadily; she had never been so complaisant a model. Meanwhile Fat Mam Etteilla came and went, communicating a monolithic calm as she burned the household rubbish. Into the fire went old picture frames, Audsley King's bloodied handkerchiefs, a chair with one leg missing, a cardboard box which when it burst slowly open revealed a compressed mass of papers tied with old ribbon. She watched them all reduce to ashes, her agreeable face reddened by the heat, patches of sweat appearing under her arms. She was like a great patient horse, gazing with drooping underlip across an empty field.

(Ashlyme studied her covertly. Had she seen the Grand Cairo since that curious meeting in Montrouge? He was not sure. Her thoughts were invisible.)

Later, old women came to sit out on their balconies, looking up at the sky like animals about to be drowned. Fat Mam Etteilla fetched down her cards, laid them out on an old baize-covered table, and predicted, "A good marriage, a bad end." The workmen next door brought down a wall, more by accident than design, and the old women, chuckling appreciatively, watched the dust belly up into the air. The light shifted secretively a degree at a time, until it had left Ashlyme's work behind. Audsley King, anyway, had evaded him again: the heat of the fire had relaxed her narrow, angular face and softened the lines about her mouth. He was reluctant to ask her to change her pose, for the comfortable crackling of the fire had induced in him a hypnotic sense of time suspended, time retrieved: so he began a new charcoal study instead. After he had been scratching away at this for a few minutes, Audsley King said, "Before I came to the city I cut off my hair. It was the first of many fatally symbolic gestures."

She contemplated this statement as if trying to judge its completeness, while Ashlyme, intrigued, looked at her sidelong and carefully said nothing.

"It was the autumn before I married," she went on. "The servants brought out all the rubbish which had accumulated in the house during the past year and burned it in the garden, just as we are doing here. Our parents looked on, while the children ran about cheering, or stared gravely into the red heart of the flames. We loved those autumn fires!"

She shook her head.

"How can I explain myself? I cut off my hair and threw it on the fire. Was it despair or intoxication? I was going to the city to begin a new life. I was going to be married. From now on I would paint what I saw, see everything I wished to see. Viriconium! How much it meant to me then!"

She laughed. She shrugged.

"I know what you are going to say. And yet . . .

"We were all going to be famous then—Ignace Retz the wood-block illustrator, elbowing his way down the Rue Montdampierre in his shabby black coat at lunchtime, Osgerby Practal, with nothing then to his name but his sudden drugged stupors and his craving for 'all human experience'; even Paulinus Rack. Oh, you may laugh, Ashlyme, but we took Paulinus Rack quite seriously then, going about his business in a donkey cart, with that sulphurous yellow cockatoo perched on his shoulder! He was thinner. He hadn't yet turned a whole generation of painters into tepid watercolourists and doomed consumptive aesthetes on behalf of the High City art collectors."

She made a sad defensive gesture.

"Once when I was ill he brought me a black kitten." She smiled. "Once," she said, "he tried to kill himself on the banks of the Pleasure

Canal. He pressed a scarf soaked in aether to his face until his legs gave way, but was pulled out of the water before he could drown. We all rather admired him for that.

"Later I understood the pointlessness of this dream, and of the people who pursued it through the smoke in the Bistro Californium, the Antwerp Estaminet. Oh, we were all going to be famous then—Kristodulos, Astrid Gerstl, 'La Divinette.' " But my husband contracted a howling syphilis and hanged himself one stifling afternoon in the back parlour of a herbalist's shop. He was twenty-three years old and had saved no money.

"I was too proud to go back to my mother. I was too determined. *Your hair was not your own to cut,* she had written to me. *It was mine. I had cared for it since you were born. What right had you to betray such a trust?* We spoke again only once before she died."

Finally she said:

"I regret none of this. Do you understand?" and was silent again. She closed her eyes. "Will somebody build up the fire? I am cold."

For a long time nothing happened in the garden. Afternoon crept toward evening; the fire burned down; the fortune-teller somnolently addressed her cards. Ashlyme sketched the strange long hands of Audsley King. (Later he was to use them as the basis of the equivocal sequence "Studies of some of my friends," fifty small oils on wood which bemuse us by their repetition of a single image differentiated only by minute changes in the background light.) Occasionally he glanced at her face. Her eyes were half closed, mimicking the exhausted trance of the invalid, while from beneath the grey papery lids she judged his reaction to her little biographical fable. He had decided to hold his tongue. He would take the story away with him and hope its meaning eventually became clear.

"One July," she said suddenly, "storms came up from Radiopolis nine days in succession, and always at the same time in the evening. We sat in the summer house, my sisters and I, watching the damp soak into the coloured wood which formed the dome of the roof." She spoke quickly and fractiously, as if she had pulled this memory across like a screen to hide something else. "In drier weather we—"

She broke off distractedly.

"My life is like a letter torn up twenty years ago," she said in a low, anguished voice. "I have thought about it so often that the original sense is lost."

The unfinished portrait attracted her attention. She got unsteadily to her feet and stumbled through the edges of the fire, the hem of her coat scattering charcoal and ashes. She took the canvas off the easel and stared intently at it. "Who's this?" she demanded. "What a travesty!" She laughed loudly and threw it in the fire. It lay there inertly in the middle of the flames, then, with a sudden dull whooshing sound, flared up white and orange. "Who is it, Ashlyme?" She whirled round and struck out at him; groaned with vertigo; fell against him, hot and fragile as a bird. He grasped her wrists. "None of it will work now," she whispered. "How could you let me die here, Ashlyme?"

This was so unfair he could think of nothing to say. He blinked helplessly at the burning portrait.

Fat Mam Etteilla, accustomed to these brief and febrile rebellions, had got patiently to her feet: now she spread her great capable arms in an elephantine gesture of comfort and tried to sweep Audsley King up in them. Audsley King, choking and weeping, avoided her with a fish-like twist. "Go back to your damned gutter!" she said. She caught sight of the tarot pack, spread out on the fortune-teller's table. "These cards will never save me now. They smell of candles. They smell of old lust." She consigned them in handfuls to the flames, where they fluttered, blackened, and finally blazed like caged linnets in a house fire in the Rue Montdampierre.

"Where is the intercession you promised?" wept Audsley King. "Where is the remission you foresaw?" And she darted away across the garden to crouch coughing desperately at the base of the wall.

Four or five of the cards, though charred at the edges, had escaped worse damage. Without quite knowing why, Ashlyme pulled them out of the fire and gave them back to the fortune-teller. He watched himself doing this, rather surprised—licking his fingers, steeling himself briefly, plunging his hand into the fire before he could think about it further—and regretted the gesture almost immediately. Fat Mam Etteilla received the cards as her due, tucked them away without comment like a handkerchief in the sleeve of her grubby cotton dress. And as soon as he saw that he had burned himself, Ashlyme felt ill and resentful. Audsley King's behaviour had caused him to act without thinking. He marched over to her.

"It was not fair to burn the portrait," he said, "or the cards. We cannot make you immortal."

She stared up at him until she had forced him to look away.

"You are only playing at this!" he shouted. "I thought you had rejected the poses of the High City." He walked off angrily, waving his arms. "You must make up your mind what you really want, if you want me to help you at all."

She coughed painfully.

"I am already dead as far as the High City is concerned," she called after him. "Why should they have even a portrait of me? They are all up there, waiting to bid for it, just like vultures!"

He forced himself to ignore this, although he knew it was probably true. He got hold of a stick and poked about with it in the fire, trying to make out which of the tarry flakes of ash had been his canvas, which the unfortunate Fat Mam's cards. Slowly his anger wore off and he stopped trembling. He blew on his smarting fingertips. When he was able to turn round again, he found the fortune-teller standing patiently behind him, supporting Audsley King in her arms like a tired child. She was too weak to cause them any further trouble. Silently they carried her inside. When Ashlyme looked down from the first landing, the fire had gone out and the corners of the garden had filled up with shadows. A small wind licked the embers, so that they blazed up briefly the colour of senna flowers, silhouetting his easel as it stood there like a small bony animal tethered and waiting for its owner.

Halfway up the stairs, a thin line of blood ran out of the corner of Audsley King's mouth. Her eyes widened; brightened; dulled. "I have such bad dreams about fish," she said drowsily. "Can't we go up another way?"

What was Ashlyme to do?

Audsley King has changed her mind, he wrote optimistically in a note to his friend Buffo, though in fact he was far from sure that she had. "*I shall come and see you immediately.*"

Unsure of his reception—after all, he had not only abandoned the astronomer during the débâcle in the Rue Serpolet, he had ignored him thereafter—he waited nervously for a reply. None came.

We must make new plans, he had written. And yet when it came to planning he found his brain full of contradictory considerations, or else as empty as a new canvas. *Audsley King must have somewhere to live, for instance, if she is coming up here. She must have money.* However distasteful it was to him, he should, he knew, go and see Paulinus Rack, with whom he could perhaps arrange such things. But the longer it took Buffo to reply to his note the less faith he had in Audsley King's change of mind—and the longer he stayed in his studio, biting his pen, listening to the rain dripping in the attic, trying to conjure up in his mind's eye a picture of the thin, intense provincial girl who had arrived in Viriconium twenty years ago to shock the artistic establishment of the day with the suppressed violence and frozen sexual somnambulism of her self-portraits.

During this period he saw very little of the Grand Cairo.

Messages more or less urgent still arrived at the studio, usually at night, and in them were named meeting places more or less remote. But the dwarf rarely turned up now *at early evening by the Haunted Gate,* or deep in the overgrown shadows of the cisPontine Quarter, where only owls now lived; so Ashlyme began to feel that he could ignore them safely. He did go to Montrouge one night—he was returning through the Haadenbosk from a dinner given by the Marchioness "L" for Mme. Chevigne, Vera Ghillera, and the cast of *The Little Humpbacked Horse*—hoping perhaps to rekindle the dwarf's enthusiasm for Audsley King. But there were no lights behind the half-completed terra-cotta façades of the civic building programme. And when he reached the tower it was dark and preoccupied.

Two or three cats ran out of a trench dug across the newly surfaced road at my feet, he wrote in his journal. *Their eyes were green and blank. Has the dwarf already left Viriconium? Or was he crouched up there in the darkness among his rusty knives and hair totems, trying to keep track of his plots against the Barley brothers?*

He had something of an answer to this a few days later in the plague zone.

On a visit to the Rue Serpolet he was forced out of his way by the attentions of the beggars in the Plaza of Unrealised Time. He found himself on the seeping periphery of Cheminor, that suburb of flaking brick walls where the streets are lined with graveyards, old churches, and boarding-houses. At night the lamps there give off an orange glare which muddles the sense of perspective and gives the blank faces of the people a suffering look. They seem to float towards you in their cheap sober clothes, then away from you again like ghosts. It is often called "the Undertakers' Quarter." Ashlyme, unencumbered by his easel for once, was making his way down an alley which opened onto the main thoroughfare of Endingall Street, when he heard the sound of running footsteps.

He popped his head out of the mouth of the alley. Up and down Endingall Street the orange lamps stretched dully away. He had the impression of a crowd of people coming quickly towards him. He withdrew his head and waited.

A moment later a small agitated figure ran past. It was the Grand Cairo. He had a leather cosh in one hand, and in the other something that looked like a long kitchen knife. He passed the mouth of the alley in a flash, the skirts of his black coat slapping his knees and his steel-toe-capped boots thudding urgently as he propelled himself down the middle of the road with his head thrown back and his breath hissing between his bared teeth. There were extensive stains on his hands, made blackish by the orange light, and on the blade of his knife. His eyes were white and staring with effort. He risked a glance over his shoulder, groaned, and ran on, looking neither right nor left.

Close on his heels came a score of *his own policemen*, waving their arms and tugging back on the leads of their enormous dogs.

It was over in an instant: one moment Endingall Street was full of the pursuit, carried on in grim silence but for the pounding of feet, the hoarse panting and choking of the dogs; the next there was only a fading whiff of Altaean Balm to suggest that the dwarf had even been there. Had he killed someone again? Why else would he be chased by his own men? Ashlyme blinked into the orange glare. Endingall Street was bounded by a high wall, purpled with soot. Over the top of it he suddenly caught sight of an ornamental obelisk, bearing the figure of a stone bird poised for flight. It was a cemetery. Had they chased the dwarf into it? For a moment Ashlyme debated going to see. Then he walked quickly off in the direction of the Artists' Quarter. By the time he found himself on familiar ground, the whole event had taken on the distant, unreal air of a scene in an old play, and he had almost convinced himself it was not the Grand Cairo he had seen, but some other very small man.

Later that evening he met Fat Mam Etteilla hurrying away from the Rue Serpolet in the direction of the High City. A fine rain had beaded her bare arms and greying hair; it gave her cheeks the same varnished appearance as the fruit on her hat. She clutched in her reddened hands the handles of an assortment of shopping bags which bulged with old clothes. She seemed withdrawn and thoughtful, heavy with determination. He walked along with her silently for a few minutes, glancing up every so often at her monumental body towering above him, and admiring what he had earlier described as her "implacable simplicity."

"How is Audsley King?" he asked. "I'm off to see her now. I expect you'll be back there soon?" When she didn't answer he went on anxiously, "Do you think she should be left alone at this time of night?"

The fortune-teller shrugged.

"I can't help her," she said, staring darkly off into the rain, "if she won't help herself. She has no faith in me or in the cards." She made a peculiar, puzzled, hopeless gesture, lifting the shopping bags for Ashlyme to see. "She told me to pack my things," she said. "That's what she's just done." She wiped the rain off her face with a sudden angry motion. Her eyes were hard and hurt.

"She's like a child," protested Ashlyme. "She doesn't mean it."

Fat Mam Etteilla sniffed. "I've packed my things, as I was told to," she said stubbornly. "You have to go where the faith is." She shook her head. "I could have helped her," she said. "She begged me to, as you well know." She walked away from Ashlyme, quickly and angrily, leaving him behind as if he reminded her too much of Audsley King. "Begged me to," she repeated, with a sort of massive dignity. "But I can't do any more if she doesn't respect my cards."

Ashlyme didn't know what to say. He struggled to keep up with her, but in her anger and hurt pride she quickly left him behind. He stood on the wet pavement feeling isolated and abandoned. "I thought I saw the Grand Cairo an hour ago," he shouted suddenly. "He seemed to be in a hurry." If he had hoped to surprise her he was mistaken. She walked on like a tired horse, her broad back moving steadily away towards the Plaza of

Unrealised Time. Eventually she looked back at him and nodded. "I knew it was you who came dressed as a fish," she said. "Oh, you could have helped her once, I give you your due for that. But you should have got her out of there while you still had the courage of your convictions." Then she was gone.

He was in the Rue Serpolet for an hour and a half, whistling and calling up at the lighted window of Audsley King's studio. A shadow moved back and forth in front of the shadow of an easel, but she would not let him in, and all he could hear was her harsh, mannish sobbing. The air was full of withered chestnut leaves, which touched his face like wet hands.

He continued to hear nothing from Emmet Buffo. Was the astronomer ignoring him out of pique? Should he go to Alves and see him anyway? He was loth somehow to make the journey. He sent another note instead.

While he wasted his energy thus, unaware that he had so little time left at his disposal, autumn, like a thin melancholy, settled itself into the plague zone. Down there it was as if the world had become as flimsy as the muslin curtains at an old woman's window in the Via Gellia: as if the actual essence of the world was too old to care anymore about keeping up appearances. With the first frosts, unknown wasting diseases had swept the Low City; and the quarantine police, unable to deal with the situation, unsure even whether the new phthisias and fevers were contagious, had panicked and begun to seal and burn the houses of the dead. For days the dusty avenues and abandoned alleyways had been full of reluctant fires, flickering at night like blue gas flames, as feeble and debilitated as the zone itself, which now crept quietly over its original boundary at the Pleasure Canal, inundating Lime Walk and the Terrace of the Fallen Leaves and stealing up towards the ponderous great houses, the banks of anemones, the tall pastel towers of the High City. Alves held out on its steep spur, eccentric and insular in a greyish sea.

As the plague tightened its grip, so the Barley brothers tried harder to become human.

If indeed they did create the city "from a handful of dust," Ashlyme told his journal, these brothers seem to have done so only in order to vandalise it. They contribute nothing. They get into the wineshops at night and steal from the barrels. When they go fishing in the Pleasure Canal it is only to fill a jam jar full of mud and stagger home at midnight as pissed as the newts they have been able to discern, always out of reach, in the cloudy water.

But if the Barley brothers felt from afar the warmth of Ashlyme's disapproval, they did not show it. They continued to grin and snigger nightly in the queue outside Agden Fincher's pie shop; they continued to hunt rats with their cudgels and Dandy Dinmont dogs among the derelict suburbs of the plague zone, taking huge hauls of these vermin from the boarded-up warehouses and empty cellars and trying to sell them for a shilling a time to astonished restauranteurs on the Margarethestrasse. *Their imagination,* complained Ashlyme, *is vile and wayward.* And as if in response to this, they invented donkey jackets, Wellington boots, and small white plastic trays covered in congealed food with which they littered the streets and gutters of Mynned.

The High City, which had recovered its heart, followed these adventures with an indulgent eye, "Besotted," as Ashlyme expressed it one day to the Marchioness "L," "by a vitality it admires but dare not emulate."

The Marchioness gave him a vague, propitiatory smile.

"I'm sure we none of us begrudge them their youth," she said. "And they do take our minds wonderfully off our present troubles!" She leaned forward. "Master Ashlyme, I fear that Paulinus Rack will have to abandon *The Dreaming Boys.*" She waved her hand in the general direction of the Low City. "In the present situation we all feel very strongly that we should have something less gloomy in the theatre. Of course, it is a pity that we shall not now see Audsley King's marvellous stage sets . . ." Here, she left an expectant pause, and when Ashlyme failed to respond, reminded him gently, "Master Ashlyme, we do so rely on you for our news of Audsley King."

"Audsley King is near to death," he answered. "She will not rest but she cannot paint. She has lost faith in her art, herself, everything. Every time I go there she has allowed herself closer to the brink." He paced agitatedly up and down the studio. "Even now she might be saved. But I will not force her to leave that place. I find that for me to act, the decision must be hers." He bit his lip. To his horror he found himself admitting, "Marchioness, I am in despair. Can *you* believe she wishes to die?"

This question seemed to take the Marchioness by surprise. She stared at him thoughtfully for some time, as if trying to assess his sincerity (or perhaps her own). Then she said meditatively:

"Did you know that Audsley King was once married to Paulinus Rack?"

Ashlyme looked at her in astonishment.

"It was a long time ago. You are certainly too young to remember. The marriage ended when Rack first made his name in the High City, with those sentimental watercolours of life in the Artists' Quarter. He called them 'Bohemian days.' At the Bistro Californium and the Luitpold Café they never forgave him for that. He had been a leading light in their 'new movement,' you see. They were all supposed to be above money and that sort of thing. They held a funeral, complete with an ornate coffin, which they said was 'the funeral of Art in Viriconium.' Audsley King was the first to throw earth on the coffin when they buried it on Allman's Heath. Later she claimed that her husband had died of syphilis: a symbolic punishment."

The Marchioness thought for a moment. "Of course," she went on, "Rack's later behaviour rather tended to confirm their opinion of him."

She got up to leave. Pulling on her gloves, she said, "You are very fond of her, Master Ashlyme. You must not allow her to bully you because of that."

She paused at Ashlyme's front door to admire the city. Sunshine and showers had filled the streets of Mynned with a slanting watercolourist's light; a bank of cloud was advancing from the west, edged at its summit with silver and tinged beneath with the soft purplish grey of pigeon feathers. "What a delightful afternoon it is!" she exclaimed. "I shall walk." But she lingered on the pavement as if trying to decide whether to add something to what she had already said. "Audsley King, you know, was a spoilt child. She has never made up her mind between public acclaim—which she sees, rightly or wrongly, as destructive of the true artistic impulse—and obscurity, for which she is not temperamentally fitted."

Ashlyme said neutrally, "She doesn't respect the judgement of the High City."

"Just so," said the Marchioness, looking out across the jumbled roofs of the Quarter. "I expect you are right." She smiled sadly. "We must hope she has more faith in yours."

When she had gone, Ashlyme sat in the studio like a stone. "Married to Paulinus Rack!" he said to himself, and, " 'Something less gloomy in the theatre'! Has no one told them up here that the world is coming to an end?" He got up suddenly and hurried out. The Marchioness had convinced him, as she had perhaps intended, that action was still possible.

THE FIFTH CARD

THE HERMETIC FEAST

A legacy will come to you from a far-off country. Light, truth, the unravelling of involved matters. In this card everything is revealed. If it comes next to No. 4 it predicts you will fall in the sea.

"I believe that the 'Waste Land' is really the very heart of our problem; a rightful appreciation of its position and significance will place us in possession of the clue which will lead us safely through the most bewildering mazes."
JESSIE L. WESTON, *From Ritual to Romance*

Afternoon was slipping away into evening as he made his way up the long hill to Alves. He saw immediately that there was something wrong. A strange flat light hung round the old towers, so that he seemed to be looking at them through dirty glass; the cries of the jackdaws as they wheeled round the dome of the derelict palace had a remote and uninflected note, as if they came from much further away; the peeling middle-class villas on the slopes below had aged since his last visit, and their overgrown gardens were full of household rubbish and decaying bricks. A dog trotted aimlessly about in the road ahead of him, sniffing the dust as it whirled round in cold circles. The hill seemed endless. Halfway up it he broke into a run. He could not have explained why.

Emmet Buffo's door was open and the damp had blown into his rooms. A stale smell came from the alcove where he did his cooking. He lay under a cheap coloured blanket in the low iron bed by the washstand. He was dead. On the floor beside him were scattered the remains of two or three meals and—as if he had dropped them and never found the strength to pick them up again—a few small ground-glass lenses of different colours.

Beneath the blanket his body had assumed an awkward posture, twisted partly on its side: it was as if it had contracted unevenly after death, curling up like an insect. One thin arm was bent behind his head, while the other hung over the side of the bed, its long, clumsily knuckled hand touching the floor. Perhaps he had been trying to turn over. He looked old. He looked, with his intelligent, tired eyes, his worn, unshaven face, and big raw ears, as defenceless, honest, and undemanding as he had ever done.

On a table by the bed were some sheets of paper which he had covered with numbered notes in a spiky, erratic hand. Though the notes were unrelated, the numbers gave them a mad air of continuity, as if they were intended as steps in a logical argument. *No one has come to visit me in my illness,* read one. *Hindering the scientist is a crime, it is murdering knowledge in the bud!* claimed another. *Why have I never received sufficient finance?* he asked himself, and answered: *Because I have never convinced them of the significance of the* stars, *among which mankind once flew.*

How long had he lain there, writing when he could, staring at the mouldy shapes on the wall when fatigue overcame him and sleep evaded him, unable to prevent himself from speculating, formulating, rationalising? *I must always remember that Art is as important as Science, and contain my impatience!*

Poor Emmet Buffo!—The world had puzzled him by its indifference, but he blamed no one.

Strewn haphazardly round the room were the curious flannel bandages in which he had swaddled himself for the "rescue" of Audsley King. Ashlyme stared dumbly at them. In his mind's eye he could see Buffo quite clearly: arguing with the women on the dusty staircase; pushing the empty handcart in erratic spurts along the Rue Serpolet in the rain; hopping from one foot to the other in the deserted observatory as he fought to free himself from the stinking confinement of the horse's-head mask. How long had he waited for Ashlyme to come and reassure him he was safe?

The observatory was in disorder. The roof lights had been left open to admit a wet, chilly air, which had stripped from the walls the last of Buffo's charts. Some crisis in his illness had prompted him to stagger in here and collapse among his telescopes: or perhaps he had simply destroyed them out of despair. Bent brass tubing littered the floor, and when he went over to examine it, Ashlyme felt the little lenses crush beneath his feet like sugared anemones. He rubbed the condensation from a pane of glass and looked out over the Low City. He could see nothing. He could feel nothing. Night was approaching. The ramshackle greenhouse seemed to rush through the twilight like a ship. He had an overwhelming sense of disaster. He knew that if he admired Audsley King, then he had loved Emmet Buffo.

He bent to the eyepiece of one of the broken telescopes.

For a second he thought he could see a vast white plain, arranged geometrically, on which were hundreds of stone catafalques, stretching away to a curved horizon. An implacable light slanted down on them, but it began to fade before he had understood the scene before him.

He heard a sound in the other room.

When he went to see what it was he found that a detachment of the quarantine police had arrived. They filled the place up. Black uniforms, blue-tinted spectacles, and huge dogs on leads gave them an air of bravado and efficiency. But behind the spectacles their eyes were harassed and nervous, and after a hurried examination of Buffo's corpse two of them began pouring oil on the bedclothes, the woodwork, and the walls above the bed. Two more pushed past Ashlyme into the observatory and set about smashing windows to create a good through draught. The rest stood about, chuckling over Buffo's underwear, riffling through his papers, and dragging the dogs off the stale food in the alcove. Despite all this they were not unkind men, and they were surprised to find Ashlyme in the house.

"What are you doing?" he demanded. "Leave those things alone! Who sent you here?"

They took him quietly aside. In cases like this, they explained, cremation was the rule: although they didn't, personally, enjoy the work. "Your father died three days ago, we don't know what of," they said. They had only just got round to him, due to pressure of work. "It's so difficult now to get places to burn properly." Recently an old woman in Henrietta Street had taken three attempts; a baker's family at the lower end of the Margarethestrasse, five: all this was very time-consuming. "These rooms should have been sealed until we arrived." They didn't know how Ashlyme had got in. It was not that they didn't admire his courage. But there was nothing he could do here now.

"He wasn't my father," said Ashlyme dully. "Why are you burning him? At least his work should be saved! Look, this is his 'exterior brain': it's not by any means an ordinary library."

"It all has to go," they repeated patiently. They were used to the protests of the bereaved. "We don't know what he died of, you see. Alves is in the plague zone now. You want to foot it while you can!"

The plague zone.

A few minutes later Ashlyme stood in the street staring up at the top of the building. A subdued, almost reluctant explosion shook it suddenly, and glass showered down from the penthouse. Strange slow blue flames issued from the upper windows, flames so pale they seemed transparent against the great black bulk of the hill behind.

"This house was always in a plague zone," said Ashlyme bitterly. "That is why all our schemes came to nothing."

All at once he was terrified that the same thing might be happening across the city at Audsley King's house: the thick oil, the smashed windows, the dilatory flames. The only person he could think of who might help him prevent that was the Grand Cairo. He ran off down the hill. When he looked back, the peculiar fire had already lost its force and he could see only a knot of dark figures in the middle of the avenue.

The High City was cold and bright under the colourless moon of autumn. The echo of Ashlyme's footsteps came back to him changed and muffled, as if from a place a long distance away. We were all accomplices to Buffo's death, he thought wildly as he ran, we are all to blame. He had no idea what he meant by this, and it gave him no relief. When at last he came to the Grand Cairo's tower in Montrouge, he was frightened to go in. All its doors and windows hung open in the pitiless light.

Inside, hundreds of the dwarf's followers had killed each other during the early part of the night. They lay mainly on the stairs and in the corridors between the hastily constructed offices and interrogation rooms, their violent and confused shadows frozen on the walls. They had not had time to prepare. Some of them clutched handfuls of hair pulled out or collars torn off during the fighting; others had knives or razors, or improvised strangling cords; most were bitten about the face and hands. Huge glittering unearthly flies, their energy dulled a little by the cold, went from wound to wound in strict rotation in the bright moonlight, making a dry, desultory buzzing as they rose and fell.

Ashlyme looked at them numbly. He got himself upstairs to a room he recognised from a previous visit, hoping to find someone there who could take him to the Grand Cairo. Attempts had been made to set it on fire. Its occupants had smashed the desk open and soaked their own coats in oil, then applied the charred garments to the flimsy partition wall, which was now full of blackened holes. They had also attempted to burn the documents which spilled out of the fireplace and across the floor. In the end they had given up and killed each other with a paper knife before the flames could take hold. Ashlyme picked up some of the documents. *Day by day our position becomes more precarious . . . The Barley brothers have named names . . . We now have a handpicked guard at every gate . . .* He threw them down again, but not before they had set up in his head a kind of hideous drone which followed him from corridor to corridor and staircase to staircase up the tower.

All the offices were the same. From a brass voice pipe Ashlyme thought he heard a whisper, but when he spoke into it there was no answer, only a long echoic sigh. He knew that he was now in the country the dwarf had spoken of so often. *Intrigue and backstabbing and great flies in everything you eat.* Ashlyme wiped his hand over his face: if he wasn't careful, he knew, he could be caught there forever. It was a country that accompanied the dwarf wherever he went; it was an atmosphere that surrounded him, miasmic and pervasive, like the smell of Altaean Balm; he had brought it with him, down from the North or the sky, and visited it on the city. *Two thousand men were thrown into fires in one day. Those people had abandoned themselves to conspiracy.*

Flies rose in clouds as Ashlyme made his way into the older places of the tower. Even there, dead men lay facedown among the orange peel and other rubbish in the gloomy carmine-lit passageways. They had daubed slogans on the walls in their own fluids as they waited to die—*Up the North, Ya bas, Go back, yellows*—their motives so tribal as to be indistinguishable from motivelessness. *We are the boys from the second floor!*

A fly settled on his wrist. Its wings were long and papery, and it seemed to have more legs than any fly he had seen in Viriconium. He shuddered and threw it off. Its eyes glittered at him.

Eventually he found his way into the Grand Cairo's suite, where for a week or more the dwarf, afraid of the plague, afraid of the Barley brothers and their informants who by now knew almost everything, afraid most of all of his own disintegrating gang, had forbidden anyone to enter. The rooms were dirty and cold, and he had allowed his cats (who, he said, were the only creatures you could trust in this life) the run of them. Just inside the door a servant was sprawled. He had been there for some days. Someone had passed a piece of stiff wire through his head from one ear to the other. A thick sour smell rose from the polished floor, where the cats had dragged chop bones and pies from among the broken crockery on the tray he had been carrying and dipped their unfastidious little tongues in the long sticky spill of "housemaid's coffee." Ashlyme went to open the windows.

When he looked out, expecting to see the High City stretching away in the moonlight, he discovered that he was staring instead across the bleak watersheds of some high plateau in the North. Rain streamed over it from a leaden sky, washing away at the aimless muddy paths which wound between the foundering cairns and ruined factories. He heard a noise like the far-off ringing of a bell. At this a few small figures appeared, ran this way and that in the mud, and then lay down. A poisonous metallic smell came up into the room. Ashlyme drew in his breath quickly, shut the windows, and turned away.

Two or three cats had run in off the balcony outside, and now accompanied him purring into the *salle* or side chamber.

White dustcloth hung off the walls in great swathes; underfoot was a muck of chewed bones, bits of cake, and fruit peel, among which Ashlyme saw books, squares of paper covered with designs half-Gnostic, half-obscene, and—to his horror—two small canvases of Audsley King's: "Making a chair in the Vitelotte Quarter" and an early gouache of "The great arch beneath the Hidden Gate," the latter slashed and daubed beyond repair. In a corner with some hanks of hair and a rusty spade lay the sheep's head which had been the centrepiece of the dwarf's banqueting table on the night he had made Fat Mam Etteilla read his future. He had flung it there in some fit of rage or pique, and now, one withered orange still stuck in its left eye socket, it stared cynically up into the blackened vault of the original room, the rafters of which had received to themselves during the Afternoon Cultures a millennium of strange smokes and incenses.

At the centre of all this stood the Grand Cairo, surrounded by a circle of shrouded furniture.

He had on dark green stockings, and a jerkin made all of green leather lozenges; on his head was a straw hat with a wide brim and a low, rounded crown, surmounted by bunches of owl feathers, ears of corn, and varnished gooseberries. Whatever he had once been, he now seemed to Ashlyme like an ancient, impudent child. In one hand he held tight to something Ashlyme couldn't quite see; while with the other he clutched the big, work-reddened fingers of the Fat Mam, who cast on him an indulgent, matronly glance. In the Plaza of Unrealised Time she had been known by a voluminous yellow satin gown: she was wearing it now. Ribbons of the same colour were tied loosely about her powerful upper arms, and on her head she bore a wreath of sol d'or.

At their feet she had arranged the five surviving cards of the fortune-telling pack which Ashlyme had pulled from the bonfire of elder boughs and old letters in the walled garden of Audsley King:

DEPOUILLEMENT *(Loss)*—A bleak foreshore. Creatures of the deep float half submerged in the ebb tide. The sky is full of owls.

THE LILYWHITE BOYS, "Lords of Illusionary Success"—Some pale children jump back and forth like frogs across a fire of sea holly and yew.

THE CITY *(Nothingness)*—A dog between two towers.

THE LORD OF THE FIRST OPERATION—In this card a monkey in a red jacket directs with his wand the antics of a man and a rat.

ECLAIRCISSEMENT (*Enlightenment,* or "The Hermetic Feast")—The doctor of this mystery lies beneath the sea. In one hand he holds a spray of rose hips, in the other a bell.

"What are you doing?" asked Ashlyme in a whisper.

The dwarf gave him a coy smile, then moved his free hand slightly, so as to show him a cake of soap filled with broken razor blades.

"Wait!" cried Ashlyme. Something appalling was going to happen. He flung himself across the room, shouting, "What about Audsley King?"

The fortune-teller raised her hand. The dwarf winked. Out of the tarot cards on the floor came an intense coloured flare of light, as if they had been illuminated suddenly from behind. Ashlyme felt it flash across his face, green and yellow, scarlet and deep blue, like light from a melting stained-glass window. There was an unbearable *newness* to it as it scoured that ancient room. Ashlyme staggered back.

"Wait!" he cried, flinging up his arm in front of his eyes, but not before he had seen the dwarf and fortune-teller begin to shrink, blasted and shrivelled by that curious glare into bundles of hair and paper ribbon which whirled faster and faster round the floor like rubbish on a windy street corner, until they toppled over suddenly and fell down into the cards with a faint cry.

The room was filled with a white effulgence so intense that he could see, through eyelid and muscle tissue, the bones of his forearm. He groaned and fell heavily on the floor.

When he was able to open his eyes again, he was alone with the cards. They had been scattered and and charred by the force of the light which still radiated from them into every corner of the room. He knelt and collected them together, hissing and blowing on the tips of his fingers. He thought he could see two new figures running between the towers of the card called THE CITY. "Wait!" he whispered, demented with fear and frustration. The light died as abruptly as it had come.

The death and defection of his only allies left him alone in a place he hardly recognised. In one night the plague zone had extended its boundaries by two miles, perhaps three. The High City had succumbed at last. Later he was to write:

A quiet shabbiness seemed to have descended unnoticed on the squares and avenues. Waste paper blew round my legs as I crossed the empty perspectives of the Atteline Way; the bowls of the everlasting fountains at Delpine Square were dry and dust-filled, the flagstones slippery with birdlime underfoot; insects circled and fell in the orange lamplight along the Camine Auriale. The plague had penetrated everywhere. All evening the salons and drawing rooms of the High City had been haunted by silences, pauses, faux pas: *if anyone heard me when I flung myself exhausted against some well-known front door to get my breath it was only as another intrusion, a harsh, lonely sound which relieved briefly the stultified conversation, the unending dinner with its luke-*

warm sauces and overcooked mutton, or the curiously flat tone of the visiting violinist (who subsequently shook his instrument and complained, "I find the ambience rather unsympathetic tonight.")

This psychological disorder of the city was reflected in a new disorder of its streets. It was a city I knew and yet I could not find my way about it. Avenue turned into endless avenue. Alleys turned back on themselves. The familiar roads repeated themselves infinitely in rows of dusty chestnut trees and iron railings. If I found my way in the gardens of the Haadenbosk, I lost it again on the Pont des Arts, and ended up looking at my own reflection dissolving in the oily water below. Though the events I had witnessed in the Grand Cairo's tower had numbed it a little, the grief and shame I felt over my friend's death was still strong. I struggled too with a rapidly growing fear for the safety of Audsley King. Everyone had deserted her but me. In this way I came eventually—by luck or destiny—to the top of the Gabelline Stairs.

Here he encountered the Barley brothers, Gog and Matey, who came reeling up from the Low City towards him with their arms full of bottles. They had been spitting on the floor all night at Agden Fincher's pie shop. As soon as they saw Ashlyme bearing down on them they gave him queasy grins and reeled off the way they had come, pushing and shoving one another guiltily and whispering, "Blimey, it's the vicar!"

But at the bottom of the stairs, near that small iron gate through which Ashlyme would have to pass if he wanted to enter the Low City, they seemed to falter suddenly. They stood in his way, sniffing and hawking and wiping their noses on the backs of their hands.

"Let me through that gate!" panted Ashlyme. "Do you think I want to waste my time with you? Because of you one of my friends is already dead!"

They stared, embarrassed, at the floor.

"Look here, yer honour," said Matey. "We didn't know it was Sunday. Sorry."

As he spoke he furtively used the sole of one turned-down Wellington boot to scrape the foetid clay off the uppers of the other. His brother tried to tidy him up—tugging at his neckerchief, brushing vainly at the mud, fish slime, and rats' blood congealing on his jacket. A horrible smell came up from him. He looked bashfully away and began to hum,

> "Ousted out of Butlins, Bilston, and Mexborough,
> Those bold Barley brothers,
> Lords of the Left Hand Thread."

"Are you mad?" demanded Ashlyme.

"We've had no supper," said Gog. He spat on his hand and plastered down his brother's reeking hair.

Ashlyme thought of Emmet Buffo, who all his life had achieved nothing but ridicule, and who now lay quiet and unshaven, surrounded by pale flames, in the iron bed up at Alves. He thought of Audsley King coughing up blood in the overcast light of the deserted studio above the Rue Serpolet. He thought of Paulinus Rack's greed, the trivial lives of Livio Fognet and Angina Desformes, the frustrated intelligence of the Marchioness "L," which had trickled away into scandal and "art."

"If you are indeed the gods of this place," he said, "you have done it nothing but harm." He made a gesture which encompassed the whole city. "Don't you see?" he appealed. "When you came down from the sky you failed us all. I have lost count of the times when you have been dragged spewing and helpless from the Pleasure Canal! It is not the behaviour of gods or princes. And while you occupy yourselves thus, you condemn us all to waste and mediocrity, madness and disorder, misery and an early death!"

He stared into their big sheepish blue eyes.

"Is this what you want? If you do, you have become worthless, and we are better off without you!"

To begin with the Barley brothers made a great show of paying attention to this speech. A nod was as good as a wink to them, implied the one; while by means of agitated grimaces, groans, and shrugs, the other tried to convey that he too knew when things had got out of hand. Easily bored, though, they were soon trying to put Ashlyme off—imitating his facial expressions, spluttering and sniggering at unfortunate turns of phrase, pushing one another furtively when they thought he wasn't looking. In the end, even as he was urging them, "Go back to your proper place in the sky before it is too late!" they eyed each other slyly and let fall a resounding succession of belches and farts.

"Gor!" cried Matey. "What a roaster!"

"Hang on! Hang on!" warned his brother. "Here comes another one!"

A foul smell drifted up the Gabelline Stairs.

Ashlyme bit his lip. Suddenly there welled up in him all the misery he had felt since his failure to rescue Audsley King. With an incoherent shout he flung himself at his tormentors, clutching at their coats and punching out blindly. Overcome with farts and helpless laughter they staggered back away from him. He heard himself sobbing with frustration. "You filthy stupid boys!" he wept. He plucked at their arms and tried to twist his fingers in their stubbly hair; he kicked their shins, which only made them laugh more loudly. He didn't know how to hurt them. Then he remembered the little knife the dwarf had given him. Panting and shaking, he tugged it from his pocket and held it out in front of him.

At this a curious change came over the Barley brothers. Their cruel laughter died. They regarded Ashlyme in horror and amazement. Then, blubbering with a fear quite out of proportion to their plight, they began to run aimlessly this way and that, waving their arms in a placatory and disorganised fashion. Penned into that cramped space which is neither High City nor Low, they made no attempt to escape up the staircase but only jostled one another desperately as Ashlyme chased them round and round, the flawed blade of the Grand Cairo's mysterious knife glinting in the light from above.

"Come on, vicar!" they urged him. "Play the white man!"

They blundered into the walls; they crashed into the gate and shook it wildly, but it wouldn't budge. Round and round they went. Their great red faces were dripping with sweat, their eyes were wide, and small, panicky sounds came out of their sagging, open mouths: and for some reason he was never able to explain, this display of weakness only offended Ashlyme further, so that he pursued them with a renewed vigour, a kind of disgusted excitement, round in circles until he was as confused and dizzy as they were.

Matey Barley, tottering about in the gloom, bumped into his brother, jumped away with a yelp of surprise, and ran straight onto the little knife.

"Ooh," he said. "That hurt."

He looked down at himself. A quick, artless smile of disbelief crossed his great big fat face, which then collapsed like an empty bag, and he started to sob gently, as if he had glimpsed in that instant the implications of his condition. He sank to his knees, his eyes fixed on Ashlyme in perplexity and awe; he took Ashlyme's bloody hand and cradled it tenderly between his own; a shiver passed through him, and he farted suddenly into the total apprehensive silence of the Gabelline Stairs. "Make us a pie, Fincher!" he whispered. Then he fell on his face and was still.

Fixed in an instant of violent expectancy, Ashlyme had no clear idea of what he had done. He would force things to a conclusion. "Quick!" he demanded of the remaining brother. "You must now accept the responsibilities of your state!" His grip on the knife became so urgent that cramps and spasms shook his upper body. "Tell me why you brought us all to this! Or shall I kill you, too?"

Gog Barley drew himself up with sudden dignity.

"The citizens are responsible for the state of the city," he said. "If you had only asked yourselves what was the matter with the city, all would have been well. Audsley King would have been healed. Art would have been made whole. The energy of the Low City would have been released and the High City freed from the thrall of its mediocrity."

He hiccuped mournfully. "Now my brother lies dead upon this stair, and you must heal yourselves." He bent down and began raking through the bottles he had dropped earlier.

Ashlyme was disgusted, but could find nothing adequate to say. "Will she die, then, despite everything?" he whispered to himself. And then, in a feeble attempt to rekindle his authority, "You have not said enough!" Gog Barley received this remark with a look of contempt. "Besides," said Ashlyme, cowed, "I did not mean to kill him. I've been with that damned dwarf too long."

"Matey was me brother!" cried Gog. He had not been able to find a full bottle. "He was me only brother!"

All intelligence deserted him. He tore his hair. He stamped his feet. He let his huge mouth gape open. He raged about in front of the iron gate, picking up bottles and smashing them against the walls where in happier times he and his brother had scratched their initials. Grinding his clumsy fists into his eyes, he roared and wept and howled his grief. And as his tears rolled down they seemed to dissolve the flesh of his cheeks, so that his tormented face shifted and changed before Ashlyme's astonished eyes.

His shapeless nose was washed away, his cheekbones melted and flowed away, as did his raw red ears and the pimples on his stubbly chin—his chin itself melted away like a piece of waterlogged soap. Faster and faster the tears welled up over his chapped knuckles, until they were a rivulet—a torrent—a waterfall which splashed down his barrel chest, cascaded over his feet, and rushed off into an unimaginable outer darkness, cleansing the god in him of the reek of dead fish and stale wine, of all the filth he had accumulated during his long sojourn in the city. So much water was needed to achieve this that it rose round Ashlyme's ankles in a black stream, full of dangerous eddies and bearing a burden of small objects washed from the god's pockets. Ashlyme bent down and dropped his knife into the stream. It was swallowed up, and he never saw it again. He dabbled his bloody hand until it was clean. At last everything earthly was washed away or else irretrievably changed. Gog Barley's filthy coat and boots were washed away on the flood: and when all was done, it could be seen that he had renewed himself completely.

He was taller. His limbs, as pliable as wax under the force of his own tears, had lengthened and taken on more-noble proportions. His hair had grown until it fell about his shoulders like a true god's, framing a face which had become slender, hawk-nosed, and finely wrought, a face full of power and humility, blessed with remote, compassionate, and faintly amused eyes.

But long before this transfiguration had completed itself, Ashlyme had shrugged and turned his back on it. What had the suffering of a god to do with him? He waded the little stream, which was gurgling into the Low City, and went out through the iron gate into the Artists' Quarter.

When he looked back he could see nothing but darkness on the Gabelline Stairs, and above that only cold flickering blue flames, as if the whole of Mynned had now been set on fire by the plague police in some grand final act of despair.

A little later he saw that his boots were quite dry. With a groan he re-membered Audsley King.

He began to run.

The hour before dawn found him in the studio above the Rue Serpolet.

A cold air spilled into it as he pushed aside the curtain at the end of the little passage. He saw straight away that it had not changed. There was the *fauteuil*, with its disordered green chenille cover and piles of brocade cushions. There were the windowsill pots, full of geraniums in hard brown earth, or small bunches of cut anemones and sol d'or. There were the silent easels, some draped, the used and unused canvases stacked against the walls, the bare grey floorboards which gave off into the still, enervated air a faint odour of dust, turpentine, geraniums, old flower water.

Paulinus Rack sat there on the floor in his overcoat. How he had found his way there Ashlyme didn't know. His face was slack and haggard, his hands were dirty; his eyes had a bruised look. Spread out in front of him tentatively, as if he hoped to read something from them, he had two or three unfinished charcoal sketches. Ashlyme could make nothing of them: they were all lines, lines going this way and that. Cradled between Rack's thighs like a sick child, and also facing the sketches, sat Audsley King. Rack's arms were wrapped round her hollow chest to comfort her; his head rested on her shoulder as though he had just that moment stopped whispering to her.

Audsley King, bundled up in her old fur coat in a last attempt to stop her substance evaporating off into the void which had always surrounded her, was staring at the sketches with a wry, amused expression, and there was blood caked in the corner of her smile.

"I was free!" Ashlyme recalled her saying once, of her arrival in the Artists' Quarter from the provinces. "I was free at last, to paint, paint, paint!"

Now painting had finally exhausted her.

She had worked desperately in those last few days, filling canvas after canvas. Most of them were simple, almost sentimental, remembered views: golden dreamy colour put down thickly with a palette knife, as—in a kind of fervid tranquillity, an astonishing balancing act of desperation and calm—she sought to recapture a level of her personality she had lost or abandoned long ago. Or had she only wanted refuge from the empty, stretched-out nights of the plague zone? The fortune-teller's cards had failed her: in opening this other door, onto the idealised landscapes of her youth, had she committed after all that act of escapism she had always so despised? Ashlyme could not be sure. He supposed that now it did not matter.

Honey-coloured stone, oak and ivy, willows and streams. Her delight poured out of them, paling the yellow lamps, overpowering the first grey suggestions of the coming dawn! A narrow road wound nowhere, choked with last year's leaves, banked with brambles and the overgrown boles of trees. Nostalgia burned out of the flat southern landscapes like a pain. And she had peopled them not with the tense, repressed, violently static figures of the self-portraits and "fantasies," but with labourers and farm people, into whose classic postures she had injected a haunted repose.

Everything is new to me, she had scrawled hastily with a piece of charcoal on the wall above them. *New or unrecognisable. What a pity I should die now.* And: *To die is as if one's eyes had been put out. One is abandoned by all. They have slammed the door and gone.*

Ashlyme read this message aloud to himself. He blinked. He passed in front of Paulinus Rack and looked down at the sketches on the floor.

"What do you see there that's so interesting?" he asked, for he could see nothing. Rack's exhausted blue eyes followed him without recognition, like the eyes of a china figure in his slack face. Suddenly there issued from his mouth an appalling noise, a low wail in which Ashlyme could discern no words; and he began to rock Audsley King to and fro, to and fro, until for an instant she seemed to reawaken and nod in time to his harsh, rhythmic sobbing. A parody of her old energy filled the thin white face; made voracious again the lines round the mouth; and animated the long hands which had been so full of power.

Ashlyme couldn't bear Rack's grief. He went to the window.

"You came here too late," he said distantly. "It's no good making that noise."

It was almost dawn, and the sky had a queer, greyish-yellow caste.

"What right have you to be here anyway?" He laughed bitterly. "Did you come to save your career with her new paintings? Or persuade her to turn *The Dreaming Boys* into something 'a little more cheerful' for the lazy old women of the High City?"

"I don't care if I never see those women again!" shouted Rack violently. He jumped up and grabbed Ashlyme by the shoulders. "I tried so many times to come here! I was afraid, but you wouldn't help me. At least leave us alone together now!"

Ashlyme sneered and pulled himself away.

"Go to the Pleasure Canal and sniff aether until you fall in," he said.

"Won't you help me?" Rack asked him in a softer voice. "I believe she's still alive."

"You're mad, Rack."

Together they carried her down into the Rue Serpolet. It was not the kind of work they were used to, so they went slowly and carefully. Outside on the pavement a crowd of people had gathered to stare into the sky.

When Ashlyme looked up it was dawn and he could see the two huge princes of the city hanging in the air above the Artists' Quarter, resplendent in their horned and lobed scarlet armour. Mounted on vast white horses, they moved through the morning sky like a new constellation. One of those princes has a wound which will never heal. His blood falls from it as a rain of white flowers onto the city beneath: which even now begins to waken from its long, grey, debilitating dream.

EPILOGUE

One day a long time afterwards, when Ashlyme was looking through a drawer for some pencils he thought he'd put there, he came across the fish's-head mask Emmet Buffo had made him wear during their doomed visit to the Rue Serpolet. He was no longer quite so afraid of it as he had been. "Absurd thing!" he thought, while for its part it eyed him lugubriously enough—fat-lipped, stupid, shedding scales. It filled him with a kind of ashamed affection for Buffo, and for himself as he had been then. It reminded him suddenly of cod and saffron, of a bright morning in the cisPontine Quarter, and the old man who lived behind "Our Lady of the Zincsmiths." He decided he would take it back where it belonged.

The old paved square was exactly as he remembered it. If it was not so warm, then it was just as sunny: the pale clear light of a late-December afternoon slanted across the cobbles and lapped the blackened hulk of the old church. The children, as before, were playing noisily at "blind Michael," and Ashlyme could hear the women laughing and squabbling in the houses. He felt suddenly elated, though he couldn't have explained why.

SELLER, announced the partly obliterated sign above the old man's shop. Ashlyme stood for a moment smiling into its small dusty window, where a ray of sun had warmed the fur of the stuffed animals until it was the colour of newly fallen oak leaves, then went inside.

Birds, stiff and silent, watched him from every shelf, their heads cocked forever intelligently on one side, their eyes made of glass. The workroom at the back had the sweet, woody smell of old books and chamomile tea. Ashlyme picked his way between bales of rag to the bottom of the stairs.

"Hello?" he called.

There was no answer, but he sensed the old man was up there: alert, shy, breathing shallowly and waiting for him to go away. "Don't be afraid," he said. "I came here once with your friend Emmet Buffo."

Silence.

Ashlyme shrugged. If he waited quietly the old man's curiosity would bring him down. Perhaps he would have another metal feather. Meanwhile he took out the fish's-head mask and unfolded it carefully. He put it down on a workbench next to the soft wire armature which would one day support the outstretched wings of a little hawk with furious eyes.

"Old man? I cannot stay for long . . ."

Wrinkling his nose, he turned over some of the rags on the floor. Among them he found a bit of heavily worked tapestry which he thought might do as a curtain. He unfolded it nervously, having learned his lesson from the last one he had picked up. It was stained yet luminous; it had been splendid once. It showed a man in the extreme yellow of age, as bald as an egg, walking between two huge buildings. The road under his feet was carpeted with the crushed husks of insects, and a shadowy figure accompanied him on his left side, a child or a dwarf mounted on a donkey. This figure, its face partly obscured by dirt, fascinated Ashlyme. He lifted the tapestry to the light so that he could see it better.

As he did so there came a loud clatter of wings from the room upstairs. Suddenly the shop seemed to be full of shadows.

A large bird had flown in through an open window, he wrote later in his journal. *I thought I heard a reedy voice speak indistinctly in the gloom. I put the tapestry down and walked quickly out into the sunshine.*

The Lamia & Lord Cromis

The Lamia &
Lord Cromis

The apologists or historians of the city—Verdigris, Kubin, Saent Saar—
tended to describe it at that time in terms of its emblems and emblematic
contradictions. *An ace in the gutter, a leopard made of flowers,* says
Verdigris in *Some Remarks to My Dog,* hoping to suggest a whole comprised of hints, causal lacunae, reversing hierarchies: *Where the city is at its
emptiest we find ourselves full.*

For Saent Saar, comfortable under the patronage of a marchioness, this
was more than enough. Less desperate perhaps, and more aware of a kind
of slippage in the city's perception of itself, certainly more conscious of his
responsibilities, he has it that *we see in her very failures of sense a twinning
of contingency and the urge to form. The city is inventing herself, in locutions
partial and accidental, like a woman rehearsing the contents of an old letter.
She lost it long ago. She may even have forgotten who it came from. If she were
to see it now, its careful phrases would surprise her by their lack of resemblance
to what she has made of them.*

Such a view, as acceptable to the Artists' Quarter as to Mynned, would
have been regarded in the provinces with fear. There they looked to the
capital, which they called "Uriconium," "Vriko," or sometimes "the Jewel
on the Edge of the Western Sea," for stability. One of its minor princes
learned the irony of this at first hand. His name was tegeus-Cromis.

He arrived at Duirinish—then a thriving fish-and-wool town on the
coast a hundred miles north of the city—towards the end of December,
and after making enquiries at a secondhand bookshop and a taxidermist's,
went in the evening to the Blue Metal Discovery, where he sat down in the
long smoky parlour at a table some way from the fire. It turned out that he

had come by horse, through the Monar passes, which at that time of the year were beginning to be icy and difficult. One or two of his fellow customers knew this; they shook their heads admiringly. One or two more, who thought they knew why he had come, watched him circumspectly while the wind drove sleet across the bleak cobbles of Replica Square. The rest—rentiers, small landowners from the Low Leedale, coming men in the fur and metal trade—watched him simply because he was a minor prince and they had never seen one before.

It had been a raw afternoon and he looked cold. Otherwise it was hard to know what to make of him. He wore a sword but carried a book *(The Hunting of the Jolly Wren)*. While he walked quickly and energetically, like a young man, when you got close you saw he was grey-haired and preoccupied, and for a moment this was unnerving. In the end they would have put it that though the steel rings on his fingers were bulky, aristocratic, cut into the very complex seals of his House, his boots were a bit cheap and dirty. They wouldn't have expected a prince's boots to be like that.

They asked him would he come nearer the fire. There was plenty of room!

But if he struck them as lonely, even diffident, he was also as perfectly unresponsive as only a minor prince can be. They were interested in him, but he was not so interested in them; they soon left him to himself, tall and polite in a heavy bice velvet cloak. Evening wore into night and he smiled faintly at the remains of his meal. He seemed to be waiting for someone.

(He was thinking: Last December I watched the early snow fall in the High City. That morning, when it looked as if the weather would improve, I sat in the Charcuterie Vivien hoping the sun would come out. Someone I had been expecting arrived, or spoke, or smiled. We were to go skating the next day if it froze. Moments like this seemed permanent but they cannot be repaired; I cannot now regenerate them. And that is not to go back very far.)

Just after midnight a boy came down from the upper rooms of the inn and began to go round from group to group in the parlour, laughing and talking animatedly. Little notice was taken of him. As far as the prince could tell he was trying to collect money—a strange, graceless-looking child fourteen or fifteen years old, who could reach out very quickly and catch a moth in one hand, then release it unharmed. Every lamp had ten or a dozen of these creatures, with their dark green and purple wings, circling it frantically: the boy was able to perform his trick again and again. At the fire they affected not to see him, though he caught a moth for each of them. They seemed uncomfortable.

"Well," said the boy loudly at last. "No one born today will ever be drowned or hanged, that's something."

Though he didn't understand the joke of this, the prince found himself laughing. A moment later the boy came over to speak to him.

"Look, watch the moth."

"You don't seem to have had much luck over there," said tegeus-Cromis when he had examined the insect; he found that he could catch it quite easily, but not without breaking its wings. "Still, they're a careful lot in the fur and metal trade."

The boy looked at him oddly, then he laughed too.

"Oh, they all know me," he said. "They all know me, my lord."

He sat down.

"I was waiting for someone, but not for you," tegeus-Cromis told him. "Do I pay you for my moth?"

"You rode over the passes on some old nag," said the boy. "I heard." He put his hand to his mouth. "Did that sound awful? I always say something like that, I don't know why. Do you ever say something you don't mean like that? I expect it's a beautiful horse, isn't it, probably a thoroughbred, and now you're hurt. I'm sorry.

"Look, here's a live one: try again. Fast but not so rough. There! You're getting the idea." He shivered. "I was in Vriko once," he said. "Artists' Quarter. Phew! That's no city for a lad like me. Six in the morning a smell so foul came up from the Yser Canal you thought it would rust the lampposts. Everything was filthy, but if we wanted a wash we had to go to the baths in Mosaic Lane. Do you know Mosaic Lane, my lord? They had some famous pictures there but you couldn't see them for dirt; the boy I was with scratched it off and saw a face just like his own. Really. Sometimes the water isn't like water at all; it smells of perished rubber."

He stared ahead thoughtfully. His hair, very dark red and cut in a "coup sauvage" once popular in the Tinmarket, made his eyes seem very large and young. Ribbons of various colours were tied to his clothes. His throat was bare, the skin smooth and olive-coloured.

"We lived in a house near Ox Lip Lane."

tegeus-Cromis laughed.

"It's a long time since the Artists' Quarter looked like that," he said. "The Yser Spa fell into its own cistern; that was the end of the murals. There's a courtyard there now with an apple tree in it, and Ox Lip Lane is all little shops which have tubs of geraniums outside them on the pavement. If you saw it now, I suppose, you'd love it."

"Would I?" said the boy quietly. "I'd hate it. It would have no soul."

"Soul!" said tegeus-Cromis, who had often thought the same thing. "I don't believe you were ever there anyway. How old are you? Thirteen?"

They smiled at one another.

For a few minutes neither of them said anything. Then the prince, looking over the ruins of his dinner for some offer he could make, held out his pewter snuffbox. The boy shook his head slowly, but after some thought pulled apart a piece of bread and ate it. He drank some wine too, tilting back his head and gasping. Someone came up from the group round the fire, put a coin contemptuously on the table in front of him, and said, "Well then?" The boy shrugged. He got up and went into the middle of the parlour, recited rapidly three times, in a high voice devoid of expression or implication,

> Johnny Jack all hung with rag dolls
> Although he is small his family is great

and began to dance in a way which managed to be both clumsy and graceful. There was no music. His big wooden shoes thudded on the bare boards; he frowned with concentration and effort, breathing noisily through his mouth. The ribbons on his arms whirled in the lamplight, leaving coloured spiral afterimages. "The effect was quite touching," tegeus-Cromis would say to him later: "But your arms are too thin." There was no applause. When he had finished, the boy simply stood where he was until he had got his breath back, then went round the parlour again, catching moths, collecting money, laughing and chattering affectedly. It had not been an entertainment, the prince saw. Put out that the boy had not come straight back to his table, he opened his book and pretended to read:

"Make him a bed of earth bark, ewe daisy, five-finger blossom."

He looked puzzledly at the cover of the book, put it down, and closed his eyes. He was tired. He saw quite clearly the great seracs collapsing up among the Monar icefields. He crossed under them, once, twice: again.

There was a red flush under the boy's cheekbones when he did come back to the table, and he was still panting a little. "I'm older than that," he said, as if they had never been interrupted. Then: "What have you come here for?"

tegeus-Cromis opened his eyes.

"What do they say by the fire?"

"To hunt. I knew that, too." He leaned forward suddenly and took the prince's hands between both of his own, which were warm and had a kind but papery touch. "Look, my dear," he said, "why let it kill you, too?" He glanced round the room. The fire had burned down, the parlour was emptying, someone was collecting the empty pots. A door opened towards the back and a smell of urine came in on a cold draught. He let go of the prince's hands and made a gesture which encompassed not just the parlour, or the inn, but the cobbled square outside it, and the town beyond that. "It belongs here. It's their responsibility. No one would want to see you killed."

At this the prince caught his cloak a bit closer round him. "Some people are coming to help me," he explained. "They should have been here by now. When the door opened, I thought that was them."

Later the boy asked him: "Which House are you from?"

"The Sixth."

"What's your emblem?"

tegeus-Cromis showed him one of the rings he wore.

"The Lamia. Here. See?"

The boy shrugged.

"It doesn't look like anything."

In the end only the potboy was in the parlour to see them get up and leave together; the prince's friends had been delayed.

The boy went in the night.

"You'll always be able to find me," he said.

In the morning the prince was woken by an altercation at the back of the inn. He had been given one of the rooms there as soon as he arrived. They were sought after because they were large, but this in itself made them seem cold and empty; and while they were supposed to be quieter than the rooms at the front, which faced Replica Square, they had the disadvantage of looking obliquely onto the stableyard. The stables, unlike the rest of the inn, were built of brick—a warm red kind more often seen in the South—and now stood bright and sharp under the blue winter sky. In the yard he could see, if he pressed one cheek against the glass and twisted his head to look out at an angle, two or three heavily laden ponies and a horse of some quality, short-coupled and powerful, with good "ends" and plenty of bone, about nineteen hands high. They were framed by an arch or passageway which further limited his vision, but which amplified the shouts and exclamations of the people gathered round them.

There had been a frost: it lay thickly on the setts in the corner of the yard the sun had not yet reached. The air was cold and transparent, giving to the scene—or that part of it the prince could see—a distinctness, a vigour, which amounted almost to gaiety. The big horse was plunging, striking out in a temper. It sent a bucket rolling across the cobbles, spilling water in a spiral in the morning light. Figures bobbed panickily under the animal's hooves, trying to secure it; or lounged laughing and giving advice; or went hurriedly to and fro across the arch waving their arms, vanishing before he was able to identify them.

One of them was dressed in a meal-coloured cloak: did the horse belong to him? tegeus-Cromis knew it did, but now everything had vanished into his breath, which lay on the cold windowpane like the bloom on a grape. He wiped it off, then, growing tired of the uncomfortable position he had to maintain to see anything, tried to open the window. When it resisted he shrugged and went back into the room, barefoot across the chilly oak floor, to the things of his he had arranged on a table by the bed—the pewter snuffbox in need of a polish, his rings scattered like dice, one or two books. The sword, which had been his father's, was propped in a corner. He dressed quickly, feeling elated for no reason.

In the south, especially in the Mingulay Peninsula where the caravans are full of fortune-tellers and their greasy tarot cards, a woman will often stunt the growth of her first child so that the lucrative career of dwarf is available to it in later life. This she does by confining it to a black oak box they call the "gloottokoma" and by feeding it discriminately, while with the help of the cards she stares paralysed into an uncertain future. The dwarf who now stood on one side of the parlour hearth, warming his deformed spine at a few newish reluctant flames, had made a great success in the arena at Uriconium as a clown and a tumbler. For a time a figure so well known on the Unter-Main-Kai that he had been painted in a red and purple doublet as "Calabacillas, Lord of Misrule" by Audsley King (then at the height of her own brief fashion), he was a founder member of both the Yellow Paper Code and the Cheminor Stilt Walkers, under whose aegis he had killed—in and out of the ring, and more or less fairly—a score of opponents larger than himself.

His name was Morgante, but he was often called Rotgob. His buckled legs gave him a gait which looked feeble, rolling, and uncertain, until you saw him run like an ape across a piece of waste ground at night, up near Allman's Heath. He had intelligent features and a sweet smile but was prone like many products of the "gloottokoma" to bouts of depression and viciousness, during which he would cry bitterly and kick out at anyone who came near him. He had attained at his full growth—when he was sixteen or seventeen years old and already had the arena crowd in the palm of his fat, undeveloped-looking little hand—a height of about four feet.

He was seen habitually in the company of the prince, and of a very tall man called Dissolution Kahn, who stood on the other side of the hearth saying in a cold voice as tegeus-Cromis entered the parlour:

"And yet you agreed. You were quick enough to agree yesterday."

"I am a liar as well as a dwarf."

"Yes," the Kahn now admitted with a remote sigh. "We all know that."

When Rotgob saw tegeus-Cromis he ran round the parlour turning somersaults and shouting, "I'm a liar as well as a dwarf! I'm a liar as well as a dwarf!" until he was out of breath. Then he started to tug at the prince's sword. "Give me that at once!" he said. "Do you want to hurt yourself?"

When the prince tried to join in this game, resisting him with a smile, he only burst into peals of fantastic laughter and jumped onto the mantelpiece, where he sat dangling his legs and staring down as if from a great height; later he took out and began to whet his own weapon, a thing halfway between an extremely long stiletto and a rather short rapier, which he kept in a startling ornamental sheath.

The prince insisted they should have breakfast with him.

Dissolution Kahn drew his chair up close and said, "We came as soon as we could."

He was a large man, and favoured clothes which he thought showed this off to best advantage: orange breeches tucked into great oxblood-coloured boots; enormous camel-hair cloaks; shirts in violet or pink lawn, with slashed and scalloped sleeves. People pointed him out as an example of an excellent horseman, and to carry him and his mail armour—which he hardly ever wore—he always preferred to have massive, ill-tempered horses. His sparse yellow hair curled anarchically round his jowled and bearded features. He had a dangerous reputation in the city, but once you knew him you became aware of his rather watery blue eyes and pendulous underlip.

"We came as soon as we could. Do you know anything for certain?"

tegeus-Cromis shook his head.

"The sign is good, and rumour makes the animal one of the Eight. But what do they know in places like this? It seems to have killed twice near Orves, leaving sign; three times at some houses on a hill near the edge of the town—a child and two women there; again the sign was good, very plain—and once, possibly, in the square behind us. They've been very nervous since then."

The Kahn shrugged. "What can you expect?" he said contemptuously.

"You'll be frightened before we're finished," predicted the dwarf. "You'll piss your pants." He crumbled some bread and ate it carefully, trying to save his teeth. "What's wrong with that?" He thought for a minute, then said: "It will be in the marsh. When do we start?"

"Until someone else is killed I can connect nothing with nothing," the prince was forced to admit. "It would be fatal to move too soon; the books are clear on that if nothing else. Old sign can mean everything or nothing. I've had it put about that I am from the Sixth House: they'll call me as soon as anything happens."

"They'll be glad to," said the Kahn.

He laughed. He got up.

"I'm going to see how they're doing with the mare," he said. "She's a bit slow to settle, that one."

When he opened the parlour door cold air blew across the breakfast table, smelling bitter and metallic and drawing the spit into their mouths.

"The marsh," said Dissolution Kahn, as if he could see it in front of him. "No stink nastier," he observed, "and it upsets her."

"Is that what I've been smelling all morning?" said the prince.

He had started to read *The Hunting of the Jolly Wren*. He looked up but the Kahn had already gone out. The dwarf swung himself quietly onto the mantelpiece, where it was warmer. "If you give me your sword I'll sharpen it," he said. "My prince."

tegeus-Cromis spent some of the days that followed with the boy who caught the moths; in the end he knew him no better.

Once they walked up to Orves and sat on the edge of the old fortifications to look out at Leedale with its fields and sheep. On the slopes below, the prince noticed several spiral lanes as steep as staircases, arranged in a complicated pattern on the hill and screened from one another by wind-eroded hedges. Damp snow had fallen. The December light, reflected back and forth between the fields and the heavy bluish sky, faded slowly, prolonging the afternoon into evening so that it seemed earlier in the year than it was. At the last minute, as the air turned grey and cold and the snow seemed to suck up the light rather than give it out, everything seemed to stand out suddenly very black and stark: the trees like fan coral, the three-storey weavers' houses, the stone walls and hanging quarries of the Leedale hillsides. Next day the snow had turned to rain; after that it was frost again.

Once he said to the boy:

"You know, the old Artists' Quarter wasn't so bad. There was always blossom on the ornamental rowan behind the railings in Mecklenburgh Square; and I can remember quite clearly the scent of black-currant gin spilled across the planished top of some corner table in the Plain Moon Café! Rack, Ashlyme, Kristodulos, they were all still alive and working in the Quarter. You felt the Yser like a warning behind you, but in the evenings they strung coloured paper lanterns across the gardens in Mynned, and everyone talked. We had all that new art, new philosophy, new thought: in those days everyone seemed to be inventing something!"

"I was never there," said the boy. "Was I?"

They laughed.

Once the boy said to him, "Let someone else get rid of it. I don't want you to be hurt," and he could only reply, "This animal, whatever it is, has fought an ancestor of mine in every generation. It killed my father, and he killed it. It killed my grandfather and he killed it. You see the implication of this. In this way, the books I have spent my life with tell me, some balance is preserved; something which would otherwise be constantly in the world is kept out of it. Much of the rest of what they tell me is opaque, I admit."

He considered this for a moment, then shrugged.

"If this is the Sixth Beast—I suspect it is—my duty's clear. I'm the scion of the Sixth House: see, it says on the ring, under the snake. The blood is another kind of book. I can't escape what's written there."

"You don't care about me, then?"

"Some texts suggest, or seem to, that if I survive the encounter the animal will never come back."

Once, he thought he understood the expression in the boy's eyes. But when he woke up he had forgotten, and that night late they called him to see a dead man in a dull house on a quiet cobbled street near the inn. The attack had taken place at the top of the house, in a small room to the walls of which were fastened some charts of the night sky done in a clever hand. An open skylight framed the fading Name Stars and admitted occasional eddies of cold air.

Two or three of the victim's neighbours—uncertain whether they had been woken by shouting or by some other noise which mimicked it—were in the room when the prince got there, wrinkling their noses at a strong, musty, but not precisely unpleasant smell. Immediately he noticed this, the prince ordered the lamps to be extinguished. He lit a small piece of orange candle he had brought with him and studied its flame intently for about thirty seconds. Whatever he saw there did not satisfy him; he made an impatient gesture. tegeus-Cromis often imagined he had made long ago some fundamentally unrealistic assumption about people, one which had undermined his judgement in that direction: but the behaviour of the Sixth Beast, inasmuch as it was clear to anyone, was clear to him. It couldn't hide itself from him.

"You can light the lamps again," he said, and, pinching the candle out abruptly, added to himself, "I would have expected better."

Everyone was impressed by his cursory examination of the victim.

This man, who was well known around the fire in the parlour of the Blue Metal Discovery, wore a heavy fur robe. Under it he was naked. His greying flesh had the consistency, the prince noted, of coarse blotting paper; ringlets covered what remained of his skull. He had tumbled over among his collection of astrological instruments and now lay among them with an embarrassed expression, as if he had fallen heavily while demonstrating it to someone. One hand still clutched a little brass orrery. The other had fetched up incongruous and waxy-looking against the skirting board some way away from the rest of the body, as though the animal had pulled it off in an afterthought. While he noticed all this, the prince seemed to concentrate on the fingernails of the hand that remained attached. Their shape he examined with great care (in fact he compared it briefly to some illustrations in a compact leather-bound directory).

As soon as he had seen enough he took the orrery away from the dead man and set it in motion. It was a delightful thing. Jewelled planets hurried round the little sun; you could hardly hear the clockwork. He was aware perhaps of the effect this had on the other occupants of the room.

"Nothing was seen?"

They had seen nothing, they said, because they had been asleep. It was the noise that had woken them. "We all thought at first it was him screaming."

"We all thought that at first."

He wanted to know next if the gatewardens had been alerted. Someone was sent to find out. Reports were to be confused for some time, but later it became clear that they had seen nothing, either, though a trail had been found quickly enough, aberrant but leading eventually out of Duirinish, of blood. "Ah," said the prince, apparently thinking of something else: "The blood." He watched the rotation of the planets through a complete cycle; another began, but was interrupted almost immediately by a commotion on the stairs.

"What a mess in here!" said Morgante the dwarf, bursting in and walking importantly round the corpse, his hands clasped in the hollow of his back, while Dissolution Kahn studied puzzledly the star charts. "This is a very unprofessional job. Who was he?"

"Someone in the fur and metal trade. The Kahn had better get our horses ready."

They left Duirinish shortly after it got light, following a difficult spoor.

After some miles, lanes and narrow greenways began to slip in all directions down the strike of the country, losing height through little identical dry valleys and nick points in the limestone terraces. The animal had got into them an hour or two before. It was cold; the wind smelled of metal; Dissolution Kahn was often obliged to be firm with his horse.

In two hours they had reached the northeast limit of Leedale. The characteristic bracken and gorse of the valley soon gave out onto poorly drained moorland where dikes had been sunk at right angles to all tracks, to keep the sheep from wandering. The dwarf sang to himself in a droning voice; at every ditch he looked down and said,

"You wouldn't like to fall in there, would you?"

By mid-morning they had crossed the last of them and entered the marsh.

It began as a few thickets of low trees, strangely shaped but still recognisable as thorn or bullace, through which meandered a river flanked by dense reedbeds a bright unnatural ochre colour. The thickets closed up; the river was soon lost, going to feed iron bogs, then quicksands of suspended magnesium or aluminium alloys, and finally sumps of thick whitish slurry marbled with streaks of mauve or oily cadmium yellow. What paths there were wound between steep-sided pits, along crumbling ridges and promontories of soft discoloured earth. The trees of the interior were of quite unknown kinds, black and burnt-orange, with smooth-barked tapering stems; their tightly woven foliage, rarely more than fifteen feet above the surface of the bog, tinted the light a frail organic pink, which seemed sometimes to be veined like the lobe of a very delicate ear. Moving furtively, as if they had been crippled, or as if they had only just learned how to breath air, frogs and small lizards floundered from sump to sump; they swam with equal difficulty, hurt perhaps by the water, and after some apparently aimless, undirected activity, always struggled to leave it at the same place they had entered. There were insects in the trees, with papery, inutile wings a foot long; they seemed to have too many legs.

At noon the trees thinned out a little.

It was bitterly cold. In the pale, slanting winter light the east wind coated everything in a transparent skin more flexible than ice but nothing like air. For thirty minutes they were able to travel along an old, abandoned road. It was foundering in the soft ground. The shadows of the trees fell distinct but washed-out across its white, tilted surface. "Who would want to make a road in a place like this?" The cold had locked up the moisture in everything—mud, stone, vegetation—so that it looked like bone and they were glad to get under the canopy again.

The horses were intractable. Disoriented by the prawn-coloured "sky," they would refuse to move, bracing their legs and trembling, then turn rolling white eyes on Dissolution Kahn who, dismounting, swore and sank to his boot-tops in the slime, releasing from it enormous acrid bubbles. By the middle of the short winter afternoon they had lost one of the ponies to quicksand. The other died after drinking from a clear pool, rapid swelling of its limbs followed by gushes of blood from the corroded glands and internal organs. Rotgob was able to save one of the loads. The other, which contained food, was lost.

Over all this presided the smell of corrupt metal. tegeus-Cromis's mouth was coated with bitter deposits; he felt poisoned, and found it difficult to speak. Though he had always known what to expect, he seemed numb for much of the day, gazing automatically at whatever presented itself to his eyes while he allowed his horse to stumble and slither about beneath him. He had slipped into a reverie in which he saw himself riding over sunny cobbles into a courtyard somewhere in the cisPontine Quarter, entry to which was gained by a narrow brick arch. It was familiar to him, though at the same time he could not remember having been there before.

Fish was being sold from a cart at one end of the square; at the other rose
the dark bulk of "Our Lady of the Zincsmiths": children ran excitedly
from one to the other in the sunshine, squabbling over a bit of pavement
marked out for a hopping game, "blind Michael." As the prince's horse
clattered under the arch he heard a woman's voice singing to a mandolin,
and the air was full of the smells of cod and saffron.

Suddenly aware of the blood and its unbearable heritage, he jerked
awake and said:

"We must get on!"

The dwarf looked at him compassionately. It was evening. They were
tired and filthy. They had long ago lost the animal's spoor.

They reached a place called on some of the prince's maps Cobaltmere
and on others Sour Pent Lay or Pent Lay. "In this case we should read *lay*
as *lake*," he told them. There they lit a fire and camped uncomfortably.
"My guts have felt bad since we got in here," Dissolution Kahn admitted.
"It's lucky there isn't much to eat." He and the dwarf were staring out
across the lay. On its shallow waters could be seen mats of a kind of tuber-
ous, buoyant vegetation which in the horizontal light of sunset had come
alive briefly with mile-long stains of mazarine and cochineal; bits of it were
drifting ashore all the time, rubbery and dull-looking. Along the far banks
were lines of shadowy knots and hummocks covered with a damp growth,
like heaps of spoil on an abandoned quarry terrace. It was easy to see that
they fascinated the dwarf, who said several times wonderingly:

"Those were buildings. This marsh was once a city."

"I know of one map that marks it as such," the prince told him,
"though I have never been shown it. Some authorities agree, but we regard them as speculative. The majority have it as a natural formation, and
on the bank there record 'blocks of stone.'"

The dwarf could not accept this.

"It was a city once," he said with quiet emphasis.

Suddenly he jumped to his feet and pinched the bridge of his nose in
imitation of the clairvoyants of Margery Fry Court.

"I see it clearly in its heyday," he exclaimed. "It was the Uriconium of
the North! I call it antiVriko, and reclaim it in the name of Mammy
Morgante, Queen of every empire of the earth!" He made a grand gesture
with his arms and a fanfaring, farting sound with his mouth. "I encompass
it on behalf of all my subjects—even this one."

"You can take the first watch, then."

An even, curious light came up from Cobaltmere once the sun had set.
It had a veiling effect. The fire seemed orange and remote. Everything else
had a soapy look, a colouration which made the prince imagine that if he
touched the dwarf or his companion they would have the texture of grey
soap. Yet it was bright enough to write by: his pen's shadow preceded it

across the page. "*The wren,*" he quoted, "*may then be hung by its leg in the centre of two hoops crossing each other at right angles.*" If he died it was hoped one of the others would take his notes back to the city to be added to the library of his House; there they would be catalogued.

"I'll take all the watches," said Rotgob. "Only some peasant would sleep, here in the Jewel of the Northern Marsh!"

He insisted on this and thereafter they would see him at intervals as they talked, moving slowly round the clearing in and out of their field of vision, humming and murmuring to himself or stopping to listen to the sound of water draining through the reedbeds. "We can only cast about for sign." "I think we are halfway down the southern shore." They could decide nothing. Dissolution Kahn fell asleep abruptly, to grunt and belch in his dreams. In the end tegeus-Cromis slept too: only to be woken sometime before dawn by the cold. He moved nearer the embers of the fire and lay there uneasily with his fingers laced beneath his head. The dwarf was still happy at that time. You could hear him yawn, rub his hands together, reassure the horses. Once he said softly but clearly, "It was a city," and gave a deep sigh.

In the morning they found him curled up with his knees thrust hard into his chest and his arms clasped round them. He had already sunk slightly into the mud. There was an expression of misery and loneliness on his face. He was shivering helplessly: for some reason he had felt compelled to tear off his clothes and throw them about. All they could get him to say was something that sounded like "Filth, filth." All at once he ran off and tried to jump into the mere; though he only managed to land with his face in it he was dead before they could pull him out.

"Be steady," said Dissolution Kahn. "There are still two of us."

Later he picked up the dwarf's short sword. "People were always offering him money for the sheath of this," he said. He studied it. "It's made of a horse's tosser, I think. They do that down in the South."

He dug a deep hole in the mud and put the dwarf in it.

"This little chap was one of the best fighters you ever saw. He was so quick."

He swallowed and stared away across the mere.

"Morgante!" he said. "Morgante!" And: "He must have been poisoned. He must have drunk the water or eaten something, to kill himself like that."

Dawn had hardly warmed the air. Now brittle flakes of snow came down, reluctantly at first and then with more vigour until Cobaltmere was obscured and the marsh around it began to look like the ornamental gardens of Harden Bosch seen through a net curtain in Montrouge. If you concentrated for a moment on the flakes that made up any part of the curtain they would seem to fall slowly, or even to be suspended: then, with the movement of flies in an empty room in summer, whirl round one another in a sudden intricate spiral before they shot apart as if a string connecting them had been cut. In this way they whirled down on the shore of the lake; they whirled down on the face of the dwarf. The prince, huddled in his cloak, touched the turned earth with his foot. He pushed some of it into the hole.

"It was the animal," he said. "I recognise the signs."

"He killed himself," repeated Dissolution Kahn stubbornly. "How could an animal kill him when he killed himself?"

"I recognise the signs."

They went on pushing earth into the hole until they could tread it down.

"Well, there are still two of us."

"I first learned about the Lamia when I was six years old," said tegeus-Cromis. "There was a musical noise in the night. They explained it to me and then I knew. . . . History's against us," he said, "and I should have come alone."

"We're here now."

The prince was easily able to identify fresh sign. They followed it and, not far from the lay, near the northern edge of the marsh, discovered an old tower. Around it the vegetation was returning to normal. Filaments of ordinary ivy crawled over the fawn stone; from cracks near the summit grew a withered bullace, its rattling branches occupied by small stealthy birds; hawthorn and elder lapped up against its base. "Books hint at the existence of a sinking tower, though they place it in the East." The prince urged his horse forward. Birds flew out of the hawthorn. He drew his sword. "I am afraid to approach too openly."

The tower, it quickly became clear, had embedded itself so far in the ground that its lower windows were rectangular slits twelve or eighteen inches high. "You won't get in there," said Dissolution Kahn. From one of them issued a smell that made him retch. He went a little nearer and sized it up, breathing heavily through his mouth, while snow eddied round his heavy, motionless figure. Eventually he shook his head and repeated,

"You won't get through there. Neither of us will. It's too small."

The prince thought he could crawl through. "I am thinner than you, and perhaps if I take my cloak off that will make things easier."

"You're mad if you go in there alone."

"What choice have I?"

"You know I would go in if I could!"

"That isn't what I meant."

The prince threw his cloak over the hindquarters of his horse, then turned and walked as fast as he could to the sunken window. "No one has been here for a hundred years," he whispered to himself. When he looked

back through the plaiting snow he could see Dissolution Kahn gazing after him in a hurt way. He wanted to say something else, but sensing the
Lamia so close to him now, and perhaps finding himself glad to take the responsibility for it after all, only managed to shout,

"Go home! I should never have brought you!"

To keep the Kahn from replying, he got down on his hands and knees
and put his face into the queer mixture of smells bellying from the slot. He
coughed; his eyes watered; against his will he hung back. He heard the
Kahn call out from a long way off—but ashamed, and anyway unable to
make sense of the words, thrust his head suddenly into the hole. Trying to
keep his sword pointed in front of him, he wriggled desperately through.
It was dark. When he stood up he hit his head on something; he didn't
think it was the ceiling. Crouching awkwardly he began to stumble about
in the dark, swinging out with his sword in all directions. This was how he
had always expected to meet the animal. Something cold dripped into his
hair and down his cheek. His feet slid on a soft and rotten surface; he fell;
the sword flew out of his hand and struck blue sparks from a wall.

He got up slowly and stood there in the dark. "Kill me, then," he said.
"I won't stop you now." His own voice sounded dull and artificial to him.
After a minute, perhaps two, when nothing had happened, he took out the
piece of candle he had been taught to use for diagnosis and lit it. He stared
in horror at its flame for a few seconds, then flung it down with a sob. The
lair, if it was one at all, was empty.

"I didn't ask for this," tegeus-Cromis said. It was something he had often repeated to himself when he was a child. He saw himself reading
books, learning these ways to recognise the Beast.

Groping about in the emptiness for his sword, he clasped its blade and
cut the palm of his hand. He squirmed backwards through the foundered
window and out into the snow, where he took a few uncertain steps, looking for the horses. They were gone. He stared at the blood running down
his sword. He ran three times round the tower, crying out. Three of his
fingers hung useless. He bound up the wound so he wouldn't have to see
it. Bent forward against the weather, he picked up in the slush two sets of
hoofprints leading back towards Sour Pent Lay. If I hurry, he thought, I
can still catch up with him. Or he may come back to look for me.

At Cobaltmere he had glimpses through the snow of long vacant mudbanks and reefs. His horse he found lying with its neck stretched out and
its head in the water. His cloak was still wrapped round its hindquarters.
Its body was swollen; blood oozed from its mouth and anus. The veins in
its eyes were yellow.

He was looking down at it puzzledly when he heard a faint cry further
along the shore.

There Dissolution Kahn sat on his great horse. She was slow to settle but full of good points—had a shoulder, he often pointed out, like the half side of a house. She arched her neck and shook her big raw head. Her bridle, which was of soft red leather—would he go heavily on her mouth with a pair of hands like his, delicate as a woman's?—was inlaid with metal filigree; her breath steamed in the cold air. The Kahn had put on his ring mail, which he had had lacquered deep blue for him some weeks before in the Tinmarket; and over that, with care to keep it spotless, a silk surcoat the same acid yellow as the mare's caparisons. He loved those colours. His hair blew back in the wind like a pennant. High above his head he brandished a sword with silver hilts. To the prince, who had lived for so long in a world of sign, it seemed for a moment that the marsh could not contain them: they were transformed into their own emblem and thus made invincible. But it was an effect of the light, and passed, and he saw that they looked quite small in front of the Beast of the Sixth House.

The Lamia!

It shook its plumage at them irritably. It broke wind. Chitinous scales rattled like dead reeds when it moved. It roared and whistled sardonically, winked a heavy lid over one bulging insectile eye. It did a clumsy sex dance on its hind hooves, and writhed its coils invitingly.

Though it did not want them, it would have them. It was determined to form words.

"Snork."

It laughed delightedly, lifted a wing, and preened. Lamia the feathered snake: a pleasant musk filled the air. Lamia! With long bent fingers it reached down to pluck the doomed man and his beautiful horse! It said distinctly:

"I am a liar as well as a dwarf."

It sent a hot stream of urine into the sodden earth. "I piss on you." It increased its size by a factor of two, staggered, giggled, regained its balance, and fell at the Kahn.

"Run! Run!" warned tegeus-Cromis.

Blood spattered the mare's caparisons: she stood bravely up to the bit. Dissolution Kahn retched and vomited: he would not run. He clung instead to his saddle, swaying and groaning, while the snow whirled down and the Lamia overshadowed him. He made himself look up. "I'll have you first," he said. He swung his big sword desperately and caught the Beast full on. It began to diminish.

"No, you see," it said.

After that it was plain he didn't know what to do. He was so tired. The mare still stood quietly up to her bit, careful not to unseat him. He dropped his sword. His mail which he had been so proud of was in shreds; strips of it seemed to be embedded in the flesh of his chest and shoulder. He kept as still as he could, in case he opened some wound, and watched the Sixth Beast shrivel up, shedding wings, scales, everything. Every facet of its eyes went dull. "Please," it said. "You know." A smell of burning hair came and went: cinders, dust, vegetable peel. Most of its limbs had withered away, leaving warty stumps which themselves soon disappeared. Iridescent fluids mixed with the water of the marsh. Mouth after mouth clicked feebly and was gone. "Please." Only when it had repeated all its incarnations would the Kahn look up. His face was pouchy and grey. He slid out of the saddle and stood like someone drunk.

"She's got ends like a church buttress, that horse," he said thickly.

He cleared his throat, peering at tegeus-Cromis as if he had never seen him before, then nodded to himself.

"You should have killed it when you had the chance," he said.

He stumbled backwards. His mouth fell open in surprise. When he looked down and saw the prince's sword sticking out of his lower belly, he whimpered. A quick violent shudder went through him. Blood plaited on his thighs. He reached down and put his hands on the sword as if he thought he might try to pull it out, then took them carefully away again.

"Why did you do that?"

"I was to be killed killing it. Who am I now?"

Dissolution Kahn sat down gingerly. He coughed and wiped his mouth.

"I never expected this," he said. 'Did you see that thing? I got away with it, and now this happens. If you helped me I could still make it out of this marsh. I could tell you what to do if you didn't know."

He laughed.

"You and all your ancestors were well fooled. It was easy to kill. Easy. Will you help me out of here?"

"What will I do now?" whispered the prince, who hadn't heard him.

Dissolution Kahn twisted round until he faced the body of the boy from the inn. He saw how thin and white it looked, how apart from being twisted at an odd angle it was unmarked by its own transfiguration, and how at this moment it looked to him like any other body. Then he leant forward, steadied the pommel of the prince's sword against its ribs, and pushed himself onto it. He grunted.

tegeus-Cromis sat by the lake until late in the afternoon, when the peculiar light began to come up from the water, his pewter snuffbox on his knee. The snow had stopped; not much had settled. *Little Johnny Jack,* he noted in the margin of one of his books: *Though he is small his family is great.* After that he could think of nothing to do. He reviewed everything he had ever done; that was nothing too. Eventually he pulled his sword out of Dissolution Kahn's belly and threw it into the mere. This did not seem to satisfy him, so he took off his rings and threw them in after it. He swung himself up onto the mare; in her saddlebags he had found a big thick cloak in which to wrap himself. Because he had avoided it all afternoon, he made himself look down at the dead boy.

"When I think of you catching moths I want to cry," he said. "You should have killed me at the inn."

The prince rode south all night, and when he came out from under the trees he would not look up in case the Name Stars should reflect some immense and unnatural change below.

VIRICONIUM KNIGHTS

VIRICONIUM KNIGHTS

The aristocratic thugs of the High City whistle as they go about their factional games among the derelict observatories and abandoned fortifications at Lowth. Distant or close at hand, these exchanges—short commanding blasts and protracted responses which often end on what you imagine is an interrogative note—form the basis of a complex language, to the echo of which you wake suddenly in the leaden hour before dawn. Go to the window: the street is empty. You may hear running footsteps, or a sigh. In a minute or two the whistles have moved away in the direction of the Tinmarket or the Margarethestrasse. Next day some minor prince is discovered in the gutter with his throat cut, and all you are left with is the impression of secret wars, lethal patience, an intelligent manoeuvring in the dark.

The children of the Quarter pretend to understand these signals. They know the histories of all the most desperate men in the city. In the mornings on their way to the Lycee on Simeonstrasse they examine every exhausted face.

"There goes Antic Horn," they whisper, "master of the Blue Anemone Philosophical Association," and, "Last night Osgerby Practal killed two of the Queen's men right underneath my window; he did it with his knife—like this!—and then whistled the 'found and killed' of the Locust Clan. . . ."

If you had followed the whistles one raw evening in December some years after the War of the Two Queens, they would have led you to an infamous yard behind the inn called the Dryad's Saddle at the junction of Rue Miromesnil and Salt Lip Lane. The sun had gone down an hour before, under three bars of orange cloud. Wet snow had been falling since. Smoke and steam drifted from the inn in the light of a half-open door;

there was a sharp smell in the air, compounded of embrocation, saveloys, and burning anthracite. The yard was crowded on three sides with men whose woollen cloaks were dyed at the hem the colour of dried blood, men who stood with "the braced instep affected only by swordsmen and dancers." They were quiet and intent, and for the most part ignored the laughter coming from the inn.

Long ago someone had set four wooden posts into the yard. Blackened and still, capped with snow, they formed a square a few metres on a side. Half a dozen apprentices were at work to clear this, using long-handled brooms to sweep away the slush and blunted trowels to chip at the hardened ridges of ice left by the previous day's encounters.

(In the morning these lads sell sugared anemones in the Rivelin market. They run errands for the cardsharps. But by the afternoon their eyes have become distant, thoughtful, excited: they cannot wait for the night, when they will put on their loose, girlish woollen jackets and tight leather breeches to become the handlers and nurses of the men who wear the meal-coloured cloak. What are we to make of them? They are thin and ill-fed, but so devout. They walk with a light tread. Even their masters do not understand them.)

An oldish man sat on a stool among the members of his faction while two apprentices prepared him. They had already taken off his cloak and his mail shirt, and supported his right wrist with a canvas strap. They had pulled the grey hair back from his face, fastening it with an ornamental steel clasp. Now they were rubbing embrocation into his stiff shoulder muscles. He ignored them, staring emptily at the blackened posts waiting for him like corpses pulled out of a bog. He hardly seemed to feel the cold, though his bare scarred arms were purple with it. Once he inserted two fingers beneath the strapping on his wrist to make sure it was tight enough. His sword was propped up against his knees. Idly he pushed the point of it down between two cobbles and began to lever them apart.

When one of the apprentices leaned forward and whispered something in his ear, it appeared that he wouldn't answer: then he cleared his throat as if he had not spoken to anybody for a long time and said,

"I've never heard of him. If I had I wouldn't give him the satisfaction. Some little pisser from Mynned?"

The boy smiled lovingly down at him.

"I will always follow you, Practal. Even if he cuts your legs off."

Practal reached up and imprisoned the boy's delicate wrist.

"If he kills me you'll run off with the first poseur who comes in here wearing soft shoes!"

"No," said the boy. "No!"

Practal held his arm a moment longer, then gave a short laugh. "More fool you," he said, but he seemed to be satisfied. He went back to prising at the loose setts.

The Mammy's man came into the yard late, surrounded by courtiers in yellow velvet cloaks who had escorted him down from Mynned. Practal had a look at them and spat on the cobbles. The inn was quiet now. From its half-open door a few sightseers—mostly costermongers from Rivelin but with a leaven of touts and sharps local to the Dryad's Saddle—watched, placing bets in low voices while smoke moved slowly in the light and warmth behind them.

The Mammy's man ignored Practal. He kicked vaguely at each wooden post as he came to it and stared about as if he had forgotten something, a tall youth with big, mad-looking eyes and hair which had been cut and dyed so that it stuck up from his head like a crest of scarlet spines. He had on a light green cloak with an orange lightning flash embroidered on the back; when he took it off the crowd could see that instead of a mail shirt he was wearing a kind of loose chenille blouse. Practal's clique made a lot of this, laughing and pointing. He gazed blankly at them, then with a disconnected motion pulled the blouse off and tore it in half. This seemed to annoy the court men, who moved away from him and stood in a line along the fourth side of the yard, ostentatiously sniffing pomanders.

Practal said disgustedly, "They've sent a child."

They had. His chest was thin and white; low down, two huge abscesses had healed as conical pits. His back was long and hollow. A greenish handkerchief was knotted round his throat. He looked undeveloped but at the same time broken down.

"No wonder he needed an escort."

He must have heard this, but he went on lurching randomly about, chewing on something he had in his mouth. Then he scratched his queer coxcomb violently, knelt down, and rummaged through the garments he had discarded until he came up with a ceramic sheath about a foot long. When the crowd saw this there was some excited betting, most of it against Practal; the Locust Clan looked uneasy. Hissing through his teeth as if he were soothing a horse, the Queen's man jerked the power-knife out of its sheath and made a few clumsy passes with it. It gave off a dreary, lethal buzzing noise and a cloud of pale motes which wobbled away into the wet air like drugged moths; and as it went it left a sharp line of light behind it in the gloom.

Osgerby Practal shrugged.

"He'll need long arms to use that," he said.

Someone called out the rules. The moment one of the combatants was cut, he lost. If either of them stepped outside the notional square defined by the posts, he would be judged as having conceded. No one was to be killed (although this happened more often than not). Practal paid no attention. The boy nodded interestedly as each point was made, then walked off, smiling and whistling.

Mixed fights were uncommon. Practal, who had some experience of them, kept his sword down out of the way of the power-knife, partly to reduce the risk of having it chopped in half, partly so his opponent would be tempted to come to him. The boy adopted a flat footed stance, and after a few seconds of uncoordinated circling began to pant heavily. All at once the power-knife streaked out between them, fizzing and spitting like a firework. The crowd gasped, but Practal only stepped sideways and let it pass. Before the boy could regain his balance, the flat of Practal's sword had smacked him on the ear. He fell against one of the corner posts, holding the side of his head and blinking.

The courtiers clicked their tongues impatiently.

"Come out of that corner and show us a fight," suggested someone from the Locust Clan. There was laughter.

The boy spoke for the first time. "Go home and look between your wife's legs, comrade," he said. "I think I left something there last night."

This answer amused the crowd further. While he was grinning round at them, Practal hit him hard in the ear again. This time the power-knife fell out of his hand and started to eat its way into the cobbles an inch from his foot, making a dull droning noise. He stood there looking down at it and rubbing his ear.

The point of Practal's sword rested against the boy's diaphragm. But the boy refused to look at him, so Practal lowered it and went back to his stool. He sat down with his back to the square while his apprentices wiped his face with a towel, murmuring encouragement in low voices, and gave him a dented flask. He held it up.

"Want some?" he called over his shoulder. The crowd appreciated this: there was some cheering even from people who had backed the other corner.

"That piss?" said the boy. "Soon I'll drink the lot."

Practal jumped to his feet so quickly he knocked the stool over.

"Fair enough then!" he shouted, his face red. "Come on!"

But nothing happened. The boy only hacked with his heel at a ridge of hard old ice the apprentices had left sticking to the cobbles in the centre of the square, while the power-knife, held negligently close to his right leg, flickered and sent up whitish motes which floated above the crowd, giving off a sickly smell. He seemed worried.

"This square has been badly set up," he said.

The court faction shifted irritably; the crowd jeered.

"I don't care about that," said Practal, and threw himself into a sustained, tight, very technical attack, controlling the momentum of the sword with practised figures-of-eight so that it shone and flashed in the light from the inn door. Practal's faction cheered and waved their arms. The boy was forced into a clumsy retreat, and when his foot caught the ridge of ice in the centre of the square he fell over with a cry. Practal brought the sword down hard. The boy smiled. He moved his head quickly out of the way, and with a clang the blade buried itself between two cobblestones. Even as Practal tried to lever it clear, the boy reached round behind his legs and cut the tendons at the back of his knee.

Practal seemed surprised.

"That's not the way to fight with a weapon like that," he began, as if he was advising his apprentice.

He let go of the sword and wandered unsteadily about the square with his mouth open, holding the backs of his legs. The boy followed him about interestedly until he collapsed, then knelt down and put his face close to Practal's to make sure he was listening. "My name is Ignace Retz," he said quietly. Practal bit the cobbles. The boy raised his voice so that the crowd could hear. "My name is Ignace Retz, and I daresay you will re-member it."

"Kill me," said Practal. "I'll not walk now."

Ignace Retz shook his head. A groan went through the crowd. Retz walked over to the apprentice who was holding Practal's mail shirt and meal-coloured cloak. "I will need a new shirt and cloak," he announced loudly, "so that these kind people are not tempted to laugh at me again." After he had taken the clothes, to which he was entitled by the rules, he re-turned the power-knife to its sheath, handling it more warily than he had done during the fight. He looked tired. One of the courtiers touched him on the arm and said coldly, "It is time to go back to the High City."

Retz bowed his head.

As he was walking towards the inn door, with the mail shirt rolled up into a heavy ball under one arm and the cloak slung loosely round his shoulders, Practal's apprentice came and stood in his way, shouting, "Practal was the better man! Practal was the better man!"

Retz looked down at him and nodded.

"So he was."

The apprentice began to weep. "The Locust Clan will not allow you to live for this!" he said wildly.

"I don't suppose they will," said Ignace Retz.

He rubbed his ear. The courtiers hurried him out. Behind him the crowd had gone quiet. As yet, no bets were being paid out.

Mammy Vooley held a disheartening court. She had been old when the Northmen brought her to the city after the War of the Two Queens, and now her body was like a long ivory pole about which they had draped the faded purple gown of her predecessor. On it was supported a very small head, which looked as if it had been partly scalped, partly burned, and partly starved to death in a cage suspended above the Gabelline Gate. One of her eyes was missing. She sat on an old carved wooden throne with iron wheels, in the middle of a tall limewashed room that had five windows. Nobody knew where she had come from, not even the Northmen whose queen she had replaced. Her intelligence never diminished. At night the servants heard her singing in a thin whining voice, in some language none of them knew, as she sat among the ancient sculptures and broken machines that are the city's heritage.

Ignace Retz was ushered in to see her by the same courtiers who had led him down to the fight. They bowed to Mammy Vooley and pushed him forward, no longer bothering to disguise the contempt they felt for him. Mammy Vooley smiled at them. She extended her hand and drew Retz down close to her bald head. She stared anxiously into his face, running her fingers over his upper arms, his jaw, his scarlet crest. She examined the bruises Practal had left on the side of his head. As soon as she had reassured herself he had come to no harm, she pushed him away.

"Has my champion been successful in defending my honour?" she asked. When she spoke, lights came on behind the windows, revealing dim blue faces which seemed to repeat quietly whatever she said. "Is the man dead?"

Immediately Retz saw he had made a mistake. He could have killed Practal, and now he wished he had. He wondered if she had been told already. He knew that whatever he said the courtiers would tell her the truth, but to avoid having to answer the question himself he threw Practal's mail shirt on the floor at her feet.

"I bring you his shirt, ma'am," he said.

She looked at him expressionlessly. Bubbles went up from the mouths of the faces in the windows. From behind him Retz heard someone say,

"We are afraid the man is not dead, Your Majesty. Retz fought a lazy match and then hamstrung him by a crude trick. We do not understand why, since his instructions were clear."

Retz laughed dangerously.

"It was not a crude trick," he said. "It was a clever one. Someday I will find a trick like that for you."

Mammy Vooley sat like a heap of sticks, her single eye directed at the ceiling.

After a moment she seemed to shrug. "It will be enough," she said remotely. "But in future you must kill them, you must always kill them. I want them killed." And her mottled hand came out again from under the folds of her robe, where tiny flakes of limewash and damp plaster had settled like the dust in the convoluted leaves of a foreign plant. "Now give me the weapon back until the next time."

Retz massaged his ear. The power-knife had left some sort of residue inside his bones, some vibration which made him feel leaden and nauseated. He was afraid of Mammy Vooley and even more afraid of the dead, bluish faces in the windows; he was afraid of the courtiers as they passed to and fro behind him, whispering together. But he had made so many enemies down in the Low City that tonight he must persuade her to let him keep the knife. To gain time he went down on one knee. Then he remembered something he had heard in a popular play, *The War with the Great Beetles.*

"Ma'am," he said urgently, "let me serve you further! To the south and east lie those broad wastes which threaten to swallow up Viriconium. New empires are there to be carved out, new treasures dug up! Only give me this knife, a horse, and a few men, and I will adventure there on your behalf!"

When tegeus-Cromis, desperate swordsman of *The War with the Great Beetles,* had petitioned Queen Methvet Nian in this manner, she had sent him promptly (albeit with a wan, prophetic smile) on the journey which was to lead to his defeat of the Iron Dwarf, and thence to the acquisition of immense power. Mammy Vooley only stared into space and whispered, "What are you talking about? All the empires of the world are mine already."

For a second Retz forgot his predicament, so real was his desire for that treasure which lies abandoned amid the corrupt marshes and foundering, sloth-haunted cities of the South. The clarity and anguish of his own hallucination had astonished him.

"Then what will you give me?" he demanded bitterly. "It is not as if I failed you."

Mammy Vooley laughed.

"I will give you Osgerby Practal's mail shirt," she said, "since you have spurned the clothes I dressed you in. Now—quickly!—return me the weapon. It is not for you. It is only to defend my honour, as you well know. It must be returned after the combat."

Retz embraced Mammy Vooley's thin, oddly articulated legs and tried to put his head in her lap. He closed his eyes. He felt the courtiers pull him away. Though he kicked out vigorously, they soon stripped him of the meal-coloured cloak—exclaiming in disgust at the whiteness of his body— and found the ceramic sheath strapped under his arm. He thought of what would happen to him when the Locust Clan caught him defenceless somewhere among the ruins at Lowth, or down by the Isle of Dogs, where his mother lived.

"My lady," he begged, "*lend* me the knife. I will need it before dawn—"

But Mammy Vooley would not speak to him. With a shriek of despair he threw off the courtiers and pulled the knife out. Leprous white motes floated in the cold room. The bones of his arm turned to paste.

"This is all I ever got from you," he heard himself say. "And here is how I give it you back, Mammy Vooley!"

With a quick sweep of the knife he cut off the hand she had raised to dismiss him. She stared at the end of her arm, and then at Retz: her face seemed to be swimming up towards his through dark water, anxious, one-eyed, unable to understand what he had done to her.

Retz clasped his hands to his head.

He threw down the weapon, grabbed up his belongings, and—while the courtiers were still milling about in fear and confusion, dabbing numbly at their cloaks where Mammy Vooley's blood had spattered them—ran moaning out of the palace. Behind him all the dim blue lips in the throne-room windows opened and closed agitatedly, like disturbed pond life.

Outside on the Proton Way he fell down quivering in the slushy snow and vomited his heart up. He lay there thinking, Two years ago I was nothing; then I became the Queen's champion and a great fighter; now they will hunt me down and I will be nothing again. He stayed there for twenty minutes. No one came after him. It was very dark. When he had calmed down and the real despair of his position had revealed itself to him, he put on Osgerby Practal's clothes and went into the Low City, where he walked about rather aimlessly until he came to a place he knew called the Bistro Californium. He sat there drinking lemon gin until the whistling began and his fear drove him out onto the streets again.

It was the last hour before dawn, and a binding frost had turned the rutted snow to ice. Retz stepped through an archway in an alley somewhere near Line Mass Quay and found himself in a deep narrow courtyard where the bulging housefronts were held apart by huge balks of timber. The bottom of this crumbling well was bitterly cold and full of a darkness unaffected by day or night; it was littered with broken pottery and other rubbish. Retz shuddered. Three sides of the courtyard had casement windows; the fourth was a blank, soot-streaked cliff studded with rusty iron bolts; high up he could see a small square of moonlit sky. For the time being he had thrown his pursuers off the scent. He had last heard them quartering the streets down by the canal. He assured himself briefly that he was alone and sat down in a doorway to wait for first light. He wrapped his woollen cloak round him.

A low whistle sounded next to his very ear. He leapt to his feet with a scream of fear and began to beat on the door of the house.

"Help!" he cried. "Murder!"

He heard quiet ironic laughter behind him in the dark.

Affiliates of the Locust Clan had driven him out of the Artists' Quarter and into Lowth. There on the familiar hill he had recognised with mounting panic the squawks, shrieks, and low plaintive whistles of a dozen other factions, among them Anax Hermax's High City Mohocks, the Feverfew Anschluss with their preternaturally drawn-out "We are all met," the Yellow Paper Men, and the Fifth of September—even the haughty mercenaries of the Blue Anemone. They had waited for him, their natural rivalries suppressed. They had made the night sound like the inside of an aviary. Then they had harried him to and fro across Lowth in the sleety cold until his lungs ached, showing themselves only to keep him moving, edging him steadily towards the High City, the palace, and Mammy Vooley. He believed they would not attack him in a private house, or in daylight if he could survive until then.

"Help!" he shouted. "Please help!"

Suddenly one of the casements above him flew open and a head appeared, cocked alertly to one side. Retz waved his arms. "Murder!" The window slammed shut again. He moaned and battered harder at the door while behind him the piercing whistles of the Yellow Paper Men filled the courtyard. When he looked up, the timber balks were swarming with figures silhouetted against the sky. They wanted him out of the yard and into the city again. Someone plucked at his shoulder, whispering. When he struck out, whoever was there cut him lightly across the back of the hand. A moment later the door opened and he fell through it into a dimly lit hall where an old man in a deep blue robe waited for him with a candle.

At the top of some stairs behind the heavy baize curtain at the end of the hall there was a large room with a stone floor and plastered white walls, kept above the freezing point by a pan of glowing charcoal. It was furnished with heavy wooden chairs, a sideboard of great age, and a lectern in the shape of an eagle whose outspread wings supported an old book. Along one wall hung a tapestry, ragged and out of keeping with the rest of the room, which was that of an abbot, a judge, or a retired soldier. The old man made Retz sit in one of the chairs and held the candle up so that he could examine Retz's scarlet crest, which he had evidently mistaken for the result of a head wound.

After a moment he sighed impatiently.

"Just so," he said.

"Sir," said Retz, squinting up at him, "are you a doctor?" And, "Sir, you are holding the candle so that I cannot see you."

This was not quite true. If he moved his head he could make out an emaciated yellow face, long and intelligent-looking, the thin skin stretched over the bones like waxed paper over a lamp.

"So I am," said the old man. "Are you hungry?" Without waiting for an answer he went to the window and looked out. "Well, you have outwitted the other wolves and will live another day. Wait here." And he left the room.

Retz passed his hands wearily over his eyes. His nausea abated, the sweat dried in the hollow of his back, the whistles of the Yellow Paper Men moved off east towards the canal and eventually died away. After a few minutes he got up and warmed himself over the charcoal pan, spreading his fingers over it like a fan, then rubbing the palms of his hands together mechanically while he stared at the lectern in the middle of the room. It was made of good steel, and he wondered how much it might fetch in the pawnshops of the Margarethestrasse. His breath steamed in the cold air. Who was the old man? His furniture was expensive. When he comes back, Retz thought, I will ask him for his protection. Perhaps he will give me the eagle so that I can buy a horse and leave the city. An old man like him could easily afford that. Retz examined the porcelain plates on the sideboard. He stared at the tapestry. Large parts of it were so decayed he could not understand what they were meant to show, but in one corner he could make out a hill and the steep path which wound up it between stones and the roots of old trees. It made him feel uncomfortable and lonely.

When the old man returned he was carrying a tray with a pie and some bread on it. Two or three cats followed him into the room, looking up at him expectantly in the brown, wavering light of the candle. He found Retz in front of the tapestry.

"Come away from there!" he said sharply.

"Sir," said Retz, bowing low, "you saved my life. Tell me how I can serve you."

"I would not want a murderer for a servant," replied the old man.

Retz bit his underlip angrily. He turned his back, sat down, and began to stuff bread into his mouth. "If you lived out there you would act like me!" he said indistinctly. "What else is there?"

"I have lived in this city for more years than I can remember," said the old man. "I have murdered no one."

At this there was a longish silence. The old man sat with his chin on his chest and appeared lost in thought. The charcoal pan ticked as it cooled. A draught caught the tapestry so that it billowed like a torn curtain in the Boulevard Aussman. The cats scratched about furtively in the shadows behind the chairs. Ignace Retz ate, drank, wiped his mouth; he ate more and wiped his mouth again. When he was sure the old man wasn't watching him he boldly appraised the steel eagle. Once, on the pretext of going to the window, he even got up and touched it.

"What horror we are all faced with daily!" exclaimed the old man suddenly.

He sighed.

"I have heard the café philosophers say: 'The world is so old that the substance of reality no longer knows quite what it ought to be. The original template is hopelessly blurred. History repeats over and again this one city and a few frightful events—not rigidly, but in a shadowy, tentative fashion, as if it understands nothing else but would like to learn.' "

"The world is the world," said Ignace Retz. "Whatever they say."

"Look at the tapestry," said the old man.

Retz looked.

The design he had made out earlier, with its mountain path and stunted yew trees, was more extensive then he had thought. In it a bald man was depicted trudging up the path. Above him in the air hung a large bird. Beyond that, more mountains and valleys went away to the horizon. No stitching could be seen. The whole was worked very carefully and realistically, so that Retz felt he was looking through a window. The man on the path had skin of a yellowish colour, and his cloak was blue. He leaned on his staff as if he was out of breath. Without warning he turned round and stared out of the tapestry at Retz. As he did so the tapestry rippled in a cold draught, giving off a damp smell, and the whole scene vanished.

Retz began to tremble. In the distance he heard the old man say, "There is no need to be frightened."

"It's alive," Retz whispered. "Mammy Vooley—" But before he could say what he meant, another scene had presented itself.

It was dawn in Viriconium. The sky was a bowl of cloud with a litharge stain at its edge. Rain fell on the Proton Way where, supported by a hundred pillars of black stone, it spiralled up towards the palace. Halfway along this bleak ancient sweep of road, two or three figures in glowing scarlet armour stood watching a man fight with a vulture made of metal. The man's face was terribly cut; blood and rain made a dark mantle on his shoulders as he knelt there on the road. But he was winning. Soon he rose tiredly to his feet and threw the bird down in front of the watchers, who turned away and would not acknowledge him. He stared out of the tapestry. His cheeks hung open where the bird had pecked him; he was old and grey-haired, and his eyes were full of regret. His lips moved and he disappeared.

"It was me!" cried Ignace Retz. "Was it me?"

"There have been many Viriconiums," said the old man. "Watch the tapestry."

Two men with rusty swords stumbled across a high moor. A long way behind them came a dwarf wearing mechanical iron stilts. His head was laid open with a wound. They waited for him to catch up, but he fell behind again almost immediately. He blundered into a rowan tree and went off in the wrong direction. One of the men, who looked like Ignace Retz, had a dead bird swinging from his belt. He stared dispiritedly out of the tapestry at the real Retz, took the bird in one hand, and raised it high in the air by its neck. As he made this gesture the dwarf passed in front of him, his stilts leaking unhealthy white gases. They forded a stream together, and all three of them vanished into the distance where a city waited on a hill.

After that men fought one another in the shadow of a cliff, while above them on the eroded skyline patrolled huge iridescent beetles. A fever-stricken explorer with despairing eyes sat in a cart and allowed himself to be pulled along slowly by an animal like a tall white sloth until they came to the edge of a pool in a flooded city. Lizards circled endlessly a pile of corpses in the desert.

Eventually Retz grew used to seeing himself at the centre of these events, although he was sometimes surprised by the way he looked. But the last scene was too much for him.

He seemed to be looking through a tall arched window, around the stone mullions of which twined the stems of an ornamental rose. The thorns and flowers of the rose framed a room where curtains of silver light drifted like rain between enigmatic columns. The floor of the room was made of cinnabar crystal and in the centre of it had been set a simple throne. Standing by the throne, two albino lions couchant at her feet, was a slender woman in a velvet gown. Her eyes were a deep, sympathetic violet colour, her hair the russet of autumn leaves. On her long fingers she wore ten identical rings, and before her stood a knight whose glowing scarlet armour was partly covered by a black and silver cloak. His head was bowed. His hands were white. At his side he wore a steel sword.

Retz heard the woman say clearly, "I give you these things, Lord tegeus-Cromis, because I trust you. I would even give you a power-knife if I had one. Go to the South and win great treasure for us all."

Out of the tapestry drifted the scent of roses on a warm evening. There was the gentle sound of falling water, and somewhere a single line of melody repeated over and over again on a stringed instrument. The knight in the scarlet armour took his queen's hand and kissed it. He turned to look out of the window and wave as if someone he knew was passing. His black hair was parted in the middle to frame the transfigured face of Ignace Retz. Behind him the queen was smiling. The whole scene vanished, leaving a smell of damp, and all that could be seen through the rents in the cloth was the plaster on the wall.

Ignace Retz rubbed his eyes furiously. He jumped up, pulled the old man out of his chair, clutched him by the upper arm, and dragged him up to the tapestry.

"Those last things!" he demanded. "Have they really happened?"

"All queens are not Mammy Vooley," said the old man, as if he had won an argument. "All knights are not Ignace Retz. They have happened, or will."

"Make it show me again."

"I am only its caretaker. I cannot compel it."

Retz pushed him away with such violence that he fell against the sideboard and knocked the tray off it. The cats ran excitedly about, picking up pieces of food in their mouths.

"I mustn't believe this!" cried Retz.

He pulled the tapestry off the wall and examined it intently, as if he hoped to see himself moving there. When it remained mere cloth he threw it on the floor and kicked it.

"How could I live my life if I believed this?" he asked himself.

He turned back to the old man, took him by the shoulders, and shook him.

"What did you want to show me this for? How can I be content with this ghastly city now?"

"You need not live as you do," said the old man. "We make the world we live in."

Retz threw him aside. He hit his head on the sideboard, gave a curious angry groan, and was still. He did not seem to be dead. For some minutes Retz lurched distractedly to and fro between the window and the wall where the tapestry had been, repeating, "How can I live? How can I live!" Then he rushed over to the lectern and tried to wrench the steel eagle off it. It would be daylight by now, out in the city; they would be coughing and warming their hands by the naphtha flares in the Tinmarket. He would have a few hours in which to sell the bird, get a horse and a knife, and leave before the bravos began hunting him again. He would go out of the Haunted Gate on his horse, and go south, and never see the place again.

The bird moved. At first he thought it was simply coming loose from the plinth of black wood on which it was set. Then he felt a sharp pain in the palm of his left hand, and when he looked down the thing was alive and struggling powerfully in his grip. It cocked its head, stared up at him out of a cold, violent eye. It got one wing free, then the other, and redoubled its efforts. He managed to hold on to it for a second or two longer, then, crying out in revulsion and panic, he let go and staggered back, shaking his lacerated hands. He fell over something on the floor and found himself staring into the old man's stunned china-blue eyes.

"Get out of my house!" shouted the old man. "I've had enough of you!"

The bird meanwhile rose triumphantly into the air and flapped round the room, battering its wings against the walls and shrieking, while coppery reflections flared off its plumage and the cats crouched terrified underneath the furniture.

"Help me!" appealed Retz. "The eagle is alive!"

But the old man, lying on the floor as if paralysed, set his lips and would only answer,

"You have brought it on yourself."

Retz stood up and tried to cross the room to the door at the head of the stairs. The bird, which had been obsessively attacking its own shadow on the wall, promptly fastened itself over his face, striking at his eyes and tearing with its talons at his neck and upper chest. He screamed. He pulled it off him and dashed it against the base of the wall, where it fluttered about in a disoriented fashion for a moment before making off after one of the cats. Retz watched it, appalled, then clapped his hands to his bleeding face and blundered out of the room, down the narrow staircase, and out into the courtyard again. He slammed the door behind him.

It was still dark.

Sitting on the doorstep, Retz felt his neck cautiously to determine the extent of his injuries. He shuddered. They were not shallow. Above him he could still hear the trapped bird shrieking and beating its wings. If it escaped it would find him. As soon as he had stopped bleeding he backed shakily away across the courtyard and passed through the arch into a place he did not know.

He was on a wide, open avenue flanked by ruined buildings and heaps of rubble. Meaningless trenches had been dug across it here and there, and desultory fires burned on every side. Dust covered the broken chestnut trees and uprooted railings. Although there was no sign at all of dawn, the sky somehow managed to throw a curious filmy light over everything. Behind him the walled courtyard now stood on its own like a kind of blank rectangular tower. He thought he was still looking at the old man's tapestry; he thought there might have been some sort of war in the night with Mammy Vooley's devastating weapons; he didn't know what to think. He started to walk nervously in the direction of the canal, then run. He ran for a long time but could not find it. Acres of shattered roof tiles made a musical scraping sound under his feet. If he looked back he could still see the tower; but it got smaller and smaller, and in the end he forgot where to look for it.

All through that long night he had no idea where he was, but he felt as if he must be on a high plateau, windy and covered completely with the dust and rubble of this unfamiliar city. The wind stung the wounds the bird had given him. The dust pattered and rained against the fallen walls. Once he heard some kind of music coming from a distant house—the febrile beating of a large flat drum, the reedy fitful whine of something like a clarinet—but when he approached the place it was silent again, and he became frightened and ran off.

Later a human voice from the ruins quite near him made a long drawn-out *ou lou lou lou,* and was answered immediately from far off by a howl like a dog's. He fled from it between the long mounds of rubble, and for a while hid in the gutted shell of a cathedral-like building. After he had been there for about an hour, several indistinct figures appeared outside and began to dig silently and energetically in the road. Suddenly, though, they were disturbed; they all looked up together at something Retz couldn't see, and ran off with their spades. While this was going on he heard feet scraping around him in the dark. There was a deep sigh. *Ou lou lou* sounded, shockingly close, and he was alone again. They had examined him, whoever they were, and found him uninteresting.

Towards the dawn he left the building to look at the trench they had dug in the road. It was shallow, abortive, already filling up with grey sand. About a mile away he found a dead man hidden by a corner of masonry that stood a little over waist high.

Retz knelt down and studied him curiously.

He lay as if he had fallen while running away from someone, his limbs all askew and one arm evidently broken. He was heavily built, dressed in a loose white shirt and black moleskin trousers tied up below the knees with red string. He had on a fish-head mask, a thing like a salmon with blubbery lips, lugubrious popping eyes, and a crest of stiff spines, worn in such a way that if he had been standing upright the fish would have been staring glassily into the sky. Green ribbons were tied round his upper arms to flutter and rustle in the wind. Beside him where he had dropped it lay a power-knife from which there rose, as it burned its way into the rubble, a steady stream of poisonous yellow motes.

They had taken off his boots. His naked white feet were decorated with blue tattoos which went this way and that like veins.

Retz stared down at him. He climbed onto the wall and looked thoughtfully both ways along the empty road. Whatever place the old man and the bird had consigned him to, it would have its Mammy Vooley. Ten minutes later he emerged from behind the wall dressed in the dead man's clothes. They were too large, and he had some trouble with the fish head, which stank inside, but he had tied on the red string and the ribbons, and he had the knife. By the time he finished all this, dawn had come at last, a lid of brownish cloud lifted back at its eastern rim on streaks of yellow and emerald green, revealing a steep hill he had not previously seen. It was topped with towers, old fortifications, and the copper domes of ancient observatories. Retz set off in the direction the trench-diggers had taken. SHROGGS ROYD, announced the plaques at the corners of the demolished street: OULED NAIL. Then: RUE SEPILE.

That afternoon there was a dry storm. Particles of dust flew about under a leaden sky.

The Luck in the head

the luck in the head

Uroconium, Ardwick Crome said, was for all its beauty an indifferent city. Its people loved the arena; they were burning or quartering somebody every night for political or religious crimes. They hadn't much time for anything else. From where he lived, at the top of a tenement on the outskirts of Montrouge, you could often see the fireworks in the dark, or hear the shouts on the wind.

He had two rooms. In one of them was an iron-framed bed with a few blankets on it, pushed up against a washstand he rarely used. Generally he ate his meals cold, though he had once tried to cook an egg by lighting a newspaper under it. He had a chair, and a tall white ewer with a picture of the courtyard of an inn on it. The other room, a small north-light studio once occupied—so tradition in the Artists' Quarter had it—by Kristodulos Fleece the painter, he kept shut. It had some of his books in it, also the clothes in which he had first come to Uroconium and which he had thought then were fashionable.

He was not a well-known poet, although he had his following.

Every morning he would write for perhaps two hours, first restricting himself to the bed by means of three broad leather straps which his father had given him and to which he fastened himself, at the ankles, the hips, and finally across his chest. The sense of unfair confinement or punishment induced by this, he found, helped him to think.

Sometimes he called out or struggled; often he lay quite inert and looked dumbly up at the ceiling. He had been born in those vast dull ploughlands which roll east from Soubridge into the Midland Levels like a chocolate-coloured sea, and his most consistent work came from the attempt to retrieve and order the customs and events of his childhood there: the burial of the "Holly Man" on Plough Monday, the sound of the hard black lupin seeds popping and tapping against the window in August while his mother sang quietly in the kitchen the ancient carols of the *Oei'l Voirrey*. He remembered the meadows and reeds beside the Yser Canal, the fishes that moved within it. When his straps chafed, the old bridges were in front of him, made of warm red brick and curved protectively over their own image in the water!

Thus Crome lived in Uroconium, remembering, working, publishing. He sometimes spent an evening in the Bistro Californium or the Luitpold Café. Several of the Luitpold critics (notably Barzelletta Angst, who in *L'Espace Cromien* ignored entirely the conventional chronology—expressed in the idea of "recherche"—of Crome's long poem *Bream Into Man*) tried to represent his work as a series of narrativeless images, glued together only by his artistic persona. Crome refuted them in a pamphlet. He was content.

Despite his sedentary habit he was a sound sleeper. But before it blows at night over the pointed roofs of Montrouge, the southwest wind must first pass between the abandoned towers of the Old City, as silent as burnt logs, full of birds, scraps of machinery, and broken-up philosophies: and Crome had hardly been there three years when he began to have a dream in which he was watching the ceremony called "the Luck in the Head."

For its proper performance this ceremony requires the construction on a seashore, between the low and high tide marks at the Eve of Assumption, of two fences or "hedges." These are made by weaving osiers—usually cut at first light on the same day—through split hawthorn uprights upon which the foliage has been left. The men of the town stand at one end of the corridor thus formed; the women, their thumbs tied together behind their backs, at the other. At a signal the men release between the hedges a lamb decorated with medallions, paper ribbons, and strips of rag. The women race after, catch it, and scramble to keep it from one another, the winner being the one who can seize the back of the animal's neck with her teeth. In Dunham Massey, Lymm, and Iron Chine, the lamb is paraded for three days on a pole before being made into pies; and it is good luck to obtain the pie made from the head.

In his dream Crome found himself standing on some sand dunes, looking out over the wastes of marram grass at the osier fences and the tide. The women, with their small heads and long grey garments, stood breathing heavily like horses, or walked nervously in circles avoiding one another's eyes as they tested with surreptitious tugs the red cord which bound their thumbs. Crome could see no one there he knew. Somebody said, "A hundred eggs and a calf's tail," and laughed. Ribbons fluttered in the cold air: they had introduced the lamb. It stood quite still until the women, who had been lined up and settled down after a certain amount of jostling, rushed at it. Their shrieks rose up like those of herring gulls, and a fine rain came in from the sea.

"They're killing one another!" Crome heard himself say.

Without any warning one of them burst out of the mêlée with the lamb in her teeth. She ran up the dunes with a floundering, splay-footed gait and dropped it at his feet. He stared down at it.

"It's not mine," he said. But everyone else had walked away.

He woke up listening to the wind and staring at the washstand, got out of bed and walked round the room to quieten himself down. Fireworks, greenish and queasy with the hour of the night, lit up the air intermittently above the distant arena. Some of this illumination, entering through the skylight, fell as a pale wash on his thin arms and legs, fixing them in attitudes of despair.

If he went to sleep again he often found, in a second lobe or episode of the dream, that he had already accepted the dead lamb and was himself running with it, at a steady premeditated trot, down the landward side of the dunes towards the town. (This he recognised by its slate roofs as Lowick, a place he had once visited in childhood. In its streets some men made tiny by distance were banging on the doors with sticks, as they had done then. He remembered very clearly the piece of singed sheepskin they had been making people smell.) Empty ground stretched away on either side of him under a motionless sky; everything—the clumps of thistles, the frieze of small thorn trees deformed by the wind, the sky itself—had a brownish cast, as if seen through an atmosphere of tars. He could hear the woman behind him to begin with, but soon he was left alone. In the end Lowick vanished too, though he began to run as quickly as he could, and left him in a mist or smoke through which a bright light struck, only to be diffused immediately.

By then the lamb had become something that produced a thick buzzing noise, a vibration which, percolating up the bones of his arm and into his shoulder, then into the right side of his neck and face where it reduced the muscles to water, made him feel nauseated, weak, and deeply afraid. Whatever it was he couldn't shake it off his hand.

Clearly—in that city and at that age of the world—it would have been safer for Crome to look inside himself for the source of this dream. Instead, after he had woken one day with the early light coming through the shutters like sour milk and a vague rheumatic ache in his neck, he went out into Uroconium to pursue it. He was sure he would recognise the woman if he saw her, or the lamb.

She was not in the Bistro Californium when he went there by way of the

Via Varese, or in Mecklenburgh Square. He looked for her in Proton Alley, where the beggars gaze back at you emptily and the pavement artists offer to draw for you, in that curious mixture of powdered chalk and condensed milk they favour, pictures of the Lamia, without clothes or without skin, with fewer limbs or organs than normal, or more. They couldn't draw the woman he wanted. On the Unter-Main-Kai (it was eight in the morning and the naphtha flares had grown smoky and dim) a boy spun and tottered among the crowds from the arena, declaiming in a language no one knew. He bared his shaven skull, turned his bony face upwards, mouth open. Suddenly he drove a long thorn into his own neck: at this the women rushed up to him and thrust upon him cakes, cosmetic emeralds, coins. Crome studied their faces: nothing. In the Luitpold Café he found Ansel Verdigris and some others eating gooseberries steeped in gin.

"I'm sick," said Verdigris, clutching Crome's hand.

He spooned up a few more gooseberries and then, letting the spoon fall back into the dish with a clatter, rested his head on the tablecloth beside it. From this position he was forced to stare up sideways at Crome and talk with one side of his mouth. The skin beneath his eyes had the shine of wet pipe clay; his coxcomb of reddish-yellow hair hung damp and awry; the electric light, falling oblique and bluish across his white triangular face, lent it an expression of astonishment.

"My brain's poisoned, Crome," he said. "Let's go up into the hills and run about in the snow."

He looked round with contempt at his friends, Gunter Verlac and the Baron de V——, who grinned sheepishly back.

"Look at them!" he said. "Crome, we're the only human beings here. Let's renew our purity! We'll dance on the lips of the icy gorges!"

"It's the wrong season for snow," said Crome.

"Well, then," Verdigris whispered, "let's go where the old machines leak and flicker, and you can hear the calls of the madmen from the asylum up at Wergs. Listen—"

"No!" said Crome. He wrenched his hand away.

"Listen, proctors are out after me from Cheminor to Mynned! Lend me some money, Crome, I'm sick of my crimes. Last night they shadowed me along the cinder paths among the poplar trees by the isolation hospital."

He laughed, and began to eat gooseberries as fast as he could.

"The dead remember only the streets, never the numbers of the houses!"

Verdigris lived with his mother, a woman of some means and education who called herself Madam "L," in Delpine Square. She was always as concerned about the state of his health as he was about hers. They lay ill with shallow fevers and deep cafards, in rooms that joined, so that they could buoy one another up through the afternoons of insomnia. As soon as they felt recovered enough they would let themselves be taken from salon to salon by wheelchair, telling one another amusing little stories as they went. Once a month Verdigris would leave her and spend all night at the arena with some prostitute; fall unconscious in the Luitpold or the Californium; and wake up distraught a few hours later in his own bed. His greatest fear was that he would catch syphilis. Crome looked down at him.

"You've never been to Cheminor, Verdigris," he said. "Neither of us has."

Verdigris stared at the tablecloth. Suddenly he stuffed it into his mouth—his empty dish fell onto the floor where it rolled about for a moment, faster and faster, and was smashed—only to throw back his head and pull it out again, inch by inch, like a medium pulling out ectoplasm in Margery Fry Court.

"You won't be so pleased with yourself," he said, "when you've read this."

And he gave Crome a sheet of thick green paper, folded three times, on which someone had written:

A man may have many kinds of dreams. There are dreams he wishes to continue and others he does not. At one hour of the night men may have dreams in which everything is veiled in violet; at others, unpalatable truths may be conveyed. If a certain man wants certain dreams he may be having to cease, he will wait by the Aqualate Pond at night, and speak to whoever he finds there.

"This means nothing to me," lied Crome. "Where did you get it?"

"A woman thrust it into my hand two days ago as I came down the Ghibbeline Stair. She spoke your name, or one like it. I saw nothing."

Crome stared at the sheet of paper in his hand. Leaving the Luitpold Café a few minutes later, he heard someone say: "In Aachen, by the Haunted Gate—do you remember?—a woman on the pavement stuffing cakes into her mouth? Sugar cakes into her mouth?"

That night, as Crome made his way reluctantly towards the Aqualate Pond, the moonlight rose in a lemon-yellow tide over the empty cat-infested towers of the city; in the Artists' Quarter the violin and cor anglais pronounced their fitful whine; while from the distant arena—from twenty-five-thousand faces underlit by the flames of the auto-da-fé—issued an interminable whisper of laughter.

It was the anniversary of the liberation of Uroconium from the Analeptic Kings.

Householders lined the steep hill up at Alves. Great velvet banners, featuring black crosses on a red and white ground, hung down the balconies above their naked heads. Their eyes were patiently fixed on the cracked

copper dome of the observatory at its summit. (There, as the text sometimes called *The Earl of Rone* remembers, the Kings handed over to
Mammy Vooley and her fighters their weapons of appalling power; there
they were made to bend the knee.) A single bell rang out, then stopped—
a hundred children carrying candles swept silently down towards them and
were gone! Others came on behind, shuffling to the rhythms of the "Ou
lou lou," that ancient song. In the middle of it all, the night and the banners and the lights, swaying precariously to and fro fifteen feet above
the procession like a doll nailed on a gilded chair, came Mammy Vooley
herself.

Sometimes as it blows across the Great Brown Waste in summer, the
wind will uncover a bit of petrified wood. What oak or mountain ash this
wood has come from, alive immeasurably long ago, what secret treaties
were made beneath it during the Afternoon of the world only to be broken
by the Evening, we do not know. We will never know. It is a kind of wood
full of contradictory grains and lines: studded with functionless knots:
hard.

Mammy Vooley's head had the shape and the shiny grey look of wood
like that. It was provided with one good eye, as if at some time it had
grown round a glass marble streaked with milky blue. She bobbed it stiffly
right and left to the crowds, who stood to watch her approach, knelt as she
passed, and stood up again behind her. Her bearers grunted patiently under the weight of the pole that bore her up. As they brought her slowly
closer it could be seen that her dress—so curved between her bony,
strangely articulated knees that dead leaves, lumps of plaster, and crusts
of whole-meal bread had gathered in her lap—was russet-orange, and
that she wore askew on the top of her head a hank of faded purple hair,
wispy and fine like a very old woman's. Mammy Vooley, celebrating with
black banners and young women chanting; Mammy Vooley, Queen of
Uroconium, Moderator of the city, as silent as a log of wood.

Crome got up on tiptoe to watch; he had never seen her before. As she
drew level with him she seemed to float in the air, her shadow projected on
a cloud of candle smoke by the lemon-yellow moon. That afternoon, for
the ceremony, in her *salle* or retiring room (where at night she might be
heard singing to herself in different voices), they had painted on her face
another one—approximate, like a doll's, with pink cheeks. All round
Crome's feet the householders of Alves knelt in the gutter. He stared at
them. Mammy Vooley caught him standing.

She waved down at her bearers.

"Stop!" she whispered.

"I bless all my subjects," she told the kneeling crowd. "Even this one."

And she allowed her head to fall exhaustedly on one side.

In a moment she had passed by. The remains of the procession followed her, trailing its smell of candle fat and sweating feet, and vanished round a corner towards Montrouge. (Young men and women fought for the privilege of carrying the Queen. As the new bearers tried to take it from the old ones, Mammy Vooley's pole swung backwards and forwards in uncontrollable arcs so that she flopped about in her chair at the top of it like the head of a mop. Wrestling silently, the small figures carried her away.) In the streets below Alves there was a sense of relief: smiling and chattering and remarking how well the Mammy had looked that day, the householders took down the banners and folded them in tissue paper.

". . . so regal in her new dress."

"So clean . . ."

". . . and such a healthy colour!"

But Crome continued to look down the street for a long time after it was empty. Marguerite petals had fallen among the splashes of candle grease on the cobbled setts. He couldn't think how they came to be there. He picked some up in his hand and raised them to his face. A vivid recollection came to him of the smell of flowering privet in the suburbs of Soubridge when he was a boy, the late snapdragons and nasturtiums in the gardens. Suddenly he shrugged. He got directions to the narrow lane which would take him west of Alves to the Aqualate Pond, and having found it walked off up it rapidly. Fireworks burst from the arena, fizzing and flashing directly overhead; the walls of the houses danced and warped in the warm red light; his own shadow followed him along them, huge, misshapen, intermittent.

Crome shivered.

"Whatever is in the Aqualate Pond," Ingo Lympany the dramatist had once told him, "it's not water."

On the shore in front of a terrace of small shabby houses he had already found a kind of gibbet made of two great arched, bleached bones. From it swung a corpse whose sex he couldn't determine, upright in a tight wicker basket which creaked in the wind. The pond lay as still as Lympany had predicted, and it smelled of lead.

"Again, you see, everyone agrees it's a small pool, a very small one. But when you are standing by it, on the Henrietta Street side, you would swear that it stretched right off to the horizon. The winds there seem to have come such a distance. Because of this the people in Henrietta Street believe they are living by an ocean, and make all the observances fishermen make. For instance, they say that a man can only die when the pool is ebbing. His bed must be oriented the same way as the floorboards, and at the moment of death doors and windows should be opened, mirrors covered with a clean white cloth, and all fires extinguished. And so on."

They believed, too, at least the older ones did, that huge fish had once lived there.

"There are no tides of course, and fish of any kind are rarely found there now. All the same, in Henrietta Street once a year they bring out a large stuffed pike, freshly varnished and with a bouquet of thistles in its mouth, and walk up and down the causeway with it, singing and shouting.

"And then—it's so hard to explain!—*echoes* go out over that stuff in the pool whenever you move, especially in the evening when the city is quiet: echoes and echoes of echoes, as though it were contained in some huge vacant metal building. But when you look up there is only the sky."

"Well, Lympany," said Crome aloud to himself. "You were right."

He yawned. Whistling thinly and flapping his arms against his sides to keep warm, he paced to and fro underneath the gibbet. When he stood on the meagre strip of pebbles at its edge, a chill seemed to seep out of the pool and into his bones. Behind him Henrietta Street stretched away, lugubrious and potholed. He promised himself, as he had done several times that night, that if he turned round, and looked down it, and still saw no one, he would go home. Afterwards he could never quite describe to himself what he had seen.

Fireworks flickered a moment in the dark, like the tremulous reflections made by a bath of water on the walls and ceilings of an empty room, and were gone. While they lasted, Henrietta Street was all boarded-up windows and bluish shadows. He had the impression that as he turned it had just been vacated by a number of energetic figures—quiet, agile men who dodged into dark corners or flung themselves over the rotting fences and iron railings, or simply ran off very fast down the middle of the road *precisely so that he shouldn't see them*. At the same time he saw, or thought he saw, one real figure do all these things, as if it had been left behind by the rest, staring white-faced over its shoulder at him in total silence as it sprinted erratically from one feeble refuge to another, and then vanishing abruptly between some houses.

Overlaid, as it were, on both this action and the potential or completed action it suggested, was a woman in a brown cloak. At first she was tiny and distant, trudging up Henrietta Street towards him; then, without any transitional state at all, she had appeared in the middle ground, posed like a piece of statuary between the puddles, white and naked with one arm held up (behind her it was possible to glimpse for an instant three other women, but not to see what they were doing—except that they seemed to be plaiting flowers); finally, with appalling suddenness, she filled his whole field of vision, as if on the Unter-Main-Kai a passerby had leapt in front of him without warning and screamed in his face. He gave a violent start and jumped backwards so quickly that he fell over. By the time he was able to get up the sky was dark again, Henrietta Street empty, everything as it had been.

The woman, though, awaited him silently in the shadows beneath the gibbet, wrapped in her cloak like a sculpture wrapped in brown paper, and wearing over her head a complicated mask made of wafery metal to represent the head of one or another wasteland insect. Crome found that he had bitten his tongue. He approached her cautiously, holding out in front of him at arm's length the paper Verdigris had given him.

"Did you send me this?" he said.

"Yes."

"Do I know you?"

"No."

"What must I do to stop these dreams?"

She laughed. Echoes fled away over the Aqualate Pond.

"Kill the Mammy," she said.

Crome looked at her.

"You must be mad," he said. "Whoever you are."

"Wait," she recommended him, "and we'll see who's mad."

She lowered the corpse in its wicker cage—the chains and pulleys of the gibbet gave a rusty creak—and pulled it towards her by its feet. Momentarily it escaped her and danced in a circle, coy and sad. She recaptured it with a murmur. "Hush now. Hush." Crome backed away. "Look," he whispered, "I—" Before he could say anything else, she had slipped her hand deftly between the osiers and, like a woman gutting fish on a cold Wednesday morning at Lowth, opened the corpse from diaphragm to groin. "Man or woman?" she asked him, up to her elbows in it. "Which would you say?" A filthy smell filled the air and then dissipated. "I don't want—" said Crome. But she had already turned back to him and was offering him her hands, cupped, in a way that gave him no option but to see what she had found—or made—for him.

"Look!"

A dumb, doughy shape writhed and fought against itself on her palms, swelling quickly from the size of a dried pea to that of a newly born dog. It was, he saw, contained by vague and curious lights which came and went; then by a cream-coloured fog which was perhaps only a blurring of its own spatial limits; and at last by a damp membrane, pink and grey, which it burst suddenly by butting and lunging. It was the lamb he had seen in his dreams, shivering and bleating and tottering in its struggle to stand, the eyes fixed on him forever in its complaisant, bone-white face. It seemed already to be sickening in the cold leaden breath of the pond.

"Kill the Mammy," said the woman with the insect's head, "and in a few days' time you will be free. I will bring you a weapon soon."

"All right," said Crome.

He turned and ran.

He heard the lamb bleating after him the length of Henrietta Street, and behind that the sound of the sea, rolling and grinding the great stones in the tide.

For some days this image preoccupied him. The lamb made its way without fuss into his waking life. Wherever he looked he thought he saw it looking back at him: from an upper window in the Artists' Quarter, or framed by the dusty iron railings which line the streets there, or from between the chestnut trees in an empty park.

Isolated in a way he had not been since he first arrived in Uroconium wearing his green plush country waistcoat and yellow pointed shoes, he decided to tell no one what had happened by the Aqualate Pond. Then he thought he would tell Ansel Verdigris and Ingo Lympany. But Lympany had gone to Cladich to escape his creditors—and Verdigris, who after eating the tablecloth was no longer welcomed at the Luitpold Café, had left the Quarter too: at the large old house in Delpine Square there was only his mother—a bit lonely in her bath chair, though still a striking woman with a great curved nose and a faint, heady smell of elder blossom—who said vaguely, "I'm sure I can remember what he said," but in the end could not.

"I wonder if you know, Ardwick Crome, how I worry about his *bowels*," she went on. "As his friend you must worry, too, for they are very lazy, and he will not encourage them if we do not!"

It was, she said, a family failing.

She offered Crome chamomile tea, which he refused, and then got him to run an errand for her to a fashionable chemist's in Mynned. After that he could do nothing but go home and wait.

Kristodulos Fleece—half dead with opium and syphilis, and notoriously self-critical—had left behind him when he vacated the north-light studio a small picture. Traditionally it remained there. Succeeding occupants had taken heart from its technical brio and uncustomary good humour (although Audsley King was reputed to have turned it to the wall during her brief period in Montrouge because she detected in it some unforgivable sentimentality or other) and no dealer in the Quarter would buy it for fear of bad luck. Crome now removed it to the corner above the cheap tin washstand so that he could see it from his bed.

Oil on canvas, about a foot square, it depicted in some detail a scene the artist had called "Children beloved of the gods have the power to weep roses." The children, mainly girls, were seen dancing under an elder tree, the leafless branches of which had been decorated with strips of rag.

Behind them stretched away rough common land, with clumps of gorse and a few bare, graceful birch saplings, to where the upper windows and thatch of a low cottage could be made out. The lighthearted vigour of the dancers, who were winding themselves round the tallest girl in a spiral like a clock spring, was contrasted with the stillness of the late-winter afternoon, its sharp clear airs and horizontal light. Crome had often watched this dance as a boy, though he had never been allowed to take part in it. He remembered the tranquil shadows on the grass, the chant, the rose and green colours of the sky. As soon as the dancers had wound the spiral tight, they would begin to tread on one another's toes, laughing and shrieking— or, changing to a different tune, jump up and down beneath the tree while one of them shouted, "A bundle of rags!"

It was perhaps as sentimental a picture as Audsley King had claimed. But Crome, who saw a lamb in every corner, had never seen one there; and when she came as she had promised, the woman with the insect's head found him gazing so quietly up at it from the trapezium of moonlight falling across his bed that he looked like the effigy on a tomb. She stood in the doorway, perhaps thinking he had died and escaped her.

"I can't undo myself," he said.

The mask glittered faintly. Did he hear her breathing beneath it? Before he could make up his mind there was a scuffling on the stairs behind her and she turned to say something he couldn't quite catch—though it might have been: "Don't come in yourself."

"These straps are so old," he explained. "My father—"

"All right, give it to me, then," she said impatiently to whoever was outside. "Now go away." And she shut the door. Footsteps went down the stairs; it was so quiet in Montrouge that you could hear them clearly going away down flight after flight, scraping in the dust on a landing, catching in the cracked linoleum. The street door opened and closed. She waited, leaning against the door, until they had gone off down the empty pavements towards Mynned and the Ghibbeline Passage, then said, "I had better untie you." But instead she walked over to the end of Crome's bed, and sitting on it with her back to him stared thoughtfully at the picture of the elder-tree dance.

"You were clever to find this," she told him. She stood up again, and, peering at it, ignored him when he said,

"It was in the other room when I came."

"I suppose someone helped you," she said. "Well, it won't matter." Suddenly she demanded, "Do you like it here among the rats? Why must you live here?"

He was puzzled.

"I don't know."

A shout went up in the distance, long and whispering like a deeply drawn breath. Roman candles sailed up into the night one after the other, exploding in the east below the zenith so that the collapsing pantile roofs of Montrouge stood out sharp and black. Light poured in, ran off the back of the chair and along the belly of the enamel jug, and, discovering a book or a box here, a broken pencil there, threw them into merciless relief. Yellow or gold, ruby, greenish-white: with each new pulse the angles of the room grew more equivocal.

"Oh, it is the stadium!" cried the woman with the insect's head. "They have begun early tonight!"

She laughed and clapped her hands. Crome stared at her.

"Clowns will be capering in the great light!" she said.

Quickly she undid his straps.

"Look!"

Propped up against the whitewashed wall by the door she had left a long brown paper parcel hastily tied with string. Fat or grease had escaped from it, and it looked as if it might contain a fish. While she fetched it for him, Crome sat on the edge of the bed with his elbows on his knees, rubbing his face. She carried it hieratically, across her outstretched arms, her image advancing and receding in the intermittent light.

"I want you to see clearly what we are going to lend you."

When the fireworks had stopped at last, an ancient white ceramic sheath came out of the paper. It was about two feet long, and it had been in the ground for a long time, yellowing to the colour of ivory and collecting a craquelure of fine lines like an old sink. Chemicals seeping through the soils of the Great Waste had left here and there on it faint blue stains. The weapon it contained had a matching hilt—although by now it was a much darker colour from years of handling—and from the juncture of the two had leaked some greenish, jelly-like substance which the woman with the insect's head was careful not to touch. She knelt on the bare floorboards at Crome's feet, her back and shoulders curved round the weapon, and slowly pulled hilt and sheath apart.

At once a smell filled the room, thick and stale like wet ashes in a dustbin. Pallid oval motes of light, some the size of a birch leaf, others hardly visible, drifted up towards the ceiling. They congregated in corners and did not disperse, while the weapon, buzzing torpidly, drew a dull violet line after it in the gloom as the woman with the insect's head moved it slowly to and fro in front of her. She seemed to be fascinated by it. Like all those things it had been dug up out of some pit. It had come to the city through the Analeptic Kings, how long ago no one knew. Crome pulled his legs up onto the bed out of its way.

"I don't want that," he said.

"Take it!"

"No."

"You don't understand. She is trying to change the name of the city!"

"I don't want it. I don't care."

"Take it. Touch it. It's yours now."

"No!"

"Very well," she said quietly. "But don't imagine the painting will help you again." She threw it on the bed near him. "Look at it," she said. She laughed disgustedly. " 'Children beloved of the gods'!" she said. "Is that why he waited for them outside the washhouses twice a week?"

The dance was much as it had been, but now with the fading light the dancers had removed themselves to the garden of the cottage, where they seemed frozen and awkward, as if they could only imitate the gaiety they had previously felt. They were dancing in the shadow of the *bredogue*, which someone had thrust out of an open window beneath the earth-coloured eaves. In Soubridge, and in the midlands generally, they make this pitiful thing—with its bottle-glass eyes and crepe-paper harness—out of the stripped and varnished skull of a horse, put up on a pole covered with an ordinary sheet. This one, though, had the skull of a well-grown lamb, which seemed to move as Crome looked.

"What have you done?" he whispered. "Where is the picture as it used to be?"

The lamb gaped its lower jaw slackly over the unsuspecting children to vomit on them its bad luck. Then, clothed with flesh again, it turned its white and pleading face on Crome, who groaned and threw the painting across the room and held out his hand.

"Give me the sword from under the ground, then," he said.

When the hilt of it touched his hand he felt a faint sickly shock. The bones of his arm turned to jelly and the rank smell of ashpits enfolded him. It was the smell of a continent of wet cinders, buzzing with huge papery-winged flies under a poisonous brown sky; the smell of Cheminor, and Mammy Vooley, and the Aqualate Pond; it was the smell of the endless wastes which surround Uroconium and everything else that is left of the world. The woman with the insect's head looked at him with satisfaction. A knock came at the door.

"Go away!" she shouted. "You will ruin everything!"

"I'm to see that he's touched it," said a muffled voice. "I'm to make sure of that before I go back."

She shrugged impatiently and opened the door.

"Be quick then," she said.

In came Ansel Verdigris, stinking of lemon genever and wearing an ex-traordinary yellow satin shirt which made his face look like a corpse's. His coxcomb, freshly dyed that afternoon at some barber's in the Tinmarket, stuck up from his scalp in exotic scarlet spikes and feathers. Ignoring Crome, and giving the woman with the insect's head only the briefest of placatory nods, he made a great show of looking for the weapon. He sniffed the air. He picked up the discarded sheath and sniffed that. (He licked his finger and went to touch the stuff that had leaked from it, but at the last moment he changed his mind.) He stared up at the vagrant motes of light in the corners of the room, as if he could divine something from the way they wobbled and bobbed against the ceiling.

When he came to the bed he looked intently but with no sign of recognition into Crome's face.

"Oh yes," he said. "He's touched it all right."

He laughed. He tapped the side of his nose, and winked. Then he ran round and round the room crowing like a cock, his mouth gaping open and his tongue extended, until he fell over Kristodulos Fleece's painting, which lay against the skirtingboard where Crome had flung it. "Oh, he's touched it all right," he said, leaning exhaustedly against the door frame. He held the picture away from him at arm's length and looked at it with his head on one side. "Anyone could see that." His expression became pensive. "Anyone."

"The sword is in his hand," said the woman with the insect's head. "If you can tell us only what we see already, get out."

"It isn't you that wants to know," Verdigris answered flatly, as if he was thinking of something else. He propped the painting up against his thigh and passed the fingers of both hands several times rapidly through his hair. All at once he went and stood in the middle of the room on one leg, from which position he grinned at her insolently and began to sing in a thin musical treble like a boy at a feast:

> "I choose you one, I choose you all,
>   I pray I might go to the ball."

"Get out!" she shouted.

"The ball is mine," sang Verdigris,

> "and none of yours,
>   Go to the woods and gather flowers.
>   Cats and kittens abide within
>   But we *court ladies* walk out and in!"

Some innuendo in the last line seemed to enrage her. She clenched her fists and brought them up to the sides of the mask, the feathery antennae of which quivered and trembled like a wasp's.

"Sting me!" taunted Verdigris. "Go on!"

She shuddered.

He tucked the painting under his arm and prepared to leave.

"Wait!" begged Crome, who had watched them with growing puzzlement and horror. "Verdigris, you must know that it is me! Why aren't you saying anything? What's happening?"

Verdigris, already in the doorway, turned round and gazed at Crome for a moment with an expression almost benign, then, curling his upper lip, he mimicked contemptuously, " 'Verdigris, you've never *been* to Cheminor. *Neither* of us has.' " He spat on the floor and touched the phlegm he had produced with his toe, eyeing it with qualified disapproval. "Well, I have now, Crome. I have now." Crome saw that under their film of triumph his eyes were full of fear; his footsteps echoed down into the street and off into the ringing spaces of Montrouge and the Old City.

"Give the weapon to me," said the woman with the insect's head. As she put it back in its sheath it gave out briefly the smells of rust, decaying horse hair, vegetable water. She seemed indecisive. "He won't come back," she said once. "I promise." But Crome would not look away from the wall. She went here and there in the room, blowing dust off a pile of books and reading a line or two in one of them, opening the door into the north-light studio and closing it again immediately, tapping her fingers on the edge of the washstand. "I'm sorry about the painting," she said. Crome could think of nothing to say to that. The floorboards creaked; the bed moved. When he opened his eyes she was lying next to him.

All the rest of the night her strange long body moved over him in the unsteady illumination from the skylight. The insect mask hung above him like a question, with its huge faceted eyes and its jaws of filigree steel plate. He heard her breath in it, distinctly, and once thought he saw through it parts of her real face, pale lips, a cheekbone, an ordinary human eye: but he would not speak to her. The outer passages of the observatory at Alves are full of an ancient grief. The light falls as if it has been strained through muslin. The air is cold and moves unpredictably. It is the grief of the old machines, which, unfulfilled, whisper suddenly to themselves and are silent again for a century. No one knows what to do with them. No one knows how to assuage them. A faint sour panic seems to cling to them: they laugh as you go past, or extend a curious yellow film of light like a wing.

"Ou lou lou" sounds from these passages almost daily—more or less distant with each current of air—for Mammy Vooley is often here. No one knows why. It is clear that she herself is uncertain. If it is pride in her victory over the Analeptic Kings, why does she sit alone in an alcove, staring out of the windows? The Mammy who comes here to brood is not the doll-like figure which processes the city on Fridays and holidays. She will not wear her wig, or let them make up her face. She is a constant trial to them. She sings quietly and tunelessly to herself, and the plaster falls from the damp ceilings into her lap. A dead mouse has now come to rest there and she will allow no one to remove it.

At the back of the observatory, the hill of Alves continues to rise a little. This knoll of ancient compacted rubbish, excavated into caves, mean dwellings, and cemeteries, is called Antedaraus because it drops away sheer into the Daraus Gorge. Behind it, on the western side of the gorge (which from above can be seen to divide Uroconium like a fissure in a wart), rise the ruinous towers of the Old City. Perhaps a dozen of them still stand, mysterious with spires and fluted mouldings and glazed blue tiles, among the blackened hulks of those that fell during the City Wars. Every few minutes one or another of them sounds a bell, the feathery appeal of which fills the night from the streets below Alves to the shore of the Aqualate Pond, from Montrouge to the arena: in consequence the whole of Uroconium seems silent and tenantless—empty, littered, obscure, a city of worn-out enthusiasms.

Mammy Vooley hasn't time for those old towers, or for the mountains which rise beyond them to throw a shadow ten miles long across the bleak watersheds and shallow boggy valleys outside the city. It is the decayed terraces of the Antedaraus that preoccupy her. They are overgrown with mutant ivy and stifled whins; along them groups of mourners go, laden with anemones for the graves. Sour earth spills from the burst revetments between the beggars' houses, full of the rubbish of generations and strewn with dark red petals which give forth a sad odour in the rain. All day long the lines of women pass up and down the hill. They have with them the corpse of a baby in a box covered with flowers; behind them comes a boy dragging a coffin lid; Mammy Vooley nods and smiles.

Everything her subjects do here is of interest to her: on the same evening that Crome found himself outside the observatory—fearfully clutching under his coat the weapon from the waste—she sat in the pervasive gloom somewhere in the corridors, listening with tilted head and lively eyes to a hoarse muted voice calling out from under the Antedaraus. After a few minutes a man came out of a hole in the ground and with a great effort began pulling himself about in the sodden vegetation, dragging behind him a wicker basket of earth and excrement. He had, she saw, no legs. When he was forced to rest, he looked vacantly into the air; the rain fell into his face but he didn't seem to notice it. He called out again. There was no answer. Eventually he emptied the basket and crawled back into the ground.

"Ah!" whispered Mammy Vooley, and sat forward expectantly.

She was already late; but she waved her attendants away when for the third time they brought her the wig and the wooden crown.

"Was it necessary to come here so publicly?" muttered Crome.

The woman with the insect's head was silent. When that morning he had asked her, "Where would you go if you could leave this city?" she had answered, "On a ship." And, when he stared at her, added, "In the night. I would find my father."

But now she only said,

"Hush. Hush now. You will not be here long."

A crowd had been gathering all afternoon by the wide steps of the observatory. Ever since Mammy Vooley's arrival in the city it had been customary for "sides" of young boys to dance on these steps on a certain day in November, in front of the gaunt wooden images of the Analeptic Kings. Everything was ready. Candles thickened the air with the smell of fat. The kings had been brought out, and now loomed inert in the gathering darkness, their immense defaced heads lumpish and threatening. The choir could be heard from inside the observatory, practising and coughing, practising and coughing, under that dull cracked dome which absorbs every echo like felt. The little boys—they were seven or eight years old—huddled together on the seeping stones, pale and grave in their outlandish costumes. They were coughing, too, in the dampness that creeps down every winter from the Antedaraus.

"This weapon is making me ill," said Crome. "What must I do? Where is she?"

"Hush."

At last the dancers were allowed to take their places about halfway up the steps, where they stood in a line looking nervously at one another until the music signalled them to begin. The choir was marshalled, and sang its famous "Renunciative" cantos, above which rose the whine of the cor anglais and the thudding of a large flat drum. The little boys revolved slowly in simple, strict figures, with expressions inturned and languid. For every two paces forward, it had been decreed, they must take two back.

Soon Mammy Vooley was pushed into view at the top of the steps, in a chair with four iron wheels. Her head lolled against its curved back. Attendants surrounded her immediately, young men and women in stiff embroidered robes who after a perfunctory bow set about ordering her wisp of hair or arranging her feet on a padded stool. They held a huge book up in front of her single milky eye and then placed in her lap the crown or wreath of woven yew twigs which she would later throw to the dancing boys. Throughout the dance she stared uninterestedly up into the sky, but as soon as it was finished and they had helped her to sit up she proclaimed in a distant yet eager voice:

"Even these were humbled."

She made them open the book in front of her again, at a different page. She had brought it with her from the North.

"Even these kings were made to bend the knee," she read.

The crowd cheered.

She was unable after all to throw the wreath, although her hands picked disconnectedly at it for some seconds. In the end it was enough for her to let it slip out of her lap and fall among the boys, who scrambled with solemn faces down the observatory steps after it while her attendants showered them with crystallised geranium petals and other coloured sweets, and in the crowd their parents urged them, "Quick now!"

The rain came on in earnest, putting out some of the candles; the wreath rolled about on the bottom step like a coin set spinning on a table in the Luitpold Café, then toppled over and was still. The quickest boy had claimed it, Mammy Vooley's head had fallen to one side again, and they were preparing to close the great doors behind her, when shouting and commotion broke out in the observatory itself and a preposterous figure in a yellow satin shirt burst onto the steps near her chair. It was Ansel Verdigris. He had spewed black-currant gin down his chest, and his cox-comb, now dishevelled and lax, was plastered across his sweating forehead like a smear of blood. He still clutched under one arm the painting he had taken from Crome's room: this he began to wave about in the air above his head with both hands, so strenuously that the frame broke and the canvas flapped loose from it.

"Wait!" he shouted.

The woman with the insect's head gave a great sideways jump of surprise, like a horse. She stared at Verdigris for a second as if she didn't know what to do, then pushed Crome in the back with the flat of her hand.

"Now!" she hissed urgently. "Go and kill her now or it will be too late!"

"What?" said Crome.

As he fumbled at the hilt of the weapon, poison seemed to flow up his arm and into his neck. Whitish motes leaked out of the front of his coat and, stinking of the ashpit, wobbled heavily past his face up into the damp air. The people nearest him moved away sharply, their expressions puzzled and nervous.

"Plotters are abroad," Ansel Verdigris was shouting, "in this very crowd!"

He looked for some confirmation from the inert figure of Mammy Vooley, but she ignored him and only gazed exhaustedly into space while the rain turned the bread crumbs in her lap to paste. He squealed with terror and threw the painting on the floor.

"People stared at this picture," he said. He kicked it. "They knelt in front of it. They have dug up an old weapon and wait now to kill the Mammy!"

He sobbed. He caught sight of Crome.

"Him!" he shouted. "There! There!"

"What has he done?" whispered Crome.

He dragged the sword out from under his coat and threw away its sheath. The crowd fell back immediately, some of them gasping and retching at its smell. Crome ran up the steps holding it out awkwardly in front of him, and hit Ansel Verdigris on the head with it. Buzzing dully, it cut down through the front of Verdigris's skull, then, deflected by the bridge of his nose, skidded off the bony orbit of the eye and hacked into his shoulder. His knees buckled and his arm on that side fell off. He went to pick it up and then changed his mind, glaring angrily at Crome instead and working the glistening white bones of his jaw. "Bugger," he said. "Ur." He marched unsteadily about at the top of the steps, laughing and pointing at his own head.

"I wanted this," he said thickly to the crowd. "It's just what I wanted!" Eventually he stumbled over the painting, fell down the steps with his remaining arm swinging out loosely, and was still.

Crome turned round and tried to hit Mammy Vooley with the weapon, but he found that it had gone out like a wet firework. Only the ceramic hilt was left—blackened, stinking of fish, giving out a few grey motes which moved around feebly and soon died. When he saw this he was so relieved that he sat down. An enormous tiredness seemed to have settled in the back of his neck. Realising that they were safe, Mammy Vooley's attendants rushed out of the observatory and dragged him to his feet again. One of the first to reach him was the woman with the insect's head.

"I suppose I'll be sent to the arena now," he said.

"I'm sorry."

He shrugged.

"The thing seems to be stuck to my hand," he told her. "Do you know anything about it? How to get it off?"

But it was his hand, he found, that was at fault. It had swollen into a thick clubbed mass the colour of overcooked mutton, in which the hilt of the weapon was now embedded. He could just see part of it protruding. If he shook his arm, waves of numbness came up it; it did no good anyway, he couldn't let go.

"I hated my rooms," he said. "But I wish I was back in them now."

"I was betrayed, too, you know," she said.

Later, while two women supported her head, Mammy Vooley peered into Crome's face as if trying to remember where she had seen him before. She was trembling, he noticed, with fear or rage. Her eye was filmed and watery, and a smell of stale food came up out of her lap. He expected her to say something to him but she only looked, and after a short time signed to the women to push her away. "I forgive all my subjects," she announced to the crowd. "Even this one." As an afterthought she added, "Good news! Henceforth this city will be called Vira Co, 'the City in the Waste.'" Then she had the choir brought forward. As he was led away Crome heard it strike up "Ou lou lou," that ancient song:

Ou lou lou lou
Ou lou lou
Ou lou lou lou
Ou lou lou
Ou lou lou lou
Lou Lou lou lou
Ou lou lou lou
Lou
Lou
Lou

Soon the crowd was singing too.

STRANGE
GREAT SINS

STRANGE GREAT SINS

"This mite's sins are nothing to some I've had to swallow," boasted the sin-eater. He was a dark, energetic man of middle height and years, always nodding his head, rubbing his hands, or shifting his weight from one foot to the other, anxious to put the family at their ease. "They'll taste of vanilla and honey compared to some."

No one answered him, and he seemed to accept this readily enough—he had, after all, been privy in his life to a great deal of grief. He looked out of the window. The tide was ebbing, and the air was full of fog which had blown in from the sea. All along Henrietta Street, out of courtesy to the bereaved family, the doors and windows were open, the mirrors covered and the fires extinguished. Frost and fog, and the smell of the distant shore: not much to occupy him. The sin-eater breathed into his cupped hands, coughed suddenly, yawned.

"I like a wind that blows off the land myself," he said.

He went and looked down at the little girl. They had laid her out two hours ago, on a bed with a spotless blue and white cover, and placed on her narrow chest a dish of salt. Gently he tapped with an outstretched finger the rim of this dish, tilting his head to hear the clear small ringing noise which was produced.

"I've been in places where they make linen garlands," he said, "and decorate them with white paper roses. Then they hang white gloves from them, one glove for each year of the kiddy's age, and keep them in the church until they fall to pieces." He nodded his head. "That's how I think of children's sins," he said. "White gloves hanging in a church."

Imagining instead perhaps the narrow cemetery behind the dunes, entered through its curious gateway formed of two huge curved whalebones, imagining perhaps the sea holly, the gulls, and the blowing sand which covers everything, the girl's mother began to cry. The rest of the family stared helplessly at her. There was another, idiot, daughter who banged her hands on the table and threw a knife into the empty grate. The father, an oldish man who delivered mackerel in a cart along the Fish Road to Eame, Child's Ercall, and sometimes as far as Sour Bridge, said dully: "She were running about yesterday as happy as you please. She were always running, happy as you please." He had repeated this every half hour or so since the sin-eater's arrival, shaking his head as if in his simple pleasure at her happiness he had somehow missed a vital clue which would have enabled him to prevent her death (or at least comprehend it). His wife touched his sleeve, rubbing her eyes and trying to smile.

It was a long vigil, as they always are. Towards morning the sin-eater heard a sound of muffled revelry in the street outside: stifled laughter, the rattle of a tambourine quickly stilled, the scrape of clogs on the damp cobbles. When he looked out he could see several dim figures moving backwards and forwards in the sea fog. He blinked. He narrowed his eyes and cleaned the windowpane with the flat of his hand. Behind him he heard the child's father get to his feet with a deep sigh. Turning back into the room he said, "They've brought the horse over from Shifnal, I think. Unless you've got one in the village."

The old man stared at him, at first without seeming to understand, then with growing anger, while outside they began to sing:

> Mari Lwyd
> Horse of frost & fire
> Horse which is not a horse
> Look kindly on our celebration.

The pallid skull of the Mari could now be seen, bobbing up and down on its pole, clacking its lower jaw energetically as the wind opened the fog up into streaming ribbons and tatters, then closed it again, white and seamless like a sheet.

"Let us in and give us some beer," called a muffled but derisive voice. The idiot daughter gave a smile of delight and stared round the room as if she had heard a cupboard or a table speak; she tilted her head and whispered. There was a clatter of hooves or clogs, or perhaps it was simply the clapping of hands. The Mari's followers were dressed in rags. They danced in the fog and frost, their breath itself a fog. The masks they wore were meant to represent the long strange lugubrious head of the wasteland locust, that enormous insect which lives in the blowing sand and clinging mud of the Great Brown Desert.

"I'll give you more than beer!" shouted the old man, his face congested with his powerful frustration and grief. "I'll give you something you won't like!" He pulled the sleeves of his shirt up above his elbows, and before his wife could stop him he had rushed out among the Mari-boys, kicking and punching. They evaded him with deft hops and skips, and ran away laughing into the mist; the idiot daughter murmured and bit her nails; the door banged emptily back and forth in the wind. The old man had to come back into the house, shamefaced and defeated.

"Leave them be," said his wife. "They're not worth it, that lot from up at Shifnal."

Distantly the voices still sang,

> Mari Lwyd
> Falls between the day and the hour
> Horse which is not a horse
> Look kindly on our feast.

The sin-eater made himself comfortable by the window again. He scratched his head. Something in the foggy street had stirred his memory. "The horse which is not a horse," he whispered dreamily.

He smiled.

"Oh, no," he said to the old man and his wife, "your little girl's sins will be like the coloured butterflies—compared to some I've tasted." And then again: "The horse which is not a horse. I never hear those words without a shudder. Have you ever been to Viriconium? Packed your belongings aboard some barge at the ruined wharfs of the Yser Canal? Watched two clouds close a slot of blue in the winter sky, so that you felt as if something had been taken from you forever?"

Seeing that he had puzzled them, he laughed.

"I suppose not. Still . . . The horse which is not a horse . . ."

To recall the momentous events of your life (he went on) is to pull up nettles with the flowers. When I think of my uncle Prinsep I remember my mother first, and only then his watery blue eyes. When I think of him I can see the high brick walls of the lunatic asylum at Wergs, and hear the echoing shouts from the abandoned almshouses round the Aqualate Pond.

I was not born in this trade. When I was a boy we lived in the broad ploughlands around Sour Bridge. We were well enough off at my father's death to have moved to the city, but my mother was content where she was. I suppose she relied on the society she knew, and on her brothers, who were numerous and for the most part lived close. I can see her now, giving tea to these red-faced yeomen in their gaiters and rusty coats who filled our drawing room like their own placid great farm horses, bringing with them whatever the season the whole feel of a November dawn—mist

in the cut-and-laid hedges, rooks cawing from the tall elms, a huge sun rising behind the bare wet lace of hawthorn. She was a woman like a china
ornament, always wary of their feet.

Uncle Prinsep was her step-brother, a very silent man who came to us
for long visits without ever speaking. Many years before, after a quarrel
with his own mother, he had let the family down and gone to live in
Viriconium. I can see now how much my mother must have disapproved
of his dress and manner (he wore a pale blue velvet suit and yellow shoes,
much out of date in the city, I suspect, but always a source of amazement
to us); but despite this, and although she often pretended to despise the
Prinsep clan as a whole, she was unfailingly kind to him. There he sat, at
the tea table, a man with a weak mouth and large skull upholstered with
fat, who gave the impression of being constantly in a dream. He was filled,
his silence informed us, with a melancholy beyond communication, or
even comprehension, which sometimes stood in the corner of his eye like a
tear. You could hear him sighing on the stairs in the morning after his
bath. He patted himself dry with a soft towel.

The other uncles disliked him; my sisters regarded him with contempt,
claiming that when they were younger he had tried to put his hands up the
back of their pinafores; but to me he was a continual delight, because he
was so often used as an example of what I would become if I didn't pay attention, and because he had once given me a book which began:

*I was in Viriconium once. I was a much younger woman then. What a
place that is for lovers! The Locust Winter carpets its streets with broken insects; at the corners they sweep them into strange-smelling drifts which glow
for the space of a morning like heaps of gold before they fade away....*

Imagine the glee with which I discovered that Uncle Prinsep had written this himself! I could not wait to fail my mother and go there.

One afternoon a little after the spring thaw, when I was eighteen or
nineteen, he arrived unexpectedly and stood on the doorstep shaking his
coat under a sky the colour of zinc. He seemed distracted, but at the tea
table his tongue was loosened at last. He talked about his journey, the
weather, his rooms in the city which he said were untenable through burst
pipes and draughts: my mother couldn't stop him talking. If there was a silence he would suddenly say, "I was in mourning for six people last May,"
causing us to look at our plates in embarrassment; or, "Do you think that
souls fly around and choose bodies to be born into?" My sisters covered
their mouths and spluttered, but I was mortified.

He couldn't hear enough, he said, about the family, and he interrogated
my mother, who had by now begun to look down at her own plate in some
confusion, mercilessly about each of the other uncles in turn. Did Dando
Seferis still go fishing when he had the chance? How was—he snapped his
fingers, he had forgotten her name—*Pernel*, his wife? How old would the

daughter be this year? When he could pursue this no further he looked round and sighed happily. "What wonderful cake this is!" he exclaimed; and, on being informed that it was a quite ordinary *kuchen*: "I can't think why I've never eaten it before. Did we always have it? How nice it is to be home!" He nudged me, to my horror, and said, "You don't get cake like this in Viriconium, young man!"

Later he played the piano and sang.

He made my sisters dance with him, but only the old country dances. To see this great fat man, face shining with perspiration, shamble like a bear to the strains of "The Earl of Rone" or "The Hunting of the Jolly Wren" moved them to even greater contempt. He told us ghost stories before we went up to bed. He managed to corner me on the stairs after I had studiously avoided his gaze all evening, to give me a green country waistcoat with some money wrapped in tissue paper in one pocket; I sat in my room looking at it and wept with fury at his lack of understanding. After we were asleep he kept my mother up, talking about their father and his political ambitions, until the small hours.

We had him for two days, during which my mother watched him anxiously. Was he drunk? Was he ill? She could not decide. Whatever it was he went back to Viriconium on the morning of the third day, and died there a week later. In keeping with her evasive yet practical nature she told us nothing about the circumstances. "It happened in someone's house," she said with a movement of her shoulders which we recognised as both protective and censorious; and she would admit nothing more.

He was brought home to be buried. The funeral was as miserable as most winter occasions. Rain fell at intervals from a low, greyish-white sky, to bedraggle the artificial flowers on the cortege and the black plumes of the funeral horses. Some of the other uncles came and stood with their hats off by the grave, while rooks wheeled and cawed overhead in the rain as if they were part of the ceremony. The cemetery was frozen hard in places, already thawing in others; and the flat meadows beyond were under a single shining sheet of water, up out of which stuck a few black hedges and trees. My sisters wept because their dresses were soaked, and after all they had not meant to be horrible to anyone; my mother was quite white, and leaned heavily on my arm. I wore with defiance a pair of yellow shoes.

"Poor Prinsep!" said my mother, hugging us all on the way home. "He deserves your prayers." But it wasn't until much later that I learned the sad facts of his death or the sadder ones of his life.

By then I could be found in the pavement cafés of Sour Bridge, with a set of my own. We favoured the Red Hart Estaminet, not just for its cheap suppers and boldly coloured art posters but because it was the haunt of visiting painters, writers, and music-hall artistes who had come from Viriconium to take the *Wasserkur* in sheds outside the town. When they weren't being hosed down with ice-cold water for their bowel disorders and gonorrhoeas, I suppose, it amused them to make fun of our scrubbed young faces, provincial romances, and ill-fitting suits.

It was at the Red Hart that I first met Madame de Maupassant, the famous contralto, by then a creature bent and diminished by some disease of the throat, with a voice so ravaged it was painful and frightening at the same moment to hear her speak. I could not imagine her on the stage—I didn't know then that to maintain her popularity in the city she still sang with deadly effort every night at the Prospekt Theatre. I thought of her as a menacing but rather vapid old woman obsessed with certain colours, who would lean over the table and say confidentially, "When I was in church as a girl I observed that flies would not pass through the lilac rays from a stained-glass window. Again, it would appear that all internal parasites die if exposed to the various shades of lavender; the doctor is disposed to try a similar remedy in my case." Or: "An honest man will admit that his most thrilling dreams are accompanied by a violet haze . . . Do you know the dreams I mean?"

I did.

One day she said, to my surprise, "So you're Baladine Prinsep's nephew. I knew him quite well, but he never spoke of a family. Don't you follow in his footsteps: all those years at a woman's feet, and never more than a smile! There's a patient man for you."

And she gave her characteristic croak of a laugh.

"I don't understand," I said. "What woman?"

Which made Madame de Maupassant laugh all the more. Eventually, I suppose, I persuaded her to tell me what my mother had kept from us, what Viriconium had always known.

"When your uncle came to the city," she said, "twenty years ago, he found the dancer Vera Ghillera at the height of her success, appearing twice nightly at the Prospekt in a ballet called *The Little Humpbacked Horse* choreographed for her by Chevigne.

"After every performance she held court in a dressing room done out with reds and golds like a stick of sealing wax. There was a tiger-skin rug on the floor. You never saw such dim yellow lamps, brass trays, and three-legged tables decorated with every vulgar little onyx box you could mention! Here they all came to invite her to supper, and she made them sit on the tiger skin and talk about art or politics instead: Paulinus Rack the impresario, ailing and thin now, like a white ghost; Caranthides, whose poems had been printed that year for the first time in a volume called *Yellow Clouds* and whose success was hardly less spectacular than her own; even Ashlyme the portrait painter came, stared at her face with a kind of irritable wonder, and went away again—his marriage to Audsley King put an end to anything like that before it could begin.

"Your uncle knew nothing about the ballet then. He saw the ballerina by chance one day, as he was looking out of his window into the street.

"He was young and lonely. He had taken rooms near the asylum at Wegs, where she went in secret once a month, wrapped in a dove-grey cloak. He soon became her most ardent admirer, waiting on the stairs outside the dressing-room door, fourteen white lilies under his arm in green tissue paper. Eventually she let him in and he had a favoured seat on one of the gilt paws of the tiger. He could be seen any night after that (though what he did in the day remained a mystery), staring up at her with a melancholy expression, taking no part in the conversation of the great men around him. She never gave him any further encouragement; she had her own affairs. In the end he died there, as uselessly as he had lived—much older then of course."

I was profoundly shocked by this, and stung, though I tried not to show it. "Perhaps the arrangement suited him," I said bravely, trying to invest the word *arrangement* with a significance it plainly did not have; and when the famous contralto had received this with the blank stare it deserved: "Anyway, he wrote a book about the city, *The Constant Imago.* He gave me a copy of it." I raised my voice and looked round at my friends. "It is my opinion that he was a great artist, genuinely in love with art."

Madame de Maupassant shrugged.

"I know nothing about books," she said with a sigh. "But it was your uncle's idea of conversation to sidle into a room along the wall like a servant, and when recognised say in a querulous voice, like this, 'I have never found it necessary to have such a high opinion of God . . .' Then he would regard his audience with that watery, fish-like stare he had, having struck them dumb with incomprehension. He was the most futile man I ever knew."

I never saw her again. She soon grew tired of her cure and went back to Viriconium, but I couldn't forget this final judgement of my uncle. If I thought of him at all after that it was with a kind of puzzled sympathy—I saw him walking at night with his head bowed, along the rainy streets near the asylum, two or three sentences of his book his only company, with the shouts of the lunatics coming to his ears like the cries of distant exotic animals; or looking dully out of his window into the orange glare of the lamps, hoping that the ballerina would pass—although he knew it was the wrong time of the month. I remembered the provincial waistcoat he had given me; somehow that completed my disappointment. Then another winter closed the pavement cafés in Sour Bridge and I forgot the author of *The Constant Imago* until the death of my mother some years later.

My mother loved cut flowers, especially those she had grown herself, and often kept them long after they were withered and brown because, she said, they had given her so much pleasure. When I think of her now she is always in a room full of flowers, watering them from a blue and white jug. All through her last illness she fought the nurse over a vase of great white marguerite daisies. The nurse said she would rather be dismissed than allow them to remain by the bed at night; it was unhealthy. My mother promptly dismissed her. When I went into the long, quiet room one afternoon to remonstrate with her over this, I found her prepared.

"We must get rid of that woman," she said darkly. "She's trying to poison me!" And then, coolly anticipating the nurse's own arguments: "You know I can't get my breath without a few flowers near me."

She knew she was wrong. She stared with a kind of musing delight at the daisies, and at me. Then she sighed suddenly.

"Your uncle Prinsep was a silly, weak man." She clutched my arm. "Promise me you'll have your own home, and not live like that on the verge of someone else's life."

I promised.

"It was his mother's fault," she went on in a more practical voice. "She was a woman of personality. And then, you see, they lived in that huge house at the back of nowhere. She attacked the servants physically if they didn't bow to her; she had her porridge fetched every morning from another village, because there it was made more nearly to her taste. This behaviour made her sons leave her one by one. Prinsep was the youngest, and the last to go—he was painstaking in his efforts to placate her, but in the end even he found it easier not to remain."

She sighed again.

"I always had a horror that I would do the same to my own children."

Before I went to take her apologies to the nurse, she said, "You had better have this. It is the key to your uncle Prinsep's rooms. You are old enough to live in Viriconium now; and if you must, you must." She held my wrist and put the key in the palm of my hand, a little brass thing, not very shiny. "One day when you were young," she said, "the wind broke the stems of the hollyhocks. They lay across the wall with all their beautiful flowers intact. While they could be of use like that the insects still flew in and out of them busily: I thought it a shame."

She hung on all that summer in the cool room, making our lives painful but unable to relax and let us go. During that time I often looked at the key she had given me. But I didn't use it until she died in the autumn: I was sure she wouldn't have wanted to know that I had gone to the city and turned it in its lock.

It turned easily enough after so many years, and I stood there confused for a moment on the threshold of Uncle Prinsep's life and my own, not daring to go in. I had lost my way by the Aqualate Pond with its curious echoes and fogs; like most people who come there I had not until then realised the extent of Viriconium, or its emptiness. But the rooms, when at last I went into them, were ordinary enough—bare grey boards with feathers of dust, a few books on the shelves, a few pictures on the whitewashed walls. In the little kitchen there was a cupboard, with some things for making tea. I was tired. There was another room, but I left it unopened and dropped my belongings on the iron bed, my boxes and cases wet with salt from passage of the Yser.

Underneath the bed with the pot for nightsoil I found two or three copies of *The Constant Imago*.

I was in Viriconium once. I was a much younger woman then. What a place that is for lovers! The Locust Winter carpets its streets with broken insects; at the corners they sweep them into strange-smelling drifts which glow for the space of a morning like heaps of gold before they fade away. . . .

After I have looked in the other room, I thought, and found somewhere to put my things, I will go to sleep, and perhaps wake up happier in the morning. After all, I am here now. So I put the book aside and turned the key again in the lock.

When he first fell in love with Vera Ghillera, my uncle had had the walls of this room painted a dull, heavy sealing-wax red; at the window there were thick velvet curtains of the same colour, pulled shut. Pictures of the ballerina were everywhere—on the walls, the tables, the mantelpiece— posing in costumes she had worn for *La Chatte, The Fire Last Wednesday at Lowth,* and *The Little Humpbacked Horse*—painted with her little chin on her hand, looking over a railing at the sea, smiling mysteriously from under a hat. The woman herself, or her effigy made in a kind of yellow wax, lay on a catafalque in the centre of the room, her strange, compact dancer's body naked, the legs parted in sexual invitation, the arms raised imploringly, her head replaced by the stripped and polished brown skull of a horse.

In this room my Uncle Prinsep had hidden himself—from me, from my mother, from Madame de Maupassant and her set, and finally from Vera Ghillera the dancer herself, at whose feet he had sat all those years. I closed the door and went to the window. When I pulled back the curtains and looked out I could see the brick walls of the asylum, tall, and finished with spikes, washed in the orange glow of the lamplight, and hear the distant, ferocious cries of the madmen behind them.

It was dawn. The Mari-dancers were long gone, off to Shifnal with their horse; and light was creeping down Henrietta Street like spilled milk between the cobbles. The sin-eater coughed and cleared his throat, yawned.

His energy had left him in the night, draining his eyes to a chalky blue colour, the colour of a butterfly on the cliffs above the sea. He let his hands fall slackly in his lap and looked at the old man, who was asleep by the hearth with his mouth open. He looked at the surviving daughter, staring intently at the table then scratching patterns on it with a spoon, tongue in the corner of her mouth. He noticed the old man's wife—laying the new fire in the grate, filling the kettle with water, making ready for the great meal of fish and potatoes which would be eaten later in the day—listening serenely to him as she went about the work, as if this were a story, not the bitter facts of his existence.

"I left Viriconium after that," he told her, "for the deserts in the North; and I never went back there." He moved his shoulders suddenly, irritated perhaps because he could no longer make these events clear enough to impress her, and he was impatient with himself for continuing to speak. "Do I miss it? No: nor Sour Bridge, with its dull farmers treading mud in the shuttered drawing rooms."

Frost, fog, the smell of the distant shore; dawn creeping down Henrietta Street like milk. He could hear the people raking up their fires, uncovering the mirrors and birdcages. They rubbed their hands briskly as they looked out at the morning. "If the wind changes later we shall have a fine day." At last they could shut the doors and get a bit of warmth! The little dead girl lay safely on the blue and white cover; it remained only for someone to eat the salt.

"One thing is odd, though," he said. "When I sat in my uncle's rooms and looked back over the decisions which had led me there, I saw clearly that at every turn they had been made by the dying and the dead; and I swore I would leave all that behind me."

He stared for a moment almost pleadingly at the woman.

"As you see, I have not."

She smiled: her child was safe; its soul was secure; she was content.

"That was where I first ate the salt," he said bleakly. "It lay on her breast as surely as it lies now on your dead daughter's. I don't know why my uncle put it there for me to find."

Later in the morning a wind from the land got up and blew light dashes of rain across the windows, but they were soon gone, and it was a fine day. Full of potatoes and fish, tired perhaps but comfortably settled in the stomach, the sin-eater picked up his bag and swung it over his shoulder. He had taken his money and put it in his pocket. Behind him at the trestle tables in the street he could hear laughter, the clatter of plates, the beginnings of music. He breathed deeply, shrugged, made a gesture with his hands, all at once, as if to convey to himself his own sense of freedom.

He was not after all that boy from Sour Bridge, or his Uncle Prinsep. A stocky, energetic man of middle height, he whistled off down Henrietta Street, ready to walk as far as he could. He looked inland, at the hills looming through squalls of rain. Soon he would climb up among them and let the wind blow those clean, childish little sins out of him and away.

LORDS OF MISRULE

Lords of Misrule

"Aid from the city is our only hope now," the Yule Greave said, looking away over the empty moorland and rough grazing seamed with tree-filled cloughs.

He was a tall man, fortyish, with weak blue eyes and a straggle of thin blond hair, who breathed laboriously through his mouth. Under the old queen, who had given him the house and the pasture that went with it, he had been known as a fighter. Every so often he would look around him as if surprised to find himself where he was, and his lower lip trembled if he talked about the city.

To give him time to catch his breath I stopped and looked back down at his house. It was built on a curious pattern like an ideogram from one of the old languages, ramified, peculiar. Much of it now lay abandoned and overgrown in a tangle of elder and hawthorn and ivy. Flung out from it were four great stone avenues, each a mile long. I wondered who had built them, and when. It seemed a pointless act out here.

"I've been forced to grub up pavements," he said. "Knock down a wall here and there. But you can see what it was like."

There were deep muddy furrows in the gateways where the stone carts went in and out. The wind came in gusts from the south and west, bringing a rainy smell and the distant bleat of sheep. The dwarf oaks on the slopes above us shifted their branches uneasily and sent down a few more of last winter's brownish withered leaves. One of the little grey kestrels of the moorland launched itself from some rocks above us, planing downwind with its wingtips ragged against the racing white clouds; it hovered for a moment, then veered off and dropped like a stone onto something in the bracken below.

"Look!" I said.

The Yule Greave stood wiping his face and nodding vaguely.

"To tell you the truth," he said, "we never thought they would come this far. We expected you to stop them before this."

I breathed in the smell of the bracken. "This is such a beautiful valley," I said.

"You'll be able to see the whole of it soon," the Yule Greave said. He started up the slope where it steepened for its final climb to the rim of the escarpment, following a soft, peaty sheep-trod through the bracken. He placed one foot carefully and heavily in front of the other, grunting at the steeper places. "I'm sorry to bring you all this way," he said. "I don't expect you're used to this sort of thing."

"I'm not tired," I said.

If I had been cold, he hardly noticed. He laughed unoffendedly.

"They'll want a report from you," he said. "Up here it's easier to appreciate the scale of the problem. As a military man you'll want to be able to judge for yourself, and not rely on the ideas of an old cutthroat."

We climbed the last few yards to the little outcrop, and at the top, when I turned, the spring sun had come out briefly; I could feel it like a poultice down the side of my jaw. Sweat poured down the Yule Greave's forehead and into his eyes. He put one hand against the rock to steady himself.

"They quarried this to build the house," he said. "A long time ago."

The rock was pale, coarse-textured, full of little quartz pebbles. Higher up in the quarried bays hung mats of ivy.

"Now you can see what I mean," he said.

I was more interested in his house, which lay like a metaphor in the wide flat valley. It was a light fawn colour. Its four vast avenues of stone thrust out from it across the old alluvial bench, black, black. What it meant I had no idea. It was one of those places where the past speaks to us in a language so completely of its own we have no hope of understanding. Puddles of water in the worn paving reflected the sky; I could see the gaps in the walls, like bites, where the Yule Greave had taken stone for the fortifications, a line of hasty revetments and trenches stretching across the valley lower down, where it sloped away to the south.

"Incredible," I said.

He pointed south, past the fortifications.

"There were dozens of places like this once," he said, "all the way down to the sea. They're overrun now."

He made an angry, miserable gesture.

"If the city won't help, why are we bothering? We don't build out here anymore: we only pull it down."

"I'm not sure I agree," I said.

I was tempted to ask him why, if he didn't want to destroy the old walls, he didn't reopen the quarry and use fresh stone, but his face was now full of a kind of savage self-hatred and self-pity, and he said,

"What's the point of discussing it?"

A retired bravo knows nothing about building. The city had made him what he was. Perhaps he knew it.

"You've heard it all before, I expect. Anyway you can see how close they've come. They'll be across the river and over the fortifications in a month, less if we don't get help. See: there, and there? You can see the sun glinting on their camps."

"Will you show me the house before I go?" I asked.

He looked at me in surprise. He was pleased to be asked, I thought, but he said, "Oh, the inside's a ruin now. We do our best, but it's all dust and mice."

He seemed reluctant to go down the hill now he had got up it. He watched the little grey hawk hovering and stooping, hovering and stooping, as it worked its way up and down the slopes of sun-warmed bracken. He took a last look at the great stone symbol which filled the valley and which he had lived in for twenty years without understanding, then began to descend slowly. New shoots, he observed, were beginning to appear green and delicately curled between the ruined bracken stems. The turf, flattened and bleached by the previous month's snow, was springing up again.

"That air!" he exclaimed, breathing ecstatically a gust of wind which brought the scent of may blossom up from the valley. Then he stopped suddenly and said:

"What's it like in the city these days?"

I shrugged.

"We have similar problems to yours," I heard myself tell him, "but not so extreme. Otherwise it is very beautiful. New buildings are springing up everywhere. The horse chestnuts are in blossom along the Margarethestrasse and in the Plaza of Unrealised Time."

I did not mention the torn political cartoons flapping from the rusty iron railings, or the Animal Mask Societies with their public rituals and increasingly unreasonable demands. But he was remembering a different city anyway—

"I suppose the place is still full of clerks and shopkeepers?" he said. "And those wonderful tarts who overcharge you in the Rue Ouled Nail?"

He laughed.

"We'll always look to Uroconium," he said sentimentally, and quoted, " 'Queen of the Empire, jewel on the beach of the Western Sea.' "

The walls that surrounded the house had already warmed to the weak sunshine, trapping a fraction of its heat to give up to the elder and ivy in the overgrown gardens. Two or three hawthorns filled the air with the scent of the may, which in that confined space seemed drugged and dangerous. Insects murmured in the little orchard and among the fruit bushes which had long ago run to bramble in the shelter of the walls. Above the garden rose the honey-coloured stone of the main building, covered in creeper and bright yellow lichens. The wind blustered round its complicated roofs.

Inside the house he had someone bring out a bottle of lemon genever, and invited me to have some.

"Foul stuff, but the best we can get out here."

We drank silently for a while. The Yule Greave seemed to sink into himself, into his own sense of abandonment and futility. "Dust and mice," he said, staring round in disgust at the high gloomy walls and the silent, massive, oppressive old furniture, "dust and rats. This is the only room we ever light a fire in." Later he began to talk about the old queen's reign. It was the common story of infighting at court and violence in the city. He had known, or said he had, Sibylle, Axonby, and even Sten Reventlow. Many of the actions in which he had taken part struck me as being little more than outrages, committed by people hardly able to help themselves, whose philosophy was that their blood was a book. He kept his souvenirs of these "little wars" in one of the upper rooms, he said. There was some peculiar stuff among it all, stuff that made you think. We could go and look at it later if I was interested.

"I'd like that if there's time," I said.

"Oh, there'll be time," he said. "It's mostly clothes, weapons, stuff we picked up in their houses. You wouldn't credit the hanks of hair, the filthy pictures they were always looking at."

He asked if I had done any fighting in the city, and I said that I hadn't. There was a silence, then he went on musingly: "The women were the worst. They would hide in doorways, and reach out for your face or your neck as you walked past. Hide themselves in doorways. They'd have bits of glass embedded in a cake of soap, do you see, and slash out at your neck or your eyes." He looked at me as if he were wondering how much more he could tell me. "Can you believe that? Women who would slash your eyes?" He shook his head. "I hated going up the stairs in those places. The lamps would all be out. You never knew what would be in a cupboard. A woman or a child, screaming at you. Or else they'd show you something foul, obscene, and laugh. The old queen would never bear them near her, not at any price."

"So I have heard," I said. "It is less of a problem now."

He chuckled.

"Old men like me cleared it up for you," he said. "We can be proud of that. I was with the Feverfew Anschluss until Antic Horn's entryists broke it up."

A little later his wife came in. By this time he had drunk most of the bottle. He stared at her with a kind of muddled resentment.

She was a tall woman, though not perhaps as tall as him, very thin and ethereal, dressed in a fashion long out of date in the city. She seemed not quite real to me, like a picture of my mother in a darkened room. I guessed she had been one of the old queen's women-in-waiting, given to him like the house and the valley in return for his loyalty in the backstreets and tavern brawls. Her hair, an astonishing orange colour, was worn long and crimped, to emphasise the height of her cheekbones, the whiteness of her skin, and the odd, concave curve of her features.

Over one arm she was carrying a piece of heavily embroidered cloth which I recognised as being part of the "mast horse" ceremony: it would be used to hide the operator of the animal's snapping jaw. I had never seen such an elaborate cloth in use. When I mentioned this she smiled and said:

"You'll have to ask Ringmer if you want to know more about this one. He was born near here, and his father worked the horse at All Hallows."

"Ringmer's father was a half-wit," said the Yule Greave, yawning and pouring himself more lemon gin.

She ignored him. "Lord Cromis, are you young men at all interested in such things in the city now?" she asked me. Her eyes were green. She had unfolded the cloth to show me a complex pattern of leaf-like shapes.

"Some are," I said.

"Because I've filled a whole gallery with them. Ringmer—"

"Have they shifted the rubble in the south avenue?" the Yule Greave broke in suddenly.

"I don't know."

"It was important to get that rubble moved today," the Yule Greave said. "I want it as infill further down the valley. We've got mud up to our ears down there: I told Ringmer this morning."

"Nobody told me that's what they were supposed to be doing," she said.

The Yule Greave muttered something I couldn't quite catch and emptied his glass quickly. He got up and stared out at the ruined raspberry canes and lichen-covered apple boughs in the garden. This left his wife and me marooned at the other end of the room with only the embroidered cloth in common. A few transparent blue and orange flames stirred round the unseasoned logs in the hearth.

"Ringmer *will* show you the rest of the horse," she said. "I'm so glad you're interested."

She folded the fabric up again, her long thin hands white in the shadows. "Sometimes I feel like wearing it myself," she laughed, holding it up against her shoulders. "It's so glorious!" I had a brief vision of her as she must have been in the days of the old queen's court—waxy and still in a stiff, grey, heavily embossed garment down to her feet, like a flower in a steel vase. Then the Yule Greave came and stood between us to tip into his glass whatever dregs remained in the brown stone bottle. He was walking heavily up some private hill again.

"Don't you want to look at the stuff I was telling you about?" he said.

"I shouldn't stay more than a few minutes," I answered. "My men will be waiting for me—"

"But you've only just arrived!"

"We have to be back in Uroconium by tomorrow morning."

"He wants to see the horse, whatever else," the Yule Greave's wife insisted.

"Oh, does he? You'd better go and show him, then," he said, looking at me as if I had let him down and then turning abruptly away. He poked so hard at the fire that one of the logs fell out of it. Smoke came into the room in a thick cloud. "This stinking chimney!" he shouted.

We left the room, the Yule Greave looking after us red-faced and watery-eyed. Her gallery, I found out, was a mezzanine floor somewhere in the west wing. The sun was just coming round to it, pouring obliquely in through the tall lanceolate windows. The Yule Greave's wife stood in an intermittent pool of warm yellow light with her hands clasped anxiously.

"Ringmer?" she called. "Ringmer?"

We stood and listened to the wind blustering about outside.

After a moment a boy of twenty or so came out of the shadows of the mezzanine. He looked surprised to see her. He had the thick legs and shoulders of the moorland people, and the characteristic soft brown hair chopped off to a line above his raw-looking ears. He was carrying a horse's head on a pole.

"I see you have the rest of the Mari," she said with a smile. "Do you think you could show Lord Cromis? I've brought the coat back with me."

It was an astonishing specimen. Usually you find the skull boiled and crudely varnished, or buried for a year to get rid of the flesh, a makeshift wire hinge for the jaw, and the bottoms of cheap green bottles for eyes. This one had been made long ago, and with more care: it was lacquered black, its jaw hinged with massive silver rivets, and somehow the inside of a pomegranate had been preserved and inserted, half in each orbit, so that the seeds made bulging, faceted eyes. It must have been appallingly heavy for the operator. The pole on which it rested was brown bone, three and a half feet long and polished with use.

"It is very striking," I said.

The boy now took the embroidered cloth and shook it out. Hooks fitted along its top edge allowed it to be gathered beneath the horse's head so that it fell in stiff folds and obscured the pole. With a quick, agile movement he slipped under it and crouched down. The Mari came to life, humpbacked, curvetting, and snapping its jaw. It predated not only the Yule Greave but his house. Time opened like a hole underneath us, and the Yule Greave's wife stepped back suddenly.

" 'Open the door for us,' " chanted the boy:

> " 'It is cold outside for the Grey Mare
>   Its heels are almost frozen.' "

"I would admit you at my peril," I said. The Yule Greave's wife laughed.

Later I went to examine some manuscripts which belonged to the house. They were kept at the other end of the mezzanine. When I looked back the Yule Greave's wife was standing next to the mast horse. Its eyes glittered, its lower jaw hung down. Her hand was resting on its back, just as it might rest on the neck of a real animal, and she was saying something to it in a low voice. I never found out what, because at that moment the Yule Greave came puffing and panting into the gallery, limping as if he had banged his leg and shouting,

"All right, come on, you've seen enough of this."

The Mari reared up for a second, bared its white teeth, then retreated into the shadows, and the boy Ringmer, presumably, with it.

At the door of the staircase which led to the Yule Greave's private room I took leave of his wife, in case, as she said, we did not meet again.

"We see so few people," she said.

"Hurry up," urged the Yule Greave. "It's quite a climb."

The staircase was so narrow that he rubbed his shoulders on the walls as he led the way up, brushing off great flakes of damp yellow plaster. His fat pear-shaped buttocks shut out the light. The little square room was right at the top of the house. From its narrow windows you could see one of the stone avenues stretching away, a sliver of brownish hillside, and a bend in the shallow stony river. The wind boomed around us, bringing quite clearly the bleat of moorland sheep.

The Yule Greave tried to open a trap door in the ceiling so that we could go out onto the roof, which was flat there. The bolts were rusted shut, but he would give up only after a lot of heaving and grunting.

"I can't understand it," he said. "I'm sorry."

He hammered at one of the bolts until he cut the heel of his hand, then his eyes watered and he began to cry. He turned away from me and pretended to look out across the hillside, where the sheep were scattered like grey rocks. "If we fail," he said, "the future will judge us very harshly." He sniffed and blinked. He looked at his cut hand, then wiped his eyes with it, leaving a smear of blood. "Now look what I've done. I'm sorry."

I couldn't think of anything to say.

The tower smelled of the old books he had abandoned to the mould in haphazard piles. I picked up *Oei'l Voirrey* and *The Death and Revival of the Earl of Rone*. I asked him if he would show me his souvenirs, but he seemed to have lost interest. He kept them in a wooden chest: a few dolls made out of women's hair and bits of mirror; some cooking implements; a knife of curious design. The damp had got at everything and made it worthless. "It's just the sort of thing we all picked up," he said. "I think there's a mask in there somewhere."

"The men of the community set out in the afternoon," I quoted, *"and, after much parading and searching, discover the Earl of Rone hidden ineffectually in the low scrub . . ."*

"You can keep the *Oei'l Voirrey* if you like," he said.

We stared down at the ancient avenue stretching away from the house, its puddled surface reflecting the white sky. His wife appeared walking slowly along it with the boy Ringmer. They were smiling and talking like ghosts. The Yule Greave watched them sadly, until I said that I would have to go.

"You must at least have something to eat with us," he said.

"I have to be in the city before morning," I said. "I'm sorry."

We went out, and I got on my horse in one of the muddy gateways. As I set off down the long avenue I thought I heard him say, "Tell them in the city that we still keep faith."

The avenue seemed barren and endless. The sun had gone in and it was raining again by the time I led my men through a break in one of the walls; and with the cold wind of spring blowing into our backs we turned north and picked our way up to the rim of the escarpment.

Up by the Yule Greave's abandoned quarries I stopped to have one more look at the house. It seemed silent and untenanted. Then I saw a stone cart move slowly down the valley towards the fortifications. Smoke came out of one of the chimneys. Above me the little grey hawk dipped and swerved on the wind. My men, sensing my preoccupation, huddled in a bay of the quarry, wrapped in their sodden cloaks and talking quietly. I could smell moorland, wet wool, the breath of the horses. Soon most of the valley was obscured by mist and driving rain, but I could see the fortifications lying across it in straight lines, and beyond them, towards the sea where a fugitive and watery sun was still shining, the light was reflected off the waiting encampments.

If I had the eyes of that hawk, I thought, I know what I would see down there, moving towards us.

One of my men pointed to the fortifications and said,

"Those walls won't last long, however well they're defended."

I found myself staring at him for a long time before answering. Then I said:

"They've already been breached. That place down there is raddled."

Even as we watched, the Yule Greave and his wife and their three children came out of the house with the boy Ringmer, and began to dance in a circle in the overgrown garden. I could hear the thin voices of the children carrying the tune, blown up the hill with the mist and the rain:

> "What time will the King come home?
> One o'clock in the afternoon.
> What will he have in his hand?
> A bunch of ivy."

Behind me someone said, "You've dropped your book, sir."
"Let it lie."

The dancer
from the dance

The Dancer
from the Dance

The city has always been full of little strips and triangles of unused land. A row of buildings falls down in Chenaniaguine—the ground is cleared for further use—elder and nettle spring up—nothing is ever built. Or else the New Men set aside some park for a municipal estate, then quarrel among themselves: a few shallow trenches and low brick courses are covered in a season by couch grass and "fat hen." Allman's Heath, bounded on two sides by empty warehouses, an abattoir, and a quarantine hospital, and on its third by a derelict reach of the canal, looks like any of them.

A few houses stare morosely at it from the city side of the canal. The people who live in them believe that insects the size of horses infest the heath. Nobody has ever seen one; nevertheless, once a year the large wax effigy of a locust, freshly varnished and with a knot of reed grasses in its mouth, is brought out from the houses and paraded up and down the tow-path. In the background of this ceremony the heath seems to stretch away forever. It is the same if you go and look from the deserted pens of the cattle market, or one of the windows of the old hospital. To walk round it takes about an hour.

Every winter years ago, little girls would chalk the ground for "blind Michael" in a courtyard off the Plaza of Realised Time. (It was on the left as you came to the Plain Moon Café, where even in February the tables were arranged on the pavement, their planished copper tops gleaming in the weak sun. You turned down by an ornamental apple tree.) Generally they were the illegitimate children of midinettes, laundry women who worked in Minnet-Saba, or the tradesmen from the Rivelin market. They preserved a fierce independence and wore short stiff blouses which bared the hollow of their backs to the grimmest weather. If you approached them properly, one of them would always tuck her chalk down her white drawers, lick the snot off her upper lip, and lead you to Orves; it was hard work to keep up with her in the steep winding streets.

Most sightseers changed their minds as soon as they saw the shadow of the observatory falling across the houses, and went back to drink hot genever in the Plain Moon. Those who kept on under the black velvet banners of the New Men, which in those days hung heavily from every second-floor window, would find themselves on the bank of the canal at Allman's Reach.

There was not much to see. The cottages were often boarded up at that time of year. A few withered dock plants lined the water's edge where the towpath had collapsed. No one was in sight. The wind from the heath made your eyes water until you turned away and found the girl standing quite still next to you, her hands hanging at her sides. She would hardly look at you, or the heath; she might glance at her feet. If you offered her money she would scratch her behind, screech with laughter, and run off down the hill. Later you might see her kneeling on the pavement in some other part of the Quarter, the wet chalk in her mouth, staring with a devout expression at something she had drawn.

Vera Ghillera, Vriko's immortal ballerina, had herself taken to Allman's Reach the day she arrived in the city from Sour Bridge. She was still a provincial and not more than a child herself, as thin and fierce and naive as any of them in the courtyard off the plaza, but determined to succeed; long in the muscle for classical dance, perhaps, but with a control already formidable and a sharp technical sense. It was the end of a winter afternoon when she got there. She stood away from her guide and looked over the canal. After a minute her eyes narrowed as if she could see something moving a great distance away. "Wait," she said. "Can you? No. It's gone." The sun was red across the ice. Long before the city knew her lyrical port de bras, she knew the city. Long, long before she crossed the canal she had seen Allman's Heath and acknowledged it.

Everyone has read how Vera Ghillera, choreographed by Madame Chevigne, costumed by Audsley King, and dancing against sets designed by Paulinus Rack from sketches attributed to Ens Laurin Ashlyme, achieved overnight fame at the Prospekt Theatre as "Lucky Parminta" in *The Little Humpbacked Horse;* how she was courted by Rack and Ingo Lympany amongst others, but did not marry; and how she kept her place as principal dancer for forty years despite the incurable fugues which compelled her to attend regularly and in secret the asylum at Wergs.

Less of her early life is public. In her autobiography *The Constant Imago,* she is not frank about her illness or how it came about. And few of her contemporaries were ever aware of the helplessness of her infatuation with Egon Rhys, leader of the Blue Anemone Ontological Association.

Rhys was the son of a trader in fruit and vegetables at Rivelin—one of those big, equivocally natured women whose voice or temper dominate the Market Quarter for years on end, and whose absence leaves it muted and empty. He had been in and out of the market since her death, a man enclosed, not much used to the ordinary emotions, not interested in anything but his own life. He tended to act in good faith.

He was shorter than Vera Ghillera. As a boy, first selling crystallised flowers round the combat rings, then as the apprentice of Osgerby Practal, he had learned to walk with a shambling gait which diverted attention from his natural balance and energy. This he retained. (Later in life, though his limbs thickened, his energy seemed to increase rather than abate—at seventy, they said, he could hardly stand still to talk to you.) He had large hands and a habit of looking at them intently, with a kind of amused indulgence, as if he wanted to see what they would do next.

His heavy, pleasant face was already well-known about the rings when Vera came to the city. Under the aegis of the Blue Anemone he had killed forty men. As a result the other "mutual" associations often arranged a truce among themselves in order to bring about his death. The Feverfew Anschluss had a special interest in this, as did the Fourth of October and the Fish-Head Men from Austonley. At times even his relations with the Anemone were difficult. He took it calmly, affecting an air of amusement which—as in other notorious bravos—seems to have masked not anxiety but an indifference of which he was rather ashamed, and which in itself sometimes frightened him. He let himself be seen about the Quarter unaccompanied, and walked openly about in the High City, where Vera first observed him from an upper room.

The Little Humpbacked Horse was history by then: she had carried a lamp in *Mariana Natesby*, overcome with furious concentration the debilitating danse d'ecole work and formalism of Lympany's *The Ginger Boy*. She had danced with de Cuevas, then past the height of his powers, and been his lover; she had had her portrait painted once a year for the oleograph trade, as "Delphine," "Manalas," and—looking over a parapet or smiling mysteriously under a hat—as the unnamed girl in *The Fire Last Wednesday at Lowth*. She had got her full growth. At work, though she was so tall, her body seemed compacted, pulled in on itself like the spring of a humane killer: but she looked exhausted when the makeup came off, and somehow underfed as she slumped awkwardly, legs apart, on a low chair in her sweat-stained practice clothes. She had forgotten how to sit. She was "all professional deformity in body and soul." Her huge eyes gave you their attention until she thought you were looking at someone else, then became blank and tired.

She never lost her determination, but an unease had come over her.

In the morning before practice she could be seen in the workmen's cafés down by the market, huddled and fragile-looking in an expensive woollen coat. She listened to the sad-sounding traders' calls in the early fog, hearing them as remote, and as urgent as the cries of lookouts in the bows of a ship. "Two fathoms and shelving!" She watched the girls playing blind Michael in the courtyard off the Plaza of Realised Time, but as soon as they recognised her walked quickly away. "One fathom!"

The first time she saw Egon Rhys she ran down into the street without thinking and found him face to face with two or three members of the Yellow Paper College. It was a fraught moment; razors were already out in the weird Minnet-Saba light, which lay across the paving stones the colour of mercury. Rhys had his back to some iron railings, and a line of blood ran vertically down his jaw from a nick under one eye.

"Leave that man alone!" she said. At ten years old in the depressed towns of the Midland Levels she had seen unemployed boys fighting quietly under the bridges, building fires on waste ground. "Can't you find anything better to do?"

Rhys stared at her in astonishment and jumped over the railings.

"Don't ask me who she was," he said later in the Dryad's Saddle. "I legged it out of there faster than you could say, right through someone's front garden. They're hard fuckers, those Yellow Paper Men." He touched the cut they had given him. "I think they've chipped my cheekbone."

He laughed.

"Don't ask me anything!"

But after that, Vera seemed to be everywhere. He had quick glimpses of a white face with heavily made-up eyes among the crowds that filled the Market Quarter at the close of every short winter afternoon. He thought he saw her in the audience at the ring behind the Dryad's Saddle. (She was blinking in the fumes from the naphtha lamps.) Later she followed him from venue to venue in the city and brought him great bunches of sol d'or whenever he won.

With the flowerboys she sent her name, and tickets to the Prospekt Theatre. There he was irritated by the orchestra, confused by the constant changes of scene, and embarrassed by the revealing costumes of the dancers. The smell of dust and sweat and the thud of their feet on the stage spoiled the illusion for him: he had always understood dancing to be graceful. When Vera had him brought up to her dressing room afterwards, he found her wearing an old silk practice top rotting away under the arms, and a pair of loose, threadbare woollen stockings out of which someone had cut the feet. "I have to keep my calves warm," she explained when she caught him staring at them. He was horrified by the negligent way she sprawled, watching him intently in the mirrors, and he thought her face seemed as hard and tired as a man's; he left as soon as he could.

Vera went home and stood irresolutely near her bed. The geranium on the windowsill was like an artificial flower on a curved stem, its white petals more or less transparent as the clouds covered and uncovered the moon. She imagined saying to him,

"You smell of geraniums."

She began to buy him the latest novels. Just then, too, a new kind of music was being played everywhere, so she took him to concerts. She commissioned Ens Laurin Ashlyme to paint his portrait. He couldn't be bothered to read, he said; he listened distractedly to the whine of the cor anglais, then stared over his shoulder all evening as if he had seen someone he knew; he frightened the artist by showing him how good an edge his palette knife would take. "Don't send so many flowers," he told her. Nothing she could offer seemed to interest him, not even his own notoriety.

Then he watched a cynical turn called *Insects* at the Allotrope Cabaret in Cheminor. One of the props used in this was a large yellow locust. When they first dragged it onto the cramped Allotrope stage it appeared to be a clever waxwork. But soon it moved, and even waved one of its hands, and the audience discovered among the trembling antennae and gauze wings a naked woman, painted with wax, lying on her back with her knees raised to stimulate the bent rear legs of the insect. She wore to represent its head a stylised, highly varnished mask. Fascinated, Rhys leaned forward to get a better view. Vera heard his breath go in with a hiss. He said loudly, "What's that? What is that animal?" People began to laugh at his enthusiasm; they couldn't see that the double entendre of the act meant nothing to him. "Does anyone know?" he asked them.

"Hush!" said Vera. "You're spoiling it for everyone else."

Poor lighting and a smell of stale food made the Allotrope a cheerless place to perform; it was cold. The woman in the insect mask, having first adjusted it on her shoulders so that it would face the audience when she did, stood up and made the best she could of an "expressive" dance, crossing and uncrossing her thick forearms in front of her while her breath steamed into the chilly air and her feet slapped one two three, one two three on the unchalked boards. But Rhys would not leave until the bitter end, when the mask came off and under it was revealed the triumphant smile, disarranged chestnut hair, and tired puffy face of some local artiste hardly sixteen years old, to whistles of delight.

Outside, their shadows fell huge and black on the wall that runs, covered with peeling political cartoons, the length of Endingall Street. "It doesn't seem much to stand in front of an audience for," said Vera, imitating the barren, oppressive little steps. "I would be frightened to go on." She shuddered sympathetically. "Did you see her poor ankles?"

Rhys made an impatient gesture.

"I thought it was very artistic," he said. Then: "That animal! *Do* things like that exist anymore?"

Vera laughed.

"Go on Allman's Heath and see for yourself. Isn't that where you're supposed to go to see them? What would you do if you were face to face with it now? A thing as big as that?"

He caught her hands to stop her from dancing. "I'd kill it," he said seriously. "I'd—" What he might do he had to think for a moment, staring into Vera's face. She stood dead still. "Perhaps it would kill me," he said wonderingly. "I never thought. I never thought things like that might really exist." He was shivering with excitement: she could feel it through his hands. She looked down at him. He was as thick-necked and excitable as a little pony. All of a sudden she was sharply aware of his life, which had somehow assembled for itself like a lot of eccentric furniture the long perspective of Endingall Street, the open doors of the Allotrope Cabaret, that helpless danseuse with her overblocked shoes and ruined ankles, to what end he couldn't see.

"Nothing could kill you," she said shyly.

Rhys shrugged and turned away.

For a week or two after that she seemed to be able to forget him. The weather turned wet and mild; the ordinary vigour of their lives kept them apart.

His relations with the Blue Anemone had never been more equivocal: factions were out for him in High City and Low. If Vera had known he was so hard put to it in the alleys and waste ground around Chenaniaguine and Lowth, who can say what she might have done. Luckily, while he ran for it with an open razor in one hand and a bunch of dirty bandages coming unravelled from the other, she was at the barre ten hours a day for her technique. Lympany had a new production, *Whole Air:* it would be a new *kind* of ballet, he believed. Everyone was excited by the idea, but it would mean technique, technique, technique. "The surface is dead!" he urged his dancers: "Surface is only the visible part of *technique!*"

Ever since she came up from the midlands, Vera had hated rest days. At the end of them she was left sleepless and irritated in her skin, and as she lay in bed the city sent granular smoky fingers in through her skylight, unsettling her and luring her out so that late at night she had to go to the arena and, hollow-eyed, watch the clowns. There while thinking about something else she remembered Rhys again, so completely and suddenly that he went across her—snap—like a crack in glass. Above the arena the air was purple with roman candles bursting, and by their urgent intermittent light she saw him quite clearly standing in Endingall Street, shivering in the grip of his own enthusiasm, driven yet balked by it like all nervous animals. She also remembered the locust of the Allotrope Cabaret. She thought,

"Artistic!"

Though on a good night you could still hear the breathy whisper of twenty-five thousand voices wash across the pantile roofs of Montrouge like a kind of invisible firework, the arena by then was really little more than a great big outdoor circus, and all the old burnings and quarterings had given place to acrobatics, horse racing, trapeze acts, etc. The New Men liked exotic animals. They did not seem to execute their political opponents—or each other—in public, though some of the aerial acts looked like murder. Every night there was a big, stupid lizard or a megatherium brought in to blink harmlessly and even a bit sadly up at the crowd until they had convinced themselves of its rapacity. And there were more fireworks than ever: to a blast of maroons full of magnesium and a broad falling curtain of cerium rain, the clowns would erupt bounding and cartwheeling into the circular sandy space—jumping up, falling down, building unsteady pyramids, standing nine or ten high on one another's shoulders, active and erratic as grasshoppers in the sun. They fought, with rubber knives and whitewash. They wore huge shoes. Vera loved them.

The greatest clown of his day, called by the crowd "Kiss-O-Suck," was a dwarf of whose real name no one was sure. Some people knew him as "Morgante," others as "Rotgob" or "The Grand Pan." His legs were frail looking and twisted, but he was a fierce gymnast, often able to perform four separate somersaults in the air before landing bent-kneed, feet planted wide apart, rock steady in the black sand. He would alternate cartwheels with handsprings at such a speed he seemed to be two dwarfs, while the crowd egged him on with whistles and cheers. He always ended his act by reciting verses he had made up himself:

> Codpoorlie—tah
> Codpoorrrlie—*tah!*
> Codpoorlie—tah! tah! tah!
> Dog pit.
> > Dog pit pooley
> > Dog pit pooley
> > Dog pit have-a-rat
> > > tah tah tah
> (ta ta.)

For a time his vogue was so great he became a celebrity on the Unter-Main-Kai, where he drank with the intellectuals and minor princes in the

Bistro Californium, strutted up and down in a padded doublet of red velvet with long scalloped sleeves, and had himself painted as "The Lord of Misrule." He bought a large house in Montrouge.

He had come originally from the hot bone-white hinterlands of the Mingulay Littoral, where the caravans seem to float like yellow birdcages at midday across the violet lakes of the mirage "while inside them women consult feverishly their grubby packs of cards." If you are born in that desert, its inhabitants often boast, you know all deserts. Kiss-O-Suck was not born a dwarf but chose it as his career, having himself confined for many years in the black oak box, the gloottokoma, so as to stunt his growth. Now he was at the peak of his powers. When he motioned peremptorily, the other clowns sprang up into the air around him. His voice echoed to Vera over the arena. "Dog pit pooley!" he chanted, and the crowd gave it him back: but Vera, still somehow on Endingall Street with Egon Rhys trembling beside her, heard, "Born in a desert, knows all deserts!" The next day she sent him her name with a great bunch of anemones. *I admire your act.* They met in secret in Montrouge.

At the Bistro Californium, Ansel Verdigris, poet of the city, lay with his head sideways on the table; a smell of lemon gin rose from the tablecloth bunched up under his cheek. Some way away from him sat the Marquis de M——, pretending to write a letter. They had quarrelled earlier, ostensibly about the signifier and the signified, and then Verdigris had tried to eat his glass. At that time of night everyone else was at the arena. Without them the Californium was only a few chairs and tables someone had arranged for no good reason under the famous frescoes. De M—— would have gone to the arena himself, but it was cold outside with small flakes of snow falling through the lights on the Unter-Main-Kai. *Discovering this about itself,* he wrote, *the place seems stunned and quiet. It has no inner resources.*

Egon Rhys came in with Vera, who was saying:

"—was sure he could be here."

She pulled her coat anxiously about her. Rhys made her sit where it was warm. "I'm tired tonight," she said. "Aren't you?" As she crossed the threshold she had looked up and seen a child's face smile obliquely out at her from a grimy patch in the frescoes. "I'm tired." All day long, she complained, it had been the port de bras: Lympany wanted something different—something that had never been done before. " 'A new *kind* of port de bras'!" she mimicked, " 'A whole new *way* of dancing'! But I have to be so careful in the cold. You can hurt yourself if you work too hard in weather like this."

She would drink only tea, which at the Californium is always served in wide china cups as thin and transparent as a baby's ear. When she had had some, she sat back with a laugh. "I feel better now!"

"He's late," said Rhys.

Vera took his arm and pressed her cheek briefly against his shoulder.

"You're so warm! When you were young did you ever touch a cat or a dog just to feel how warm it was? I did. I used to think: It's alive! It's alive!"

When he didn't respond she added, "In two or three days' time you could have exactly what you want. Don't be impatient."

"It's already midnight."

She let his arm go.

"He was so sure he would be here. We lose nothing if we wait."

There things rested. Fifteen minutes passed, perhaps half an hour; de M——, certain now that Verdigris was only pretending to be asleep to taunt him, crumpled a sheet of paper suddenly and dropped it on the floor. At this Rhys, whose affairs had made him nervous, jumped to his feet. The Marquis's mouth dropped open weakly. When nothing else happened Rhys sat down again. He thought, After all, I'm as safe here as anyone else in the city. He was still wary, though, of the poet, whom he thought he recognised. Vera glanced once or twice at the frescoes (they were old; no one could agree on what was represented), then quickly down at her cup. All this time Kiss-O-Suck the dwarf had been sitting slumped on a corner of the mantelpiece behind them like a great doll someone had put there for effect years before.

His legs dangled. He wore red tights, and yellow shoes with a bell on each toe; his doublet was made of some thick black stuff quilted like a leather shin guard and sewn all over with tiny glass mirrors. Immobility was as acceptable to him as motion: in repose his body would remember the gloottokoma and the hours he had spent there, while his face took on the look of varnished papier-mâché, shiny but as if dust had settled in the lines down the side of his hooked nose down to his mouth, which was set in a strange but extraordinarily sweet smile.

He had been watching Vera since she came in. When she repeated eventually, "He was so sure he could be here," he whispered to himself: "I was! Oh, I was!" A moment later he jumped down off the mantelpiece and blew lightly in Egon Rhys's ear.

Rhys threw himself across the room, smashing into the tables as he tried to get at his razor which he kept tucked up the sleeve of his coat. He fetched up against the Marquis de M—— and screamed, "Get out of the fucking way!" But the Marquis could only stare and tremble, so they rocked together for a moment, breathing into one another's faces, until another table went over. Rhys, who was beginning to have no idea where he was, knocked de M—— down and stood over him. "Don't kill me," said de M——. The razor, Rhys found, was tangled up with the silk lining of his sleeve: in the end he got two fingers into the seam and ripped the whole lot down from the elbow so that the weapon tumbled out already open, flickering in the light. Up went Rhys's arm, with the razor swinging at the end of it, high in the air.

"Stop!" shouted Vera. "Stop that!"

Rhys stared about him in confusion; blinked. By now he was trembling, too. When he saw the dwarf laughing at him he realised what had happened. He let the Marquis go. "I'm sorry," he said absentmindedly. He went over to where Kiss-O-Suck had planted himself rock steady on his bent legs in the middle of the floor, and caught hold of his wrist.

"What if I cut your face for that?" he asked, stroking the dwarf's cheek as if to calm him down. "Here. Or say here. What if I did that?"

The dwarf seemed to consider it. Suddenly his little wrist slipped and wriggled in Rhys's grip like a fish; however hard Rhys held on, it only twisted and wriggled harder, until he had let go of it almost without knowing. (All night after that his fingers tingled as if they had been rubbed with sand.)

"I don't think she would like that," said Kiss-O-Suck. "She wouldn't like you to cut someone as small as me."

He shrieked; slapped Rhys's face; jumped backwards from where he stood, without so much as a twitch of intent, right over the table and into the hearth. Out of his doublet he brought a small jam jar which he put down in the centre of the table. It contained half a dozen grasshoppers, a grey colour, with yellowish legs. At first they were immobile, but the firelight dancing on the glass around them seemed to invigorate them, and after a moment or two they started to hop about in the jar at random.

"Look!" said the dwarf.

"Aren't they lively?" cried Vera.

She smiled with delight. The dwarf chuckled. They were so pleased with themselves that eventually Egon Rhys was forced to laugh too. He tucked his razor back up his sleeve and stuffed the lining in after it as best he could. Thereafter strips of red silk hung down round his wrist, and he sometimes held the seam together with his fingers. "You must be careful with that," said Vera. When she tapped the side of their jar, one or two of the grasshoppers seemed to stare at her seriously for a moment, their enigmatic, horsey little heads quite still, before they renewed their efforts to get out, popping and ticking against the lid.

"I love them!" she said, which made Egon Rhys look sidelong at the dwarf and laugh even louder. "I love them! Don't you?"

The Marquis watched incredulously. He got himself to his feet and with a look at Ansel Verdigris as if to say "This is all your fault" ran out onto the Unter-Main-Kai. A little later Rhys, Vera, and the dwarf followed. They were still laughing; Vera and Rhys were arm in arm. As they went out into the night, Verdigris, who really had been asleep, woke up.

"Fuck off, then," he sneered. His dreams had been confused.

The day they crossed the canal they were followed all the way up to Allman's Reach from the Plain Moon Café. The mutual associations were out: it was another truce. Rhys could distinguish the whistles of the Fish-Head Men, January the Twelfth, the Yellow Paper College (now openly calling itself a "schism" of the Anemone and publishing its own broadsheet from the back room of a pie shop behind Red Hart Lane). This time, he was afraid, the Anemone was out too. He had no credit anywhere. At Orves he made the dwarf watch one side of the road while he watched the other. "Pay most attention to doorways." Faces appeared briefly in the cobbled mouths of alleys. Vera Ghillera shivered and pulled the hood of her cloak round her face.

"Don't speak," warned Egon Rhys.

He had a second razor with him, one which he no longer used much. That morning he had thought, It's old but it will do, and taken it down off the dusty windowsill where it lay—its handle as yellow as bone—between a ring of his mother's and a glass of cloudy water through which the light seemed to come suddenly when he picked it up.

Though he was careful to walk with his hands turned in to the sides of his body in such a way as to provoke no one, he had all the way up the hill a curious repeating image of himself as somebody who had *already* run mad with the two razors—hurtling after his enemies across the icy treacherous setts while they stumbled into dark corners or flung themselves over rotting fences, sprinting from one feeble refuge to another. "I'll pen them up," he planned, "in the observatory. They won't stop me now. Those bastards from Austonley . . ." It was almost as if he had done it. He seemed to be watching himself from somewhere behind his own back; he could hear himself yelling as he went for them, a winter gleam at the end of each wildly swinging arm.

"We'll see what happens then," he said aloud, and the dwarf glanced up at him in surprise. "We'll see what happens then." But the observatory came and went and nothing happened at all.

By then some of the Austonley men were no longer bothering to hide, swaggering along instead with broad grins. Other factions soon fell in with them, until they formed a loose, companionable half circle ten or fifteen yards back along the steep street. Their breath mingled in the cold air, and after a few minutes there was even some laughter and conversation between the different parties. As soon as they saw he was listening to them they came right up to Rhys's heels, watching his hands warily and nudging each other. The Yellow Paper kept itself apart from this: there was no sign of the Anemone at all. Otherwise it was like a holiday.

Someone touched his shoulder and, stepping deftly away in the same movement, asked him in a soft voice hardly older than a boy's, "Still got that old ivory bugger of Osgerby's up your sleeve, Egon? That old slasher of Osgerby Practal's?"

"Still got her there, have you?" repeated someone else.

"Let's have a look at her, Egon."

Rhys shrugged with fear and contempt.

It was bitterly cold on the canal bank. Vera stood listening to the rush of the broken weir a hundred yards up the reach. Sprays of scarlet rose hips hung over the water like necklaces tossed into the frozen air; a wren was bobbing and dipping among the dry reeds and withered dock plants beneath them.

"I can't see what such a little thing would find to eat," she said. "Can you?" No one answered.

The sound of the weir echoed off the boarded-up housefronts. Men from a dozen splinter groups and minor factions now filled the end of the lane to Orves, sealing it off. More were arriving all the time. They scraped heavily to and fro on the cinder path, avoiding the icy puddles, blowing into their cupped hands for warmth, giving Rhys quick shy looks as if to say, "We're going to have you this time." Some were sent to block the towpath. Presently the representatives of the Blue Anemone Ontological Association came out of one of the houses, where they had spent the morning playing black-and-red in a single flat ray of light which slanted between the boards and fell on a wooden chair. They had some trouble with the door.

Rhys brandished his razors at them.

"Where's the sense in this? Orcer Pust's a month dead; I put Ingarden down there with him not four nights ago—where was the sense in that?"

Sense was not at issue, they said.

"How many of you will I get before you get me?"

The representatives of the Anemone shrugged. It was all one to them.

"Come on, then! Come on!" Rhys shouted to the bravos in the lane. "I can see some bastards I know over there. How would they like it? In the eyes? In the neck? Facedown in the bathhouse tank with Orcer Pust?"

Kiss-O-Suck the dwarf sat down suddenly and unlaced his boots. When he had rolled his voluminous black trousers up as far as they would go he made a comical face and stepped into the canal, which submerged him to the thighs. He then waded out a few yards, turned round, and said quietly to Rhys, "As far as they're concerned you're as good as dead already." Further out, where it was deeper, probing gingerly in the mud with his toes, he added, "You're as good as dead on Allman's Heath." He slipped: swayed for a moment: waved his arms. "Oops." Shivering and blowing he climbed out onto the other side and began to rub his legs vigorously.

"Foo. That's cold. Foo. Tah." He called, "Why should they fight when they've only to make sure you go across?"

Rhys stared at him, then at the men from the Anemone. "You were none of you anything until I pulled you out of the gutter," he told them. He ran his hands through his hair.

When it was Vera's turn, the water was so cold she thought it would stop her heart.

Elder grew in thickets on the edge of the heath as if some attempt at habitation had been made a long time ago. Immediately you got in among it, Vriko began to seem quiet and distant; the rush of the weir died away. There were low mounds overgrown with nettle and matted couch grass; great brittle white-brown stems of cow parsley followed the line of a foundation or a wall; here and there a hole had been scraped by the dogs that swam over in the night from the city—bits of broken porcelain lay revealed in the soft black soil. Where brambles had colonised the open ground, water could be heard beneath them, trickling away from the canal down narrow aimless runnels and trenches.

It was hard for the dwarf to force his way through this stuff, and after about half an hour he fell on his back in a short rectangular pit like an empty cistern, from which he stared up sightlessly for a moment with arms and legs rigid in some sort of paralytic fit. "Get me out," he said in a low, urgent voice. "Pull me out."

Later he admitted to Vera:

"When I was a boy in the gloottokoma I would sometimes wake in the dark not knowing if it was night or day, or where I was, or what period of my life I was in. I could have been a baby in an unlit caravan. Or had I already become Kiss-O-Suck, Morgante, 'the Grand Little Man with the crowd in the palm of his hand'? It was impossible to tell: my ambitions were so clear to me, my disorientation so complete."

"I could never get enough to eat," said Vera. "Until I was ten years old I ate and ate."

The dwarf looked at her whitely for a moment.

"Anyway, that was how it felt," he said, "to live in a box. What a blaze of light when you were able to open the lid!"

Elder soon gave way to stands of emaciated birch in a region of shallow valleys and long spurs between which the streams ran in beds of honey-coloured stone as even as formal paving; a few oaks grew in sheltered positions among boulders the size of houses on an old alluvial bench. "It seems so empty!" said Vera. The dwarf laughed. "In the South they would call this the 'plaza,' " he boasted.

"If they knew about it they'd come here for their holidays." But after a mile or so of rising ground they reached the edge of a plateau, heavily dissected into a fringe of peaty gullies each with steep black sides above a trickle of orange water. Stones like bits of tile littered the watershed, sorted into curious polygonal arrays by the frost. There was no respite from the wind that blew across it. And though when you looked back you could still see Vriko, it seemed to be fifteen or twenty miles away, a handful of spires tiny and indistinct under a setting sun.

"This is more like it," said Kiss-O-Suck.

Egon Rhys blundered across the entangled grain of the watershed, one peat hag to the next, until it brought him to a standstill. The very inconclusiveness of his encounter with his rivals, perhaps, had exhausted him. He showed no interest in his surroundings, but whenever she would let him he leaned on Vera's arm, describing to her as if she had never been there the Allotrope Cabaret—how pretty its little danseuse had been, how artistically she had danced, how well she had counterfeited an animal he had never imagined could exist. "I was amazed!" he kept saying. Every so often he stood still and looked down at his clothes as though he wondered how they had got dirty. "At least try and help yourself," said Vera, who thought he was ill.

The moment it got dark he was asleep; but he must have heard Kiss-O-Suck talking in the night because he woke up and said,

"In the market when my mother was alive it was always, 'Run and fetch a box of sugared anemones. Run, Egon, and fetch it now.'" Just when he seemed to have gone back to sleep again, his mouth hanging open and his head on one side, he began repeating with a kind of infantile resentment and melancholy, "'Run and fetch it now! Run and fetch it now! Run and fetch it now!'"

He laughed.

In the morning, when he opened his eyes and saw he was on Allman's Heath, he remembered none of this. "Look!" he said, pulling Vera to her feet. "Just look at it!" He was already quivering with excitement.

"Did you ever feel the wind so cold?"

A cindery plain stretched level and uninterrupted to the horizon, smelling faintly of the rubbish pit on a wet day. The light that came and went across it was like the light falling through rainwater in empty tins, and the city could no longer be seen, even in the distance. To start with it was loose uncompacted stuff, ploughed up at every step to reveal just beneath the surface millions of bits of small rusty machinery like the insides of clocks; but soon it became as hard and grey as the sky, so that Vera could hardly tell where cinders left off and air began.

Rhys strode along energetically. He made the dwarf tell him about the other deserts he had visited. How big were they? What animals had he seen there? He would listen for a minute or two to the dwarf's answers, then say with satisfaction, "None of those places were as cold as this, I expect," or: "You get an albino sloth in the South, I've heard." Then, stopping to pick up what looked like a very long thin spring, coiled on itself with such brittle delicacy it must have been the remains of some terrific but fragile dragonfly: "What do you think of this, as a sign? I mean, from your experience?" The dwarf, who had not slept well, was silent.

"I could go on walking forever!" Rhys exclaimed, throwing the spring into the air. But later he seemed to tire again, and he complained that they had walked all day for nothing. He looked intently at the dwarf.

"How do you explain that?"

"What I care about," the dwarf said, "is having a piss." He walked off a little way and gasping with satisfaction sent a thick yellow stream into the ground. "Foo!" Afterwards he poked the cinders with his foot and said, "It takes it up, this stuff. Look at that. You could water it all day and never tell. Hallo, I think I can see something growing there already! Dwarfs are more fertile than ordinary people." (That night he sat awake again, slumped sideways, his arms wrapped round his tucked-up knees, watching Vera Ghillera with an unidentifiable expression on his face. When he happened to look beyond her, or feel the wind on his back, he shuddered and closed his eyes.)

"When I first saw you," Vera told Egon Rhys, "you had cut your cheek. Do you remember? A line of blood ran down, and at the end of it I could see one perfect drop ready to fall."

"That excited you, did it?"

She stared at him.

He turned away in annoyance and studied the heath. They had been on it now for perhaps three, perhaps four days. He had welcomed the effort, and gone to sleep worn out; he had woken up optimistic and been disappointed. Nothing was moving. The dwarf did not seem to be able to give him a clear idea of what to look for. He had thought sometimes that he could see something out of the corner of his eye, but this was only a kind of rapid, persistent fibrillating movement, never so much an insect as its ghost or preliminary illusion. Though at first it had aggravated him, now that it was wearing off he wished it would come back.

"My knee was damaged practising to dance Fyokla in *The Battenberg Cake*. That was chain after chain of the hardest steps Lympany could devise; they left your calves like blocks of wood. It hurt to run down all those stairs to help you."

"Help me!" jeered Rhys.

"I'm the locust that brought you here," she said suddenly.

She stood back on the hard cinders. One two three, one two three, she mimicked the poverty-stricken skips and hops which pass for dance at the Allotrope Cabaret, the pain and lassitude of the dancer who performs them. Her feet made a faint dry scraping sound.

"I'm the locust you came to see. After all, it's as much as *she* could do."

Rhys looked alertly from Vera to the dwarf. Ribbons of frayed red silk fluttered from his sleeve in the wind.

"I meant a real insect," he said. "You knew that before we started."

"We haven't been lucky," Kiss-O-Suck agreed.

When Rhys took hold of his wrist he stood as still and compliant as a small animal and added, "Perhaps we came at the wrong time of year."

Something had gone out of him: Rhys gazed down into his lined face as if he was trying to recognise what. Then he pushed the dwarf tenderly onto the cinders and knelt over him. He touched each polished cheek, then ran his fingertips in bemusement down the sides of the jaw. He seemed to be about to say something: instead he flicked the razor into his hand with a quick snaky motion so that light shot off the hollow curve of the blade. The dwarf watched it; he nodded. "I've never been in a desert in my life," he admitted. "I made that up for Vera. It sounded more exotic."

He considered this. "Yet how could I refuse her anything? She's the greatest dancer in the world."

"You were the greatest clown," Rhys said.

He laid the flat of the razor delicately against the dwarf's cheekbone, just under the eye, where there were faint veins in a net beneath the skin.

"I believed all that."

Kiss-O-Suck's eyes were china-blue. "Wait," he said. "Look!"

Vera, who had given up trying to imitate locust or danseuse or indeed anything, was en pointe and running chains of steps out across the ash, complicating and recomplicating them in a daze of technique until she felt exactly like one of the ribbons flying from Rhys's sleeve. It was a release for her, they were always saying at the Prospekt Theatre, to do the most difficult things, all kinds of allegro and batterie bewilderingly entangled, then suddenly the great turning jump forbidden to female dancers for more than a hundred years. As she danced she reduced the distinction between heath and sky. The horizon, never convinced of itself, melted. Vera was left crossing and recrossing a space steadily less definable. A smile came to Kiss-O-Suck's lips; he pushed the razor away with one fat little hand and cried:

"She's floating!"

"That won't help you, you bastard," Egon Rhys warned him.

He made the great sweeping cut which a week before had driven the razor through the bone and gristle at the base of Toni Ingarden's throat.

It was a good cut. He liked it so much he let it pass over the dwarf's head; stopped the weapon dead; and, tossing it from one hand to the other, laughed. The dwarf looked surprised. "Ha!" shouted Rhys. Suddenly he spun round on one bent leg as if he had heard another enemy behind him. He threw himself sideways, cutting out right and left faster than you could see. "And this is how I do it," he panted, "when it comes down to the really funny business." The second razor appeared magically in his other hand and between them they parcelled up the emptiness, slashing wildly about with a life of their own while Rhys wobbled and ducked across the surface of the desert with a curious, shuffling, buckle-kneed, bent-elbowed gait. "Now I'll show you how I can kick!" he called.

But Kiss-O-Suck, who had watched this performance with an interested air, murmuring judicially at some difficult stroke, only smiled and moved away. He had the idea—it had never been done before—to link in sequence a medley of cartwheels, "flying Dementos," and handsprings, which would bounce him so far into the smoky air of the arena, spinning over and over himself with his knees tucked into his stomach, that eventually he would be able to look *down* on the crowd, like a firework before it burst. "Tah!" he whispered, as he nerved himself up. "Codpoorlie, tah!"

Soon he and Rhys were floating too, leaping and twirling and wriggling higher and higher, attaining by their efforts a space which had no sense of limit or closure. But Vera Ghillera was always ahead of them, and seemed to generate their rhythm as she went.

Deserts spread to the northeast of the city, and in a wide swathe to its south.

They are of all kinds, from peneplains of disintegrating metallic dust—out of which rise at intervals lines of bony incandescent hills—to localised chemical sumps, deep, tarry, and corrosive, over whose surfaces glitter small flies with papery wings and perhaps a pair of legs too many. These regions are full of old cities which differ from Vriko only in the completeness of their deterioration. The traveller in them may be baked to death, or, discovered with his eyelids frozen together, leave behind only a journal which ends in the middle of a sentence.

The Metal-Salt Marshes, Fenlen Island, the Great Brown Waste: the borders of regions as exotic as this are drawn differently on the maps of competing authorities, but they are at least bounded in the conventional sense. Allman's Heath, whose borders can be agreed by everyone, does not seem to be. Neither does it seem satisfactory now to say that while those deserts lie outside the city, Allman's Heath lies within it.

The night was quiet.

Five to eleven, and except where the weir agitated its surface, the canal at Allman's Reach was covered with the lightest and most fragile web of ice. A strong moon cast its blue and gamboge light across the boarded-up fronts of the houses by the towpath. They don't look as if much life ever goes on in them, thought the watchman, an unimaginative man at the beginning of his night's work, which was to walk from there up to the back of the Atteline Quarter (where he could get a cup of tea if he wanted one) and down again. He banged his hands together in the cold. As he stood there he saw three figures wade into the water on the other side of the canal.

They were only ten yards upstream, between him and the weir, and the moonlight fell on them clearly. They were wrapped up in cloaks and hoods, "like brown-paper parcels, or statues tied up in sacks," he insisted later, and under these garments their bodies seemed to be jerking and writhing in a continual rhythmic motion, though for him it was too disconnected to be called a dance. The new ice parted for them like damp sugar floating on the water. They paid no attention to the watchman, but forded the canal, tallest first, shortest last, and disappeared down the cinder lane which goes via Orves and the observatory to the courtyard near the Plain Moon Café.

The watchman rubbed his hands and looked round for a minute or two, as if he expected something else to happen. "Eleven o'clock," he called at last, and though he couldn't commit himself to a description which seemed so subject to qualification as to be in bad faith, added: "And all's all."

A YOUNG MAN'S
JOURNEY TO
VIRICONIUM

A YOUNG MAN'S JOURNEY TO VIRICONIUM

On the day of the enthronement of the new archbishop, the "badly decomposed" body of a man was found on the roof of York Minster by a TV technician. He had been missing for eight months from a local hospital. He had fallen, it was said, from the tower; but no one had any idea how he had come to be there. I heard this on the local radio station in the day; what excited me about it was that they never repeated the item, and no mention of it was made either on the national broadcasts later in the day, or in the coverage of the ceremony itself. Mr. Ambrayses was less impressed.

"A chance in a thousand it will be of any use to us," he estimated. "One in a thousand."

I went to York anyway, and he came with me for some reason of his own—he paid visits to a secondhand bookshop and a taxidermist's. The streets were daubed with political slogans; even while the ceremony was going on, council employees were working hard along the route of the procession to paint them out. The man on the roof, I discovered, had been missing from an ordinary surgical unit, so I had had the journey for nothing, as Mr. Ambrayses predicted. What interested us at that time was any event connected with a mental or—especially—a geriatric home.

"We all want Viriconium," Mr. Ambrayses was fond of saying. "But it is the old who want it most!" That night on the way home he added,

"No one here needs it. Do you see?"

The 11:52 Leeds stopping train was full of teenagers. The older boys looked confused and violent in their short haircuts, faces and jaws thrown forward purple and white with cold; the girls watched them slyly, shrieked with laughter, then looked down and picked at their fingerless gloves. They stuck their heads out of the windows and shouted, 'Fuck off!' into the rush of air. Later when we got off the train we saw them hopping backwards and forwards over a metal barrier in the sodium light; unfathomable and energetic as grasshoppers in the sun. Sensing my disappointment Mr. Ambrayses said gently, "On occasion we all want to go there so badly that we will invent a clue."

"I'm not old," I said.

Mr. Ambrayses had lived next door to me for two years. At first I was only aware of him when I was trying to watch the news. A body under a coloured blanket, slumped at the foot of a corrugated iron fence; the camera moving in on a small red smear like a nosebleed cleaned up with lavatory paper, then as if puzzledly on to helicopters, rubble, someone important being ushered into a building, a woman walking past the end of a street. Immediately Mr. Ambrayses's low appreciative laughter would come "Hur hur hur" through the thin partition wall, so that I lost the thread. "Hur hur," he would laugh, and I felt as if I was watching a television in a foreign country. He liked only the variety shows and situation comedies.

His laughter seemed to sensitise me to him, and I began to see him everywhere, like a new word I had learned: in his garden where the concrete paths, glazed with rain, reflected the sky; in Marie's café, a middle-aged man in a dirty suede coat, with jam on his fingers—licking at them with short dabbing licks like a child or an animal; in Sainsbury's food hall with an empty metal basket in the crook of his arm, staring up and down the tinned-meat aisle. He didn't seem to have anything to do. I saw him on a day-trip bus to Matlock Bath, wearing one sheepskin mitten. His trousers, which were much too large for him, so that the arse of them hung down between his legs in a gloomy flap, were sewn up at the back with bright yellow thread as coarse as string. The bus was full of old women who nodded and smiled and read all the signs out to one another as if they were constructing or rehearsing between them the landscape as they went through it.

"Oh, look, there's the 'Jodrell Arms'!"

". . . the 'Jodrell Arms.' "

"And there's the A623!"

". . . A623."

The first time we spoke, Mr. Ambrayses told me, "Identity is not negotiable. An identity you have achieved by agreement is always a prison."

The second time, I had been out buying some Vapona. The houses up here, warm and cheerful as they are in summer, become in the first week of

September cold and damp. Ordinary vigorous houseflies, which have crawled all August over the unripe lupin pods beneath the window, pour in and cluster on any warm surface, but especially on the floor near the electric fire, and the dusty grid at the back of the fridge; they cling to the side of the kettle as it cools. That year you couldn't leave food out for a moment. When I sat down to read in the morning, flies ran over my outstretched legs.

"I suppose you've got the same problem," I said to Mr. Ambrayses. "I poison them," I said, "but they don't seen to take much notice." I held up the Vapona, with its picture of a huge fly. "Might as well try again."

Mr. Ambrayses nodded. "Two explanations are commonly offered for this," he said:

"In the first we are asked to imagine certain sites in the world—a crack in the concrete in Chicago or New Delhi, a twist in the air in an empty suburb of Prague, a clotted-milk bottle on a Bradford tip—from which all flies issue in a constant stream, a smoke exhaled from some appalling fundamental level of things. This is what people are asking—though they do not usually know it—when they say exasperatedly, Where are all these *flies* coming from? Such locations are like the holes in the side of a new house where insulation has been pumped in: something left over from the constructional phase of the world.

"This is an adequate, even an appealing model of the process. But it is not modern; and I prefer the alternative, in which it is assumed that as Viriconium grinds past us, dragging its enormous bulk against the bulk of the world, the energy generated is expressed in the form of these insects, which are like the sparks shooting out from between two huge flywheels that have momentarily brushed each other."

A famous novel begins:

I went to Viriconium in a century which could find itself only in its own symbols, at an age when one seeks to unify one's experience through the symbolic events of the past.

I saw myself go on board an airliner, which presently rose into the air. Above the Atlantic was another sea, made of white clouds; the sun burned on it. The only thing we recognised in all that immense white space was the vapour trail of another airliner on a parallel course. It disappeared abruptly. We were encouraged to eat a meal, watch first one film and then another. The captain apologised for the adverse winds, the turbulence, of what had seemed to us to be a completely tranquil journey, as if apologising for a difficult transition from childhood to adolescence.

In Viriconium the light was like the light you only see on record covers and in the colour supplements. Photographic precision of outline under an empty blue sky is one of the most haunting features of the Viriconium landscape. Ordinary objects—a book, a bowl of anemones, someone's hand—seem to be lit in a way which makes them very distinct from their background. The identity of things under this light seems enhanced. Their visual distinctness becomes metonymic of the reality we perceive both in them and in ourselves.

I began living in one of the tall grey houses that line the heights above Mynned.

You can't just fly there, of course.

Soon after my trip to York I got a job in a tourist café in the town. It was called the Gate House, and it was attached to a bookshop. The idea was that you could go in, look round the shelves, and leaf through a book while you drank your coffee. We had five or six tables with blue cloths on them, a limited menu of homemade pastries, and pictures by local artists on the walls. Crammed in on the wooden chairs on a wet afternoon, thirteen customers seemed to fill it to capacity; damp thickened in the corner by the coats. But it was often empty.

One day a man and a woman came in and sat down near one another but at separate tables. They stared at everything as if it was new to them.

The man wore a short zip-fronted gabardine jacket over his green knitted pullover and pink shirt; a brown trilby hat made his head seem small and his chin very pointed. His face had an old but unaged quality—the skin was smooth and brown, streaked, you saw suddenly, with dirt—which gave him the look of a little boy who had grown haggard round the eyes after an illness. He might have been anywhere between thirty and sixty. He looked too old for one and too young for the other: something had gone wrong with him. His eyes moved sorely from object to object in the room, as if he had never seen a calendar with a picture of Halifax town centre on it, or a chair or a plate before; as if he was continually surprised to find himself where he was.

I imagined he had come up for the day from one of the farms south of Buxton, where the wind sweeps across the North Staffordshire Plain and they sit in their old clothes all week in front of a broken television, listening to the gates banging.

He leaned over to the other table.

"Isn't it Friday tomorrow?" he said softly.

"You what?" answered the woman. "Oh, aye, Friday defnitely. Oh, aye." And when he added something in a voice too low for me to catch: "No, theer's no fruit cake, no, they won't have that here. No fruit cake, they won't have that."

She dabbed her finger at him. "Oh, no, not here."

Tilting her head to one side and holding her spoon deftly at an angle so that she could see into the bottom of her coffee cup, she scooped the half-melted sugar out of it. While she was doing this she glanced round at the other customers with a kind of nervous satisfaction, like an Eskimo or an Aborigine in some old TV documentary—the shy, sharp glance which tells you they are getting away, in plain view, with something that is unacceptable in their own culture. It was done in no time, with quick little licks and laps. When she had finished she sat back. "I'll wait till teatime for another," she said. "I'll wait." She had cunningly kept on her yellow-and-black-check overcoat, her red woollen hat.

"Will you have a cup of coffee now?" she asked. And seeing that he was gazing in his sore vague way at the landscapes on the walls, "Theer watercolours those, on the wall, I'd have to look to be certain: watercolours those, nice."

"I don't want any coffee."

"Will you have ice cream?"

"I don't want any ice cream, thank you. It cools my stomach."

"You'll be better when you get back up there, you'll get television on. Get sat down in front of that."

"Why should I want to watch the television?" he said quietly, looking away from a picture of the town bridge in the rain. "I don't want any tea or supper, or any breakfast in the morning."

He put his hands together for a moment and stared into the air with his solemn boyish eyes in his delicately boned dirty face. He fumbled suddenly in his pockets.

"You can't smoke in here," said the woman quickly. "I don't think you can smoke in here; I thought I saw a sign which said no smoking because there's food about, you see, oh, no: they won't have that in here."

When they got up to pay me he said,

"Nice to have a change." His voice was intelligent, but soft and clouded, like the voice of an invalid who wakes up disoriented in the afternoon and asks a new nurse the time. "It's a day out, isn't it?" They had come over by bus from a suburb the other side of Huddersfield which he called Lock Wood or Long Wood. "Nice to have a change," he repeated, "while the weather's still good." And before I could reply: "I've got a cold, you see, really it's bronchial pneumonia, more like bronchial pneumonia. I've had it for a year. A year now or more: they can't help you at these Health Centres, can they? My lungs seem inside out with it on a wet day—"

"Now get on," the woman interrupted him.

Though his voice was so low they could have heard nothing, she grinned and bobbed at the other customers as if to apologise for him.

"None of that," she said loudly to them.

She pushed him towards the door. "I'm not his wife, you know," she said over her shoulder to me, "oh, no, more his nurse-companion, I've managed for two years. He's got money but I don't think I could marry him."

She was like a budgerigar bobbing and shrugging in front of the mirror in its cage.

I looked out of the window half an hour later and they were still standing at the bus stop. Nothing could ever come of them. The meaning of what they said to one another was carefully hidden in its own broken, insinuatory rhythms. Their lives were so intricately repressed that every word was like a loose fibre woven back immediately into an old knot. Eventually a bus arrived. When it pulled away again he was in one of the front seats on the top deck, looking down vaguely into the florist's window, while she sat some rows back on the other side of the aisle, wincing if he lit a cigarette and trying to draw his attention to something on part of the pavement he couldn't possibly see from where he was.

When I told Mr. Ambrayses about them he was excited.

"That man, did he have a tiny scar? Beneath the hairline on the left side? Like a crescent, just visible beneath the hair?"

"How could I know that, Mr. Ambrayses?"

"Never mind," he said. "That man's name is Doctor Petromax, and he once had tremendous power. He used it cleverly and soon stood the thickness of a mirror from what we all seek. But his nerve failed: what you see now is a ruin. He found an entrance to Viriconium in the lavatory of a restaurant in Huddersfield. There were imitation quarry tiles on the floor, and white porcelain tiles on the walls around the mirror. The mirror itself was so clean it seemed to show the way into another, more accurate version of the world. He knew by its cleanliness he was looking into one of the lavatories of Viriconium. He stared at himself staring out; and he has been staring at himself ever since. His courage would take him no further. What you see is a shell; we can learn nothing from him now."

He shook his head.

"Which café was that?" I asked him. "Do you know where it is?"

"It would not work for you, any more than it did for him, though for different reasons," Mr. Ambrayses assured me. "Anyway, it is known only by the description I have given."

He said this as if it was remote, on no map. But a café is only a café.

"I think I recognise it. In the steam behind the counter is a photo of an old comedian. Two men with walking sticks and white hair smile feebly at a round-shouldered waitress!"

"It would not work for you."

———

"That man's name is Dr. Petromax."

Mr. Ambrayses loved to preface his statements like this. It was a grammatical device which allowed him to penetrate appearances.

"That boy," he would say, "knows two incontrovertible facts about the world; he will reveal them to no one."

Or:

"That woman, though she seems young, dreams at night of the wharfs of the Yser Canal. By day she wears beneath her clothes a garment of her own design to remind her of the people there, and their yellow lamps reflected with such distinctness in the surface of the water."

On a steep bank near my house was a domestic apple tree which had long ago peacefully reverted amid the oaks and elder. When I first drew his attention to it Mr. Ambrayses said, "That tree has no name in botany. It has not flowered for ten years." The next autumn, when the warm light slanted down through the drifting willow-herb silk, hundreds of small hard reddish fruits fell from it into the bracken; in spring it bore so much blossom my neighbours called it "the white tree."

"It bears no flowers in Viriconium," said Mr. Ambrayses. "There, it stands in a courtyard off the Plaza of Realised Time, like the perfect replica of a tree. If you look back through the archway you see clean wide pavements, little shops, white-painted tubs of geraniums in the sunlight."

"That man's name is Dr. Petromax."

Rilke describes a man for whom *in a moment more, everything will have lost its meaning, and that table and the cup, and the chair to which he clings, all the near and commonplace things around him, will have become unintelligible, strange and burdensome,* and who nevertheless only sits and waits passively for the disaster to be complete. To an extent, I suppose, this happens to us all. But there was about Dr. Petromax that vagueness which suggested not just injury but surrender, a psychic soreness about the eyes, a whiteness about the mouth, as if he was seeing the moment over and over again and could not forget it no matter how he webbed himself in with the aboriginal woman in the yellow coat. He did no work. He went constantly from café to café in Huddersfield; I had no means of knowing why, although I suspected—quite wrongly—at the time that he had forgotten which lavatory the mirror was in, and was patiently searching for it again.

I followed him when I could, despite Mr. Ambrayses's veto; and this is what he told me one afternoon in the Four Cousins Grill & Coffee Lounge:

"When I was a child my grandmother often took me about with her. I was a quiet boy already in poor health, and she found me at least as easy to manage as a small dog. Her habits were fixed: each Wednesday she visited the hairdresser and then went on to Manchester by train for a day's shopping. She wore for this a hat made entirely out of pale pink, almost cream feathers, dotted among which were peacock eyes a startling brown-red. The feathers lay very dense and close, as if they were still on the breast of the bird.

"She loved cafés, I think because the life that goes on in them, though domestic and comfortable, can't claim you in any way: there is nothing for you to join in. 'I like my tea in peace,' she told me every week. 'Once in a while I like to have my tea in peace.'

"Whatever she ate she coughed and choked demurely over it, and for some time afterwards; and she always kept on her light green raincoat with its nacreous, gold-edged buttons.

"When I remember Piccadilly it isn't so much by the flocks of starlings which invaded the gardens at the end of every short winter afternoon, filling the paths with their thick mouldy smell and sending up a loud mechanical shrieking which drowned out the traffic, as by the clatter of pots, the smell of marzipan or a match just struck, wet woollen coats hung over one another in a corner, voices reduced in the damp warm air to an intimate buzz out of which you could just pick a woman at another table saying, 'Anyway, as long as you can get about,' to which her friend answered immediately,

" 'Oh, it's something, isn't it? Yes.'

"On a rainy afternoon in November it made you feel only half awake. A waitress brought us the ashtray. She put it down in front of me. 'It's always the gentleman who smokes,' she said. I looked at my grandmother sulkily, wondering where we would have to go next. At Boots she had found the top floor changed round again, suddenly full of oven gloves, clocks, infrared grills; and a strong smell of burning plastic had upset her in the arcades between Deansgate and Market Street.

"Along the whole length of the room we were in ran a tinted window, through which you could see the gardens in the gathering twilight, paths glazed with drizzle giving back the last bit of light in the sky, the benches and empty flower beds grey and equivocal-looking, the sodium lamps coming on by the railings. Superimposed, on the inside of the glass, was the distant reflection of the café: it was as if someone had dragged all the chairs and tables out into the gardens, where the serving women waited behind a stainless-steel counter, wiping their faces with a characteristic gesture in the steam from the *bain marie,* unaware of the wet grass, the puddles, the blackened but energetic pigeons bobbing round their feet.

"As soon as I had made this discovery a kind of tranquillity came over me. My grandmother seemed to recede, speaking in charged hypnotic murmurs. The rattle of cutlery and metal trays reached me only from a great distance as I watched people come into the gardens laughing. They were able to pass without difficulty through the iron railings; the wind and rain had no effect on them. They rubbed their hands and sat down to eat squares of dry Battenburg cake and exclaim 'Mm' how good it was. There they sat, out in the cold, smiling at one another: they certainly were a lot more cheerful out there. A man on his own had a letter which he opened and read.

" *'Dear Arthur,'* it began.

"He chuckled and nodded, tapping a line here and there with his finger as if he was showing the letter to someone else, while the waitresses went to and fro around him, for the most part girls with white legs and flat shoes, some of whom buttoned the top of their dark blue overalls lower than others. They carried trays with a thoughtless confidence, and spoke among themselves in a language I longed to understand, full of ellipses, hints, and abrupt changes of subject, in which the concrete things were items and prices. I wanted to go and join them. Their lives, I imagined, like the lives of everyone in the gardens, were identical to their way of walking between the tables—a neat, safe, confident movement without a trace of uncertainty, through a medium less restrictive than the one I was forced to inhabit.

" 'Yes, love' I would say to introduce myself. 'Thank you, love. Anything else, love? Twenty pence then, thank you, love, eighty pence change, next please. Did Pam get those drop earrings in the end, then? No, love, only fried.'

" 'I think it's just as well not to be,' they might reply. Or with a wink and a shout of laughter, 'Margaret's been a long time in the you-know-where. She'll be lucky!'

"At the centre or focal point of the gardens, from which the flower beds fell back modestly in arcs, a statue stood. Along its upraised arms drops of water gathered, trembled in the wind, fell. One of the girls walked up and put her tray on a bench next to it. She buried her arms brusquely in the plinth of the statue and brought out a cloth to wipe her hands. This done, she stared ahead absently, as if she had begun to suspect she was caught up in two worlds. Though she belonged to neither her image dominated both of them, a big plain patient girl of seventeen or eighteen with chipped nail varnish and a tired back from sorting cutlery all morning. Suddenly she gave a delighted laugh.

"She looked directly out at me and waved. She beckoned. I could see her mouth open and close to make the words 'Here! Over here!'

"She's alive, I thought. It was a shock. I felt that I was alive, too. I got up and ran straight into the plate-glass window and was concussed. Someone dropped a tray of knives. I heard a peculiar voice, going away from me very fast, say: 'What's he done? Oh, what's he done now?' Then those first ten or twelve years of my life were sealed away from me neatly like the bubble in a spirit level—clearly visible but strange and inaccessible, made of nothing. I knew immediately that though what I had seen was not Viriconium, Viriconium nevertheless awaited me. I knew, too, how to find it."

People are always pupating their own disillusion, decay, age. How is it they never suspect what they are going to become, when their faces already contain the faces they will have twenty years from now?

"You would learn nothing from Dr. Petromax's mirror even if you could find it," Mr. Ambrayses said dismissively. "First exhaust the traditional avenues of the research." And as if in support of his point he brought me a cardboard box he had found among the rubbish on a building site in Halifax, the words *World Mosaic* printed boldly across its lid. But my face was down to the bone with ambition.

Old people sit more or less patiently in railway carriages imagining they have bought a new bathroom suite, lavender, with a circular bath they will plumb-in themselves. April comes, the headlines read, BIBLE BOY MURDERED; KATIE IN NUDE SHOCK. The sun moves across the patterned bricks outside the bus station, where the buses are drawn up obliquely in a line: from the top deck of one you can watch in the next a girl blowing her nose. You don't think you can bear to hear one more woman in Sainsbury's saying to her son as she shifts her grip on her plastic shopping bag with its pink and grey Pierrot, "Alec, get your foot off the biscuits. I shan't tell you again. If you don't get your foot off the biscuits, Alec, I shall knock it straight on the floor."

April again. When the sun goes in, a black wind tears the crocus petals off and flings them down the ring road.

"I can't wait," I told Mr. Ambrayses.

I couldn't wait any longer. I followed Dr. Petromax from the Blue Rooms ("Meals served all day") to the Alpine Coffee House, Merrie England, the Elite Café & Fish Restaurant. I let him tell me his story in each of them. Though details changed, it remained much the same: but I was certain he was preparing himself to say more. One day I kept quiet until he had ended as usual, "Viriconium nevertheless awaited me," then I said openly to him:

"And yet you've never been there. You had the clue as a child. You found the doorway but you never went through it."

We were in the El Greco, at the pedestrian end of New Street. While he waited for the waitress he stared across the wide flagged walk, with its beech saplings and raised flower beds, at the window of C&A's, his sore brown eyes full of patience between their bruised-looking lids. When she came she brought him plaice and chips. "Oh, hello!" she said. "We haven't seen you for a while! Feeling any better?" He ate the chips one by one with his fork, pouring vinegar on them between every mouthful, only afterwards scraping the white of the plaice off its slippery fragile skin until he had the one in a little pile on the side of the plate and the other intact, glistening slightly, webbed with grey, in the middle. His dirty hands were as deft and delicate as a boy's at this. Once or twice he looked up at me and then down again.

"Who told you that?" he said quietly when he had finished eating. "Ambrayses?"

He put down his knife and fork.

"Three of us set out," he said. "I won't say who. Two got through easily, the third tried to go back halfway. On the right day you can still catch sight of him in the mirror, spewing up endlessly. He doesn't seem to know where he is, but he's aware of you.

"We lived there for three months, in some rooms on Salt Lip Road behind the Rue Serpolet. The streets stank. At six in the morning a smell so corrupt came up from the Yser Canal it seemed to blacken the iron lampposts; we would gag in our dreams, struggle for a moment to wake up, and then realise that the only escape was to sleep again. It was winter, and everything was filthy. Inside, the houses smelled of vegetable peel, sewage, perished rubber. Everyone in them was ill. If we wanted a bath we had to go to a public washhouse on Mosaic Lane. The air was cold; echoes flew about under the roof; the water was like lead. Sometimes it was hardly like water at all. There were some famous murals there, but they were so badly kept up you could make furrows in the grease. Scrape it off and you'd see the most beautiful stuff underneath, chalky reds, pure blues, children's faces!

"We stuck it for three months. We knew there were other quarters of the city, where things must be better, but we couldn't find our way about. At first we were so tired; later we thought we were being followed by some sort of secret police. Towards the end the man I was with was ill all the time; he started to hear the bathhouse echoes even while he was in bed; he couldn't walk. It was a hard job getting him out. The night I did it you could see the lights of the High City, sweet, magical, like paper lanterns in a garden, filling up the emptiness. If only I'd gone towards them, walked straight towards them!"

I stared at him.

"Was that all?" I said.

"That was all."

His hands had begun to tremble, and he looked down at them. "Oh, yes. I was there. What else could have left me like this?" He got up and went to the lavatory. When he came back he said, "Ambrayses has a lot to learn about me." He bent down, his eyes now looking very vague and sick, as if he was already forgetting who I was or what I wanted, and quickly whispered something in my ear: then he left.

As he walked across the street he must have disturbed the pigeons, because they all flew up at once and went wheeling violently about between the buildings. As they passed over her an Indian woman, who had been sitting in the sunshine examining a length of embroidered cloth, winced and folded it up hurriedly. Though they soon quietened down, coming to rest in a line along the top of the precast C&A façade, she continued to look frightened and resentful—biting her lips, making a face, moving her shoulders repeatedly inside her tight leather coat, from the sleeves of which emerged thin wrists and hands, powdery brown, fingernails lacquered a plum colour.

The older Asian women fiddle constantly with their veils, plucking with wrinkled fingers at the lower part of their faces. In the bus station they lift their feet—automatically looking away from him—to let the cleaner run his brush along the base of the plastic banquette. They have features as coarse and wise as an elephant's but underneath they are in a continual nervous fidget.

The furniture in Mr. Ambrayses's front room, inert great drop-leaf tables and sideboards with stained, lifting veneers, was strewn with the evidence he had accumulated: curled-up grainy photographs, each a detail enlarged in black and white from some colour snap until, its outline fatally eroded and its context yawing, it reached monstrous or curious conclusions; articles cut from yellowed newsprint found lining the drawers of an empty house; cassettes furred with dust, which when you played them gave out only the pure electric silence of the machine, punctuated once or twice by feral static; his notebooks, where in a clear hand he had written, *Each event, struck lightly against its own significance, can be excited into throwing off a spark; it is this energetic mote which lies at the heart of metaphor—and of life;* or: *The lesson we learn too late is that we cannot have only by wanting.* Then on another page, *Nothing impedes us; we need only learn to act.*

He preserved the circulars, bills, Christmas cards, charity appeals, and small parcels which came through his letterbox for the previous tenants of the house. Almost as if by accident a little of this lost or random communication was addressed to him, from Australia: he gave it pride of place. This was how I learned that his daughter had married and emigrated there several years before.

"She was ungrateful," he would say, avoiding my eyes and staring at the television. (A car drove slowly out of some factory gates, then faster through a housing estate and onto an empty road.) "She was an ungrateful girl."

Two chimney sweeps called to see him the Wednesday after I had talked to Dr. Petromax in the El Greco. He was out.

"Is he expecting you?" I asked them.

They didn't seem to know. They waited patiently in the garden for me to let them in—a large awkward boy in Dr. Martin's boots, and a man I took to be his father, much smaller and more agile in his movements, who said: "You've a fair view here anyhow. You can see a fair way from here." The boy didn't answer but stood as if marooned on the concrete path which, like a mirror in the rain, reflected one or two thick yellow crocus buds. Piles of red bricks, rusty brown conifers, the conservatory with its peeling paint, the shed door held closed by a spade, everything else that afternoon was dark; it was more like October than April. "We're used to working in town." The boy looked warily at the rain, rubbed some of it into the stubble on his bony, vulnerable skull. He seemed to cheer up.

"You'll have a few accidents in these lanes then," he said. "With tractors and that."

Later he brought the brushes in, and, glancing away from me shyly, spread two old candlewick bedspreads on the lino to protect it. He knelt with a kind of dreamy conscientiousness in Mr. Ambrayses's tiled hearth, like a child fascinated by everything to do with fire: arranged the canvas bag over the fireplace; fixed it there with strips of Sellotape which he bit carefully off the roll; pushed each extension of the brush up through the bag until the smell of soot came into the room, rich and bitter, and he was forced to stop suddenly.

"There's still three exes here," said his father. "It'll go three more."

"No it won't," said the boy, stirring and pummelling away at the chimney.

"I'll go and look."

When he came back he said, "I can hear it rattling at the top."

"It might be rattling but it's not going up."

They stared at one another.

"I can hear it as plain as day; there's something at the top. I can fair hear it, plain as day, rattling against it."

At this the boy only pummelled harder.

"Has plenty come down?" his father asked.

"Aye."

"That's all we can do then."

The boy pulled the brush gently back into the room, disassembling the extensions one by one while the man stood looking down at him breathing heavily, hands on hips, watching in case he had fetched the obstruction out. They ripped the bag off, revealing the fireplace choked to three-quarters of its height with soot: nothing else. The boy screwed the Sellotape up contemptuously into a glittering sticky ball. He invited me to look up the chimney, but all I saw was a large dark recess, much rougher than I had imagined it would be, blackened and streaked with salts, like a cave.

"The fact is," he said to me, "I don't know how your friend keeps a fire there at all."

When I told Mr. Ambrayses this he said anxiously, "Was Petromax with them?"

I laughed.

"Of course he wasn't. Is he a sweep?"

"Never let anyone in here," he shouted. "Describe them! That boy: were his hands big? Clumsy, and the nails all broken?"

"How else would a chimney sweep's hands be?"

He ignored this and, as if preoccupied by the answer to his first question, whispered to himself, "It was only the sweeps." Suddenly he got down on his back among the hair clippings and screwed-up bits of paper on the floor, pulled himself into the hearth, and tried as I had done to look up the chimney. Whatever he saw or failed to see there made him jump to his feet again. He went round the room pulling cupboards open and slamming them shut; he picked up one or two of the postcards his daughter had sent him from Australia, stared in a relieved way at the strange bright stamps and unreal views, then put them back on the mantelpiece. "Nothing touched," he said. "You didn't let them touch anything?" When I said that I hadn't, he seemed to calm down.

"Look at these!" he said.

He had used up an entire pack of Polaroid film, he told me, photographing three pairs of women's shoes someone had thrown into a ditch at the top of Acres Lane where it bends right to join the Manchester Road. "I noticed them on Sunday. They were still there when I went back, but by this morning they had gone. Can you imagine," he asked me, "who would leave them there? Or why?" I couldn't. "Or, equally, who would come to collect them from a dry ditch among farm rubbish at the edge of the moor?" The pictures, which had that odd greenish cast Polaroids sometimes develop a day or two after they have been exposed, showed them to be flimsy and open-toed: one pair in black suede, an evening shoe with a brown fur piece; one made of transparent plastic bound at the edges in a kind of metallic blue leather; and a pair of light tan sandals with a crisscross arrangement of straps to hold the upper part of the foot.

"They were all size four," said Mr. Ambrayses. "The brand name inside them was Marquise: it was a little worn and faded but otherwise they seemed well-kept."

All at once he dropped the photographs and went to look up the chimney again.

He whimpered.

"Never let anyone in here!" he repeated, staring helplessly up at me from where he lay. "You have a lot to learn about Petromax."

Two or three days later he locked up his house and went to Hull, to look, he said, for a rare book he had heard was there. The door of his garden shed banged open in the wind half an hour after he had gone, and has been banging since.

If Mr. Ambrayses was, as I now believe, the other survivor of the experiment with the mirror—the one who, sickening in that slum behind the Rue Serpolet, heard even in his sleep echoes of a voice in the deserted bathhouse, and who, dragged delirious and sweating with wrecked dreams through the freezing back lanes on their last night, never saw the ethereal lights of the High City—why was his memory of Viriconium the reverse of Petromax's?

It seems unlikely I will ever find out.

Petromax avoids me now he has set his poison in me. I see him around Huddersfield, but his wife keeps close to him. If they notice me they go up another street. They often have a child with them, a girl of about ten or eleven whose undeveloped legs stick out of the hem of a thick grey coat however warm the weather. She dawdles behind them, or darts away suddenly into a shop doorway, or she stops in front of the Civic Centre and refuses to walk with them, making a grunting noise as if she is suppressing a bowel movement. You can see that this is only another formalised gesture: they are a family, and her effort not to belong is already her contribution.

Petromax's mirror, if anyone wants to know, is in the lavatory of the Merrie England Café, a little further down New Street than the El Greco, between the Ramsden Street junction and Imperial Arcade.

Go straight through the café itself, with all its cheap reproductions of Medieval saints and madonnas, *Mon Seul Desir,* all those unicorns and monkeys, where the iron lamp fittings and rough plaster bring you close to the Medieval soul in its night "untainted by any breath of the Renaissance," and you find on the left a doorway made to look like varnished oak. The steps are painted cardinal red; for a moment they appear wet. Go down them and the warm human buzz of traffic and conversation fades, distance dilutes the familiar scraping hiss of the espresso machine. There behind the pictogram on the neat grey door, above the sink with its flake of yellow soap and right next to the Seibel hand dryer, is Petromax's mirror. It is smaller than you would think, perhaps eighteen inches on a side.

How did they force themselves through? The mere physical act must have been difficult. You can picture them teetering on the sink, as clumsy and fastidious as the elephant on the small circus chair. Their pockets are stuffed with whatever they think they might need: chocolate, Tekna knives, gold coins, none of which in the last analysis will prove to be any good. They have locked the door behind them (though Petromax, who goes through last, will open it again, so that things remain normal in the Merrie England up above), but every sound from the kitchen makes them pause and look at one another. They try an arm first, then a shoulder; they squirm about. At last Petromax's feet disappear, kicking and waving. The soap is stuck to the sole of his foot. The lavatory is vacant. "Well, that's it, isn't it?" says a voice from the corridor. "It's for the kids really, isn't it?"

Mr. Ambrayses was right: the mirror is of no use to me. I went down there; I stood in front of it. Except perhaps myself, I saw no one trapped and despairing in it. When Petromax whispered me its location, did he already know I would never dare go through, in case I found Viriconium as he found it?

A couple with two children live on the other side of me to Mr. Ambrayses. The day he went to Hull they came out and began to dig in their garden with a kind of excited, irritable energy. A gusty wind had got up from the head of the valley, rattling the open windows, blowing the net curtains into the room. They had to shout to make themselves heard against it, while the children screamed and fell over, or killed worms and insects.

"Do you really want this dug up?"

"Well, it hasn't done very well."

"Well, say if that's it. Do you want it dug up or not?"

"Well, yes."

It didn't seem like gardening at all. The harder the wind blew the faster they worked, as if they were in some race against time to dig a shelter for themselves. "A spider, a spider!" bellowed the two little boys, and the father humoured them with a kind of desperate calm, the way you might in the face of an air attack or a flood. He is a teacher, about thirty years old, bearded, with a blunt manner meant to conceal diffidence. "Is it going to break, this storm?" I heard him say to his wife. It was hard to see what else he could have said, unless it was "this stuff." Soon after that they all went back in again. The wind buzzed and rustled for a while in my newspaper-stuffed fireplace, but it was dying down all the time.

Viriconium!

ABOUT THE AUTHOR

M. JOHN HARRISON is the award-winning author of eight previous novels and four collections of short stories. His fifth novel, *In Viriconium,* was shortlisted for the Guardian Fiction Prize, and his sixth, *Climbers,* won the Boardman Tasker Award. His most recent novel, *Light,* was awarded the James Tiptree Jr. Award and shortlisted for the 2002 Arthur C. Clarke Award.

EXPLORE THE WORLDS OF DEL REY AND SPECTRA.

Get the news about your favorite authors.
Read excerpts from hot new titles.
Follow our author and editor blogs.
Connect and chat with other readers.

Visit us on the Web:

www.Suvudu.com

Like us on Facebook:

www.Facebook.com/DelReySpectra

Follow us on Twitter:

@DelReySpectra

For mobile updates:

Text DELREY to 72636.

Two messages monthly. Standard message rates apply.

DEL REY SPECTRA